The Abruzzo Trilogy

Foreword by Alexander Stille

IGNAZIO SILONE

The Abruzzo Trilogy

Fontamara
Bread and Wine
The Seed Beneath the Snow

TRANSLATED FROM THE ITALIAN BY ERIC MOSBACHER
REVISED BY DARINA SILONE

STEERFORTH ITALIA
AN IMPRINT OF STEERFORTH PRESS · SOUTH ROYALTON, VERMONT

LIBRARY OF CONGRESS CATALOGING-IN-PUBLICATION DATA

Silone, Ignazio, 1900–1978.
[Novels. English. Selections]
The Abruzzo trilogy / Ignazio Silone ; translated by Eric Mosbacher ;
translation updated and revised by Darina Silone.
p. cm.
Contents: Fontamara — Bread and Wine — The seed beneath the snow.
ISBN 1-58642-006-2 (alk. paper)
1. Abruzzo (Italy) — Fiction. I. Mosbacher, Eric, 1903- II. Silone, Darina. III. Title.

PQ4841.I4 A6 2000
853'.912—dc21   00-061882

Manufactured in the United States of America

FIRST EDITION

CONTENTS

FOREWORD

Ignazio Silone's Novels of Exile

DURING THE SUMMER of 1930 a sick, penniless Italian anti-fascist exile living in Switzerland under an assumed name began to write a novel about the plight of the peasants in his native region of the Abruzzo. "Since, in the doctor's view I had only a short time to live, I wrote hurriedly to construct to the best of my ability that village in which I put the quintessence of myself and the district in which I was born, so that at least I might die among my own people," he wrote much later. It took the author, who adopted the pseudonym Ignazio Silone, two years to find a publisher for *Fontamara*. A small Zurich press published it in German translation, but the book spread with astonishing speed around the world, selling more than a million and a half copies in twenty-seven languages. Appearing on the eve of the Spanish Civil War, when the world was beginning to take sides for or against fascism, the novel had a galvanizing effect on public opinion. Its publication was a central event in Alfred Kazin's memoir, *Starting Out in the Thirties,* and had an equally strong impact on other major critics such as Edmund Wilson, Malcolm Cowley, and Irving Howe. "In the light of *Fontamara,* oppression, misery and injustice took on a luminous quality," Kazin wrote, adding that the book "expressed the necessity of some urgent, personal act of solidarity." The late Italian writer Niccolò Tucci once said that he became an anti-fascist the day he started reading *Fontamara*. "I realized I could not continue the life I was leading," he said. Tucci quit his job in the Italian diplomatic corps and emigrated to the United States. Silone's second novel, *Bread and Wine*, was perhaps an even bigger success, and during World War II the U.S. Army printed its own unauthorized version of the books and distributed them to the Italians when the Allies occupied Italy after 1943.

After the war, Silone acquired another set of readers with a brooding memoir describing his romance and disillusionment with communism that appeared in the volume *The God That Failed*, together with essays by other writers such as Arthur Koestler, Andre Gide, and Richard Wright. Silone had been a youthful leader and founding member of the Italian Communist Party, served on its central committee, and witnessed firsthand the gradual ascendancy of Stalinism during the 1920s. He had the foresight and courage to break with the Party in 1931, before the major show-trials in Moscow, giving up politics for life as a writer. Having opposed fascism from the beginning and broken with communism early on, Silone became — like Orwell, Malraux, and Camus — something of a secular saint, widely revered as a figure of rare intellectual and moral courage.

In recent years, however, troubling evidence has begun to surface in Italy that Silone may have acted as an informant for the Fascist police. These documents in no way diminish the value of his published work, which appeared after he broke off ties with the police. In many ways, they help us understand the turning point of Silone's life — the crisis that led to his decision to abandon active politics for writing. Indeed, his novels, which have often been read simplistically as straightforward calls for social justice and expressions of Christian socialism, now appear more complex and problematic. The best reaction to the "Silone case" should be a return to the reading of Silone's books, which stand as some of the finest political novels of the twentieth century.

Silone once wrote that he had spent his life "writing and rewriting the same book, the single book that every writer has within him that is the image of his soul." Silone's book was essentially the story of his early life and of the political odyssey that led him into and out of communism. He was born in 1900 with the name Secondino Tranquilli, in the small town of Pescina in the southern region of the Abruzzo, an area with a few vast feudal estates and a large number of peasants eking out a subsistence living from a harsh, unforgiving terrain. The town is described in *Fontamara* as "about a hundred shapeless one-story houses, on either side of a long, steep street, battered by the wind and rain." Most of the peasants lived in a single room with their chickens, pigs, and donkeys and the animals' presence was generally welcome, an important source of heat during the winter. "It was, in short, a village like many others, but to those who were born and grew up here, the cosmos," Silone wrote.

Although he was the son of a small landowner, Silone was a precocious rebel who identified with the *cafoni*. As a boy, Silone witnessed an incident in which a local nobleman set his dog on a peasant woman, who was knocked to the ground and left battered. When the peasant had the temerity to take the nobleman to court, no witnesses would testify on her behalf. The woman lost the suit and was stuck with the legal costs. The judge, a family friend of the Tranquillis, explained that, while he regretted the injustice, he had no choice but to follow the facts presented at trial. The episode symbolized the dramatic shortcomings of "liberal" pre-Fascist Italy, in which the formalities of law and democracy were easily manipulated by the established powers.

Silone's father died when he was eleven and his mother was killed in the devastating earthquake that levelled his town and the surrounding area in 1915.

In minutes, the earthquake had reduced aristocrats, landholders, and farmers into mere mortals shivering near the rubble of their former houses. "An earthquake achieves what the law promises but does not in practice maintain — the equality of all men," Silone wrote. He was horrified to see a close relative stealing from an earthquake victim buried in the rubble. In *Bread and Wine*, the novel's hero describes a similar experience: "To grow up requires a whole life, but to become old, one night like that is enough."

To grow up in this corrupt reality and not be compromised by it was intensely difficult, as Silone's novels make clear. A doctor in Silone's area used to say: "People who are born in this district are really out of luck. . . . There's no halfway house; you've got either to be rebel or become an accomplice." The doctor rebelled and became an anarchist, making Tolstoyan speeches to the poor. "His post as panel-doctor was finally taken away from him, and he literally died of hunger," Silone wrote.

Silone also rebelled. At the age of sixteen he and two other boys led a group of peasants in storming the local police station to protest the arrest of three local residents. For twenty-four hours he and his group were the masters of Pescina. Waiting for the inevitable, the arrival of the authorities to restore order, one of the boys suggested: "Couldn't we take advantage of the fact that the whole village is asleep to make socialism?"

Not long afterward, Silone moved to Rome and became a full-time political activist, rising rapidly within the socialist youth movement. In 1921 he was part of the radical wing of the Socialist Party that chose to split off from the more cautious, reformist majority and form the Italian Communist Party, which hoped to create a Bolshevik Revolution in Italy. Instead, Mussolini seized power in 1922. Under the political persecution that followed, the Communists were forced underground and, with many top leaders in prison, the young Silone assumed more and more important responsibilies within the party. He enjoyed so much trust and respect, that the head of the party, Palmiro Togliatti, brought Silone with him to Moscow for a series of high-level meetings at the Kremlin at the height of the power struggle between Stalin and Trotsky.

At these meetings, Silone and Togliatti refused to vote to condemn Trotsky because they were not allowed to examine the evidence. But on returning to Germany, Silone was shocked to read that the executive of the Communist International had unanimously passed the resolution condemning Trotsky.

Disillusioned by the brutal mendacity of communism, which began to appear more and more like "red fascism," Silone began to withdraw from active party politics, claiming severe illness. Indeed, in a state of severe depression, he began psychoanalysis at the Swiss clinic of Carl Jung. It was during this period, in the spring of 1930, that Silone found the way out of his crisis, by beginning the novel *Fontamara*.

In the foreword, he describes the world of his childhood:

> For twenty years I knew the monotony of that sky, circumscribed by the amphitheater of mountains that surround the area like a barrier with no way out: for twenty years I knew the monotony of the earth, the rain, the wind, the snow, the saints' days, the food, the worries, the troubles, and the poverty – the everlasting poverty handed down by fathers who inherited it from grandfathers, in the face of which honest toil had never been of any use. The harshest injustices were of such long standing that they had acquired the naturalness of the rain, the wind, and the snow. The life of men, of the beasts of the field, and of the earth itself seemed enclosed in an immovable ring, held in the viselike grip of the mountains and the changes of the season, welded into an unchanging natural cycle as in a kind of never-ending imprisonment.

What makes *Fontamara* so distinctive, however, is that Silone's lyric evocation of the millennial condition of the southern peasant is alloyed with a rich component of irony and ferocious humor. At one point, for example, he explains the cosmological world of the local peasants:

> At the head of everything is God, the Lord of Heaven. Everyone knows that. Then comes Prince Torlonia, lord of the earth.

Then come Prince Torlonia's guards.
Then come Prince Torlonia's guards' dogs.
Then, nothing at all.
Then, nothing at all.
Then, nothing at all.
Then come the *cafoni*. And that's all.

Silone, however, does not offer a sentimental picture of the *cafoni*, who are often portrayed ironically. Before fascism did away with democracy, the local peasants were happy to sell their votes to a local lawyer, Don Circostanza, known as the Friend of the People, who paid them not only for their own ballots but also for those of their dead relatives who continued to vote decades after their deaths. (As a result, Fontamara acquires a regional reputation for the extraordinary longevity of its people.)

The *cafoni* frequently worsen their own position by wrangling among themselves. At one point, Silone writes that the minute they work themselves out of debt with a good harvest, they spend the proceeds suing one another in petty disputes: "The same never-ending lawsuits are handed down interminably from generation to generation, involving never-ending expense and leaving in their wake an ineradicable trail of rancor and resentment, all to establish the ownership of a thicket of thorns. The thicket may burn down, but the litigation continues more acrimoniously than ever."

Into this world of seemingly timeless misery, fascism arrives, adding a new arrogance and cruelty to the already feudal conditions of the area, removing what few traditional rights the peasants enjoyed.

The action in *Fontamara* begins when, one evening, a man arrives in Fontamara, waving a petition that he insists the people sign. After being assured it is not a new tax and involves paying no money, some of the farmers sign the document. The following day, they discover that much of the water from the stream that feeds their land has been diverted to irrigate the land of Don Carlo Magna, a businessman with close ties to the government in Rome who is taking over the local economy.

When the Fontamarans protest against losing their water, the local lawyer (the Friend of the People) offers to intervene on their behalf and then tricks them by negotiating a compromise in which both Fontamara and Don Carlo Magna receive three-quarters of the water. Ignorant of fractions, the Fontamarans fall for the trick, only to realize in the days that follow that they are still losing most of their water.

The increasingly desperate condition of the *cafoni* forces them into increasingly extreme measures, burning down Don Carlo Magna's warehouse and starting an underground newspaper.

Already in *Fontamara*, however, Silone's revolutionary impulses are beginning to be tempered by a return of religious faith — a theme that becomes increasingly important in his work.

Silone's religion is very much the primitive Christianity he encountered in the Abruzzo, which consists of an elementary solidarity with others. In his autobiographical memoir, *Uscita di Sicurezza* (Emergency Exit), Silone recounts an important lesson he received from his own father when they saw a "small, barefoot, ragged little man" being led off to jail in leg irons. When the young Silone laughed at the man's odd, limping gait, his father reacted with fury, dragging him from the scene by the ear. "Never make fun of a man who's been arrested! Never!" his father said. When the boy asked why, his father replied: "Because he can't defend himself. And because he may be innocent. In any case, because he's unhappy."

The most popular religious figure in the area was Saint Giuseppe da Copertino, a peasant saint always depicted with a large piece of white bread — the unattainable dream of the local *cafoni*. Although poor in Latin, San Giuseppe shows his devotion by performing somersaults in celebration of the Virgin Mary. In *Fontamara*, Silone recounts a local legend: when San Giuseppe ascended to heaven, God encouraged him to ask for anything he wanted.

> But San Giuseppe da Copertino did not dare confess
> what he really wanted. He feared that his immoderate

wish might arouse the Lord to anger. Only after much
insistence on the Lord's part, only after He gave his
word of honor that He would not be angry, did the
saint confess what he most wanted.

"Oh Lord," he said, "a big piece of white bread."

And the Lord was as good as His word and did not
grow angry, but embraced the *cafone* saint, and was
moved and wept with him.

This Abruzzese Christianity, however, often regarded the official Church authorities with as much suspicion as the government authorities, their frequent allies in sharing power. In
Fontamara, Silone tells a fable about the pope's growing closeness
to the Fascist regime after signing the Lateran Treaty of 1929. In
the story, Christ wants to do something for the peasants of the
Abruzzo but when he suggests dividing up the land more equi-
tably the pope objects that this will upset the government. When
Jesus insists the peasants must get something, the pope decides to
give them a plague of lice, so that the peasants' constant itching
will distract them from their hunger.

In *Fontamara*, Silone's Christianity has the righteous anger of
Christ throwing the money-changers out of the temple, railing
against the Pharisees and insisting on the fundamental equality of
humankind. The Christian and revolutionary themes come together at the end of the novel when the main character, Berardo
Viola, allows the police to beat him to death rather than betray a
fellow prisoner, who is trying to organize political opposition to
the regime. While this may seem melodramatic to contemporary
readers, it was hardly so for readers of the 1930s and 1940s: Silone's
own brother, Romolo, died in a Fascist prison in 1932 after having
undergone severe beatings.

Fontamara was written at a time when Silone still hoped for a
popular rebellion against fascism. His next two novels, *Bread and
Wine* (1937), and *The Seed Beneath the Snow* (1941), were written
at a time when fascism appeared to be virtually triumphant. The
main character of both books, Pietro Spina, is a Communist

leader from the Abruzzo, who is an idealized version of Silone. In the two novels, Spina becomes Silone's vehicle for describing his own spiritual journey from international communism to his own anomalous brand of Christian socialism, from which he emerged as "a socialist without a party a Christian with a Church."

At the beginning of *Bread and Wine*, Spina returns to his home region after years as a political exile despite being ill and hunted by the Fascist police. In order to elude arrest, Spina disguises himself as a priest, hiding out in a small village in order to recuperate. The local peasants, whose town is too poor to support a parish, are thrilled to have a priest in their midst. Spina, who resists performing the functions of a priest but must maintain his disguise, is taken as a kind of saint, whose very reluctance is seen as a further sign of saintly humility. And yet, the deception bears fruit: he finds himself growing into his role, entering into the intimate life of the village and acting as a source of comfort in the lives of the peasants. Gradually, he begins to see that the abstract ideology of communism is light years from the concrete, day-to-day troubles of the villagers and from their rather superstitious, primitive form of Christianity.

For example, Spina takes a room in the house of an elderly woman who sees the presence of a priest in her house as protection against the evil eye and consults a sorceress to try to prevent his departure.

The local peasants are a closed, suspicious lot, who, like the ancient Greeks, live in fear that any success they might enjoy could provoke the envy of fate. Spina, disguised as Don Paolo Spada, learns a lesson about envy from a peasant named Magascià.

> "What's the crop looking like?" Magascià asks the man on the donkey.
> "Bad," the man answered.
> "He's expecting a good harvest," Magascià whispered in the priest's ear.
> "Then why did he say the opposite?"
> "To save himself from envy," Magascià explained.

"And what's your crop looking like?" asked the priest.

"Disastrous," he said.

Magascià made the sign of the cross.

"Are you afraid I might envy you?" said Don Paolo.

"Envy's the in air here," Magascià explained.

At the same time, the extreme concreteness of the peasants make them resistant to ideology in general, fascist as well as communist.

There is a wonderful satirical scene in *Bread and Wine*, where the schoolmistress of the town tries to proselytize for the Fascist regime by reading aloud from a newspaper. At a certain point, she reads:

> "We have a leader for whom all the nations of the earth envy us," she read. "Who knows what they would be prepared to pay to have him in their country . . ."
>
> Magascià interrupted. As he disliked generalities, he wanted to know exactly how much other nations would be willing to pay to acquire our leader.
>
> "It's a manner of speaking."
>
> "There's no such thing as manners of speaking in commercial contracts," Magascià objected. "Are they willing to pay for him or not? And if they are willing to pay, what are they offering?"
>
> The schoolmistress repeated angrily that it was merely a manner of speaking.
>
> "So it isn't true that they want to buy him, then," Magascià said. "And if it isn't true why does it say that they want him?"

At another point, the schoolmistress reads an article about how the "rural revolution" has succeeded on all fronts. The peasants are surprised to learn of a revolution that they themselves have supposedly achieved. "What revolution did we make?" they asked. "This term is to be understood in a moral sense," she replies.

When they press her to be more specific, she answers: "The rural revolution has saved the country from the communist menace."
"Who are the communists?" Grascia asked.
"To become a communist you have to trample on the crucifix, spit in Christ's face, and promise to eat meat on Good Friday." Rather than being put off by this description, the peasants are eager to know more about the meat — an unheard luxury among the *cafoni*. "Where do they get the meat from? Do they get it for nothing or do they have to pay for it?" When the schoolmistress is unable to reply, one of the peasants responds: "As usual, you don't know the most important thing."

Part of their resistance to the schoolteacher, however, derives from her being a woman, as one of the peasants explains by quoting a local proverb: "When woman teaches man, children are born hunchbacked."

Spina gradually realizes that his project for organizing a rebellion in the Abruzzo is virtually impossible but finds that he is serving an important role in the village by serving as a priest, albeit a false one. People come to him with their troubles, hoping to be able to confess their sins. Although Spina avoids doing formal confessions, the townspeople unburden themselves just the same and clearly derive relief and spiritual contact from the priest. Thus Spina, who had rejected religion years ago for communism, finds himself drawn back into the religious world of his childhood. Silone later wrote that "Pietro Spina was not a man who sought God but was pursued by God."

While *Bread and Wine*, is Silone's attempt to blend socialism and Christianity, the book has often been read superficially as a simple call to social justice and religious piety. Pietro Spina is seen both as a figure of uncompromising integrity and courage and as a faithful portrait of Silone. The recent revelations of Silone's relationship with the Fascist police during the 1920s show Silone to have been a much more complicated figure and allow us to see how much more complicated the novel is as well. *Bread and Wine* is, among other things, a story of intrigues, betrayals, and disguises. This dimension of the novels comes into sharper relief when seen against the background of the new information that has been emerging in recent years about Silone's life.

Starting in 1997, two Italian historians, Dario Biocca and Mauro Canali, began turning up documents that strongly suggest that Silone acted as an informant for the Fascist police during his years as a Communist leader and before starting his career as a writer. The most important documents are a series of letters Silone appears to have written between 1929 and 1930 to Guido Bellone of Rome police headquarters, the man responsible for investigating subversive groups in Italy. The letters are clearly those of an informant to his police handler, and are signed with the code name Silvestri. The informant's true identity can be deduced from a number of details that are clearly from Silone's life in the late 1920s: his depression, the clinic in Switzerland where he took refuge during his crisis, his disillusionment with communism, the gradual return of his religious faith, and his desire to begin life over as a writer.

Moreover, there are other government documents that explicitly link Silone to Police Commissioner Bellone. A signed letter from 1928 by the chief of the secret police to Mussolini himself states that "the Inspector General of Public Security Commissioner Guido Bellone has received a telegram from Basle from Tranquilli, Secondino [Silone's given name] — one of the Communist leaders — giving notice of his arrival in Italy. The conversation with him could be interesting."

Silone's defenders acknowledge the authenticity of these documents but some have tried to argue that Silone had entered into dialogue with Bellone after Silone's brother, Romolo Tranquilli, was arrested in 1928 on suspicion of taking part in a terrorist bombing and was trying to gain his release.

However, researchers Biocca and Canali have found archival documents attributed to the informant "Silvestri" dating back to 1924, long before the arrest of Silone's brother. One police report, dated October 7, 1924, states "Silvestri has been named the head of the Italian Communist movement for France, Belgium, and Luxemburg, and therefore will be moving to Paris at the beginning of October." Silvestri's cirumstances match Silone's in this period in considerable detail.

Subsequently, other Silone defenders have hypothesized that Silone was a double agent, writing mostly harmless and generic reports while trying to gain information from the police on behalf of the Italian Communist Party. Unfortunately, there is no trace of this in the archives of the Italian Communist Party, and Silone and the other high-level Communists from that time are now dead. Moreover, if there was nothing improper about his relationship with the Fascist police, why did Silone never mention it during his own lifetime?

Furthermore, when reading the full range of documents that have now been published it is difficult to see them all as generic and harmless. In one, for example, the informant tells the police about a group of Communist railway workers who help smuggle party propaganda into Italy. The group was promptly dismantled. Silvestri also provided detailed information about the people who acted as go-betweens for those sending money to Communists from abroad, giving names, descriptions, and bank information.

It is also true, however, that Silone, as a member of the Central Committee of the Communist Party, could have given Commissoner Bellone far more information than he did. Silone appears in his final letters like a reluctant informant caught in a trap from which he tries to extricate himself.

For example, in July of 1929 Silvestri writes to Commissioner Bellone:

> You understandably complain about the infrequency of my letters: our relations can remain regular and frequent only if they change their nature and character. At the point I have reached in my moral and intellectual formation, it is physically impossible for me to maintain the same relations with you as ten years ago. . . . The first thing to eliminate, because it leaves me either indifferent or humilated, is money. But we can speak about that in person with greater ease.

The arrest of Silone's brother must have made Silone's position unbearable. On the one hand, Romolo Tranquilli, emulating his older brother, was sacrificing himself for a Communist cause in which Silone no longer believed and, in fact, was actively betraying. At the same time, Silone must have been reluctant to sever all ties with the Fascist police and avoid any possible retribution against his brother.

Then in April of 1930, Silvestri writes an extraordinary letter in which he makes a final break and in which one can clearly hear the voice of the mature Silone:

> My health is terrible but the cause is moral. . . . I find myself in an extremely painful point in my existence. A sense of morality, which has always been strong in me, now overwhelms me completely; it does not permit me to sleep, eat, or have a minute's rest. I am at a crossroads in my life, and there is only one way out: I must abandon militant politics completely (I shall look for some kind of intellectual activity). The only other solution is death. Continuing to live in a state of ambiguity has become impossible, is impossible. I was born to be an honest landowner in my hometown. Life has thrown me along a course from which I now want to leave. I am conscious of not having done great harm either to my friends or to my country. Within the limits of the possible, I always tried not to do harm. I must say that you, given your position, have always behaved like a gentleman. And so, I write you this last letter with hopes that you will not try to prevent my plan which will be carried out in two phases: first, eliminate from my life all falsity, doubleness, ambiguity, and mystery; second, start a new life, on a new basis, to repair the evil that I have done, to redeem myself, in order to do good for the workers and the peasants (to whom I am bound with every fiber of my heart) and for my country. . . .

If you are a believer, pray to God that he give me the
strength to overcome my remorse, to begin a new life,
and to live it for the good of the workers and of Italy.

Yours,
Silvestri

At first glance, the revelation of Silone as informant seems a
radical negation of everything he stood for as a writer. He once
wrote, "No word and no gesture can be more persuasive than the
life and, if necessary, the death of a man who strives to be free,
loyal, just, sincere, distinterested. A man who shows what a man
can be."

On closer examination, however, the ambiguity of Silone's
own life to some degree helps us to see the considerable ambiguity of his work — one of the elements that has kept it from becoming stale and dated like so much other political fiction. The
hero of *Bread and Wine*, Pietro Spina, although potrayed hero-
ically, is also a man of multiple identities, who, while trying to do
good, deceives virtually everyone he meets. At a certain point,
Spina falls in love with a woman who opens herself to him because she believes him to be a celibate priest. Spina feels guilty
for misleading the woman and, unintentionally, causes her death.

Moreover, the denouement of the novel is Spina's meeting
with a young man from the area who confesses to him about
having been a police informant. It is difficult, under the current
circumstances, not to read this chapter as a kind of indirect confession on Silone's part.

After being arrested and beaten by the police, the young man,
Luigi Murica, is persuaded to give them information. Initially, he
provides only generic reports, but then is pressured by police to
give more detailed information. He compensates for his betrayal
by working even harder than ever, allowing him, for a time, to
function on two levels at the same time. "An insuperable abyss
opened up between my apparent and my secret life," the young
man tells Spina. "Sometimes I managed to forget my secret. . . .
But I was deceiving myself. When my new comrades admired my

courage and my activity they reminded me that in reality I was betraying them."

At various points, Murica tries to extract himself from this hell,
but fails.

> I tried to get away from them and cover my tracks
> several times. . . . Once I moved, but they had no dif-
> ficulty in tracking me down to my new address. For a
> time I tried to quiet my conscience by writing harm-
> less, phony reports that told them nothing. . . . I tried
> to deceive the police by telling them I had left the cell
> because my comrades no longer trusted me. But they
> had other informers who satisfied them of the oppo-
> site. Finally I became obsessed with the idea that my
> situation was irremediable. I felt condemned. There
> was nothing that I could do. It was my destiny.

Spina asks why the young man did not explain the truth to his
comrades. "The truth of the matter was this. Fear of being discovered was stronger in me than remorse. What was I to tell my girl if
my deception were revealed? What would my friends say? That
was the thing that haunted me. I feared for my threatened reputation, not for the wrong that I was doing."

Eventually, Murica can take no more and flees Rome to return to his hometown in the Abruzzo and work beside his father
as a peasant. Here, he confesses to an elderly local priest (a real
priest, not Spina) who helps him recover his inner equilibrium.
"He taught me that as long as one is alive, nothing is unre-
deemable," Murica tells Spina. "He explained to me that, though
evil must not of course be loved, nevertheless good is often born
of it, and that perhaps I should never have become a man but for
the infamies and errors through which I had passed."

Certainly this confession sounds very much like an echo of the
final letter Silone writes to Commissioner Bellone, announcing
his plan to "first, eliminate from my life all falsity . . . second, start
a new life . . . to repair the evil that I have done, to redeem myself,
in order to do good."

Interestingly, Spina forgives Murica his betrayal and then shows the ultimate trust in him by revealing his true identity as Pietro Spina, a leader of the party Murica has informed against. Murica honors Spina's trust, and not only does not betray him, but behaves with great courage at the end, sacrificing himself for others.

The Seed Beneath the Snow — Silone's personal favorite among his novels — completes the trilogy written during his years of exile in Switzerland. It picks up Spina's story where it left off at the end of *Bread and Wine*. Having revealed his identity at Murica's funeral, Spina is forced into hiding again, taking refuge in the stable of a local peasant. Rather than proving himself to be a trustworthy friend, the peasant, known as Sciatàp (a corruption of "shutup," one of the few English words Sciatàp recalls from his time in New York), uses Spina to extort money from Spina's grandmother. The grandmother seeks help from her son, Bastiano, Pietro Spina's uncle, who does not want to compromise himself by helping his reckless nephew.

Thus, like *Bread and Wine*, *The Seed Beneath the Snow* is a story of betrayal and redemption. Published in 1941, when Europe appeared to be losing the war against Fascism and Nazism, the redemption in the book is purely spiritual rather than political. Spina's grandmother, while having no interest in Pietro's political ideas, risks everything by hiding and trying to save her fugitive grandson. She works to obtain a pardon from the government, which he refuses to accept, preferring to live like a hunted animal in a stable with a deaf-mute. The friendship he establishes with the mute, Infante, and with other characters, shows Spina that life is worth living even under the worst conditions when the political situation appears lost.

The Seed Beneath the Snow completes the arc of Silone's personal transformation from communism to his own personal brand of Christian socialism. These books are document one of the great epic battles of that century: the clash between communism and fascism. Silone was in a unique position to describe it, having lived intimately inside both worlds and, as his own personal drama makes clear, his struggle to free himself from the grip of these two great totalitarian systems and find a human, ethical, and spiritual space that was independent of them. The fact that this was an intensely and painfully lived personal experience breathes life into these novels and gives them a remarkable currency and freshness even as the politics of the twentieth century acquire the patina of history.

Alexander Stille

FONTAMARA

NOTE

on the Revision of Fontamara

*T*O EXPLAIN THE ORIGIN AND meaning of the changes I made in *Fontamara* on the occasion of its first publication in Italy after the fall of Fascism, I must say something about the relations between me and my books. I identify myself completely with Hugo von Hofmannsthal's claim that writers are a human category for whom writing is more difficult than it is for anyone else. The reason for this becomes plain to me whenever I am on the point of finishing a book. Finishing it seems to me to be an arbitrary and painful act, an act against nature, at any rate my nature. I live in a close communion with the characters in my stories that cannot be broken from one day to the next; I go on thinking about them and letting my imagination play with them, and thus the book goes on living and growing inside me and changing even after it has appeared in the bookshop windows.

Apart from this natural predisposition of mine, additional circumstances were at work in the case of *Fontamara*. I wrote it in 1930 when I was a refugee from the Fascist police in Davos, Switzerland. Since I was there alone, unknown, and living under a false name, writing became my only defense against loneliness and isolation, and since in the doctors' view I had only a short time to live, I wrote hurriedly, in an indescribable state of anxiety and distress, to construct to the best of my ability that village in which I put the quintessence of myself and the district in which I was born, so that at least I might die among my own people.

Later, for better or worse, life gained the upper hand, and one of its surprises was that that desperate refuge in writing became my secret home for the rest of my long exile. Though some critics take a different view, there is no break or rupture between that first book of mine and its successors. The story of Pietro Spina in *Bread and Wine*, of Rocco in *A Handful of Blackberries*, of Andrea in *The Secret of Luca* derive from the Mystery Man who makes his first appearance toward the end of *Fontamara*.

There was no plan behind that, for such persistence is part of my nature. I can say more. If it were in my power to change the mercantile laws of literary society, I might well spend my life perpetually writing and rewriting the same story in the hope of at last understanding it and making it understood, just as in the Middle Ages there were monks who spent their whole lives painting and repainting the Savior's face, always the same face, yet always different.

Thus a number of years later, when I was able to return to my country and had to concern myself with the first edition of *Fontamara* to be produced by an Italian publisher, I was not a little surprised when I reread it. Contrary to what might be supposed, my embarrassment was not the result of comparing the book with the reality that I now once more had before my eyes, but between the 1930 story and the developments it had undergone inside me during all the years in which I had gone on living in it. To return to the painting simile, I retouched the picture here and there. Some characters have become more distinct and others have receded into the background. But they are the same characters and it is the same story.

Ignazio Silone
Rome, 1960

FOREWORD

*T*HE STRANGE EVENTS I AM about to describe took place in the course of a summer at Fontamara.

That was the name I gave to an old and obscure village in the Marsica, north of the reclaimed Lake Fucino in a valley halfway up between the hills and the mountains. Later I discovered that other places in southern Italy were already known by that name, sometimes with minor variations, and, what was more serious, that the strange things that I faithfully record in this book also happened at a number of other places, though not at the same time or in the same sequence. But that did not seem to me to be a good reason for keeping quiet about them. There are plenty of names — Maria, Francesco, Giovanni, Lucia, Antonio, and many others — that are common enough, and the really important things in life, birth, love, pain, and death, are common to everyone, but people do not stop talking about them for that reason.

Well, then, in many ways Fontamara is just like every other rather remote southern Italian village between the plain and the mountains, away from the highways and therefore a little poorer and more abandoned and backward than the rest. But Fontamara also has characteristics of its own. Poor peasants, who make the soil productive and suffer from hunger — fellahin, coolies, peons, muzhiks, *cafoni* — are alike all over the world: they form a nation, a race, a church of their own, but two poor men identical in every respect have never yet been seen.

To anyone going up to Fontamara from the Fucino plain the village stands out against the gray, bleak, arid mountainside as if it were on a flight of steps. The doors and windows of most of the houses are easily visible from below; there are about a hundred shapeless, irregular hovels, nearly all of one floor only, blackened by time and worn by wind and rain and fire, with dilapidated roofs made up of tiles and scrap of all sorts.

Most of them have only a single opening that serves as door, window, and chimney. They generally have dirt floors and unplastered walls; inside, men, women, children, goats, chickens, pigs, and donkeys live, sleep, eat, and procreate their kind, sometimes in the same room. The exceptions are about a dozen houses belonging to small landowners and an old manor house, now empty and almost falling to pieces. The upper part of Fontamara is dominated by a church with a bell tower and a small terraced square reached by a steep street that passes through the whole village and is the only one along which carts can pass. Narrow alleys lead off it, most of them short, steep, and stepped, with roofs nearly touching one another and making it hardly possible to see the sky.

To anyone looking at it from a distance, from the Fucino region, the village looks like a flock of dark sheep and the bell tower looks like the shepherd. In short, it is a village like many others; but to those born and bred there, it is the universe, for it is the scene of universal history — births, deaths, loves, hates, envies, struggles, and despair.

But for the strange events that I am about to describe, there would be no more to say about Fontamara. I spent the first twenty years of my life there, and that is all I should have to say about it.

For twenty years I knew the monotony of that sky, circumscribed by the amphitheater of mountains that surround the area like a barrier with no way out; for twenty years I knew the monotony of the earth, the rain, the wind, the snow, the saints' days, the food, the worries, the troubles, and the poverty — the everlasting poverty handed down by fathers who inherited it from grandfathers, in the face of which honest toil had never been of any use. The harshest injustices were of such long standing that they had acquired the naturalness of the rain, the wind, and the snow. The life of men, of the beasts of the field, and of the earth itself seemed enclosed in an immovable ring, held in the viselike grip of the mountains and the changes of the season, welded into an unchanging natural cycle as in a kind of never-ending imprisonment.

First came the sowing, then the spraying, then the reaping, then the gathering of the grapes. And then? The same thing over again. Sowing, hoeing, pruning, spraying, reaping, the gathering of the grapes. It was always the same song, always the same refrain. Always. Years passed, years added up, the young grew old, the old died, and sowing, hoeing, spraying, reaping, and gathering the grapes went on. And then? Back again to the beginning. Each year was like the previous year, each season like the one before, each generation like its predecessor. It has never occurred to anyone at Fontamara that this ancient way of life might change.

At Fontamara there are only two rungs on the social ladder: the lowest, that of the *cafoni*, which is at ground level, and that of the small landowners, which is just a little higher. The tradesmen are divided between the two: the less impoverished, who have a small shop or a few tools, are a little way up; the rest are at rock bottom. For generations the *cafoni*, the unskilled workers, the day laborers, the poor tradesmen, have suffered incredible privations and sacrifices trying to climb that lowest step of the social ladder, but only rarely have they succeeded. The height of good fortune is to marry a small landowner's daughter. But, if it is borne in mind that there is land around Fontamara where a man can sow a hundredweight of wheat and sometimes not harvest more than a hundredweight, it will be appreciated that it is not uncommon to relapse from the painfully acquired status of small landowner to that of *cafone*.

(I am well aware that in the current usage of my country *cafone* is a term of derision and contempt, but I use it in this book in

the confident belief that when suffering ceases to be shameful in
my country it will be a term of respect, perhaps actually of honor.)

At Fontamara the better-off *cafoni* have a donkey or sometimes
even a mule. In the autumn, after struggling to pay off last year's
debts, they have to borrow to buy the small amount of potatoes,
beans, onions, and corn flour necessary to avoid starving to death
during the winter. Thus for most of them life consists of a heavy
chain of small debts incurred to avoid starvation and the exhausting labor necessary to pay them off. When an exceptionally
good harvest puts some unexpected cash into their pockets, it is
generally spent on lawsuits. At Fontamara there are no two families that are not related. In mountain villages everyone generally
ends up related to everyone else; every family, even the poorest,
has interests that are shared with others, and for lack of wealth it is
poverty that has to be shared. So at Fontamara there's not a family
that does not have some lawsuit pending. In bad years litigation
dies down, of course, but as soon as there's a little cash in hand to
pay the lawyer, it flares up again. The same never-ending lawsuits
are handed down interminably from generation to generation, involving never-ending expense and leaving in their wake an ineradicable trail of rancor and resentment, all to establish the
ownership of a thicket of thorns. The thicket may burn down, but
the litigation continues more acrimoniously than ever.

There has never been any way out. Laying aside twenty *soldi* a
month, thirty *soldi* a month, in summer actually a hundred *soldi* a
month, might result in savings of about thirty lire by autumn. But
they would disappear immediately; there would be interest to be
paid off, or the lawyer or the priest or the pharmacist. Then next
spring the same thing would begin all over again. Twenty *soldi*,
thirty, a hundred a month. And then again back to the beginning.

Down on the plain many things changed, of course — at any
rate, in appearance — but nothing changed at Fontamara. The
villagers watched the changes taking place below as if it were a
play that had nothing to do with them. The mountain land they
had to work was as barren and stony as ever, and there was as little
of it as before, and the climate was still unfavorable. The draining

of Lake Fucino, carried out about eighty years ago, benefited the districts on the plain but not those in the mountains, because it resulted in a marked reduction in temperature throughout the Marsica that actually ruined the traditional crops. The old olive groves were completely destroyed. The vineyards are often affected by disease and the grapes no longer fully ripen. They have to be hurriedly gathered at the end of October to avoid being frozen by the first snowfalls, and the wine they yield is as sour as lemon juice. For the most part those who produce it are condemned to drink it.

Exploitation of the very fertile soil uncovered by the draining of the lake would have largely compensated for this havoc but for the fact that the Fucino basin was subjected to a colonial régime. The great wealth it yields annually enriches a privileged minority of local people while the rest migrate to the capital. For, in addition to a vast expanse of land in the Rome area and the Maremma, the thirty-five thousand acres of the Fucino belong to the so-called princely family of Torlonia, who arrived in Rome at the beginning of the last century in the wake of a French regiment. But that is another story, and to cheer the reader after this description of the sad fate of the people of Fontamara, one day perhaps I shall write an edifying life of the Torlogne family (Torlogne was their original name), which will certainly make much more entertaining reading. The obscure history of Fontamara is that of a monotonous calvary of land-hungry *cafoni* who for generation after generation have sweated blood from dawn to dusk to increase the size of a small plot of barren land and have not succeeded in doing so, while the fate of the Torlognes was the precise opposite. None of them have ever touched the soil, even for pleasure, but their holdings have extended into a lucrative realm of many tens of thousands of acres.

They arrived in Rome in wartime, and speculated on the war. Then they speculated on the peace, and then on the salt monopoly, the troubles of 1848, the war of 1859, the Bourbons of the Kingdom of Naples and their downfall; later they speculated on the House of Savoy, then on the democratic régime, and then on the dictatorship. Thus they gained thousands of millions of lire without taking off their gloves. After 1860 a Torlogne managed to pick up shares cheaply in a Neapolitan-Franco-Spanish finance company that had constructed the outlet for the draining of Lake Fucino but that found itself in difficulties because of the collapse of the Neapolitan kingdom. The king of Naples had granted the company a ninety-year lease on the reclaimed land, but in return for Torlogne's political support of the weak Piedmontese dynasty this was extended to perpetuity and he was given the title of duke and later that of prince. In other words, the Piedmontese dynasty gave him something it did not possess. The Fontamaresi looked on at this performance down in the plain, and in spite of its novelty, they found it natural enough, since it was in harmony with traditional abuses of power. But in the mountains life continued as before.

There was a time when one could escape to America. Before the war, some Fontamaresi actually tempted fate in Argentina and Brazil. But those who managed to accumulate some banknotes between their vest and their shirt (on the side of the heart) and returned to Fontamara in a few years lost their small savings on the parched and barren soil of their native place and relapsed into the old lethargy, preserving like a vision of Paradise lost the memory of a life glimpsed at beyond the sea.

But last year the life of Fontamara, which had been stagnant since time immemorial, was shaken to its foundations by a series of unexpected and incomprehensible events. No publicity was given to them at the time, and it was not till some months later that rumors began to trickle out to other parts of Italy and even abroad, where I, to my misfortune, have been forced to take refuge. Thus Fontamara, a place not even on the map, became the subject of strange conjectures and arguments. I was born and bred in the area and had been away for many years, but that did not prevent me from disbelieving these tales, from regarding the things that were alleged to have happened in Fontamara as imaginary and utterly fantastic, invented out of thin air for questionable motives, like so many other stories, and attributed to that remote spot because that made them more difficult to check. Some attempts I made to get direct news failed. Yet not a single day passed on which I did not return in my imagination to that place that I knew so well, and did not think about it and long to know what had happened to it. And then a strange thing happened. One evening, when I was feeling particularly homesick, to my great surprise I found three *cafoni*, two men and a woman, sitting outside my front door, leaning against it and almost asleep. I recognized them at once as coming from Fontamara. They rose and followed me into the house. I recognized their faces by the light of the lamp. One was a tall, thin old man with a gray, stubbly face; the others were his wife and son. They came in, sat down, and began to talk. Then I recognized their voices, too.

The old man spoke first. Then his wife took up the tale, then the man again and then his wife, and while she was talking, I fell asleep — and this was the most extraordinary phenomenon — without losing the thread of what she was saying: as if her voice came from the deepest depths of my being. When dawn broke and I awoke, the man was talking again.

What they said is in this book.

But, first, two points must be made clear. To the foreign reader, who will be the first to read it, this tale will be in striking contrast to the picturesque vision of southern Italy often conjured up in tourist literature. In some books, of course, southern Italy is a blessed and beautiful land in which the peasants go caroling joyfully to work, echoed prettily by a chorus of country girls dressed in traditional costume, while nightingales trill in the neighboring wood.

But no such marvel has ever happened at Fontamara.

Its people dress like the poor do all over the world. There is no wood at Fontamara. The mountainside is parched and bare — like the greater part of the Apennines, in fact. The birds are few and timid — because of the pitiless way in which they are hunted — and there are certainly no nightingales. There is not even a word for nightingale in the local dialect. The peasants don't sing in chorus, or even alone. They don't sing even when drunk, let alone on their way to work. They don't sing; they swear. They swear to express any strong feeling, whether joy, or anger, or even religious devotion. There is not much imagination even in their swearing. They merely swear by the two or three saints they know, always using the same crude oaths.

In my youth the only person who used to sing in Fontamara was a cobbler, and he knew only one song, and that dated back to the beginning of our first war in Africa and began like this:

> Oh, Baldissera,
> Beware of the blacks . . .

The repetition of this piece of advice every day of the year, from morning to night, delivered in a voice that became more and more lugubrious as the cobbler grew older, in the course of time gave rise to a widespread fear among the young people of Fontamara that General Baldissera, whether from foolhardiness, absence of mind, or sheer negligence, might perhaps end up trusting the blacks after all. Many years later we learned that this had actually happened before we were born, with catastrophic results.

The second point is this: in what language ought I tell this story?

Do not imagine for one moment that the inhabitants of Fontamara talk Italian. To us Italian is a language learned at school, like Latin, French, or Esperanto. To us it is a foreign language, a dead language, a language whose vocabulary and grammar developed without any connection with us or our way of behaving or thinking or expressing ourselves.

Of course, other southern *cafoni* before me have spoken Italian and written it, just as when we go to town we wear shoes and collars and ties. But one glance at us is sufficient to reveal our uneasiness. The Italian language cripples and deforms our thoughts, and cannot help giving them the flavor of a translation. But to express himself a man should not have to translate. If it is true that to be able to express yourself well in school Italian you have first to learn to think in it, the effort that it costs us to talk that kind of Italian obviously means that we can't think in it. In other words, to us that kind of Italian culture is still school culture.

But since I have no other way of communicating what I have

to say (and expressing myself is now an absolute necessity to me), I shall make the best job I can of translating, into the language that we learned at school, what I want everyone to know: the truth about what happened at Fontamara.

Even though we tell the story in a borrowed tongue, the way of telling it will, I think, be our own. That at least is one of the arts of Fontamara. We learned it when we were children, sitting on the doorstep, or around the fireplace in the long nights of winter, or by the hand loom, listening to the old stories to the rhythm of the pedal.

The art of storytelling — the art of putting one word after another, one line after another, one sentence after another, explaining one thing at a time, without allusions or reservations, calling bread bread and wine wine — is just like the ancient art of weaving, the ancient art of putting one thread after another, one color after another, cleanly, neatly, perseveringly, plainly for all to see. First you see the stem of the rose, then the calyx, then the petals. You can see from the beginning that it is going to be a rose, and for that reason townsfolk think our products coarse and crude. But have we ever gone to town and tried to sell them? Have we ever asked townspeople to tell their story in our way? No, we have not.

Let everyone, then, have the right to tell his story in his own way.

Ignazio Silone
Davos (Switzerland)
Summer 1930

I

*O*N THE FIRST OF JUNE last year Fontamara went without electric light for the first time. It remained without electric light on the second, the third, and the fourth of June. So it went on for days and months. In the end we got used to moonlight again. A century had elapsed between the moonlight era and the electric era, a century that included the olive oil age and the paraffin age, but one evening was sufficient to plunge us back from electric light to the light of the moon.

Young people don't know the story, but we old folk know it. All the innovations the Piedmontese brought us southern peasants in the space of seventy years boil down to two: electric light and cigarettes. They took the electric light away again, and as for cigarettes, those who've smoked them may choke for all we care. A pipe has always been good enough for us.

Electric light had come to be accepted as a natural phenomenon at Fontamara, just like moonlight. In the sense that nobody ever paid for it. Nobody had paid for it for many months. What were we to pay for it with? Recently the district collector hadn't even come around delivering the monthly bills and warnings for those who were in arrears. We used the pieces of paper he distributed for domestic purposes. The last time he came around he was lucky to escape with his skin. He was lucky not to be laid out by a bullet on his way out of the village.

He was very careful. He came to Fontamara when the men were at work and only women and children were about. You can never be too careful. He was extremely polite. He would deliver his pieces of paper with an idiotic, conciliatory grin.

"Take one for heaven's sake," he would say, "it won't do you any harm; a bit of paper always comes in handy about the house."

But politeness wasn't enough. One day — not in Fontamara, for he pretty soon gave up setting foot in the place, but down below in our local town — a carter gave him a pretty plain hint that the shot that had been fired had probably been aimed not so much at him, Innocenzo La Legge, personally as at taxes in general. But if the shot had hit its mark, it wouldn't have been the taxes that would have been done away with, but he, Innocenzo La Legge. So he didn't come anymore, and nobody missed him. The idea of starting legal proceedings against the inhabitants of Fontamara he did not consider a practical one.

"There's no doubt that legal proceedings would be highly effective if it were possible to seize and sell lice," he said once. "But even if there were a legal way of doing that, who on earth would buy them?"

The light was to have been cut off on the first of January. Then it was to have been the first of March, and then the first of May. Then people started saying, "It's not going to be cut off, after all. They say the queen's against it. It won't be cut off, you'll see."

On the first of June it was cut off.

The women and children who were at home were the last to notice it. But we men on our way back from work did notice it. Some of us had been at the mill and were coming back by the main road; some had been up near the cemetery and were coming back down the mountainside; some had been at the sandpit and were coming back along the ditch; and others, who had been day laboring, were coming back from all over the place.

As darkness fell and lights went on in the neighboring villages and Fontamara remained in darkness, getting lost in shadow and mist and becoming indistinguishable from the rocks and thickets and dunghills, we immediately realized what had happened. It was a surprise and yet it wasn't.

The children thought it a tremendous joke. Our children don't have many diversions, so when an opportunity comes their way they take full advantage of it — the passing of a motorcyclist, the coupling of two donkeys, or a chimney on fire, for instance.

When we got back we found poor General Baldissera shouting and cursing in the middle of the street. During the summer he used to mend boots until late at night by the light of the street-lamp in front of his house, and now there was no light. A crowd of children had surrounded his table, upset his nails and knives and prizer, his wax and hemp and pieces of leather, and turned his bucket of filthy water over his feet. He was swearing at the top of his voice by all the saints of the neighborhood, and he wanted to know what he'd done at his age, half blind as he was, that he should be deprived of the light of the streetlamp; and what would Queen Margherita have thought of such an outrage?

It was difficult to imagine what she would have thought.

Of course, a lot of women were there, complaining bitterly. There's no point in mentioning names. They were sitting on the ground in front of their houses, feeding their babies or delousing them, or they were busy cooking, and they were lamenting as if someone had died. They wept over the cutting off of the electric light as if their wretchedness was going to be worse in the dark.

Michele Zompa and I stopped at the table that had been put in the street outside Marietta Sorcanera's bar, and then Losurdo arrived with the she-ass he had taken to stud; and then Ponzio Pilato appeared with his sulfur bellows on his back; and then Ranocchio and Sciarappa, who had been hoeing; and the next to turn up were Barletta, Venerdì Santo, Ciro Zironda, Papasisto, and some others who had been to the sandpit; and we all started talking about the electric light and the taxes, the new taxes, the old taxes, the local taxes, and the state taxes, repeating the same

old things because these things don't change. Meanwhile a
stranger had arrived without our noticing it. A stranger with a bicycle. It was difficult to decide who he might be at that time of
day. We consulted one another with our eyes. It was really extraordinary. He wasn't the electric light man, and he wasn't the
man from the district office or the local magistrate's court. He was
a very smart young man. He had a delicate, shaved face and a
little pink mouth, like a cat. The hand with which he held the
handlebar of his bicycle was small and clammy, like the under-
side of a lizard. On one finger he had what looked like a big mon-
signor's ring. Also he wore spats. An extraordinary apparition at
that time of day.

We fell silent. The little popinjay had obviously come to announce a new tax. About that there could be no possible doubt.
Nor could there be any doubt that he was wasting his time. It was
obvious that he had come all this way for nothing, and that his
papers were destined for the same fate as Innocenzo La Legge's.
The only question was: what was there on which another tax
could be put? We racked our brains and exchanged glances, but
no one could think of anything. Could they put a tax on moonlight, perhaps?

Meanwhile the stranger had asked two or three times in that
nanny goat's voice of his if someone could direct him to the house
of the widow of the heroic Sorcanera.

Marietta was there, on the threshold of her bar, obstructing the
door with her pregnancy, her third or fourth since her husband's
death in the war. In addition to a pension he had left her a silver
medal, but probably not the three or four pregnancies. Because of
his glorious death (as it is called), since the war she had frequently
had dealings with persons of consequence. She had several times
been taken to Rome, shown to the authorities, had her photograph
taken, been wined and dined and made to trot past the balconies
of the *palazzi* with hundreds of other widows. But because of her
pregnancies they had stopped sending for her.

"Why don't you marry again?" we asked her. "If you don't like
widowhood, why don't you marry again?"

"Because I'd lose my pension as a hero's widow," she said. "That's the law. So I'm forced to remain a widow."

Some of the men agreed with her and thought she was quite right. But the women hated her.

However that might be, she knew how to deal with persons of consequence. She made the stranger sit at the table. He produced some big sheets of paper and laid them on the table.

At that we looked at one another and our last doubts vanished. There they were on the table (the papers about the new tax). The only question was what the new tax was on.

Meanwhile, the stranger had started talking. We could tell at once he was a townsman. We picked up a few words here and there, but what the new tax was on eluded us completely. Could it be on moonlight, perhaps?

In the meantime it was getting late. There we were, with our tools, our hoes and picks and forks and shovels, the sulfur bellows and Losurdo's she-ass. Some of us went off. Women's voices could be heard calling their husbands to come home. Venerdì Santo, Barletta, and Papasisto went off. Sciarappa and Ranocchio went on listening to the townsman's rigmarole for a little longer, and then they went off too. Losurdo wanted to stay, but the she-ass was tired and persuaded him to go.

That left three of us, including the townsman, who went on talking. Every now and then we looked at one another, but none of us understood — I mean, understood what the new tax was on.

Eventually the man stopped talking. He turned to me — I was nearest to him — held out a white sheet of paper, gave me a pencil, and said, "Sign."

Why should I sign? What had signing got to do with it? I hadn't understood ten words of his whole rigmarole, but even if I had, what was there to sign for? I looked at him calmly and didn't even answer.

The man turned to the *cafone* next to me, put the sheet of paper in front of him, handed him the pencil, and said, "Sign. You'll be doing yourself a service."

He didn't answer either, but looked blankly at the man, as if he

were a tree or a rock. So the man turned to the third *cafone*, put
the sheet of paper in front of him, held out the pencil, and said,
"You sign first. After that, the others will sign, too, you'll see."

He might have been talking to a brick wall. Nobody breathed
a word. But as we hadn't the slightest idea what it was all about,
why should we sign?

So we stood there, staring at him in silence. At that, he lost his
temper, and from his tone of voice we thought he must be insulting us. We waited for him to start telling us about the new tax,
but he went on talking about other things. At one point he took a
small whip that was attached to the frame of his bicycle and
started shaking it at me, nearly touching my face with it.

"Damn you, you dog, you worm," he yelled at me. "Why don't
you speak? Why won't you sign?"

It takes more than that to make me lose my patience, so I told
him we weren't fools, we'd understood perfectly, and all his talk
would never persuade us he hadn't come about a new tax. "So get
a move on and tell us what the tax is," I said, feeling bored.

He looked at me as if I had been talking Hebrew.

"We talk, and we don't understand one another," he said, discouraged. "We talk the same language, and we don't talk the
same language."

That was true, and who doesn't know it? It's hard for a townsman
and a *cafone* to understand each other. When he talked, he was a
townsman; he couldn't help being a townsman, he couldn't talk in
any other way. But we were *cafoni*. We understood everything as *cafoni* — that is, in our own way. I've noticed thousands of times in
my life that townsmen and *cafoni* are two different things. When I
was young, I was in Argentina, on the pampas. I talked to *cafoni* of
all nationalities, from Spaniards to Indians, and we understood one
another as if we were at Fontamara. But there was an Italian
townsman who came to see us on Sundays, sent by the consulate,
and when we talked to him, we didn't understand one another; in
fact, we often understood the opposite of what he was saying. On
our hacienda there was actually a Portuguese deaf-mute, a peon, a
cafone from that part of the world. Well, we understood each other

without talking. But we couldn't make head or tail of what that Italian from the consulate said.

So I wasn't surprised when the stranger started up all over again, explaining that he had not been talking about taxes, that he had nothing whatever to do with taxes, that he had come to Fontamara for a completely different reason, and that there was nothing to pay, absolutely nothing.

By this time it was late and it had got dark, so he started striking matches. He showed us the sheets of paper, one by one. They really were blank. They were not tax demands, which are always black on white. They were completely blank. Something was written at the top of one sheet only. The man lit two matches and showed us what it was. It said: "The undersigned, of their own free will and volition, have given their signatures to the Hon. Pelino in enthusiastic support of what is stated above."

The man assured us that he was the Hon. Pelino.

"Don't you believe me?" he asked me.

"Maybe," I said. "Everyone has a name."

He explained that the sheets of paper, when duly signed, would be sent to the government. He had been given them by his superiors. Identical sheets of paper had been taken to other villages by colleagues of his. They were not especially for Fontamara; they were for all the villages. They constituted, in fact, a petition to the government, a petition for which many signatures were required. It was true that he didn't have the petition with him and didn't know what was in it. It would be written by his superiors. All he had to do was to collect the signatures, and all the peasants had to do was to sign. To each his own duty.

"The time when *cafoni* were ignored and despised is gone forever," he explained. "There are new authorities in office now, who hold the peasants in high esteem and wish to give consideration to their views. So I appeal to you to give me your signatures. Show your appreciation of the honor that the authorities have done you in sending an official here to discover your wishes."

This argument made a certain impression on Marietta, though we were still suspicious. But meanwhile, General Baldissera had turned up and he had heard the last few words.

"Very well," he said, with no more ado (you know what these cobblers are). "If the honorable gentleman assures me that there's nothing to pay, I'll sign first."

He did sign first. Then I signed, though (now I can admit it) I took the precaution of signing my dead father's name. After all, I said to myself, you never can tell, it's better to be on the safe side. Then Ponzio Pilato, who was next to me, signed, and then Zompa and then Marietta. But what about the others? How could their signatures be obtained at that time of night? At that hour it was impossible to go from door to door collecting them. But the Hon. Pelino had an idea. We should dictate to him the names of all the inhabitants of Fontamara and he would register them. And that is what we did. There was a lively argument in one case only, that of Berardo Viola. We tried to explain to the Hon. Pelino that Berardo wouldn't have signed on any account, but his name was put down too.

"We'd better not tell him," Marietta suggested. "It'll be far wiser to tell him nothing whatever about it."

The second sheet was filled with names and the stranger had already struck thirty or forty matches when he noticed something on the table. It seemed to fascinate and horrify him. But there was nothing on the table. He lit a match and examined it carefully. He bent over it and nearly touched it with his nose. Then, pointing a finger at something, he began to shriek at the top of his nanny goat's voice, "What's this? To whom does this filthy thing belong? Who dared put it on the table?"

He was obviously looking for trouble. Nobody answered. General Baldissera prudently went home. The stranger repeated his question four or five times, and struck three matches at the same time to make a better light. Then we saw something on the table — something moving. It was nothing very terrible, but it was something.

Ponzio Pilato got up first, bent over, looked at it, spat on the ground, and said, "It's not mine."

I tried to explain to the stranger that in these parts sheep were the only animals that had to be branded on the back with their owner's name. This was not required in the case of other creatures. But the man's absurd indignation showed no sign of subsiding.

Marietta bent over the table, too, took a prolonged look at the insect, which by this time had reached the middle of the sheet of paper covered with names, took it in the palm of her hand, and threw it into the middle of the street.

"What an extraordinary thing," she exclaimed. "I think it's a new kind. Darker, longer, and with a cross on its back."

This had a strange effect on Michele Zompa — just imagine it, a quiet old man like that. He turned to Marietta and started almost shouting, "What? Did it really have a cross on its back? Was it really a new kind?"

And then he told us a story we already knew, as a matter of fact, though we had forgotten it. In the beginning all the different kinds of animals were created immediately after man, and they included lice, of course, and God decided that a new kind of louse should appear after every big revolution. But to explain his excitement Zompa told us something else.

"Last winter I had a dream," he said. "I told the priest about it, but he forbade me to tell anyone else. But now that it has appeared, if Marietta isn't lying, now that it has appeared, I can speak, perhaps it's actually my duty to speak."

We gathered around the table and Zompa went on, "You remember that after peace was made between the Pope and the government the priest explained to us from the altar that a new age was beginning for the *cafoni*, too. The Pope was going to obtain from Christ many graces that the *cafoni* needed. That night I saw the Pope talking with Jesus in my dream. Jesus said, 'In order to celebrate the conclusion of this peace it would be as well to distribute the land of the Fucino among the *cafoni* who cultivate it, as well as the landless *cafoni* of Fontamara on the mountain.'

"The Pope replied, 'O Lord, Prince Torlonia would not agree to that. And the prince is a good Christian, too.' Jesus said, 'In order to celebrate the conclusion of this peace it would be well to exempt the *cafoni* from the payment of taxes.'

"The Pope replied, 'O Lord, the government would not agree to that. The members of the government are good Christians, too.'

"Jesus said, 'To celebrate this peace it would be well to grant an abundant harvest, above all to the *cafoni* and the small landowners.' The Pope replied, 'O Lord, if the *cafoni* have an abundant harvest, the prices of agricultural produce will fall and that will be the ruin of many merchants; they, too, being good Christians, deserve consideration.' And Jesus was grieved at not being able to do anything for the *cafoni* without doing harm to someone else.

"And so the Pope said, 'O Lord, let us go and see for ourselves. Perhaps it may yet be possible to do something for the peasants that will displease neither Prince Torlonia nor the government nor the rich.'

"So on the night of the Conciliation Christ and the Pope came flying over the Fucino and all the villages of the Marsica. Christ went in front, with a large bag on His shoulders, and behind Him came the Pope, who had permission to take from it whatever might benefit the *cafoni*.

"In every village the Holy Visitors saw the same thing, and what else was there for them to see? The *cafoni* were grumbling, cursing, squabbling, and worrying, not knowing which way to turn for food or clothing. And the Pope was afflicted in his heart at what he saw. So he took from the bag a whole cloud of a new kind of lice and released them over the houses of the poor saying, 'Take them, my beloved children, and scratch yourselves. Thus, in your moments of idleness you will have something to distract your thoughts from sin.'"

That was Michele Zompa's dream. Everyone interprets dreams in his own way, of course. Many people use dreams to play the lottery. Many use them to read the future. All I think them good for is to send you to sleep. But Marietta Sorcanera, who is a pious woman, thought otherwise. Anyway, she burst into tears and said, between her sobs, "Oh, it's true, it's true. Who would there be to keep us from sin if there were no Pope to pray for us? Who would be there to save us from damnation?"

By this time it was late, and we wanted to go home. Suddenly, I felt the whole exhaustion of the day. Why waste more time on all this idle talk? But the Hon. Pelino had his own ideas.

"You're making a laughingstock of me," he shouted, brandishing his riding whip at Zompa and Sorcanera. "You're making a laughingstock of me. You're mocking the authorities. You're mocking the government and the Church."

And he said a lot of other silly things in the same strain that none of us understood.

"The government will put you in your place," he said. "The government will punish you. You'll hear more about this from the authorities."

He'll go on talking, but in the end he'll shut up, we thought to ourselves. He'll have to shut up and let us go home. But he went on. He wouldn't shut up.

"Don't you know that if I denounced you you'd get at least ten years?" he shouted at Michele. "Don't you know there are many spending years in jail for saying things far less harmful and seditious than what you've just said? What world are you living in, man? Do you or do you not know what has been happening in the last few years? Don't you know who's master now?"

He was like an infuriated cockerel. Zompa's pipe had gone out, but he went on sucking it for a bit. Then he spat on the ground and answered patiently.

"Listen," he said. "In town many things happen. In town at least one thing happens every day. They say that every day a newspaper comes out and reports at least one happening. How many happenings does that make at the end of the year? Hundreds and hundreds. And after several years thousands and thousands. How on earth can a poor worm of a *cafone* know about everything that's happened? It's impossible. But things that happen are one thing, the people in command are another. Things change every day, but the authorities are always the same."

"And the hierarchy? What about the hierarchy?" the stranger asked.

At that time we didn't yet know what that strange word meant.

The man had to repeat it over and over again, and explain it in different terms.

Michele patiently explained to him our ideas on the matter.

"At the head of everything is God, the Lord of Heaven. Everyone knows that. Then comes Prince Torlonia, lord of the earth.

"Then come Prince Torlonia's guards.

"Then come Prince Torlonia's guards' dogs.

"Then, nothing at all.

"Then nothing at all.

"Then nothing at all.

"Then come the *cafoni*. And that's all."

"And the authorities, where do they come in?" the stranger exclaimed more angrily than ever.

Ponzio Pilato interrupted to explain that the authorities were divided between the third and fourth categories, according to the pay. The fourth category (that of the dogs) was immense.

The Hon. Pelino rose to his feet. He was quivering with rage. He said, "I promise you you'll hear more of this." He jumped on his bicycle and off he went.

We didn't take any notice of him. We said good night to one another and went off home. But as I groped my way in the dark up the steps of the Vicolo de Sant'Antonio, I heard the sound of stones being thrown and smashing glass. At the top of the steps I made out the shadowy figure of a man whom I recognized at once because of his powerful physique.

"Brà," I called out. "What in heaven's name are you doing?"

"Giovà," Berardo answered, "what's the good of the lamps if there's no light?"

I went home, where my supper was waiting — it was cold by now — and Berardo continued on his rounds.

2

NEXT DAY AT DAWN AN extraordinary thing happened that put the whole of Fontamara in an uproar.

A poor, thin spring rises from beneath a heap of stones at the entrance to Fontamara and forms a puddle. A few paces away, the water burrows into the stony soil and disappears, to reappear later in the form of a more abundant stream at the bottom of the hill. The stream makes a number of bends and then flows in the direction of the Fucino. The *cafoni* of Fontamara have always drawn their water from it, to irrigate the few fields they possess down in the valley, which are the village's meager wealth. Furious quarrels about sharing the water break out every summer. In years of drought these sometimes end in stabbing frays, but the flow of water doesn't increase because of that.

The custom with us at that time of year is for the men to get up early in the morning, at half past three or four, when it's still dark. They drink a glass of wine, load their donkeys, and take the road down to the plain in silence. To avoid wasting time and to get there before the sun is high they eat their breakfast on the way. Breakfast? A crust of bread with an onion or a red pepper or a bit of cheese.

The last Fontamara *cafoni* to go down the hill on June 2 on their way to work met a gang of roadmen who had come from the local town with picks and shovels to divert the wretched stream (so they said) from its course between the fields and vegetable plots it had irrigated since time immemorial and send it in the opposite direction, so that it first skirted some vineyards, and then watered some land that did not belong to Fontamara at all, but to a wealthy landowner from the local town called Don Carlo Magna. He belongs to one of the oldest families in our part of the world, now through his own fault greatly in decline, and he got his nickname Magna because at whatever time of day anyone calls on him and says, "Is Don Carlo at home?" the maid always answers, "Don Carlo *magna*, he's at the table, but you can see madam if you like." And indeed it is the mistress who rules the roost in that household.

For a moment or two we thought the roadmen were getting a rise out of us, which the people of the local town (not all of them, of course, but the usual idlers and loafers) never miss an opportunity of doing. A whole day wouldn't be enough to describe all the tricks they have played on us in the last few years. The most disgraceful hoax of all, the famous story of the donkey and the priest, will give some idea of the kind of thing they did.

There has not been a priest at Fontamara for the past forty years; the parish revenue is not sufficient to support one. So the church is generally open only on great feast days, when a priest comes from the local town to say mass and preach the gospel. Two years ago the people of Fontamara sent a last appeal to the bishop to send us a parish priest. A few days later, contrary to all our expectations, we learned that our prayer had been granted and that we were to prepare to celebrate the priest's arrival. Naturally we did our best to give him a proper reception. We may be poor, but we know how to behave. The church was given a thorough cleaning. The road leading to Fontamara was mended and in some places actually widened. A big triumphal arch was put up on the entrance to the village and decorated with flowers and drapings. The doors of the houses were decorated with green branches. When the great day arrived, the whole village turned out to meet the new priest. After walking for a quarter of an hour we saw a strange-looking crowd coming toward us. There were no priests or representatives of the authorities among them, nothing but strange types and many young hooligans. We went on to meet them in procession, carrying the banner of San Rocco, singing hymns and reciting the rosary. In front walked the elders, among them General Baldissera, who was to make a short speech, and the women and children brought up the rear. When we were near the people from the town, we divided into two ranks along either side of the road to welcome our priest.

General Baldissera went ahead, waving his hat and shouting excitedly, "Blessed be Jesus! Blessed be the Virgin Mary! Blessed be the Church!"

At that moment the strange crowd of townspeople also divided, and the new priest, in the shape of an old donkey, adorned with colored paper to represent sacred vestments, advanced toward us, urged on by kicks and the throwing of stones.

Jokes of that kind are not easily forgotten, even if the town loafers constantly think up new ones. So our first thought was that the diversion of the stream was a practical joke too. After all, it would be the end of everything if men started interfering with the elements created by God, and diverted the course of the sun, the course of the winds, and the course of the waters established by God. It would be like hearing that donkeys were learning to fly, or that Prince Torlonia was no longer a prince, or that *cafoni* were no longer to suffer from hunger — in other words, that the eternal laws of God were no longer to be the laws of God.

But the roadmen without further ado put their hands to their picks and shovels to dig the new streambed. That seemed carrying the joke a little too far. A boy, Papasisto's son, rushed back to Fontamara, telling everyone he met on the way.

"Hurry, hurry, we must tell the *carabinieri*, we must tell the mayor, there's not a moment to lose," he shouted.

There were no idle men in the village. In June there's far too much work in the fields. So the women had to go. Well, you know

what women are like. The sun was high before we even started.
The whole village was in an uproar. Women repeated the news to
each other from one alley to the next; even those who already
knew had it repeated ten times by everyone who passed their
door. But no one moved. As always at that time of day, I was in the
house of poor Elvira, the dyer, whose mother had just died and
whose father had been paralyzed since the accident at the quarry.
I was helping Elvira look after the old man, who was grumbling
and cursing and, as usual, to his daughter's great distress, kept
saying he wanted to die. When I heard what the roadmen were
doing I refused to believe it. In short, no one would budge. No
one wanted to go. No one "could" go. Some had children who
couldn't be left, others had chickens or a pig or a goat, or had to
do the washing or prepare the sulfur for spraying the vines, or get
the sacks ready for the threshing. As usual, nobody "could" go.
Everyone wanted to mind her own business. But then Marietta
volunteered to go, "because I know how to talk to the authorities,"
and she was joined by another woman, better not to mention her
name, who, although her husband had been in America for ten
years, was pregnant too — it was hard to believe that her husband
could have been responsible for that at such long range.

Michele's wife came to see me and said in a state of great agitation, "Can we allow Fontamara to be represented on a question
affecting the whole village by two women who, with all due respect, are no better than whores?"

"Matalè, you go," Elvira said to me. "We can't allow such a disgrace to the village."

It would have been an affront to us all. So we hurried along to
see Lisabetta Limona and Maria Grazia and persuaded them to
come with us. Maria Grazia persuaded the Ciammaruga woman
to join us, and she persuaded Cannarozzo's daughter, who in turn
persuaded Filomena and the Quaterna woman.

We had all gathered outside the church and were ready to go
when Ponzio Pilato's wife started making a frightful row — because
we hadn't asked her.

"You want to go behind our backs, do you?" she screamed.

"You want to put yourself forward at the expense of all the rest, do you? Do you suppose my husband's land doesn't need water?"

So we had to wait while she got dressed. But instead of hurrying, she went and fetched Filomena Castagna, Recchiuta, Giuditta Scarpone, and the Fornara woman, and persuaded them to come. Old Faustina, whose husband has been in prison for twenty years, wanted to come, too, but we said to her, "What do you want to come for? Your husband has no need of water."

"But supposing they release him?"

"You've been waiting for him for twenty years, and still they don't release him. And even if they did, where would he raise the money to buy back the land?"

"What you really mean is that you don't want to be seen with me," the old woman flung at us, and shut herself up in her house so as not to be seen weeping.

At last about fifteen of us were ready to go, but there was another wait outside Baldissera's shop while Marietta tarted herself up. Eventually she appeared in her Sunday best, wearing a new apron, a coral necklace, and the dead hero's silver medal on her breast. So when at last we left the village, the sun was high and the heat was stifling. At that time of day not even dogs go places if they can help it. The dust was blinding.

When the roadmen saw us approaching, making a clamor and raising a cloud of dust, they were terrified and fled through the vineyards.

When Lisabetta Limona saw this, she decided that we had obtained the desired effect and wanted to turn back, but Marietta, who was wearing her new apron and had curled her hair, said we ought to go on all the same, because the men were not acting on their own initiative, after all, but on orders from the town hall. She knew all about official ways. We started arguing about what to do, and we were just deciding to go back when Marietta cut the argument short.

"If you're frightened, we'll go on alone," she said, meaning herself and the other woman who was in the same state as she; and off the two of them went in the direction of the town.

"We cannot possibly allow Fontamara to be represented by two women who, with all due respect, are two whores," we said to one another, and off we went behind them.

On the road across the plain the heat was like a furnace. The air was almost black. We went on like a flock of sheep with our tongues hanging out. I don't know where some of us got the strength to complain.

We stopped for a short rest in the shade of the cemetery wall. We could see the graves of some *cafoni* who had made money in America. They hadn't made enough money to buy a house and land and live better, but enough to pay for a tomb that put them on a level with the gentry when they were dead. It was stifling even in the shade.

By the time we reached that town it was nearly midday. We were covered in white dust from the road and looked as if we had been to the mill. Our appearance in the town hall square caused quite a panic. Certainly it can't have been reassuring. Shop-keepers came scurrying nervously out of their shops and hurriedly put down their shutters, and some fruit sellers in the middle of the square made off with their baskets on their heads. In a moment windows and balconies were crowded with anxious onlookers. Some terrified clerks appeared at the door of the town hall. Were they expecting us to try to take it by storm? Actually we were ad-vancing on it in a compact group, but without any definite plan of action. Then a rural guard called out from one of the town hall windows, "Don't let them in. They'll fill the place with lice."

That broke the spell, and everyone burst out laughing. All those who a moment before had been frightened out of their wits and were making off — the shopkeepers who had put down their shutters, the fruit sellers who had taken to flight with their bas-kets on their heads — came back and started jeering at us. Dis-concerted, we huddled against the wall just by the town hall door. The rural guard, success going to his head, started telling incredible stories at the top of his voice about the people of Fontamara and their lice. Everyone in the square was now roaring with laughter. A gentleman on a balcony opposite was laughing so much that he was holding his belly with his hands as if to prevent himself from bursting. A watchmaker taking down his shutters again was laughing so much that he was almost weeping. More clerks had appeared at the town hall door and were joined by women who worked there, and they were all laughing noisily.

"Aren't you ashamed of yourself?" I said, without raising my voice, to one of these women who was standing close to me.

"Why should I be?" she answered, laughing.

"Shame to those who laugh while others weep," I tried to explain to her. "Shame to those who laugh in times of misfortune."

But she didn't understand. In any case, we were at a loss what to do. On the way Marietta had kept saying we should leave it to her, but faced with all those laughing people even she was flummoxed. Had it been only the rural guard, it would have been easy to put him in his place, for it hadn't been only on others that he had seen lice when he was a boy. But all those respectable people were there. Also we felt intimidated because we were dirty, sweaty, and covered in dust, and that is not the way to present oneself at the town hall.

A clerk took pity on us and asked, "Whom do you want to see? What do you want?"

Marietta pressed forward and said, "We want to talk to his Worship the mayor."

At this the clerks at the door looked at each other in amazement.

"What is it you want?" some of them asked again.

"To talk to the mayor," four or five of us replied, losing patience.

At this the clerks all burst out laughing again like half-wits. They repeated what we said at the top of their voices.

"Did you hear that? They want to talk to the mayor," they said, and once more laughter spread to the square, the windows, the balconies, and the dining rooms of the neighboring houses. Then, as it was midday, women started calling their husbands from windows and balconies to tell them that the pasta was nearly ready, and the clerks came streaming hurriedly out of the town hall, and one of them shut the door.

Before he left, the clerk who had been least rude to us said, "Do you really want to talk to the mayor? Wait here, then. You may have to wait for some time."

Not till later did we realize the deceitfulness of that remark. At the moment our attention was attracted by a drinking fountain we could see in a corner of the square. What with the dust and the heat of the sun, we were parched. Cabbage leaves, potato peelings, and other kitchen refuse floated on the water in the basin of the fountain; it was like a soup tureen full of soup. As we were all thirsty but everyone couldn't drink at once, a squabble broke out around the fountain about who should drink first. Marietta's claim to priority because she felt faint was not admitted. Eventually, after a great deal of pushing and shoving, a kind of order was established. Several of us drank, and then it was the turn of a girl with a sore on her lip. We wanted her to drink last, but she held on to the tap and wouldn't let go. Then it was Marietta's turn, but the water suddenly gave out. We waited, thinking it a momentary interruption, but the water didn't come back, the fountain was dead. When we turned to go away, a gurgling sound told us that the water had suddenly come back. Then there was another outburst of squabbling, and two girls seized each other by the hair. Eventually order was restored, but the water suddenly gave out again. Again we waited, but it didn't come back. The way it behaved was really extraordinary. Nothing like it had ever happened at the spring at the entrance to Fontamara. On the other side of the square the rural guard and the watchmaker were watching us and laughing.

It may seem stupid of me to waste time telling you this in view of the far graver events that happened later. But I can't get out of my mind that extraordinary business of the water that disappeared in the face of our thirst. What happened was this. Because it didn't come back we moved away, but then it suddenly came back again. And this happened three or four times. When we went back, the water suddenly disappeared, the fountain dried up. But as soon as we moved away, the fountain started gurgling again and cool water flowed abundantly. We were parched, but could not drink. All we could do was look at the water from a distance. As soon as we approached, it gave out again.

After it failed yet again about a dozen *carabinieri* appeared on the scene. They surrounded us and asked us threateningly what we wanted.

"To talk to the mayor," we replied.

And we all shouted our indignation, because derision and threats were now added to injury.

"They want to steal our water."

"It's an unheard-of sacrilege. They ought to be hanged for it."

"We'd rather sacrifice our blood than the water for our land."

"If there's no more justice, we'll see to it ourselves."

"Where's the mayor?"

"The mayor?" the commander of the patrol started shouting. "Don't you know there's no such thing as a mayor any longer? Nowadays the mayor is called the *podestà*."

We didn't care what the head of the district was called, but it must have mattered a great deal to educated people, or the clerks wouldn't have laughed at us so much for asking to see the mayor and the *carabiniere* warrant officer wouldn't have gotten so angry. Educated people are pedantic and get very angry about words.

The warrant officer ordered four *carabinieri* to escort us to the *podestà*. Two walked in front of us and two behind. The strange procession through the streets of the town attracted curious onlookers, and we were derided with shameful words and gestures, because of that special taste that town errand boys have always had for ridiculing *cafoni* from the mountains. To our embarrassment we realized that the Sorcanera woman enjoyed widespread notoriety among them; and to make matters worse, she started answering them back with coarse language of her own. Maria Grazia nearly fainted, and Limona and I had to support her and help her along. "O Jesus," we said, "what sins greater than those of others have we committed that You should punish us like this?" With those *carabinieri*, two in front and two behind, we were like a flock of sheep that had been caught and were being impounded.

"Matalè," Limona said to me, "let's go back to Fontamara, let's go home. Why do we have to put up with this? It's crazy, Matalè."

The *carabinieri* made us cross the main street and then a lot of minor streets that we didn't know. We came to the house of the old mayor, Don Circostanza, but to our great surprise the *carabinieri* went on. We were very surprised to discover that the mayor was no longer Don Circostanza. Then we thought the *carabinieri* were taking us to the house of Don Carlo Magna, but they went straight on without stopping. Soon we were outside the town again, among the kitchen gardens. Clouds of dust rose from the sunbaked road.

"Now the *carabinieri* are making fools of us," we said to one another. "The mayor can't be anyone but Don Circostanza."

Workmen were eating their lunch in the shade of the hedges, and others were resting, with their heads on their folded jackets and their hats over their faces. The *carabinieri* did not conceal their ill humor.

One of them said rudely, "Why did you have to come just at lunchtime? Couldn't you have come later?"

"And what about us?" we replied. "Aren't we human beings too?"

"You're *cafoni*," the man said. "Flesh used to suffering."

"What sins have we committed that are greater than yours? Don't you have mothers and sisters at home? Why do you talk to us like that? Just because we're badly dressed?"

"That's not the reason, but you're *cafoni*, you're used to suffering."

The *carabinieri* took us along a path encumbered with building materials — bricks, lime, beams, and sheets of metal — and it was difficult to advance in a group. We came to the gate of a recently built villa that belonged to a man from Rome known throughout the area, and even at Fontamara, as the Contractor. The villa was adorned with flags and brightly colored paper lanterns as if for a party. Women were busy sweeping and beating carpets in the yard. The *carabinieri* stopped right outside the gate, and not one of us could repress amazement.

"What? Has that brigand been made mayor? That stranger?"

"Since yesterday," one of the *carabinieri* said. "The telegram arrived from Rome yesterday."

"When strange things start happening there's no stopping them," was my comment.

When the Contractor arrived in our part of the world three years before, no one knew who he was or where he was born. He looked like an ordinary traveling salesman and put up at an inn where people passing through stay. He started buying apples in May when they are still on the trees and the *cafoni* need cash. Then he started buying onions, beans, lentils, tomatoes. Everything he bought he sent to Rome. Later he started breeding pigs, and then he went on to horses, too. In short, he ended up being involved in everything — chickens, rabbits, bees, animal skins, roadworks, land, bricks, timber. He was to be seen at all the fairs and markets and his appearance created an uneasiness of a new kind. At first the old landowners regarded him with contempt and refused to have any dealings with him, but one by one he brought them to heel. There wasn't an important deal in which he didn't come out on top. Where could he be getting all that money from? The old landowners' suspicions were aroused and they actually denounced him to the *carabinieri* as a forger, but his banknotes were genuine. In fact, it was discovered that behind him there was a bank that supplied him with the money he needed. This discovery became known even at Fontamara, and for a time there was a great deal of talk about this strange and novel fact, which no one, not even General Baldissera, could understand. It was the first of a series of new and incomprehensible facts with which we were confronted. We knew, partly from our own experience but more from what we had picked up from others, that a bank could be used for keeping money, or sending it back to Italy from America, or changing it into the currency of another country. But what had a bank to do with business? How could a bank be interested in pig breeding, house building, tanning hides, or making bricks? Many strange things followed that strange beginning.

The extraordinary speed with which he grew rich was the talk of the whole neighborhood, and to explain it someone said, "The truth of the matter is that he has discovered America in our part of the world."

"America?" exclaimed those who had been there. "America's a long way away and is quite different."

When this conversation was reported to the Contractor, he said, "America's everywhere. All you need is to have eyes to see it."

"But how comes it that a stranger sees something in the place where we were born that we never saw before he appeared on the scene?"

"America lies in work," he also said, wiping the sweat from his brow.

"But don't we work?" someone asked.

"Those who work hardest are the poorest," he said.

But, leaving talk aside, there was no doubt that this extraordinary man had discovered America in our part of the world. He found a recipe for turning even thorns into gold. Some claimed that he had sold his soul to the devil in exchange for wealth, and they may have been right. In any event, after the *carabiniere* inquiry into his paper money his prestige increased enormously. He represented the bank. He had a big banknote factory behind him. The old landowners started trembling in his presence. In spite of all that, it was inconceivable to us that they should have actually surrendered to him the position of mayor (or *podestà*, which to us was the same thing).

As soon as the women who were sweeping in the courtyard saw us they hurried to fetch Rosalia, his wife. A few moments later she appeared, raging like a fury. She was an elderly woman, dressed in town fashion, with a long, skinny body and a head like a bird of prey.

"Go away! Go away," she began shrieking at us. "What do you want here? Can't we be masters even in our own home? Don't you know there's a luncheon today to celebrate my husband's appointment? No one invited you. Go away! My husband isn't here, and when he comes back, he won't have time to waste on you. If you want to talk to him, go to the brickworks."

"We brought these women here because they want to present a

petition to the mayor," one of the *carabinieri* explained.

"We want justice," Marietta yelled, pushing herself forward. "That's what the authorities are for — justice!"

She was repeating things she had often heard when dealing with the authorities in her capacity as a hero's widow.

"The water was given us by God," she yelled.

The Contractor's wife's vanity was flattered. "My husband's at the brickworks," she informed us.

The *carabinieri* showed us the way to the brickworks and left us. "We've got to go and have our lunch," they said. "We advise you to behave yourselves."

We had a lot of trouble finding our way to the brickyard, where about twenty workmen and some carters were loading bricks. They stopped work and greeted us with cries of astonishment.

"Where do you come from?" they said. "Are you on strike? What strike?"

That showed how unreassuring we must have looked.

"Where's your master?" several of us asked. "We want justice from him."

"Justice? Ha, ha, ha!" the workmen answered with a laugh. "How much is that a pound?" they wanted to know.

"Listen to me," an older workman with a kind voice said. "Listen to me. Go back to Fontamara. You can't argue with the devil."

In any event, the Contractor wasn't there. He had been there, but had left again, the workmen said. He might have gone to the electric sawmill, but probably had already left again. It would be best to look for him at the tannery. But that was a long way away.

We didn't know which way to turn and stood indecisively in the middle of the road. The heat was stifling. We had dust in our eyes; our clothes and hair were filthy and covered with dust; our teeth, mouths, throats, and breasts were full of scorching sand; we were practically unrecognizable. We were parched, famished, and exhausted.

"It's all your fault, damn you, damn you," Lisabetta Limona started yelling at Marietta.

This was the signal for a very painful scene. We split up into squabbling little groups of two or three. Ponzio's wife actually went for me.

"You dragged me here," she yelled. "I didn't want to come, I had plenty to do at home, I've no time to waste gallivanting about the streets of the town."

"Are you going mad?" I replied. "The sun must have gone to your head."

Giuditta and Cannarozzo's daughter grabbed each other by the hair and ended up on the ground. Maria Grazia tried to rescue the Cannarozzo girl, but the Recchiuta woman flung herself on her, and all four ended up on the ground in a cloud of dust. Fortunately the shrieks were worse than the blows that everyone gave and received. In particular, Marietta, caught between Michele's wife and the Limona woman, yelled as if she were being flayed alive, but all she lost was a tuft of hair and her new apron, which was torn to shreds. Some brickyard workers intervened and put an end to the struggle, but not to the exasperation. Heat, thirst, fatigue, humiliation, had reduced us to tears.

"We were wrong to follow that witch," the Limona woman said, pointing to Marietta. "The Contractor has nothing to do with the diversion of the stream. Why did we come here?"

"He's authority," Marietta shouted, "and only authority can decide."

"Let us go and see Don Carlo Magna," said Zompa's wife. "They're diverting the stream to his land, so he's responsible for the outrage."

We resumed our calvary, exhausted and disheartened. Some of us wept. "Why did we have to do this? Why did we have to do this?" several women kept repeating at the top of their voices, like a litany. "Why did we have to do this?"

"We'll get the rest of what's coming to us at home this evening," the Limona woman kept saying. "You'll see what beatings up there'll be when our husbands find out how we've spent the day."

"Did we come here for fun, by any chance?" I pointed out. "We came for the sake of our families, for the sake of the land."

"You'll see what beatings up there'll be," said Lisabetta Limona, and went on wailing.

The gate of Don Carlo Magna's house is as big and wide as that of a church, wide enough to admit carts at harvesttime, and there's a big courtyard paved with cobbles. As we couldn't all go into the house, most of the women waited at the gate and three of us went on. The usual arrogant and suspicious maid opened the door.

"Can we see Don Carlo for a moment?" I asked.

"Don Carlo?" the woman said. "You want to see him now? Have you brought payments in kind? Will you see madam?"

At that moment the lady of the house, Donna Clorinda, appeared. She recognized us immediately.

"Carmè," she said to the maid, "who let these people in?"

"After stealing our water what else do you want?" Zompa's wife exclaimed. "Do you want our wine as well?"

Donna Clorinda didn't and couldn't understand, and she showed us into the big kitchen.

"Don Carlo's in the dining room," she said by way of apology.

Hams, salami, sausages, bladders of lard, thick clusters of sorb apples, garlic, onions, and mushrooms hung from the kitchen ceiling. On the table was half a lamb, still bleeding, and the smell coming from the oven made us feel faint.

"What is it?" the lady of the house said to me harshly. "Did the other vagabonds standing at the gate come with you, too? What has happened?"

Donna Clorinda wore a black dress with a lot of lace on her breast and a kind of black bonnet. Looking her in the face and listening to her voice, you could see why her local nickname was the Crow. She was the real master of the house. She dealt with the tenant farmers, paid the workmen, decided what should be bought and sold. Otherwise, her husband, a weak and timorous man who lived only for having a good time, womanizing and gambling, eating and drinking, would long since have dissipated what remained of the fortune left him by his father, Don Antonio, who in spite of his wealth and advanced years died while guiding a plow. It has been well said that there are those who make money

and those who enjoy it. Don Carlo Magna had married late, and
his wife had been able to save only what was left over from the
shipwreck. His forebears had accumulated vast estates by buying
up at bargain prices properties confiscated from dioceses and
monasteries that good Christians would not dare to touch, but
little of them was left. At one time he had owned nearly the whole
of the Fontamara district, and those of our girls he fancied were
forced to go into service in his house and submit to his whims.
But now all that remained was the land brought by his wife as part
of her dowry, which she had insisted on keeping in her own
name. It was also well known that in return for ruling the roost
she shut one eye to her husband's principal vice, the one that
brought discord and dishonor to a number of *cafone* families. The
standard reply that the maid had given for many years past to
callers who asked for him was a device of her mistress that enabled her to keep an eye on every detail of his affairs.

"Do you want to take our water, too, now?" I said to her.
"Aren't you satisfied with reducing us to poverty? Do you want us
to go out begging for alms?"

"Water is God's to give and to take away," Lisabetta Limona
said. "You can't take water away from land it has always watered.
It's a sacrilege, it's a sin against creation, for which you'll have to
answer to the Almighty on His eternal throne."

By the time we had finished telling her about the water,
Donna Clorinda was as pale as if she were going to faint. Her rigid
jaws betrayed the effort she was making to avoid bursting into
tears of rage.

"That devil," she muttered to herself. "That devil."

She did not mean her husband.

"He really has made a pact with the devil," she said to us. "No
law restrains him. If he stays here a few more years, he'll eat us all
alive, together with our houses, our land, our trees, and our mountains. He'll destroy us all. He and his infernal bank will force us all to
go out begging for alms. And then he'll help himself to our alms."

Thus, to the accompaniment of lamentations and abuse, we
learned that a week previously the famous land belonging to Don

Carlo Magna toward which the Fontamara stream was to be diverted had been bought up cheaply by the Contractor, who would undoubtedly sell it again at a higher price after providing it with irrigation.

"That man really has discovered America in our part of the world," I couldn't help saying. "*Cafoni* have to cross the sea to find America, but that brigand has discovered it here."

"Doesn't the law apply to him, too?" Zompa's wife asked. "Don't God's laws apply to him?"

"God's laws don't apply to the devil," I said, making the sign of the cross.

"Now they've made him *podestà*," Donna Clorinda went on. "The new government is in the hands of a band of brigands. They call themselves bankers and patriots, but they're real brigands, with no respect for the old landowners. Just imagine, it's only a day since that bandit became *podestà*, and two typewriters have already vanished from the town hall. You can take it from me, before a month is out the doors and windows will have vanished too. The road sweepers are paid by the district, but this morning some of them started working as laborers at the brickworks. Roadmen paid out of public funds are digging the ditch that will take water to the land that brigand has robbed my husband of. Do you know the district messenger, Innocenzo La Legge? Well, he has become the Contractor's wife's servant. I met him this morning carrying a big basket of vegetables, walking behind her with lowered head, like a dog. And this is only the beginning. Believe me, at this rate that brigand will devour us all."

All we gathered from this agitated speech was that the day of reckoning had come for the old landowners too. Must I admit that this added a slight flavor of sweetness to all the bitterness? You know what the saying is: he who swallows a sheep later brings up the wool.

"Now the old thieves have someone to rob them," we explained to our fellow villagers waiting outside.

"Do we have to go on looking for the Contractor?" some of them loudly protested. "Is there to be no end to it?"

"If we've counted up to thirty we can count up to thirty-one," said Marietta. "Are we to go home empty-handed after all we've been through?"

So off we went again to the *podestà*'s villa. After all that walking my knees were aching, as they do on Good Friday, when one does the stations of the cross on one's knees without ever getting up. My feet were burning and I was dizzy.

On the way we met La Zappa, a Fontamara goatherd who was looking for the Contractor too. He had been grazing his goats when a rural guard had come and told him to go away, because that bit of pasture was to be plowed by order of the Contractor.

"Does the pasture belong to the Contractor?" the goatherd said with a laugh. "In that case he must own the very air we breathe."

He was not a very bright lad, but that time he was right. The rural guard had probably been pulling his leg. Pasture has always been common to all. That has always been so in our mountains, all the way to Apulia. Every year in May, after the Foggia fair, an endless stream of sheep come to spend the summer in our mountains, and they stay there till October. They say that that was so even before the birth of Christ. So many things have happened since — wars, invasions, struggles between popes and kings — but pasture has always been common to all.

"If the Contractor thinks he can touch pastureland, he must have gone out of his mind," we said. "Either that, or the rural guard was trying to fool the people of Fontamara."

The maid was waiting at the gate of the Contractor's villa. She was frantic.

"The master hasn't come back yet," she wailed. "They've been at the table for half an hour, the lunch party's for him, and he hasn't come back yet."

"We shan't go away till we get satisfaction," we announced.

Some of us sat down on the grassy border of the path and others on a pile of bricks.

The smell of food reached where we were waiting. The maid kept us fully informed about the progress of the meal. Don Circostanza had already proposed a toast. Then came a detailed description of the various dishes. She expressed herself in diminutives: little onions, delicate little sauces, little mushrooms, little potatoes, and delicate little savors and flavors.

The meal must have been nearing its end, because the effects of the wine were already becoming perceptible. Don Circostanza's powerful voice dominated everyone else's. The windows were wide open, and snatches of talk reached us. At one moment a violent argument arose about the Almighty. The opinions of Don Abbacchio, the priest, were diametrically opposed to those of the pharmacist. Someone asked Don Circostanza what he thought.

"The Almighty?" he exclaimed. "But it's obvious. The Almighty is an adjective."

Everyone laughed, peace was restored, and harmony prevailed once more.

Then the drunken voice of Don Abbacchio was heard, intoning as if in church, "In the name of bread, salami, and good white wine. Amen."

An outburst of laughter greeted the priest's sally.

There was a pause, and Don Abbacchio again intoned, "*Ite, missa est.*"

This signaled the end of the meal.

The men, in accordance with the usual practice, began trooping downstairs to relieve themselves in the garden.

Don Abbacchio, fat and puffing, with veins standing out on his neck and with a beatific expression on his purple face and his eyes half closed, was the first. He was so drunk that he could hardly stand, and he relieved himself against a tree, leaning his head against it to prevent himself from falling.

Next came a lawyer, the pharmacist, the tax collector, the post office official, the notary, and others we didn't know. They went and relieved themselves behind a pile of bricks.

Then came the lawyer Don Ciccone, with a young man whom he supported by holding his arm; he was dead drunk, and we saw him collapse onto his knees in his own urine behind the pile of bricks. At that moment the maid, who had been standing beside us keeping a lookout, signaled the Contractor's arrival.

I hurriedly made the sign of the cross and gripped the rosary I had under my apron. He approached, talking animatedly to some workmen; he was in working clothes, with his jacket over his arm, a level in one hand, and a double ruler sticking out of his trouser pocket. His shoes were white with lime and his trousers and shoulders were dirty with chalk and gypsum. Anyone who didn't know him would never have suspected that he was now the richest man in the district and the new mayor. Though he noticed us, he went on arguing with his workmen, shouting at them.

He briefly acknowledged our greeting by touching the brim of his hat with two fingers.

"I've no time to waste," he announced straightaway.

"Nor have we," we answered. "All we want is justice."

"Talk to me about that sort of thing at the town hall, not here," he said.

"You weren't at the town hall," I said, but my voice was trembling.

"No, because I've got no time to waste," he answered angrily. "I like work, not idling."

"You discovered America in our part of the world," I said, clutching my rosary in one hand, "but you mustn't believe that no one ever worked before you did."

Marietta came forward to explain what we wanted, but he ignored her and went on railing at the workmen who were with him.

"If the carter isn't more careful and goes on breaking tiles, I'll give him the fragments as his wages. What? He wants last month's pay? What cheek! Is he afraid I'll run away? Instead of thanking me for giving him work in the middle of a slump. The cement workers don't want to work ten hours a day? They say a ten-hour day is too much? I'm the boss and I work twelve hours a day."

"You may have discovered America in this part of the world," I shouted at him, "but you've no right to take advantage of it, you've no right to think that because we're poor we're lazy."

"Rosalia," he called out in the direction of the villa, and his wife promptly appeared on the balcony. "Rosalia, has the architect brought the plans? What? He hasn't? Does the man think I pay him for filling his belly? Has the station master brought the clearing papers? He hasn't? I'll have the rogue transferred to Calabria. Did the police chief come? You sent him away? Why did you send him away? Because of the luncheon? What luncheon? Oh, you mean the one for my appointment. I'm sorry, I've no time, I can't come, I've got to find the police chief. The guests will be offended? Oh, no, they won't, you can depend on it, they won't be offended. I know them. Give them drink, give them plenty of drink, and they won't be offended. Don't worry, I know them."

His way of behaving and talking was terrifying. We listened openmouthed.

Really, I said to myself, if that brigand stays here another two years he'll lay his hands on everything.

"Wait here, you women," La Zappa called out, and ran after him.

We saw them disappear behind a house that was being built and waited for them to come back. We were dazed, intimidated, and also a bit fascinated.

Meanwhile, the drunken guests had gathered on the balcony of the villa. The most conspicuous was the lawyer Don Circostanza, with his bowler hat, his spongy, porous nose, his huge, protuberant ears, and his belly at the third stage. Lawyers in our part of the world keep a special pair of trousers for banquets, called concertina trousers, or sometimes gentlemen's trousers, because they have three rows of buttons instead of one, so that they can be let out as required. Needless to say, on this occasion they were all at the third stage.

As soon as Don Circostanza saw us, he opened his arms in a broad, expansive gesture of greeting.

"Long live my Fontamaresi," he exclaimed. "What is it? What is the matter? What is troubling you?"

"The donkey's death is the master's sorrow," I replied. "But, if it doesn't disturb your Worship's digestion, we want to appeal for your aid."

Don Circostanza, also known as the Friend of the People, had always made a show of special benevolence for the people of Fontamara; he was our patron and protector, and telling you about him would make a long story in itself. He had always been our defender, but also our ruin. All the lawsuits of the people of Fontamara passed through his hands, and for the past forty years most of the chickens and eggs produced at Fontamara had ended up in his kitchen.

In the old days, when only those who could read and write had the vote, he sent a writing master to Fontamara who taught the *cafoni* how to write their surnames and Christian names. The result was that he always had the unanimous vote of the people of Fontamara, who, being unable to write any other name, could not have voted for anyone else even if they had wanted to. This was followed by a period in which the death of Fontamara males of voting age was notified, not to the town hall, but to Don Circostanza, who contrived to keep them alive on paper and let them vote for him at every election. Whenever this happened, the family of the still-living departed received a gratuity of five lire. Thus the Losurdo family, who had seven of these living dead, were paid thirty-five lire each time, and the Zompa, Papasisto, Viola, and other families who had five were paid twenty-five. We — to cut a long story short — had two dead who were still alive on paper though in reality they were in the cemetery (one son, God rest his soul, was killed in Tripoli and another was killed at the quarry); they, too, voted loyally for Don Circostanza at every election, and we were paid ten lire each time. In the course of the years the number of these living dead mounted up and provided a modest and trouble-free source of revenue for the impoverished people of Fontamara, and furthermore it was the only occasion on which, instead of paying, we were paid.

This advantageous system, as the Friend of the People constantly assured us, was known as democracy, and thanks to the loyal and assured support of our dead, Don Circostanza's democracy triumphed at every election. Though we had sometimes been badly let down by Don Circostanza, who often quietly swindled us for Don Carlo Magna's benefit, we had never had the courage to drop him in favor of another patron, chiefly because he had a hold on us through our dead who, thanks only to his influence, were not completely dead and benefited us every now and then to the extent of five lire a head, which was not wealth, but was better than nothing. One result of this was, among other things, that on paper Fontamara had a number of centenarians that was entirely disproportionate to its size, and for some time this made us celebrated throughout the area. Some attributed it to the water, others to the air, and others again to the simplicity of our diet, not to say our poverty; and, according to Don Circostanza, many prosperous residents in the neighborhood who suffered from gout or liver or stomach troubles were openly envious of our health and longevity. The number of living dead in Don Circostanza's pay grew to such an extent that even when many *cafoni* started voting against him, resenting his barefaced support of our worst exploiter, Don Carlo Magna, he was still assured of a substantial majority.

"The living betray me," Don Circostanza reproached me bitterly, "but the blessed souls of the departed remain faithful to me."

Then, when nobody was expecting it, he suddenly stopped paying us the fee for the service rendered to him by our dead, on the hardly credible pretext that elections had been abolished, and we did not know what to think. We talked about it for months and could not resign ourselves to the situation. How could we admit that all our dear departed had suddenly become useless and were dead completely and forever? Every now and then some poor widow or mother would go to Don Circostanza to claim the five-lire compensation for a dead husband or son. But he refused even to receive them; the mere mention of our living dead made him lose his temper, and he would slam the door in our face. The result was that fewer and fewer Fontamaresi insisted on that ancient privilege. General Baldissera used to say that it was not enough to be in the right if you lacked the education to see that you got it. One day he himself returned to Fontamara in a state of high excitement, claiming that the age of the living dead had returned, or so it had seemed to him, because in the local town he had seen a procession of men in black shirts marching in formation behind little black flags, and both the flags and the men's chests were decorated with skulls and crossbones. "Were they our dead?" Marietta asked, thinking of her dead and the five-lire fee. But General Baldissera had not positively identified any Fontamaresi.

"Long live my Fontamaresi," Don Circostanza called out to us from the balcony of the Contractor's villa.

This reassured us not a little. Hearing his voice, we no longer felt alone. We were so tired and disconsolate that we mistook the old humbug for an angel from heaven.

"The presence of these good women of Fontamara," he said to the gentlemen who were with him on the balcony, "enables us to complete the telegram we have decided to send to the head of the government."

He took a piece of paper from his pocket, changed the wording, and read out at the top of his voice: "Authorities and people, united in fraternal harmony, applaud the appointment of the new *podestà*."

But when we saw that the guests were beginning to say good-bye to Signora Rosalia and were about to leave without taking any notice of us and without waiting for the Contractor to return, we lost patience. We blocked the gateway, determined not to let anyone pass until our case had been heard and we had an assurance that the stream was not to be diverted.

"Thieves, thieves," we yelled. "You should be ashamed to treat poor people like this. We're human beings too. We've been tramping around since this morning without anyone listening to us. God will chastise you. God will punish you."

Two or three of the more impatient spirits started picking up stones and throwing them at a second-floor window. Others, excited by the sound of smashing glass, made for a pile of bricks just by the gate. The drunks who were in the garden on their way out took fright and fled back into the villa, and the maid hurriedly closed the shutters of the other windows. There was a moment of panic among the guests.

"It's revolution," the clerk of the district started shouting. "Send for the police."

But at that moment we heard the Contractor's voice behind us. It was strangely calm.

"What are you doing with my bricks?" he said with a laugh. "Those bricks are mine, and you can't take them even to stone me with. Besides, there's no need to stone me. I'm here to give you all the explanations you want."

We put back the bricks and went into the garden at the Contractor's invitation. We stood on one side and the Contractor and his drunken guests, not all of whom had yet overcome their fear, on the other. The Contractor's calmness took us aback.

"Perhaps he's not a man but a demon," Maria Grazia whispered to me, clutching my arm. "Look at him. Don't you think he's a demon?"

"Perhaps he is," I replied. "Otherwise how could he have discovered America in a place like this? He's not more educated than Don Circostanza, and he doesn't work harder than our men."

"He must be a demon," Maria Grazia repeated, and we hurriedly and surreptitiously made the sign of the cross.

Marietta stepped forward, put her hand on her heart just at the height of the medal, and described in carefully chosen words the rascality of the roadmen who wanted to divert the course of the Fontamara stream.

"It's a sacrilegious act," she said. "We are sure that you gentlemen will see that the roadmen are duly punished for this outrage," she concluded.

"If it were an outrage," the Contractor replied without hesitation, "you can rest assured that I should take appropriate action to deal with it. As long as I am *podestà* there will be no outrages. But I regret that in this instance you are badly informed, there's no question of an outrage." Turning to the clerk of the district, he said, "You explain to them what it is all about."

The secretary of the district, shy, intimidated, and obviously drunk, emerged from the group of guests; he removed his straw hat before beginning to speak.

"There's no question of an outrage," he stammered. "On my word of honor. Under the new government outrages can no longer occur. Outrages? Never. That is a forbidden word. On the contrary, what is taking place is a perfectly legal act; actually it's a favor that the authorities have decided to confer on Fontamara."

He looked around with a smile as he said the word "favor," and then took a sheet of paper from his pocket and went on more rapidly, "Here is a petition bearing the names of all the peasants of Fontamara — in other words, your husbands, all of them, without a single exception. It calls on the government 'in the higher interests of production' to have the stream diverted from land inadequately cultivated by the people of Fontamara to land belonging to the local town 'whose landowners are able to devote more capital to it.' There may be some things you women are unable to understand."

He wanted to go on, but we interrupted. We knew how on the previous evening a certain Hon. Pelino had written down the names of the men of Fontamara on blank sheets of paper.

"Swindlers! Forgers! Cheats!" we started yelling. "You study all the laws only to swindle the poor. That's a phony petition."

The Contractor tried to get a word in, but we wouldn't let him. Our patience was at an end.

"We won't hear any more," we yelled. "We won't hear any more. All your speeches are traps. We've had enough of them. The water's ours and ours it must remain. We'll burn down the villa, as sure as Christ was born."

Our words exactly expressed our state of mind, but it was Don Circostanza who calmed us down.

"These women are right," he began shouting, leaving the others and walking toward us. "They're ten times right, a hundred times right, a thousand times right."

We fell silent. Our confidence was restored. Don Circostanza was defending us, and we knew him to be a great lawyer. His voice caused a truly inexplicable childish emotion in us. Some of us were unable to restrain our tears.

"These women are right," the Friend of the People went on. "I have always defended them and I always shall. What is it that these women really want? What they really want is to be respected."

"That's true," Marietta interrupted, and ran and kissed his hands.

"They want to be respected, and we must respect them," Don Circostanza went on, making a threatening gesture in the direction of the distinguished gathering. "These women deserve our respect. They are not being insolent. They know the law is against them, alas, and they don't want to go against the law. What they want is a friendly agreement with the *podestà*. They are appealing, not to the head of the district, but to the public benefactor, the philanthropist, the man who discovered America in our poor country. Is an agreement possible?"

When Don Circostanza finished his speech on our behalf, we thanked him and some of us kissed his hands in gratitude for his fine words; our compliments made him preen himself. Then various suggestions were made. One was made by Don Abbacchio, another by the notary, and another by the tax collector, but they were all impossible, because they did not take into account the meager amount of water in the stream and the needs of irrigation.

The Contractor said nothing. He let the others do the talking, and smiled, with a cigar that had gone out in a corner of his mouth. It was Don Circostanza who found the solution.

"These women claim that half the stream is not enough to irrigate their land. They want more than half; in any event, that is how I interpret their wishes. So there is only one possible answer. The *podestà* must be left three-quarters of the water of the stream, and the three-quarters of the remainder must be left to the people of Fontamara. Thus both parties will have three-quarters, that is, each will have a little more than half. I appreciate," he went on, "that my proposal will inflict great hardship on the *podestà*, but I appeal to his heart as a philanthropist and public benefactor."

The guests, having recovered from their fear, surrounded the Contractor and implored him to make this sacrifice on our behalf. After a great deal of persuasion he ended up giving in.

A sheet of paper was hurriedly produced. I saw the danger immediately.

"If there's anything to pay, you can count me out of it," I hastened to say.

"There's nothing to pay," the Contractor said at the top of his voice.

"Nothing to pay?" Zompa's wife whispered to me. "If there's nothing to pay, it must be a swindle."

"If you really want to pay, there's nothing to stop you," I pointed out.

"Not if they threaten to put my eyes out," she replied. "But if there's nothing to pay, it must certainly be a swindle."

"Then it would be better if you did pay," I said.

"Not if they put my eyes out," she insisted.

The notary scribbled the terms of the agreement on a piece of paper, and after the Contractor and the secretary of the district had signed it, Don Circostanza added his signature as the representative of the people of Fontamara.

Then we set off for home. Actually, not one of us had understood what the agreement consisted of.

"What luck there was nothing to pay," Marietta kept repeating. "What luck."

3

ON THE DAYS THAT FOLLOWED, an escort of two armed
guards was provided for the roadmen, who went on digging
the channel that was to take part of our water to the land bought
by the Contractor. But exactly how much water?

"You worry about your own affairs and let others compromise
themselves," every woman at Fontamara told her husband. "Don't
get mixed up with the guards and bring ruin to your family."

Everyone waited for others to compromise themselves, and on
the way to work in the morning and on the way home at night
everyone passed by the guards in silence and in fact tried to look
the other way. Thus no one compromised himself. But there
was bitterness in our hearts, and in the evening, sitting on the
threshold of our houses with our soup plates on our knees, we
talked about nothing else. How could we possibly think about
anything else?

"When misfortunes begin, who can stop them?" we said to one
another. "Perhaps the worst is still to come."

We weren't educated enough to understand how the water
could be divided into two parts of three-quarters each. Even the

women who had agreed to the arrangement disagreed about what it actually meant. Some said the water would be shared out equally, others that Fontamara would keep more than half, that is, three-quarters, and Michele Zompa tried to persuade us that the three-quarters referred to the phases of the moon, that is, that the stream would irrigate the land of the people of Fontamara for three phases of the moon and the Contractor's land for the following three phases, and so on indefinitely.

Not one of us was educated enough to solve the problem, because we had been taught little except how to write our names, and we were afraid of consulting some educated person, not wishing to add expense to injury. So every evening, while we ate our supper sitting on the threshold of our houses with our soup plates on our knees, from one end of the alley to the other there was no talk of anything but of this new swindle. The same old theories were trotted out over and over again. That it was a swindle was certain, but exactly what sort of swindle? As usual, one Saturday evening General Baldissera made one of his fiery and extravagant speeches about wickedness striking down the innocent but being overtaken in the end by the infallible sword of justice.

"I'll go myself," he started shouting. "I'll go myself and recall the truth to those who have forgotten it."

However, his ardor never went beyond words, not only because of his age but also because of his timidity. In his youth in Fossa, where he had practiced his cobbler's trade, he had learned manners from an old baron who had gone down in the world and on Sunday afternoons and holidays employed him in the ancient and dignified office of Sunday footman. The job was unpaid, but it was gratifying and not in the least tiring, since it consisted solely of following the baron at a respectful distance on his afternoon walk. The baron had been reduced to extreme poverty and often did not have enough money to buy food, let alone employ a servant; he lived in a corner of his old and dilapidated baronial mansion. His last creditors had long since sold up all the furniture and movable objects, leaving him only a four-poster bed and an armchair. So he was reduced to the most complete solitude and was

looked down on by everyone. But he would never give up his
Sunday afternoon walk, which the honor of his house prevented
him from taking unaccompanied. Many years had passed since
then, but our Baldissera still remembered every detail of what the
decayed nobleman had said and done on every occasion, and
often he actually invented things and attributed them to him, and
those were his best stories. But we let him tell them, because they
were obviously a great comfort to him.

General Baldissera was poor enough himself; perhaps he was
the poorest of all the inhabitants of Fontamara, but it hurt his
pride that this should be known, and he resorted to a variety of
little tricks to conceal the hunger from which he had suffered for
many years. Among other things, he would seize on the most far-
fetched excuses to leave Fontamara on Sundays, and in the
evening he would come back, actually hungrier and more sober
than ever, but with a toothpick between his teeth and reeling
slightly, like someone who has been eating meat and drinking to
the point of tipsiness, wanting to look like a man able to spend
money and satisfy his whims.

In this state of simulated insobriety he would describe in detail
the bold arguments and courageous encounters he had had with
prominent personalities in the local town, most of them creditors
of the dead baron.

"Oh, if only you could have seen me, if only you could
have heard me," he would say, his features transformed by self-
satisfaction.

Two or three of his old friends knew that all this was complete
invention, but we kept the secret to avoid hurting him and de-
priving him of the only pleasure he had in his wretched existence.

The row about the water also brought us the honor of a totally
unexpected visit from Don Abbacchio, the priest. He arrived at
Fontamara one evening, sweating and panting, in a trap drawn by
a fine horse, and he sent for some of the elders among us, desiring
to talk to us about a grave matter.

"You see what sacrifices I make for you?" he said. "I came here
because I have more regard for you than for myself. For heaven's

sake, don't take on the Contractor," he warned us in a voice as grim as when he talked to us about hell in his sermons. "He's a terrible man," he went on. "A demon such as he has never before been seen in our part of the world. Be patient, that is the best course you can adopt. All you can do is pray."

"If he's possessed by a devil, why don't you exorcise him?" old Zompa interrupted.

Don Abbacchio made a gesture of helpless resignation.

"Perhaps he's not just possessed by a devil, perhaps he's a real devil. The Church can do nothing about it. You are too ignorant to understand these mysteries."

"A real devil?" I said.

"Giovà," the priest replied, "perhaps he's Satan himself."

"Then why hasn't he got horns and cloven feet?" I objected.

"Oh, Giovà," the priest said, "that is no longer the practice. Satan is cunning."

The priest's words made a deep impression on us, and this was further increased when Baldovino told us that he had heard from the coachman that the horse and trap used by Don Abbacchio to come to Fontamara actually belonged to the Contractor. We had never before heard of a devil's actually having a priest in his service, and we were too ignorant to understand how such a thing could be possible. So, instead of quarreling with the devil each one of us thought of grabbing for his own benefit and at the expense of everyone else in the village the biggest possible share of the little water that would be left. There were still some weeks to go before irrigation time, but arguments and rows began immediately.

At that time most of us were going to the Fucino for the reaping. We had to get up before dawn and be in the marketplace in Fossa before sunrise and wait for someone to offer us work. I can't tell you how humiliating that was. At one time only the poorest *cafoni* were forced to offer themselves in the public square in that way, but bad times had come for everyone. The land we small landowners had was mortgaged up to the hilt and yielded hardly enough to pay the interest, so in order to survive we, too, had to go and offer ourselves as day laborers. The landlords and big tenant farmers immediately took advantage of the greater supply of labor in the market to reduce the wages, but, however low they were, there were always *cafoni* forced by hunger to accept them; and some actually got to the point of offering to work without the pay being fixed in advance; they were willing to accept anything at all. From the square at Fossa to the Fucino was another six to ten miles, depending on where the work was, and that was on top of the two and a half miles we had walked to Fossa; and the same distance had to be covered again to get home in the evening, so that every night I was completely exhausted and at the end of my tether.

"I'm not getting up tomorrow morning," I would say to my wife. "Matalè, I can't stand on my feet anymore, I want to die."

But at three o'clock next morning as soon as the cock crowed I woke my son, we drank a glass of wine, and off we tramped again behind the donkey.

On the way to the Fucino and on the way back quarrels about the water grew more violent every day. Things began to look serious between me and Pilato, my brother-in-law, as neither of us was willing to sacrifice himself for the other, and both of us went to work accompanied by our sons. When we met, we no longer greeted each other, but the glances we exchanged made it obvious that a quarrel could not be avoided.

Going down to Fossa with my son one morning, we caught up with Pilato just when he was talking to the roadmen.

"Listen, what matters is that you leave enough water for my beans," he was saying. "The others can go to hell."

Whom could he have been referring to except me?

"You'll be in hell first," I shouted, going for him with my billhook.

Berardo Viola and the two guards rushed to intervene, and that day violence was avoided. But for the next few days Berardo came with me to the Fucino to prevent a repetition of the incident. He was able to act as peacemaker in this matter of the water for the simple reason that he no longer had any land, whether irrigated or not, and owned nothing that had to be shared with

other *cafoni*. Several years before he had sold to Don Circostanza
a good plot of land his father had left him to meet the expenses of
a lawsuit and pay for a passage to America. At the time he was
thinking of emigrating and, if things went well for him, never
again returning to Fontamara. He was sickened by the treachery,
as he called it, of a man from Fossa whom he had believed to be
his friend. He had met the man during his military service and
had subsequently shared bread with him on many occasions and
struck up a close friendship with him. He went to his defense in a
brawl that suddenly broke out one day near Fossa and hit several
heads rather hard, after which he returned to Fontamara, feeling
pleased at having done his friend a service without being identified. But this good friend of his got himself out of trouble by
giving his name to the *carabinieri*. Berardo was deeply hurt, and
for some days was uncertain how to retaliate. But, as he basically
liked the man, he decided never to see him again and leave for
some faraway place. Neither his mother's appeals nor our advice
made any difference. "If you have land, why go to America?" we
said to him. "I'm not staying here," he replied. "It stinks here. I
can't breathe here." The only one to encourage him to go was
Don Circostanza. "If you stay here," he kept telling him, "you'll
die in prison." So Berardo sold his land, paid hush money to the
men he had hurt at Fossa, and bought a passage to America with
what remained. But before he left, a new law (that Don Circostanza perhaps already knew about) put a stop to emigration.
And so Berardo had to stay at Fontamara like a dog freed from its
chain that does not know what to do with its liberty and keeps circling desperately around its empty plate.

But no one blamed him for that. How can a peasant resign
himself to the loss of his land? That land had belonged to Berardo's father, and Berardo himself had worked on it since the age
of ten. In our part of the world, and perhaps elsewhere too, the relationship of a peasant to his land is a serious thing, like that between husband and wife. It's a kind of sacrament. It's not enough
to buy land to make it yours. It becomes yours in the course of
years, with toil and sweat, sighs and tears. If you own land, on

stormy nights you don't sleep; even if you're dead tired, you don't
sleep, because you don't know what is happening to your land;
and next morning you rush to go and see. If someone takes your
land, it's always rather as if he were taking away your wife, even if
he pays hard cash for it, and even when a piece of land is sold, it
keeps the name of the former owner for a long time.

So everyone understood Berardo's torment. Maria Rosa, his
mother, seeing how much her son was suffering because of the
useless sacrifice of that land and knowing how violent and impul-
sive he was, asked me one day to go with her to see Don Circostanza. She took him a cockerel and a dozen eggs as a present,
and when she arrived in his presence, she kissed his hand, went
down on her knees in front of him, and implored him to restore
the land to her son, who would pay for it by giving him part of the
produce for a number of years. But Don Circostanza would not
hear of it. He explained that he had bought the land, not to cultivate it, but to exploit the *pozzolana* in the subsoil, and he threatened to call the *carabinieri* if we did not go away. (In fact,
nowadays there is a huge deep pit there in which workmen are
busy with picks and wheelbarrows.) As a conciliatory gesture Don
Circostanza said that, if Berardo wanted a job, he could have one
as a laborer in the pit. But that would have been adding insult to
injury, and we were too discreet even to mention it to him.

That pit, that crater that grew bigger and bigger and deeper
and deeper, smoldered like a volcano in Berardo's breast. "One
day he'll do something crazy," we said. "He'll come to a bad end,
like his grandfather." And poor Maria Rosa, his mother, secretly
arranged a novena to San Giuseppe da Copertino and sold two
sheets to have candles lit in the saint's presence so that her son
might be saved.

But one day, as we learned later, Berardo unexpectedly presented himself at the lawyer's, swept aside the maid, who tried to
send him away on the pretext that her master was out, and
searched for him in every room before finding him hiding, terrified, behind some curtains.

"Sir," he said very calmly (in fact, respectfully, as he later told us), "you have several times assured me that I shall die in prison. Don't you think that the time for me to go there has come?"

The lawyer must have realized that his life was hanging by a thread, but he tried to smile.

"Why are you in such a hurry?" he managed to stammer out.

"Because it would be a unique opportunity to go there with a clear conscience."

"Are you still thinking about that land?" said the lawyer. "Why haven't you tried some other kind of work?"

"Why don't trout fly? And why don't sparrows swim?" Berardo replied. Then he added threateningly, "I'm a *cafone*, and I want land."

"There's another piece of land of a different kind," Don Circostanza then said. "I'm surprised you didn't think of it yourself. Sit down and listen to me. Above Fontamara, in the Serpari district, a grazing ground has formed in a hollow between the rocks. It belongs to the district and is hardly ever used, perhaps by an occasional goat, but that's all. It's good land, and if you're willing to work it, I'll have it assigned to you cheaply."

That was how Don Circostanza extricated himself. The district granted Berardo that piece of uncultivated land in the Serpari district at a very low price, and he had some land of his own again. But clearing it involved backbreaking labor that Berardo had to do early in the morning and late at night as well as on Sundays and holidays, because if he were to buy seed and live with his mother he had to go on day laboring like the other *cafoni*. In the morning when we saddled our donkeys to go to the fields we saw Berardo coming down from the mountain with his mattock on his shoulder, and he would follow behind us; and in the evening, when we had finished our supper and were going back into the house to go to bed, we saw Berardo setting out for the mountain.

"You're killing yourself," we said. "You mustn't abuse your strength, you'll end up killing yourself."

"Either the mountain will kill me or I'll kill the mountain," he replied with a laugh.

"Don't talk like that," Michele Zompa warned him. "You can

act as you please, but don't tempt the mountain with words."

But basically everyone liked Berardo. He had his faults, particularly when he was drunk, but he was honest and genuine and he had been very unfortunate, and for that reason we all hoped he would make good with that piece of land. So on the day he told us he had sown a sack of corn in the Serpari district (where in human memory, nothing had ever been sown before), we rejoiced with him and drank to his health. "I've tamed the old mountain," he said with a smile. Perhaps we rejoiced too soon, or too much; perhaps by so doing we tempted the mountain, as Michele feared.

What happened two months later is well known. True, old people talk of similar happenings in the past, but as everyone believes only what he sees with his own eyes, this was something that we shall not easily forget; and there are some things that are best told briefly, because thinking about them doesn't help. Well, then, it rained for three days in succession, and the rain was not exceptionally heavy; the top of the mountain above Fontamara was wrapped in a big black impenetrable cloud that concealed everything. At dawn on the third day a huge flood of water came down from the mountain in the Serpari direction with a roar like that of an earthquake, as if the mountain were collapsing, carrying away Berardo's field like a starving man emptying a plate of soup. The soil was carried away down to the rock and the little green corn plants were scattered all over the valley. Where the cultivated field had been there was an enormous pit, a kind of crater.

Nowadays those who don't know these things or have forgotten them are often unfair to Berardo, preferring to explain his destiny by recalling that of his grandfather, the famous brigand Viola, the last brigand in our part of the world to be executed by the Piedmontese. But throughout his life Berardo struggled against this destiny, and no misfortune seemed to get him down for long.

But can one win against destiny? The worst of it — and it's a point that must not be overlooked — was that when we saw the flood coming down the mountain that day everyone was terrified but no one seemed surprised, Berardo least of all. We were all in the square in front of the church, and he was in the middle of us.

"Well, that's it. That's it," he said. "Of course, of course," and that was all. His mother was by his side, clinging to his shoulder, overcome with terror, her face ashen like that of a corpse, clinging to him like Mary at the cross; and he looked at the mountain and kept saying, "Well, that's it. That's it. Of course, of course."

According to the very old, who still remembered his grandfather, he had certainly inherited from the latter his great physical strength. He was tall, as sturdy as the trunk of an oak tree, with a short, bull-like neck and a square head, but he had kind eyes; he kept his child's eyes after he grew up. It was incomprehensible — absurd, in fact — that a man as strong as that should have the eyes and the smile of a child.

What ruined him was friendship, as we have already mentioned. To help a friend he would have pawned his shirt. "If he's really going to end up like his grandfather," his mother said, "if he's really going to die on the gallows, it won't be because of money, but because of friendship."

Because of his physical superiority, his influence on the young men of Fontamara easily put that of their fathers in the shade. It would take too long to describe his feats; one of them, the most absurd, will do. One evening he carried a donkey on his back to the top of the bell tower of our church. But generally he used his strength for less amusing purposes. When we heard of some new act of violence, we could always tell if it was Berardo's doing. He left unrequited no wrong that came to us from the local town. In response to the famous occasion when we were sent a donkey instead of a priest, the pipes that take water to Fossa were broken in several places. Another time the concrete mile markers stones along the national highway were smashed over an area of ten miles. Signposts indicating directions and distances for drivers generally did not remain in position for long. And so, when the electric light failed at Fontamara for the first time, Berardo said nothing, but two evenings later all the lamps along the roads connecting the local town with neighboring villages were smashed.

"Don't argue with the authorities," was Berardo Viola's bitter doctrine. "The law is made by townsmen," he explained. "It is applied by judges, who are all townsmen, and it is interpreted by lawyers, who are all townsmen. How can a peasant expect justice?" He had no difficulty in answering those who asked whether it was wrong to argue with employers when they reduced wages. "It's a waste of time," he said. "Day laborers who argue with an employer are wasting their time. The pay will be reduced in any case. An employer is never affected by argument; he acts in accordance with his interests. The only thing that stops him from cutting wages is his realizing that it doesn't always pay him. Why not? It's quite simple. They cut the lads' pay for weeding in the cornfields from seven lire to five. The lads did as I told them. They didn't complain, but instead of moving the weeds, they simply covered them over with soil. The little the employers thought they'd gained by cutting the pay they'll lose ten times over in a few weeks' time when threshing begins. If they cut the threshers' pay, there's no point in protesting or arguing. There isn't just one way of reaping, there are ten ways, and each way corresponds to a different rate of pay. If the pay's good, the yield will be good. If it's bad, the yield will be bad."

If someone asked him whether we shouldn't protest now that the Contractor wanted to rob us of our water, he answered in the same way.

"Set fire to his tannery, and he'll give you back your water without arguing. If he doesn't understand, set fire to his timberyard. And if that isn't sufficient, blow up his brickworks. And if he's a fool and still doesn't understand, burn down his villa at night while he's in bed with Donna Rosalia. That's the only way to get back your water. If you don't do as I say, the day will come when he'll take your daughters and sell them in the marketplace. And I don't blame him, because what are your daughters worth anyway?"

Such was the bitter doctrine of Berardo Viola.

But he argued like that only because he had no land, and the lack of it burned him up inside. He argued like a man with nothing to lose. Others were in a different position. With the loss of his land and his struggle to make both ends meet by doing the

most varied jobs according to the season, working now as day laborer, now as woodcutter, now as charcoal burner, now as bricklayer's laborer, he had descended to a level lower than the other
peasants, and he had no right to expect anyone to imitate him. So
whenever he interfered in our discussions, he only increased the
confusion, and no older man listened to him, even to contradict
him. The only exception was General Baldissera, who took a
point of view diametrically opposed to his and was inclined by nature to useless arguments. But Berardo changed the attitude of all
the young men of Fontamara by his wild talk, and still more by
his example.

Actually so many unemployed young men had never before
been seen. At one time they started going away to look for work as
soon as they were sixteen. Some went to Latium, some to Apulia,
and the more adventurous tried their luck in America. Some left
their fiancée for four, six, or even ten years, the girl swore fidelity,
and they married on his return. Others married the day before
leaving and, after a single night together, stayed away for four, six,
or even ten years and on their return found themselves fathers of
quite big children, sometimes several of different ages. But the
ban on emigration meant that young men were forced to stay at
Fontamara, with the result that work grew scarcer for everyone.
The impossibility of emigrating meant the impossibility of laying
aside the money that would have enabled them to keep the small,
debt-ridden paternal property going, to make the necessary improvements, buy a new donkey to replace an old or dead one, or
buy a bed in order to be able to marry. But, being young, they
didn't give vent to their discontent in grumbling and complaints.
They didn't even show any sign of realizing the harshness of their
lot. Instead, they gathered on their frequent days of leisure, and
under the influence of the one among them who was the oldest in
years but the youngest in sense, they tended to plan to do things
that were entirely without rhyme or reason.

In winter their favorite meeting place was Antonio La
Zappa's shed, where the breath of the goats made the air a little
warmer. Those who went there were Spaventa's son, Della Croce,

Palummo, Raffaele Scarpone, Venerdì Santo, my son, Pilato's son, and a few others, and Berardo would turn up whenever some especially daring act was being organized. No one else was admitted to this society, which the girls of Fontamara called the vice club. The name was more justified than appeared at first sight, because later it became known that acts of indecency took place between these young louts and the goats, and this abomination went on for a long time because, as always happens in such cases, the owners of the goats were the last to hear about it. But those who had entrusted their goats to Antonio La Zappa ended up taking them away, and the vice club broke up. The boys met elsewhere, behind the church or on the ruins of Don Carlo Magna's old mansion, or at Marietta's bar, where they waited for Berardo. If he didn't turn up, it meant a wasted day. They talked or played, but that was merely a way of killing time until his arrival; if he invited them, they followed him openmouthed, without losing a word he said.

But what most surprised us older men was seeing a young fellow like Berardo, who was now nearing thirty, letting himself be looked after by his mother, who was no longer young, and showing no intention of taking a wife.

"There's no woman who can tame him," his mother used to say. "I know him; it was I who made him, after all. He's not a marrying man."

"But he can't stay like that forever," I replied. "A man needs a wife. You ought to talk to him."

"It's not God's will," she replied with sadness and resignation. "That's obvious after what has happened. Otherwise, how do you explain all that water that came down from the mountain?"

"That wasn't the first flood," I replied, "and it won't be the last."

"God intended him to be a brigand," she stubbornly concluded. "That's the Violas' destiny. It's obvious."

That was how old Maria Rosa talked. She spent most of the day, and in summer most of the night as well, on a stone outside the entrance to her home, which was really a cave with brick walls. There she sewed and spun and awaited the return of the son whom she admired and praised in terms not usually heard from mothers. Being unable to boast about his wealth, she thought it natural and inevitable that he should excel at least in misfortune.

"The Violas are not family men," she said, with sadness mingled with pride. "They are not made to sleep between sheets. They are not men who can be satisfied with a single woman. During the nine months that I carried Berardo he kicked me all the time. My belly was black and blue from his kicking."

All this would have been no concern of mine had it not been for Elvira, the daughter of my sister, Nazzarena, who died the year before, may her soul rest in peace. At Fontamara she was regarded as Berardo's girl, though the two had probably never exchanged a word. But when the girl went to church or to the fountain, Berardo grew pale and held his breath at the sight of her, and the way he followed her with his eyes left no doubt about his feelings. And, as it wasn't long before Elvira's friends told her about the intense interest that Berardo took in her, and as she didn't object or change her time or route when she went out, it meant that she did not dislike him. That's all that there was between them. But the people of Fontamara regarded them as betrothed and thought this natural enough, since he was the strongest man and she was the prettiest girl in the whole neighborhood. There may perhaps have been still-prettier girls in town, but no one as pretty as she had been seen in Fontamara for a long time. Apart from that, she was gentle and refined, of medium height, with a sweet, calm face, and no one had ever seen her laugh loudly, or make a noise, or show agitation in public, or weep. She was extremely modest and reserved, like a little Madonna. No one dared swear or use coarse words in her presence. One day when Palummo's son forgot himself, it was only with great difficulty that he was rescued from Berardo's anger. Her friends promptly told her about this, and next day she, who never spoke to a young man in the street, apologized to him when she met him. "It was my fault," she said. On top of this, it was known that she had quite a good dowry: one thousand lire in cash and a complete trousseau, with sheets, pillowcases, tablecloths, nightdresses, blankets, everything to match, a new kneading trough, two walnut chests of drawers, and a double brass bedstead, already bought and paid for. So what was Berardo waiting for?

One day I plucked up courage and mentioned the subject. This was after the flood.

"But how can you expect me to marry a girl with a dowry if I have no land?" he replied with tears in his eyes. "How can you possibly expect me to do such a thing?"

There was so much strain and desperation in his voice that I did not insist. Asking him about Elvira was a certain way of sending him into a rage. On winter evenings, when there was no work to do and the old drank and the young talked to their wives, Berardo would sit up till late at night arguing with General Baldissera about the differences between townsmen and peasants and about the three laws — the priests' law, the employers' law, and the law of custom — banging the table in a way that made Marietta's bar shake but left the old general, a supporter of the "old and unchanging order," completely unmoved. So it could be supposed that Berardo had relinquished all claim to Elvira. But one day the news spread that she had been asked for in marriage by Filippo il Bello, the roadman. Berardo started raging like an infuriated bull. He dashed to the man's house, but he wasn't there. Someone said he must be at the quarry, and he dashed there and surprised him weighing gravel. Without even asking whether it was true that he had proposed to Elvira, he picked him up as if he were a feather and bumped him about a dozen times on a gravel heap, and stopped only when the other workmen intervened.

After that, no other suitor for Elvira's hand presented himself. But Berardo went on avoiding her.

One day my wife complained at length about this to Maria Rosa, and the old woman unexpectedly said, "Let us go and see."

I helped Maria Rosa lock up her cave and we took a shortcut to Elvira's house, a stony, narrow, deep path made long ago by a flood. We went into the big dark room that was paved with cobblestones, and could just make out the chimney at one end and at the other a low bed on which poor old paralyzed Damiano lay.

"Damià," Maria Rosa said to him, after observing him with open disgust, "Damià, who put the evil eye on you?"

Elvira rose on our arrival and lit an oil lamp, and other faces and hands appeared out of the darkness; it is the custom that those who have nothing to do pay visits to houses where someone is seriously ill, and they stay there for hours and hours, sometimes actually for whole days at a time. In the dark corners of the room women were feeding their babies and others were knitting socks, or telling stories about illnesses, misfortunes, and deaths. Meanwhile Elvira had resumed her place beside the bed and was bending over her father, using a long towel to wipe the sweat from his face, the never-ending, inexhaustible river of sweat.

"Damià," Maria Rosa repeated, looking suspiciously at the women visitors one by one, "who put the evil eye on you?"

A woman's voice replied out of the darkness, recalling a dream that Nazzarena, Elvira's mother, God rest her soul, had when Elvira was born. "I give you the most beautiful of my doves," the Virgin Mary had said, "but you and your husband will pay for it with great suffering."

I called Elvira, and she and Maria Rosa and I sat on the threshold so as to be able to talk at ease. This was probably the first opportunity that Maria Rosa had had to observe the girl so closely and admire her sweetness. I saw the old woman's eyes slowly brighten, as if she were making a very pleasant discovery, and then they suddenly moistened with emotion.

"My daughter," she said, taking the girl's hand in both of hers, "I don't know if you know the story of the Violas. Theirs is a strange destiny that no one has yet explained. Berardo's grandfather died on the gallows."

At that, the girl went pale, and her tender hand trembled in the rough woody hand of the old woman.

"That is no reason to despise them, I think," she murmured.

"Berardo's father died in Brazil," the old woman continued. "How he died we never knew. Every month he used to send me money to lay aside with a view to buying a certain piece of land.

In the end I was able to buy it, but after that he did not write again, and then came the notification of his death. But how he died we never knew."

"There's no dishonor in that, it seems to me," Elvira said.

"Berardo has no land," Maria Rosa went on. "He is very strong, his strength is that, not of a man, but of a bull. There has never been a man as strong as he at Fontamara. He is strong enough to lift a donkey on his back and carry it to the top of the bell tower, but he cannot overcome destiny, and his destiny is a sad one."

"Do you think ours is any better?" said Elvira, pointing to her sick father.

"So you love him as much as that?" Maria Rosa exclaimed, as if she were deeply shocked.

Elvira blushed, and her reply was readier than I expected.

"With your permission," she said, "I shall answer that question only if it is put to me by your son."

She said this in such a humble and moving way that Maria Rosa was left with nothing to say.

"She's an extraordinary girl," I said to the old woman on the way home. "And she has a good dowry. She could be Berardo's salvation."

"You mean his ruin," his mother said crossly.

I did not attach any importance to what she said, because she tended by nature to see everything in gloomy colors, but I told the whole story to my husband.

I have never liked interfering in other people's affairs, but Damiano's illness forced me to keep an eye on Elvira, who was my sister Nazzarena's only daughter. So one evening on the way back from the Fucino with Berardo I broached the subject.

"Elvira is nearly twenty-five," I said, "and in our part of the world, that's getting on. Also her father is ill, as you know, and can't help her with her weaving and dyeing. Apart from anything else, she ought to get married to have some help and someone to look after her."

Berardo said nothing.

"If you don't marry her," I concluded, "the girl has a perfect right to marry someone else."

Berardo flared up. "Change the subject," he said in a way that permitted no reply.

Next morning I waited for him in the square, but he didn't turn up. I went to his house to find out whether he was angry with me, and found his old mother in tears.

"Berardo's going mad," she said. "He'll end up like his grandfather. He didn't sleep all night. At two o'clock he got up. 'It's too early for the Fucino,' I said. 'I'm not going to the Fucino,' he said. 'Where are you going?' I said. 'To Cammarese,' he said. 'Why are you going to Cammarese if there's work at the Fucino?' I said. 'Because the pay's better,' he said. 'Since when have you bothered about that?' I said. But he took some bread and an onion and off he went."

The news of his departure spread rapidly and caused great surprise, though a *cafone* who lives by day laboring is under no obligation to remain in his village, even when there's plenty of work, if he can earn more somewhere else. But we were even more surprised when he came back the same evening.

Four or five of us, including Marietta, Baldissera, and old Zompa, were standing in the street, and as it happened, we were talking about him. He must have made up his mind to get himself some land as quickly as possible, we were saying, but how was he to manage that if he earned barely enough to keep himself alive?

"He'll do twice as much work," Marietta said. "He'll find some night work."

"And ruin his health," I said. "All the land he'll get will be a plot in the cemetery."

No one dared suggest he should give up Elvira.

"Wandering around from place to place is no good," old Zompa said. "A tree that's often transplanted doesn't bear much fruit."

Berardo's unexpected reappearance made us suspect for a moment that the news of his departure had been a leg-pull, but then we noticed that he was in his Sunday best and had a bundle under his arm. Why had he come back?

"They think up something new every day," he said. "Now you have to have a passport to go to Rome."

"Why?" Baldissera asked. "Isn't it part of Italy any longer?"

Berardo's story was very confused.

"I was at the station," he said. "I had already bought my ticket when a patrol of *carabinieri* came in and started asking everyone for their papers and the reasons why they were traveling. I told them the truth, which was that I was going to Cammarese to find work. 'Where's your identity card?' they said. 'What identity card?' I said. 'You can't get work without an identity card,' they said. What did they mean by identity card? I could get no clear explanation. They made me get a refund for my ticket and threw me out of the station. So I decided to walk to the next station and take a train from there. As soon as I had bought my ticket, two *carabinieri* turned up and asked me where I was going. I told them I was going to Cammarese to find work. 'Your identity card,' they said. 'What identity card?' I said. 'What have identity cards got to do with it?' 'You can't get work without an identity card,' they said. 'That's the new regulation governing internal migration.' I tried to persuade them I wasn't going to Cammarese for internal migration, but just to find work. But it was no use. 'We have our orders,' they said, 'and we can't allow any workingman going to work in another area to get into a train without an identity card.'

"They saw to it that my fare was refunded and put me out of the station. But I couldn't swallow that story about identity cards. I went into a tavern and struck up a conversation. 'What? You don't know what an identity card is?' a carter said to me. 'During the war we never talked about anything else,' he said. And here I am back again after wasting a whole day."

The person on whom Berardo's story made the biggest impression was General Baldissera, who fumbled among his papers and produced a printed sheet.

"They talk about papers here too," he said in consternation.

Indeed they did. The Federation of Tradesmen and Artisans peremptorily required General Baldissera to provide himself with cobbler's papers.

"Elvira had a letter just like that a few weeks ago too," Marietta said. "Freedom of labor no longer exists. They wrote and said that if she wants to go on exercising the trade of dyeing she must pay a tax and get papers."

Those letters and what had happened to Berardo made us suspect that we were being had.

"What has the government got to do with the cobbler's or the dyer's trades?" I said. "What has the government to do with a *cafone*'s going from one province to another looking for work? Those are private affairs, and the government has other things to worry about. Such interferences with personal liberty are possible only in wartime, but now we are not at war."

"How do you know?" General Baldissera interrupted. "How do you know? How do you know whether we are at peace or at war?"

That question made a big impression on everyone.

"If the government insists on everyone's having papers, it must mean that we're at war," the general continued in lugubrious tones.

"War against whom?" Berardo asked. "How can we be at war without anyone knowing anything about it?"

"How do you know?" said the general. "How can an ignorant, landless *cafone* like you possibly tell? It's the *cafoni* who fight wars but the authorities who declare them. When the last war broke out, did anyone at Fontamara know whom it was against? Pilato insisted it was against Menelik, and Simpliciano said it was against the Turks. Not till much later did we discover it was only against Trento and Trieste. There have been wars that nobody knew whom they were against. A war is such a complicated thing that a *cafone* can't possibly understand it. He sees an infinitesimal part of the war — identity cards, for instance — and that makes a tremendous impression him. Townsmen see more — barracks and munition factories, for instance. The king sees the whole country. Only God sees all."

"Wars and epidemics," old Zompa said, "are government devices to reduce the number of *cafoni*. It's obvious there are too many of us again."

"But are you going to get your papers?" I asked Baldissera, to cut short the discussion.

"Of course," he replied, "but you can rest assured that I shan't pay for them."

So, in spite of our different ways of expressing ourselves, it could be said that basically we were in complete agreement.

That evening there was a great deal more talk about the war, and there wasn't a single household in which it wasn't discussed.

Everyone asked everyone else whom it was against, and nobody knew the answer. General Baldissera, sitting outside Marietta's bar, patiently explained the situation as he saw it to everyone who consulted him, and that made him happy.

"You want to know whom we're at war with? I haven't the slightest idea. The notice doesn't say. All it says is that the papers must be paid for," he said to everyone.

"Pay, pay, always pay," the *cafoni* would comment.

Next day the general bewilderment was increased by the unexpected arrival of Innocenzo La Legge.

There must have been a very grave reason indeed for Innocenzo to have risked another visit to Fontamara, for well-justified apprehension had kept him away for months; he would certainly not have come of his own accord. He had a moment of panic when he got as far as the bar and saw people hurrying toward him from every direction. Marietta offered him a stool just in time to save him from collapsing to the ground.

"Excuse me, excuse me," he started saying in a tiny little trickle of a voice. "Don't be afraid. What is there to be afraid of? You're not afraid of me, are you?"

"Speak up. What's it all about?" said Berardo in a not very encouraging tone of voice.

"Now listen to me," Innocenzo La Legge went on. "Now listen to me. Let me make it perfectly clear from the outset that what I've come about has nothing whatever to do with taxes. I swear by all the saints in heaven that there's nothing whatever to pay. May God strike me blind if it has anything to do with taxes."

There was a short pause, just sufficient to enable God to take stock of the situation. Innocenzo remained in possession of his sight.

"Go on," Berardo said.

"Well, you remember that one evening a warrant officer of the militia came here? A certain Hon. Pelino? You remember? Excellent, excellent. It gives me great pleasure to hear that. Well, the Hon. Pelino made a report to the authorities in which he said that he had noted that Fontamara was a hotbed of enemies of the present government. Don't be alarmed, there's nothing to be afraid of. The Hon. Pelino reported word for word certain speeches made here in his presence against the present government and against the Church. He must certainly have misunderstood what you said, there can be no doubt about that. But the authorities have decided to take certain steps in relation to Fontamara. Nothing serious, I assure you, and there's nothing to pay, there's nothing whatever to pay. The whole thing's a lot of nonsense, the sort of nonsense to which townsmen attach great importance but of which sensible persons, *cafoni*, take no notice at all."

Innocenzo did not know what steps had been decided on in relation to Fontamara. He was merely the district messenger, and all he knew was that he must communicate the decisions of the district to those concerned; that was all he knew or wanted to know. The first decision that it was his duty to communicate was that the ancient curfew law had been reimposed on Fontamara. No one in the village was allowed outdoors after vespers, and everyone must remain at home until dawn.

"And is our pay to be the same?" Berardo asked.

"How does pay come into it?" Innocenzo replied.

"How pay comes into it? If we can't leave home before dawn," Berardo explained, "it means we shan't get to the Fucino, where we work, until just before midday. If we're to get the same pay as before for only a couple of hours' work, hurrah for the curfew law."

"And what about irrigation?" said Pilato. "How are we to regulate the irrigation at night if we have to stay at home?"

For a moment Innocenzo La Legge was nonplussed.

"You haven't understood," he then said, "or if you'll excuse me for saying so, you're pretending not to have understood, just to torment me. Who said that you've got to change your way? You're still *cafoni*, and you can do your work when it suits you. But the

Contractor is now the *podestà*, and you can't prevent him from acting as *podestà*. And I'm the district messenger, and you can't stop me from doing my job. To protect himself against protests and complaints by the other authorities, the Contractor in his capacity as *podestà* has decided that you're to stay at home at night. I, as the district messenger, bring you his orders. You *cafoni* will naturally do as you please."

"And the law? What about the law?" General Baldissera exclaimed indignantly. "Is that how the law is to be treated? Is the law the law, or isn't it?"

"Excuse me," said Innocenzo, "but what time do you go to bed in the evening?"

"As soon as it gets dark," the nearsighted old cobbler replied.

"And what time do you get up in the morning?"

"About ten, because there's so little work and I'm so weak."

"Very well, then," said Innocenzo, "I appoint you to see that the law is observed."

We all burst out laughing, but Baldissera was upset, and as by this time it was nearly dark, he went off home to go to bed.

Innocenzo was delighted at his unexpected success and recovered his self-assurance. He lit a cigarette and began to smoke in a way we had never seen before. Instead of letting the smoke come out of his mouth, he kept his mouth shut and let it out of his nostrils, not out of both at the same time, which was something we could do, but first out of one nostril and then out of the other.

He took advantage of the admiration and surprise that this caused to impart to us the *podestà*'s second decision concerning Fontamara. This was that a notice must be put up in all public places saying:

POLITICAL DISCUSSION
FORBIDDEN HERE

The only public place in Fontamara was Marietta's bar. Innocenzo handed her an order signed by the *podestà* informing her that if political discussion took place in her bar she would be held responsible.

"But no one in Fontamara even knows what politics are," Marietta correctly pointed out. "No one has ever talked politics in my bar."

"Then what is it that you talk about that causes the Hon. Pelino to go back to town in such a fury?" Innocenzo asked with a smile.

"Oh, we talk about all sorts of things," Marietta explained. "Prices, wages, taxes, and laws; today we talked about identity papers, the war, and internal migration."

"Those are the things that according to the *podestà*'s order you're not allowed to talk about any longer," Innocenzo said. "That doesn't apply only to Fontamara; the same order has been distributed all over Italy. Taxes, wages, prices, and laws may no longer be discussed in public places."

"So we're not allowed to argue about anything at all," Berardo concluded.

"Exactly, Berardo, you've understood perfectly," Innocenzo said with satisfaction. "All argument is prohibited; that is the meaning of the *podestà*'s decision. There must be no more argument, it must be eliminated. What good does it do, after all? Can a hungry man live on argument? It's useless, and must be done away with."

When Berardo agreed with him, Innocenzo was so delighted that he accepted his proposal that the notice to be put on the wall should be corrected in the interests of clarity, and he himself wrote out in our presence on a large piece of white paper the following amended wording:

ALL ARGUMENT STRICTLY
PROHIBITED
by Order of the Podestà

Berardo supervised the placing of this notice high up on the wall outside the bar. His compliance astonished us. As if his attitude were not sufficiently clear, he added, "Anyone who touches that notice had better look out."

Innocenzo shook his hand and wanted to embrace him. But his enthusiasm was somewhat diminished when Berardo went on,

"What the *podestà* has now ordered is what I've always said. My principle has always been that you don't argue with an employer. All the *cafoni's* troubles come from arguing. A *cafone* is a donkey, a donkey that argues, and that's why our life is a hundred times worse than that of real donkeys, which don't argue (or at any rate pretend not to). A donkey will carry a load of one hundred fifty, or two hundred, or two hundred twenty pounds; it won't argue, but won't carry any more. A donkey requires a certain amount of straw, but doesn't argue. You can't get from it what you can get from a cow or a goat or a horse. No amount of talk or argument will move it, it just doesn't understand (or pretends not to understand). But a *cafone* argues. A *cafone* can be persuaded. He can be persuaded to go without food, he can be persuaded to give his life for his master, he can be persuaded to go to war, he can be persuaded that in the next world there's a place called hell, though he has never seen it. You only have to look about you to see the consequences."

What Berardo said was not new to us, but it terrified Innocenzo La Legge.

"Your donkey won't put up with missing its meals," Berardo went on. "It says, 'If I get my food, I work; otherwise I don't work.' Or rather it doesn't actually say anything of the sort, because that would be arguing; it just naturally acts that way. Just imagine what would happen if the eight thousand peasants who cultivate the Fucino, instead of being donkeys that argue — in other words, donkeys that can be tamed and persuaded, that is, made to fear the *carabinieri*, the priests, and the judges — just suppose they were completely unreasoning beasts of burden. Prince Torlonia would have to beg for his living. That was a nice dark road you came along, my good Innocenzo, and very soon you'll be going home the same way. What prevents us from bumping you off? Answer me that."

Innocenzo tried to stammer something in reply, but couldn't. He looked as pale as death.

"What might stop us," Berardo went on, "is an argument about the possible consequences of murder. But you, Innocenzo, wrote in your own hand on that piece of paper that henceforth all argument is prohibited by order of the *podestà*. You have yourself broken the thread on which your safety depended."

"Just a moment," Innocenzo managed to stammer out. "Just a moment. You say you're against argument, but it seems to me, if you'll allow me to say so, that you argue only too much. All you've been saying was nothing but an argument. I've never heard a donkey — I mean, an unreasoning *cafone* talk like that."

"If arguments favor only the employers and the authorities," I asked Berardo, "why has the *podestà* decided to prohibit all argument?"

Berardo remained silent for a moment. Then he said, "It's late, I've got to get up at three in the morning to go to the Fucino. Good night."

And off he went.

That was how arguments with him always ended. He would make long speeches, go on ranting for hours like a preacher, saying the most absurd and violent things that came into his head in a tone that permitted no reply, and then, when he had finished, someone would ask him a question, and he would be embarrassed and go away without answering.

That night Innocenzo La Legge stayed at Fontamara. Perhaps because of Berardo's threats, perhaps because of a sudden indisposition, he preferred to spend the night at Marietta's bar. I must say that this was not the first time that it happened. In fact, it happened so often that we said, "They could get married. Why don't they get married?"

"If I marry again," Marietta explained, "I lose my war widow's pension. That's the law."

Some men thought she was quite right, but the women disagreed.

4

OWARD THE END OF JUNE the news spread that representatives of the *cafoni* of the Marsica were to be summoned
to a big meeting at Avezzano to hear the decisions on the Fucino
question made by the new government in Rome.

The news was brought us by Berardo, and you could tell by his
eyes how hopeful it made him. We talked about it a great deal,
and it made a great impression on us, because previous governments had never admitted that there was such a thing as the Fucino question, and ever since elections had been abolished, Don
Circostanza, who had used to talk about it a great deal, had forgotten its existence. There was no doubt that there was a new government in Rome, because we had heard it being talked about for
some time. This might also have been confirmation that there
had been or was going to be a war, because only war can get rid of
old rulers and establish new ones; thus in our part of the world, as
old people tell, the Bourbons took over from the Spaniards and
the Piedmontese from the Bourbons. But no one at Fontamara
yet knew where the new government came from or what nation-
ality it was.

All a poor *cafone* can do when faced with a new government is to say, "May the Lord have mercy on us." It's the same as when big clouds gather on the horizon in summer; it doesn't depend on the *cafoni* but on God Almighty whether they bring rain or hail. But it seemed strange that a representative of the new government should want to talk to us on familiar terms. We were rather incredulous, but General Baldissera was not.

"We're going back to the old days," he explained, "when there were none of the present-day barracks and prefectures and sub-prefectures between the royal palace and the humble homes of the *cafoni*, and once every year the rulers disguised themselves as paupers and went to the fairs to listen to the grievances of the poor. But now, if what they say is true, we are returning to the old ways, which should never have been abandoned."

Michele Zompa was just as optimistic, but for different reasons. "A government based on elections is always in awe of the rich who manage the elections," he said, "while a one-man government can overawe the rich. Can there be jealousy or competition between a ruler and a *cafone*? That's an absurd idea. But there can easily be jealousy between a king and a Prince Torlonia."

The hope that in a redivision of the land of the Fucino he might at last get some for himself kept Berardo from contradicting the ideas of others, as was normally his bad habit.

"Every government always consists of thieves," he argued. "But if a government consists of a single thief instead of five hundred, it's better for the *cafoni*, of course, because the appetite of a big thief, however big it may be, will always be less than that of five hundred small and hungry thieves. If they're going to share out the Fucino land again, Fontamara must insist on its rights."

This possibility, which seemed quite near, filled Berardo with an excitement that he was unable to conceal, and he couldn't talk about anything else.

"The Fucino land is the promised land," he kept saying. "You can sow a sack of wheat and reap ten. It's fine, rich soil, there are no stones, it's perfectly flat, and it's safe from flooding."

We all knew that, of course. But we also knew that the people of Fontamara, living on the mountain, had always been denied the right to be considered dwellers on the old lakeside, and so we had been excluded from exploitation of the reclaimed land.

"Excluded?" Berardo objected violently. "But at the height of the working season we go there, don't we?"

"Yes, but as laborers, not tenant farmers," Zompa pointed out. "In the same way you might be sent for to work as a laborer in the garden of the royal palace."

"But if they need us as laborers there," Berardo replied, clenching his fists threateningly, "why can't they rent us land there too?"

We had been appealing for that right for years, but were only laughed at for our pains. "You're mountain people, and if you want land you must find it in the mountains," they said.

But one Sunday morning a truck arrived at Fontamara, making an infernal din, and stopped in the middle of the square. A driver dressed like a soldier got out and started shouting at those who were attracted by the noise.

"Get in," he called out. "I'm taking you to Avezzano," he said, pointing to the truck.

"What does it cost?" old Zompa asked cautiously.

"It doesn't cost anything, it's free," the man said. "I'm taking you there and back for nothing. Hurry up, get in, unless you want to be late."

"It costs nothing?" said Zompa, scratching his nose and shaking his head.

"Why?" the driver asked him. "Would you prefer to pay?"

"Oh, no, heaven forbid," Zompa said hastily. "But if it's free, it must be a swindle."

The driver took no more notice of him and went on shouting, "Hurry up, hurry up, late arrivals get the worst seats."

Berardo appeared and jumped on the truck without further ado, looking more cheerful than he had looked for as long as anyone could remember.

That ended the hesitation of the others. But who was to go? There happened to be about a dozen *cafoni* still at Fontamara that morning. The others had gone to work, because the Church has always allowed us to work on Sundays in summer when there is a great deal to do. But no one could blame the new government for not knowing that reaping begins at the end of June. How can a government be expected to know when it's reaping time?

On the other hand, it would have been absurd, just for the sake of not losing a day's work, to stay away from a meeting at which the Fucino question was to be settled for our benefit.

The old hope of getting a share of the good, rich, fertile soil of the plain, of which Don Circostanza had talked to us so often, particularly at election time, was rekindled. "The Fucino to those who cultivate it," was Don Circostanza's slogan. It should be taken away from the prince and his phony tenant farmers, rich peasants, lawyers, and other professional men, and given to those who made it yield its produce, that is, the *cafoni*. So as we climbed onto the truck we were filled with great excitement at the thought that the redivision of the Fucino was to take place at Avezzano that very day, and that the government had sent that truck to ensure that the *cafoni* of Fontamara should get their share at last. So the few of us who were there that day climbed on board without further ado. Those who did so were Berardo Viola, Antonio La Zappa, Della Croce, Baldovino, Simpliciano, Giacobbe, Pilato and his son, Caporale, Scamorza, and myself. We were sorry we didn't have enough time at least to change our shirts, but the driver kept shouting at us to hurry.

But at the very last moment, just when we were ready to go, he said, "And what about the pennant?"

"What pennant?" we asked.

"According to my instructions, every party of peasants must have a pennant," he explained.

"But, excuse me, what is a pennant?" we asked in embarrassment.

"A pennant is a flag," the man explained with a laugh.

We didn't want to make a bad impression on the new government, particularly at the ceremony at which the Fucino question was to be settled, so when Teofilo, who kept the keys of the church, suggested we should take the banner of San Rocco, we agreed immediately. He went to the church and fetched the banner with Scamorza's help, but when the driver saw them coming back, struggling with a ten-yard-long pole to which the huge blue-and-white banner with San Rocco's picture painted on it with a dog licking his wounds was attached, he objected to taking it on his truck. But it was the only flag we had at Fontamara, and on Berardo's insistence he eventually gave in.

"It will be an extra amusement," he said.

Three of us had to take it in turn to hold it erect while the truck was in motion, and it was a great strain. It seemed not so much a flagpole as the mast of a ship in a gale. It must have been visible from a great distance, because we saw *cafoni* working in the fields making gestures of astonishment, and women went down on their knees and made the sign of the cross.

The truck dashed madly downhill with little regard for the continual twists and turns, and we were tossed about like calves on the way to market, but it made us laugh. The unaccustomed speed added to the sense of adventure, and when we reached the last turning and suddenly found ourselves faced by the vast Fucino plain with its ripe, golden crops divided by rows of huge poplars, emotion took our breath away. The Fucino had a new look — that of the promised land. At this point Berardo took over, and with the extra strength given him by his enthusiasm he single-handedly raised and waved the banner with the picture of the holy pilgrim and the pious dog.

"Land, land," he started shouting, as if he had never seen such a thing in his life before.

At the entrance to the first village we came to on the plain the driver said, "Sing the anthem."

"What anthem?" we asked in embarrassment.

"My instructions are that when passing through every inhabited place the peasants shall sing the anthem and show signs of enthusiasm," the driver explained.

But we didn't know any anthem, and in any case by now we were in a line of other trucks packed with *cafoni*, as well as a great

many horses and traps, cars, motorcycles, and bicycles, all going
in the same direction. Our huge blue-and-white banner with the
picture of the saint caused amazement when people caught sight
of it, immediately followed by interminable silly laughter. The
flags that everyone else had were black and no bigger than a
pocket handkerchief, and in the middle there was a picture of a
skull and crossbones, like that to be seen on telegraph poles with
the inscription DANGER OF DEATH: they were not by any means
more handsome than ours.

"Are they the living dead?" asked Baldovino, pointing to the
men in black carrying those funereal-looking flags. "Are they the
souls bought by Don Circostanza?"

"They're the souls bought by the government," Berardo explained.

Because of that banner we had a violent scuffle at the entrance
to Avezzano. A group of youths in black shirts were waiting for us
in the middle of the road, and they immediately told us to hand it
over. We refused, because it was the only one we had. Our driver
was ordered to stop, and the youths tried to confiscate it by force.
But by now we had become very irritated by all the laughter, and
we reacted energetically, and quite a number of those young men's
black shirts turned gray as a result of contact with the dusty road.

Our truck was surrounded by shouting people, including
many youths in black shirts as well as a large number of *cafoni*
from villages near Fontamara who recognized us and greeted us
vociferously. We stayed on the truck, standing silently around our
banner, determined not to accept any more insults. Suddenly we
saw the fat, sweating, and panting form of Don Abbacchio
making his way toward us through the throng with some *carabinieri*, and we were all convinced that he was coming to San
Rocco's aid. But we were mistaken.

"Do you think this is carnival time?" the priest shouted at us.
"Is this how you compromise the agreement between the Church
and the state? When will you Fontamaresi stop your contuma-
cious and provocative behavior?"

At that we let the *carabinieri* take possession of the banner without lifting a finger to prevent them. Berardo was the first to give in. If a priest renounced San Rocco, why should we remain loyal to him at the risk of compromising our rights to the Fucino?

We were taken to a big square, where we were given a good position in the shade behind the Law Courts. Other groups of *cafoni* were placed against the various buildings around the square. Squads of *carabinieri* took up positions between one group and the next. *Carabiniere* dispatch riders on bicycles crisscrossed the square in every direction. When each new truck arrived, the *cafoni* were told to get off and were conducted by *carabinieri* to prearranged places in the square. All this seemed to be in preparation for a big festival. At one point a *carabiniere* officer crossed the square on a horse. Berardo thought the horse magnificent. We were thrilled, and admired everything.

Immediately after this a dispatch rider arrived and handed out orders to the various squads of *carabinieri*. Berardo made us admire the swiftness of the movements.

A *carabiniere* detached himself from one squad and made an announcement to the *cafoni*. It was as follows: "Permission to sit on the ground has been granted."

We sat on the ground. We were as obedient as schoolchildren. We went on sitting on the ground for about an hour, and then the arrival of another dispatch rider caused a great stir. A group of authorities appeared at the corner of the square.

"Stand up, stand up," the *carabinieri* told us. "Shout at the top of your voices: long live the *podestà*. Long live honest administrators. Long live administrators who do not rob."

We jumped to our feet and shouted, "Long live the *podestà*, long live honest administrators, long live administrators who do not rob."

The only one of these honest administrators whom we recognized was the Contractor. As soon as they had left, we were able to sit down again with the *carabinieri*'s consent. Berardo began to feel that the ceremony was becoming a little protracted.

"And what about the land?" he asked the *carabinieri* at the top of his voice. "When are they going to tell us about the land?"

A few minutes later another dispatch rider caused renewed excitement.

"Stand up, stand up," the *carabinieri* told us. "Shout more loudly: long live the prefect."

The prefect passed in a shining automobile, and again we were able to sit down with the *carabinieri*'s consent.

No sooner had we settled ourselves than they made us stand up again.

"Shout as loudly as you can: long live the minister," they said.

A huge automobile followed by four motorcyclists crossed the square in a flash, while we shouted as loudly as we could, "Long live the minister. Hurrah!"

Then we sat down again with the *carabinieri*'s consent. The *carabinieri* on duty were relieved for lunch, and we opened our sacks and ate the bread we had brought from home.

Berardo kept assuring us that the minister was just going to send for us. "He's studying our case now, you'll see, and he'll be sending for us at any time now. We'd better finish eating quickly."

At about two o'clock the pantomime was resumed. First the minister flashed by, then the prefect, and then the honest administrators. Each time we had to rise to our feet, show signs of joy, and utter shouts of enthusiasm.

Eventually the *carabinieri* told us, "You are free now. You can go."

They had to repeat this in different words.

"The celebrations are over. You can leave now, or you can have a look at Avezzano first. But you have only one hour. You must all be gone one hour from now."

"And the minister? And the Fucino question?" we asked in astonishment. "What sort of farce is this?"

No one would listen to us, but we couldn't leave in total ignorance of what had happened.

"Come with me," said Berardo, who knew his way about Avezzano quite well, having been to prison there a couple of times.

His expression and his voice had changed.

"I don't care if I go back to prison," he said to us, "but first I'm going to satisfy my curiosity. Come with me."

We came to the door of a big building on which many flags were flying.

"We want to see the minister," Berardo said abruptly to the *carabinieri* on guard at the door.

The *carabinieri* fell on him as if he had uttered a blasphemy and tried to drag him inside, but we held on to him, and there was a scuffle. A lot of people appeared from inside the building, among them Don Circostanza, obviously drunk, with his concertina trousers at the third stage.

"Let no one fail in respect to my Fontamaresi," he shouted. "Treat my Fontamaresi well."

The *carabinieri* let go of us, and Don Circostanza came among us and wanted to embrace and kiss us one by one; he was particularly affectionate toward Berardo.

"We want to see the minister," we told the Friend of the People.

"The minister has gone," he replied. "Urgent business, you understand, an affair of state."

"We want to know how the Fucino question had been settled," Berardo interrupted dryly.

Don Circostanza had us conducted by a *carabiniere* to the Fucino administrative offices, where a clerk patiently explained to us how the Fucino question had been settled.

"Has the new government considered the question?" Berardo asked.

"Yes, and settled it in a manner satisfactory to all concerned," the clerk answered with a false smile.

"Why weren't we called in to the discussion? Why were we left outside in the square?" Berardo exclaimed. "Aren't we human beings too?"

"Be reasonable, the minister could not discuss the matter with ten thousand persons. But he discussed it with your representatives," the clerk replied.

"Who was our representative?" I asked.

"The Hon. Pelino, warrant officer in the militia," was the reply.

"How is the land to be divided up? How much is to go to the people of Fontamara? When will the division take place?" Berardo asked impatiently.

"The land is not to be divided up," the clerk replied. "On the contrary, the minister and the representative of the *cafoni* decided that small tenant farmers must as far as possible be eliminated. Many of them were granted land because they were ex-servicemen, but that is not right."

"Agreed," Berardo rudely interrupted. "A man's having done war service does not mean that he knows how to work the land. The important thing is knowing how to work the land. The Fucino to those who cultivate it, that's Don Circostanza's principle. The people of Fontamara — "

"That is precisely the principle that the minister has adopted," the clerk continued with that deceptive smile of his. "The Fucino to those who cultivate it. The Fucino to those with the means to cultivate it or have it cultivated. In other words, the Fucino to those with sufficient capital. The Fucino must be freed from the burden of poverty-stricken small tenant farmers and granted to wealthy farmers. Those without substantial capital have no right to rent land in the Fucino. Is that clear?"

He told us this as unconcernedly as if we had asked him the time. His face was as impassive as a beet.

"It's all perfectly clear," we replied.

It was all perfectly clear. The streets were full of lights. It was late, but the streets were as bright as if it were daytime. (Everything was perfectly clear.) Why all this? we wondered. There was a strange carnival look about Avezzano. I saw people enjoying themselves in the cafés and inns, singing and dancing and calling out senseless, useless things in a painful, exaggerated kind of gaiety. I had to make an effort to believe in the reality of what had happened, and I wondered whether everyone was behaving like this as a joke, or had they all gone mad without realizing it?

"The townspeople are enjoying themselves," Berardo said furiously. "The townspeople are enjoying themselves, they're eating and drinking, flaunting it in the face of the *cafoni*."

A party of drunken youths passed by, singing to the accompaniment of ribald gestures. What they sang was:

> My hair and thy hair
> Ah, ah, ah!

An armless, legless man, on wheels, drawn by a dog, kept rapidly approaching passersby and begging them for alms.

The first party of youths was followed by another, and some of them were the young men in black shirts with whom we had had the scuffle for the banner of San Rocco on our arrival. When they recognized us, they started shouting, "Hurrah for San Rocco," and they followed this up with whistles and shouts. Then they formed a ring and began dancing around us, singing an indecent song to the accompaniment of obscene gestures that were a parody of lovemaking. The song said,

> My legs and thy legs
> Ah, ah, ah!

We let them. We had no more spirit to react. We no longer understood anything. We were bewildered and humiliated.

The youths left us.

"You're not in the least amusing, you're too stupid," they said. Their gaiety was nauseating.

Berardo was exasperated and made as if to grab one or two of them and give them what they deserved.

"Not now, not now," I implored him, holding him by the arm. "Don't you see how many *carabinieri* there are about?"

We remembered the truck that was to take us back to Fontamara, and we went to the place the driver had indicated.

"Why are you so late?" a garage hand said to us. "Your truck has gone."

He started abusing us, telling us we were both stupid and arrogant. But the idea of having to tramp all the way back to Fontamara was so disheartening that it left us immune to further insults. We stayed by the garage door like a flock of sheep without a sheepdog.

We had noticed a gentleman had been following us for some time, and he now approached us. He was well dressed, and I remember that he had red hair and a red mustache and a scar on his chin.

"You are from Fontamara?" he said to us. "Do you realize that the authorities are afraid of you? They know you are against the new government."

We let him talk. We had other things on our mind.

"You're quite right," he went on. "You're quite right to rebel. Things can't go on like this. Come with me, let us talk more quietly."

He went off down a side street, and we followed him like sheep. A young man who looked half workman and half student followed behind us and smiled at us two or three times as if he had something to say to us. The red-haired gentleman led the way to a lonely, deserted tavern, and we followed him inside. The young man who had been following us hesitated, but came in too and sat at a table close to ours.

The red-haired gentleman ordered wine and looked mistrustfully at the young man. Then he resumed in an undertone the speech he had been making in the street.

"Things can't go on like this. The discontent of the *cafoni* is at its height. But you are uneducated, you need an educated man to guide you. Don Circostanza has talked to me about you with a great deal of sympathy. He wishes you well, but he does not want to compromise himself and has to be careful. If you need me, I'm at your disposal. If you have plans, ask my advice. You understand me?"

The way this unknown gentleman put himself completely at our disposal would have seemed suspicious to anyone not in our frame of mind. But it was the first time that a townsman had ever talked to us confidentially like this. We let him go on.

"I understand you," he went on. "It's enough for me to look in your eyes to understand you. The *carabinieri* said you were to leave Avezzano within an hour, but you're still here. I understand you. You want to strike a blow at the authorities. It's obvious, you can't deny it. And why am I here? To help you, to advise you, to sacrifice myself with you. You understand?"

Actually we did not understand. Pilato was about to say something, but Berardo signaled him to say nothing.

"Very well," the stranger went on. "I'm an enemy of the government too. Perhaps what you want to tell me is that you want to strike a blow at the authorities, but you lack the means, you have no arms. But it's easy to get them, nothing is easier."

We hadn't yet said anything, but the townsman went on of his own accord. He kept asking questions and answering them himself.

"You may say that words are one thing and deeds another. Well, put me to the test. If you will wait for me here for a quarter of an hour, I'll bring you what you need and tell you how to use it. You don't believe me? You doubt what I say? Well, then, wait for me here."

He rose, shook hands with us all, paid for the wine he had ordered, and left.

As soon as he had gone the young man who was sitting on the bench next to ours came over and said, "That man is a policeman. He's an *agent provocateur*. Be careful. He'll bring you a bomb or something and then have you arrested. Go away before he comes back."

We left Avezzano, taking a path through the fields to avoid meeting the *provocateur*. The young man who had warned us against him wouldn't leave us alone, but followed us and kept muttering incomprehensible things to us, until Berardo lost patience with him. After twice telling him to mind his own business and clear off, he picked him up and threw him in a ditch.

Hungry, thirsty, and with bitterness in our hearts, we tramped back by the road along which we had sped that morning, full of hope and with our fine banner of San Rocco flying in the breeze. We plodded on in silence. There were no words to express how sick at heart we felt.

We reached Fontamara at midnight, in a state you can imagine. At three o'clock we were up again to tramp to the fields, because reaping had begun.

5

THE DISTRICT HAD A wooden fence built around the grazing ground that had been appropriated by the Contractor.

The idea was to put an end to the grumblings of the *cafoni*, who doubted that anyone had the right to take possession of land that had been common property for thousands of years. But the grumbling did not stop, and one night the fence went up in flames.

"The wood was too dry," Berardo explained. "It caught fire in the sun."

"You mean the moon. It caught fire at night," I pointed out.

The Contractor had another fence built at the expense of the district and appointed an armed district road sweeper to keep guard on it. But could a road sweeper guard a grazing ground that from the beginning of creation had experienced everything: wars, invasions, shepherds' quarrels, wolves, and brigands? The fence went up in flames a second time, actually in the road sweeper's presence. He distinctly saw flames coming out of the ground and burning down the whole fence in a few minutes. As is obligatory in the case of every miracle, he immediately described the incident to Don Abbacchio, and then to everyone else who would listen.

Don Abbacchio decided that the fire was unquestionably of supernatural origin and therefore the work of the devil, whereupon
we decided that the devil was not so black as he was painted. The
Contractor, concerned for the prestige of the public authorities
but unable to have the devil arrested, had the road sweeper sent
to prison instead.

We wondered whether the devil or the Contractor would win.
(We were all against the Contractor, but the only open partisan of
the devil was Berardo.)

One evening, just when it was getting dark, some of us Fontamara women were talking about this while waiting in the little
square outside the church for our men to come back from the Fucino. Those with me were Maria Grazia, the Ciammaruga woman,
Filomena Castagna, the Recchiuta woman, and Cannarozzo's
daughter, and as usual we were sitting on the low wall that over-
looks the valley. We were looking down toward the plain, which
was already in shadow. The valley below Fontamara, which is divided in two by the dusty main road, was silent and deserted, and
the road that zigzags up to Fontamara was silent and deserted too.
Our men were going to be late, because at reaping time they don't
work by the clock. I also remember that Maria Cristina, wearing
black because of her husband's recent death, was winnowing the
small amount of wheat that had been gathered from her field. No
one could possibly foresee what was going to happen, and we were
saying the same sort of things that we said every day.

"What shall we give our men to eat next winter," I said, "if
there are no beans because there's no water?"

"And what shall we sow in the autumn if we have to eat all the
wheat because there's no corn?" said Filomena.

"These misfortunes will pass like so many others have passed,
God willing," the Recchiuta woman said confidently. "How
many times have we said that things could not go on? And yet
they did go on."

In a corner of the square some boys and girls were playing
sheriff: the sheriff isn't allowed to go on foot, he has to go on
horseback, and the girls had to take turns at being the horse. Then

twilight fell, and the first fireflies appeared. A little girl (I think it was one of Maria Cristina's daughters) came and asked me if it was true that fireflies looked for grains of wheat to make bread for hungry souls in purgatory; she had some grains of wheat in the open palm of her hand.

Meanwhile, without our noticing it at first, a monotonous, regular hum became audible in the silence; at first it was rather like that of a beehive, then it was more like that of a threshing machine. It was coming up from the valley, but we couldn't tell what it was. No threshing machines were to be seen, and all the threshing floors were empty, and besides, threshing machines came up the valley only toward the end of reaping time. Suddenly the noise grew more distinct, and a truck full of men appeared at the first bend of the road leading up to the village. Immediately afterward a second truck appeared, and then a third. Then five trucks were coming up to Fontamara. But then another appeared, and another. We couldn't tell how many there were altogether, there may have been ten, or fifteen, or twelve. Cannarozzo's daughter exclaimed that there were a hundred, but she couldn't count. The first had reached the last bend at the entrance to Fontamara while the last was still at the bottom of the hill. So many trucks had never been seen before. None of us had imagined so many trucks existed.

Alarmed by the unprecedented din made by such a large number of vehicles, the whole population of Fontamara — that is, the women and children and old men who were not at work in the fields — hurried to the square outside the church, and everyone had a different explanation for the sudden and unexpected appearance of all these vehicles making for Fontamara.

"It's a pilgrimage," Marietta exclaimed excitedly. "Nowadays rich pilgrims don't go on foot, they go by car. It's a pilgrimage to our San Rocco."

"But today isn't San Rocco's day," I pointed out.

"It must be a car race," said Cipolla, who had done his military service in town. "Some drivers must have challenged one another to see who can go fastest. You see car races in town every day."

The sound of the trucks grew louder and louder and more and more alarming, and on top of it there were the savage cries of the men on board them. A sharp crackle of shots, followed by the falling of glass from the big window of the church, turned our curiosity to panic.

"They're firing, they're firing at us, they're firing at the church," we started yelling.

"Get back, get back," Baldissera shouted to us women who were nearest the parapet. "Get back, they're firing."

But who were these men who were firing? Why were they firing? And why were they firing at us?

"It's war, it's war," said Baldissera in a state of exaltation, "it's war."

By why war? And why war against us?

"It's war," Baldissera kept saying. "God alone knows why, but it's war."

"If it's war, we must say the war litany," Teofilo the sacristan said, and started reciting *"Regina pacis, ora pro nobis"* when a second volley riddled the church facade and scattered bits of plaster over those of us who were near the door.

The litany was interrupted. The whole thing was senseless. War? But why war? Giuditta had convulsions, and we women crowded around her like a herd of crazy nanny goats. Everyone was yelling incoherently. Baldissera alone repeated gravely and impassively, "There's no help for it, it's war, there's no help for it, it's destiny. Every war begins like this."

Maria Rosa, Berardo's mother, had a good idea.

"Let us ring the church bells," she said. "When the country's in danger, the church bells must be rung. That has always been done."

But Teofilo was so terrified that he could not stand on his feet. He handed the keys to us. Elvira, who came hurrying into the square at that moment, came with me toward the bell tower to ring the alarm, but just before we got there, she hesitated.

"Has there ever been a war against women?" she said.

"I've never heard of one," I replied.

"Well, then," she said, "these men haven't come against us, but against our menfolk. We had better not ring the alarm. If we do, the men will think it's a fire and hurry home, and then they'll meet these people."

Elvira was certainly thinking of Berardo, and I thought of my husband and my son. So we stayed in the bell tower without touching the ropes.

From the top of the bell tower we saw the trucks stop at the entrance to Fontamara, and a large number of men armed with rifles got out. Some stayed behind with the trucks, and the others came toward the church.

At our feet the women, children, and old men of Fontamara had finished repeating the litanies and started the supplication. Teofilo the sacristan said the supplication in a quivering voice, and the others chanted the response: *"Libera nos, Domine."* Elvira and I, kneeling at the top of the bell tower, joined in the response in a whisper: *"Libera nos, Domine."* No one knew what was going to happen next. Teofilo went through all the supplications possible, and to all of them we responded: *"Libera nos, Domine."*

"Ab omni malo." "Libera nos, Domine."
"Ab omni peccato." "Libera nos, Domine."
"Ab ira tua." "Libera nos, Domine."
"A subitanea et improvisa morta." "Libera nos, Domine."
"A spiritu fornicationis." "Libera nos, Domine."

None of us could imagine what horror was going to happen next. Teofilo had gotten to the supplication against cholera, famine, and war when the column of armed men emerged onto the square, yelling and waving their arms. Their number dismayed us. Elvira and I instinctively retreated into a corner so as to be able to see without being seen.

There may have been about two hundred of them. In addition to their rifles, each had a dagger at his belt. They were all disguised as death's heads. The only ones we actually recognized were the rural guard and Filippo il Bello, the roadman, but the others were not unfamiliar to us and did not come from far away. Some of them actually looked like *cafoni*, but the landless kind who go out working for landowners, earn little, and live by sneak thieving. Others, as we discovered later, were dealers, the kind to be seen at markets, as well as tavern dishwashers, barbers, coachmen at private houses, and itinerant musicians. Idlers and cowards in the daytime, they fawn on the landowners in exchange for the privilege of taking it out on the poor. Unscrupulous toadies who used to come to us with Don Circostanza's orders for the elections and now came with rifles to wage war on us. Men without family, without honor, without faith, treacherous people, poor, but enemies of the poor.

A little fat man with a tricolor sash around his belly marched at their head, and Filippo il Bello preened himself at his side.

"What are you talking about?" the little man with the tricolor sash said to Teofilo the sacristan.

"I'm praying for peace," the terrified little sacristan replied.

"I'll give you peace," the little fat man said with a laugh, and made a sign to Filippo il Bello, who approached Teofilo and, after hesitating for a moment, slapped his face.

Teofilo put his hand to his cheek, looked all around, and asked timidly, "What was that for?"

The man with the tricolor sash started reviling him. "Coward, coward," he said. "Why don't you react? You're a coward."

But Teofilo stayed motionless and silent; he was more surprised than anything else. In the crowd of women, children, and old and disabled men with whom he was confronted, the little fat man could not see anyone who could be provoked to better effect, so after a brief consultation with Filippo il Bello he said contemptuously, "I see there's nothing to be done."

Then he turned to the crowd and called out in a shrill voice, "Go home, everyone."

When no one from Fontamara was left in the square, he turned to the man in black and said, "Split up into parties of five, carry out a thorough search of every house, and confiscate all the weapons you can find. Quickly, before the men come back."

The square emptied in a moment, and by now it was dark. But from our hiding place we could see the men splitting up into parties of five and disappearing into the dark houses.

"It will be difficult to search all the houses without electric light," I pointed out.

"My father's in bed, and he'll be terrified. I'd better go home and light the lamp," Elvira said, preparing to go down from the top of the bell tower.

"No, stay here," I said to her. "They can't do any harm to your father."

"But what weapons can they be looking for?" Elvira asked. "We haven't any guns. Luckily Berardo isn't here."

"I suppose they'll take the scythes and pruning hooks," I said. "Those are all the weapons we have."

But the sudden screams of Maria Grazia, whose house was next to the bell tower, followed immediately afterward by desperate shrieks from Filomena Castagna and Carracina and others in houses farther away, accompanied by the sound of furniture being upset, chairs being broken, and glass smashed, quickly showed us what kind of arms those men were after.

Immediately beneath us Maria Grazia yelled like an animal about to have its throat cut, and through the open door we had a confused view of one woman's desperate struggle against five men; several times she managed to struggle free, and once she actually reached the door, but she was caught, held by the legs and shoulders, and flung to the ground, where her clothes were torn off and she was held by four men with her arms open and her legs apart so that the fifth could take her. She screamed like a beast at the slaughter. When the first man had finished, his place was taken by another, and her martyrdom began all over again, and so it went on until all resistance ended; her groans grew so feeble that we could no longer hear them.

Elvira beside me saw the whole thing. How could I prevent it? It all happened beneath our eyes, only fifteen yards away. The terrified creature clung to me with her arms around my neck, and I could feel her trembling as if she were having convulsions. It was as if the bell tower and the whole earth beneath us were trembling. I held her tight to prevent her from falling, from tumbling

down the wooden stairs and attracting the attention of the armed
men to our hiding place. She gazed with enormous, staring eyes
at the room from which the five men emerged, where Maria
Grazia's martyred body lay, and I was afraid she would go out of
her mind. I shut her eyes with my hands as one does with the
dead. Then my own strength failed, my legs gave away, and we
collapsed in the dark side by side.

I remember nothing of that terrible night except what I have
just tried to tell you. Sometimes it seems to me that I know
nothing and remember nothing of the whole of my life except
what happened before my eyes that night. My husband can tell
you the rest if he wants to.

We men on our way back from the Fucino of course knew
nothing of all this. If only they had rung the bells. A number of
men from Fontamara, including Berardo, had met on the road
and were coming back together. Others were following a short distance behind us. When we saw the long row of trucks and the
militiamen at the entrance to the village, Berardo said, "It must be
because of the fence. The Contractor must have thought it was
burned down by someone from Fontamara. Where would he get
an idea like that from?"

Among the militiamen guarding the trucks there were some
who knew Berardo personally and were afraid of him and were
very embarrassed at his arrival, but they wouldn't tell us why they
had come to Fontamara, or perhaps they didn't really know. They
merely told us to wait. When the second party of *cafoni* arrived,
they escorted us to the middle of the village, where the other
militiamen were drawn up in a square under the command of a
little fat man with a tricolor sash around his belly, aided by the
roadman, Filippo il Bello.

In the middle of the square we were surprised to see Baldissera,
Teofilo the sacristan, Cipolla, old Braciola, Anacleto the tailor,
and one or two others who had not been out to work. They were
standing there silent and motionless, pale and resigned, like prisoners of war.

"What's happening?" asked Berardo, but no one answered.

As we approached, the square opened and then it closed behind us. Berardo looked at me as if he did not know whether to laugh or be angry. We tried to get Baldissera to tell us what had happened before our arrival, and he came up to me and muttered in my ear, "It's absolutely unheard of," and then he went up to Berardo and muttered the same thing in his ear, and then he went to the others and did the same. "It's absolutely unheard of," he repeated. This wasn't very clear, but it was certainly extraordinary, because in the past, even when confronted with the most terrible events, he had always been able to quote previous examples in history. For the first time in his life he admitted that something had happened that was beyond his comprehension.

The square of militiamen opened again to admit a third group of men who had come back from work, including Pilato, Losurdo, Michele Zompa, Testone, Uliva, Gasparone, and a few lads. The latter looked at us as if the whole thing were our fault, but in the face of that large number of armed men even they did not dare to protest.

"When strange things begin to happen there's no stopping them," Zompa said to me.

I implored Berardo to keep calm and say nothing and not compromise us all. I told him that if he absolutely had to, he could do crazy things on his own account later, but not now in the faces of all those rifles.

Then more *cafoni* arrived to keep us company, including Maria Grazia's future husband. No one yet knew anything about what had happened, and no one spoke. We all looked at one another. We all realized that for some reason still unknown to us we were faced with the authorities, and no one wanted to compromise himself more than anyone else. Everyone thought of himself, and every now and then someone else would arrive. It was hard to imagine what the little fat man had in mind. Was he proposing to take us all to prison? That was unlikely and practically impossible. We could put up with standing and waiting for a while in the middle of our village square, but there were not enough of those armed men to carry us off to the town and put us in prison.

Besides, we knew those men in black shirts. To give themselves courage they had come at night. Most of them stank of wine, and yet, if we looked at them straight in the eye, they looked away. They, too, were poor men, but poor men of a special kind: landless, jobless or with many jobs, which is the same thing, and averse to hard work. Too weak and cowardly to rebel against the rich and the authorities, they preferred serving them in order to be able to rob and oppress other poor men, *cafoni*, small landowners. When you met them in the street in daylight, they were humble and obsequious, but at night and in groups they were evil, malicious, treacherous. They have always been in the service of authority and always will be. But recruiting them into a special army, giving them a special uniform and special arms, was a novelty. Such are the so-called Fascists. There was another explanation for their boldness. Physically each one of us was a match for at least three of them. But what did we have in common? What link was there between us? We were all born at Fontamara, and here we were all together in the village square; that was what we *cafoni* had in common, and that was all. Apart from that, everyone thought of himself, of the best way of extricating himself from that square of armed men, never mind what might happen to those left behind; each one of us was a family man and thought of his family. Perhaps only Berardo thought differently, but he had neither land nor wife.

By now it was late.

"Well?" Berardo called out threateningly. "Shall we get a move on?"

The little fat man was impressed by Berardo's tone of voice.

"The examination will now begin," he announced.

Examination? What examination? Were we at school?

A gap of about a yard appeared in one side of the square, and the little fat man and Filippo il Bello took up positions on either side of it, just as shepherds do in sheepfolds at milking time.

Then the examination began.

The first to be summoned was Teofilo the sacristan.

"Long live who?" the little fat man with a tricolor sash asked him peremptorily.

Teofilo seemed to fall from the clouds.

"Long live who?" the representative of the authorities repeated impatiently.

Teofilo, terrified, turned and looked at us as if to draw inspiration from the sight, but we were no wiser than he. And as the poor fellow continued to show signs of not knowing what to answer, the little man turned to Filippo il Bello, who was holding a big open book in his hands, and said to him, "Put him down as refractory."

Teofilo went off in dismay. The next to be called was Anacleto the tailor.

"Long live who?" the little fat man asked him.

Anacleto, who had had time to think replied, "Long live Mary."

"Which Mary?" Filippo il Bello asked him.

Anacleto thought for a moment, seemed to hesitate, and then said, "Our Lady of Loreto."

"Put down refractory," the little man said contemptuously.

But Anacleto was not resigned to failure. He declared himself ready to substitute Our Lady of Pompeii for Our Lady of Loreto, but he was sent away with a flea in his ear. The next to be called was old Braciola. He, too, had his answer ready.

"Long live San Rocco," he said, but even that did not satisfy the little man, who ordered the roadman to write down "refractory."

Next it was Cipolla's turn.

"Long live who?" he was asked.

"Excuse me, but what do you mean?" he plucked up courage to ask.

"Answer sincerely what is in your mind," said the little man. "Long live who?"

"Long live bread and wine," was Cipolla's sincere reply.

But he, too, was put down as refractory. We were all awaiting our turn, and no one could guess what reply to his strange question the representative of the authorities wanted.

Our chief worry, of course, was whether there would be anything to pay if we gave the wrong answer. None of us knew what
"refractory" meant, but the most probable meaning was that there
was something to pay. In short, one pretext was as good as another
to impose a new tax on us. So far as I was concerned, I tried to get
as close as possible to Baldissera, hoping to get some good advice
from him, as he was the best educated of us and knew how to behave. But he looked at me with a compassionate smile, as one
who knew all the right answers, but for himself alone.

"Long live who?" the little man asked.

The old cobbler took off his hat and called out, "Long live
Queen Margherita."

The effect was not at all what he expected. The militiamen
burst out laughing, and the little fat man said, "She's dead.
Queen Margherita's dead."

Baldissera was dumbfounded.

"Dead?" he exclaimed. "Queen Margherita dead? Impossible!"

"Put down constitutionalist," the little man said to Filippo il
Bello with a contemptuous smile.

Baldissera went away crestfallen, shaking his head at this sequence of inexplicable events. He was followed by Antonio La
Zappa, who, on instructions from Berardo, called out, "Down
with thieves."

This provoked a general protest from the men in black, who
took it as a personal affront.

The little fat man told Filippo il Bello to put him down as an
anarchist.

La Zappa went off laughing, and it was Spaventa's turn.

"Down with vagabonds," he called out, arousing more protests
in the examiners' ranks. He, too, was put down as an anarchist.

"Long live who?" the fat man asked Della Croce.

He, too, was a pupil of Berardo's and refused to wish long life
to anyone or anything. So he replied, "Down with taxes."

In the interests of truth it must be stated that this time the
men in black and the little fat man did not protest. But Della
Croce, too, was put down as an anarchist because, as the little

man explained, there were certain things that one does not say.

A bigger impression was made by Raffaele Scarpone, who almost shouted in the face of the representative of the law, "Down with your paymaster."

The little man was dumbfounded, as if sacrilege had been committed, and wanted to have him arrested, but Raffaele had been careful to say these words only after emerging from the square, and in two bounds he vanished behind the church and wasn't seen again.

Caution was resumed when it came to Losurdo's turn.

"Long live everyone," he said with a smile, and it was difficult to imagine anything more prudent, but it was not appreciated.

"Put down liberal," the little man said to Filippo il Bello.

Uliva showed a maximum of goodwill by calling out, "Long live the government."

"What government?" Filippo il Bello asked.

Uliva had never heard that there was more than one government, but out of politeness he replied, "The legitimate government."

"Put him down as perfidious," the little fat man said.

Pilato, whose turn came next, thought he'd take a chance. He, too, replied, "Long live the government."

"What government?" Filippo il Bello asked in alarm.

"The illegitimate government."

"Put down scoundrel," the little fat man ordered.

No one had yet managed to give a satisfactory reply, and the freedom of choice of those who had still to be examined was becoming increasingly restricted. But the really important point — that is, whether a wrong answer involved paying something and, if so, how much — was still obscure. Only Berardo showed complete disregard for this, and he amused himself by suggesting impudent replies to his young friends on the basis of "down with" instead of "long live" so-and-so or such-and-such.

"Down with the bank," Venerdì Santo shouted.

"What bank?" Filippo il Bello asked him.

"There's only one, and it gives money only to the Contractor," Venerdì knowledgeably replied.

"Put down communist," the little fat man said.

Gasparone, who called out, "Down with Torlonia," was put down as communist too. On the other hand, Palummo, who very politely replied, "Long live the poor," was put down as socialist.

At that moment Berardo's mother, Maria Rosa, whom we had seen coming down the alley and going into Maria Grazia's house, which is at the beginning of the slope behind the church, appeared on the other side of the square.

"Berardo, where is Berardo?" she shouted. "Do you know what these brigands have done in our houses? Do you know what they have done to the women? And our men? Where are our men? Where is Berardo?"

Berardo immediately understood, or at any rate thought he understood. In a bound he was facing Filippo il Bello, who was standing there livid with fear. Berardo seized him by the collar, spat in his face, and said to him, "Where's Elvira? What have you done to Elvira?"

By now old Maria Rosa had reached the threshold of the church, gone down on her knees, and was calling out, "Our Lady, protect us, intercede for us, because our men are useless."

Before she had finished, a stroke of the big bell made us all look up to the bell tower.

Next to the bell we all saw a strange vision, the ghost of a tall, slim young woman, with a face as white as snow and her hands clasped to her bosom. For a moment the vision took our breath away. Then it vanished.

Filippo il Bello was seized with panic. "It's Our Lady, it's Our Lady," he started yelling. The other men in black were just as panic-stricken. "Our Lady, Our Lady," they started yelling too.

The square melted away, and the militiamen fled precipitously to the trucks that had been left at the entrance to the village, and the little man went with them.

We heard the engines being started up. Then we saw the

trucks being driven at speed down the hill with their headlights on. We didn't manage to count them, but it was a long procession.

At the bottom of the hill, at the last bend before the main road, the procession came to a halt. The holdup lasted for more than half an hour.

"Why have they stopped? Do they want to come back?" I asked Berardo.

He laughed. "Perhaps Scarpone knows why they stopped," he said.

(Next day we learned that the first truck had crashed into a tree trunk that had been placed across the road and had overturned. Several men were injured, including the little man with the tricolor sash.)

By the time the trucks started up again it was late.

"Shall we go to bed or wait a little longer before going to work?" I asked Berardo.

"First of all, we must see who's in the bell tower," Berardo replied.

Berardo believed in the devil, but not in Our Lady. If he had seen the devil in a vision, he would have believed it unquestioningly, but he had no faith in a vision of Our Lady. We climbed the tower and were astonished to find my wife and Elvira. The girl had fainted away again, and it was a long time before she came to.

What were we to do? We couldn't wait up there for daylight, but it was no easy task to get her down the steep bell tower steps in the dark. I went first and held her feet, with Berardo following, holding her by the shoulders.

Down the square Elvira was no better; she did not answer our questions and could not stand on her feet.

It was I, I don't deny it, who said to Berardo, "Listen, if you have counted to thirty, you can count to thirty-one."

He picked her up in his arms with the ease of a shepherd carrying a newborn lamb and vanished in the dark in the direction of her house.

6

MARIA ROSA, BERARDO'S mother, came to see me next morning.

"Have you seen my son?" she asked. "Did he sleep here? I stayed awake all night waiting for him."

I was surprised by what she said, but I did not tell her what it made me think.

The poor old woman struggled back up the alley, and I saw her going to Scarpone's door to ask him whether he had seen Berardo.

Later, when I was saddling the donkey, Maria Rosa passed my door again, and, to excuse her son, said, "Berardo's not a bad man, but he was born under an unlucky star, poor fellow. What a hard destiny is his."

But as I went around behind the bell tower on my way to work, whom should I run into but Berardo.

"I was just coming to see you," he said in a new and strange voice and without looking me in the face. "I want to talk to you."

"You mother's looking for you all over the village," I said to him reproachfully, giving the donkey a shove to make it hurry up.

But Berardo took no notice of this and started walking beside me, guessing from my tone of voice that I knew everything.

"Don't be angry with me," he suddenly burst out. "What has happened was bound to happen."

"I think you're attributing too much to destiny," I interrupted.

"That isn't true," he protested vigorously, gripping my arm. "You know it isn't true. You know I've not had an easy life. You know I've never let things take their course."

Then, after a short pause, he added, almost in an undertone, but firmly, "And now I'm less resigned than ever."

"What are you proposing to do?" I asked.

"I shall marry her," he said, "but first of all I must put myself on my feet again as quickly as possible and get some land. I think you'll agree with that."

"That's not easy nowadays, and you know it, Berardo," I said. "It's not easy, you've tried it a couple of times and you haven't succeeded."

"I shall try again," he said vigorously and with unusual optimism. "I shall try again, and you'll see, this time I'll succeed. It isn't just for myself this time. It's not only my life that's at stake this time, and I feel ten times stronger than ever before. You'll see."

I was going to tell him that reestablishing oneself with a bit of land at Fontamara wasn't easy, and didn't depend on strength, or determination, or need, but when I looked at his face, as I had not yet done that morning, I suddenly felt enormous compassion for him, as if I had seen the whole of his sad future in a flash. And this affected me so much that I tried to hide my inexplicable perturbation.

"May God's blessing be upon you, Berardo," I muttered. "That's all I can say. May the Lord help you."

He must have seen how affected I was, because he seemed to be affected too. He hurriedly said good-bye and went back to fetch his mattock.

All that day I could think of nothing but Berardo and his desperate need to get some land, and to get it quickly, for without it his pride prevented him from marrying Elvira, though now he had to marry her. To understand this attitude you have to bear in mind the wretched state of landless *cafoni* in our part of the world in the last few years. At Fontamara and the neighboring villages most *cafoni* have small holdings that they own or rent, or sometimes both. Those who have no land are few, and they are despised and looked down on by everyone. Because land was cheap at one time, a laborer who had none was regarded as stupid, idle, and lacking in character, and this was nearly always true. But then things changed. In our part of the world those who had a little land no longer increased their holdings and laborers no longer acquired any; on the contrary, some small landowners actually relapsed to the state of *cafoni*. But, though times had changed, attitudes had not, and the landless *cafone* was regarded with contempt.

True, in many respects Berardo was an exceptional *cafone*, and no one dared show disrespect to him, because his poverty was not the result of laziness or ignorance but of misfortune and destiny. Nevertheless, though he generally behaved like a proud and upright man, the idea of marrying a girl like Elvira while he was landless made him feel inferior and unworthy.

All day long, while mowing the hay in a field belonging to Don Carlo Magna, I thought about Elvira's plight, and I decided that the only way out would be for Berardo to get a job in town, one of those heavy jobs that townsmen won't do and are better paid than work in the country. If he did this for five or six months, he might be able to save enough to buy himself something when he returned. But to whom could one turn for advice without risking being fooled and swindled again? Not the priest, or the landlord, or the lawyer. We had been disillusioned by recent events.

Even Baldissera was useless. He was more disturbed than anyone else by the extraordinary things that had been happening for some time past. The old ceremonious world in which he had gone on believing was dead and buried, and the things that happened now were completely crazy and incomprehensible.

The militia had come to Fontamara and violated a number of women — an abominable outrage, though in itself not incomprehensible. But they had done it in the name of the law and in the presence of an inspector of police, and that was incomprehensible.

At the Fucino the rents of the small tenants had been increased and those of the big ones reduced, and that was natural enough, as it were. But the proposal had been made by a representative of the small tenants, and that was not at all natural.

On a number of occasions, we were told, so-called Fascists had beaten up, injured, and sometimes killed persons who had done nothing wrong in the eyes of the law, merely because they were a nuisance to the Contractor, and that too might seem natural enough. But those who did the injuring and killing were rewarded by the authorities, and that was inexplicable.

In short, if one looked one by one at each of the disasters that had afflicted us for some time past, it could be said that none of them was unprecedented and that there were many examples of them all in past history. But the way they happened to us now was new and absurd, and we could see no explanation.

The small amount of wheat that should have come to Fontamara after the harvest now in progress had been bought up by the Contractor in May, when it was still green, for 120 lire a hundredweight. At the time, that seemed to us to be an opportunity too good to miss, and we were surprised that the Contractor, who was usually so farsighted, should risk buying wheat in May, when no one could foresee the market price. But we needed the cash, and we sold him the wheat while it was still green without bothering our heads about it too much, and the *cafoni* in neighboring villages did the same. But at reaping time the mystery was solved. The government made a special law in favor of homegrown wheat, and the price suddenly jumped from 120 to 170 lire a hundredweight. The Contractor must obviously have known in May that that law was coming. He made a clear profit of fifty lire on every hundredweight of our wheat before it was even harvested. So all the profit from the cultivation of our wheat went to him. All the profit from the plowing, the winnowing, the reaping, the threshing, the whole profit of a year's sweat and toil, had gone to that stranger who had nothing to do with the land. The *cafoni* cleared and plowed the land, hoed, reaped, and threshed, and when the whole job was done, a stranger came in and took the profit.

Could we protest? We could not even protest. It was all legal. The only thing that would have been illegal would have been for us to protest.

For a long time past all the thefts the *cafoni* had suffered had been legal. If the old laws did not suffice, new ones were made.

"I'm not staying here," Berardo kept saying in torment. "I must go away. But where?"

His suffering was obvious to all. He was no longer the same man, he didn't laugh or joke, and he avoided people. Everyone could tell that there was a thorn in his heart, and that his heart was bleeding.

"The only person that can help you is Don Circostanza," I was forced to admit. "He has a great many connections."

Berardo, Scarpone, and I were owed a small sum of money by Don Circostanza for replanting some vines in an old vineyard of his behind the cemetery that had been half uprooted by a flood, and one Sunday morning we went to see him to get our money and give Berardo a chance to ask his advice and help.

"Only the Friend of the People can help you," I said to Berardo.

Don Circostanza received us with great cordiality. He shook hands with us and made us sit down.

"How many days' work do I owe you?" he asked.

He owed Berardo fifteen days' work and Scarpone and me twelve each — not a difficult sum for an educated man like Don Circostanza to work out. But his face suddenly darkened, and for several minutes he remained silent. He strode up and down his office two or three times, looked out of the window, and listened at the keyhole to make sure no one was listening. Then he came over to us and said in low tones, "It's dreadful, you can't imagine how the government is persecuting us. It makes a new law against us every day. We're no longer free even to handle our own money."

What he said made a certain impression on us. So the government was beginning to persecute gentlemen too?

"You have only to say the word, your Worship," said Berardo in a tone of voice he had dropped for some time past, "and all the *cafoni* will revolt."

"There's no question of that," Don Circostanza said in alarm. "What we're up against is outrage of a more subtle kind. Look, there are the three envelopes I had prepared for you. One for each of you, with the pay agreed on."

In fact, there were three envelopes on the desk.

"I prepared them in precise accordance with the agreed terms," he went on. "I did not withhold a single *centesimo*. Do you believe me?"

Why should we not believe him?

Once more he gratefully shook our hands.

"Well," he went on. "I have been sent a copy of the new labor contract for the agricultural laborers of the province. To me it was a terrible and unexpected blow. Read it. Read it for yourselves."

Mistrustfully I took the newspaper that Don Circostanza handed me, and on his insistence I read aloud some passages he had marked with a red pencil. According to what the newspaper said, the current wages for agricultural workers aged between nineteen and sixty — that is, us — had been reduced by 40 percent.

"Isn't it weird? Isn't it dreadful?" he interrupted. "Go on, that is not all."

The newspaper went on to say that land-betterment work — the planting or replanting of vineyards, olive groves, and orchards; the making of dung heaps; the filling in, clearing, or digging of ditches; weeding; and road making — came into a special category with a view to the relief of unemployment, and as such was to be paid at a rate lower than the above, the permissible reduction being up to 25 percent.

"Isn't it intolerable?" Don Circostanza went on. "Why should the law intervene between employers and *cafoni*? What will become of our liberty if this sort of thing goes on?"

The swindle was obvious. This was a new trick to rob us in the name of the law. Don Circostanza had always been a master of such devices. One of the smart things he did was to buy up, at a third or quarter of their face value, promissory notes *cafoni* were unable to meet, and he made them pay off the debt by working for him, with the result that they worked without wages and he got the work done for a pittance. So before going to his office that day we had a small examination of conscience and made quite sure that none of us had any promissory notes outstanding, not even any very small ones that had slipped our memory. But this time it was a different swindle.

"There are the three envelopes," Berardo pointed out. "Let us take them and that will be that."

He made as if to take the envelopes, but Don Circostanza, who had been expecting this, prevented him.

"What?" he shouted, changing his voice and expression. "How dare you behave so outrageously in my house?"

I intervened to prevent Berardo from compromising himself.

"He is not behaving outrageously," I said. "We worked at an agreed wage for a certain number of days. There's no difficulty in working out what we are owed, and we can go on being on the same friendly terms as before."

"And the law?" the lawyer shouted at me. "What about the law? Do you know what the penalties are for flouting a law like that? No, you do not, you are ignorant men, you do not know, but I do, and I have no intention of going to prison for your sake."

"The law of Moses says, 'Thou shalt not steal,'" I pointed out.

"The law of Moses is valid before the judgment throne of God, but here below it's government's law that prevails. In any case, it's not my responsibility to see that it is obeyed. If you're not satisfied, I shall have no alternative but to call the *carabinieri*."

This last sentence produced a strange effect, and I had the impression that Don Circostanza himself thought he had gone too far. To Berardo it was like a slap in the face and he leaped to his feet, but I went over to him, and he understood and returned to his seat. There was an embarrassed silence.

"I don't want to say anything that could be misunderstood," the lawyer muttered. "But my life is difficult too."

In saying that he may have been telling the truth. On his office wall there was a big photograph of his son, who was killed in the war, and next to it there was one of his wife, who was in a mental hospital; and you had only to look at him to see that he was no longer the prosperous, jovial man he used to be. But was that any reason for him to persecute us, who were far worse off? So why should we grieve for him?

"When the shepherd is in a bad way, so are the sheep," he added, as if in response to our thoughts.

Berardo was fuming and raging inside like a man who cannot and does not even want to escape from his chains. He was demoralized and humiliated, and dared not look in Scarpone's direction.

"How much does it come to?" he muttered between his teeth.

Don Circostanza was astonished at Berardo's unusual compliance and had the bad taste to express pleasure at it.

"I do not say this in any spirit of reproach, but if you had always shown the good sense that you're showing now, you'd be much better off," he said.

He went over to the desk, picked up Berardo's envelope, and withdrew the money. He took a pencil and a sheet of paper and started calculating.

"First of all," he said, "we must deduct forty percent in accordance with the law. From the remainder, also in accordance with the law, we must deduct twenty-five percent for the relief of unemployment. That leaves thirty-eight lire for Berardo. My dear Berardo, I'm sorry, but it's the government's fault."

Fifteen days' hard work had earned him the pittance of thirty-eight lire.

Don Circostanza then took my envelope and withdrew the money. When he had finished his sums, thirty-four lire remained for me. He then performed the same operation on Scarpone's envelope.

Thirty-four lire for twelve days' work. The amount was so absurd that it suggested sorcery. Was it worth going on tilling the soil only to be fobbed off and swindled like this? Berardo was silent and his mind was certainly elsewhere, and Scarpone looked at him as if he could not believe his eyes: his amazement at Berardo's behavior prevented him from being angry with Don Circostanza, who, to show that he bore us no ill will, made the magnanimous gesture of calling the maid and offering us a glass of wine.

Alas, we accepted it. When we were on the point of leaving, I signaled Berardo that he should stay behind as we had agreed.

"I want to talk to you," Berardo said to the lawyer as he accompanied us to the door. "I need some advice."

I promised to wait for him outside in the street, and I made Scarpone come with me — he was expecting, or rather hoping for, a sudden resurgence on Berardo's part and wanted to stay with him to give him a helping hand.

"Berardo's no longer a boy," I said to him reproachfully, "and it's time he started thinking about his own affairs."

"You people who have always thought about your own affairs are not much better off," Scarpone replied scornfully.

Outside in the street we met Baldovino Sciarappa, who was cursing his wife at the top of his voice and blaming her for their ruin, and the poor woman was imploring him to keep quiet and postpone arguments and reproaches and beatings until later, in the intimacy of the home. But her appeals served only to exasperate her husband further.

Baldovino rented a small plot of land from Don Carlo Magna, and that day he had paid the rent. But to his astonishment Donna Clorinda had found it insufficient, because the year before his wife had brought along two dozen eggs as a present in addition to the rent; and in accordance with the law of custom, the lady now claimed two dozen eggs in addition to the rent in cash. As a matter of fact, the unhappy idea of making the present the year before had been Baldovino's, but his wife had handed over the eggs without explaining that they were a special and exceptional gift, with the result that Baldovino insisted that it was his wife's fault. So in accordance with the law of custom that year, and the next year, and every year ever afterward, as long as Baldovino lived and his son lived after him, the lady would insist on her claim to those two dozen eggs in addition to the rent.

One thing, in any event, was clear. New laws in favor of the landlords were made every day, and the only old laws to be abolished were those that favored the *cafoni*; the others remained. And that was not all. In accordance with an old custom, Donna

Clorinda, like other old landlords' wives, had a wooden ring in her kitchen to measure the eggs that tenants brought her as presents, and she systematically rejected those small enough to pass through the ring. Now, that ring dated back to a time when, heaven knows why, hens laid much bigger eggs, and the occasions on which the lady refused small eggs and insisted on their being replaced by bigger ones grew more and more frequent. But was it the *cafoni*'s fault if hens no longer laid big eggs? And in any case, those eggs were gifts.

Berardo rejoined us with a letter in his hand, looking fairly pleased with himself.

"He promised to help me," he said. "He wrote a letter for me to a friend of his in Rome."

"Oh? You believe the promises of the Friend of the People?" Scarpone asked with a contemptuous laugh.

"No," Berardo replied, "but I think he believes it to be in his own interest to see that something is done for me."

Berardo, in spite of everything, was still liable to self-deception, and after this he was to be seen smiling and joking again. It was a long time since he had been to Marietta's bar, but that evening he put in a brief appearance. Unfortunately he walked in just when Americo was talking about Elvira. He was certainly not saying anything bad about her, but he was talking about her. Berardo, as if he had remembered some piece of business that the two of them had to discuss, politely asked him to step outside for a moment into the kitchen garden behind the bar, and a few minutes later he brought him back with one ear and his mouth bleeding, and he asked Marietta to wash him carefully with cold water and vinegar.

Teofilo the sacristan had been making a collection with a view to asking Don Abbacchio to say a mass at Fontamara. The collection had raised about ten lire, but Don Abbacchio replied that the price of masses had gone up and that he would not come unless he was sent at least another ten lire. With a great deal of difficulty, another ten lire were scraped together, one copper at a time, with one or two curses thrown in as well, and one Sunday morning Don Abbacchio duly appeared.

To attract the men as well as the women, he announced that in his sermon he would talk about San Giuseppe da Copertino. In fact, the church was full, and when he heard about the sermon, Berardo came too. The church was pretty dilapidated and the walls were peeling in many places as a result of the shots fired through the big window of the facade by the men in black. The only really beautiful thing in the church was the picture of the Eucharist on the altar. Jesus, with a piece of white bread in His hand, was saying, "This is My body, white bread is My body, white bread is the Son of God, white bread is truth and life." Jesus was not talking of the dark bread that *cafoni* eat, or of the tasteless substitute for bread that is the consecrated wafer of the priests. Jesus had in His hand a piece of real white bread and was saying: *"This* (white bread) *is My body,* which is truth and life." What He meant was that he who has white bread has Me (God). He who does not have white bread, who has only dark bread, is outside the grace of God, does not know the truth, has no life. He lives on garbage, like pigs and donkeys and goats. For those who have no white bread, who have only dark bread, it is as if Christ had never been, as if the Redemption had never taken place, as if Christ were still to come. And how were we not to think of our wheat, cultivated with so much labor and bought up by the bank in May when it was still green and then resold at a much higher price? We had cultivated it in the sweat of our brow, but we were not to eat of it. We were to eat dark bread. Yet Christ on the altar, saying, "This is My body," pointed, not to a loaf of dark bread, but to a fine golden loaf of white bread.

And the words of the Lord's Prayer, "Give us this day our daily bread," certainly did not refer to dark bread, but to white bread; and the bread in the verse of the Sacrament, "O living bread of heaven," is not coarse dark bread, but white.

When Don Abbacchio came to the reading of the gospel, he turned to us and preached us a little sermon about San Giuseppe da Copertino. We knew the story, but we always liked hearing it again. For this saint was a *cafone* who became a monk but never managed to learn Latin, and whenever the other monks recited the psalms, he gave praise to Our Lady by turning somersaults wherever he might be, even in church. Our Lady must have been delighted at the innocent spectacle, and to encourage and reward him she gave him the gift of levitation, and after that he had no difficulty in somersaulting all the way up to the ceiling. He died at an advanced age, after a life of severe privations, and it is said that when he appeared before the heavenly throne, God, who knew him by repute and wished him well, because Our Lady had talked about him so often, embraced him and said, "I will give you whatever you want. Don't be afraid to ask for whatever you like."

The poor saint was utterly bewildered by this offer.

"May I ask for *anything?*" he asked timidly.

"You may ask for anything," the Almighty encouraged him. "I give the orders here. I can do whatever I like here. And I am really fond of you. Whatever you ask for will be granted."

But San Giuseppe da Copertino did not dare confess what he really wanted. He feared that his immoderate wish might arouse the Lord to anger. Only after much insistence on the Lord's part, only after He gave His word of honor that He would not be angry, did the saint confess what he most wanted.

"O Lord," he said, "a big piece of white bread."

And the Lord was as good as His word and did not grow angry, but embraced the *cafone* saint, and was moved and wept with him. And then, in His voice of thunder, He summoned twelve angels and gave orders that every day from morning till evening for all eternity, *per omnia saecula saeculorum*, they should give San Giuseppe da Copertino the best white bread that was baked in Paradise.

That was the true story of San Giuseppe da Copertino as handed down from father to son in our part of the world, though of course no one can guarantee the correctness of every detail. Nevertheless, we Fontamaresi liked it and never tired of hearing it. But Don Abbacchio used it only as a pretext and went on to rebuke us for our turbulence and indiscipline, and he threatened us with divine punishment if we did not mend our ways. We listened in silence, as we generally do to such exhortations, until Don Abbacchio had the bad idea of reproving us for nonpayment of taxes.

"Pay, pay, always pay," Berardo Viola interrupted at the top of his voice and walked out of the church. All the other men followed him one by one, leaving the women and children behind.

Don Abbacchio saw how the land lay, quickly finished the service, took off his chasuble and surplice, and emerged from the sacristy in a bad temper.

He was not a bad man, but he was weak and timid and not to be trusted in serious matters. He was certainly not a shepherd capable of risking his life to protect his flock from wolves, but he was sufficiently well educated in his religion to explain that, since God had created wolves, He had granted them the right to devour a sheep every now and then. We used him for the sacraments, but we knew by experience that we could not look to him for aid or advice in the misfortunes that came to us as a result of the malice of the rich and the authorities. You remember the saying: "Take note of what the priest preaches and not of what he does." So we could put no more trust in him than in anyone else.

On the way out of the sacristy he came across Baldissera, standing with his back against the wall, slowly (very slowly, so that nobody should see) rubbing himself against it to kill possible insects.

"How are you?" the priest said to him for the sake of saying something.

"Very well, very well indeed," the general replied with a bow.

But the men standing about in the square waiting for the women to come out of church gave him more varied and less obsequious replies.

"It seems to me," the priest remarked in angry tones, "that you forget that it was God who said, 'Thou shalt earn thy daily bread in the sweat of thy brow.'"

The unlucky priest did not realize he had put his foot in a hornets' nest. Five or six men answered him, until Berardo's voice prevailed.

"If only the world were regulated according to that saying," he said.

"Why do you say that? You think that it is not?" the priest said to him in surprise.

"If only, if only I earned my daily bread in the sweat of my brow," Berardo said. "What actually happens is that for the most part I earn the daily bread of those who do not work."

"It is possible to be useful in society without tilling the soil," the priest replied in embarrassment.

"What does that sentence say?" Berardo went on stubbornly. "It says, 'Thou shalt earn thy daily bread.' It does not say, as happens in reality, thou shalt earn the Contractor's pasta, coffee, and drinks."

"I am concerned with religion and not with politics," the priest said. He was by now thoroughly annoyed, and made as if to go.

But Berardo held him by the arm and stopped him, to the general amusement.

"What does that sentence say?" Berardo repeated. "It says: 'in the sweat of thy brow.' It does not say, as happens in practice, with the blood of thy lungs, with the marrow of thy bones, with thy very life."

"If you had entered the Church, you would have made an excellent preacher," Don Abbacchio replied in all seriousness, and with that he had the last laugh, and off he went. On his arrival he had held out two fingers to everyone who wanted to shake his hand, but on his departure he held out one finger only.

"In years of plenty a priest is all right," Michele Zompa said. "He celebrates mass, triduums, and novenas, baptizes and gives Holy Communion and extreme unction and accompanies the dead to the cemetery, and in a year of plenty all those things are fine, like grated cheese on macaroni. But in times of famine, what can a poor priest do?"

When there's famine, there has always been only one way out for the *cafoni* — that is, devouring one another.

At Fontamara there were hardly two families that were still on speaking terms. Violent quarrels broke out for the most trivial reasons. They began during the daytime among the women and children and flared up again in the evening when the men came back from work. They would be about a bit of yeast borrowed and not returned, or a brick, or a barrel, or a piece of wood or corrugated iron, or a hen, or a bit of straw. When there's poverty, reasons for quarreling turn up a dozen times a day. But for us the reason of reasons was the water of the stream.

The roadmen eventually finished digging the new streambed, and on the day when the water was to be divided all the *cafoni* of Fontamara who were concerned with irrigation turned up, plus Baldissera and the usual idlers.

At the spot where the water was to be divided two sluice gates had been constructed to make it possible to control the part of it that was to go on flowing in the old streambed and the part that was to go to the Contractor — that is, the mysterious three-quarters each.

The gentry's bad conscience was demonstrated from the outset. About a hundred *carabinieri* arrived from the local town and drew up along the side of the road, and a squad came toward us and with the aid of kicks and shoves made us move back from the stream toward the vineyards. We let it happen because we had never seen so many *carabinieri*.

"It's war," said Baldissera, on whom this made a big impression. "It's real war."

"It's war against the *cafoni*," Michele added. "There are too many of us."

Scarpone was frantically looking for Berardo.

"Something has got to be done," he said. "Where's Berardo? Has no one seen Berardo?"

His absence was more demoralizing than the presence of those armed men.

Scarpone took me aside. He almost had tears in his eyes.

"You know where Berardo is," he said. "Tell me where he is and I'll go get him at once. He can't stay away on a day like this, it's impossible."

I didn't tell him where Berardo was.

"I don't know," I replied. "I really don't know. Perhaps he'll turn up later."

Soon afterward two squads of militia arrived. Some of these men had been to Fontamara before, on the evening of the examination; and behind them came a distinguished company consisting of the Contractor, the notary, Don Circostanza, the now-notorious little man with the tricolor sash around his waist, Don Cuccavasio, Don Ciccone, Don Pomponio, Don Abbacchio, the Hon. Pelino, some gentlemen whom we didn't know, and finally Filippo il Bello and Innocenzo La Legge, trying to look as inconspicuous as possible.

Don Circostanza came straight over and shook hands with us all and advised us for our own sake to have confidence in him. He would do everything for us that he possibly could, though he did not conceal the fact that our cause was almost lost. We ourselves had compromised it by our excesses.

"Where's Berardo?" he asked. "Keep him away, I beg of you."

It was arranged that we should appoint a committee of elders to observe the division of the water. It consisted of Pilato, Losurdo, and myself. The other *cafoni* were allowed to stand on the road behind a cordon of *carabinieri*.

All those spectators of such different kinds spread over a big area, all staring at the same thing, reminded one of an open-air circus; or, if one looked at the people of Fontamara and the *carabinieri*, of an investigation into some revolting murder at the scene of the crime, as if the remains of the body were between the two sluice gates. But the whole scene also recalled the ceremony that takes place when a new cross is erected in the open country: the celebration of a calvary.

"Where's Berardo?" Filippo il Bello asked me quietly.

"He's just coming," I replied, and I saw him grow pale.

The notary advanced toward us and read out the agreement between the Contractor and the people of Fontamara on the division of the stream.

"It is simple and perfectly clear," he said. "Three-quarters of the water will flow to the new channel made by the district and three-quarters of the rest will continue to flow to the old bed."

"No," Pilato immediately and rightly objected. "The agreement says three-quarters each, and nothing else. That's half each. That is, three-quarters goes to us and three-quarters to the Contractor. Each gets the same."

"No, no, no," Losurdo shouted. "That's not what it says at all. It says we must have three-quarters of the water, and the rest, if there is any, though it's possible that there won't be, since there's very little water, is to go to the Contractor, but even that's unfair to us."

"Three-quarters each is sheer deviltry," I said, losing patience. "Nothing so extraordinary has ever been heard of. The truth of the matter is that the water belongs to Fontamara, and so it must remain."

Our fellow villagers who were on the road, surrounded by *carabinieri*, realized from our shouts and gesticulations that the division of the water was about to take place to our disadvantage, and they started making an uproar. Scarpone in particular yelled like a soul in hell, aided and abetted by his usual gang of harebrained young men.

"Since the inhabitants of Fontamara have adopted a provocative attitude and even the members of their own committee of elders are not in agreement among themselves," the Contractor announced, "I avail myself of my powers as head of the district and appoint as representatives of Fontamara the Hon. Pelino, decurion of militia, and Don Circostanza. Are there any objections?" he asked the gentlemen surrounding him.

"That is in accordance with the law," Don Circostanza declared on our behalf.

"A perfectly legal step," the others chimed in.

"Very well, then, let us carry on," the Contractor said impatiently. "I've no time to waste."

The man's effrontery was unbelievable. He acted the whole thing himself; he was the accused, the prosecutor, the judge, and the people.

Six *carabinieri* fell on us and pushed and shoved us back to where the other Fontamaresi were, while Don Circostanza shouted to us, "Stay calm, have confidence in me."

From behind the cordon of *carabinieri* we had only an imperfect view of what was happening down by the stream. To tell the truth, I was not displeased with this, because it absolved me of any responsibility to the other *cafoni*.

We had a confused view first of the notary, then of an architect, and then of four roadmen approaching the stream with shovels.

Then the Hon. Pelino and Don Circostanza were to be seen having a series of discussions with the architect.

The high shoulder of the road and the big crowd of *carabinieri* and dignitaries around the two technicians who were to regulate the division of the water prevented us from seeing how that damned three-quarters each was to be applied. But there was a place about a hundred yards farther down where the old streambed made a sharp bend between Barletta's and Papasisto's vegetable plots from which we would be able to see distinctly how much our water was to be diminished and how much of it was to remain. So our eyes were glued to that spot, and we tried to guess what the authorities and our representatives were deciding a few paces away from us.

Scarpone was the first to see that the water level was sinking. No one supposed we were going to be left with as much water as before, but when we saw it actually sinking, we all started shouting and cursing the Contractor and the distinguished company. Slowly the level of our water subsided until it filled only half the streambed, but it did not stop there.

"Thieves, thieves, thieves," we yelled. Many women went down on their knees and raised their fists to heaven, shouting the most dreadful curses they could think of.

"May they lose as much blood as the water they are robbing us of."

"May they weep as many tears as the water they are robbing us of."

"May toads be born in their bellies."

"May sea serpents be born in their bellies."

"May none of them ever see their wives and children again."

The *carabinieri* who were nearest and distinctly heard these curses were terrified and implored the women to stop.

"That'll do, that'll do, for heaven's sake, stop," they said, but this only encouraged the women to go on.

"May they die in the wilderness."

"May they end up in everlasting fire."

"Jesus, Joseph, Sant'Anna, and Mary, do this grace for my soul."

Meanwhile the water level at that part of the stream that we could see continued to sink until the stones, the tufts, and the weeds at the bottom emerged.

"*Consummatum est,*" we heard Don Abbacchio say.

"All our water, all our water, they've taken all our water," we started yelling again. Scarpone and Venerdì Santo, backed up by the other young men, went for the *carabinieri* who were keeping us on the road, and the *carabinieri* defended themselves with their rifle butts and struck out blindly, shouting, "Keep back, keep back."

Don Circostanza managed with great difficulty to make his voice heard above the hubbub.

"Keep calm, keep calm," he shouted. "I'm here to defend your interests. Leave it to me. Don't be reckless, don't compromise yourselves."

He walked toward us along the shoulder of the road and made one of his usual speeches, and believe it or not, we listened to him.

"Have you lost confidence in me? That's why things are going badly with you. Do you think shouting and violence will do you any good?"

Then he turned to the Contractor and said, "The dissatisfaction of these people is justified. A compromise must be found. The people of Fontamara are good people and deserve to be respected. The district has met the expense of the two sluice gates. What has happened has happened. That is a saying of Christ's. '*Quod factum est, factum est.*'"

"Are you trying to steal my job?" Don Abbacchio said with a laugh, in which the distinguished company joined.

"A date could be fixed on which all the water of the stream could be returned to Fontamara," Don Circostanza went on.

"That would reassure them. Their loss is legal, but it would not be eternal. Let someone make a proposal."

"Fifty years," said the Contractor.

A howl of indignation on our part received this shameless proposal, and even those who had not heard it joined in.

"We'd rather be flayed alive," we yelled. "We'd rather all go to jail. Thief, thief."

Don Circostanza managed to restore silence. He turned to the Contractor and said, "Fifty years is too much. There must be a shorter term."

"Forty years," Don Abbacchio suggested.

The Hon. Pelino suggested thirty-five, and the notary twenty-five. There was a tremendous uproar. Each new proposal was received with yells of protest, and as always happens, those who had not heard it joined in too. On the other hand, what good did hearing do? Every word spoken by these gentry, every one of their gestures, stank of fraud. Eventually the little man with the tricolor sash joined in and ordered the *carabinieri* to move us still farther away. This was no easy task for them, but the kicks and shoves that we received and returned resulted in our losing from sight what was going on near the sluice gates.

At one point we saw the notary with a sheet of paper in his hand.

"There's the paper," Scarpone shouted, with the anger of one who has finally seen the swindle with his own eyes.

Baldissera could not see as far as that.

"They've produced the paper?" he said anxiously. "In that case the betrayal is complete."

We saw the gentlemen gathering around the piece of paper and standing and talking for a few minutes, and eventually they exchanged bows, handshakes, and congratulations, but we were too far away to hear what they said.

Later we were told that the loss of the water would last for ten lusters, and that this proposal had been made on our behalf by Don Circostanza, but not one of us knew how many months or years ten lusters were.

7

THERE WAS A GREAT DEAL OF discussion at Fontamara
about how long ten lusters were. Baldissera maintained that
it was ten centuries.

"Couldn't it be ten months?" Marietta tried to suggest, but no
one took any notice of her.

In any event, what it meant in the short term was famine for
Fontamara. The fields at the bottom of the hill that were no
longer watered by the stream looked more desolate every day. On
top of it, as if the Almighty were in league with the Contractor,
there had been no rain since the end of May.

The crops were slowly being burned up. Big cracks appeared
in the dry, parched soil. From a distance only Pilato's and Ranocchio's cornfields appeared to be an exception, but it was in appearance only. The corn grew tall, but the ears were small and
few and the grains were tiny and thin. At best the crop would
serve as forage for animals. Michele Zompa's, Baldovino's, and
my fields, which were sown with beans, were in an even worse
state: the beans looked like weeds burned by the sun; Barletta's,
Venerdì Santo's, Braciola's, and Papasisto's vegetable plots looked

as if a torrent of molten lava had flowed over them.

The reason why this meant famine for Fontamara was that, whereas the yield of the other few fields we owned or rented normally served to pay rent and taxes and other expenses, the irrigated fields provided us with food, wheat for bread making, and vegetables for soup. The theft of our water condemned us to a winter without bread or soup. Was such a thing possible? None of us even tried to resign himself to the prospect. But to whom were we to turn?

The ten-lusters swindle, coming on top of the three-quarters-each swindle, had opened the eyes even of the blind. On both occasions we had been hoodwinked by the man on whom we had always relied to protect our interests. So there was no one to whom we could turn. It isn't easy to explain what that meant to us, both collectively and individually. A poor village like Fontamara was bound to feel as helpless and vulnerable as a worm on the surface of the earth without the patronage of a member of the "gentry," preferably a lawyer, to whom every villager felt he could turn in case of need, to get justice against the wiles of a neighboring village, or to find a job, or if he wanted to emigrate, or to get a few days' leave for a soldier, or to seek advice on the occasion of a death or a marriage, and so on and so forth.

An inhabitant of Fontamara would never dare present himself at a public office, even to ask for such a simple thing as a birth certificate, for instance, without being accompanied by Don Circostanza. If he had gone there alone, he would have been kicked out, like a dog out of church. Baldissera remembered that when the Rome-Pescara railway line was first opened, the people of Fontamara would go to the Fossa station armed, not only with enough money to pay the fare, but also with one of Don Circostanza's visiting cards. However, in the course of time, traveling by train became more commonplace and the trains more crowded, with the result that this custom gradually fell out of use, and *cafoni* actually traveled to Rome secretly, without so much as even mentioning it to Don Circostanza. But in all other respects a poor *cafone* who lacked a patron felt like a sheep without a shepherd.

In the memory of the oldest inhabitants of Fontamara things had not always been like this. At one time there had been three or four big landowners, including the bishop, who owned and managed everything themselves on the basis of two or three simple laws that were well known to everyone. People were not well off — in fact, they were very badly off, but everything was simple. Complications and swindles began, according to the old, when the Piedmontese arrived. Every day they made a new law and set up a new office, and to enable people to find their way about in all this lawyers became necessary. Nominally the law was made independent of the landowners and was supposed to be the same for everyone, but to apply it, dodge it, turn it to your own advantage, the importance of lawyers and their numbers grew. At the same time the old type of landowner and the old type of priest decayed, as was shown by Don Carlo Magna and Don Abbacchio.

When I was a boy, there were only two lawyers in Fossa, and they also acted as notaries; now there are eight lawyers and four notaries, without counting the lesser rogues who take arbitration cases. In order to make a living all these lawyers are obliged every week to devise new plots, encourage quarrels that will lead to litigation, and drag out to eternity the most insignificant cases. Because of the lawyers, quarrels that in the old days were patched up informally now last for years, cost vast sums of money, and leave long trails of hate and rancor in their wake. Because of the lawyers, relations between families have grown more and more mistrustful. They insinuate themselves everywhere. And how are they to be gotten rid of? Their gestures, their tone of voice, their way of dressing and greeting one, their way of eating and drinking, seem to be specially devised to strike the imagination of the poor. Every *cafone*'s ambition is to have a lawyer as godfather; and in church on confirmation day every lawyer is surrounded by dozens of *cafone* children accompanied by their mothers in their Sunday best.

The only *cafoni* who stay outside this system of patronage are the landless ones, those with nothing to protect, with nothing to lose or gain, that is, unless they are scoundrels, in which case they have more need of a patron than anyone else. But this patronage is of course never exercised against the rich.

How many times had Don Circostanza swindled us in the past, but how were we to manage without him? Also he always behaved in a friendly, cordial way toward us, he always shook hands with everyone, and when he was drunk, he actually embraced us and asked us to forgive him, and we always did forgive him. But with the three-quarters-each swindle followed by the ten-lusters swindle he had gone too far.

No one could reconcile himself to the loss of the water — that is, to dying of hunger — but no one knew how to get the water back. Pilato and Michele Zompa wanted us to sue the Contractor, but I and others opposed this. We knew only too well what happens in such cases: they last for tens or even hundreds of years, they go from one court to another, from one appeal to another, they swallow up the resources of whole villages, and they end up leaving things exactly as they were. And even if we did take the Contractor to court, to whom were we to entrust our case? To Don Circostanza? He would merely think up another swindle like the three-quarters-each and the ten-lusters swindles. Better not talk of it. Yet no one could resign himself to the loss of the water. No one could resign himself to the loss of his whole crop. No one could get used to the idea of a winter without bread or soup.

"We've reached the end," Zompa kept saying. "You'll see, one of these days the Almighty will lose patience, there'll be an earthquake, and that will be that."

"When the government's laws are no longer observed and those whose job is to see that they are observed are the first to violate them, it's time to return to the law of the people," Baldissera replied angrily.

"What is the law of the people?" he was asked.

"God helps those who help themselves," said Baldissera, who had ended up adopting the hard doctrine of Berardo Viola.

There could be no denying the truth of what Baldissera said, but it offered no solution to our plight. Besides, Baldissera only talked like that; he was incapable of killing a fly.

Berardo, however, said nothing. The poor chap was no longer himself. His mind was elsewhere. His silence baffled and perplexed the young men who considered him their leader. They regarded his absence on the day the waters were divided as a betrayal, and there was more resentment against him than against Don Circostanza. He now lived the life of a recluse, and he was hardly ever seen. Previously he had gone too far one way; now he went too far the other. All plans to claim our rights left him cold.

"So much the worse for you," he said. "I have no land to irrigate." He also said, "I'm no longer a boy, I have my own affairs to think about."

He now had only one idea in his head: to go away, emigrate, work like a beast of burden, work twice as hard as anyone else, and so come back to Fontamara after six months or a year, buy a bit of land, and marry. It was impossible to talk to him about anything else. He was a changed man. I was one of the few who sympathized with him.

"I'll go away, work ten hours a day, twelve hours a day, even fourteen hours a day," he kept telling me, "and I'll come back with a thousand lire in my pocket. Ten lire is not a great deal, but it'll be the average wage. If I work more than the others, I'll be able to earn more, and as for spending it, I'll tighten my belt to the last hole."

Every now and then he would go and see Don Circostanza to find out if the lawyer had yet had a satisfactory answer from Rome; and he would go and see him in the evening, so that his fellow villagers wouldn't know, thus avoiding painful arguments. The lawyer seemed genuinely to want to see him leave as soon as possible and gave him good advice, and congratulated him on every visit on his decision to save money, marry, and settle down.

"There's no better way of getting rid of bees in one's bonnet," Don Circostanza told him in almost paternal tones, imitating the way in which priests talk. "A wife, a few children, a home, a little money put aside tame young men like you much better than fear of the *carabinieri*. I too," he added in confidential tones, "behaved pretty wildly when I was a bachelor."

This confession made Berardo forget all the swindles that had gone before and reinforced him in his new ideas, and eventually the Friend of the People sent for him urgently one evening and introduced him to a traveling salesman from Rome who gave him some hints on job-finding in the capital.

"And if the *carabinieri* make me get off the train?" Berardo asked.

"You mustn't tell them you're looking for work," the stranger explained, laughing at such a foolish idea. "Tell them you're going to Rome on a pilgrimage, or to visit a relative dying in the hospital."

Berardo asked me to lend him a hundred lire, and I did so, on condition he take my son with him, and he agreed.

On the evening before he left I went to see him, because I wanted to talk to him about my son. I found him in Elvira's dyeing shop, sitting at the foot of the bed on which poor Damiano was lying.

"If it's heavy work I don't want my son to work more than ten hours a day," I started telling Berardo, "and I don't want you to stay at taverns frequented by bad women."

But I was interrupted by the arrival of Raffaele Scarpone. Three other young men were with him, but waited outside.

Raffaele went straight up to Berardo and said, "Revolution has broken out at Sulmona."

"What sort of revolution?" Berardo said with some irritation. "What do you mean, what sort of revolution?"

"Have the confetti manufacturers revolted?" Berardo said with a laugh.

"A *cafone* revolution has broken out at Sulmona," Scarpone said in the tones of someone who wants to leave joking aside.

"Who told you?" Berardo asked mistrustfully.

Scarpone hesitated, and then said, "Baldissera."

"And who told Baldissera?"

"That's a secret," Scarpone replied.

"Then it isn't true," Berardo announced, and turned to me to resume the interrupted conversation.

Scarpone went outside and told Venerdì Santo, who was one of those waiting there, to go get Baldissera.

While we waited, no one spoke. In a corner of the room Elvira was preparing vegetables for the soup.

Baldissera had to be persuaded, but eventually he arrived. He greeted Damiano ceremoniously, and then he told us this:

"I went to Fossa today to buy some sole leather, and in the square I ran into Donna Clorinda coming out of church. As you know, when I was a boy I worked in her house, and we have always been on friendly terms, and when we meet, we stop and talk. 'Sant'Antonio himself must have sent you to me,' Don Carlo Magna's wife said to me quietly. 'Drop in and see me for a moment, because I've got to talk to you.' Knowing my duty, but not having the slightest idea what it was all about, I went to see her as soon as I had bought my leather. 'Have you heard the great news?' she said as soon as she opened the door. 'Revolution has broken out at Sulmona. *Carabiniere* reinforcements have been sent for, from here and from all around.' According to what she told me, there seems to be a kind of Contractor at Sulmona too who has reduced everyone to ruin. The revolution began in the market square three days ago, and is still going on. 'Can it be that the day of reckoning has come for our brigand too?' the lady said, referring to our Contractor. I said nothing. 'For two months I have been keeping the candles lit night and day in front of the statue of Sant'Antonio so that something might happen to him, but nothing has happened yet,' she whispered in my ear. As I still said nothing, she started talking more openly. 'This is the time to act,' she said. 'The *carabinieri* have gone to Sulmona. Hatred of the Contractor is widespread. Everything depends on making a start, giving a signal, and only the people of Fontamara can give it. When I met you just now outside the church I realized at once that you have been sent by Sant'Antonio.' I explained that I had come to town just to buy a bit of sole leather, but the lady thought otherwise. 'No, it was Sant'Antonio himself who sent you,' she insisted. 'During my prayers this morning the saint directed me. He said, "I can do nothing for you. Only the people of Fontamara can give that brigand the lesson he deserves." And then outside the church I met you.'"

Don Carlo Magna's wife also hinted to the old cobbler that if the people of Fontamara needed anything, such as gasoline or arms, for instance, they could have it, provided they applied through some trustworthy person.

"Well, what do you say to that?" Scarpone said to Berardo as soon as Baldissera had finished.

"What do you say about it?" Berardo replied.

"Before coming here, some of us got together. In their name, and in the name of those waiting outside, I tell you we must follow the Sulmona example and must not refuse anyone's aid," Scarpone said vigorously.

He had already worked out a plan for a night raid, beginning with the destruction of various enterprises belonging to the Contractor.

"And why all this?" said Berardo, as if lost in a reverie.

"Are you living in the moon, man?" Scarpone exclaimed. "Have you forgotten all the wrongs that the Contractor has done us? Can't you see that there's no other way out for us? Don't you realize that there will be nothing but stones to eat at Fontamara next winter?"

Berardo let him talk. Then he turned to Baldissera and, with the same impassivity and assumed naïveté as before, said, "If Donna Clorinda has a grudge against the Contractor, why does she appeal for aid to Sant'Antonio? Hasn't she got a husband? And if Sant'Antonio shares the lady's feelings, why docs he appeal to the people of Fontamara? Hasn't he any angels handy?"

Then he turned to Scarpone and went on in the same tone, "If you burn down the Contractor's property, do you suppose we shall be able to live on the ashes next winter? If the workmen now employed at the Contractor's cement works and brickworks and tannery lose their jobs, do you suppose the people of Fontamara will benefit?"

Then he changed his tone and said what he really felt.

"All these things are no concern of mine," he said. "Our situation is bad enough in all conscience. Every man must look to his own affairs. In the past I troubled myself too much about things that didn't concern me. The result is that at the age of thirty I own nothing but the straw bed on which I sleep. Now I'm not a boy any longer and I've got my own affairs to think about. So leave me in peace."

"It's not we who don't leave you in peace," Scarpone replied. "It's the Contractor who doesn't leave us in peace."

Berardo listened, shaking his head. He knew all those arguments, which he had used hundreds of times in discussions with other *cafoni*. But now he wasn't a boy any longer, he no longer had only himself to think about. He was no longer in a position to risk his life and liberty. Now he had to think differently. Just when the whole village had come around to his point of view, he had changed his mind.

"Listen," he said in a tone of voice that left no more doubt possible. "I've no intention of going to prison for the sake of your water and your land. I've got my own affairs to worry about."

Scarpone and Baldissera got up and walked out.

When he was outside, Scarpone raised his voice, so that we too should hear, and said to the young men waiting there, "Berardo's afraid."

What would happen now? To the young men of Fontamara Berardo was a demigod. They would have been willing to face death under his leadership, but it was easy to see that without him nothing would happen.

All this time Elvira had been standing silently near the fireplace. Throughout the argument she hadn't taken her eyes off Berardo, and she had listened to him, at first with curiosity, as if she doubted whether he was serious, then with astonishment, and finally, when no more doubt was possible, with anxiety and concern, though without daring to interrupt or contradict him in the presence of others.

But when Scarpone and Baldissera had left, she could restrain herself no longer and said to him reproachfully, "If it's on my account that you're behaving like this, you might remember that what first attracted me to you was my being told that you used exactly the opposite arguments."

When he heard that Elvira, too, was against him, he could not repress an angry gesture and nearly let out some terrible expletive, but instead he turned on his heel and left without even saying good night.

When I got home, I found my wife and son waiting for me.

So that the boy should not cut too bad a figure in Rome my wife had given him a suit of mine that was a little too big for him around the shoulders, but otherwise fit quite well. Actually it was probably about ten years old, but it was the best we had in the house. My wife sewed a scapular of San Giuseppe da Copertino in between the material and the lining of the collar as a protection against misfortunes. A knapsack with food for the first few days was already hanging behind the door; it contained a loaf, a couple of onions, some tomatoes, a handful of almonds, and some sheep's milk cheese. I gave the boy a letter of recommendation from Don Circostanza to be used in case of need; it was in very general terms and was a couple of years old, and I had already used it several times, but it might still come in handy.

My wife was worried by the rumors of revolution she had heard, and asked me what truth was in them.

"Never mind what happens," I said to my son, "you try to go to sleep, because tomorrow you've got to leave before dawn."

We all tried to go to sleep, or pretended we were asleep, but none of us succeeded. At about two o'clock all three of us were still awake when we heard chimes of the church bell. The first and second chimes were pretty loud and distinct, and the others were like a distant echo of them.

"Did you hear?" my wife exclaimed in alarm, turning toward me.

"It must be Our Lady," I replied. "Let's try to go to sleep."

That was an evasive reply. All three of us went on listening, holding our breath, but we heard nothing more.

Perhaps half an hour later there were two or three more chimes, fainter than the first.

"Did you hear?" said my wife in alarm.

"It must be the wind," I replied. "Let's try to go to sleep."

But the air was still, and it could not have been the wind. In any case, even the strongest north wind had never rung our church bell.

A little while afterward there was another chime, which we heard only because we were listening.

"It must be an owl," I said, for the sake of saying something.

"Can an owl ring a church bell?"

"If it's not an owl, it must be a weasel," I said.

"What can a weasel be doing in the bell tower?"

"If it isn't a weasel, it must be a witch," was the only answer I could think of.

At that moment few people could have been asleep in Fontamara, and all those who had been kept awake by the unusual chiming of the bell were making the same conjectures and having the same arguments as we were. But everyone minded his own business and no one got up to go and see who was in the bell tower.

My son will tell you what happened next.

8

AT FOUR O'CLOCK IN THE morning Berardo and I left Fontamara and set off to Fossa to catch the train to Rome.

Berardo was in a black mood and did not even answer my good morning, but to avoid any unpleasantness right at the beginning I pretended not to notice.

"Did you hear the bell last night?" I asked, trying to start a conversation. I might have been talking to a brick wall.

When we got to the chapel of Our Lady of the Flood, I tried again.

"Did you hear the bell?" I asked.

He didn't answer.

He walked quickly, taking enormous strides, and I had to make an effort to keep up with him.

As we entered Fossa we were surprised to hear the whistle of a train, and we ran to avoid missing it, but it was a goods train, and there was a long wait before ours came in.

After we'd been in the waiting room for half an hour Scarpone suddenly appeared in the doorway. He was pale and distraught.

Berardo pretended not to see him. He turned his back and

started reading a notice on the wall with exaggerated interest.

But Scarpone went straight over to him and said, "Teofilo has hanged himself."

Berardo did not raise his eyes from the notice.

"Baldissera found him this morning on the bell tower stairs," Scarpone went on. "The bell rope was tied around his neck. The body was still warm. He must have been struggling on the rope all night, and no one went to his aid."

"May he rest in peace," Berardo said without turning his head.

"I went to see Don Abbacchio," Scarpone went on, as if incredulous of Berardo's indifferences. "I've just come from his house. He began by abusing me for waking him so early, and then he refused to come and give the absolution. 'How can you refuse the blessing to a sacristan who has served the Church all his life?' I asked him. 'A man who hangs himself goes to hell,' he replied, 'and a sacristan who hangs himself goes to the bottommost pit.'"

"May he rest in peace," Berardo repeated without turning a hair.

"We must put Teofilo in the middle of the church," Scarpone went on, "and keep him there for twenty-four hours, so that Christ, Our Lady, San Rocco, Sant'Antonio, San Giuseppe da Copertino, San Berardo, and all the other saints may have time to see him. Let them see the straits to which we are reduced."

"May he rest in peace," Berardo said again.

Our train came in.

"Don't go," Scarpone suddenly burst out.

"Why not?" Berardo replied in surprise.

"Don't go," Scarpone begged him.

Berardo went toward the train, and reluctantly I followed him. Behind us came Scarpone, shaking his head and with tears in his eyes.

"The *carabinieri* will be coming to Fontamara today because of Teofilo," Scarpone said. "Berardo, don't go, don't leave us, you can go tomorrow."

But we went.

Throughout the journey we didn't exchange a word. Berardo

sat opposite me and spent the whole time looking out the window, as if he were concentrating on a single idea.

Watching him, I could see that he would stop at nothing to gain his ends. No scruple would restrain him. If he thought it might serve his purpose, he would have had no hesitation in throwing me out the window. The set of his jaws was frightening. If he's hungry, he'll eat me, I said to myself.

Through the window we saw mountains, fields, houses, gardens, orchards, streams, hedges, horses, cows, sheep, villages pass by, and then land and yet more land.

"What a lot of land," Berardo muttered between his teeth.

Suddenly we noticed that two *carabinieri* had entered the carriage and were asking questions of all the passengers.

"Where are you going?" they abruptly asked us too.

"On a pilgrimage," Berardo replied, producing a letter from Don Abbacchio with the parish stamp on it.

The *carabinieri* wished us a safe journey.

Berardo smiled.

Before getting out at the Rome station he tightened his shoelaces and spat in the palm of his hands like a man preparing to face a heavy task.

At Rome we put up at the Inn of the Good Thief, which had been recommended to Berardo by the traveler he met at Don Circostanza's office. On the door there was a sign representing the three crosses of Calvary, from which it might have been supposed that the place took its name from the celebrated thief who was crucified on Christ's right hand and recognized Him before he died and was rewarded with the great promise: "Today thou shalt be with Me in Paradise." But, as we learned later, the place was actually named after the owner, who had served several terms of imprisonment for theft and in the evening of his life had thrown in his lot with the Fascists and had taken part in a large number of punitive expeditions against enemies of the regime, specializing in patriotic robberies from cooperatives and workers' organizations. These meritorious services were eventually rewarded at a solemn patriotic ceremony at which the chief of police personally bestowed on him the title of Good Thief.

Next morning we presented ourselves at the office that was to give us work on a reclamation scheme. A porter in uniform sent us to the third floor, where there was a corridor in which a lot of people were waiting. We joined the line. Our turn came at about midday, and only then did we discover that we had been waiting, not on the third floor, but on the fourth.

We returned the next day and went to the third floor, where we waited for three hours, sitting on a bench, the two of us alone. A large number of people passed, but no one took any notice of us. The people we asked answered irritably. Eventually we were sent to the fifth floor, where we waited for two hours before being told to apply somewhere else.

That was how we spent the third day. At the next place to which we went they said, "Have you got your cards?"

"What cards?" we answered in surprise.

I produced the old letter from Don Circostanza that my father had given me, but the clerk laughed at me.

"That's no use," he said. "You have to have a card."

We were taken to a window where a clerk gave us two pieces of paper on which he stuck twelve stamps, one for each month of the year.

"Thirty-five lire," he said.

"Pay, pay, always pay," Berardo grumbled.

Thirty-five lashes would not have hurt us more. We paid the thirty-five lire and went back to the first office with the two pieces of paper.

"Here are our cards," we said.

"You have done your duty," the clerk replied. "Go to the employment office tomorrow and have yourself registered as unemployed and as volunteers for work on public reclamation schemes."

So ended the fourth day.

I must say Berardo was not at all annoyed at these long, drawn-out procedures. In fact, he insisted that they were natural.

"The more difficult it is to get a job, the better paid it will be," he kept assuring me.

In the afternoon, when the offices were shut, he took me for walks all over the city.

"Look, look," he exclaimed the first time we came across a building with the word BANK written up outside it. For some minutes he gazed at it as if entranced.

"That's where the Contractor gets his money from," he whispered in my ear.

But then we came across another bank, and then another and another and another, and in the end we stopped counting them. Which was the Contractor's? It was impossible to say. In the middle of Rome, where we expected to find San Pietro's, there was nothing but banks.

"Look, look," Berardo exclaimed each time he spotted another one.

Each bank building was grander than the last, and some had domes, like churches. Around them there was a great coming and going of people and cars.

Berardo gazed at them in wonder.

"But they have domes," I pointed out, "perhaps they are churches."

"Yes, but the god worshiped in them is a different one," Berardo replied with a laugh. "The god that now reigns over this world is Money, and that applies to everyone, including even priests like Don Abbacchio, who nominally worship the God in heaven. Perhaps our ruin," Berardo added, "was to have gone on believing in the old God while a new one now reigns over the world."

Berardo stopped to drink at every fountain, just as our donkeys do on the way to the Fucino in the morning. But we also came across splendid ones that flung huge jets of water up to incredible heights in the air, and those you couldn't drink from.

"What a waste of water," Berardo complained. "If only we had all that water at Fontamara."

One morning he bought a colored shawl, a comb, and a hair clasp from an itinerant vendor.

"I'll send them to Elvira as soon as I can," he said to me, making an effort to pronounce her name. "Do you think they'll suit her?"

"Of course," I replied, and added the usual phrase about everything suiting a pretty girl.

"Do you really think she's pretty?" he said. "When you're in love everything gradually changes its meaning," he also said.

Berardo very much enjoyed sitting on benches in the avenues and public gardens.

"Sit down," he would say to me. "It seems incredible, but it's free."

He would listen attentively to the conversation of strangers sitting on our bench or neighboring ones.

"You never know," he said. "There's always a chance we might overhear someone saying he's looking for a good, strong, reliable workman, preferably from the Abruzzi mountains, in short, someone who isn't work-shy."

When we got back one evening we found that a crowd had gathered outside our inn. A wheel had come off a military forage cart, which had overturned and was lying on its side against a wall, and several men were trying to lift it, but as often happens in towns, they were more noisy than effective. Berardo pressed forward, took off his coat and hat, bent under the cart, went down on his knees, crept underneath it, and then, taking the weight on his back, slowly righted it and held it up, enabling the driver to put back the wheel, to the admiration of the onlookers.

This incident restored some of his old talkativeness.

"Donna Clorinda keeps two candles lit in front of the statue of Sant'Antonio to destroy the power of banks. Isn't it absurd?" he said to me that evening.

But I was in no mood for an argument. I realized he wanted to return to the argument he had had with Scarpone on the evening before we left, which was still burning him up inside, but there was little for him to discuss with me.

"Harebrained excesses are all very well so long as you're young," he said. "Roasting chestnuts in the fire makes sense, but what's the use of burning down the Contractor's villa? What good does it do?"

He seemed to need to go on talking, so I let him.

"It's not a question of courage, don't you see?" he said. "How can Scarpone think I'm afraid? It's not a question of courage. If there's a chance to risk my life to earn a little more than others, you'll see. I feel I've got the strength to do what no one has ever done before. You'll see. Tomorrow we'll get to work, and as soon as we start, you'll see, and the others will see, too, and so will the engineers."

"I wonder how Teofilo's funeral went off," I said to distract him from these ravings. The interruption greatly displeased him.

"Courage has nothing to do with it, and neither has the use of force," he went on rudely. "Has the Contractor ever used force against us? He has not. He used neither courage nor strength; he used cunning, and that's how he got the stream. He didn't even take it; the people of Fontamara gave it to him. First they signed a petition to the government, then they agreed to the three-quarters-each swindle and then to the ten-lusters swindle. What else should the Contractor have done? He acted correctly, in his own interests."

That was how wrongheaded he had become.

"The price of land is bound to drop," he went on, revealing his innermost thoughts. "Without water there's bound to be a big drop in the price of land, and it will have to be cultivated differently."

He already knew the piece of land he wanted, but he wouldn't tell me where it was.

On the morning of the fifth day we went to the employment office, and after we had waited in front of a window all the morning, we were asked, "What province do you come from?"

"Aquila," we promptly replied.

"In that case you must apply to the Aquila office."

"Where's that?"

The clerk burst out laughing. He repeated our question to the other clerks, with the result that his hilarity spread to the whole office. When quiet returned and the clerk had wiped away the tears that came from his having laughed so much, he explained to us that the Aquila office was at Aquila.

But we had no desire to make the tour of Italy.

"We've been to too many offices," Berardo announced energetically. "We came to Rome with a lawyer's recommendation to be sent to do reclamation work and not to make the stations of the cross."

The clerk slammed the window in our face, and our calvary continued.

One of the residents at the Inn of the Good Thief was Don Achille Pazienza, a lawyer from the Abruzzi. We did as the Good Thief suggested and immediately applied to him for aid and advice, and next day, the sixth of our stay in Rome, he summoned us to an audience in his bedroom, which was next to ours and was just as small, dark, dirty, and untidy. He received us lying flat on his bed; he was a poor little old man who suffered from catarrh, had a ten-day beard, wore a yellow suit and white canvas shoes, and had a straw hat on his head, a bronze medal on his chest, and a toothpick in his mouth; that was how he caparisoned himself to receive us. Under the bed there was a chamber pot full of urine. On the darkest wall there was a phosphorescent, yellowy green portrait of a frightening head, under which was the word DUCE.

"The consultation fee is ten lire," Don Pazienza began by saying.

"All right," I replied impulsively.

"Ten lire in advance," he added.

We handed over the ten lire.

"Ten lire each," he said.

We handed over another ten lire.

He rose from the bed and left the room without saying another word. We heard his cough making its way along the corridor and then slowly going down the staircase, stopping for a few minutes on the ground floor, where the Good Thief was lying in wait, and then going out into the street and vanishing into the tavern opposite.

We had to wait for nearly an hour before the cough reappeared, crossed the street again, slowly and laboriously mounted the staircase, lingered for a moment outside our door, and then came in, bringing with it a small French loaf, half a salami, and half a bottle of red wine.

"Yours is a very bad case," he announced after resuming his horizontal position, though we had not yet told him what we wanted from him.

"How much money have you left?" he asked, after a pause for meditation.

We put all the money we had left into Berardo's hat. Including the small change, it amounted to about fourteen lire.

"Your case is insignificant and actually hopeless," he announced in disappointment.

After another pause for meditation he said, "Couldn't you have more money sent from Fontamara?"

"Of course," Berardo promptly replied, though he was well aware of the opposite.

"And perhaps a teeny-weeny chicken? And a bit of cheese? And some honey, which is very good for coughs?" he added.

Berardo, who had never tasted honey in his life, hurriedly replied, "Of course."

"Your case is perfectly simple and straightforward," Don Pazienza announced with a large, horsey smile that displayed all his yellow teeth. "Tell me about it," he then said.

Berardo explained why we had come to Rome.

The lawyer rose, fetched a stick that looked just like an old umbrella handle, brandished it like a warrior setting out for the wars, and said, "Follow me."

We followed him. The first stop was at a telegraph office, where the lawyer composed the following telegram: "Urgently require two hundred lire twenty pounds cheese four pounds honey some chickens."

"To whom shall I address it?" he said. "Which of you has the richer family?"

"Address it to my father, Vincenzo Viola," replied Berardo, whose father died when he was a boy.

Don Pazienza was just handing in the telegram when Berardo said, "Sir, don't you like peaches?"

"Do I not?" the lawyer replied. "They're excellent for coughs."

So a request for twenty pounds of peaches was added to the telegram. The lawyer took a copy, and said, "Pay and follow me."

Out next stop was at the trade union employment office from which we had been sent away the day before. Don Pazienza left us in the corridor, but through a window we could see him engaged in animated conversation with the head of the office, to whom he showed a copy of the telegram sent to Fontamara, pointing out the most significant phrases. The head of the office must have had some strong objections to make, because the lawyer grew pale and came hurrying over toward us.

"Is Fontamara cheese for grating or for eating?" he wanted to know.

"When it's fresh it's for eating and when it's hard it's for grating," Berardo replied, to the great satisfaction of the lawyer, who hurried back to the head of the office with this reassuring reply.

Evidently there were no more serious hitches, as the lawyer came back and told us that matters were in hand. The office would apply for the necessary documentation — that is, birth certificates, police records, and certificates of good conduct — and as soon as these arrived our names would be put on the unemployed register. A reclamation job would follow. The office would send for us in due course.

On our seventh day in Rome we had only four lire left. We bought four pounds of bread, and that left us with a *centesimo*.

"It won't be long now before they send for us," Berardo kept assuring me to reassure himself.

He was still far from giving up hope.

Thus he would suddenly be seized with a strange idea while lying on his bed, and we would have to dash outdoors.

"A gentleman in the street might stop us," he explained, "and say, 'Excuse me, are you by any chance looking for a job? Would thirty lire a day do to begin with, in addition to meals, of course? You can start tomorrow if you like.'"

We went as far as the avenue and sat on the first bench we came to, listening to the conversations all around us. But after a while Berardo would suddenly have another idea.

"Very likely Don Achille Pazienza is looking for us and getting angry because he can't find us. 'Just when I've found them a good job, they disappear,' he's probably saying."

After that, to be on the spot when we were sent for, and also because we had no great desire to go out walking on an empty stomach, we no longer left the inn. Whenever we heard footsteps we rushed to the door, and whenever we saw the postman coming we hurried down to the ground floor, where the Good Thief was lying in wait.

Don Pazienza was on tenterhooks just as much as we were, though with the difference that we were waiting to be sent for to work, while he was waiting for a money order and an appetizing food parcel from Berardo's father. All three of us spent the day lying on our beds, and all three hurried downstairs at the slightest sound.

On the way up again mutual recriminations grew more bitter every day.

"You have an unnatural father," the lawyer said to Berardo. "Why does it take him such a long time to send two hundred lire?"

"Is there work or isn't there?" Berardo replied. "If there is, why don't they send for us? If there is, why all these formalities?"

"Never mind about the parcels," the lawyer went on. "Parcels are slow, of course, especially if the contents are a bit fragile, but a telegraphic money order arrives the same day. Your father is a selfish man."

"Why do you need a birth certificate to get a job?" Berardo replied. "If someone is looking for a job, it's obvious he was born. Nobody wants a job before he's born."

After three days of fasting and useless waiting Berardo and I stopped going downstairs whenever the postman came. We lay on our beds from morning to night and got up only to drink water occasionally from the tap in the lavatory. Don Pazienza was much more persistent and optimistic. Three times a day, whenever the postman arrived, we heard his cough rising from his bed, leaving the room, and slowly going downstairs to the ground floor and after a while slowly and laboriously coming up again, lingering for a moment near the keyhole of our room, and then uttering fresh imprecations against Fontamara.

"Berardo Viola," the poor old man gasped, "your father's a scoundrel. Your father's the ruin of me, Berardo Viola, your father's the death of me. I haven't eaten for three days," he shouted, "because of your father."

Berardo did not reply. He had relapsed into silence. He spent hours lying on the bed with his hands behind the back of his head, staring at the ceiling.

"What shall we do?" I said. "We can't go on forever without eating."

Berardo did not reply.

Once he said, "They say that when my grandfather was in the mountains he once went without food for three weeks and drank nothing but water."

Another time he said, "What day is it today?" Then he went on, "By now Elvira must be back from the pilgrimage she was going to make to Our Lady of Perpetual Succor. She was going to make it on foot, with poor Maria Grazia, to obtain pardon."

"Elvira has no need of any pardon," I said. "She'll just want to accompany Maria Grazia."

On the afternoon of the fourth day of our fast we had a thrill. It must have been about five o'clock in the afternoon when we heard confused cries from Don Pazienza and the Good Thief outside on the staircase.

"Victory, victory," the lawyer exclaimed, and burst into a patriotic song:

> Oh, where are victory's golden wings?
> God made her slave of Rome.

When the two reached our door they flung it wide open without knocking and walked in, the Good Thief waving a telegram for Berardo and the lawyer holding two bottles of wine by the neck.

"Berardo Viola," he exclaimed, "your father is a gentleman. The money order has arrived."

"Really?" Berardo exclaimed in amazement, almost beside himself with joy. How could he believe that his father, who had been dead for twenty years or more, had sent him a money order? After fasting for four days he was obviously a little unhinged.

While the lawyer poured out some wine to celebrate the happy occasion Berardo took the telegram, opened it, read it, read it again, looked us in the face, folded it, and put it in his pocket without saying a word.

"What is it?" I asked.

Berardo didn't answer; in fact, he certainly didn't even hear me. There was a terrifying look on his face, and the whites of his eyes were bloodshot.

"What is it?" I repeated in the most affectionate tone I could manage.

Berardo lay on the bed again, still without speaking. The Good Thief and Don Pazienza went off in consternation.

I sat beside Berardo and repeated in an undertone, "What is it, what has happened? Has someone died?"

He didn't answer, and I don't know how I realized that someone at Fontamara had died.

At about eight o'clock the same evening there was an unusual commotion in the room next to ours — which, as I have mentioned, was occupied by Don Achille Pazienza — who came to our door and said, "The head of the trade union employment office came to see me. Your papers have arrived. Your certificate, signed by the *podestà*, says: 'Conduct, worst possible from the national point of view.' With a certificate like that you can't be given a job. Also, the police have been notified. You'll never get a job."

He slammed the door and went away.

Five minutes later the door was opened again.

"Your room has been let," the Good Thief announced. "You have half an hour to clear out."

By the time we left the Inn of the Good Thief it was dark.

"What shall we do?" I asked Berardo.

What could he say? He didn't answer.

Because I was so hungry my legs were weak and I had a bad

headache. Every now and then I thought I was going to collapse. In the street people turned to look at us, and they moved aside when we approached as if they were afraid. And Berardo really looked alarming.

We kept coming across stalls loaded with watermelons, surrounded by all sorts of people making a din to show how cheerful they were, and over some of the stalls there were arches of colored lights. Couples were dancing in the gardens of the inns: they had certainly had dinner.

"We might ask for soup at some monastery," I suggested, but Berardo didn't answer.

We found ourselves near the station, without meaning to. In the square there was a large number of *carabinieri*, militiamen, and police who were stopping passersby and searching them. A young man looked at us in amazement, and then stopped in front of us.

"Good evening," he said to Berardo with a smile.

Berardo looked at him mistrustfully and didn't answer.

"I was just thinking about you," the young man went on. "If I hadn't met you, I should have gone to Fontamara tomorrow to look for you."

"I haven't got a *centesimo*," Berardo said. "If you're looking for someone to swindle, you'd better try someone else."

The young man burst out laughing. He looked half student, half workman. He was tall, thin, and well but not smartly dressed, and his voice and the way he looked at you did not invite suspicion. But we were not in a very trustful frame of mind.

"Do you remember the last time you were at Avezzano?" the young man said to Berardo. "You remember the tavern to which the policeman with red hair and a scar on his chin took you and some other men from Fontamara? You remember? No, you've forgotten who put you on your guard against him."

Berardo looked carefully at the young man and recognized him.

"Buy us something to eat," I said to him, fearing that Berardo was going to let the opportunity slip.

The young man took us to a café close by and ordered us ham and eggs.

"Is that for us?" Berardo said suspiciously. "And who's going to pay? We haven't got a *soldo* left."

To reassure him the young man had to go to the counter and pay the bill in advance, while Berardo looked at me as if to say the fellow must be mad.

"What's all this activity by the *carabinieri* and the militia about?" Berardo asked the young man after we had eaten something.

"It's the search for the usual Mystery Man," he replied.

What he meant was not very clear to us.

"For some time past," the young man explained in an undertone, "an unknown person known as the Mystery Man has been a threat to public order. In every case heard by the Special Tribunal there is talk of a Mystery Man who prints and distributes clandestine newspapers denouncing scandals, inciting workers to strike and citizens to disobey. People who are caught in possession of these illegal newspapers always say they got them from the Mystery Man. At first he was mostly active in the neighborhood of certain factories, but then he began to favor the outskirts of cities and soldiers' barracks, and then he also turned up at universities. He has been reported to have been in different provinces and even on the frontier on the same day, and the cleverest detectives have been put on his trail, but so far they have failed to catch him. Several thousand persons have been arrested, and several times the government has believed that the Mystery Man was among them. But after brief interruptions the clandestine press has always reappeared and the Mystery Man's activities have again been mentioned in court proceedings. For some time past he seems to have been extending his activities to the Abruzzi."

"The Abruzzi?" Berardo exclaimed.

"Yes, he has been reported at Sulmona, Prezza, Avezzano, and other places also. Wherever the *cafoni* revolt he appears."

"But who is he? Is he the devil?" Berardo asked.

"Perhaps he is," the man from Avezzano replied with a laugh. "But he's a good devil."

"If only he could be shown the way to Fontamara," Berardo added.

"He knows it already," was the answer in an undertone.

At that moment a policeman, followed by a party of militiamen, walked into the café and came straight toward us.

"Passports or identity cards," the policeman said abruptly.

While he examined the cards Berardo and I had gotten from the trade union office and the identity card, passport, and many other documents produced by the man from Avezzano, the militiamen searched the café.

Our papers seemed to be in order and the policeman was just going away when the militiamen came toward us with a parcel wrapped up in a piece of cloth that they had found under the hat stand. At the sight of the contents the policeman and the militiamen leaped in the air as if they had been bitten by a tarantula, and they rushed at us, shouting, "Whom does this parcel belong to? Who left it there?"

Without even listening to what we said they surrounded us and dragged us off to the police station.

Berardo thought we had been taken for thieves and that the parcel found on the floor contained stolen property, so on the way to the police station he kept shouting, "Us, thieves? You ought to be ashamed of yourselves. You're the thieves. We're the robbed, not the robbers. The trade unions that took thirty-five lire from us are thieves. Don Pazienza, who took twenty lire from us, is a thief. Us, thieves? The Contractor's a thief, but you'd never dare arrest him."

More and more arrested persons from different parts of the city kept arriving at the police station to which we were taken.

"The hunt for the Mystery Man goes on," the man from Avezzano explained in an undertone to Berardo, who eventually realized that we were not suspected of robbery and calmed down.

After the completion of some formalities we were put in a dark cell in which there were two other prisoners already. Berardo and I exchanged smiles of satisfaction. We were assured of a roof over our heads and meals next day. So far as the more distant future was concerned, there would be time to think about that later.

Half the space of the cell was taken up by a raised concrete block a little higher than an ordinary pavement, and this served as a bed. In a corner there was a stinking hole the purpose of which was even more obvious. The two prisoners who had arrived before us were curled up in a corner, their heads resting on their jackets, which they had folded up to serve as a pillow. I promptly imitated them: I took off my jacket, folded it, and stretched out on the concrete with the jacket under my head. But Berardo and the man from Avezzano began an animated conversation, striding up and down the cell. The man from Avezzano spoke in a low voice, perhaps out of mistrust of our two unknown companions, but Berardo had difficulty in doing the same. In any event, all I heard of what passed between them was what Berardo said.

"I don't find this story about the Mystery Man at all convincing," he said. "Is he a townsman or a *cafone*? If he's a townsman and goes to the Abruzzi, he must have some ulterior motive."

The man from Avezzano laughed.

"But townsmen are well off," Berardo insisted. "Townsmen are well off because they exploit the *cafoni*. Yes, I know, there are townspeople who are badly off too. Don Pazienza, for instance, is not exactly living in the lap of luxury. But he's not a real townsman, he's an Abruzzese who has gone to live in town."

Sometimes Berardo lowered his voice too, and then I lost the thread, but I could tell from their gestures that they did not agree. When it would probably have been wiser to lower his voice, Berardo flared up, enabling not only our two cell companions to hear what he said but probably also those in neighboring cells.

"You mean to tell me that that parcel found in the café contained newspapers? And that they arrested all those people because of a lot of wastepaper? What is a parcel of paper worth?"

The man from Avezzano advised him to talk more quietly and Berardo agreed, but soon started shouting again.

"What? Townsmen and *cafoni* unite? But townsmen are well off and *cafoni* are badly off. Townsmen work less and earn more, they eat well, drink, and don't pay taxes. It's enough to see how much they make us pay for cloth and hats and boot leather.

We're like worms. Everyone exploits us. Everyone tramples on us. Everyone swindles us. Even Don Circostanza, the Friend of the People, swindles us."

The man from Avezzano listened patiently.

"I don't understand," Berardo insisted, "I don't understand why townsmen should want to print a newspaper to distribute free to the *cafoni*. Why doesn't the Mystery Man mind his own business? But perhaps he's a paper merchant and prints newspapers as a way of marketing his wares."

The man from Avezzano tried to make him lower his voice.

"Are all these people you talk about who go to prison mad?" I also heard Berardo say. "And if they're not mad, what are they after? And all those people you have mentioned who went and got killed by the government, what were they after? Is getting yourself killed a way of promoting your interests?"

So far as I could tell, the stranger was trying to tackle Berardo at his most sensitive spot, which was his pride. He said, "That other *cafoni* should not understand certain things is understandable. But a man like you?"

He countered every argument that Berardo produced by saying, "But a man like you. You yourself don't believe what you're saying. A man like you."

He must have realized that most of the arguments that Berardo was producing were arguments against himself. The hopes he had had when he left Fontamara had vanished. The possibility of looking after his own affairs, of finding work, and buying a plot of land no longer existed. Every way was closed.

The *podestà* had classified us as persons of reprehensible conduct and so, as Don Pazienza had assured us, every way was closed. Berardo must have felt his old way of thinking reviving within him more vigorously than ever. The arguments he kept producing to the man from Avezzano were his last stand.

The conversation must later have turned to other countries, actually including Russia, because I heard Berardo say, "Russia? Tell me the truth, is there really such a place as this Russia there's so much talk about? Everyone talks about it, but no one has ever been there. *Cafoni* go everywhere, to America, Africa, France, but no one has ever been to Russia."

On some things Berardo was immovable, as on the subject of freedom, for instance.

"Freedom to speak in public?" he exclaimed contemptuously. "But we're not lawyers. Freedom of the press? But we're not printers. Why don't you talk about freedom to work, freedom to own land?"

Then, without realizing it, I must have dropped off to sleep out of sheer exhaustion. I must have been asleep for some time when Berardo woke me. He was sitting at my feet, and the man from Avezzano was sitting beside him. I was surprised they were still awake and still talking. The man from Avezzano was telling him his life story, all about his childhood and youth.

They no longer disagreed. You could tell from the way he spoke and his gestures that Berardo's resistance had ceased. The old Berardo had come back.

"What's happening?" I asked sleepily. "Why aren't you asleep?"

"We've been asleep only too long," Berardo replied with a laugh.

It was a long time since I had heard him laugh, and his laughter was so extraordinary that it frightened me. From the way they were talking and smiling I realized that Berardo had struck up a friendship with the stranger, and since I knew what friendship could mean to him, I immediately had a strange feeling that he was lost.

Then, speaking softly, he said something to me that I shall never forget. What he said was, "I thought that life no longer had any meaning for me, but perhaps it may yet have a meaning."

He paused for a moment, and then added, "Perhaps it's beginning to have a meaning only now."

"Have you found work?" I asked.

"Work? What work?" he answered.

"Have you forgotten that we came to Rome to look for work?" I said.

"Go to sleep," Berardo said. "We'll talk about it in the morning."

I dropped off to sleep again.

When I woke up, it was daylight. Berardo was striding up and down the cell like a caged lion. The man from Avezzano was lying beside me, but was not asleep.

He was lying beside me as if he had been waiting for me to wake up.

"Do you trust Berardo?" he asked me quietly.

"Yes," I replied.

"All the *cafoni* should trust him," the man from Avezzano went on. "You must tell them that at Fontamara. All the *cafoni* should trust him. He's an extraordinary man. What has happened to him was bound to happen. Perhaps there's not another *cafone* like him in all Italy. You must repeat at Fontamara what I'm telling you now. You must do what Berardo tells you to do. Today or in the next few days both of you will certainly be released and sent back to Fontamara. My fate will be different. Forgive me if I don't talk to you about it now; Berardo will tell you about it at Fontamara. The first thing to do is to make things up between Berardo and Scarpone. Berardo knows the rest."

At eight o'clock they gave us a bowl of coffee. Berardo stopped striding up and down the cell and said to the warden, "I want to talk to the inspector immediately."

"Wait your turn," the warden replied contemptuously, slamming the door in his face.

This exchange did not escape the man from Avezzano, who looked at Berardo with terror in his eyes. He dared not ask for an explanation, but the fear of betrayal was evident in his eyes.

At nine o'clock all three of us were taken to a police inspector's office.

Berardo stepped forward and said, "Sir, I'm ready to tell everything."

"Out with it, then," said the inspector.

"The parcel of clandestine newspapers found in the café near the station belongs to me. It was I who had them printed. I'm the Mystery Man."

9

So the Mystery Man had been caught at last, and he was a *cafone*. As soon as they heard the news, journalists and high state officials came hurrying to the police station where we were held.

The police had hunted him all over the city, but is there such a thing as a mystery townsman? Every townsman is registered, cataloged, rubber-stamped, known to the authorities. But the *cafoni*? Who knows the *cafoni*? Has there ever been a government that has known the *cafoni*? And could they ever register, catalog, rubber-stamp, supervise, and know every *cafone*?

In short, there was nothing strange about the Mystery Man's being a *cafone*. Every now and then Berardo was dragged from the cell to be shown to some new official who wanted to interrogate or merely see the *cafone* Mystery Man with his own eyes. In the evening they took the precaution of separating us and putting us in different cells, but during the next few days they resumed sending for all three of us for interrogation.

The inspector wanted to know many things from Berardo: where the clandestine printing press was, for instance, who the printer was, and whether there were other accomplices. But Berardo did not answer. To show the inspector his determination to say nothing he bit his lips till the blood flowed. He was in a worse state after each interrogation. After the first one there was only one dark blue bruise under his right eye, but later he was almost unrecognizable; his lips, nose, ears, and eyebrows bore the marks of the violence to which he was subjected. But still he would not speak. Not being able to bite his lacerated lips, he gritted his teeth to show his determination to say nothing.

One evening I, too, was sent for, for a "special session."

"Out with the truth," the inspector said.

I told him the truth, but he would not believe me.

I was taken to a cellar, thrown on a wooden bench, and strapped to it with my hands behind my back. And suddenly it was as if a rain of fire were falling on me, as if my back had been opened and fire were being poured into it, as if I were falling into a bottomless pit.

When I came to, blood was coming from my mouth and forming a little pool on the bench. I tasted it with the tip of my tongue and swallowed a little, because my throat was burning.

Next day the man from Avezzano was released.

Berardo and I were put back in the same cell, together with an individual who looked just like a policeman. I whispered my suspicions about him in Berardo's ear.

"I don't care," he replied. "I've already said everything I had to say."

But when I told him that the man from Avezzano had been released, his reaction was unexpected.

"Oh?" he said with a smile. "Well, then, now we must see about getting out of here ourselves. This game's all right if it doesn't last too long."

But if it was easy to begin the game, ending it was much more difficult.

When Berardo told the inspector that his first confession had been bogus, the inspector burst out laughing and sent him back to the cell, saying, "Either you tell everything you know or you'll come to a bad end."

Next day Berardo had another special session. There was something atrocious about his special sessions. He defended himself. He was incapable of receiving a blow without returning it. To tie his hands and feet, eight or nine policemen were needed. That evening he pretended to be resigned to the torture without reacting, but while one policeman was tying a rope around his knees he sank his teeth into the back of the man's neck and clamped them so firmly that the other policemen had to hammer his jaws to make him let go, and eventually they dragged him back to the cell by his legs and shoulders like Christ when He was taken down from the cross.

"Now he's out there and I'm in here," Berardo said to me next day. "After all, at bottom he's a townsman too. Now he's out there having a good time while I'm letting myself be killed for his sake. Why shouldn't I tell everything?"

The prisoner whom we suspected of being a policeman pricked up his ears.

The next time we were called to the inspector's office I wasn't sure whether Berardo was right or not to tell everything that the man from Avezzano had told him just for the sake of being released.

"Are you ready to tell everything?" the inspector asked.

Berardo nodded almost imperceptibly. Because of his maltreatment he could hardly stand, and his face was unrecognizable.

The inspector opened a drawer and showed Berardo a newspaper with the headline in big letters:

LONG LIVE BERARDO VIOLA

"In this newspaper," the inspector said, "in this badly printed sheet, there's a report about the treatment to which the police have rightly subjected you from the day of your arrest until today. As you say you are willing to tell everything, begin by telling us how you managed to transmit this report from your cell to the editors of this underground journal."

Berardo didn't answer.

"In this newspaper," the inspector went on, "there's a great deal about Fontamara. It mentions the diversion of a stream, a grazing ground, the Fucino question, the suicide of a man named Teofilo, the death of a woman named Elvira, and other similar happenings. The source of this information could obviously be only someone from Fontamara. Explain how this came about."

Berardo didn't answer. He gazed as if he were hypnotized at the small, badly printed sheet that the inspector had placed in front of him on which his name and Elvira's were printed, on which the words "Long Live Berardo Viola" were printed in big letters.

"Speak up, then," said the inspector.

"No, sir, that's impossible," Berardo said, strangely moved. "Now I prefer to die."

The inspector went on urging him to talk, but in spirit Berardo was already elsewhere. He no longer saw the inspector or heard him. He let himself be led back to the cell like someone who has just made his will and is on the point of death. But the struggle was not over yet.

That night neither of us slept. Berardo held his head between his hands as if it were about to burst. He decided to confess, changed his mind, again decided to confess, and then changed his mind again. He held his head between his hands as if to stop it from bursting. Why should he stay in prison? Why should he die in prison at the age of thirty? For the sake of honor? For the sake of an idea? When had he ever bothered about politics? That was how we spent the night. That was how Berardo Viola spoke to me and to himself, while the other occupant of the cell tried to catch every word. The struggle continued.

"What is the point of living now that Elvira is dead? If I turn traitor, everything will be lost. If I betray," he said, "Fontamara will be damned forever. If I betray, centuries will pass before another such opportunity arises. And if I die? It will be the first time that a *cafone* dies, not for himself, but for others."

That was his great discovery. That was the discovery that opened his eyes, as if a blinding light had flashed in the cell.

I shall never forget his appearance and his voice when he said those last words.

"It will be something new," he said. "Something completely new, and an example. The beginning of something entirely new."

Then, suddenly remembering a highly important fact, he added, "Ever since I was a boy they said I would die in prison."

This belief gave him a great sense of peace. He lay on the concrete block like a felled tree, a tree ready for the burning.

The only other thing he said was, "My greetings to my friends when you see them again."

Those were the last words I heard spoken by Berardo.

Next morning we were separated for the last time; and two days later I was sent for by the inspector, who was in an unusually gentle mood.

"Berardo Viola committed suicide last night," he said. "He hanged himself in despair from the window of his cell. There's no doubt about what happened, but no one was present and there's no evidence. Evidence is indispensable. If you are willing to sign a statement certifying that your fellow villager hanged himself, you will be released today."

On hearing that Berardo Viola had been killed I burst into tears.

The inspector wrote something on a sheet of paper and I signed it without reading it. I would have signed anything, even my own death sentence.

Then I was taken to the office of the chief of police.

"Were you a friend of the deceased Berardo Viola?" he asked.

"Yes, sir."

"Do you confirm that the deceased had always had suicidal tendencies?"

"Yes, sir."

"Do you confirm that the deceased had recently had serious love trouble?"

"Yes, sir."

"Do you confirm that the deceased was confined in the same cell as you and took advantage of the fact that you were asleep to hang himself from an iron bar?"

"Yes, sir."

"Bravo," the inspector, who was present at this interrogation, said to me on the way out, and offered me a cigarette.

Then I was taken to the Law Courts, to the office of a judge. And there the refrain was repeated.

"Were you a friend of the deceased Berardo Viola?" the judge asked me.

"Yes, sir; yes, sir; yes, sir."

He, too, asked me to sign something, and let me go.

At midday I was released, taken to the station, and put on a train with compulsory traveling papers. My mother and father can tell you the rest.

10

WHEN MY SON ARRIVED at Fontamara the Mystery Man had already told us most of the things he has just told you.

To old Maria Rosa the news was a terrible blow, though she had foreseen it. All night Fontamara resounded with her lamentations.

"Poor son of mine," she cried, "forgive me for bringing you into the world with such a hard destiny. And may your poor bride forgive me for ensuring her own ruin by betrothing herself to you."

Many women sat on stones placed outside the grief-stricken mother's cave and said the prayers for the dead.

"He ended up like his grandfather," Maria Rosa lamented, and wept. "How many times was he not warned? It was foreseen ever since his childhood. The Violas don't die at home like other human beings. No one knows why, but they don't die of coughs or fevers. They can't stay in bed or sit by the fire, they can't sit still on a chair. No one has ever known why."

Among us was Maria Grazia, the unfortunate young woman who had been mishandled that night by the representatives of the

law when they came to examine Fontamara, and she told us the
story of Elvira's pilgrimage and pious death.

At first no one had understood why Elvira had insisted on
joining Maria Grazia on that wearisome penance, and some
thought it was merely to accompany her friend. But after walking
all day long, after climbing the steep, stony, dusty valley of Forca
Caruso and making their way through the endless gorge of San
Venanzio, when the two young women entered the shrine of Our
Lady of Perpetual Succor, Maria Grazia had immediately understood the purpose of Elvira's pilgrimage. "Holy Mother of God,"
Elvira had said as soon as she arrived in the presence of the sacred
image, "I ask you only one thing: to intercede for Berardo's salvation. In return I offer you the only poor thing that I possess, that is,
my life. I offer it to you without hesitation, without qualification,
and without regret." As soon as she had said these words Elvira
had been seized with a high fever; she had begun to burn like a
bundle of dry sticks to which a match has been put. "I offer you
my life," Elvira had repeated to the sacred image and, feeling that
her offer had been accepted, added in a more subdued voice,
"The only grace for which I ask is that I may die at home." And
the Virgin Mary had granted her that grace. She had returned
home, put her few affairs in order, entrusted her sick father to an
aunt, gone to bed, and died.

"And was Berardo saved?" a woman murmured.

"Perhaps he was," old Maria Rosa replied. "No one can tell."

"Dying in prison is a strange way of being saved," the other
women said quietly.

"No one can tell," his mother repeated. "My poor son, who
was not born to own land, wanted at all costs to own land. He was
never able to sit still on a chair, but he wanted to set up a household. He never tolerated injustice and was born for friendship,
but he wanted only to look after his own affairs. I'm his mother,
and I can't repeat the incredible, the sacrilegious things he said
before he left for Rome. He was really prepared to do anything for
the sake of getting what he wanted. All for the love of a woman.
Perhaps her death saved him."

"Dying in prison is a strange way of being saved," the other woman again muttered between her teeth.

"No one can tell," his mother went on, with anger in her voice. "Perhaps Berardo's salvation was to be restored to his destiny. The salvation of the Violas has never been of the same kind as that of other Christians. The Violas don't die like other people. They don't die of coughs or fevers, with a pot full of piss under the bed. They can't stay in bed. Didn't your elders ever tell you how his grandfather died? And no one has ever found out how his father died."

"What's this about a paper we're supposed to print?" the Limona woman asked.

"That's another strange thing," a girl answered. "I heard Scarpone talking about it, but I didn't understand a thing."

"When strange things begin to happen, who can stop them?" I said. "Let us leave these things to the men."

My son arrived just when about a dozen of us had gathered around a box and some other things the Mystery Man had brought us for the purpose of publishing a *cafone* newspaper, actually the first *cafone* newspaper ever printed. On the box there were the words DUPLICATING MACHINE.

We had innocently put the box on Marietta's table in the middle of the street and, as I said, about a dozen of us were discussing what sort of newspaper we were to make. It was a strange thing to be doing, though we didn't realize it.

Maria Grazia, who had the best handwriting and was to write the sheet, was there, and so was Baldissera, who knew about grammar and apostrophes. So was Scarpone, to whom the Mystery Man had explained how the box worked.

The first thing we discussed was the title to be given to the newspaper. Baldissera wanted the sort of thing they have in towns, like *The Messenger*, *The Tribune*, or something of that kind, but Scarpone, who had inherited Berardo's ways, told him to shut up.

"Ours is not to be an imitation newspaper. This is to be the first *cafone* newspaper ever published," he announced firmly.

Michele suggested a good title, *The Truth*, which meant a great deal, but Scarpone turned up his nose at it.

"*The Truth?*" he exclaimed. "Who knows the truth?"

"We don't, but we want to," Michele replied.

"And when you've found it, what are you going to do with it?" said Scarpone. "Make soup?"

That was his way of arguing.

Losurdo also had a good idea; the title he suggested was *Justice*.

"You must be out of your mind," Scarpone said. "Justice has always been against us."

With us justice has always meant the *carabinieri*. Having to do with justice has always meant having to do with the *carabinieri*. Falling into the hands of justice has always meant falling into the hands of the *carabinieri*. So that was not a suitable title.

"But I mean real justice," Losurdo said angrily. "Justice that would be the same for everyone."

"That you'll find in Paradise," said Scarpone.

What answer could there be to that?

Marietta's suggestion was *The Cafoni's Bugle*. But no one took any notice of her.

"What are we to do?" Scarpone said.

"But we've got to decide on a title," Marietta said. "Why don't you suggest something?"

"I have. It's *What Are We to Do?*"

We looked at one another in surprise.

"But that's not a title," Baldissera objected. "That's not a title. We want a proper title to put at the head of the newspaper, don't you see? In beautiful handwriting, don't you see?"

"Well, then, write at the head of the newspaper in beautiful handwriting: *What Are We to Do?*" Scarpone replied. "And that will be your title."

"But that's a ridiculous title," Baldissera again objected. "If a copy of our newspaper gets to Rome, everyone who sees it will burst out laughing."

Scarpone lost his temper. This was to be a *cafone* newspaper, the first *cafone* newspaper of all time. It was to be a handwritten newspaper, and what people might think of it in Rome was a matter of total indifference to him.

Eventually Baldissera was persuaded, Scarpone's proposal was accepted.

While Maria Grazia began writing out the title we went on to discuss the first article.

Maria Grazia wrote with her head bent to one side, like a schoolgirl, and the whole thing seemed like a children's game. It's strange, I said to myself, it's strange how many new things are happening all at once.

Zompa said, "The first piece of news, you'll all agree, must be this: they have killed Berardo Viola."

Scarpone agreed, but proposed an addition, "They have killed Berardo Viola, what are we to do?"

"But 'what are we to do?' is already in the title," Michele pointed out.

"That's not enough," Scarpone replied. "It must be repeated, otherwise the title's no good, and we had better drop it. 'What are we to do?' must be repeated in every article. They have taken away our water, *what are we to do?* Don't you see? The priest refuses to bury our dead, *what are we to do?* They violate our women in the name of the law, *what are we to do?* Don Circostanza is a scoundrel, *what are we to do?*"

At that we all saw Scarpone's idea and agreed with it.

There was another slight argument about Berardo's name. Baldissera thought Viola should be written with two Ls, and Michele thought one was enough. But Maria Grazia said she could write it in a way that left it in doubt whether there was one L or two, and that settled the argument.

When I realized that there was nothing else to discuss, I went off home to spend some time alone with my son, because I thought I had lost him but had found him again.

Late that evening Scarpone brought me a parcel of thirty copies of the newspaper *What Are We to Do?* to distribute at San Giuseppe, where I knew a lot of people. Next day other

Fontamaresi were to distribute it in other neighboring villages. Altogether five hundred copies had been made.

When my wife saw these sheets, she made a grimace.

"Now we're going to be just like Innocenzo La Legge, distributing sheets of paper," she said.

"They mention Berardo's name, that's the only reason," I explained.

"When strange things begin to happen, no one can stop them," my wife replied.

"You're right, it's not our job. But they mention Berardo's name. That's the only reason."

My wife's family lives at San Giuseppe, and we had the idea of celebrating my son's release by going to San Giuseppe, all three of us. That was our salvation.

We went there in the afternoon, and in half an hour I distributed the newspaper to everyone we met in the street. At about nine o'clock, after having supper and drinking a glass of wine with our relatives, we left to go back to Fontamara. When we were halfway we heard some shots in the distance.

"Which saint's day is it?" asked my wife, wanting to know from which village the shots were coming.

It was difficult to tell. San Luigi's day was over and Santa Anna's had not yet come.

As we went on, the shots became more frequent.

"Anyone would think they were coming from Fontamara," I remarked. At that moment a carter from Manaforno, coming from the Fossa direction, passed by.

"Hey, Fontamaresi," he called out without stopping, "at Fontamara there's war."

We went on.

"War? Why war?" we asked one another. "War between Fontamaresi? Impossible. War by the Contractor against Fontamara? Again? But why?"

Every now and then the firing died down, but then started up again more vigorously than ever. As we went on, it became more and more obvious that it was coming from Fontamara and that the shots were rifle shots.

"What are we to do?" we asked one another in dismay.

That was Scarpone's question: "What are we to do?"

The question was easier to ask than to answer.

Meanwhile we kept on our way. Just where the road to Fontamara and the road to Fossa meet, Pasquale Cipolla suddenly appeared.

"Where are you going? To Fontamara? Are you mad?" he shouted, and hurried on in the direction of Fossa.

We ran after him.

"But what's happening at Fontamara?" I shouted. "What's all that firing?"

"It's war, it's war," Cipolla replied. "War against the *cafoni*, against the newspaper."

"And the others, what has happened to them?" I asked.

"Those who could, fled. Those who could, escaped," Cipolla replied without stopping.

"Did Scarpone get away?" my son asked.

"May his soul rest in peace," Cipolla replied, making the sign of the cross.

"And what about Venerdì Santo?"

"May his soul rest in peace," Cipolla replied, again making the sign of the cross.

"And Pilato?" I asked.

"He went up into the mountains."

"And General Baldissera?"

"May his soul rest in peace."

"Who else is dead?"

In the distance we heard the clatter of horses' hooves approaching. It might have been the *carabinieri* from Pescina going to Fontamara, so we fled into the fields. We lost Pasquale Cipolla in the dark. We have had no news of him since.

Nor have we had news of any of the others, of these who died or those who escaped, or of our house or of the land.

Now we are here. The Mystery Man helped us to get out of the country, and that is how we arrived here, abroad. But it's obvious that we can't stay here.

What are we to do?

After so much anguish and so much mourning, so many tears and so many tricks, so much hate and injustice and despair, what are we to do?

BREAD AND WINE

AUTHOR'S NOTE

1962

*A*WRITER SOMETIMES HAS the experience of seeing a
stranger reading a book of his. An incident of the kind
that happened to me many years ago made an impression on me
that I still remember, perhaps because of a combination of circumstances that I did not realize at the time.

I was in a train on the way from Zürich to Lugano, in an empty
compartment, when an elderly woman got in. She was modestly
dressed, and after a brief nod she sat opposite me, next to the
window. As soon as she had settled down she took a book from her
traveling bag and opened it at a page marked by a narrow ribbon.
As I still had some newspapers and periodicals I wanted to look at
I took no more notice of her, but after a while my attention was
drawn by the colored jacket of her book, and I realized that it was
the German version of a novel of mine published a couple of
years previously, *Brot und Wein*. I put aside my newspapers and
periodicals and started observing her with curiosity.

She was neatly and simply dressed, with no ornament whatever about her person, as is still the rural custom in that country,
particularly in the Protestant cantons. In spite of her gray hair,
her cheeks were pink and her features were still regular and

fine; her expression was intelligent, open, and agreeable; she must certainly have been beautiful when she was young. I imagined her to be a retired schoolmistress or a doctor's wife; very probably she was a strong, well-balanced woman who had not been spared her share of suffering.

On the pretext of putting away some of my papers I stood up to see how far she had gotten in the novel. She was reading a chapter I remembered well, for it had caused me a good deal of trouble. From that moment, though I pretended to be still looking at a newspaper, in my mind I followed her reading page by page, I might almost say line by line.

She remained apparently impassive, though once or twice she shut her eyes for a moment or two, only to resume her reading. It was a strange sensation to be faced with a stranger to whom I was secretly telling a long story. Fortunately that edition of my novel did not include the author's photograph, for if she had recognized me I should have been greatly embarrassed. In fact a strange uneasiness came over me. The page she was reading did not satisfy me at all; indeed, at that moment it struck me as actually stupid. Why had I written it? If I had foreseen that a person like this was going to read the book, I said to myself, I should certainly have cut that page, as well as others, besides giving much thought to certain expressions. Why, I said to myself, do most authors have in mind colleagues and critics who read a hundred books a year instead of strangers to whom the book may have a personal message?

Perhaps I had never before felt so immediately and so acutely the privilege and the responsibility of being a writer, though, I may say, these feelings were not new to me. I recalled the embarrassment caused me a year before by a letter written to me by an Italian worker in the name of a group of his comrades who like him were refugees in Switzerland. They had been discussing a sentence in my book and, not having been able to agree about its meaning, had decided to ask the author. It was a sentence I had written quite casually . . .

The woman got out before I did, and for the rest of the journey I went on thinking about the great dignity and power of literature and the unworthiness of most writers, including myself. At any rate, my determination to subject *Bread and Wine* to a critical rereading dated from that occasion.

I had written it *ex abundantia cordis* immediately after the Fascist invasion of Abyssinia and during the great Moscow trials staged by Stalin to destroy the last vestiges of opposition. It was difficult to imagine a more depressing combination of negative events. General Graziani's inhuman treatment of Ethiopian soldiers and civilians, the euphoria of many Italians at the conquest of an empire, the passivity of most of the population, and the impotence of the anti-fascists were news that filled me with a deep sense of shame. On top of that were my horror and disgust at having spent the years of my youth in the service of a revolutionary ideal that was turning out to be nothing but "red fascism," as I then called it. As a result, my state of mind was more inclined to overemphasis, sarcasm, melodrama than to calm narration. I must add that I was not greatly deceived by the book's exceptional and to me entirely unexpected success, for I was well aware that the success of a book can sometimes owe more to its defects than to its merits. But had I the right to go back and revise it? There was no lack of examples, including illustrious ones, pointing to an affirmative answer, but at the time I was inclined to think that a book once published belonged no longer to the author but to the public.

Later, however, I was to see the question in a different light, for after the fall of Fascism it became possible for the first time for my books to be published in Italy. Was I to let slip the opportunity provided for me by a delay that in all other respects had been painful and prejudicial to me? With a clear conscience I took advantage of it to revise the books I had published in exile: *Fontamara, Bread and Wine,* and *The Seed Beneath the Snow.*

As critics have noted, the structure, the moral essence, the vicissitudes of the characters have remained unchanged; but these books have been stripped of secondary or nonessential material and the basic theme has been deepened. No vanity can prevent me from admitting that my experience confirms the existence of a similarity between writing and the other arts in the sense that the former too is learned and improved by practice.

In this connection I have also had occasion to confess that, if it depended on me, I should gladly spend my life writing and rewriting the same book: the single book that every writer has within him that is the image of his soul and of which his published works are only more or less rough fragments.

Should I now mention the lessons that it seems to me I have learned? The first is that a writer with a strong sense of social responsibility is more exposed than anyone else to the temptation of overemphasis, of the theatrical and the romantic, and of a purely external description of things and facts, while in every work of literature the only thing that matters is obviously the development of the interior life of the characters. Even the landscape and other things by which they are surrounded are worthy of mention only to the extent that they are involved in the life of the spirit. And, since pathos cannot be eliminated from human life, I feel that a touch of irony is required to make it acceptable.

Another thing that has grown in me in the course of years is an aversion to all forms of propaganda. Of all the talk about the so-called commitment of artists, what remains? The only commitment that deserves respect is that of a personal vocation. Besides, everyone knows that the artist cannot sacrifice art to efficacy without also sacrificing efficacy. As for style, it seems to me that the supreme wisdom in telling a story is to try to be simple.

If I have refrained from making the slightest concession to the literary fashions that have sprung up in the meantime and are already on the wane; it is not from prejudice. I consider it foolish to judge whether a writer is modern by the technical expedients he uses. To hold that literature can be reviewed by formal devices is a timeworn illusion of rhetoric. I feel even greater repugnance for the fashion for erotic descriptions adopted not only by wary scribblers who pander to the bad taste of the public, but also by writers of talent. In my opinion there is nothing more false than to justify the literary commercialization of eroticism in the name of freedom, while I remain convinced that it cannot be countered efficiently by censorship or any other bureaucratic means, only by the disgust that springs from a serious and profound sense of life.

I

DON BENEDETTO, SITTING on the low garden wall in the shadow of a cypress, was reading his breviary. His black priest's habit absorbed and prolonged the shadow of the tree. Behind him his sister sat at her loom, which she had placed between a box hedge and a rosemary bed, and the shuttle bobbed backward and forward through the warp of red and black wool, from left to right and from right to left, to the accompaniment of the rhythm of the treadle that lifted the warp cords and of the lamb that lifted the warp.

She interrupted her work to look with ill-concealed anxiety at a vehicle that stopped at the bottom of the hill. But it was only an ox-drawn cart, and she went back to her work, disappointed.

"They won't be long now, you'll see," she said to her brother.

He shrugged his shoulders, simulating indifference.

On the right were the railway and the Via Valeria that led between fields of hay, wheat, potatoes, beets, beans, and corn to Avezzano, then rose to Colli di Monte Bove, before coming down to Tivoli and ending up, like all rivers that flow down to the sea, by leading to Rome. On the left was the provincial road, with vineyards and fields of peas and onions on either side, climbing straight up into the mountains, making for the heart of the Abruzzi, the region of beech trees and holm oaks and the last wild bears, and leading to Pescasseroli, Opi, and Castel di Sangro.

The priest's sister kept the shuttle bobbing backward and forward without losing sight of the road down below in the valley. But nothing was to be seen except everyday persons and things, and there was no sign of what she was waiting for.

A young peasant woman with a baby in her arms, riding a small donkey, came down the provincial road, which was as stony and winding as the bed of a dried-up stream. In a small field behind the cemetery a bareheaded old peasant was tracing brown lines with a small wooden plow drawn by two donkeys. Life seen from the priest's garden was like an ancient, monotonous pantomime.

That day was Don Benedetto's seventy-fifth birthday. It was a warm afternoon at the end of April, the first really warm day after a severe winter. Sitting on his low garden wall, he too raised his eyes from his breviary every so often and looked down at the valley, awaiting the arrival of some of his former pupils. They would be coming separately, from the right and from the left, from the direction of the town and from that of the mountain villages, from where life had scattered them at the end of their student days. But would they be coming?

At that time of day the few houses of the village of Rocca below Don Benedetto's garden seemed uninhabited. In the midst of the huddle of poor houses was a narrow square with grass growing between the cobbles, and at the other end of it was the low porch of an old church with a big rose window over it. The houses, the streets, the square itself looked as if they had been abandoned. A beggar in rags crossed the square and went off without stopping. A little girl appeared in a doorway and stood there, looking. Then she hid behind a hedge and stayed there, peeping out from behind the bushes.

"Perhaps I should have bought some beer," the priest's sister said. "And you might have shaved, as it's your birthday."

"My birthday? It's a fine time for birthdays, to be sure. Tamarind will be good enough for the young men," Don Benedetto said. "That is, if they turn up."

Tamarind came in bottles from town, while Matalena Ricotta, with strawberries, mushrooms, and eggs, came from the mountains.

Don Benedetto put his book down beside him on the wall and began looking at the work on the loom. What a disappointment it would be to Marta, his sister, if the young men did not turn up. She had sent out the invitations without telling him, but that morning had revealed the secret to make sure he stayed at home the whole afternoon. But supposing no one turned up? To disguise their anxiety the two tried not to look at each other.

"Do you know that Sciancalla has gone back to barter?" Marta said. "He won't take anything for his charcoal but onions and beans nowadays."

"For several days I've been having heartburn again after every meal," Don Benedetto said. "Bicarbonate of soda has tripled in price."

Bicarbonate of soda came from town, like insecticides and safety razor blades.

"Safety?" his sister said. "If you shave with one of those things you cut yourself worse than with an old-fashioned cutthroat."

"Safety is always relative," said Don Benedetto. "The Department of Public Safety would be well advised to call itself the Department of Public Danger, after all. When you come to think of it, however, my former pupils will prefer wine, they're not boys any longer."

The former pupils whom Don Benedetto was expecting had in fact finished their schooling soon after the Great War, so by now they must be thirty or more. Marta rose from her loom and went to the kitchen to fetch the refreshments she had prepared for the young men and put them on the granite table in the middle of the garden, between the tomatoes and the sage. Her action was perhaps a propitiatory rite, to get the young men to hurry.

"At any rate Nunzio will come," she said. "He's bound to."

"He's a doctor," said Don Benedetto. "He's very busy."

Marta went back to her loom and threw the shuttle full of black wool between the threads of the warp.

"Do you know they've changed the commissioner at the town hall?" she said. "Another stranger, of course. It seems that there are also going to be other changes because of this new war in Africa."

"Wartime is career time," Don Benedetto said.

Transfers and changes always came from town; commissioners, inspectors, controllers, bishops, prison governors, corporation speakers, preachers for the spiritual exercises were sent from town with up-to-date "directives." Newspapers, popular songs — "Tripoli bel suol d'amore," "Valencia," "Giovanezza," "Faccetta nera" — gramophones, the radio, novels, bromide paper, picture postcards also came from the town. From the mountains there came the poor Capuchin friar Brother Gioacchino with his bag for alms and Sciatàp for the Tuesday market; and Magascià arrived with salt and tobacco every Saturday, and sometimes Cassarola the wise woman appeared with her herbs and badger hair and snakeskins against the evil eye; and at the end of November the pipers arrived for the Advent novena — "Ye suffering and afflicted, open your hearts to hope, for the Savior is about to be born."

"Have you heard that Clarice has become engaged to a mechanic at the sugar refinery?" Marta said. "Marrying in wartime is like sowing among thorns."

The warp cords of the loom got tangled and Marta had to get up to free them.

"There are lucky women who are born with a talent for becoming war widows," Don Benedetto said. "Poets are made, but war widows and bishops are born. Mind you, I'm not saying that with reference to Clarice, who seems to be a rather innocent creature."

"Clarice has a good dowry, good land, hemp land," Marta said.

"Does the mechanic want to leave the refinery and grow hemp?"

"On the contrary," Marta explained, "it's Clarice who wants to sell the land. Hemp is no good anymore."

There used to be a demand for it, but no longer; it was considered expensive, primitive, and crude.

"Cloth made of homewoven wool is no good anymore either," Don Benedetto said. "Nor are we."

"Neither are shoes made to measure," said Marta, "nor solid wooden furniture. Artisans' workshops are closing down one after the other."

"And we're not wanted anymore either," Don Benedetto repeated.

Factory products were smarter and cheaper. Those who could shut up shop and went to town, and the old were left alone to wait for death.

Marta had to get up to turn the beam of the warp at the bottom of the loom. That had been exactly what Monsignore had said. "Your brother's primitive crudity, my dear lady, cannot possibly be tolerated in a school to which the richest, that is to say, the best families in the diocese send their sons," he had said. There was no denying that Monsignore was neither primitive nor crude and, knowing Don Benedetto to be unambitious and resigned so far as his career was concerned, he had dismissed him on the pretext of poor health.

Since then Don Benedetto had lived in seclusion with his sister in his little house above Rocca dei Marsi, with his old books and his garden. As he was by nature placid and taciturn, there had been little to prevent his rapidly acquiring a local reputation as a misanthropic and cantankerous eccentric and perhaps also something of a simpleton. But the few in whom he sometimes confided knew that his country shyness concealed a liberty of spirit and a liveliness of mind that in his station in life were positively foolhardy. The result was that it was rather compromising to allow it to be known that one was a friend of his. Imagine, then, what his relatives, his brothers, his cousins, and sisters-in-law, thought of him. Had all those sacrifices to keep him at the seminary been worthwhile if he was going to end up like this? They actually hated him for not having the prestige with the authorities that they expected of him and for having been reduced to living like a hermit instead of being able to use influence on their behalf at a time when honest work was of no use whatever in the absence of recommendations and backing in high places. As a consequence of this the last meeting with his relatives in the office of the notary at Fossa had ended with a very painful scene.

"You wretch," an old aunt called him at one point. "Don't you realize why we made such sacrifices for the sake of having a priest in the family?"

"Undoubtedly your purpose was to attract the Lord's goodwill toward you," Don Benedetto replied.

He should never have said it. That naive reply sounded deliberately provocative to these worthy Christians, and only the notary's intervention saved him from their legitimate anger. After that he did not see them again. Being deprived of the society of everyone except his aged sister, his affections had settled on some former pupils whose fortunes in the complicated and contradictory vicissitudes of their careers he tried to follow. He had no one else in the world. Marta had invited some of them, those who lived nearest and those to whom he was most attached, to come to their old schoolmaster's hermitage at Rocca on the occasion of his seventy-fifth birthday. She had asked them to bring others whose addresses she did not know, and she was very worried that the refreshments she had prepared might not be sufficient and that the dozen glasses of different shapes and sizes lined up on the granite table might not be enough. But the opposite possibility, that no one might come, alarmed her even more. She went on with her weaving, and between one shuttle and the next kept looking at the road in the valley and the paths along which the guests would have to come.

"At any rate Nunzio is bound to come," she said.

"If those boys are late, it's because the trains and buses don't arrive on time," Don Benedetto said. "As foreigners don't come to our part of the world, what would be the point of punctuality?"

From Rocca dei Marsi the land sloped gently down to the huge basin of the former lake of Fucino, now reclaimed and the estate of a prince. It was a huge green chessboard of young wheat, cut by canals and long rows of poplars, surrounded by a big circle of gently sloping hills, on nearly every one of which there was a small village, an assortment of houses that looked like a manger scene, or a smoke-blackened ancient township with a cluster of towers or surrounded by a high wall or with houses dug into the slope like caves. They were places with ancient names and ancient stories, but many had been destroyed in the last earthquake and badly rebuilt. Behind the ring of hills the mountains rose steeply, furrowed by floodwater and torrents, and at that time of year still covered with snow.

Marta stopped weaving and went back into the house.

"Where are you going?" Don Benedetto asked.

"I'll be back in a moment," she said.

She went up to the second floor and sat by the window overlooking the valley. The confused noises that floated up toward Rocca at sunset only increased the feeling of the village's solitude and remoteness. Some women in black shawls, dirty and old before their time, appeared in the dark doorways of their houses. Others, with handkerchiefs tied under their chins and brass pots on their heads, returned slowly from the fountain. A woman dressed in black crossed the little square and went into the church, holding by the hand, and almost dragging, a little girl in a yellow dress. An old *cafone* passed by, sitting on a donkey and kicking it. But soon the narrow roads and alleys emptied again and Rocca resumed the appearance of a village of the dead.

"They're coming," Marta called out from the window. "Nunzio's coming."

Don Benedetto promptly rose to his feet, attracted not only by the announcement of his guests' arrival but also by a hubbub coming from the road. It was not easy to see what it was about. All that was visible at first was a long cloud of dust spreading from the road into the neighboring vineyards and vegetable plots. Then a flock of sheep emerged from the cloud, a little river of yellow waves advancing slowly along the road, and behind it a donkey loaded with the usual equipment of a shepherd: the straw canopy, the saucepan bag, the milk pails, and cheese molds. Behind the donkey came the shepherd himself, surrounded by some big white dogs, and behind him there was a small open car with two young men in it who were shouting themselves hoarse, wanting the shepherd and his flock to move over to the left and make room for them to pass, but with no apparent effect. The shepherd either ignored them completely or gesticulated vigorously, perhaps to indicate that he was deaf and dumb and could not hear them, but in any event that they should leave him in peace. But since even a deaf-mute ought to be able to understand that a car cannot dally forever behind a flock of sheep, the young men yelled at him more vigorously than ever, and they might easily have passed from words to deeds but for the shepherd's escort of three big, ferocious-looking dogs wearing spiked collars. One of the young men in the car, who was in the uniform of an officer of militia, kept standing up at the steering wheel and threatening the deaf-mute in words and gestures, calling on him to make the flock move over to the right and leave room for the car to pass.

The shepherd, surrounded by his dogs, remained unmoved, making equally expressive gestures to indicate his inability to understand what the fuss was about. This had been going on for some time when Don Benedetto advanced to meet the flock, made his way through the cloud of dust, and cordially greeted both the shepherd and the two former pupils of his who were in the car.

"Welcome, welcome," he called out. Then he turned to the shepherd and said politely, "These are two friends of mine who are coming to see me."

The shepherd suddenly regained the power of speech and shouted angrily at the young men in the car, "Why didn't you say you were coming to see Don Benedetto?"

He gave an order to the dogs, and in a flash the flock had reformed itself lengthwise and moved over to the right, leaving plenty of room for the car to pass. But the two young men had not yet recovered from their amazement at the behavior of the pretended deaf-mute.

"What's the rascal's name?" Concettino insisted, turning to

Don Benedetto. "I'll settle him for the rest of his life."

Meanwhile, Marta had come out smiling and full of compliments.

"In spite of his black shirt this young man isn't a coal heaver, but just Concettino Ragù, remember?" Don Benedetto explained to his sister "And of course you know Nunzio Sacca, he's a full-fledged doctor now. They're good lads, both of them."

To Concettino he said with a laugh, "I've reached the age of seventy-five and have never yet acted as an informer, and it's too late to start now." He took his two former pupils by the arm and led them toward his garden.

But the shepherd, no doubt believing himself to be entirely in the right, went on standing in the middle of the road shouting, "Why didn't you say you were coming to see Don Benedetto?"

"Sit down and rest," said Marta, to divert the young men's attention from the shepherd. "The others won't be long now."

But Concettino could not swallow the insulting behavior of the bogus deaf-mute. His amazement actually prevented him from being angry.

"What's his name?" he insisted.

"Forgive him," Marta said with an imploring smile. "He's not a bad man. He's a poor fellow with an enormous family. Actually he's one of the most decent shepherds in the neighborhood."

"My dear fellow," Don Benedetto, who probably would have preferred to avoid giving this explanation, said, "there's no need for me, who takes no interest in politics, to tell you what your uniform means to the poor. The day on which the tongues of those who pretend dumbness are loosened will be a terrible one, and I hope you will be spared it."

Concettino looked at Nunzio as if to say: you see, here we are, was it really worthwhile coming? Nunzio tried to change the subject.

2

"WE CAME TO SEE YOU in your retreat," said Nunzio, "to show you that you are not alone, that your former pupils . . ."

"*Deus mihi haec otia fecit*," Don Benedetto replied with a smile, his voice betraying an obvious willingness to respect the conventions. "Now sit down and rest," he went on. "Not there on the ground, that is not grass but thyme; and this is basil, *Ocymum suave*, and farther along that is parsley, *Apicum petroselinum*, as you must know, and that at the side is mint. Ancient and honest things. Sit here."

The three men, slightly embarrassed, sat on a wooden bench under a graceful, silvery olive tree. The old man sat between his former pupils, and Marta asked for permission to return to her loom.

"I still have a few minutes' more work," she said. "By the time I've finished perhaps there'll be some more arrivals."

For a short while the only sound in the quiet garden was the alternating rhythm of Marta's loom, the rhythm of the treadle, the shuttle, and the comb. The air was bathed in delicate green light, between the trees it was brightened by beams of gilded dust, and the gentle odors of the aromatic herbs seemed to emanate from that light.

"How peaceful it is here," said Nunzio.

"Tell me some news," the old priest said. "I never see anyone here. What is Luigi Candeloro doing? I haven't heard of him for a long time."

"He died of typhus in Libya two years ago," Nunzio said. "Didn't you know? After he qualified as an engineer he couldn't find a job, and he ended up joining the Corps of Civil Engineers and going to Libya; for the sake of earning a living he would have been willing to go anywhere, even to hell itself, so he told me. He died a fortnight before sailing for home to marry a cousin of mine."

The old man shook his head sadly. After a short silence he asked again, "What has happened to Battista Lo Patto? Does he still paint?"

"He plays *scopone*,"* Concettino replied. "At scientific *scopone* he's unbeatable."

"Doesn't he ever vary his program?" the old man asked.

"Yes, on Sundays."

"What does he do on Sundays? Does he work?"

"On Sundays he plays billiards."

"And Antonio Speranza? How is his shop doing?"

"Well," Nunzio said, "for ten years he struggled with promissory notes falling due and fines for rotten sardines, rancid olive oil, moldy pasta, and inaccurate scales. In the end he too wanted to make his fortune, so he got into debt on a huge scale and promptly went bankrupt. So now he can't go out in the evening because of the creditors that are after him to beat him up. But he's even more afraid of the *carabinieri*."

"And poor Carlo Caione? Is he still ill?"

"He died of tuberculosis and left a wife and two young children," Nunzio said.

"Has his wife any money at least?"

"No, but she's beautiful," Concettino said.

---

*A card game.

The old man fell silent, weary and disheartened. Marta's loom stopped too. The first twilight shadows were gathering on the Fucino. Don Benedetto said almost in an undertone, "Excuse these questions. It's not inquisitiveness, I assure you. I'm very lonely here, and I often think about you. I never see anyone here." Then he added, "Where is Di Pretoro? Still with the railway?"

"He was sacked some time ago," Concettino said. "He was the best of us at Latin, that I don't deny, but in my opinion he was always muddleheaded, half a socialist. To be a good socialist, in my opinion, you have to be a millionaire. In any event, he had a casual affair with a poor little seamstress in his village who owned nothing in the world except her sewing machine. I don't blame him in the least for that. Let him who is without sin, as the saying is. But the little woman realized the kind of man he was, and very sensibly immediately presented him with a son, and like a fool he married her. She has regularly presented him with a child every year since. So after four years of marriage he has five children, including the one that arrived in advance. Meanwhile he was dismissed from the railway because of his antinational ideas — another luxury that the idiot permitted himself. Now, anyone who is fired by the railway can't get a job in any other public administration, that's obvious. But as private firms have to recruit staff from public employment exchanges, which are obliged by law to reject political suspects, there could be little doubt about what would happen to him. On the other hand, pride forbids him to do manual work. After all, you don't study for ten years to finish up as a carpenter. So he's permanently unemployed. As for his wife, she's always either pregnant or feeding the latest arrival, so she can't do any sewing. So very often there's nothing for them to eat. Then he can think of nothing better to do than to go to the tavern and drink on credit, and when he's drunk he goes home and beats his wife and children until the neighbors intervene and restore peace. And you know what people say? They say, that's how the pupils of the priests' school end up."

Don Benedetto looked in turn at each of his young guests, obviously taken aback at the relative indifference with which they related such painful facts.

"Couldn't you help him?" he asked them.

"I saved him from banishment, but perhaps that was a mistake," said Concettino. "At Ponza, or wherever it might be, he would at least have been paid an allowance, and meanwhile his wife would have had a rest."

Don Benedetto struggled to his feet. There was a great weariness in his pale, lean face. He paced up and down in the garden once or twice and then went silently into the house.

Meanwhile Marta had finished her weaving, but she remained bent over her loom as if her back ached. After a few moments she pointed to the work she had done, which was still around the beam, and said to the two young men, "This blanket is my birthday present to Don Benedetto."

She always referred to him as Don Benedetto, with detachment and respect.

"My dear lady," Nunzio said, "you make a present to your brother every day. You made him the gift of your life."

Marta blushed to her temples and shook her head vigorously.

"No," she said. "On the contrary, what should I do without him?"

She was taller and slimmer and rather more bent than her brother, and she actually looked older, though in fact she was ten years younger. Her brow, eyes, and mouth still bore the traces of a faded beauty. She rose from her loom and sat on the bench between the two visitors.

"Don't think that we're unhappy because we're lonely," she said quietly to avoid being overheard by her brother. "But what makes life bitter is the hostility, the suspicion that surrounds us nowadays."

"You know very well that that is Don Benedetto's own fault, unfortunately," said Concettino. "Do you think there's any hope of a change of heart?"

"Frankly I have no idea," Marta said. "Don Benedetto is not a man who confides his sorrows. The little I know I hear from third parties. But what harm have we done to anyone to deserve these tribulations?"

"The past is the past," Nunzio said. Then, turning to Concettino, he added, "Can nothing be done?"

"It depends on him," Concettino said. "On his goodwill."

"Talk to him," Marta said imploringly.

Don Benedetto reappeared on the threshold carrying a bundle of yellowed papers.

"Did you receive my suggestion for the blessing of the flag?" Concettino asked him. "It would be a suitable occasion for remedying past misunderstandings."

"Yes," Don Benedetto replied. "I received it."

"Do you agree to bless the flag?"

"Of course not."

"Why? Why insist on your own ruin? Why not take the opportunity to rehabilitate yourself?"

"Rehabilitate myself?" Don Benedetto said in surprise. "Why do you address me as if I were a senile delinquent?"

Concettino muttered something inaudible.

"You see," Don Benedetto said to him, "I'm a poor old man, full of fears and failings. But also I'm an old-fashioned Christian and, believe me, I cannot act against my conscience."

"So to you blessing the national flag, the flag of the party in power, is a sin against your conscience?"

"Yes, one of the gravest. It's idolatry."

"But others . . ." Concettino exclaimed.

"I know what you're going to say," Don Benedetto said. "But idolatry is a sin against the spirit, never mind who practices it."

"Excuse me," Marta exclaimed imploringly, with her eyes full of tears. "I don't understand you. Is this friendly behavior? Is this the way to celebrate a birthday?"

The old lady's bright eyes, which were moist with tears, and her heartbroken voice affected everyone.

"Signorina Marta is right," said Nunzio, who was the most embarrassed. "We came here, not to argue, but to demonstrate our affection for our old schoolmaster."

"Whatever may have been said was of course dictated solely by friendly feelings," Concettino said apologetically.

"I do not doubt it," Don Benedetto said with a smile, tapping his shoulder. "Why should we argue? I often think of you, you know. It's no effort, I have no one else to think about."

"What are those old papers?" said Nunzio, thinking he had found a peg on which happy memories could be hung.

Don Benedetto was still holding the bundle of yellowed papers he had brought from his study a short while before, and his hands were trembling slightly.

"They actually concern you," he said. "This morning I found the old photograph that was taken when we all said good-bye to one another fifteen years ago, do you remember? I also found the last essays you wrote for me. The subject was 'Say sincerely what you want to be and what meaning you want to give to your life'; and I reread your essays, Caione's and Di Pretoro's and Candeloro's and Lo Patto's and the others' whose sad fortunes you have told me about. Well, I confess in embarrassment and humility that I am beginning to feel completely bewildered. I am even beginning to doubt that it's worthwhile seeking an explanation. As a nineteenth-century Frenchman, who, like you, was educated by priests, said, perhaps the truth is sad."

Don Benedetto had dropped his voice, and he spoke gravely and also hesitantly, like someone who is listening in the first place to himself, as if there were a censor inside him, or as if he were a nearsighted man moving about among unknown objects and were fearful of hurting, not himself, but them. He started talking about some of the yellowed sheets of paper he held in his hands.

"In considering such compositions after so many years, all sorts of allowances must of course be made," he said. "They are full of literary frills in the manner of Carducci, Pascoli, D'Annunzio. Besides that, there are the naïvetés peculiar to pupils of a school run by priests, and there are the illusions of the age. There are echoes of the tumultuous armistice that had recently been concluded. But, underneath all that, underneath the frills and flourishes and plagiarisms, in several of you there seemed to me

to be something vital and personal that coincided with the observations that I had been able to make of each one of you during the
years of lower and upper school; and that something was by no
means commonplace. Now, what happened to the something
later, when you went out into the world? I am referring to the
news you gave me just now about some of your classmates and,
without wishing to offend you, I am also referring to both of you.
You must be between thirty-two and thirty-five if my arithmetic is
not at fault, and you already look like cynical and bored old men.
Seriously, that makes me wonder what is the point of teaching.
You realize that to me that is no idle question. When a poor man
who has lived with the idea of making decent use of his life
reaches an age such as I have reached today, he cannot avoid
asking himself what has been the result of his efforts, what the
fruits of his teaching have been."

"School is not life, my dear Don Benedetto," Concettino said.
"At school you dream, in life you have to adapt yourself. That is
the reality. You never become what you would like to become."

"What?" Nunzio said ironically to his friend. "Is that how an
activist talks? A Nietzsche fan?"

"Never mind literature, we were talking about serious things,"
Concettino said.

Marta was on tenterhooks. She suddenly rose and went toward the table on which there were a number of bottles and a
dozen glasses.

"Do you think any others will still be coming?" she said. The
poor woman was trembling as if she had a fever.

"They certainly intended to come, but they must have been
prevented," Concettino said evasively.

Marta made as if to take the superfluous glasses back into the
kitchen.

"Leave one for Don Piccirilli," Don Benedetto said.

"We didn't invite him," said his sister. "You know very well I
left him out on purpose."

"For that very reason he will not fail to appear," Don
Benedetto said. Then, turning to the two young men, he went on,

"You remember Piccirilli? He was the only boy in your class who wanted to go into the Church. His family were small landowners who couldn't afford to let him go on with his studies, so he had himself accepted without fee by the Salesians, studied theology, and took orders. But no sooner was he ordained than he left the Salesians and went back to his family. That certainly wasn't very handsome behavior toward his benefactors. Now he has a parish not far from here, but he's not satisfied, he would like to be a teacher at the seminary and a canon. To ingratiate himself with the bishop he acts as his secret informer. 'Secret' is just a manner of speaking, because we all know it. He never fails to turn up wherever he thinks something might be said that should be denounced to the diocesan curia. So you can imagine that he does me the honor of frequent and cordial visits."

Meanwhile it was getting dark in the garden, and Marta had difficulty in filling the glasses. Also a cool breeze was coming from the mountains, and Don Benedetto had a fit of coughing.

"We had better go indoors," Marta said.

The two young men helped her to take the bottles and glasses inside. On the ground floor one big room served as kitchen, workroom, and living room, as with the peasants. Marta lit a big lamp with a yellow shade and some candles, which she put in the corners of the room. A pleasing odor of quince and walnuts hung in the air.

"It's delightful here," said Nunzio, looking all around. "Nothing has changed."

A yarn windle hung on a nail on the door; a distaff was propped against the doorpost; majolica plates with a floral design were on the shelves of the sideboard, copper pots and pans hung on the fireplace wall, and red rows of peppers, brown rows of sorb apples, and bunches of garlic and onions hung from the huge hood of the fireplace. In what was probably Marta's working corner there was a small recess with a little Madonna made of colored plaster surrounded by paper lilies.

"Sit down and drink," Marta said.

There was a knock at the door, and in came Don Piccirilli.

Don Benedetto received him standing with his back to the fire-place. The newcomer went toward him and offered him his con-gratulations. Don Benedetto returned the embrace and invited him to join the others.

"Sit down and drink," he said. "There's a glass ready for you."

Don Piccirilli was plump and well nourished, and he had an expansive and jovial air. He explained that he was late because he had had to finish a little article for the diocesan journal.

"It's called 'The Scourge of Our Time,'" he explained. "I don't want to boast, but I think it has come out rather well."

"I congratulate you," Don Benedetto said. "What is it about? The war or unemployment?"

"Those are political issues," Don Piccirilli replied dryly. "The diocesan journal deals only with religious questions. From the purely spiritual point of view the scourge of our time, in my opinion, is immodesty in dress. Are you not of that opinion?"

"The scourge of our time," Don Benedetto calmly replied, looking him in the eye, "is — do I have to tell you? — insincerity between man and man, the pestilential Judas Iscariot spirit that poisons relations between man and man. Forgive me if in speaking like this I am failing in the duties of hospitality."

Don Piccirilli made a grimace that was intended to be a smile. "In my parish in recent years, thanks be to God, enormous spiri-tual progress has been made," he said. "Enormous," he repeated with emphasis. "The number of confessions has increased by forty percent and that of communions by thirty percent. I don't want to boast, but I don't know of any parish that can equal that."

"But why do you talk of spiritual progress in terms of figures and percentages like a baker?" Don Benedetto said with irony and contempt.

Concettino made a gesture of despair, as if to say, here we go again; and Nunzio had a violent and very unnatural fit of coughing. But the biggest sufferer in this situation was poor Marta. Her hopes of a reconciliation between her brother and the author-ities were collapsing before her eyes, and she could hardly restrain her tears. Hoping to reintroduce at any rate a little conventional cordiality into the occasion, she took from her brother's hand the old photograph in which he was surrounded by his pupils and put it over the fireplace where it was well in the light.

"Do you recognize each other in the photograph?" she asked, trying to speak in as natural a voice as possible. "I bet it won't be easy."

The visitors immediately gathered around, each trying first to pick out himself and then expressing surprise at not recognizing one or another former classmate. Don Benedetto stood out in the midst of his pupils like a hen surrounded by its chicks. To judge by appearances, the brood had been pretty heterogeneous. The only thing they all had in common seemed to be the way their hair was cut. The smallest boys squatted cross-legged in the front row and the others were arranged in three rows behind them. Concettino was among the small boys in the front row. His head was shaved, like the others, and he had a small, dark, gray face, with a catlike expression. After all these years only his eyes were still the same; his cowlick and his goatee beard now made him look like a musketeer in a provincial theater — something that no one would have expected fifteen years before. But Nunzio Sacca had changed little, apart from the fact that loss of hair over his temples made his forehead look bigger. He was standing behind Don Benedetto in the photograph, and he was recognizable by the long thin neck between his rather narrow shoulders, his deepset eyes, and the shy and absent-minded manner that he had preserved.

"Who were your favorite pupils?" Concettino suddenly asked Don Benedetto.

"Those who had most need of me, of course," Don Benedetto replied without hesitation.

"Names, names, names," his three ex-pupils demanded in chorus, their curiosity aroused.

Don Benedetto looked perplexed. Then he said, "Where is Pietro Spina now? What has happened to him?"

In the photograph Pietro Spina was standing next to Don Benedetto, who had one hand on the boy's shoulder. Spina had a lean, ashen, sullen look on his face and his tie was askew. After a time, as no one answered, Don Benedetto repeated his question. "Does none of you have news of Pietro Spina? Where is he living now?"

The three young men looked at each other in embarrassment. Perhaps at the bottom of her heart Marta had still been nursing some illusions, but now she sat down on a stool with the air of someone who has finally abandoned hope. Nunzio went toward her and gave her a smile of brotherly sympathy, while Don Benedetto seemed to have noticed nothing. He turned to Concettino and said, "If I remember correctly, Pietro Spina was your best friend at school. You admired him so much, you might almost have been in love with him. Where is he now? What news do you have of him? What is he doing?"

"How should I know? Am I my brother's keeper?" Concettino answered, avoiding Don Benedetto's eyes.

At this reply the old man, who was standing by the fireplace, went so pale that he seemed about to faint. Slowly he walked toward Concettino, put one hand on his shoulder, and, looking him in the eyes, said in a low voice, almost with tears in his eyes, "My poor fellow, is this what you have come to? You don't know what a terrible thing you have just said."

In the painful silence that followed Don Benedetto left the young officer and went and sat in the farthest corner of the room in an armchair under the recess with the image of the Madonna surrounded by colored paper decorations.

"Yes, it's true," he said, "Pietro Spina was in a way my favorite pupil. You remember him? He was not satisfied with what he found in the textbooks, he was insatiable, restless, and often undisciplined. He worried me, I feared for his future. Was I wrong, perhaps? I don't know if you remember, but the severest punishments he had during his school years were nearly always the result of his protesting at what he considered to be undeserved punishments imposed on one or another of his fellows. That was one side of his character. He was devoted, perhaps too devoted, to his friends. If his superiors made a mistake, he protested. No consideration of expediency could ever make him hold his peace. Isn't that right, Concettino? Wasn't he like that?"

Don Benedetto sought among the yellow papers for the last essay written at school by Pietro Spina.

"Listen," he said, "this is Spina: 'But for the fact that it would be very boring to be exhibited on altars after one's death, to be prayed to and worshiped by a lot of unknown people, mostly ugly old women, I should like to be a saint. I don't want to live in accordance with circumstances, conventions, and material expediency, but I want to live and struggle for what seems to me to be just and right without regard for the consequences.' Fifteen years ago, when I read that confession," Don Benedetto went on, "though I did not doubt the boy's sincerity, I did not know to what extent he might have been carried away by rhetoric. At the time he was devouring the lives of the saints. He had been an orphan for several years, and family misfortunes had reinforced his tendency to meditation."

Don Piccirilli had been impatiently waiting for the old man to pause, so that he could interrupt.

"In 1920 Spina wanted to be a saint," he said. "Very well. But in 1921 he joined the Young Socialists, who were atheists and materialists."

"I am not interested in politics," Don Benedetto said dryly.

"You are not interested in atheism, the struggle against God?" the young priest asked curiously.

Don Benedetto produced a slight ironic smile.

"My dear Piccirilli," he said slowly, almost articulating each syllable separately, "he who does not live according to expediency or convention or convenience or for material things, he who lives for justice and truth, without caring for the consequences, is not an atheist, but he is in the Lord and the Lord is in him. You can teach me many things, Piccirilli, how to get on in the world, for instance, but I was your master in the use of language, your master in the science of words, and please note that I am not afraid of them."

He paused, and then added prayerfully, and in a voice that was serene again, "Can't one of you give me news of Pietro Spina? Where is he now?"

Nunzio eventually decided to tell what he knew.

"He was arrested at the beginning of 1927," he said, "and we heard that he was deported to an island, the island of Lipari. A year later he escaped and took refuge in France."

"That I knew," said Don Benedetto. "His grandmother, Donna Maria Vincenza, told me."

"After about a year he was expelled from France and went to Switzerland," Nunzio went on. "There the same thing seems to have happened, and he went to Luxembourg. After some time he was expelled from Luxembourg too, and went to Belgium. How he manages to live I have no idea, but he's probably hungry. I have also heard from an uncle of his that he suffers from lung trouble."

"What a wretched fate," Marta said. "How could he choose it deliberately? Do you think he's mad?"

"He's a puzzle to me, too," Nunzio said. "It's a pity, because he really was the best of us all."

"Can't his relatives help him?" Marta asked again. "They're rich, after all. Who knows how much his grandmother, Donna Maria Vincenza, must suffer on his account."

Don Benedetto was staring at the ground.

"Don't imagine it's anything new," he said. "On the contrary, it's a boring old story that is repeated over and over again. Vultures have holes, and birds of the air have nests; but the Son of Man has not where to lay his head."

Marta was trembling, and she looked imploringly at her brother. The three young men rose to their feet.

"It's late," they said. "We must go."

The farewells were brief, almost laconic. Marta tried in vain to take Concettino aside.

"It's late," he said to excuse himself.

Don Benedetto and his sister accompanied their guests to the fork in the road. Don Piccirilli took the track to the left toward the mountains, and Concettino and Nunzio went off in their car along the Via Valeria.

The old man and his sister watched them disappear in silence.

As they left Rocca Concettino muttered to Nunzio without looking at him, "Pietro's back in Italy. He returned surreptitiously from Belgium. The police have warned us, they're on his trail already. He may have been arrested already. But what can I do if he's mad?"

"Can't you help him? He's one of us, after all."

"If he's mad, what can I do? He had the luck to be abroad, and he could have stayed there."

"Can't you help him?"

"How? That's the difficulty. I've got to watch my own step. You're wrong if you think my position is a hundred percent secure."

3

ONE MORNING AT DAWN Dr. Nunzio Sacca was called to the bedside of a sick man. A young man from Acquafredda called for him with a horse and trap. The doctor was still full of sleep when he appeared at the door of his house, carrying the bag with his first aid kit. After looking at the young man he said, "We know each other, I think."

"I am Cardile Mulazzi of the Mulazzi family of Acquafredda," the young man said. "Yes, we know each other. Forgive me for coming so early, I'll explain. My grandfather used to have Monsignore's old mill and land, it was good land, expensive land. For three years my father rented a vineyard belonging to your family. Do you remember? Then came misfortunes, quarrels, illnesses. Two brothers are in Brazil and do not write."

"Yes, yes, we know each other," the doctor said. "Who's the patient?"

The narrow, deepset village streets were still dark; the roofs were barely caressed by the gray light of dawn. Some peasants were loading donkeys outside their front doors before going to work in the country. The wheels of the trap rumbled on the newly graveled road. The horse walked; they were going into the wind, and there was rain in the wind. The doctor pulled his hat down over his brow and turned up his coat collar. Having just gotten out of bed, he felt cold.

"At the end of April rain is good," Cardile said. "When I was a boy you made a speech in the square at Acquafredda, for the Church and for the people. Do you remember? The word LIB-ERTY was on the banner. Our families were on the same side. It was immediately after the war, and liberty was permitted. Then the Church was not for the government, but for the people. We were on the same side. After that the wind changed."

The doctor looked at the young man curiously.

"What a strange speech," he said, but he did not seem to be displeased.

"There's a reason for it," Cardile said. "You'll see."

"What reason?" asked the doctor.

At the fork in the road by the station four *carabinieri* were waiting. Why so early? One of them recognized Dr. Sacca and saluted him. The trap left the village, driving into the rain. The road sloped gently downward, and the horse began to trot.

"Now," Cardile went on, "women and old people are still for the Church and we, of course, look after our own affairs. My father is sixty, and is a prior of the Confraternity of the Holy Sacrament. You can check that for yourself, if you want to. On Sunday mornings he sings at mass, and on Good Friday and Corpus Christi he walks in the procession in a red cassock and makes the responses to the *Oremus*. Every year we give two barrels of wine to the parish for masses. All our dead are buried in the Chapel of the Holy Sacrament in Acquafredda cemetery, on the right as you go in. All this does not mean that we are any better than others, but I have a reason for recalling these things. In short, what I mean is that we are on the same side."

"We know each other," the doctor said. "We know each other. Who's the patient? Someone in your family?"

The trap left the national highway and went up a side road full of puddles between newly plowed fields. The road wound its way uphill in a series of big zigzags. A light, whitish mist hung over the skeleton-like branches of the apple trees. The horse resumed walking without instructions from its master.

"Nevertheless there are many ways of knowing one another," Cardile said. "We peasants get to know people through the land they own and through testimonials. But is that a way of getting to know people? You work, buy, sell, rent, and you have to have papers and testimonials. If you go abroad to work you have to apply to many offices, and you need recommendations. Is that a way of getting to know people?"

"I agree," the doctor said. "But now tell me where you're taking me. Surely you didn't wake me before dawn just to make all these speeches?"

"We shall soon be there," Cardile said. "I must ask you to be patient for a little while longer. What I am telling is not just idle chitchat."

The trap reached the top of the hill together with the first rays of a sickly sun. The horse was sweating, but started trotting again of its own accord. The road had degenerated into a country track overlooking the whole village. Smoke from the chimneys spread a bluish pall over the gray and black huddle of houses.

"I left home at sixteen." Cardile went on. "My father would have had plenty of work for me, but I was bored, and I went to France with other young men from the locality. I worked at l'Estaque, near Marseilles, where an underground canal was being excavated. One day someone told me that someone from my part of the world had turned up, an educated person. It'll be someone who wants something from me, I said to myself. My papers were in order, I'd paid what I had to pay, so what could he want? Anyway, the man came to the tavern where we ate, sat down, said he had been away from the Marsica for several years, and started talking about the land and the people here and the way they lived, and about his village in the Fucino. The same thing happened on the evenings that followed. We went out to the wharf at l'Estaque, sat on the ground and talked till late, and it became a habit. I gave up going dancing or to the movies. I

liked his company. I had never had a friend like that. I don't know
if I've made myself clear. In the daytime I worked in the tunnel. It
was an eight-hour day, but everyone did two or three hours' over-
time to earn more. But when the eight hours were up I stopped,
knowing that the man whom I enjoyed talking to was waiting for
me at the wharf. What did we talk about? We talked about men,
and about the land, and about life. We argued, and we also joked
and laughed. Here's someone, I said to myself, with whom I have
nothing to do, either for work or for papers or testimonials or anything else, who did not approach me as a priest or teacher or a
propagandist, people who know everything and are paid to persuade others. Here, I said to myself, is someone who approaches
me as a man. Then one bad day he left and I didn't hear from him
again. I felt immediately that I was missing something. Then I
heard that he had been denounced by the Italian consulate and
expelled from France."

"I can imagine who he was," the doctor said. "But why are you
talking to me about him?"

"I don't want to be misunderstood," said Cardile. "I'm talking
about myself. It's obvious that there's nothing special about me. I
was born a peasant, and a peasant I shall remain. A peasant lives
according to custom, and carrying a knife in one's pocket isn't the
only custom, there are also others."

The horse and trap met two *carabinieri* coming down from the
mountains. They recognized the doctor and saluted him.

At that moment it started to rain again.

"Two years ago," Cardile said, "coming back with my barrow
from the Feast of San Bartolomeo on the Magliano road, I came
across a dog that had been run over by a car and had had its leg
broken. It was howling by the roadside in a pitiful manner. I put
the dog in the barrow, tied up its leg, and took it home. Two
months later a carter from La Scurcola came and took it back because it was his dog. I mention this to tell you what the customs
are. Last summer I found a lame sheep on the road and took it
back and put it in the shed between the cow and the donkey; later
its owner came and took it back. That is the custom, mine and

other people's. Well then, last night that man whom I met at l'Es-taque knocked at my door. At first I didn't recognize him."

"Is Pietro Spina here? Are you taking me to him by any chance?" Dr. Sacca asked in alarm.

Cardile drew the trap to the side of the road and stopped, and the two men jumped down. Cardile tied the horse to an elm tree and covered it with a woolen blanket. The doctor looked all around him with a worried expression on his face. The rain had died down and was moving away toward Tagliacozzo, but big black clouds that had been held in reserve were moving up from Avezzano. The country looked deserted. The two went on talking beside the trap.

"Well then, that man knocked at my door," Cardile said, "but he refused to come in, though he was in a pretty bad state and was feverish. So we went for a short stroll. We went down a lane out-side the village and sat under a tree. After talking a little about l'Estaque he started telling me that he had returned to Italy sur-reptitiously and had had a miraculous escape from being arrested by the police in Rome. As a result he had lost contact with his party friends and would not be able to approach them again for some time without risking being caught. He said that for several days he had been wandering in the mountains in the rain but could not go on, because he had a high fever. After a great deal of hesitation he had decided to come to ask me to hide him for a few days until he felt better. He said, 'You are a worker, and it is for the party of the workers that I came back to Italy; don't give me away.' Last night I hid him in a shed, and now I'm wondering what can be done for him. Can we leave him to die like that?"

"He had only to stay where he was, abroad," the doctor said irritably.

"But now he's here. I found him on the doorstep, as one might find a dog or a sheep, a dying animal. Can he be allowed to die like that?"

"He has nothing to lose, he's alone. I have a wife and children. Our political ideas are not the same," replied the doctor.

"But excuse me, this is not a matter of politics," Cardile said. "He's a dying man. In the catechism, which they made me learn by heart when I was a boy, it said: the works of mercy are these: to give drink to the thirsty, to clothe the naked, to give shelter to pilgrims, and to succor the sick. It did not say: to succor the sick that are of the same way of thinking as you. It just said to succor the sick. I don't know whether I'm mistaken or not."

"And was it he who sent you to me? Did he tell you he knew me?" the doctor asked.

"He said he was at school with you, but that I was not to fetch you in any circumstances," Cardile said. "That's the truth."

They went on talking for some time next to the horse and trap. A peasant passed with a donkey with a load of wood and eyed them suspiciously. A little later an old woman passed with a goat. Cardile did not know whether to tell the doctor the whole truth. Eventually he made up his mind.

"He didn't want me to fetch you, on my word of honor," he said. "On the contrary, last night he said to me, 'I came back to my country for the party of the workers, and if I ask you for help it's because you're an honest worker. But Dr. Sacca is an intellectual who has his career to worry about, and on top of that he frequents the diocesan curia and to ingratiate himself with the authorities might be capable of handing me over to the militia.' I tell you that though I do not believe it. He was also totally opposed to my getting in touch with any of his relatives. He said he considered himself dead to his family, as if he had entered a monastic order. There was only one person who would not be afraid of helping him, and that was a priest who had been his schoolmaster, but now he was too old, and he didn't want to expose him to any risks. That was how we left things last night. As you can imagine, I couldn't sleep because of him. But at about three o'clock I dozed off and had a nightmare, I thought he had died. I went to see immediately, and found he was worse. So then I came and fetched you without asking his opinion again. It would be our duty to help him even if he were only a sheep."

The doctor was leaning against one of the shafts and was looking anxiously all around him as if he were feeling sick. Finally he plucked up courage.

"We must make sure he leaves immediately," he said. "I'll try
to persuade him. If he needs medicine, I'll give you a prescription
in the name of some member of your family. May the Lord direct
us out of this."

"He's down there," Cardile said, "in the shed behind that
walnut tree. It's a shed my father uses in summer. You can go
there alone while I stay here on guard."

In the shed behind the walnut tree the doctor found an old
man who looked like a groom huddled on the floor. This upset
him, because Cardile had not told him that anyone else would be
there.

"Where's the patient?" he asked dryly.

"Nunzio, what are you doing here?" the man said. "Whom are
you looking for?"

"Cardile said there was someone here who was ill," said the
doctor, even more upset at being addressed by name.

"I'm sorry," the man said, rising to his feet. "I explicitly forbade
him to send for you."

Only then did the doctor recognize his former classmate
Pietro Spina, and surprise took his breath away.

"Is it you?" he barely managed to stammer out. "What a state
you're in."

The big, wide-open, deepset eyes and handsome broad forehead
were the only features of his former classmate that he recognized.

"You're my age and you look sixty," he said. "What's wrong
with you?"

Pietro smiled. No, his premature aging was not the result of
any strange disease, he explained. Must he reveal his secret? Before returning to Italy, to change his appearance and make him
unrecognizable to the police, he had for several weeks treated his
face with a mixture based on tincture of iodine, thus producing
the wrinkles and coloring of premature old age.

"I found the recipe in the life of an old Russian revolutionary,"
he said, "and it's capable of the most widespread application.
When the supreme ambition of the average young Italian ceases
to be to become the lover of an American or Swiss tourist and he

turns to more serious aims, it will perhaps be necessary to open artificial disfigurement parlors for the daintiest dandies to take the place of the present beauty parlors."

Nunzio gazed at his disfigured contemporary with astonishment and pity. Pietro had never been a handsome youth, but his impetuosity and frankness often caused his face to be lit up by an internal fire that made him attractive to women. How could political sectarianism have driven him to mutilate himself in this barbarous fashion?

"But the police recognized you in spite of the state to which you have reduced yourself," the doctor said. "The whole countryside here is being combed by *carabinieri* and militia who are looking for you."

"No, the police did not recognize me," Spina said. "I was denounced to police headquarters. If I managed to get away it was because they distributed copies of an old photograph of mine everywhere. In any case, I had no intention of staying in Rome, but in some province in southern Italy."

The resemblance of all this to the plot of a cheap thriller abruptly recalled Nunzio to the childish and dangerous situation in which he had recklessly allowed himself to be involved. The distant sound of a truck on the national road made him start.

"Don't be frightened," Pietro said to him with a smile. "Sit down. How are things with you? I've heard some things about you. I know that you're married and have children, that you're a success in your profession, and that you enjoy the respect of the authorities. I congratulate you. Are you a *commendatore* yet? What? No? What an appalling injustice."

"I'm going," Nunzio said. "Why should I sit down? Do you think I want to compromise myself with you, to argue with you, to listen to your wild ideas?"

Spina motioned to him to calm down. "I know you've always been a rabbit," he said. "Go away, it upsets me to see you quivering with fear. If they haven't made you a *commendatore* yet, and you're certainly itching to be one, let me suggest to you an infallible method of becoming one. Just hurry away and denounce me."

"Don't be offensive," said Nunzio. "Only a lunatic would mistake common sense for cowardice. Besides, I was sent for as a doctor. I didn't come here to argue with you, but to see what you need."

"Physician, cure thyself," said Pietro. "I assure you that I'm in a better state than you. You may not believe me, but I repeat that it wasn't I who sent for you."

Nunzio seemed to be seized with sudden compassion and sat down beside him. "Weren't you safe abroad?" he asked. "Why did you come back to this dreadful country, into the lion's jaws? If you're in love with freedom, why didn't you stay in a free country?"

"I came back in order to be able to breathe," Pietro said, making the gesture of filling his lungs. "You see, even when I was abroad the reality in which I lived my mental life was here, but gradually that reality became a dream, an abstraction. I had a real need to feel the ground beneath my feet again."

"The greatest revolutionaries," Nunzio said, "your masters, Mazzini, Lenin, Trotsky, who plotted for their ideas for decades, spent whole lifetimes in exile. Why can't you?"

"Perhaps you're right," Spina said. "I'm a very bad revolutionary. To hell with politics, tactics, strategy. What I mean is, I don't know how to preserve myself in the hope of one day playing a big role. In any event, I'm not going abroad again. You see, Nunzio, I'm just like the wines of our part of the world: they are by no means to be despised, but take them to a different climate and they're no good at all, while other men and other wines seem to be especially made for export."

"And if they catch you?" Nunzio asked.

"I admit that prison is rather disagreeable," Spina said. "You can take it from me that I shan't go there of my own accord. But if they take me there by force, what can I do about it?"

"In short, you don't want to go abroad again?"

"No."

"In that case," the doctor said, "it's no concern of mine, I wash my hands of it."

"I'm delighted to hear you expressing yourself in biblical sim-
iles," Pietro said ironically. "I see that something remains of your
education by priests."

"What remains with you is the fanaticism," Nunzio said. "You
no longer believe in God, but instead you believe in the prole-
tariat, and with the same obsessiveness."

Pietro made a gesture as if to forbid him to speak of things of
which he could have not the slightest understanding.

"Yesterday evening," he said, "to avoid the *carabinieri* and
militia I walked the whole length of the path halfway up the
Monte della Croce, and I saw in the distance the school at which
we spent eight years together. The flower beds that we looked
after must still be in the garden. Do you remember my geraniums? The big dormitory where we slept in neighboring beds, so
close that we could talk until late at night without the prefect
noticing it, must still be on the third floor. Do you remember the
fantastic plans we used to make?"

"To me you seem to be recalling prehistory," Nunzio said.

"When we went out into the world," Pietro went on, "we
found ourselves in a society that was totally unforeseen, and each
one of us had to make his choice — to submit or to put his life in
jeopardy. Once upon a time there may have been middle ways,
but for our generation, after that war, they were closed. How
many years have passed since then? Barely fifteen, and anyone
who saw the two of us here now would never imagine that up to
the age of twenty our lives ran parallel and we nursed the same
dreams for the future."

Nunzio seemed nervous and upset. "It's true that we now belong to two different parties," he said.

"Two different humanities," Pietro corrected him. "Two different races. I know of no other terms to express what I am trying
to say. In my present situation, in which I am practically in your
hands, to pretend an esteem for you and those like you that I do
not feel would cost me an effort of which I am not capable. Besides, the day of reckoning is not yet. You may go."

"There are many other things of which you are not capable,"

Nunzio said. "You are not capable of understanding that the ordinary person generally doesn't have any choice at all. The conditions in which he lives are prefabricated for him. If they are not to his liking, the best he can do is to wait for them to change."

"And if they don't change of their own accord, who is to change them?" said Pietro. "Oh, how pitiful is an intelligence used only to make excuses to quiet the conscience. At least do me the favor of going away."

Pietro went back into the shed and sat wearily on a donkey saddle. The doctor remained uncertain for a moment, then went up to him and said, "Let me at least examine your chest. I can get you medicines through Cardile."

Reluctantly Pietro bared his neck. There was a grotesque contrast between his prematurely aged head, which was the color of vulcanized fiber, and his slender, clean, slightly bent chest, which was white and graceful, like that of an adolescent. The doctor bent over him, tapped, and put his ear to each of his ribs, checked the frantic hammering of his heart, tried to listen from every side to the painful panting of the lungs. The examination exhausted Pietro's slight physical resistance, and he slowly slipped from the saddle and lay outstretched on the straw-covered floor, shutting his eyes. Nunzio was seized with a sudden feeling of warmth and fellowship.

"Listen, Pietro," he said, "let's get things straight, you mustn't die."

He sat next to him on the straw and started unburdening himself, telling him about the illusions, the disappointments, the miseries, the lies, the intrigues, the boredom of his professional life.

"We live the whole of our lives provisionally," he said. "We think that for the time being things are bad, that for the time being we must make the best of them and adapt or humiliate ourselves, but that it's all only provisional and that one day real life will begin. We prepare for death complaining that we have never lived. Sometimes I'm haunted by the thought that we have only one life and that we live it provisionally, waiting in vain for the day when real life will begin. And so life passes by. I assure you that of all the people I know not one lives in the present. No one gets any benefit from what he does every day. No one is in a condition to say: on that day, at that moment, my life began. Believe me, even those who have power and take advantage of it live on intrigues and anxieties and are full of disgust at the dominant stupidity. They too live provisionally and spend their lives waiting."

"One mustn't wait," Pietro said. "Those who emigrate spend their lives waiting too. That's the trouble. One must act. One must say: enough, from this very day."

"But if there's no freedom?" Nunzio said.

"Freedom is not a thing you can receive as a gift," Pietro said. "One can be free even under a dictatorship on one simple condition, that is, if one struggles against it. A man who thinks with his own mind and remains uncorrupted is a free man. A man who struggles for what he believes to be right is a free man. You can live in the most democratic country in the world, and if you are lazy, callous, servile, you are not free, in spite of the absence of violence and coercion, you are a slave. Freedom is not a thing that must be begged from others. You must take it for yourself, whatever share you can."

Nunzio was thoughtful and troubled. "You are our revenge," he said. "You are the best part of ourselves. Pietro, try to be strong. Try to live and to endure. Take real care of your health."

"Nunzio," Pietro said with difficulty, "if my return to Italy served only to make you talk like that, I should be satisfied. That is how you used to talk during the nights at school while the rest of the dormitory was asleep."

Cardile appeared at the door of the shed. He was soaked to the skin.

"It's still raining, and there's not a soul to be seen," he said.

The doctor and he went aside and conferred for a moment. Then Nunzio said to Pietro, "For the time being you'll stay hidden here. You must spend the whole day lying down, and Cardile will bring you what you need. Meanwhile we'll find you somewhere more comfortable."

"I shan't go abroad again," Pietro said.

"I'm afraid you couldn't even if you wanted to," the doctor said. "You're in no condition for a long journey. We must find you a safe and quiet hiding place for a few months. Afterward you can do what you like."

When he was left alone Pietro clambered up a stepladder to the hayloft above the shed. That was his sanatorium.

4

$\mathcal{A}$T LAST HE COULD REST, comforted by the warmth of his fever. This was his first chance to relax since returning to his country.

"I feel I'm in a manger scene," he said to Cardile.

For that idea to have been complete he should have had an ass and a cow for company. The ass and the cow were there, but down below in the shed, as well as a horse, and only at night, because during the daytime they had to earn their hay. When they came back they were tired, and the outlaw upstairs was asleep. The straw encouraged him to sleep. There was no sound to disturb him. Behind the loft there was a brook, and at night its babbling was his lullaby. Nymphs emerged from it in the dark and told him forgotten stories of his childhood. Memories made him drowsy. When Cardile arrived with food and medicines he opened his eyes, ate, swallowed his pills, and then sank back into the straw and dropped off to sleep again. Cardile came twice a day. He would arrive with the ass or the horse, dismount, remove the animal's load, tie it by the halter to a ring fixed in the wall, look around, and then come up to the loft. Pietro recognized every one of his movements. His visits lasted no longer than was strictly necessary.

"Any news?"

"No, nothing. Be patient."

He was in no hurry. There was a big unframed window in the loft through which the hay was put after the threshing, and he could stay in the shade and see a large expanse of fields through the wide opening; fields of young green wheat, low vines, and apple and almond trees in blossom. He could also see a stretch of the national road in the distance. One evening a long procession of carts passed by with little lights hanging between the wheels, going to some fair. Pietro closed his eyes and went to the fair with them.

"Aren't you bored?" Cardile asked him.

No, he wasn't. He found it difficult to explain his state of mind. He was struck by the naturalness of the things about him, things in their proper place, not in the fictitious world, the fictitious countryside of the haunted imagination of an émigré. His own sick body was like a natural object among other natural objects, a thing just like other things, a pile of stiff bones. It was not a central or basic thing in relation to other things, but a concrete, limited thing, a product of the earth. His body lay on the straw between a loaf of bread and a bottle of wine, which was the usual breakfast that Cardile brought him. The straw was yellow, the bread brown, the wine red.

"Bring me some colored pencils and I'll paint you a picture," he said to Cardile.

But one evening Cardile arrived panting and out of breath.

"What? Are you still here? Am I to believe my eyes?" he said.

"Where did you think I was?"

"Dr. Sacca has just heard you were arrested at a hotel at Avezzano."

"Well, it depends on whom he got the information from."

"An officer in the militia, a friend of his."

"In that case," Pietro said seriously, "most probably it's true."

"To the glory of the militia," said Pietro, raising the bottle.

"The militia is always right," Cardile said. "Have another."

The bottle was quickly drained.

"Couldn't you bring me a newspaper?" Pietro asked.

"I'm sorry, but I've never bought a newspaper in my life," said Cardile. "Newspaper readers in Acquafredda can be counted on the fingers of one hand. I don't want to do anything that might arouse suspicion."

Pietro did not insist. He had with him some crumpled notebooks containing Lenin's notes on the agrarian revolution. These would have been incriminating if they had been found in the event of a casual search by the militia, but he had not wanted to get rid of them, thinking they might be useful for a closer study of the southern Italian problem, particularly if he were forced to remain out of the active struggle for some weeks. But, leafing through them in his idleness in the hayloft, he found himself unable to go on reading them; they might have been written in Chinese. The fact was that he had always been bored by theory.

One day Dr. Sacca made Cardile a speech about vitamins, the conclusion of which was that Pietro needed a more substantial diet. The result was that henceforth he was regularly given two loaves of bread and a double quantity of wine every morning. Every now and then Cardile managed to steal some cheese and salami from home; for Pietro these occasions were Lucullan feasts.

Cardile came to the shed at dawn and sunset to look after the animals or to take them out to work in the fields and bring them back as required. Pietro recognized each of his movements, when he piled the manure or spread the straw, when he only half closed the door because he would be coming back very soon, and when he shut it. The animals' drinking trough was a short distance away. It consisted of a big wooden tub into which water flowed from an iron pipe fixed to a dry stone wall. The wall served to protect the fountain. Water flowed out of a slit in one side of the tub and continued its way downhill, forming the brook that Pietro heard babbling at night.

One morning, after Cardile's usual visit, Pietro could no longer resist the temptation to take a bath. It was a fine morning, the sun had just risen, and the apple and cherry trees glistened with dew. Down on the plain peasants were busy with the spring sowing and winnowing the young wheat, but on the hillside there was no one to be seen. Pietro had no difficulty in following the tracks of the animals and finding the drinking trough. The water was light green in color and very cold. Pietro had just taken off his shirt and was unlacing his shoes when a young peasant woman appeared carrying a pail. There had been no sound of footsteps, as the girl was barefoot; she had obviously come to draw water. Pietro hurriedly put on his shirt again.

"Excuse me," he said, trying to smile.

"Are there no fountains near your house?" the girl said disdainfully. "Why do you trespass on other people's property?"

"I'm on a pilgrimage," he said. "I'm simply passing through."

He tried to placate the girl by politeness.

"Would you like me to help you fill the bucket?" he said.

"Spring has never been a time for pilgrimages," she said. "In Christian countries people go on pilgrimages in August or September. In spring they work."

"I made a vow," said Pietro. "You certainly know what a vow is. Actually it's a matter of conscience."

She was a robust, self-confident young woman, not easy to intimidate; she had thick eyelashes and the strong shoulders, neck, and thighs of a woman who does heavy work, but her delicate nose, her lively and ironic eyes, and her slender ankles meant that she was by no means ordinary in appearance.

"Can't I help you?" Pietro said. "I'm in no hurry, you know."

She looked hard at him and supported his gaze without embarrassment.

"Perhaps you live in these parts?" he said. "I'm delighted to see that you're in no hurry either."

Her only answer was to plunge the pail into the trough and pull it out full. Before going away she turned to Pietro as if she were trying to think of something to say.

"Good luck," she ended by saying in a friendly tone that affected him deeply. Why that greeting and that sudden change of tone?

He followed her with his eyes until she disappeared from

sight, and then quickly went back to the loft, where he took up a
position behind the big window. He stayed there with his eyes
fixed on the path down which she had disappeared. The path
led through an orchard, and beyond it, above the treetops, the
roof of a farmhouse was visible. Was that where she lived? Pietro
stayed motionless at his post all day, and the hours passed
without his noticing them. Time stood still. In the afternoon,
when he suddenly saw her reappear, carrying a pail in one hand
just as in the morning, he thought that perhaps it was a halluci-
nation. All the same, he hurried down the ladder and went to
meet her. But he had the sense to arrive at the trough as if he
were coming down from the top of the hill.

"Still here?" the girl said, pretending surprise. "Have you forgotten your vow?"

"I've been waiting for you to come back," he honestly admitted.

"Were you sure I was coming back?" she said. "What nerve."

"No, I certainly wasn't sure. I was afraid you might not come
back, but I hoped that you would," he said. "I've been thinking
about nothing else all day."

"Where have you been, if I may ask?" she said.

"Up in the woods," he said. "I've spent the whole time looking
in the direction of your house on the other side of the orchard."

"Did you spend last night in the woods too?" the girl asked.
"It's not very comfortable at this time of year. What do you do if it
rains?"

"I'm waiting for you to offer me a better place," Pietro said.
Now he had laid his cards on the table. The girl did not answer,
but waited for him to go on.

"Is there anyone else in the house?" he asked. His voice was
trembling, and he tried hard to smile politely to mitigate the
crudeness of the question.

"Yes, my mother-in-law," the girl said.

"At some time of night mothers-in-law generally go to sleep,"
Pietro said.

For a moment the girl defended herself by resorting to irony.

"Really," she said with a laugh. "That's not bad for a pilgrim."

After a moment she added, "Also there's the dog. It sleeps in the daytime, it takes it in turn with my mother-in-law."

"So I'll expect you here, then," said Pietro. "It's nice warm weather, but don't keep me waiting too long."

"Are you in such a hurry?" the girl said provocatively.

"Being alone gets on one's nerves," Pietro said.

The girl threw caution to the winds and laughed aloud. "You could tell your beads," she said.

"I'll expect you as soon as it's dark," he said. "Don't keep me waiting."

How interminable are the hours that precede a romantic appointment.

Cardile was later than usual that evening. A peasant's day is regulated by the weather, and it would have been foolish not to take full advantage of a sunny day in April. Pietro was impatient.

"You look much better," Cardile said. "I'm delighted that the air in my shed has done you good."

"Yes, I feel much better," Pietro said. "But last night I hardly slept a wink because of a dog's barking. Who lives in that house beyond the orchard?"

"A young woman cousin of mine, with her mother-in-law," Cardile said. "Her husband now works at the sugar refinery."

"What sort of people are they?" Pietro asked.

"Not to be trusted," Cardile said. "We're hardly on speaking terms."

"Excuse me, I'm tired," Pietro said. "I hope that dog will let me sleep tonight."

No sooner had Cardile left than he climbed down from the loft and made straight for the water trough, without worrying about hiding the direction from which he came. The girl was there already.

"You make yourself sought after," she said.

"I saw a man over there near the shed, and that held me up," he said.

"That was my cousin," she said. "You did well to avoid him."

"What sort of person is he?" he said.

"Not to be trusted," said the girl.

"It's just as well that you're different," he said.

"How do you know I am? Are you sure it'll be all right?"

"Did your mother-in-law give you permission to go out?" he asked.

"I told her I had an errand to do in the village," she said. "I mustn't be late; I've got to say good night to her when I get back."

On the ground there was a big bottle, propped up against the tub.

"I've brought you something to drink," she said.

"Thank you," he said. "We'll drink afterward. It's not wine I'm thirsty for at the moment."

"Is it a long time since you've been with a woman?" she said. "Be gentle with me, please. No, don't you see the ground's wet here? It's cleaner over there, under the tree."

"What's your name?" Pietro asked.

"Margherita," she said. "And what's yours? No, don't tell me, please, it would be another lie."

"Do you think I've been telling you lies already? Do you think I'm a liar?" he said.

"You're not a pilgrim," the girl said with a smile.

"You're quite right," he said. "But that wasn't a lie, it was manner of speaking."

The two were lying on the grass, and a little of the warmth of the day still lingered in the air. At the bottom of the hill the village was a cluster of faint lights.

"It's good here," Pietro said.

"Would you like to bet that I can guess your name?" the girl said.

"Why?" said Pietro. "If you guess right, it's not worth the trouble, because I know my name already; if you guess wrong, it's a silly waste of time. Do you like wasting time?"

"During the past few days," the girl said, "the *carabinieri* have been to every house and told everyone that there's a fugitive in the area. They said that if he turned up and asked for food or lodging we were to pretend to do as he asked and inform the police immediately."

"Have you denounced me already?" Pietro asked.

"The *carabinieri* said that the man is an enemy of the government and that the person who denounced him would get a reward," the woman went on. "They talk about you a great deal in the village, your real name's Pietro."

"Doesn't the reward tempt you?" Pietro said. "Or do you prefer another one, from me?"

Margherita's reaction was abrupt. She withdrew the arm on which Pietro's head was resting, adjusted her clothing, and sat up.

"Forgive me," Pietro said. "I'm an idiot."

"Do you think," she said, "that a woman does not betray a man only if she hopes to sleep with him?"

"You're right," Pietro said. "Please forgive me."

"You may not believe me," Margherita said, "but if I had come across a woman who was a fugitive from the police like you I should not have behaved differently."

"I believe you, Margherita, forgive me," Pietro said.

"Would you like to know who taught me to be like that?" said Margherita. "When I was a little girl we hid a man who had escaped from prison in our house for several months. He was a man in distress, a stranger. My father often used to tell us that to honorable people the first of the works of mercy is to help the persecuted."

She paused for a moment, and then went on, "You may certainly think it strange to hear me talking of honor at this moment."

"You talk of it in the sense that I respect most," Pietro said seriously. "Every part of the body can be said to have its own honor. But for too long people believed that the most important kind of honor was between the legs."

"Pietro, let us be truthful," said Margherita. "What's the point of fiddling with words? It's better to say nothing."

Their two faces gradually moved closer to each other.

"Your lips taste like a child's," said Margherita. "Is it true you were born near here, in the Fucino area? I've heard it said."

"What else have you heard?" said Pietro.

"That you come from a well-off family, that you lost your parents in the earthquake, and that you're a bit mad," Margherita said. "Why do you lead such a desperate life?"

"Because of what you mentioned a few moments ago, Margherita," Pietro said. "I have a certain sense of honor."

"Would you like to send a message to your grandmother?" Margherita said. "I could go and see her. They say she's a real lady."

"I've given up my blood relatives for many years past," Pietro said. "It's disagreeable, but I think one must start with that."

"How can you possibly do such a thing?" Margherita said. "What a strange idea. You're not a foundling, after all."

"The only relationship I now respect," Pietro said, "is that between minds. Like that which has just been born between us."

"Pietro, let me think for a moment about what you've just said. Yes, I have the same feeling about you now. Pietro, listen, I want to suggest something to you."

The girl rose to her feet and tidied her hair. Then she held out her hand to help him to his feet.

"Let us say good-bye without making love," she said resolutely. "After what we've just said to each other it seems to me to be the right thing to do. Do you agree? That's how I want it. But what's this?" she exclaimed. "You haven't tasted my wine yet."

Pietro raised the bottle and took a long drink.

"It's strong," he said. "Have some too."

Margherita helped herself as generously as Pietro had. The gurgling of the wine mingled with the babbling of the brook. The duet continued until the wine was finished.

"How much was there?" Pietro asked.

"Three liters," said Margherita. "Now I must go."

"I'll come with you as far as the orchard," Pietro said.

"That wouldn't be wise," Margherita said. "Our dog is let off the chain at night and it might go for you."

They parted without saying good-bye. Only when he saw her disappear at the end of the path was Pietro overcome with sadness; he sat down on the ground and started to weep. His return to the hayloft was difficult for other reasons. In his absence some idiot had changed the whole layout of the place. The door, for instance, had been moved and made smaller, and the ladder was simply impossible to find. Also dawn arrived earlier than usual, before the effect of the wine had worn off. Cardile found him huddled in the manger.

"What on earth are you doing here?" he said. "Why didn't you sleep up in the loft?"

"A huge rat kept disturbing me," Pietro said, rubbing his eyes. "It didn't frighten me, but I didn't want to waste time arguing with it."

"The bottle I brought you yesterday must have gone to your head," Cardile said with a smile.

After attending to the animals he went up into the loft to fetch the daily ration of hay. Meanwhile Pietro tried to decipher a very puzzling letter from Nunzio, an almost impossible task in which he was interrupted by exclamations of surprise from the floor above.

"How extraordinary," Cardile exclaimed. "I can't believe my eyes."

He came hurrying down the ladder with the bottle he had brought the evening before. It was full.

"What did you get drunk on last night if this bottle's still full?" Cardile wanted to know.

Pietro's surprise was no less, but it was of briefer duration, because of his innate tendency to remain impassive in the face of the strangest natural phenomena.

"What on earth am I to make of this?" Cardile said.

"Well," said Pietro, "it seems to me that this is an obvious refutation of the old proverb according to which it is impossible to have a full bottle and a tipsy wife or friend. All that can be done, it seems to me, is to take cognizance of the fact."

"I don't understand," Cardile said.

"Your bewilderment does not surprise me," Pietro said. "You are a peasant, and agriculture is based on proverbs. But truth, fortunately, is greater than proverbs."

Those words served to end the discussion, but not to convince Cardile, who kept looking suspiciously at the bottle and shaking his head. So Pietro was able to go back to trying to elucidate Nunzio's letter. It mentioned in sibylline terms a strange plan for living safely in a mountain village for two or three months, long enough to restore someone's health. What did the person concerned think of the idea? The details were glossed over or incomprehensible, but Pietro decided that a change of air was urgently required and that the burden must be removed from Cardile's shoulder, so he accepted. One of the things he did not realize was that he was to leave immediately.

Hardly had he dropped off to sleep in the straw that evening than he heard a voice downstairs calling him.

"Pietro, Pietro, come down," it said.

Groping in the dark, Pietro managed to lift the latch in the trapdoor and look down. Nunzio was down below between the donkey and the cow, holding a lantern and calling him.

"Bring whatever you need," he said. "You're leaving immediately."

As soon as Pietro joined him Nunzio showed him in the feeble light of the lantern a big bundle of ecclesiastical clothing.

"It's a complicated setup," Nunzio said, "and, to tell the truth, it's not really to my taste at all."

Pietro was speechless. He had not realized from the letter that the plan was that he should disguise himself as a priest.

"I have a horror of carnivals and dressing up," he said. "Even when I was a boy I never wore a mask."

"Given the situation," Nunzio said, "we failed to think of anything safer."

Pietro went on stubbornly shaking his head.

"It's a long time since I left the Church, but disguising myself as a priest is repugnant to me, it's an act of irreverence that is inconsistent with my character."

This scruple pleased Nunzio.

"If we didn't know you," he said, "if we had thought there was the slightest chance of your making improper use of this disguise, we shouldn't have offered it to you."

The clothing of Pietro in his priestly attire took place immediately in the dim light of the oil lamp. The horse was asleep, and the cow created the impression of not realizing what was happening, for it squatted on the straw and shut its eyes. But the donkey remained on its feet and looked. This attentiveness on its part ended by upsetting the doctor, who took it by the halter and made it face the other way. It allowed itself to be moved, but then turned its head and went on gazing at this strange man who had come down from the hayloft and was now putting on a long, black cassock with a long row of little buttons in front.

"Don't forget that the habit does not make the monk," Nunzio said.

But Pietro was in no mood for joking and went on muttering incomprehensibly.

To distract him Nunzio improvised a short, semiserious consecratory speech.

"These garments," he said, "are derived from primitive mystery religions, from the priests of Isis and Serapis, as you know. In the Catholic Church they were adopted by the first monastic communities, to try to safeguard Christian values from worldly contamination so that the essential charismatic virtues might be preserved for a minority living outside society and in opposition to society. Thus rites survive the age in which they are born and pass from one religion to another, from one society to another. Now, here are you, a man initiated into the new revolutionary mysteries, into the mysteries of revolutionary materialism, donning the black garments that for thousands of years have been symbols of sacrifice and supernatural inspiration." An involuntary smile came into Pietro's eyes.

"Don't talk nonsense," he said.

"I don't understand," Nunzio went on in the same tone, "why Lenin did not introduce similar clothing, or at any rate the tonsure, for the personnel of the Comintern, to distinguish the agent, depository, and interpreter of the sacred texts from the simple proletarian or *cafone.*"

Time was pressing. Cardile was waiting outside with the horse and trap.

"You will stop at my office," Nunzio said, "where you will have a bath and have your hair cut, and I shall take an X ray."

"Promise to come and see me," Pietro said.

"All right," Nunzio said. "What will you call yourself?"

Pietro thought for a moment. Then he suggested, "Spada. What do you think of it?"

"All right," said Nunzio. "We'll call you Don Paolo Spada."

"Why Don Paolo?"

"Pietro Spada is too close to your real name. So, Reverend Don Paolo Spada, let us go. Have you forgotten nothing? Have you your tricorn, your breviary, your beads, your scapular, the special instructions for your sacred mission?"

"Let us go," said Don Paolo Spada. *"Procedamus in pace."*

5

"THE HORSE DOESN'T LIKE going out at night," the driver said. "I must say I don't blame it."

"Nor do I," said Don Paolo. "But I missed my train. I was delayed by the bishop."

"Monsignore ought to buy himself a watch," said the driver. "How can he send his priests around at night in this appalling weather?"

It had stopped raining a short time before, but it was windy and the air was as cold as in winter.

"Are you cold? Shall I raise the hood?" the driver asked.

"It's all right as it is, provided the rain holds off," said Don Paolo.

The road was dark and lonely. The sound of the horse's hooves aroused the dogs in their kennels. Occasionally an inquisitive face appeared at a window that was still lit. The driver was sitting on his box, smoking his pipe. An occasional shake of the reins was sufficient to keep the horse trotting. The man turned to Don Paolo and said, "How much do you charge for a funeral service? I'm just asking out of curiosity."

"Are you thinking of dying soon?" Don Paolo replied.

"Not for the time being," the man said, and touched a certain part of his body. "But I should like to know, for purposes of comparison."

"Forget it," Don Paolo said. "Comparisons are odious."

"Do you know this part of the world?" the man asked.

Don Paolo did not answer. This was the neighborhood where he was born, from which he had been banished about ten years previously, his native country that was forbidden him. He felt his heart beating, and he was sweating in spite of the coldness of the night. Behind him was Monte Velino, its two summits still covered with snow, and in front of him, covering the whole semicircle of the horizon, was the mountain barrier surrounding the Fucino basin, standing out against the snowy night sky like the gloomy battlements of a closed world. The cab came to a big village in which recently built houses and villas alternated with huddles of muddy huts and piles of rubble. The place was badly lit, and the darkest stretches of roadway coincided with the widest and deepest puddles. At a bend in the road the cab was abruptly halted by two *carabinieri*, who promptly let it go on when they saw that the only passenger was a priest.

"Good evening, Father," they said.

"*Pax vobiscum*," the priest replied.

At the end of the village the road was being repaired and the horse started walking. Don Paolo held tight in the jolting vehicle to avoid ending up between the wheels. It was an effort, but it was also a distraction. As soon as the road returned to normal the driver turned toward him and said, "Do you believe in this new war in Africa?"

"A priest, if he believes at all, believes in God," Don Paolo replied. "That in itself is a great deal."

"What I wanted to know," the driver said, "was whether you think the new war will be profitable."

"Not to those who die," said Don Paolo.

The driver took this as a witticism, and laughed. But what he really wanted to know was something else, as he explained in different terms. "Do you think there are plenty of pickings there? Is there gold there? Plenty of gold?"

"So wars are just if there are plenty of pickings, in your opinion?" Don Paolo said.

"In everybody's opinion," the driver said. "Do you expect the poor lads to die for nothing? Do only the English have the right to steal?"

"I'm sleepy," said Don Paolo. "Leave me in peace."

The road had been recently graveled. They were close to Don Paolo's birthplace. The cab jolted in space and time. In this locality Don Paolo knew every bridge, every vineyard, every brook, every tree. At the crossroads before Orta there was an old tavern. Acquasanta, the landlady, was lowering the shutters, and a girl was helping her. Could Acquasanta's daughter have grown that much? The wheels of the cab sank in the gravel and turned with difficulty. They rounded a bend and the first houses of Orta suddenly appeared only a few yards away; there was the electric streetlamp on the dark wheelwright's shop at the entrance to the village. Don Paolo shut his eyes. He didn't want to see. The first to notice the cab's arrival was the wheelwright's mastiff. It barked two or three times, as usual, and then listened behind the door, growling to itself uncertainly and interrogatively. The cab passed the shop, nearly grazing the door, whereupon the mastiff let out a protracted, high-pitched howl, to which the bitch guarding the vegetable plot behind the church responded in alarm. Don Paolo kept his eyes shut, but he could tell from the sound of the wheels when the cab reached the cobbles of the small Orta square. The bitch started barking hysterically, woke her young that were sleeping in the kennel together with the puppies, and jumped against the gate of the vegetable plot. One by one the other village dogs were aroused, including those over by the mill, those at the civil engineers' storerooms, and those at the carters' stables.

"What on earth is happening?" the cabman exclaimed. "What sort of a place is this?"

Thirty or forty dogs were howling, growling, and barking in every alley and every courtyard. They were still barking when the cab left the last houses behind, and then one by one they fell silent. When Don Paolo opened his eyes again the cab had stopped by a fountain with a big drinking trough for animals. On the fountain there was a bronze plaque with the words: ERECTED AT THE EXPENSE OF THE SPINA FAMILY.

"Wait a minute, I'm getting out too," Don Paolo said to the driver.

He got out, took some water in the hollow of his hand, and drank. Then he wiped his burning brow with his wet hands. There was no more gravel on the road, and the horse could start trotting again. Don Paolo sat with his back to the driver, so as to be able to see the last village lights. There were still lights in about a dozen scattered windows. Then one went out up on the hill, then another down below near the mill, then another in the direction of the stream, and then another up on the hill. Don Paolo could recognize every house, every chimney, every window, every garden. What had become of his grandmother, old Donna Maria Vincenza? Was she still alive? Did she ever think about him? Had she been troubled by the authorities? What had become of Faustina? Did she remember him? Was she married? He felt like a visitor from another world. The cab passed close to an old pozzolana quarry that had belonged to his father. As a boy he had played hide-and-seek with the children of the men who worked there. Halfway up the hill he recognized "his" vineyard, the last remnant of his father's estate. The fig trees were still in their place, but where were the cherry trees? Where was the walnut tree? His uncle, to whom the vineyard had been handed over, must have had them cut down. Don Paolo's eyes filled with tears. Then the wind rose and turned east, and the trees rustled. Don Paolo bent his head and really went to sleep.

The driver woke him at Fossa dei Marsi, outside the Girasole hotel. He was expected. A woman took charge of his suitcase.

Before taking his departure the driver asked a favor of Don Paolo. "Couldn't you write me a good recommendation?" he said.

"A recommendation to whom and for what?"

The driver thought for a moment, and then said, "At the

moment I can't exactly say, but there'll be plenty of occasions when it'll be bound to come in handy. You could give me a general recommendation."

"But I don't know you," the priest said. "Good night."

He must have been dazed and exhausted, for he had no memory whatever of his arrival at the inn.

6

DON PAOLO WOKE EARLY but stayed in bed late. Nunzio had given him some typed "Notes on How a Priest Should Conduct Himself Outside His Diocese." Don Paolo came from the diocese of Frascati and was going to the Marsi diocese to convalesce in the mountain village of Pietrasecca. The notes indicated the major difficulties he might encounter and gave instructions on how to cope with them. Don Paolo read and reread them. The carter who was to take him up to Pietrasecca was coming to fetch him in the afternoon, so he took his time dressing and spent the whole morning in his room. He noted with pleasure that there was a washbasin. After roughing it in the hayloft, a washbasin in his room offered him real luxury. It also showed the progress that had been made in his country. Over the washbasin there was a notice in beautiful handwriting saying: GENTLEMEN ARE REQUESTED NOT TO URINATE IN THE WASHBASIN BECAUSE OF THE SMELL. In fact the washbasin stank.

Don Paolo looked at himself in the mirror. His hair had been cut very short in Nunzio's office. With his shaved head and in his black cassock he looked grotesque. He almost burst into tears.

The cassock had twenty-eight buttons in front. The idea of having
to do up or undo twenty-eight buttons every time he put it on or
took it off plunged him into despair. Fortunately he discovered
that it was sufficient to unbutton it only from the neck to the waist
to take it off over his head or to drop it to his feet. These feminine
gestures put him in a good humor. But other difficulties arose. He
was disturbed at the idea that he would have to raise the cassock
every time he wanted to take something from his trouser pockets.
Wasn't it ridiculous to have to raise one's cassock in public? But
later he discovered an opening near the pockets through which
the trouser pockets could be reached. Oh well, being a priest was
not so difficult after all. When he went out onto the landing he
ran straight into the landlady, the widowed Berenice Girasole.
The reception the old woman gave him was rather alarming. She
had evidently suffered some sort of calamity; her tearful expression and her sighs boded nothing good for Don Paolo.

"It was providence that sent you," she said, kissing his hand.

"No, it was the doctor," said Don Paolo, slipping away.

Opposite the hotel there was a clothes store. To keep himself in
countenance he pretended to look at one of the windows, but a
burst of laughter from some youths who were standing about drew
his attention to the merchandise on display, which consisted of
women's underwear and brassieres. He fled, and did not stop until
he reached a hat shop. His reflection in a big mirror in the window
showed him an even more disastrous version of himself than that
which he had seen in the hotel bedroom. How horrible. Tired and
disheartened, he went back to the hotel. By now it was lunchtime.

"Would the Reverend Father like spaghetti?" the landlady in-
quired.

"Heaven forbid," said Don Paolo. "Anything but spaghetti."

Fortunately the landlady had other guests to serve.

The dining room walls were lavishly adorned with colored pages
from a well-known illustrated weekly reproducing stirring incidents
such as a train being saved from certain disaster by a signalman's
daughter, an airplane being attacked by an eagle, and cages of a
menagerie being broken in the middle of a town, enabling wild

beasts to escape and chase terrified passersby. There were about a dozen other guests in the dining room, and Don Paolo had the feeling that they were all watching him and talking about him. He tried not to raise his eyes from his plate. When coffee was served Signora Berenice sat at his table to tell him her troubles. She wore no corset, her huge breasts were flopping, and she was perspiring profusely after the hard work of serving lunch. When she mentioned providence again, Don Paolo rudely interrupted.

"I'm sorry," he said, "but I do not belong to this diocese. I came here solely to rest and recuperate."

The woman was offended and upset, and she fell silent. Don Paolo took advantage of her dismay to go and sun himself in front of the hotel. Five or six youths were sitting around a small table and snoozing, with their hats on and cigarette stubs between their lips. At another table a little farther away other young men were playing cards and scattering yellow spittle like butterflies in the dust all around them. Nearly all of them wore the government party emblem in their buttonholes. Among them an old man in a broad-rimmed hat who looked like a retired actor was playing cards too and was puffing and blowing over his coffee. When he saw the strange priest he gave the signal against the evil eye.

"Iron, iron," he called out.

The sleepers awoke immediately and they too took the precaution that was called for. Don Paolo recognized the rite and was about to respond with some profanity, but held his peace, because the behavior of these idlers confirmed him in his priestly role. This gave him pleasure, so he stayed where he was. Opposite the hotel were the beflagged headquarters of the government party and the municipal portico with a medallion of King Umberto with the usual big mustache. A lean doorkeeper was seated outside the entrance; he too had an impressive handlebar mustache. He was surrounded by flies, and every now and then he cleared his throat and spat in a wide arc that reached the very middle of the small square. The strange priest's presence attracted to the hotel a number of beggars escorted by swarms of flies. A cripple who came bounding along on crutches begged for alms in the

name of them all. Don Paolo fled back into the hotel where, however, the landlady was on the watch. She seized him by the arm,
held him firmly, and started again in a tearful voice, "In the name
of Our Lady of Sorrows I implore you to listen to me," she said in
a heartbroken voice. "There's a dying girl here, my only daughter,
she's dying, don't be heartless."

"I'm sorry," said Don Paolo, at the limits of his patience. "I
have already told you, and I now repeat, that I do not belong to
this diocese and that I am not authorized to undertake the cure of
souls in these parts."

"Not even in urgent cases?"

"In no circumstances whatever."

Berenice could no longer restrain her tears. "Very well," she
said, "but at least let me talk to you. You might be able to give me
some advice. The girl is on the point of death and is not willing to
confess to the priest here, because he's a relative. Don't you understand that? When I told her a strange priest had arrived here, she
was overjoyed. Jesus Christ sent him to me, she said immediately."

"I'm sorry," Don Paolo said. "If it's so urgent, why don't you
send for the priest of a neighboring parish?"

"It may be too late," said Berenice. "And also it would be noticed, and the result would be a scandal. People would ask why
the family priest had not been sent for."

"I'm sorry," Don Paolo said.

Berenice could not stifle her heartrending tears. "How can a girl
be left to die without a priest and without a doctor?" she sobbed.

"Why without a doctor?" Don Paolo asked. "What is this story?"

Berenice was afraid she had said too much, and looked all
around her in alarm.

"Can I speak under the seal of silence?" she said.

Don Paolo indicated that she could. Speaking in an undertone,
and without ceasing to weep, she told him what had happened.

"The girl isn't married and was going to have a baby. To avoid
being dishonored and dishonoring her family she tried to get rid
of it by herself. Do you follow me? The law forbids that, as you
know. If a doctor or midwife or anyone else helps a woman to get

rid of it, it means imprisonment. That often happens, you have only to read the newspapers. There are some who come to an even worse end. The daughter of the notary at Fossa was four months gone and drank some bleach. A local girl who was in domestic service with the *podestà* went to Tivoli and drowned herself. My poor girl tried to get rid of it by herself. She had no choice but to risk death or face dishonor. She risked death, and she's dying. Can you imagine a poor mother's situation? I can't tell a doctor, because he'd report it, inquiries would be made, there'd be a trial, and the whole thing would come out. And the girl doesn't want the parish priest to be sent for, because he's a relative. Of course she has sinned, but there is forgiveness for everyone. Didn't Christ die on the cross for everyone?"

Don Paolo was baffled. This was a case not foreseen in the instructions Nunzio had given him.

"I sympathize with you, but I do not know what to advise you," he said.

The poor priest's eyes were full of tears. Berenice noticed this. She signed to him to come with her as if she wanted to tell him something else, and he obediently followed her. She led the way up to the second floor. Slowly and noiselessly she opened the door of a small room. It was in semidarkness and smelled of disinfectant. In a corner, under a big black crucifix, there was a small white iron bed.

"Bianchina," Berenice said quietly. "Look who has come."

Something moved in the bed. A thin, pointed, ashen, childish little face, distorted by pain, appeared among the thick black hair scattered on the pillow. When Don Paolo realized that Berenice had gone it was too late. He stayed by the door, rooted to the spot. Several minutes passed like that. He was about to tiptoe out again, but he was stopped by the dying girl's big, wide-open eyes. How was he to explain to a human being on the point of death that he was not like other priests? He was utterly at a loss, he was paralyzed. The dying girl went on looking at him with her big, feverish eyes.

"Courage," he said, trying to produce a smile.

Slowly he tiptoed toward her, bent over her, kissed her hand. Her big eyes filled with tears. The light blanket showed the outline of her slender, dying body, her breasts that stood out like two lemons, her emaciated legs. "My dear girl," he said, "I know everything. Please tell me nothing, don't abase yourself, don't renew your sufferings. You have no need to confess. You are confessed already."

"Will you give me absolution?" she said.

"You are forgiven," said the priest. "Who could fail to forgive you? You have done penance, and it has been too hard."

"If I die," the girl said, "where shall I go?"

"To the cemetery," said the priest, "like everyone else."

"Shall I be saved?"

"Certainly, but don't be in a hurry to go, try to postpone your departure," he said in a forced humorous tone.

He was holding the girl's hand between his two hands. His hands were burning.

"You're feverish too, are you ill perhaps?" she said.

Don Paolo nodded. "Yes, I'm ill too," he said with a smile, "I too am doing penance."

At that moment a voice called out from the street, "Where's that priest who's going to Pietrasecca?"

Don Paolo wanted to go, but the girl held him back with one hand.

"Don't go so soon," she said. "When shall I see you again?"

"I shall think about you," said Don Paolo.

"I don't believe you," the girl said. "You have other things to think about."

"Don't you believe me? Why don't you believe me?" Don Paolo said.

He bent over her and looked her closely in the eyes. Silently the two looked at each other for some moments. Don Paolo was filled with a great pity. "Why don't you believe me?" he said.

"Yes, now I believe you," said the girl. "I've never believed anything so much. You have extraordinary eyes that don't lie. I've never seen eyes like yours."

BREAD AND WINE ❖ *241*

"I shall think about you," Don Paolo said.

The sound of an angry voice came through the window, "Is that priest coming or not?"

"Now I must go," Don Paolo said. "Don't be afraid, you are forgiven. What will not be forgiven is this evil society that gave you the choice between death and dishonor."

Old Magascià was sitting in the doorway of the hotel. He had finished his soup and was dipping his bread in his wine. He was a big, bearded man, broad chested and massively built, and his left sleeve hung empty from his shoulder. "Let us be off," he said to Don Paolo. "We have a long way to go."

He made the priest take his place beside him. The two-wheeled cart moved off slowly, drawn by a donkey that advanced at a walking pace. Magascià was returning to Pietrasecca with the weekly supply of salt and tobacco.

"It's not a vehicle fit for a priest," he said. "Still less for a convalescent priest."

"It doesn't matter," Don Paolo said. "How long ago did you lose your arm?"

"Two years ago come Candlemas," said Magascià. "But what's the use of complaining? God sends flies to plague old donkeys." Then he went on, "Had you met Berenice before? And do you know her daughter? That's a girl who gets herself talked about."

The priest did not reply.

Magascià tied the reins to the brake and lit his pipe. "There's no need to hold the reins," he said. "The donkey has come this way once a week for the past ten years and never makes a mistake. She knows where to stop and drink, where to relieve herself, and how long every climb and every downward slope takes." Magascià had bought a new hat at Fossa, and he was wearing it on top of his old one. "Her name is Bersagliera," he went on, indicating the poor, skinny beast that was pulling the cart. "'Bersagliera' ought to mean that she moves fast, but she's old now."

"We all grow old," said the priest.

"A donkey's a lucky beast," said Magascià. "A donkey generally works till it's twenty-four, a mule till it's twenty-two, and a horse

till it's fifteen. But man, poor devil, goes on working till he's seventy or more. Why did God take pity on animals and not on men?
But He can do what He likes, of course."

No sooner had they left the town behind than the road started
to mount. To the priest the mountains, valleys, hills, and streams
were old acquaintances. The places they passed through still bore
signs of the earthquake; they looked like poor smashed and crum-
bling beehives that had been only partly reconstructed. On the
road they met a small *cafone* family, husband, wife, and baby all
on the same donkey; the woman's breast was uncovered and she
was feeding the baby.

"What's the crop looking like?" Magascià asked the man on
the donkey.

"Bad," the man answered.

"He's expecting a good harvest," Magascià whispered in the
priest's ear.

"Then why did he say the opposite?"

"To save himself from envy," Magascià explained.

"And what's your crop looking like?" asked the priest.

Magascià made the sign of the cross. "Disastrous," he said.

"Are you afraid I might envy you?" said Don Paolo.

"Envy's in the air here," Magascià explained.

Every now and then they came across stonebreakers sitting on
the ground by the roadside near piles of stones, breaking the biggest
stones with hammers. Magascià's cart went through the village of
Lama dei Marsi. Ox horns were fixed to the walls of houses and
hovels as a protection against the evil eye, and groups of silent old
men and women and swarms of half-naked children were at the
doorways. As they left the village they passed a chapel dedicated to
the Madonna. Magascià made the sign of the cross and said to Don
Paolo, "It's a chapel dedicated to the Madonna delle Rose in
memory of a miracle in days gone by. That year roses bloomed,
cherries ripened, and ewes lambed in January. Instead of rejoicing
people were terrified, of course. Were not such blessings the har-
bingers of disaster? Sure enough, cholera came that summer."

"Why was the chapel built?" Don Paolo said.

"To keep the Madonna quiet," Magascià explained. "You know that better than I do." Then he went on, "This year things look good too. Not in my case, of course, I mean it looks as if it's going to be a good year in general, as if other people's crops are going to be good. Who knows what disasters are in store?"

Beyond the chapel the road wound its way between two hills, crossed a bridge, and entered the gorge of Pietrasecca, which at first was wide and then narrowed between steep slopes of gray rock. In flat areas formed of alluvial deposits between the rocks were tiny cultivated fields, small farms measured not in acres but in *canes* or *cups*. More of these tiny fields were to be seen clinging like sticking plaster to the mountainsides. The cart advanced slowly. The road, which skirted a rocky streambed, was marked by deep ruts, like railway lines. As they climbed, the sides of the valley were more and more rent and riven and poorer and poorer in vegetation. A herd of goats that were nibbling one by one at a few blades of new grass growing between the rocks turned their bearded faces toward the strange priest traveling in the salt and tobacco cart. When the slope grew steeper Magascià got out to lighten the load.

At a bend in the road they came to small villa in Renaissance style built in a space partly dug out of the living rock. The doors and windows were barred.

"It was built by Don Simone Scaraffa, a local man who made good," Magascià explained. "Haven't you heard of him? He spent thirty years in Brazil and made a lot of money as a coffee planter, and he came home to enjoy being envied by us, that's why he had the villa built. But envy prevailed. During the first week he lived in it he went raving mad and had to be sent to Santa Maria di Collemaggio, the Aquila lunatic asylum, and he's still there. Was it worth the trouble?"

Farther along they came to a wooden cross planted in a cairn of stones with a date inscribed on it.

"That's where Don Giulio, the Lama notary, was robbed and murdered," said Magascià. "At the postmortem they found he had been stabbed in the heart seven times. The person who did him that evil service was never discovered. Don Giulio lent out money at thirty percent. After his death usury disappeared."

The first houses of Pietrasecca appeared in the distance.

"It looks like the end of the world," said the priest, seized with a shivering fit.

"It's a village of adversity," said Magascià. "It has twice been destroyed by floods and once by earthquake."

"How many people are left there?" the priest asked.

"About forty families. Those who can go down to the plain," said Magascià. "Those who can, leave."

They came to another cairn of stones by the roadside with a wooden cross and a date on it.

"That's where . . ." Magascià began.

"I'm not interested," Don Paolo said irritably. "It's where some other disaster happened."

"How do you know?"

"You tell me about nothing but disasters. Are you trying to frighten me?"

Magascià laughed aloud. "Not even the devil himself could frighten a priest," he said. "Aren't you priests the administrators of death?"

When they reached Pietrasecca it was twilight. Don Paolo saw in front of him about sixty cracked and smoke-blackened little houses, a number of them with doors and windows barred, no doubt having been abandoned. The village seemed to have been built in a kind of funnel dug out of the end of the valley. Only two decent houses were to be seen. One of them, just beyond the bridge, was Matalena Ricotta's inn, where the priest was to stay; the other, at the end of the village, was bigger and older; it occupied a large area surrounded by a low wall and was the patrician home of the Colamartini family, the only old house in Pietrasecca that had survived the floods and the earthquakes. Beyond there was a small church, with a bell tower and a porch facing the valley.

"Are services held there?" Don Paolo asked.

"There has been no parish priest here for the past thirty years,"

Magascià said. "A priest rarely comes here. It's a poor village. How could we support a priest?"

The little land there was between the rocks around the village was split up into a large number of small fields. The fields were so small and the stone walls that separated them were so numerous that they looked like the foundations of a destroyed town. Immediately beyond the village the gorge closed in to form a barrier, and no road led beyond. Two streams of water that came down the mountainsides met at the bottom of the valley and formed a rivulet that divided the village into two parts connected by a wooden bridge. Don Paolo looked around and could not conceal his alarm.

"You don't like it?" said Magascià.

"I don't understand why villages are built in such stupid places," said the priest. "If one had to escape from here, what choice would there be? It's not a village but a trap."

"It lacks all conveniences," said Magascià. "The only advantage is that the authorities take little notice of us."

Outside the inn there was a spring. A boy with a bleeding nose was bending over it and washing himself, and the water was quite red. Under the bridge a group of women and girls were kneeling at the edge of the rivulet, washing and beating clothes. When they caught sight of the priest they stopped as if they had been put under a spell.

Magascià drove the cart to the front door of the inn, where an old woman, the landlady, was waiting. She was short, thickset, and wore several heavy petticoats. A very dignified old gentleman with a sporting gun on his shoulder appeared on the scene and welcomed the priest to his poor village. Magascià introduced him. "This is Don Pasquale Colamartini," he said.

Don Paolo excused himself, explaining that he was dead tired.

The woman took him straight to the room that had been prepared for him. "What would you like for dinner?" she asked.

"Nothing," said Don Paolo. "All I want is to go to sleep."

In the darkness of the little room he heard a woman's voice calling her child, who was still out playing with other bigger boys.

"I'm coming, Mama, I'm just coming."

7

ONE SUNDAY MORNING A young donkey that had been bought at the last fair was christened in the space between the inn and the Pietrasecca bridge just under Don Paolo's window. A young man held the donkey by the halter while an old peasant beat it with a wooden cudgel. After each blow the two men shouted into the beast's ears, "Garibaldi."

That was the name that had been chosen for it. To the *cafoni* the name of Garibaldi meant strength and courage. The christening ceremony was protracted because naturally it took time to convince the donkey that that was its name. The man beat it on the rump without anger, without impatience, without resentment, but hard, as if it were a mattress, and after each blow he and the young men shouted into the beast's ears, "Garibaldi."

The donkey looked at them, and after each blow it shook its head. The man beat it on the rump, every blow on a different rib, and when he had completed the circuit he started all over again. Dozens and dozens of times the heroic name of Garibaldi resounded in the open space of Pietrasecca, alternating with the sound of the blows on the donkey's rump. Eventually the man grew tired and said to the youth, "That'll do. It must certainly know it by now."

To make sure the youth took a handful of straw, went to the wooden bridge, and called out from a distance, holding up the straw, "Garibaldi."

The donkey trotted toward him.

"Yes, now he knows it," the youth said.

Don Paolo was in bed, burning with fever. The journey had exhausted him. The reiterated invocation of the name of Garibaldi that came to him through the window surprised and alarmed him. Was it possible that the Republican Party could be so strong in such a remote village?

He asked the landlady what was happening.

"Nothing out of the ordinary," Matalena explained. "Old Sciatàp is christening his new donkey."

Old Sciatàp was known by that name throughout the valley. He had been christened by blows, just like his donkey. As a young man in America he had worked as general handyman to a fellow villager, one Carlo Campanella, who sold coal in winter and ice in summer on Mulberry Street, in New York. This fellow villager, who at Pietrasecca had been Carlo Campanella, in New York had become Mr. Charles Little-Bell, Ice and Coal, and he treated his employee as a beast of burden. Whenever the poor beast complained Mr. Little-Bell shouted at him, "Sciatàp."

It seems that in English *sciatàp** means "be quiet." When Sciatàp returned to Pietrasecca after several years' residence in America that was the only English word he knew, and he kept repeating it on every possible occasion, irrespective of its appropriateness or lack of it. His wife hardly dared open her mouth, because he immediately put his finger to his lips and shouted at her, "Sciatàp."

Thus the word ended by becoming part of the valley dialect. It was the only word of English known at Pietrasecca, the only element of modern and foreign culture that had entered the humble, ancient peasant tradition.

---

*Pronounced "shut up."

Don Paolo was curious to see the man, so he got out of bed and went to the window. Sciatàp and the donkey were making their way down toward the stream by an alley beside the bridge. At the beginning of the alley there was an old sign with the words: RUBBISH MUST NOT BE TIPPED HERE. But at that very spot there was a great pile of rubbish, broken dishes, kitchen refuse, and other garbage. Don Paolo smiled. Any kind of nonconformity was pleasing to him, and not everyone could print clandestine leaflets, after all.

Matalena had given him her own bedroom on the second floor. A huge double bed occupied three-quarters of it, barely leaving space for a small table, a chair, and an enameled iron washbasin. Over the bed there was a crucifix; Christ's limbs were twisted and emaciated, and His face was that of a poor hungry *cafone*. On the bedside table there was a small blue and white statuette of the Blessed Virgin in the act of crushing the serpent's head.

Meanwhile Don Paolo was no better. The mountain air did not bring about the rapid improvement for which he hoped. He stayed in bed nearly all day without being able to rest properly. The days and nights were interminable. The air was warm and heavy. The smell of cabbage and dried salt cod that floated up from the kitchen made him feel sick. To complete the priestly setup Nunzio had provided him with some devotional books, a breviary, the *Eternal Maxims* of Sant'Alfonso Maria dei Liguori, the *Introduction to the Devout Life* of St. François de Sales, a *Life of San Camillo de Lellis*, a seventeenth-century Abruzzo saint, a *Life of San Giovanni Bosco*, a Piedmontese saint of the end of the nineteenth century, a *Life of San Gabriele dell'Addolorata*, and a manual of liturgy. To distract himself Don Paolo started browsing in these books, reading passages here and there, just as he would have done with anything else in print, whether it was a thriller or a prospectus for some chemical product. Some of this literature he had read before, either at home as a boy or in his years at school, and many of those pages and illustrations roused long-forgotten memories. Symbols and memories of childish terrors slowly reemerged from the deepest levels

of his mind, and so the day came when he felt himself more and
more attracted by those sacred books and ended by reading
them every evening until his eyes grew tired. That was the state
of mind he was in when he wrote his first letter to Nunzio. This
was his only way of communicating with anyone without lying,
though caution obliged him to sign himself as Paolo Spada.
"I'm particularly grateful to you for the reading matter," he
wrote. "What a strange and haunting impact it makes. I seem to
have picked up the thread of my earlier life."

In addition to the books, the extreme weakness to which his
illness had reduced him helped to take him back to his adolescence, when he had been ill a couple of times; as an only son and
because of his weak constitution he had always been looked after
by his mother, grandmother, aunts, and the maid, and had been
surrounded by an atmosphere of warm feminine affection. Though
chance had forced him to take refuge in an environment several
grades lower, from the social point of view, than that in which he
had grown up, all the signs of life that reached him during the day
at Pietrasecca between one period of reading and the next came
from women and children, since all the grown men were out at
work on the mountain or in the valley. Don Paolo had to use the
little strength he had left to defend himself against old Matalena's
impetuous warmth of heart.

"Saving your reverence, I could be your mother," she said to
him. "Let me treat you like a son."

"If you don't stop it, I shall leave," Don Paolo said. "I've no intention of returning to childhood."

Matalena considered the presence of a priest in her inn a
blessing, and she continually found pretexts to come and make a
fuss over him. As long as there was a priest in the house it could
be considered to be protected against misfortune. Fear of disaster
kept her perpetually on tenterhooks. The skull of a cow with two
big curved horns was fixed solidly on the roof at the point where
the two eaves met.

Don Paolo asked what the horns were for.

"They're a protection against the evil eye," Matalena explained, making the sign of the cross, "but only against the evil eye, they're no use against any other misfortune."

Sure enough, cow horns had not prevented Matalena's house from collapsing like many others in the 1915 earthquake.

"It was bigger than this house," Matalena told him several times. "My husband, God rest his soul, worked in Argentina for six years in order to be able to build it. He sent all the money back to me to pay the builders and carpenters. The house had been finished for barely three months when it collapsed, and I was buried in the cellar for a week. Actually I didn't know it was an earthquake, I thought it was the evil eye, and that only my house had collapsed. You can imagine my despair. When they cleared away the rubble on top of the cellar after a week and made an opening through which I could crawl out, I didn't have the courage. 'Let me die here,' I called out, 'I don't want to go on living.' I really had no more desire to live. But they reassured me. 'Nearly the whole village has collapsed,' they shouted down the hole, 'nearly the whole of the Marsica has been destroyed, thirty districts have been razed to the ground and fifty thousand dead have been counted so far.' It was true. It hadn't been a private evil eye, but a visitation of God. What does the proverb say? Everyone's misfortune is no one's misfortune. In the meantime my husband, God rest his soul, had had to come back to Italy to serve in the war, and no harm came to him, thanks be to God. After the war he went straight back to Argentina and worked for another five years to save money to rebuild the house. Just when it was finished and he was coming back to enjoy it, he stopped writing. After six months of worrying I was sent for by the local district. I thought it was for a new tax. In any event, I went there, and the clerk said to me, 'Your husband has been killed in an accident. He was run over by a car.' I burst into tears and exclaimed, 'There you are, envy struck him because he was coming home to enjoy the new house.'"

Every time she told this story the poor woman had a protracted fit of weeping.

"A car accident is a misfortune that can happen to anyone," Don Paolo said to put an end to it.

"Has it ever happened to you?"

"No."

"And why not?" said Matalena. "If you, as a priest, genuinely don't believe in the evil eye, why do you wear black? Why, saving your reverence, do you conceal your legs?"

But Matalena's extravagances were not sufficient to distract Don Paolo from his gloomy mood. Nunzio did not answer his letters, but every two or three days sent him an envelope full of newspaper cuttings with the most important political news. This was not enough to stop him from fretting. How long would he have to remain in this Siberia? Matalena's uninterrupted chatter soon acquired the monotony and naturalness of the sounds of the wind and the stream. Apart from that, Matalena was a pious woman who was proud of observing Wednesdays and Fridays and dedicating March to San Giuseppe, May to the Blessed Virgin, June to the Sacred Heart, and November to the dead. She had long since passed the canonical age and went about the house unkempt, untidy, and with her corset undone. She took great pains over the priest's meals, and after every one of them waited for compliments that never came. Don Paolo had never been a gourmet, and in any case there was not much variety on the Pietrasecca menu; bread dipped in wine was still what he liked best. But every morning Matalena came up to his room to ask what she should cook for him that day, and this was a daily torment to him. One day he lost patience and told her to give him what all the other inhabitants of Pietrasecca generally ate. Matalena was offended by this, and so did exactly as he asked. For breakfast she gave him a piece of corn bread and an onion, for lunch another big piece of the same bread with raw peppers seasoned with oil and salt, and for dinner a big helping of bean and potato soup. This diet lasted for only two days because, apart from the soup in the evening, Don Paolo's digestion could not stand it. The incident came to the *cafoni*'s ears and caused them a great deal of amusement. It's easy to say that one should live like the poor. Matalena exploited her victory and reverted to the morning consultations. She had inflexible ideas about the treatment and cure of lung trouble.

"The best medicine for it is new-laid eggs," she said.

She kept a dozen chickens in the garden behind the inn, and whenever an egg was laid she took it straight to the sickroom. If a chicken was late in laying Matalena would look for it, chase it, grab it, and feel it to find out if an egg was really there. After making sure, she called up to the priest from the garden, "Don't be impatient, it won't be long now."

Don Paolo's confinement to his bed did not prevent him from following the life of the village. It was a primitive one. In the morning a woman named Chiarina came to the inn with a nanny goat, and Matalena took a bowl and milked it until she had drained it to the last drop. By this time the men had gone to work, and the women combed their hair at an open window or outside in the street, so as to get rid of the lice out of doors. At midday a woman named Filomena Sapone arrived at the inn with lettuce from her garden and a baby in her arms. She sat in the doorway of the inn, uncovered her breasts, and the baby did not wait to be asked. Filomena was the first to ask Don Paolo to confess her, but the priest replied coldly that he did not have permission to do so. This reply became generally known and caused great disappointment. There was a great deal of discussion about it in every family, at the baker's, the cobbler's, the carpenter's, and the barber's. Matalena actually went and consulted Don Pasquale Colamartini, but the answer she got silenced her.

"If you annoy him, he'll end up going away."

In the space between the inn and the wooden bridge the biggest boys practiced marching and premilitary exercises. One day a quarrel broke out about who the current enemy was, for everyone complained that the enemy was changed too often. A deputation of three boys came and consulted Don Paolo in his room.

"Who's the enemy now?" they asked.

"What enemy?" the priest said in surprise.

"The hereditary enemy," one of the boys explained.

The priest did not understand, or pretended not to understand.

"There are two sides in our exercise," the boy explained. "The Italians are on one side and the hereditary enemy is on the other.

For a long time our teacher said the hereditary enemy was France and Yugoslavia. Then she said it was Germany. Then she said it was Japan. This morning she said, 'Children, the new hereditary enemy is England.' But in our schoolbook there's a chapter called 'The Agelong Friendship Between England and Italy,' so we don't know where we are. Which is wrong, our teacher or the book?'"

"The book," Don Paolo said. "It was printed last year, so it's out of date."

"Very well, then," said the boys. "Let us destroy the English hereditary enemy."

"The English don't fight on land, but on water," the priest said.

So the boys decided to fight in the stream. Don Paolo watched the battle from his window. The new hereditary enemy was rapidly defeated, but both sides emerged drenched to the skin.

The village boys constituted a kind of community apart, with its own laws, its own rites, and its own dialect. It had its own champions at stone throwing, jumping over the stream, lizard hunting, and pissing against the wind. Mothers shouted at their sons from morning till night, and the air often resounded with the most terrible curses, but these were so frequent that no one took any notice.

In the afternoon, if it was fine, the women did their chores in the street. They hung out their washing, or peeled potatoes, or darned, or mended, or deloused and scratched their children. The few who had nothing to do came and sat on the stones outside the inn. They were little barefoot women, dressed in rags and with greasy hair, with the dim-witted expression of milked nanny goats. One of them was an old woman named Cesira, who was worn out with hunger and childbearing and perpetually complained of strange pains. The chief topic of conversation was childbearing. Annunziata was about to have her fourteenth. Lidovina had already had eighteen. The first was always the hardest; the others found the way made ready for them. One of the women, Annina, who was pregnant, touched her belly and said, "Here's the head, here's one foot, and here's the other. It must be a boy, because it sometimes kicks me."

"That's in the hands of God," said Cesira. "God acts in accordance with our sins. Every pain is a visitation from heaven."

When the women dropped their voices it was obvious that they were talking about the priest. What tales did Matalena make up to satisfy their curiosity? It was difficult to imagine. All the priest could hear was a querulous mumbling. The only thing that changed was the weather. The sultry heat was several times interrupted by short and violent downpours.

Don Paolo vented his ill humor in the notes he wrote to Nunzio. "I feel like a chunk of rotten meat surrounded by a swarm of flies," he wrote. "I shan't be able to stand this for long." He could not rest, either sitting or standing or reading or writing.

A swarm of half-naked children completely covered in mud played from morning to night around a puddle created by the overflow from the fountain. They fled only on the appearance of Signorina Patrignani, the schoolmistress.

In fine weather most women, waiting for their husbands to come home in the evening, cooked their soup in the street in a brass pot or gasoline can placed on a tripod over a fire surrounded by stones. The smell of beans being cooked filled the whole valley.

As soon as it got dark Signorina Cristina Colamartini arrived at the inn. The deep silence that fell as soon as she arrived indicated the respect in which she was held, and enabled Don Paolo to hear her solicitously asking how he was and making recommendations and giving advice to Matalena on how he should be treated. Then she would hurry away. Don Paolo had not seen her yet, but Matalena had told him that she had studied music for many years in a convent and was about to leave to take the veil.

"She's not a woman, she's an angel," Matalena said of her, though she did not spare poisonous darts for the rest of the family. At home she had to look after her ninety-year-old grandmother as well as her parents and an aunt who were very old themselves. Her brother, an idler and a good-for-nothing, was nearly always away. "If you're interested you can ask Magascià," Matalena said. "He has the most amazing stories about him."

"I'm not interested," the priest assured her.

Cassarola, the wise woman, was a less engaging and more troublesome character. At first she had feared that the priest's appearance on the scene would involve a reduction in her power and prestige, but she was reassured when she heard that he did not have permission to administer the sacraments. One day she presented herself to him to offer him her magic herbs as a cure for the cough. He refused them. She was a revolting hag, with a snub nose and protruding blubber lips. To show the priest how religious she was she started mumbling prayers, exorcisms, and responses in barbarous Latin and unbuttoned her blouse at the neck to show him the medallions, scapulars, crosses, and rosary that she had hanging from her neck as well as the sacred tattoos with which her arms were covered.

"God rules over good, but not over evil," she announced with confidence. "Otherwise why is it that he does not cure his priests when they are ill? Why don't you pray to God and rise cured from your bed?"

To get even with her Don Paolo offered a piece of advice of his own. "Go to the devil," he told her.

Fortunately the old woman had other clients. Antonia, the dressmaker, had a little girl who was ill. Cassarola prescribed a glass of wine for her every morning.

"But she's only three," her mother said.

"Is she three already?" Cassarola said. "In that case you can give her a glass of wine in the evening too."

Matalena's principal activity in her capacity as the priest's guardian and nurse was to explain to everybody over and over again why he was unable to administer the sacraments.

"Not even if he's paid double?"

"Not even then."

"Not even if he's paid triple?"

"Not even then."

"Not even if he's offered his own price on credit?"

"We don't give credit."

The limited religious needs of the people of Pietrasecca, their baptisms, marriages, and funerals, were the responsibility of Don

Cipriano, the parish priest of Lama, but the older he got the rarer his visits had become, with the result that a tacit compromise had gradually been arrived at between the blind laws of nature and the instincts of the local people, whose religious services had come to be concentrated in short periods of the year.

Marriages were celebrated in October and November, and children were born between May and July. It was a kind of conscription from which there were very few exemptions. Many babies died in the first few months. It was a periodic massacre of the innocents.

On Sunday mornings a number of women went down to Lama for mass. They wore black shawls over their shoulders and black handkerchiefs on their heads, because showing their hair would have been immodest, and black shoes and stockings. From his window Don Paolo watched them going and coming back. The oldest walked with their beads in their hand, letting them run slowly between thumb and first finger. When they were overtaken by the horse and trap in which Don Pasquale and Signorina Cristina went to mass they bowed very respectfully. But there were occasions on which the lack of a parish priest was felt acutely; not even Matalena's watchfulness saved Don Paolo from some disagreeable incidents.

A peasant woman, Teresa Scaraffa, dreamed one night that the baby she was expecting was going to be born blind. Early next morning the poor woman came to see Don Paolo and went down on her knees at his bedside. "I dreamed my baby is going to be born blind. Only you can save it," she said.

"I'm sorry, my poor woman, but I can do nothing," the priest replied.

The woman started weeping and imploring him. "I don't want my baby to be blind. Why should others be able to see and not he?"

Her round yellowish face made her look like an old sheep. Don Paolo tried to get the idea out of her head, but without success.

"I dreamed it," she said. "I saw it with my own eyes. If you don't help me, the child will be blind."

She would not go away. Don Paolo was very conscious of the fact that if he pretended to say prayers or carry out exorcism in

one case the inn would immediately be besieged by other appli-
cants whom it would be impossible to refuse. They would all say
that, as he had helped Teresa Scaraffa, he must help them too.
The news would reach the villages down on the plain. Apart from
behaving like a fraud and a clown, he would end up attracting the
attention of the authorities.

So he called Matalena and said to her, "Please see this woman
out of my room, if necessary by force. I'm not interested in her
dreams."

At this Teresa rose like a fury and started yelling, "Why should
my baby be blind? Why should other babies be able to see and
not mine?"

Teresa waited for a reply, and Don Paolo coldly repeated that
he could do nothing, but in vain. Again the woman went down on
her knees with her face on the floor, and she began hitting it with
her head and tearing out her hair. She actually pulled out whole
chunks of it and screamed the most senseless things.

"Why should he be blind? Why? Tell me why. At least I want
to know why. Others will be able to see and he won't. Others will
go to school and he won't be able to. Others will rob him and he
won't notice it. Others will mock him and he won't be able to see
them, and when he's grown up no woman will have anything to
do with him."

Then she rose to her feet and seemed suddenly to have
calmed down.

"Now I know what to do," she said. "I'll throw myself out of the
window, and he'll die with me."

The woman made for the window, and in her frantic, hysterical state Don Paolo had no doubt that she would throw herself
out of it. She was on the windowsill when a cry from the priest
stopped her. "I'll do what you ask," he said. "What do you want
me to do?"

Matalena hurried to fetch the keys of the church, which
were kept in the Colamartini house, and then she went to the
church and fetched a glass of holy water. Don Paolo was silent
and humiliated.

Teresa held out her swollen belly to the priest.

"The head must be here," she said, "the eyes must be there."

At the place Teresa indicated the priest twice made the sign of the cross, once for each eye, and he moved his lips as if he were praying.

"Now he'll be all right," the woman said with relief. "It won't happen now. Thank you."

She went away, but came back a little later with a dead hen.

"You again?" the priest exclaimed angrily.

The woman showed him the hen.

"I can't accept it," Don Paolo replied. "Priests cannot accept gifts."

The woman protested. "In that case it's no use," she said. "If you don't take the hen the grace won't work and the child will be born blind."

"Grace is free," Don Paolo said.

"There's no such thing as free grace," the woman said.

To cut things short she walked out, leaving the expiatory sacrifice on the table.

This happened on a Saturday. That was the day on which Magascià went down to Fossa with his cart to fetch the weekly supply of salt and tobacco. Don Paolo immediately sent for him and gave him a letter to post to Nunzio. "I've had enough," he wrote. "I'm not staying here. I'm leaving for Rome as soon as my temperature's normal."

8

HE WAS SITTING ON A BENCH under a rowan tree, writing to Nunzio. Instead of a desk he had on his knees a three-cornered box that Matalena used to avoid wetting her feet and her skirts when doing her washing at the stream. A pleasing smell of fresh bread came from the baker's.

"Though you haven't answered me, I'm writing to you again to save me from talking to myself and making people who see me think I've gone crazy. If this lasts much longer, my lungs may get better, but at the expense of my brain. This is not a harmless bit of playacting . . ."

A procession of ants was coming down the tree trunk and making its way along the ground. Every ant carried a load. He watched the procession for a time, and then went back to his writing:

"If only I could go to sleep here and wake up next morning, saddle the donkey, and go to the vineyard. If only I could go to sleep and wake up, not just with healthy lungs, but with the brain of an ordinary man, free of all abstractions. If only I could go back to ordinary, real life. Digging, plowing, sowing, reaping, earning a living, and talking to the other men on Sundays. Obeying the law that says: thou shalt earn thy daily bread in the sweat of thy brow. When I come to think of it, perhaps the real cause of my distress is my defiance of the ancient law, my way of living in cafés, libraries, and hotels, my having broken the chain that for centuries linked my forefathers to the soil. Perhaps I feel an outcast, not so much because of my disobedience to the arbitrary decrees of the party in power, but because of my infringement of the older law that said: thou shalt earn thy living in the sweat of thy brow. I have ceased to be a peasant, but I have not become a politician. It is impossible for me to return to the soil, but still more impossible to return to the world of illusions in which I have been living up to now. Strange thoughts are coming to me. Please listen."

He was still writing when a girl from Fossa dei Marsi arrived at Pietrasecca in Magascià's cart.

"The inn's over there, on the right beyond the bridge," the carter explained.

The girl came hurrying along and said to Matalena, "Is there a Don Paolo Spada staying here?"

Matalena was jealous of her priest, and before answering the stranger she said, "Why do you ask?"

"He saved me when I was on the point of death, and I want to thank him."

"The Don Paolo who's staying here is not a doctor but a priest," said Matalena.

"Perhaps he's neither a priest nor a doctor but a saint," said the girl. "I was on the point of death, he came, he touched my hand, and I was saved."

Matalena was proud of having a priest at her inn, but the idea of having a saint who actually performed miracles while still living disturbed and upset her.

"Yes, he's a real saint," she said, to avoid appearing to be unable to recognize a saint when she saw one. "He's staying here doing penance, like a true man of God. For that reason, I'm not sure that he will be willing to see you. You see, he's from a different diocese."

"Perhaps he's actually more than a saint," the girl from Fossa said. "I have an idea he might be Jesus Himself."

This was too much for Matalena, who sat down on a stool and murmured, "Are you mad? What makes you think he might be Jesus Himself? Why should Jesus come to my inn? Isn't He in heaven on His Father's right hand?"

Matalena spoke softly, so that her second-floor lodger, if he were really He, should not overhear her doubting words.

"It would not be the first time that Jesus has disguised Himself and come down to earth to see how the poor are living," the girl from Fossa replied. Then she added in a little trickle of a voice, "Have you noticed whether his hands and feet are pierced? That is the surest way of telling. Never mind how much he disguises himself, if he is really He, he could not get rid of the stigmata."

Matalena was suddenly seized with unspeakable excitement. She was not prepared for such a happening. Heavens, what was she to do? His evening meal was ready; it consisted of two eggs and a lettuce salad. She blushed at the sight of that meager repast. Two eggs and a salad for the Son of God? How disgraceful. One ought at least to kill a lamb. But supposing he was not He?

"What makes you suppose that perhaps it is He? What gave you the idea? Tell me the truth, are you mad?" said Matalena, seized with doubt.

"I recognized him by his voice," the girl replied. "When he appeared he took my hand and before I had time to say anything he said, "Courage, I know everything." I realized at once that that was no human voice. I know men, they don't talk like that. I have an uncle who's a priest, he's the parish priest of Fossa, he doesn't talk like that."

"Tell me what to do if he's really Jesus," Matalena said. "Should I warn Don Cipriano? Tell the *carabinieri?*"

A copy of police regulations was displayed on the inn door, but the arrival of Jesus was not an eventuality foreseen in them.

With bated breath the two women tiptoed up to the second floor and knocked at the door. There was no answer. Slowly they opened it. The room was empty. Matalena thought she was going to faint.

"He's gone," she said.

The two women looked at each other in consternation. Then they heard a cough in the garden, and they dashed there immediately. Don Paolo was sitting on a bench under the little rowan tree with some sheets of paper in his hand.

"Who wants me?" he said.

The two women approached timidly.

"I'm Bianchina," the girl said. "Bianchina Girasole, from Fossa dei Marsi, Berenice's daughter. Don't you recognize me? Don't you remember me?"

"I'm delighted to see that you're alive," Don Paolo said, with a smile. "I've often thought about you."

"So you kept your promise?" Bianchina exclaimed, radiant with joy.

"Don't you believe me?"

"I believe you," said Bianchina. "I was on the point of death and abandoned by everyone, and you came and touched my hand and saved me."

Don Paolo had another fit of coughing. The sun had set, and the cold shadows of night were mounting from the bottom of the valley. He rose, and the two women followed him to his room. He was tired, and sat on the edge of the bed. Bianchina stayed near the door, but then plucked up courage and said in a tremulous voice, "Please show me your hands."

Don Paolo smiled. "Do you want to tell my fortune?" he asked.

Bianchina carefully examined his hands. There was no trace of stigmata, no trace of the crucifixion. He was not Jesus. He was a saint, but not Jesus.

"All the better," Bianchina said, looking pleased. " I prefer you to be a man."

"Did you think I was a ghost?" Don Paolo said with a smile.

Matalena too sighed with relief and went back to her kitchen. The two remained silent for a moment.

"I see that you're ill," the girl said. "Is there anything I can do for you?"

"No, thank you," said Don Paolo.

The girl's pretty face looked even prettier against the dark rectangle of the door. Perhaps her neck was rather thin, and her red mouth was rather big, and when she laughed it was perhaps rather too big, but the liveliness of her eyes and gestures and her outspokenness and candor gave her an almost childish naturalness and charm.

"My mother wants to throw me out," she said with a grimace of annoyance.

"Why?"

Bianchina sought for words. "She thinks I'm the dishonor of the family. Perhaps she's right. If I like a man, I can't resist him. You agree with my mother, of course."

"I don't know," said Paolo. "I've never been a mother."

Bianchina burst out laughing, but quickly relapsed into gloom.

"Even if my mother were willing to put up with me I couldn't go on living at home," she said. "The atmosphere's too stuffy. Didn't you notice it?"

"What do you want to do?" said the priest.

"Isn't there anything I can do for you?"

"It seems to me that you ought to be thinking about yourself," said the priest. "What will you do if your mother throws you out?"

"I don't know," Bianchina said. "There's nothing I can do. If I knit, I drop the stitches. If I sew, I prick my fingers. If I try gardening, I hit my feet with the mattock. The nuns taught me how to make sweets and to do embroidery and the Gregorian chant. Could I go and sing the *Magnificat* and *Salve Regina* on the variety stage?"

"But if there's nothing you can do, what would you do for me?" the priest asked.

"Anything, provided I could stay near you."

"Meanwhile," said the priest, "where are you going to stay tonight?"

It was an awkward problem. Don Paolo sighed, and Bianchina had tears in her eyes.

"There's an old school friend of mine here at Pietrasecca, Cristina Colamartini. She's a little saint too. Perhaps she'll help me. Do you know her?"

This was just the time when Cristina paid her daily visit to the inn. Matalena told her of Bianchina Girasole's arrival, and she appeared in the doorway of the sickroom, which had been left open. Bianchina fell on her neck and embraced her at length. "How beautiful you've become," she kept repeating.

Matalena produced a second chair, and Cristina was able to sit down and tidy her ruffled hair. So far Don Paolo had only heard her voice, and now he was able to note that the rest of her harmonized perfectly with it. She was a really lovely creature. Her face was thin and pointed, but perfectly shaped, and she was tall and slender. She wore a black pinafore with a high neck and long sleeves, like a schoolgirl, an impression accentuated by her jet black hair, which was parted in the middle, slightly waved at the temples, and gathered at the back of the neck in a large knot of tiny curls. She said good evening to the priest and apologized for disturbing him.

"What? You haven't met yet?" Bianchina said. "This is Cristina, and she was my first love. We spent three years together at the same convent school. She was at the top of the class and I was at the bottom, of course, but that was another reason for liking each other." Then she went on, "There's always a time in life when you go back to your first love. And this," she said to Cristina, pointing to Don Paolo, "is a saint to whom I owe my life."

Don Paolo took no notice of what Bianchina was saying because he was enchanted by Cristina. A girl like this at Pietrasecca? He could not believe his eyes. Her face and hands had the pallor of white roses, but there was nothing in nature to compare with the light of her eyes and the grace of her smile.

"We're tiring Don Paolo with our chatter," Cristina said, blushing and rising to leave.

"I'm coming with you," said Bianchina. "You wouldn't want to leave me alone with a priest, would you? I'll come back in the morning," she added, turning to Don Paolo. "You haven't answered the question I asked you yet."

Don Paolo's change of mood did not escape Matalena's notice though she did not guess the real reason for it.

"Magascià came and told me some strange stories about that girl," she said, but she did not go on, because he was not listening.

"I feel much better," he said. "It's extraordinary, but I feel almost completely well again."

However, he hardly slept that night. He earned a severe rebuke from Matalena when she brought him his breakfast.

"You look terrible," she said. "People will think I don't look after you properly."

The priest was staring out the window.

"I'm surprised Donna Cristina put that girl up for the night after all the talk there has been about her and her brother," she said.

Through the open window the priest saw Cristina leaving her house. He hurriedly dressed and went downstairs. "Good morning," he said with a smile. "Good morning. You're out early."

"I'm delighted at having a chance to talk to you for a moment before Bianchina appears," Cristina said. "You have no idea of the enormous influence over her that you have acquired."

"She has too much imagination," Don Paolo said apologetically.

"Yes, she has had some terrible experiences," Cristina said. "She told me some frightening things about herself last night. They kept me awake all night. Believe me, you're the only person who can save her now."

"Will Bianchina agree to be saved? In what sense?" Don Paolo said.

"You can point out the right path to her."

Don Paolo did not conceal his doubts. "Will Bianchina follow that path alone and unaccompanied? I certainly cannot accompany her," he said.

"You will accompany her with your thoughts," Cristina said. "Perhaps that will be sufficient. You have no idea of the impact made on her during her illness by your simple promise to think of her sometimes. She told me that she has lived in the company of your thoughts ever since."

"I have in fact often thought about her," the priest admitted. "But may I go on? You do not know it, Signorina, but my character is already excessively inclined to fixed ideas."

This confidence visibly embarrassed Cristina. "What I meant," she said with a blush, "was that you should remember her in your prayers."

Bianchina came hurrying along with her hair flying in the wind. "What are you two plotting against me?" she said.

"I must go and get breakfast for the rest of the family," Cristina announced. "I'll see you later."

Don Paolo invited Bianchina to keep him company for a while in the garden next to the inn.

"Come and sit here," he said.

"I hope you have thought about what I asked you," the girl said. "Can I do anything for you?" Then she went on, "I don't want to go back to the empty life I've lived so far. I want at least to see you every now and then. But I don't want to be a parasite."

"Yes, I need you," Don Paolo said.

"Really?" Bianchina exclaimed, jumping to her feet. "Will you take me with you when you go back to your diocese?"

"I need you immediately," he said.

"Aren't you afraid of scandal? In a little place like this everything is known immediately."

"I'm not asking you for what you are now imagining."

"It's all I have," said Bianchina.

"You have many other things," Don Paolo said.

"You think so? What, for instance?"

"Listen to me seriously," Don Paolo said. "I need to send someone to a friend of mine in Rome on a personal and rather delicate mission. You are the only person whom I can ask to do this for me."

"Why am I the only person?"

"You're the only one I can trust."

"Are you pulling my leg? Forgive me, I don't mean to doubt what you say, but look, no one has ever talked to me like that before. I've never expected anyone to trust me."

"But I trust you."

"Is this trip to Rome for something important?"

"Very important indeed," said Don Paolo. "But unfortunately I can't tell you what it is. There are secrets about which priests cannot speak. Don't you trust me?"

"I'd throw myself into a fiery furnace for you," Bianchina said seriously. Then she added, "Is it a matter of secrets of the confessional?"

Don Paolo nodded.

"Now, listen to me carefully, Bianchina," he said. "You must tell no one that you're going to Rome on my account. Not even Cristina or your mother. You must think up some excuse."

"Making up lies is one of my few specialties," said Bianchina. "But it's the first time I've had to do it for a priest. Are there such things as holy lies, then?"

"They're not real lies, but stratagems," said Don Paolo.

"Will you think about me while I'm away?"

"Yes, I promise," Don Paolo said.

"You won't be unfaithful to me with Cristina?"

"Don't talk nonsense."

Don Paolo withdrew to his room to write out the message the girl was to take. He dashed it off at once. "We can't go on nursing illusions," was his conclusion.

9

DON PAOLO WAS TORN between worrying about Bianchina, who left unsuspectingly for Rome on the risky business of restoring contact with his clandestine organization, and an ardent desire to see Cristina again, for the girl completely captivated him. To aggravate his anxiety, on the days that followed Cristina did not reappear at Matalena's inn. Had she perhaps realized that she had lit a dangerous flame in Don Paolo? Did she want to resist temptation? He found an excuse to send Matalena on a voyage of exploration. No, Cristina's thoughts were elsewhere, for the day when she was to leave for the convent had been approaching. Her family seemed resigned, her outfit was ready, the Mother Superior had been informed. But on the eve of her departure Cristina's old grandmother, who had always opposed the idea, had succeeded in persuading Don Pasquale to talk to the girl. The conversation between father and daughter had been painful.

"Your grandmother is right," he said. "You know the state to which we are reduced. I can't count on your brother. He's an idler and a good-for-nothing, and we don't even know where he is. If you go too I shall be left alone with your grandmother, your mother, and your aunt, three old women who are incapable of any kind of work, and we shall be left to end our lives in the care of some servant girl who will rob us of the little we have left."

After a long fit of weeping Cristina ended by giving in. "Father," she said, "I shall do nothing against your will."

Her father was very fond of her, and was not irrevocably opposed to her vocation; all he asked her, therefore, was to postpone it.

"If God wants you, He will provide," he said.

For once the people of Pietrasecca were unanimously on the grandmother's side. The general opinion was that a daughter belonged primarily to her family and only secondarily to the Church. Don Paolo had already heard strange stories about Cristina's grandmother, who terrorized the Colamartini household. She wanted Cristina to get married. Almost nothing was left of the family heritage, and only a good marriage could save it, but that was an argument that Don Pasquale could not put to his daughter, who sadly and silently and uncomplainingly went on with the housekeeping. She looked after the chickens, made the beds, swept the rooms and the staircase, helped her aunt and her mother in the kitchen, ironed the linen, and looked after the bees in the garden. She went out rarely, and then only for a few moments. But one morning, when Don Paolo was in Matalena's garden, she suddenly appeared with a bunch of chives to transplant. Don Paolo was delighted. The morning light wrapped the girl as if in a golden veil. Some bees buzzed around her head as around a flower, and to the priest the flower looked incredibly beautiful, though rather pale. He plucked up courage and said to her, "Forgive me if I'm indiscreet, but are you perhaps unhappy at not yet having left for the convent?"

Cristina smiled. "Don't think me discourteous," she said, "if I answer you with three words that I was taught as a child and have not forgotten: *Jesus autem tacebat.* Perhaps those words impressed me more than anything else in the Bible. Jesus taught us to be silent under torment."

"Is secular life a torment to you?" Don Paolo said. "Cannot abandoning one's family be equivalent to a flight?"

Cristina looked at the priest a trifle uncertainly. Was he playing the part of devil's advocate in order to put her to the test?

"True flight," she said, "is distancing oneself from God. Those who are distant from God are distant from their fellows."

"Cannot one live a decent life with one's family?" Don Paolo asked. "Cannot one meditate and pray at home?"

"We are not called on to be bold, but to be docile and let ourselves be helped," Cristina said. "I read this morning in a book written by a French nun: 'Does the newborn babe raise itself to the mother's breast? Or does not the mother take the little one and bend gently over it to feed and comfort it?' We are all like newborn babies of the Church who is our mother."

These were conventional arguments. Don Paolo and Cristina hardly knew each other. The priest's answer was conventional too.

"I do not propose to embark on a theological discussion with you," he said. "But here we are in a country of great poverty in the economic respect and even greater poverty in the spiritual respect. If a *cafone* succeeds in mastering his animal instincts he becomes a Franciscan friar; if a girl succeeds in freeing herself from servitude to her body, she takes the veil. Don't you think that that is the source of many evils? Don't you think it is better to live and struggle among one's fellows than to shut oneself up in an ivory tower?"

"He who has faith and is absorbed in prayer is never separated from his fellows," Cristina said. "Only the soul that does not know God is a leaf detached from the trees, a solitary leaf that falls to the ground, shrivels, and rots. But the soul that is given to God is like a leaf attached to the tree. Through the sap that nourishes it, it communicates with the branches, the trunk, the roots, the earth. Don't you believe that?"

Don Paolo smiled. Apart from anything else, having to express himself in language compatible with his ecclesiastical habit put him at an obvious disadvantage.

"But you know these things better than I do," the girl went on with a smile. "Is the examination over?"

"I assure you it was not intended to be an examination," said

Don Paolo. "During my first few days here I found the enforced solitude very trying, but now I'm beginning to endure it. I now have leisure to think about certain things that it is not easy to think about when leading an active life. I should like to discuss them with you."

"One must let oneself be carried along by silence," Cristina said with a smile, "like an unconscious man carried along by a deep stream. Only then does God speak to us."

She shook hands with Don Paolo and said cordially, "I hope we shall meet again. I too like talking to you."

Don Paolo went back to his room, sat down at the little table, took a notebook, and wrote in it "Conversations with Cristina." After thinking for a short time he began to write: "Never has lying been so repugnant to me as it is now. As long as it's a mere matter of deceiving the police, well and good, it may even amuse me. But what torment it is to deceive Cristina, to engage in playacting with her, to hush up what I would like to say if I could talk to her freely. My dear Cristina, I shall talk to you freely in this notebook. At least here I shall have no need to pretend."

Conversation with Cristina was also conversation with himself. "It seems to me that things have come to a head. I can't go on like this. Perhaps that's why I'm ill."

The hand with which he was writing stopped. He rose and went over to the window. The Colamartini house seemed uninhabited; its gray, compact outline stood out against the black mountain. It looked like a fortress. Which was Cristina's room? Don Paolo went back to the table and started writing again: "Staying in this little village, contact with these primitive people, meeting this girl, have taken me back to myself as I was fifteen years ago. In this lovely Cristina I have found many features of my own adolescence, I might almost say a portrait of myself, an embellished and idealized portrait, a female version, of course, but basically a reflection of what I myself felt and thought at that time: the same infatuation with the absolute, the same rejection of the compromises and pretenses of ordinary life, even the same readiness for self-sacrifice. When I passed through my native village at night I saw once more the haunts of selfishness and hypocrisy from which I fled. I felt like a dead man revisiting the scenes of his life. The only sound I heard was the barking of dogs, which seemed to me to be a faithful transcription of the thoughts of most of the inhabitants of the village who were asleep at that moment. No, I do not in the least regret having cut myself off from that. The cause of my pain is the question of whether I have been faithful to my promise."

He remembered his first joining a socialist group. He had left the Church, not because he doubted the correctness of its dogmas or the efficacy of the sacraments, but because it seemed to him to identify itself with a corrupt, petty, and cruel society that it should have combated. When he first became a socialist that had been his only motive. He was not yet a Marxist; that he became later after joining the socialist fold. He accepted Marxism "as the rule of the new community." In the meantime had that community not itself become a synagogue? "Alas for all enterprises the declared aim of which is the salvation of the world. They seem to be the surest traps leading to self-destruction." Don Paolo decided that his return to Italy had been basically an attempt to escape that professionalism, to return to the ranks, to go back and find the clue to the complicated issue.

These thoughts gave him no peace. At meals he was silent and more distracted than ever. Matalena tried talking to him, but in vain; he might have been deaf. To her great offense and sorrow he took not the slightest notice of what he was eating. As soon as he had finished his coffee he went out into the garden, sat on the bench under the rowan tree, and started writing again, with the notebook resting on his knees: "Is it possible to take part in political life, to put oneself in the service of a party and remain sincere? Has not truth for me become party truth and justice party justice? Have not the interests of the organization ended up getting the better of all moral values, which are despised as petit bourgeois prejudices, and have those interests not become the supreme value? Have I, then, escaped from the opportunism of a decadent Church only to end up in the Machiavellism of a political sect? If these are dangerous cracks in the revolutionary consciousness, if they are ideas that must be banished from it, how is one to confront in good faith the risks of the conspiratorial struggle?"

Don Paolo reread what he had written and realized that all he had done was to write down a series of questions. Meanwhile a flock of sparrows and some wild pigeons had started hopping and fluttering about him as in an aviary. At one point some women who were watching the scene from a distance decided that he was talking to them; the poor priest, having no one else to talk to, was in fact talking to himself. The women immediately hurried to the inn to spread the news of this marvel.

"Your priest," they said to Matalena, "is talking to the birds, just like San Francesco di Assisi."

"Yes," she replied, "he's a saint, a real saint."

10

"WE OUGHT TO SEE EACH other more often," Don
Paolo, overcoming his shyness, said to Cristina. "Believe me, talking to you does me good."

"My father has made the same suggestion," the girl said with a
smile. "He says that so far we have been very inhospitable toward
you. If you knew about our family troubles, you would forgive us."

"So far I've had to spend nearly all my time in bed," Don Paolo
said, "but during the remainder of my stay at Pietrasecca I shall be
very willing to allow myself to be spoiled, if not by your family,
then by you."

Meanwhile the fresh air of Pietrasecca had restored some of its
lost naturalness to Don Paolo's face. It was still dark and shadowed, but the wrinkles had vanished.

"I don't want to boast, but you look twenty years younger than
when you arrived here," Matalena said.

Cristina came to an agreement with Matalena about some
improvements to be introduced into the care of her guest. The
girl had a real genius for creating beauty out of nothing, and it
was marvelous to see how Don Paolo's room became cool, fresh,

and flower-filled at her hands. As Don Paolo's talks with her grew more frequent they became more frank and sincere. At first Don Paolo still felt inhibited by having to avoid arousing suspicion about his identity, but as he became more familiar with Cristina's ingenuousness his worries on that score diminished. He let himself go in stories about his youth, his village, his first studies, his early religious experiences, and his first steps in real life, taking care only to make the background of his memories his own diocese and not that of the Marsi. Without realizing it, he ended up infusing life into his fictitious role, nourishing it with the still-vivid memories of his youth. There was so much spontaneity, sincerity, and warmth in his talk that Cristina was quite carried away by it.

Once she said to him, "If I were to write down what you say and read it to someone without disclosing anything about you, I bet the verdict would be that a boy of eighteen was responsible for it."

Their liking for each other made them more conciliatory in the arguments that sometimes broke out between them. What Don Paolo dared not say to her he confided to his diary, with tender expressions of love. He often postponed writing in his diary until late at night. He would write a phrase and then cross it out, write it again and again cross it out.

One morning when he opened his window he saw Cristina standing on a little balcony on the second floor of her house. She immediately smiled and greeted him with a slight motion of her head, and then withdrew. He had the impression that she greeted him as if she had been waiting for him to appear. This was the first time he had seen anyone on that balcony, which faced his window and was always closed. But perhaps new life was beginning for it. In fact that morning Cristina had put two pots of geraniums on it. This novelty did not escape the sharp eyes of Matalena, who was openly critical.

"I don't see why she puts geraniums on a balcony that never gets any sun," she said.

"I expect she's trying an experiment," said the priest. "There's no need to discourage her."

"I didn't think Donna Cristina was a girl who tried experiments," Matalena said.

But the frequent waterings to which Cristina henceforth subjected the two pots increased Matalena's concern.

"What on earth is the matter with Donna Cristina?" she said. "With all that water and no sun those geraniums will die."

She also noticed that Don Paolo's small worktable had been moved over to the window. This took her breath away.

"You always used to complain about the draft," she said. She realized what was up, but did not dare call it by its real name. So she restricted herself to saying, "I never imagined that a priest would encourage certain whims."

Matalena was not jealous, but she was upset and alarmed. Her attitude to her priest was of complete traditional respect, and not even in her dreams would she have tolerated any ambiguity in her own feelings toward him. Also she was old, and had accepted the fact. But Don Paolo was "her" priest, "her" protector, and not the protector of others, not even of the Colamartini family. She started feeling that a closer friendship with Cristina might induce the priest to accept hospitality in the Colamartini house. Faced with this threat, she defended herself by every means in her power. Thus that very same day she refused a hare that Cristina wanted to give her to cook for Don Paolo. It was a way of telling the girl that her little game had been discovered.

"Thank you, but he doesn't like game," she said dryly, rejecting the gift.

Cristina seemed to fall from the clouds. "Couldn't you ask him?" she said. "Perhaps you're mistaken."

"It's not necessary," said Matalena. "Besides, he's my guest, and if he wants anything it's up to me to provide it."

"He's only your lodger," Cristina said. "And my father is perfectly entitled to give a present to anyone he chooses."

But it probably struck her that it would not be very becoming to continue with that conversation, and so she hurried away before Don Paolo, whose footsteps she heard on the stairs, made his appearance.

Innocent though Cristina was in the matter, it was actually she who was in the wrong. It was not correct to say that to Matalena Don Paolo was an ordinary lodger. Without his realizing it, his importance to her had grown from day to day. To her it mattered little that he refrained from exercising his ministry at Pietrasecca, since that in no way detracted from the sacred nature of his presence. On the contrary, as he did not administer the sacraments the divine investiture that was in him was inaccessible to the other inhabitants of Pietrasecca and remained concentrated and intact, as it were, in his mere presence. As a result his exorcising efficacy could be only reinforced.

She felt differently about him from day to day; sometimes she felt she was his nurse, and sometimes she felt like an orphan or a widow; and, strangely enough, as time passed she felt more and more often like an orphan rather than a widow or a nurse. In his encounters with her Don Paolo prudently adopted the expedient of not understanding.

"I can't imagine this house without you," she began saying more and more often. "I couldn't live without your protection, without it, the evil eye and envy would afflict the house immediately, while as it is they keep away out of respect for your consecrated presence."

But she was not naive enough to imagine that Don Paolo was likely to remain inactive for long in this poor mountain village, and a crazy plan began to develop in her primitive mind; a plan, that is, to keep "her" priest at Pietrasecca and through him dominate the whole valley.

"Why don't you have yourself transferred here by the Pope?" she said to him on the evening after her breeze with Cristina. "Do you know the Pope personally?"

"Why should I be transferred here?" said Don Paolo.

"The climate is good, and if you leave you'll be ill again, so it would be much better for you to be transferred here. You could administer the sacraments, hold confessions, conduct baptisms and funeral services. There's no need to worry about the valley being a poor one. If you stayed here, I'd see about meeting your expenses."

"One more word on that subject," Don Paolo said coldly, "and I'll leave at dawn tomorrow morning."

"You haven't understood," Matalena said. "All I'm worried about is your health. We'll discuss it another day; there's plenty of time, after all."

"There's less time than you think," said the priest.

This reply left Matalena openmouthed with surprise and horror.

Next day the arrival of a smart carriage in the space outside the inn aroused the curiosity of the whole village. Had someone come to see Don Paolo? No, the visitor was an unknown ecclesiastical dignitary, tall and thin and with distinguished manners, who made straight for the Colamartini house. His uniformed coachman, who stayed behind and guarded the carriage, was immediately sur-rounded and interrogated by curious villagers, to whom he ex-plained that the prelate had been Signorina Cristina's confessor and spiritual director at school. Had he come to take the young lady away? The coachman didn't know. After a couple of hours the prelate reappeared, accompanied only by Don Pasquale, and he wanted to greet Don Paolo before leaving. The conversation took place at the inn door, while Don Pasquale stood deferentially and silently to one side.

"Signorina Colamartini has talked to me about you with a great deal of respect," he said to Don Paolo. "While passing through the Marsica I came up here to Pietrasecca in response to the prayers and entreaties of the Mother Superior and the nuns, who are very fond of Signorina Colamartini and are sad that she is not yet among them."

Don Paolo was obviously very embarrassed; he stood with his back to the wall, clutching his breviary to his chest. He restricted himself to replying that he had remained completely aloof from any discussions that might have taken place in the Colamartini household.

"Quite right," said the prelate. "I too on the occasion of this visit refrained from exercising any pressure on the young lady. I merely thought it my duty to find out why she has postponed fol-lowing a vocation the genuineness of which is beyond all doubt."

"Signorina Cristina," Don Paolo said, "can also be very useful at Pietrasecca."

"If one takes account of her purely human qualities, that is certainly true," replied her spiritual director. "However, bearing in mind her truly exceptional sensibility and intelligence, I do not see how those gifts can be adequately employed in such a primitive place. But in Signorina Cristina there is also something else. Have you not noticed it? She is one of those predestined creatures who on this earth already bear on their brow, as the biblical phrase has it, the name of the Lamb."

"Signorina Cristina has made a deep impression on me too," Don Paolo said. "Nevertheless I would not say it was wrong for her to remain among such needy people. Nothing would prevent her from devoting part of the day to prayer and meditation. The religious vocation does not necessarily involve living in a convent."

The spiritual director was touched to the quick and was about to reply, but the coachman respectfully pointed out that it was getting late.

After the prelate's departure Don Pasquale went back into the inn to thank Don Paolo for his sensible remarks and made the mistake of talking to him in Matalena's presence. Among other things, he apologized in genuinely regretful tones for not having invited Don Paolo to his house. "But if you knew our family troubles . . ." he said. Don Paolo felt obliged to interrupt. "Your apologies are completely unnecessary," he said. "I did not come here on a visit, but on doctor's orders."

Don Pasquale went on apologizing, however. "You do not know the tradition in these parts," he said. "The custom in the Abruzzi, particularly in small places, is that inns are only for traders. Other travelers, including complete strangers, are generally entertained in private houses."

"I appreciate that tradition," Don Paolo said, "but it really is not applicable in my case. I did not come to Pietrasecca just for a night or two."

"The difficulty, I assure you, was not the length of your stay," Don Pasquale replied. "In the old days guests sometimes stayed for whole seasons. But now we have three ailing old ladies in the house and no servants."

The conversation continued at the same courteous level and eventually concluded in an invitation to Don Paolo to call at the Colamartini house next day. He accepted with alacrity.

Immediately after Don Pasquale's departure, however, he had to cope with Matalena, whom he had never seen in such an agitated state.

"I hope you didn't believe a single word of what that old man told you," she said in a voice changed by emotion.

"He created an impression of being a perfect gentleman," Don Paolo replied.

"That's what he appears to be," Matalena said, "but would you like to know what's behind it?"

The priest avoided encouraging tittle-tattle, but that evening it provided a rich and piquant accompaniment to his modest dinner. Of the three old women who lived in the Colamartini house, Matalena told him, the oldest, Cristina's grandmother, was a wicked and unscrupulous tyrant. "She isn't a woman, she's a she-devil," Matalena declared. As a young woman she had been the terror of the valley. This was not the first time Don Paolo had heard her talked of in such terms. The second old lady, her daughter-in-law, Cristina's stepmother, was not ill, according to Matalena, but was simply an imbecile. Her intelligence was that of a five-year-old. Don Pasquale had married her after his first wife's death solely for the sake of her dowry, on which the whole family lived. Don Pasquale might perhaps have been telling the truth in saying that the third old lady, his sister, was ill, but in fact nothing had been seen of her for several years; she might have been buried alive. This unfortunate woman was the same age as Matalena, who remembered her as a girl, when she had been very attractive and much sought after. There had been no lack of young men of good family in neighboring villages who had asked for her hand, but her mother, that she-devil incarnate, had made it a condition that she should have no dowry. She had no intention of allowing the family property, which was reserved for Don

Pasquale as the firstborn, to be divided up. Some suitors would actually have accepted the girl without a dowry, but she had refused to get married on those terms, which her pride would not permit. And so on and so forth. Matalena unburdened herself of all the secret resentments against the Colamartini family that were nourished by the poor. The priest listened in disgust, but did not dare to interrupt her.

"Does Signorina Cristina know all these stories?" he asked at one point.

"I can't say whether she knows every detail," Matalena replied. "But the religious little prig breathes that atmosphere, and she must certainly at least know the very unedifying stories about her brother Alberto."

Cristina's brother had the reputation of being a rogue with no redeeming features. He had not been seen at Pietrasecca since his father had refused to recognize the signature on some promissory notes that the young man had forged. But to Don Paolo not the least curious item in that flood of uncheckable and spiteful gossip was that in the course of it Bianchina's name cropped up. When Signorina Girasole had turned up at the inn and asked for him Matalena had not known who she was. Not till several hours later had Magascià revealed to her that the girl had been Alberto Colamartini's lover. Magascià knew many secrets. It was not surprising if the old slyboots, going backward and forward between Pietrasecca and Fossa and stopping at the Girasole hotel, heard the most shocking stories. According to him, young Colamartini had for some time enjoyed free board and lodging at Berenice Girasole's hotel as well as the use of her daughter. A situation worthy of an Oriental potentate. Signora Berenice had persuaded him to marry young Bianchina, but the Colamartini family would not hear of it. Subsequently there had been talk of Signorina Girasole's being gravely ill. When she reappeared after being confined to her bed for some time, she was much thinner.

"That's enough for my headache," Don Paolo said, rising from his table. "Good night."

At the prearranged time he walked hesitantly through the gate of the Colamartini house. Don Pasquale and Cristina received him in a big, half-dark room on the ground floor. Three thin little old ladies in old-fashioned clothes were seated around a heavy walnut table. They had been put on display there for his benefit. An odor of honey and the graveyard hung in the air. Though Cristina smiled at him, Don Paolo was seized with a cold sweat; Cristina did the introducing.

"My grandmother, my aunt, my mother," she said.

She immediately helped her aunt and her mother into the next room. Her grandmother remained. Under her small white bonnet her head looked like that of a hairless vulture. Her face was shrunken and wrinkled like that of a mummy.

"Where do you come from?" she asked the priest in a shrill, unsteady voice.

"From Frascati," Don Paolo said with a shudder.

"Have you brothers or sisters?"

"No, I'm an only son."

"In that case it was wrong of you to become a priest," the old lady said. "Very wrong."

Don Paolo tried to excuse himself.

"My vocation," he said.

"The Church cannot desire the destruction of families," the old woman announced. "Without families there can be no Church or anything else."

The old lady raised her head in his direction.

"Why don't you say mass?" she asked. "Have you by any chance been suspended *a divinis?* Don Benedetto was punished in that way too."

Don Paolo was very embarrassed. Cristina gave him a smile of commiseration, but he took no advantage of her aid.

"What did you say?" the old woman asked the priest.

"Nothing," he replied.

The old lady made a sign to her granddaughter, who hastened to help her into the next room.

"You must excuse us," Don Pasquale said to his guest, inviting him to sit in an armchair and taking a seat beside him. "Ever since we have had no servants," he went on, "we have used this room as living room, kitchen, and dining room."

The whole of one wall was covered with copper pots and pans and covers and molds. There were two big grated windows through which the garden was visible, and at the bottom of the garden there were some beehives.

Cristina brought a tray with a bottle of Marsala and two glasses. At one end of the table she resumed the work that had been interrupted by Don Paolo's arrival. She was ironing tablecloths and napkins, folding them and putting them in wicker baskets.

Don Pasquale poured out the Marsala.

"Last Sunday at Rocca dei Marsi Cristina and I met Don Benedetto," Don Pasquale said. "He kept pressing us for news about you."

"About me?" Don Paolo said. "Strange."

"Why are you surprised?" Cristina asked. "Wasn't it he who recommended you to come and convalesce at Pietrasecca?"

"Of course," Don Paolo said. After thinking for a moment he added in an embarrassed voice, "My only surprise, in one way, is that he does me the honor of remembering me."

"So far from forgetting you," Cristina said, "I had the impression that you're his chief preoccupation at present."

"But not the only one," Don Pasquale pointed out. "There were some other visitors there, and the conversation turned to a former pupil of his, a notorious character named Pietro Spina. Well, Don Benedetto actually had the courage to defend him. But, as you know the individual in question, that is something you won't appreciate."

"He didn't just defend him," Cristina said, "he delivered a tremendous eulogy of him."

"Using the most shocking arguments," Don Pasquale went on. "That saddened me greatly, the more so as Don Benedetto is an old family friend and morally is a saintly man."

Cristina finished her ironing and set about lighting the fire. She knelt in front of the fireplace and blew hard to make it catch. The wood was not seasoned and merely smoked.

Don Pasquale tried to bring the conversation around to Cristina's future. The family point of view, he said, was naturally not impartial, but what would be the attitude of a disinterested third party?

"Certainly not mine," Don Paolo hastened to say. "I too have an interest in your daughter's remaining at Pietrasecca."

Cristina laughed wholeheartedly and, as the fire flared up just at that moment, the reflection of the flames concealed her blushes.

"Even the wolves don't want me," she said jestingly.

"Real or metaphorical wolves?" Don Paolo said.

Her father then described a curious incident in her childhood. "Cristina was still in the cradle," he said, "and as she was very fond of lambs and it was warm in the sheepfold in winter, one evening we left her alone for several hours in her pram among the sheep. Well, a wolf got into the sheepfold, the whole flock started bleating frantically, and I dashed there with my gun and the dogs, but the wolf had gone."

"Was Cristina asleep?" Don Paolo asked.

"No, she was sitting up in her pram and calling her mother. She had not been frightened by the wolf, no doubt taking it for a bad dog that wanted to eat the sheep."

"Perhaps the wolf realized she was still a baby and decided to come back for her when she was bigger," Don Paolo said.

"It won't be able to catch me if it waits much longer," Cristina said with a laugh. "There are strong iron bars on convent windows."

This reminder promptly changed Don Pasquale's mood.

"That's how the Colamartini family will come to an end," he said bitterly. "A wastrel son and a nun for a daughter."

The three remained silent for a moment in the half-dark kitchen. Cristina went upstairs to put away the ironing.

"It's sad to be present at the end of one's own family," said Don Pasquale.

In that room how would it have been possible to think about anything else?

"The fate of the family does not seem to me to depend on Signorina Cristina's decision," Don Paolo said.

"No, it doesn't, you're perfectly right, of course," Don Pasquale said. "At the point we've reached the end is inevitable."

"One can at least end with dignity."

"You cannot possibly appreciate what a bad end the Colamartini family is facing."

"Perhaps it isn't right to talk of good and bad as inevitable."

"In our case it is. Believe me, even the outward decorum of the family no longer depends on me."

"There are desperate circumstances in which family decorum should perhaps be cast aside."

"If I were alone I might well be capable of that," said Don Pasquale, raising his voice. "But I can hardly put the three old ladies you met just now out to grass on the mountainside."

As he said this his eyes filled with tears.

"Forgive me," said Don Paolo.

"I have four pieces of land left, two planted with vines and two of them arable," Don Pasquale said. "Up to a few years ago the wine from the vineyards yielded about seven thousand lire. Now, after the phylloxera and other calamities and restoring the vineyards at great sacrifice and expense, the yield is only a few hundred lire. If I bought wine at market instead of making it from my vines, it would cost me three times less."

The old man rose and fetched from a drawer a greasy and worn old account book, swollen with receipts and promissory notes.

"Look," he said, "the yield from the arable land is hardly sufficient to pay the men's wages, though these have gone down to four or five lire a day, which is not very much. And I have to pay the taxes. For several years I have been wondering why I go on cultivating that land."

"It's the slump," Don Paolo said for the sake of saying something. "Everyone talks about it everywhere."

"It's bankruptcy," Don Pasquale said. "But for the family pride that prevents me from selling land that has belonged to the Colamartinis for centuries, I should have gotten rid of it years ago in my own interest. Land no longer pays. I have an old house near Lama that is now used as a stable, and I've let it. Would you like to know what I've had to spend to fulfill the legal requirement? Exactly six times more than the wretched rent. You think I'm exaggerating? There are no fewer than fourteen charges to be set against it. Here's the list: stamp duty, transcription charge, tax on numbering agreement, notary's fee, registration tax, tax for copying agreement, charge for formal transfer of lease, copies for registrar and parties to the agreement, various costs and postages, receipt stamps . . ."

"What you are saying seems to me to confirm that private property has had its day," Don Paolo said. "Are you not of that opinion?"

"I don't know," said Don Pasquale. "Before being reduced to this state I resorted to many expedients, some of which were not very dignified, and I've thought about it night and day. Well, Father, I don't know what to do."

"How do small landowners fare?"

"As I do. The difference is that they and their families sweat blood on their plots of land all the year round. That does not prevent every *cafone* from aspiring to be a small landowner, though the few who achieve it are worse off than the others. Actually land needs an unlimited amount of money."

"If cultivating the soil doesn't pay," Don Paolo said, "why were farm laborers who wanted to expropriate it gunned down?"

Don Pasquale's manner changed immediately.

"Those shootings were justified," he hastened to say, "but that doesn't mean that they were sensible or that they solved anything. The landowners who keep cultivating their land are simply madmen obsessed by a fixed idea. Besides, what else can they do? A farm laborer can become an industrial worker, but for a landowner there's no way out."

"Are laborers any better off?"

"They are in a bad way too. If they stay here and go on hacking away at the soil it's only because emigration has been stopped," Don Pasquale said. "All the same, they're better off than I am. Flesh used to suffering doesn't feel pain."

"I have the impression," Don Paolo said, "that times are getting harder and harder, and that only men of that sort will survive. For the reason you have just mentioned: it's flesh used to suffering."

Meanwhile Cristina had finished putting away the linen and came back to keep the two men company. It was Don Pasquale's turn to rise. Behind the house there was a shed with two cows, a heifer, and a horse. He excused himself for a few minutes and went to look after the animals.

"Another drop of Marsala?" said Cristina.

"Thank you," Don Paolo said. "It's excellent."

"My father will have told you the landowners' tale of woe," Cristina said.

"Signorina Cristina," Don Paolo said. "I cannot tell you how much it grieves me that your life is so hard."

"Do you perhaps suppose that that is why I want to take the veil?"

Don Paolo did not reply.

"It isn't," Cristina said. "My vocation is real, I assure you. But honesty compels me to add that it is certainly also convenient. But for that special summons from Jesus, how should I manage if I stayed here?"

"You would have the other possibility that life offers most women," Don Paolo said. "You could become a good wife and mother of a family."

"In the state to which good families are reduced," Cristina said, "that seems to me to be much more difficult than dying at the stake."

"You don't have a very high opinion of good families."

"What I mean is that this seems to me to be a particularly difficult time in which to reconcile the duties of one's station in life with those of one's soul."

"A Christian woman should not put the duties of her station in life on the same level as those of her soul."

"If she abandons secular life, she certainly shouldn't. But everyone who remains in the world has a station in life that imposes obligations."

"But if, as you admit, the duties of one's station become irreconcilable with those of one's soul, surely the only course is to dismiss the former out of hand."

"Following the example of Pietro Spina, perhaps?" Cristina

exclaimed. "Do you realize that you're repeating the arguments used by Don Benedetto last Sunday?"

"Perhaps it will surprise you, Signorina Cristina," Don Paolo said in an ironic tone, "but I do not consider the comparison with Spina outrageous."

"But the official teaching of the Church seems to me to be different," said Cristina. "Social inequalities were also created by God, and we must humbly respect them. . . . But I wonder why our talks always end up in an argument. Undoubtedly it's my fault, I'm obstinate and presumptuous. Let us change the subject."

The armistice was of brief duration.

"Have you any news of Bianchina?" Cristina asked.

"I heard a curious thing," Don Paolo said. "I heard there was a love affair between her and your brother Alberto."

"Again?" Cristina exclaimed angrily. "Didn't it end some time ago? It's really scandalous."

Argument flared up again. Don Paolo had for some time been aware of a sense of irritation, and it now had another excuse to show itself.

"There would be a very simple way of ending the scandal," he said. "Let them get married. That would settle everything."

Cristina's face hardened. "Impossible," she said coldly.

The priest pretended not to understand. "Impossible? Why impossible?" he said.

"My grandmother and my father would consider it a disgrace, not only to themselves, but to their forefathers," Cristina said firmly. To put an end to the discussion she added, "Please let us talk about something else."

"It's not a matter of forefathers, but of Alberto and Bianchina," Don Paolo insisted. "If the two are in love, that would be the honorable course to take."

"Family honor is not a matter for discussion," Cristina said angrily.

"So even you have these strange medieval ideas?" the priest exclaimed with pretended surprise. "Even you?"

"Yes, of course, even me," said the girl, accepting the challenge.

"Who are the Girasoles? Where do they come from? As for Bianchina, let me just remind you of the rather special circumstances in which you made her acquaintance."

"I have not in the least forgotten them," Don Paolo said. "But what would you say if your brother Alberto were not entirely extraneous to the girl's illness?"

"How dare you," Cristina exclaimed, jumping to her feet as if to reject a personal insult.

"I beg your pardon," Don Paolo said.

Without hesitating he made a slight bow of farewell and walked to the door. Cristina, pale and trembling, watched him leaving and made not the slightest move to detain him.

II

URING THE PRIEST'S absence Matalena secretly sent for Cassarola, the wise woman, who arrived dragging her feet and complaining about mysterious aches and pains in various parts of her body.

"I urgently need your aid," Matalena said to her. "Envy is trying to rob me of my priest."

"I don't understand," Cassarola said. "Do you own a priest?"

Matalena whispered into the woman's ear the cause of her anxieties.

"I don't understand," the wise woman said. "Perhaps it's because I haven't had anything to eat yet."

Matalena offered her bread and cheese and a glass of wine; she waited for a short time and then asked again, "Is there no sure way of keeping Don Paolo here?"

"Your cheese is salty," said the wise woman, spitting on the ground.

Matalena hastened to offer her another glass of wine.

"Now please be quick," she said, "because he might come back at any moment."

"Now, let me see," Cassarola began. "Do you sleep together?"

Matalena made a display of genuine indignation.

"Is that what you think?" she exclaimed. "At my age, and with a man in holy orders?"

"That is what I might have thought," the wise woman said. "But if you had, he would certainly have left long ago. But why do you want to keep him here? For money?"

"No, for protection. Without him the house will fall down. What am I to do?"

"Be patient, let me think."

Matalena filled the woman's empty glass and encouraged her to think quickly.

"I can't live without him," Matalena insisted. "I'm as frightened as if I were a little girl."

"Frightened of what?"

"Of everything."

Cassarola shut her eyes. She breathed with difficulty and complained again about her mysterious aches and pains.

"Give me something to drink," she muttered. "My throat's dry."

"Would you like a glass of cold water?"

"Do you think I'm a cow? Unfortunately I'm not a cow."

Matalena brought a full jug of wine to the table and put it next to the woman's glass, but she drank straight from the jug. She took several long swallows.

"We'll tie him up like a Bologna sausage," she announced with a leer when she had finished.

"No, I only want him to stay here."

"But I tell you he'll obey the two of us as meekly as a child, and through him we'll have control of the whole valley, and the souls in purgatory, and exorcisms."

"And natural disasters," Matalena added, "and subterranean forces."

"To begin with," Cassarola said, "you must put seven of your hairs in every plate of his soup. That's only the beginning. The hairs must of course be black, not dyed."

"I don't think he'll like them."

"He doesn't have to eat them, all that matters is to make sure they're cooked with his soup."

"Are there words to be said during the cooking?"

"I shall say them. Have you a picture of a woman?"

"No. Only of Our Lady of the Rosary."

Cassarola made a grimace of disgust and resumed complaining about her aches and pains. She picked up the jug and took several more long gulps.

"Then you must take a sheet of paper and draw a picture of a woman yourself. It doesn't have to be complete, it's enough to put in the holes. Listen carefully to what I'm saying and don't interrupt. You must draw nine holes on the sheet of paper to represent the nine holes in the body. Then you must put the drawing under his pillow."

"But he'll notice it and he'll ask for an explanation."

"Then you must put it under his mattress. Couldn't you get me some of his hair?"

"I'll try his comb in the morning," Matalena said.

No sooner had Cassarola gone than Matalena took the additional precaution of lighting an oil lamp and putting it in the presence of Our Lady of the Rosary. While standing on a chair to adjust the lamp she trembled all over with anxiety. Then she spoke into one of the Blessed Virgin's ears. "Holy Mother of God," she said, "I commend this poor priest of mine to you. Make him stay here. If you do, I shall keep this lamp alight for a whole year."

These precautions served to calm her down a little. She took a chair and put it outside the inn and sat on it to await Don Paolo's return. The heat of the day was beginning to lessen. A pleasant breeze came from the mountain, with a good smell of elder and cut grass. Fortunately she did not have to wait as long as she had expected.

"How was it?" she asked him. Her voice was as timid as if she had been asking for alms.

The priest did not answer. There was a strange expression on his face. He seemed both pleased and upset. Behind him a mendicant friar appeared, covered in dust and mud. The bag on his shoulder was nearly empty.

"Few alms?" Don Paolo said.

"Not even enough to pay for the sandal wear," the Capuchin replied.

He remained standing humbly by the door. The feet in his worn sandals looked black and deformed because of the scars and swellings. Matalena offered him a glass of wine, but he refused. The priest's presence intimidated him and he did not know what to say, or whether to stay or go. He had several times been reported to the Provincial Father by parish priests for his familiarity with the *cafoni* and his fondness for wine.

"Drink, Brother Gioacchino, drink, don't be shy," Matalena said, but her insistence only increased his embarrassment.

"Everyone serves the Lord as best he can," he said. "Some by words, some by charity, some by sanctity. My lot has been having to walk. I'm a donkey of the Lord's, the Father Superior says."

Don Paolo smiled. The Capuchin, whose eyes were those of a submissive *cafone*, hardly dared glance at him.

"Why do people give fewer alms? Are they less religious?" Don Paolo asked.

"Down on the plain they now have insurance, which is an invention of the devil," the monk said. "If I ask for something for San Francesco so that he may protect the crop against hail, they answer that it's insured already. Then he'll protect you against fire, I say. But they say they already have fire insurance. But how comes it that in spite of all those insurances they still live in fear? What is it they're afraid of?"

"Poor people always live in fear," said Matalena. "If you have a house, an earthquake happens. If you're healthy, illness comes. If you have a plot of land, a flood comes. There's envy in the air."

"Once upon a time every trade had its own saint," the monk said. "The cobblers had San Crispino, the tailors Sant'Ombono, the carpenters San Giuseppe. Nowadays every trade has its own union. But people are no safer than they were before. The fear remains."

"Is life better in a monastery?" Matalena asked.

"You live badly there too, but you have security," the monk said. "You have no family life, but you have no fear either. Also there's hope."

"What hope?" Don Paolo said.

The monk pointed to the sky.

"It's not a way for everyone," said Matalena. "We can't all be monks or nuns."

"Do you know what holds you back?" the monk said. "Greed for property. It holds you back like a chain holds a dog. Once upon a time the devil became flesh in women, but now he's incarnated in property."

"And no longer in women?" Matalena said. "Brother Gioacchino, there you may be wrong."

"Woman has lost her power," the monk said. "Nowadays it's property that leads to perdition."

"Do the poor get saved?" Matalena asked. "It doesn't seem to me that they get saved."

"Those who covet property are not saved," the monk said. "They are the false poor. Look, I speak out of family experience. After a bad year in which the whole crop was lost my father had to sell a vineyard behind the village castle. He ruined the rest of his life for the sake of buying it back; he grew mean, bad tempered, and quarrelsome, and died without ever managing to buy it back. Then my brother wanted to buy it back, and because of it he committed murder and ended up in prison. My other brother went to Brazil, intending to come back with enough money to buy it back, but he barely succeeded in making a living out there. Meanwhile that vineyard passes from hand to hand. Every three or four years it passes into new hands. How many souls is it sending to perdition?"

"What sort of vineyard is it?" said Matalena. "Is it a bewitched vineyard? A bad-woman vineyard?"

"It's a perfectly ordinary vineyard," said the monk. "It's a vineyard just like any other."

"Does it yield more than other vineyards?" Matalena asked. "Why does your family want just that vineyard?"

"It belonged to our family for generations," said the monk. "Otherwise it's exactly like all other vineyards."

"In the end every woman is exactly like all other women," Matalena said. "But if the devil intervenes . . ."

"Nowadays," the monk went on, "when my work of collecting alms takes me in that direction and I see that vineyard in the distance, I make the sign of the cross as if I were in the presence of the devil."

"Do you often go in that direction?" Don Paolo asked.

The monk nodded. "I know I'm wrong to do so," he said. "When one embraces the religious life and abandons the world one should go far away from one's home. It's not enough to change one's name if the water, the stones, the grass, the plants, the dust on the road are those of one's birthplace. One should go far away."

"I went far away," the priest confessed in a low voice. "But I couldn't stand it, and I came back."

"Perhaps one should go to some place from which one can't come back."

The monk said this in such gloomy tones that Don Paolo had to restrain himself from flinging his arms around him.

"Drink," he said, and poured him out a glass of wine. This time he accepted. He drank slowly, after wiping his chapped lips with the back of his hand.

"It must be Fossa wine," he said to Matalena.

"Yes, it is," she said.

"It must be from the district halfway up the hill, above the pozzolana quarry," he went on.

"Since you like it, have some more," said the priest, smiling, filling his glass.

"Thank you," the monk said. "It's a wine that's worth getting to know."

Don Paolo felt happy. He found this poor monk very touching.

"Come on, don't stay standing at the door," he said. "Come and sit at my table. Matalena, bring us a bottle."

"A whole bottle?" exclaimed the monk, taken aback.

"Why not? If we feel like it, we'll have another one when we've finished it," said the priest. "I'll take full responsibility."

"Your health," said the monk, raising his glass. Then, turning to Matalena, he said, "Couldn't you give me a piece of bread, please? It helps one to drink," he explained to the priest.

He broke the bread and gave some to Don Paolo.

"There's nothing better than wheat bread dipped in red wine," he went on. "But one's heart must be at peace," he added with a smile.

Don Paolo grew cheerful. Matalena had never seen him like this.

"What are you smiling at?" the monk asked him.

"One day we'll do the devil in," Don Paolo confided in his ear. "Yes, one day we'll do him in, that loathsome old enemy of man."

"How?"

"By abolishing the private ownership of land."

"Do you mean that land will belong to everyone? Including the vineyards?"

"Land, vineyards, woods, quarries, canals, everything."

"Do you mean you believe in revolution?"

"I don't believe in anything else," Don Paolo whispered in his ear. "Meanwhile drink, Brother Gioacchino, drink and be merry."

"Do you believe in the Kingdom? In this world?"

"*Sicut in coelo et in terra, amen.*"

"Who will make this revolution in your opinion? The Church?"

"No. The Church, as usual, will bless the revolution, but only after others have made it."

"Who will make it, then? God Himself?"

"No. You know the old rule: God helps those who help themselves."

"Who will make it, then?"

"The poor," the priest said in a serious voice. "That is, of course, the poor who are uncontaminated by greed for property."

The monk looked all around and then whispered in Don Paolo's ear, "Have you by any chance heard of someone called Pietro Spina?"

"Why do you ask?"

"He thinks the same way as you do," the monk said. "At any rate, so they say."

"Have you met others on your rounds who think in that way?" the priest asked.

"Yes," the monk said in an undertone, "but secretly."

"To your health," Don Paolo said, laughing. "Drink and be merry, Brother Gioacchino. Let us make a revolution that will do in that loathsome old devil once and for all."

Matalena listened in openmouthed astonishment. What strange things to hear from the lips of churchmen. She waited for the two to stop talking before asking the monk whether some natural disaster was in store.

"My husband is dead," she said, "and if my house is carried away by a flood, who will rebuild it for me?" Her voice was that of a terrified little orphan girl.

"We shall have worse than that," the monk blurted out.

His face darkened, and he said no more. Matalena made the sign of the cross and murmured in terror, "Worse?"

"What shall we have, then?" Don Paolo said in friendly fashion, to induce the monk to speak up.

"One night while I was praying in my cell," the monk said, without daring to look the priest in the face, "I looked in the direction of Rome. The horizon was as black as pitch, and there was a red specter peeping between the clouds."

"That sounds very plausible," Don Paolo said with a smile.

Matalena was reassured, for the menace in the sky was directed, not at Pietrasecca, but at Rome. The bottle was now empty, and the monk took his departure, because evening was falling and he hoped to be put up in the Colamartini stable, as on other occasions.

"I hope we meet again," he said to Don Paolo. "If not here, up there."

"Up there? Where? On the mountain? In the woods?" the priest asked.

"In heaven," the monk said with a smile.

"In case of need I shall get in touch with you sooner," the priest said.

"You'll find me on the road," said the monk.

Don Paolo watched him going away. He walked briskly, with a

light, dancing stride. The gate leading to the Colamartini house was open. The monk climbed the three steps that led up to the front door and pulled at the bell. As no one answered it, he sat down at the threshold and waited patiently. A small mouse peeped out of a clump of rosebushes. It was as brown as the monk's habit. For a few moments the mouse and the monk looked at each other in friendly fashion, but their attention was averted by the creaking of the front door.

"I'm sorry," Don Pasquale said. "My daughter is not feeling very well."

12

THE ARRIVAL OF A LETTER from Bianchina in Rome put Don Paolo in a state of unusual excitement, though there was nothing sensational in it; the contents were almost commonplace. The trip had gone off well, she wrote. She had had no difficulty in finding the person to whom she had been sent, she had not seen anyone else the whole time, and so she had been able to have a look at the city. She might be coming back very soon, and she would certainly be bringing back plenty of reading matter for him. The effect of this brief message on Don Paolo was almost miraculous. He suddenly felt reinvigorated. The end of his enforced isolation was in sight. He would be having some serious discussions with the party, but discussion was better than soliloquy.

From that moment he tried to get away from the tedious female atmosphere by which he was surrounded; he forgot Cristina, and sought out the company of men. Before leaving Pietrasecca he wanted at least to get to know them better. But during the daytime they were dispersed all over the valley, and they came back only after sunset, in small groups, walking behind their loaded donkeys. From the garden of the inn he watched them climbing up the valley, weary, hungry, and ragged, with that typical forward-leaning gait of theirs that was the result of using the mattock, of working bent over the soil, and also of habituation to servility, to uninterrupted subjection. Now that he felt better, Don Paolo went out to get away from the complaints of Matalena, who was living in fear of his departure, and the complaints of the other women, who darned and mended and deloused themselves outside the inn, and also to get away from the breviary, the *Eternal Maxims*, the ghosts of his youth who, he thought, had vanished, but had gathered around him, taking advantage of his solitude and his physical debility.

One afternoon he crossed the wooden bridge and took the narrow road that led down to the valley. He felt like a machine that had been repaired and was now resuming its usual motion, its usual rhythm. Once more he felt an instinct that was part of his nature, the urge to be sociable. In his isolation he had been out of his element, a fish out of water. He sat on a wall by the roadside and waited. It was natural for him to wait. As a boy he had waited after catechism in the evening in the square at Orta for other boys, nearly all the sons of poor people, to join him and play games. Later in Rome, when he was a member of a socialist students' group, he had waited for some worker at the gate of the Tabanelli works, outside Porta San Giovanni, or at the gasworks outside Porta San Paolo, to spend the evening with him. At l'Estaque he had waited for Cardile. He knew how to wait.

The first to appear that evening were old Sciatàp and his son, walking a few paces behind their donkey, which was loaded with brushwood. When he saw the priest Sciatàp stopped.

"I've been waiting to talk to you for a long time," he said, "but they said you had the cough, and I didn't want to trouble you."

"The cough's better now," Don Paolo said.

"I want to talk to you about my son," the old man went on. "He wanted to join the *carabinieri* or the militia, but they turned him down. Couldn't you write a letter of recommendation?"

"Do you really want to be a *carabiniere*?" the priest asked the young man.

"I certainly do," he said. "People speak ill of them out of envy. They don't do much work, and they're well paid."

"But that's not the point," said the priest. "You're a worker. If you become a *carabiniere* your superiors may order you to fire at dissatisfied *cafoni*. That has already happened not far from here, at Sulmona, Pratola, and Prezza, as you probably know."

Sciatàp instantly agreed with this.

"Don Paolo's right," he said. "If you want to live at all well you have to sell your soul. There's no other way."

The way his father put it made the boy laugh.

"Is there no other way?" said Don Paolo. "Is it impossible to live well and stay honest?"

"Do you know the story of the devil and the cat?" Sciatàp said. "Once upon a time there was a big devil who lived in a cave. He was dressed in black, wore a top hat, and had many rings on his fingers, just like a banker. Three *cafoni* went to see him and asked him what was required to live well, without working. "What is needed is a soul, an innocent soul," the devil replied. The *cafoni* went away, took a cat, swaddled it like a newborn baby, and took it to the devil. "Here's a soul, a really innocent soul," they said, and in return the devil gave them a book of instructions on how to live well without working. But while they were on their way home the cat started meowing, the devil discovered he had been cheated, and the magic book went up in flames in their hands. A cat's no use. What is required is a soul, a real, human soul."

"Very well," the lad said, "I'll do what everyone else does, of course. Meanwhile my application has not been accepted. There are too many applications."

"That's the trouble, there are too many souls," said Sciatàp. "The earthquake and epidemics and the war weren't much use. There are still too many souls."

"What is left to a man who sells his soul?" the priest asked.

The two *cafoni* looked at him in surprise. What a strange question to come from a priest. As if there were any doubt.

"There's always a way of putting things right while life lasts," said Sciatàp. "What's the Church for? Does the Church forbid the *carabinieri* to open fire? In the procession at Fossa on Corpus Christi day there are always four *carabinieri* in full dress uniform in the place of honor behind the Sacrament. You said that at Pratola the *carabinieri* opened fire on poor people. Afterward they must have confessed. But the *cafone* they shot are dead, and who confessed for them? In this world they suffered from cold and in the next they are suffering from fire."

"I'm sorry," Don Paolo said, "but I don't know to whom I could recommend you. I don't know any *carabiniere* officers."

Meanwhile the donkey had gone on ahead.

"Garibaldi," the old man shouted angrily after it.

But the donkey took no notice and went on its way.

"It won't listen to me because it's hungry and it's not far to the stable," Sciatàp explained to the priest. "When it's hungry it even forgets its own name."

Sciatàp and his son wished him a good evening and hurried after the donkey, and Don Paolo went and sat down again.

Next to appear was a drunken *cafone* on a donkey. The man kept slipping from one side to the other, and every time he righted himself he struck and kicked the beast.

"Will you go straight or not?" he kept saying.

Immediately after him came a number of *cafoni* accompanying Magascià and his cart. Magascià stopped the cart and said, "We've been to market."

"Did you get good prices?" asked the priest.

"Prices have fallen," Magascià said. "They imposed price control. We didn't want to sell, but we had to, or they would have confiscated our produce."

"Country prices are subject to price control, but not town prices, which have risen," said a man standing by the cart.

"Giacinto was arrested by the *carabinieri*," Magascià said, "for rebellion. When he heard about the price control he wanted to go back to Pietrasecca without selling."

The cart set off again, and Don Paolo joined the men on their way home. Next to Magascià was a man named Daniele, a tall fellow with an old hat askew over his bearded face.

"Daniele had a sick donkey that certainly won't live another month," Magascià confided to the priest. "He took it to market and sold it to a Fossa woman as a healthy one."

"I'll confess next Easter," Daniele said. "God will forgive me."

The whole group laughed with pleasure at Daniele's smartness. A youth named Banduccia who looked as if he were drunk was walking behind the cart, holding on to it in order to keep on his feet.

"Banduccia," Magascià confided to the priest, "went to a tavern at Fossa, ate, drank, offered a round of drinks to everyone present, and then went out into the garden as if to relieve himself, but he jumped the wall and got away without paying."

"I'll confess at Easter too," Banduccia said. "God will forgive me."

Again everyone laughed. Don Paolo shuddered.

"When Signora Rosa Girasole, the landlady, realized I'd gone," Banduccia said, "she tried to make Biagio pay my share, on the grounds that he came from Pietrasecca too. Poor Signora Rosa made a bad choice. If other customers hadn't intervened he would have smashed up the whole place. He picked up a log and threw it at her; if it had hit her she would have been done for."

Biagio was the strongest and most violent *cafone* in the valley, and Don Paolo had already heard him talked of with great admiration.

"He's been to prison for acts of violence three times already," another man said approvingly. "He's a man who makes himself respected."

"Handing it out's no disgrace, what's disgraceful is taking it," said Banduccia.

"The first time he went to prison was for breaking his father's arm with a chopper," said Magascià. "'He broke my arm, but I'm delighted he's so strong,' the old man told me. 'He'll make himself respected in life, at any rate by people as poor as himself.'"

Other men recalled other brave deeds of Biagio's, but Don Paolo stopped listening. Among the group of *cafoni* around Magascià's cart there was also a young man with a rather strange appearance.

He was barefoot, poorly dressed, tall, and thin. A big tuft of hair on his forehead gave him a wild look that contrasted with his eyes, which were those of a tame dog. He took no part in his companions' jokes and sallies. Don Paolo smiled at him, and he smiled back and moved closer to him. When the group crossed the wooden bridge and broke up Don Paolo took him by the arm and detained him.

"I should like to talk to you," he said to him quietly. "I should like to hear what you think about certain things."

The young man smiled at him and went off toward the hovel in which he lived. This was in the farthest corner of the village, among a group of sheds and pigsties. The path that led to it was a foul-smelling ditch that served as a drain for manure. Don Paolo followed the young *cafone*, who turned every so often and looked at the priest without speaking, but with gratitude in his eyes.

"I should like to talk to you as man to man," Don Paolo said. "Forget for a moment that I'm wearing this habit and that you're a simple *cafone*."

The young man's home was rather like a pigsty. You had to bend down to get into it; the door also served as chimney. In the darkness and stench inside it was just possible to make out a straw bed stretched out on the cobbled floor and a goat ruminating on some filthy straw. The reek of manure and filthy rags was too much for Don Paolo, who sat at the entrance while the young man prepared his evening meal.

"There's a country," Don Paolo started saying in an undertone, "a big country in the east of Europe, a vast plain cultivated with wheat. A vast plain, populated by millions of *cafoni*. In that country in 1917 . . ."

The young *cafone* cut a few slices of corn bread, sliced two tomatoes and an onion, and offered the priest a piece of bread with that seasoning. He still had traces of soil on his swollen and scarred hands. The knife with which he cut the bread was obviously used for all purposes. Don Paolo shut his eyes and tried to swallow the food to avoid offending him.

"There's a country," he began again, "a big country in which the *cafoni* in the country struck up an alliance with the workers in the town."

Meanwhile Matalena had been going from house to house looking for her lodger.

"Have you seen him?" she asked everyone. Eventually she found him.

"Your dinner has been ready for an hour," she said. "I was afraid something had happened to you."

"I'm not hungry," said Don Paolo. "Go back to the inn, because I want to go on talking to this friend of mine."

"Talking to him?" Matalena exclaimed. "But haven't you noticed that the poor lad is a deaf-mute and only understands a few signs?"

The deaf-mute was sitting at the entrance to his den next to the priest. Don Paolo looked him in the face and saw realization of the mistake of which he had been the cause slowly dawning in his eyes.

"It doesn't matter," the priest said to Matalena, "go back to the inn, I'm not hungry."

The two stayed where they were, and the one of them who had the gift of speech was silent too. Every so often they looked at each other and smiled. The gray light of evening faded and was followed by the darkness of night. As soon as it was dark torpor descended on the village. But for the stench coming from the hovels and sheds the valley might have been uninhabited. After a time Don Paolo rose, shook the deaf-mute by the hand, and wished him good night. He had to grope in the dark like a blind man.

The only door that was still open and lit was that of the inn. There were always some who came to drink or play cards and stayed late. There was nowhere else to go in the village. The furniture of the bar consisted of two greasy tables, a few chairs with no straw left on them, and a wooden bench next to the fireplace. In a corner under the staircase that led to the first floor were piled provisions for the whole year, consisting of sacks of potatoes, beans, and lentils. There was nearly always a saucer of salted roast chickpeas on one of the tables to make the customers thirsty. A picture of Our Lady of the Rosary had been hanging on the wall for so long that it had become part of the place. Customers chewed chickpeas, drank, chewed tobacco, drank again, and continually spat on the floor, so that when Don Paolo came in he had to be careful not to slip.

An old man named Fava was always squatting by the fireplace, staring fixedly at the floor with a sad, stupefied expression on his face. He was perpetually chewing the cud and never talked to anyone. He was the first to arrive and the last to leave, by which time he was so drunk that he could hardly stand. His daughters came to fetch him, his sons came to fetch him, and his wife came to fetch him, but he refused to budge.

"There's wine at home," his wife said. "Why don't you drink the wine from our vineyard?"

"I don't like it," he said with a grimace of disgust.

Matalena had had to exchange some wine with Fava's wife.

"Now we have the wine you like, so stay at home," his wife said.

"I don't like it," he said.

And he went back to the inn every night and spent the little money that he earned. His wife ended up holding Matalena responsible.

"You mustn't give him anything to drink," she said. "If he wants to drink, let him come home."

It made no difference. Fava went to the inn every evening, always to the same place.

When Don Paolo arrived after talking to the deaf-mute there were only two peasants playing cards.

"When I saw you talking to the deaf-mute," one of them said, "I thought it was a miracle, but it was only a mistake."

Don Paolo sat down at the table with the two men.

"It wasn't a miracle and it wasn't a mistake," he said.

"The deaf-mute is very intelligent," the other man said. "Perhaps God deprived him of speech and hearing as a punishment."

The two resumed their game of cards.

That evening Don Paolo was not sleepy. A strange restlessness made him talkative.

"*Cafoni* have been complaining ever since the world began, but have been resigned to their fate. Will that always be the case?" he said.

"If one could die of hunger we should have been dead long ago," one of the card players said.

"Don't you think that one day things might change?" Don Paolo asked again.

"Yes, when the patient's dead the doctor arrives," the other man said.

Don Paolo grew reckless.

"Haven't you ever heard that there are countries in which things are different?"

This time Matalena answered.

"Yes," she said. "There are countries that are different from ours. God put the grass where there are no sheep and sheep where there's no grass."

"I see," Don Paolo said. "Good night."

The two men went on with their game. Later one of them said to Matalena, "Your priest seems a decent fellow, but he's also a bit crazy."

"You don't understand him," said Matalena. "He's too educated for you."

"Yes, he's educated," the other man said, "but he's a bit crazy, too. Why doesn't he say mass?"

"He doesn't belong to this diocese."

"What difference does that make? Mass is the same everywhere. It's that he's a bit crazy."

13

NEXT DAY WAS A HOLIDAY, and in the evening the bar was crowded with drinkers and card players, as on great occasions. Many stood, because there were not enough chairs, and others played *morra** outside. Don Paolo stayed in his room, bent over the small table, busy with some sheets of paper that bore the heading: ON THE INACCESSIBILITY OF THE CAFONI TO POLITICS. But because of the noise coming up from the bar he could not concentrate. He heard people coming and going, the noise made by the chairs, the calls made by the *morra* players, the sudden flaring up of arguments followed by shouts, bangs, oaths, and the sound of chairs and tables being overturned.

"Please be quiet," Matalena implored. "Don Paolo's upstairs resting."

But her appeals were in vain, for how can one enjoy oneself without making a noise?

A strange squabble arose among three or four young men who were playing *settemezzo*, because of one of the cards. The most im-

---

Morra, a gambling game played with the fingers only — unlike other games mentioned here, which are card games.

portant card at *settemezzo* is the king of coins.* Matalena had only two packs, and in both the king of coins was so worn and consequently so easily recognizable that a fair game was impossible. To avoid quarrels Daniele, one of the players, proposed that they substitute another card for it, the three of goblets,† for instance. The easily identifiable king of coins would have the value of the three of goblets, and the three of goblets, which was indistinguishable from the rest, would have the value of the king of coins.

"Impossible," another player, Michele, announced. "It would be impossible even if we all agreed to it."

"Why?" Daniele wanted to know.

"But it's obvious," a third player, Mascolo, insisted. "Whatever happens, the king of coins remains the king of coins. No matter how dirty, marked, or worn he may be, he's still the king of coins."

"But it's enough if we all agree," Daniele said. "It'll be a better game if no one knows who has the king of coins."

"It's not sufficient for us to agree," Michele insisted. "The rules are the rules."

"You say it would be a better game?" Mascolo declared. "Perhaps it would be, but it wouldn't be the real game."

Sciatàp, who was at the other table, the old men's table, and had heard the argument, said, "Let's ask Don Paolo. A priest knows as much as the devil."

"You can't," said Matalena. "He's resting."

But Don Paolo, who heard his name being mentioned, appeared at the top of the stairs.

"Did someone ask for me?" he asked.

The argument stopped immediately, and everyone offered the priest a drink. He thanked them all and tried to excuse himself, but in the end he had to agree to go around the room touching every glass with his lips, in accordance with the custom.

"Who wanted me?" he asked at the conclusion of this rite.

Sciatàp explained what the argument was about, and ended, "Now tell us who's right."

Denari, a suit in the Italian pack.
†*Coppe*, another suit in the Italian pack.

"It's not a matter of sacred images," the priest said, laughing.
But Sciatàp cut off his way of retreat.

"A priest knows as much as the devil," he said.

Don Paolo picked up the king of coins.

"Do you think that this card has a value in itself or just the value that has been given to it?" he asked Michele.

"It's worth more than the other cards, because it's the king of coins," Michele replied.

"Has this card a fixed or variable value?" the priest asked again. "Does the king of coins have the same value in all games, at *tressette*, *briscola*, and *scopa*, or does it vary?"

"It varies according to the game," said Michele.

"And who invented those games?" the priest asked.

No one replied.

"Don't you think that games were invented by players?" the priest suggested.

A number of men immediately agreed. Games had obviously been invented by players.

The priest concluded, "If the value of this card varies according to the fantasy of the players and what they agree on, it seems to me that you can do what you like with it."

"Well said, bravo," many of those present called out.

Don Paolo was flattered by his success. He turned to Sciatàp. "Once upon a time there was a man here at Pietrasecca who was called Carlo Campanella, and now there's a man in New York who's called Mr. Charles Little-Bell, Ice and Coal. Is there only one of him or are there two?"

"He's the same man," a number of men answered.

"If a man can change his name, why can't a playing card?" the priest asked.

"A king is always a king," Michele said.

"A king is a king only as long as he remains on the throne," Don Paolo said. "A king who no longer reigns is no longer a king, but an ex-king. There's a country, a big country, from which the sun comes to us, that had a king, let us call him a big king of clubs, who ruled over millions of *cafoni*. When the *cafoni* stopped obeying him he ceased to reign, he was no longer a king. Not far away from us, in the direction in which the sun sets, there's a country where another king used to reign, let us call him a king of goblets or coins. When his subjects stopped obeying him he ceased to reign, ceased to be king and became an ex-king. Now he's an emigrant, which is a thing that any of you might be. So play *settemezzo* in any way you like, and good night to you."

Don Paolo handed back the king of coins to Daniele, said good night to everyone again, and went up to his room, followed by the acclamation of drunks.

But for the next few days the dethronement of the king of coins led to a long trail of comment among the *cafoni* of Pietrasecca.

The village schoolmistress, Signorina Patrignani, came and complained to the priest in person.

"It was impossible to teach today in the top class," she said. "The boys would talk of nothing but that business of the king of coins and the three of goblets, and they kept repeating what you said in the bar last night without having understood it."

The schoolmistress wore the emblem of the government party on her breast. She sighed deeply between one sentence and the next, and the tricolor emblem tossed about like a small boat on a stormy sea.

"These peasants are very ignorant," she said, "and when they listen to educated people such as ourselves they nearly always understand the opposite of what is meant."

She had just received the latest number of *News from Rome*, the broadside that was intended to be displayed on the school door. It was her custom before putting it up to read and explain the most important items to the *cafoni* gathered in Matalena's bar. The news spread among the *cafoni* that the priest was going to attend that evening, and so the bar was fuller than usual. Some of those who turned up the priest had never seen before. In a short time about thirty ragged individuals were squatting in a huddle on the floor. Don Paolo sat at the foot of the stairs leading to the second floor and so could look nearly everyone in the face. The smell of manure and dirty clothing that rose from the throng took one by the throat.

They were submissive and diffident people with dazed-looking faces on deformed and contorted trunks, faces misshapen by hunger and illness, and among them were several wild and violent youths. The older men, the notables such as Sciatàp, Magascià, and Grascia, stayed standing by the door.

In the strange priest's presence the schoolmistress was unusually nervous and talkative. She told the audience to pay careful attention and not to be afraid to ask for explanations of difficult words. Then she started reading *News from Rome* in a loud and piercing voice.

"We have a leader for whom all the nations of the earth envy us," she read. "Who knows what they would be prepared to pay to have him in their country . . ."

Magascià interrupted. As he disliked generalities, he wanted to know exactly how much other nations would be willing to pay to acquire our leader.

"It's a manner of speaking," said the schoolmistress.

"There's no such thing as manners of speaking in commercial contracts," Magascià objected. "Are they willing to pay for him or not? If they are willing to pay, what are they offering?"

The schoolmistress repeated angrily that it was merely a manner of speaking.

"So it isn't true that they want to buy him, then?" Magascià said. "And if it isn't true, why does it say that they want him?"

Sciatàp also wanted some specific information. Would it be a cash or credit transaction?

The schoolmistress glanced at the priest as if to say: now you see the kind of people we have to deal with in this village.

The next item concerned the rural population.

"Who are the rural population?" asked one of the throng sitting on the floor.

"You are," the schoolmistress replied, losing her patience. "I've told you that hundreds of times."

Some members of the audience burst out laughing.

"We were the rural population and didn't know it," they said.

The schoolmistress went on reading, "The rural revolution has attained its objectives all along the line . . ."

"What line?" someone asked. "The railway line?"

"Are we the rural population?" Sciatàp asked. "Is the rural revolution the revolution we made?"

"Exactly," said the schoolmistress. "I congratulate you on your intelligence."

"What revolution did we make?"

"The expression is to be understood in a moral sense," the schoolmistress explained.

Sciatàp did not want to appear ignorant and pretended to understand, but Magascià was not satisfied.

"That sheet of paper is sent us by the government," he said, "and it says that the rural population, that is the *cafoni* according to what you say, have made a revolution, and that that revolution has attained its objectives. What objectives have we attained?"

"Spiritual objectives," said the schoolmistress.

"What spiritual objectives?"

The schoolmistress flushed, grew flustered, and there was general confusion. Then she had a brilliant idea, imposed silence, and, while you could hear a pin drop, she announced, "The rural revolution has saved the country from the communist menace."

"Who are the communists?" said Grascia.

The schoolmistress was safe. She had no more need to think. "I've told you before, but now I'll tell you again," she said. "The communists are wicked people who choose to meet at night in town sewers. To become a communist you have to trample on the crucifix, spit in Christ's face, and promise to eat meat on Good Friday."

"Where do they get the meat from?" Sciatàp wanted to know. "Do they get it for nothing or do they have to pay for it?"

"I don't know," the schoolmistress said.

"So what it boils down to is that, as usual, you don't know the most important thing," said old Grascia.

The schoolmistress turned to Don Paolo as if to give him a chance to speak and thus come to her rescue, but the priest seemed absorbed in contemplation of the cobwebs on the ceiling.

"As I disagree, I'm going," Grascia announced.

The schoolmistress invited him to say what he disagreed with, but the old man went off without replying.

Don Paolo overtook him in the open space in front of the inn.

"Well done, I congratulate you," the priest said to him.

"I only said it to infuriate the woman," Grascia said. He found it intolerable that a woman should try to instruct men.

"When woman teaches man children are born hunchbacked," he explained.

It was a sultry night. Gusts of sirocco coming up from the valley along the little stream gave one a slightly queasy feeling. The small crowd had gathered to listen to the schoolmistress and they now quickly dispersed. Near the wooden bridge, where they stopped to talk, Don Paolo and Grascia were joined by Sciatàp, Magascià, and Daniele.

"Before going to bed we ought at least to wet our whistle," the priest suggested.

"If it's a matter of obeying a precept of the Church, we have no possible objection," said Magascià.

Don Paolo gave Sciatàp some money to pay Matalena for a bottle of wine. Meanwhile Grascia had started inveighing against the schoolmistress again.

"There's nothing worse than a hen trying to lay down the law to a cock," he said.

"Here, have a drink," said Sciatàp.

He had brought a glass for Don Paolo, but the priest refused it.

"It's better straight from the bottle," he said.

Grascia could not get his fixed idea out of his head.

"One of us ought to do her the kindness of giving her a baby," he said. "We might even draw lots for the job."

"Who are you talking about?" asked Magascià.

"The schoolmistress."

"Leave the wretched woman alone," Magascià said. "Everyone earns a living as best they can."

"Have a drink and pass the bottle," Daniele said to him. "We'll draw lots another evening. You're not in a hurry, are you?"

"No, I can wait," Grascia said.

"Perhaps I may be leaving in a few days' time," Don Paolo said. "I'm feeling much better. But before I go I should like to have a better idea of your way of thinking."

"That's soon said," said Daniele. "We're just tillers of the soil and don't have much to think about."

"Even a *cafone* thinks sometimes," the priest said. "To begin with, why don't you tell me what you think about the situation, Daniele?"

"What situation?" said Daniele.

"The general situation."

"The general situation of Pietrasecca? Are you asking whether I think Pietrasecca would be better off if it were situated somewhere else? I must admit I've never considered it. This village has always been here."

"You haven't understood me," said the priest. "I was referring to living conditions in general, here and elsewhere in Italy. What do you think of them?"

"I don't think of them," said Daniele. "You know, everyone has his own worries."

"Everyone is plagued by his own fleas," said Sciatàp. "Are you saying we should worry about other people's too?"

"Everyone has his own little bit of land," said Grascia. "Everyone thinks day and night about his own little bit of land. If it rains too much, or hails, or doesn't rain at all. Italy is an endless number of plots of land, mountains, hills, plains, woods, lakes, marshes, beaches. If you had to think about them all, you'd go mad. Man's brain isn't big enough. All we can do with our little brain is to think about our own bit of land."

"And sometimes," said Sciatàp, "our brain isn't even big enough for that. And in any case what's the good of thinking? Hail comes just the same."

"You haven't understood me," said the priest. "I want to know what you think about this government."

"Nothing," said Daniele.

The others agreed. "Nothing," they said.

"What?" said the priest. "Though you're always grumbling?"

"Everyone has his own troubles," said Magascià. "That's all that interests us. At most you worry about your neighbor's. You look at your own vineyard or your own plot of land; you look through the door or the window of your house if the door or the window is open; when you eat your soup sitting at the front door in the evening you look at your own plate."

"Everyone has his own fleas to plague him," said Sciatàp, "and no doubt the government has its own fleas too. Let it do what we do, scratch itself. What else could we suggest to it?"

"You haven't understood me," said the priest. "I want to know what you think about taxes, prices, military service, and other laws."

"Drink," Grascia said to him. "Father, you obviously have time to waste. No, I don't mean to be rude. What I mean is that all these questions are superfluous. Everyone knows what we think about some things."

"On taxes, military service, and rents we all think the same," said Daniele. "Even the most timid and resigned, and even the most sanctimonious. There's nothing new or secret about that. It would be really strange if we thought otherwise."

"Drink and pass the bottle," Grascia said.

"It's empty," said Daniele.

Don Paolo offered to pay for another, but the men objected. "It's our turn," they said. "We know how to behave." They all contributed, and Daniele went to the bar and came back with a full bottle.

"You drink first," he said to the priest. "It will serve as a grace."

"You grumble," Don Paolo said, returning to the theme, "but you remain obedient and resigned."

"We are born and grow up with the same ideas," said Sciatàp. "What are our oldest memories? Of our old folk grumbling. What are our children's of their childhood? Of our grumbling. We used to think things couldn't get worse, but they got worse. Even the blind and deaf-and-dumb know it. I've never met anyone who thought otherwise."

"Even the authorities know it," said Magascià. "Do you know what the *podestà* of Fossa said in his last speech in the square? 'I don't ask you not to grumble,' he said, 'but at least do so at home and not in the public square and not in the corridors of the town hall. At least show a little decency.' And in the end he was quite right. You must have a sense of decency. What's the use of grumbling?"

"I don't agree," said Grascia. "If it doesn't do anything else it at least saves you from exploding."

"Drink, and pass the bottle," Daniele said to him.

"But don't you think that one day your troubles might end?" the priest asked.

"Are you talking about the next life, about life after death?" Grascia asked. "Are you talking about Paradise?"

"No, I'm talking about this world," Don Paolo insisted. "Don't you think that one day the landowners might be expropriated and their land given to the poor? Don't you think that the country might be run by people such as yourselves? Don't you think that your sons and grandsons might be born free?"

"Yes, we know that dream," said Grascia. "Every so often we hear about it. It's a beautiful dream, there's none more beautiful."

"But unfortunately it's only a dream," said Magascià.

"A beautiful dream," said Sciatàp. "Wolves and lambs will graze together in the same field. Big fish will no longer eat little fish. A lovely fairy story. Every so often we hear about it."

"So you think that in this world damnation is eternal?" the priest said. "Don't you think that one day laws might be made by you in favor of all?"

"No, I don't," said Magascià. "Don't let's have any illusions."

"If it depended on me, I'd abolish all laws," said Grascia. "That's where all evil comes from."

"It's a dream," said Sciatàp. "A beautiful dream."

"If it depended on me, I'd replace all existing laws with one single law," Grascia said. "There's just one single law that would be enough to stop everyone from complaining, believe me. It would give every Italian the right to emigrate."

"Impossible," said Daniele. "Who would stay here?"

"It's a dream," said Sciatàp. "A beautiful dream. It would be like abolishing stable doors."

"Drink, and pass the bottle," Magascià said to him.

"It's empty," said Sciatàp. "Shall I get another?"

"No, it's late," Don Paolo said. "I'm feeling rather tired."

Back in his room, he took from his suitcase the notebook in which he had written, ON THE INACCESSIBILITY OF THE CAFONI TO POLITICS, and sat down at the table. He remained sitting there for a long time with his head between his hands. Eventually he began writing. "Perhaps they are right" was his first sentence.

14

WHEN DON PAOLO TOLD Matalena that he was going to Fossa next day she took it as an announcement of impending catastrophe. She barely had the strength to ask him when he was coming back.

"I don't know," he replied with exaggerated indifference. "I may come back just to fetch the things I'm leaving here for the time being."

At that moment Teresa Scaraffa happened to pass by on her way to draw water from the fountain.

"Teresa," Matalena called out. "For the love of heaven keep an eye on the place for a few minutes, I'll be back directly."

"What's the matter with you?" Teresa exclaimed in alarm, but she got no answer.

Matalena, unkempt and in bedroom slippers as she was, started running. Breathlessly she climbed the alley and the steps that led to the cave where Cassarola lived. The wise woman was lying on a sack of corn leaves, complaining about her aches and pains and feeding bits of bread to a goat.

"What's the matter?" she exclaimed when she saw Matalena. "Is your house on fire?"

"He's going," Matalena barely managed to gasp with the little breath she had left.

"That's your fault," the wise woman retorted. "So I poke the fire and you put it out. Why did you provoke a quarrel between him and Donna Cristina?"

"You know why. It certainly wasn't out of jealousy."

"Only a hen's brain like yours could entertain the suspicion that Don Pasquale would invite the priest to stay with him. You ought to know who rules the roost in that house."

Matalena was easily persuaded that she was in the wrong, and she began to snivel.

"What can we do now?"

"We must try to repair the blunder if it isn't too late. If you want to tie someone, it's no use going against nature. Even a priest is made of flesh and blood."

Matalena hurried back to the inn and smartened herself up. She combed her hair, changed her apron, and put on a pair of shoes.

"Please, please, wait here a little longer," she said imploringly to Teresa. "I've got to go and see Donna Cristina."

To Matalena calling out of the blue at the Colamartini house like this was very much against the grain. Over and above her dismay at the priest's departure, there was a special reason for her reluctance. At her last encounter with Cristina she had been extremely rude, and since then the two had not seen each other. Fortunately it was her father who opened the door. Did he know why the priest wanted to hasten his departure from Pietrasecca? No, he knew nothing about it. Then Cristina appeared; she had been unwell for the past few days, and knew even less.

Cristina walked back to the gate with Matalena.

"Perhaps both of us have been at fault," Matalena said humbly. "Perhaps we both could have done more to keep Don Paolo here."

"What could we have done?" Cristina asked.

"Perhaps you offended him without meaning it," Matalena said. "He was very fond of you, and still is."

"How is he?" Cristina asked. "Is he leaving without having completely recovered?"

"During these last few days he has lost all that he had previously gained," said Matalena.

"I'm very sorry to hear it," said Cristina.

Don Paolo was punctual for the appointment next morning. It was a fine morning, and the fresh smell of wet grass was coming down from the mountain. There had not been such a bright morning for a long time. While old Colamartini put the mare between the shafts and slowly adjusted the traces, the bit, and the blinkers, Cristina came and greeted the priest.

"Are you leaving already?" she said. "For good?"

"I don't know," said Don Paolo, embarrassed. "I'm leaving my things here. I may come back, or I may send someone for them."

His irritation with the girl had vanished, though a certain annoyance and disappointment remained. But the fact of the matter was that his mind was elsewhere. He no longer felt like an invalid. The girl, however, looked run down.

"Donna Cristina has been unwell," Matalena had told him that morning while he was having his breakfast. "She has been very ill."

"I didn't know," the priest had said.

"She was in bed for a week," Matalena had added. "I hope it wasn't your fault."

"My fault?"

"She's a very sensitive girl, and she was very fond of you. Haven't you noticed that the geraniums on the little balcony have withered?"

Don Paolo received this statement with a certain amount of irritation.

"We're ready," Don Pasquale announced.

"Bon voyage," said Cristina. "I hope we shall see you again soon."

"I hope so too," said Don Paolo.

Cristina was going to say something else, but the trap moved off. For a short time the two men remained silent, almost embarrassed.

"The mare's name is Diana," Don Pasquale said. "I bought her fifteen years ago to go hunting. Happy times that won't return."

The shape of the trap, with its high seats and four wheels, the front ones small and the back ones big, the mare's harness, the embroidered cushions on which the two men sat, and even their clothes also belonged to other times.

A man riding a donkey behind a number of other donkeys approached them from the opposite direction. The donkey the man was riding was small, and his feet nearly touched the ground; he was looking toward the stream and took no notice of the trap as it passed by.

"He leases a small plot of land from me and hasn't paid the rent for three years," Don Pasquale said to the priest. "Whenever we meet he looks the other way."

The trap overtook a cart going down to the valley loaded with sacks of grain. The carter was walking behind the cart; he had applied the brake and was acting as a counterweight.

"A good crop?" Don Paolo asked.

"This is the whole of it," said the carter. "It's all there, and I've got to take it to the landlord before the bailiff comes and seizes it."

The rusty coloration of the valley gradually turned grayish as they approached the Fucino plain. The stubble of recently reaped fields formed yellow patches on the sloping countryside. Tall cones of hay were visible in the distance, with men moving around them like ants. Women passed with babies in their arms, looking like the madonnas in the churches, dark and ill-tempered madonnas taking their lunch to the men who were busy threshing. The heat of the day began to make itself felt.

The horse's head was surrounded by a swarm of little flies. The unpaved road was bad. In a field a party of militiamen were squatting outside a tent, with their rifles between their knees. All the heat of the midday sun seemed to be concentrated on a small donkey standing motionless in the middle of the road. "Look, it's just going to burst," Don Paolo said. Some donkeys loaded with sacks of flour were coming from the Fossa mill. A group of *cafoni* with bundles under their arms were going in the direction of the station. Even in the midday heat people going away wore everything they had, as if they were fugitives, as if they were never going to return.

Don Pasquale spotted a friend standing at the door of a shop, and he stopped the trap and made him get in. He was Don Genesio, who worked at the tax office.

"That's not an occupation that is generally highly thought of," remarked Don Paolo.

"That's true," said Don Genesio. "To the *cafoni*, particularly the most backward ones in the valleys, every official is a big parasitic insect."

"And they're not entirely wrong," said Don Pasquale. "What does Rome do to remedy our plight? It sets up new offices, and then capitalists from other parts infiltrate behind them and act as masters."

"Priests too are considered more or less to be parasites," said Don Genesio. "And that in spite of the fact that people know they can't do without either the one or the other."

"In what sense do they consider us to be parasites?" Don Paolo asked. "Do they put us on a par with flies and fleas? If so, they would have no difficulty in doing without us."

"I can't really say for certain," said Don Genesio. "Perhaps they equate us with the cow horns they put on their houses to protect them against the evil eye, or something of the sort. But there's no cause for alarm, they believe they can't do without us."

Don Pasquale and Don Genesio engaged in an animated conversation about family matters and transfers of property and mortgages, while Don Paolo seemed absorbed in his own thoughts. Every now and then the distant sound of liturgical singing came down from the hills. Parties of pilgrims were coming down the mountain roads and joining forces on the highway.

"They're going to the Holy Martyrs at Celano," Don Genesio said. "They'll be on the road all day."

Don Pasquale dropped the priest in the little square outside the Girasole hotel at Fossa and went off immediately, perhaps to avoid meeting Signora Berenice, who hurried forward to greet the priest and kissed his hand with profound respect.

"There's someone waiting for you in the dining room," she said.

"Where's your daughter?" Don Paolo asked anxiously.

"I'll send for her immediately," Berenice said. "She came back yesterday from Rome, where she found a good job, thank heaven."

"I'm delighted to hear it," said Don Paolo.

In the dining room he found Cardile waiting for him, sitting at a table with half a liter of wine in front of him. They greeted each other cordially.

"I was expecting to see the doctor too," Don Paolo said.

"I'm sorry, but he couldn't come," said Cardile.

"Will he be coming this evening? Or tomorrow morning?"

"No, I don't think he will," Cardile said.

"If he can't come here, I'll go and see him," said Don Paolo. "I need his help to find somewhere else to go. If I stay at Pietrasecca I'll die of boredom. I have an idea I want to put to him."

"Listen," Cardile said, embarrassed. "We can't count on him any longer."

"Why not? Did he tell you that himself?"

"Yes."

"Is he afraid?"

Berenice brought Don Paolo some wine and went back to her kitchen.

"He's in a difficult position," Cardile said. "War to the death has broken out between him and other doctors about the headship of the local hospital. He's not a bad man, but his whole future's at stake. The slightest suspicion would be sufficient to ruin him."

Bianchina appeared at the door of the inn like a sudden luminous apparition because of her white dress.

"Don Paolo," she exclaimed joyfully.

The priest went over toward her.

"How are you?" he said. "How did the trip go?"

"Exactly according to plan," she said.

Her mother, who was setting the tables, looked pleased.

"Tell me about it later," Don Paolo said, pointing to the girl's mother, who might have overheard them.

He did not know what excuse the girl had invented to explain her trip to Rome. She had lost the slightly disreputable, gypsylike look she had had when she came to Pietrasecca, and she seemed better from every point of view. Raising her voice slightly so as to be sure that her mother could hear, she began telling the priest all about the basilicas and museums of Rome. But as soon as her mother vanished into the kitchen she dropped her voice and said, "I've brought back some papers for you, I've hidden them in the garret."

"What are they about?" Don Paolo asked.

"I don't know, they're in a closed envelope," Bianchina said. "Since you trusted me, for once I respected a secret. I'll bring them to your room."

"All right," Don Paolo said. He turned to Cardile and asked him to order lunch for him too. "But no spaghetti, please. I'll be back in a few minutes," he said.

On the second floor Bianchina handed him a big yellow envelope. "Thank you," he said. "We'll see each other later." He went into the room that had been reserved for him and shut the door. His hands trembled as he opened the envelope. This was the first communication from "foreign headquarters" that had reached him since his return to Italy. The envelope contained copies of three voluminous reports as well as a laconic note asking him to give his opinion of the documents immediately. He restricted himself to reading the titles of the reports. These were: "The Leadership Crisis in the Russian Communist Party and the Duties of Fraternal Parties," "The Criminal Complicity with Imperialist Fascism of Oppositional Elements on the Right and on the Left," and "The Solidarity of All the Parties of the International with the Majority of the Russian Communist Party." He put the papers in an attaché case and went down to the dining room. Throughout the meal he hardly spoke.

"Bad news?" Cardile said.

"Very bad indeed," Don Paolo said. "Special service from Byzantium," he added a moment or two later, with a grimace.

"I don't understand," said Cardile.

"Neither do I," Don Paolo said. "But I'm surprised to see that you ordered spaghetti."

"Do you really dislike spaghetti as much as that?" Cardile said. "I don't see why."

The rest of the meal passed in silence. Only at the very end did

Don Paolo say, "Perhaps I'll go back to Rome tomorrow."

"So by and large the time you spent here served some purpose," said Cardile.

"Yes, I think I've gathered a fistful of flies," Don Paolo said. "Where did you leave the trap?"

"Quite near here," Cardile said. "Unfortunately I have to go back at once to avoid arousing suspicion at home. When shall I see you again?"

Don Paolo accompanied him to the trap. When the time came to say good-bye Cardile embraced him. "You know where I live," he said. "Also you know where my hayloft is."

The usual idlers were gathering outside the Girasole hotel, as it was coffee time. There were grown men with week-old beards in shirtsleeves and slippers, with their trousers and collars undone, and youths with long, well-oiled hair. Some of the latter were surrounding an elderly man who was gesticulating with the masklike expressiveness of an aged provincial actor.

"Who's that?" Don Paolo asked Berenice.

"That's our greatest lawyer, Marco Tullio Zabaglia, known as Zabaglione," she replied.

The priest had heard the name before.

"Wasn't he once the socialist leader in these parts?" he asked.

"Yes, but he's a decent person all the same."

Zabaglione noticed the priest standing at the door of the hotel and introduced himself.

"I am the lawyer Zabaglia," he said. "It's an honor to meet you. Signora Berenice has sung your praises to me. I know all about you. Excuse me, but are you from the curia?"

"What curia?" said Don Paolo.

"The episcopal curia. The reason I ask is that I very much want to know whether the clerical speakers for the departure of the conscripts have been chosen yet, and who will be coming here."

"They will be chosen during the next few days," Don Paolo said. "Who they will be? The usual ones, of course."

Don Paolo found himself talking to a man whom as a boy he had always heard talked of with hatred by the landowners and admiration and respect by the poor. Zabaglione's local fame was based on his forensic eloquence. If it was known that he was going to plead at a criminal trial the cobblers' and tailors' and carpenters' shops emptied, the concierges abandoned their lairs, and everyone who could went to listen to him. Many of his famous speeches had become proverbial. During the first years of the dictatorship he had had to make tremendous efforts to cause his rhetorical feats to be forgotten. He had transformed his old Mazzini-style beard, which he had worn since he was a young man, into a Balbo-style goatee; and he shortened and thinned his hair, changed the way he knotted his tie, and tried, though vainly, to lose weight. But if these were the most visible and hence the most painful sacrifices to which the former tribune of the people had had to subject himself, there was no counting the minor, everyday mortifications that he had to endure, such as having to sacrifice his ideas, being careful in what he said about the government, and breaking off relations with his suspect friends. In spite of the undeniable determination he had put into all this, he had not succeeded in completely rehabilitating himself, and he was consistently left out in the cold by the new institutions.

What had caused him the greatest suffering in recent years had been having to be silent on the numerous occasions on which he could have stirred the minds of the people, "raising them to the level of events," as he put it. As a result incidents of historical importance had been utterly wasted, and that was the greatest misfortune that could happen to a civilized country.

"Will you do me the infinite honor of coming to my house for coffee?" Zabaglione said to the priest. "Some friends of mine would very much like to meet you."

"Thank you, but I can't," Don Paolo said. He went back into the hotel, and then abruptly turned and retraced his steps. "It's not as late as I thought," he said to Zabaglione. "I shall be delighted to come with you."

15

To REACH THE LAWYER'S house they first had to make their way through the old part of the town, with its dark and ancient alleys bearing the names of saints and local benefactors and silent little squares enclosed by stone houses blackened by time. Next they came to the new quarter, built on garden-city lines after the earthquake. The streets and avenues were too big for local needs, and the new street names recorded glorious dates in the history of the government party. Heroic slogans, written in charcoal, chalk, tar, or painted in various colors or actually standing out in relief, carved in wood or stone or even forged in bronze, were to be seen on the fronts of houses and on fountains, trees, and garden gates.

"Here we are," the lawyer announced.

Outside his house a party of bricklayers were squatting on the ground, with chunks of bread, knives, and red and green peppers to help it down. They greeted the lawyer cordially. The house was surrounded by a perimeter wall topped by glass fragments. In the garden, kneeling on the gravel, a little man was tidying up around a bed planted with flowers in the three colors of the Italian national flag. A refined and attractive lady with hair curled by tongs appeared on the threshold; this was Zabaglione's wife.

"Kiss the Father's hand and get us some coffee," her husband said.

The lady kissed the priest's hand and withdrew to the kitchen. Three skinny girls, dressed in dark clothing and as pale as plants that had grown up in the dark, appeared in the entrance hall. These were Zabaglione's daughters.

"Kiss the Father's hand and leave us," their father said.

The girls kissed the priest's hand, made a slight curtsy, and disappeared too.

"I send my daughters to mass every Sunday," Zabaglione said. "If you don't believe me, ask Don Angelo, the Fossa priest. What would become of women without the restraint of religion? Their mother goes with them, of course."

A sharp smell of cat urine filled the drawing room. Worn blue curtains hung from the windows, and the walls were almost completely hidden by shelves full of dusty books. An unidentified plaster bust, perhaps of some ancestor, surrounded by numerous yellowish photographs presided over the desk.

"Take a seat," the lawyer said cordially. "I feel I know you, because, as I mentioned before, I have heard you very highly spoken of."

Without too much beating around the bush the priest brought the conversation around to the subject closest to his heart.

"About fifteen years ago," he said, "I was concerned with the organization of Catholic peasants. Our organizations, like the socialist organizations, were subsequently dissolved. Hence we are in a similar situation from one point of view. What is the present state of mind of former members of the socialist leagues in these parts?"

Zabaglione suddenly became reserved and started tidying the papers on his desk. The silence grew painful.

To encourage him to talk, Don Paolo made up a story about the situation in his own diocese. He talked of a serious crisis in wine production and of growing popular restlessness. The corporations were empty shams in which no one believed any longer.

"And what is the situation here?" he said. "What do the former members of the red leagues think? Are they still socialists?"

"They never were," said the lawyer.

"But most districts were in the hands of your red leagues," said the priest. "Or is my memory at fault?"

"Your memory is perfectly correct," said the lawyer. "But the point is that those leagues were not political. The poor peasants, the people whom we call *cafoni* here, joined the league for the sake of company and protection. To them socialism meant getting together. The ideal of the boldest spirits among them was to have work and be able to eat their fill. To have work and be able to sleep peacefully without having to worry about next day. Beside the bearded portrait of Karl Marx in our league premises at Fossa there was a picture of Christ in red clothing as the Redeemer of the poor. On Saturday evenings *cafoni* came and sang "Brothers Arise, Comrades Arise," and on Sunday mornings they went to mass to say amen. The essential task of a socialist leader was writing letters of recommendation. Nowadays the recommendations are written by others; my recommendations have lost their value, because the *cafoni* no longer take any interest in me. That is what the change of régime means to them."

"But weren't there any real socialists?" the priest wanted to know.

"The only socialist in this part of the world was, so to speak, myself," said Zabaglione. "Yes, there were one or two groups that were a little more vigorous, and they suffered severely as a result. The survivors avoid meeting or being seen together."

"But grave events such as happened elsewhere did not happen here," said Don Paolo. "Why was there so much restraint?"

Zabaglione was silent for a moment. "Here, too, shameful things happened," he said. "On the nineteenth of January 1923 — it's a date I cannot forget — a gang of political innovators raided the house of the head of the league at Rivisondoli, and all twenty-two of them raped his wife. It took them from eleven at night till two in the morning. Just an incident. Some of our *cafoni* took refuge at that time in France or in America. Those who remain, as you know, are no longer called *cafoni*, but members of the rural population."

"But oppositional elements must still exist," Don Paolo said. "There must be some who look back with regret to the days when it was possible to meet freely."

"There are not many left here," Zabaglione replied, "but I must say I liked socialism myself. As you are a priest, may I confess one of my weaknesses to you? Well, then, socialist theories left me indifferent, but I liked the socialist movement, just as I liked women. The best speeches I ever made were about socialism . . ."

To the priest's intense annoyance, just when the conversation was becoming more confidential, other visitors arrived. They were Don Genesio, whom the priest had already met, the chief of the municipal guards, and Don Luigi, the pharmacist. The chief of the guards wore a magnificent uniform worthy of a prewar general.

"How many guards do you have under your command?" Don Paolo asked him.

"For the time being only one," he replied. "It's a poor district you see, and it's growing very slowly."

Don Luigi was a handsome man, with mustache and hair in the style of King Umberto.

"Father," he said, "I assure you that I send my wife to mass every Sunday. If you don't believe me, ask the parish priest. In my opinion religion is to women what salt is to pork. It helps to maintain the freshness and the flavor."

Don Genesio had smartened himself up; he too was carefully combed and brilliantined. As was to be expected, he too sent his wife to mass every Sunday.

"The news that the bank has closed its doors has begun to reach its customers in the valley," Don Luigi said. "Just now I met Don Pasquale Colamartini of Pietrasecca, and he seemed to have gone out of his mind. All that was left of his half-witted wife's dowry was deposited in the bank, and he didn't know it was sailing through a minefield."

Zabaglione sighed. "In the old days the failure of a bank would have led to a magnificent lawsuit," he said.

"Have you ever heard of a notorious individual named Pietro Spina?" the commander of the guard asked.

Don Paolo started browsing through an album of picture postcards.

"He belongs to the Spina family of Rocca dei Marsi, and he's a crazy revolutionary," the man went on. "It seems that he went abroad and came back to Italy to commit murders. The police have been looking for him for three months. He was reported to our area, too for it seems that he wanted to set fire to the sheaves of corn on the threshing floors. But today we had news that he was arrested in Rome."

"That's another fine trial that will be wasted," Zabaglione said.

"What do you say?" asked the commander of the guard.

"A little penal servitude will do him good," said Zabaglione.

"Did you say Spina of Rocca dei Marsi?" Don Luigi asked. "I know the family. I was at the university with Don Ignazio Spina, the boy's father. He was a good man, he died in the earthquake. That's another old family that's going to the dogs."

"How is it known that he wanted to set fire to the sheaves of corn?" Don Paolo asked. "Has he been seen in these parts at threshing time?"

"He has never been seen in these parts, either now or in previous years," the commander of the guard said. "He has always done his propaganda in towns. But during this threshing season there have been some red inscriptions on walls saying, LONG LIVE PIETRO SPINA. That has never happened before, and it shows that he must have been in this part of the world."

"Do you think he came here to write his own name on the walls?" the priest asked.

"No, he didn't do it, but his followers did," said the commander of the guard.

"Oh, his followers," Don Paolo blurted out. "Are there any rebellious *cafoni?*"

He was on the point of forgetting to be cautious when one of the lawyer's daughters came in and served the coffee.

"No sugar for me," Don Paolo said.

"No, there are no rebellious *cafoni*, but there's a great deal of unrest among the young," the commander of the guard admitted.

"The things they say under the pretext of corporatism are enough to make one's hair stand on end."

"The new generation is the dangerous one," said Don Luigi. "How shall I put it? It's the generation that presents the accounts. It takes literally the claim that corporatism means the end of capitalism, and it wants the destruction of capitalism."

"That's the cause of all the trouble," said Zabaglione. "Taking theories literally. No régime ought ever to be taken literally, otherwise where would it end? Have you read today's papers? In Russia the death penalty has been reintroduced for adolescents. Why? Probably because they take the Soviet constitution literally. There ought to be a rule that a country's constitution is a matter that concerns only lawyers and the most trustworthy of the older generation, and that it must be strictly ignored by the young."

The commander of the guard agreed.

"As you know," he said, "I was made responsible for the setting up and supervision of the public library. What need there is of a library here I really do not know. Those who want to read books ought to buy them, in my opinion. But the order was given, the books arrived from Rome, and the library was opened. One might have expected the books to have been properly censored, but instead what happened? Juveniles came and asked for the early works of the head of the government and started saying: 'Look, here it says that the Church, the monarchy, and capitalism must be overthrown.' I tried to explain that those books were written for grownups and not for children, and that at their age they ought to be reading fairy tales. But there was no way of putting them off. In the end, with the agreement of higher authority, I had to withdraw those books from circulation and hide them in a locked cupboard."

"Too late," said Don Luigi. "My son tells me that someone on his own initiative copied out extracts from those books, which are circulating among the young. Some of them meet at the Villa delle Stagioni on the other side of the stream to read and discuss them. My son says there's going to be another revolution to carry out what those books say . . ."

"Are they young peasants?" Don Paolo asked.

"No," said the commander of the guard, "they are three or four young students. The authorities know all about them, and when the right time comes they'll put a stop to their little game."

Zabaglione shook his head.

"The greatest of evils is when the young start taking seriously what they read in books," he said.

Don Paolo and the pharmacist left Don Zabaglione's house together.

"You said you knew Pietro Spina's father in his student days," the priest said. "Was he as mad as his son?"

"We met in Naples," Don Luigi said. "We were Republicans, like most students at that time. Giuseppe Mazzini was our god, and Alberto Mario his living prophet. Then we returned to the Marsica, and he married very soon after. He came to see me a few years later, and he had changed out of all recognition. I shall never forget what he said. 'The poetry has finished and the prose has begun,' he said. I'm genuinely sorry about his son."

"Did you also know Don Ignazio's wife?" the priest asked.

"I met her a couple of times with her husband," said Don Luigi. "She was an excellent lady."

"What was it that your friend complained about, then?"

"Certainly not his wife," Don Luigi said, "but all the petty rivalries, jealousies, envies and self-interest of provincial life."

"It seems to me," the priest said with a smile, "that you are justifying the rebellion of that young man, what's his name? I mean young Spina."

"No," Don Luigi said. "His revolt is illusory and is therefore to be deplored. I can feel nothing but compassion for the unfortunate young man. Now the authorities complain that my son Pompeo is inciting his friends and talking about another revolution. I certainly don't approve of what he says, but neither do I want him to be taken seriously and mishandled. Now he's at the poetry stage, I say, and later on he'll have a regular job and he'll marry and settle down and he'll reach the prose stage."

"What would happen if men remained loyal to the ideals of their youth?" Don Paolo asked.

Don Luigi raised his arms to high heaven as if to say that it would be the end of the world.

"The time always comes," he said, "when the young find that the bread and wine of their home have lost their flavor and they look elsewhere for their nourishment. Only the bread and wine of the tavern at the crossroads of the great highways can assuage their hunger and their thirst. But man cannot spend all his life in taverns."

16

THE PRIEST SAW IN THE distance an old gentleman leaning against a streetlamp as if he had been suddenly taken ill, and then he recognized him as Don Pasquale Colamartini. Quickly he said good-bye to the pharmacist and hurried to his assistance. The old man seemed to be semiconscious and hardly recognized the priest until he collapsed in his arms.

"Courage," Don Paolo said to him. "Courage."

The old man was gasping for breath, his pallor was corpselike, and he was unable to speak. The priest helped him, one step at a time, as far as the trap, and it was even more difficult to help him onto the box and put the reins in his trembling hands.

The old man's eyes were full of tears. "It's the end," he managed to say.

"Isn't there anyone here who could go back to Pietrasecca with you?" Don Paolo asked. "Haven't you a friend here who could go with you?"

The old man shook his head. "There's no one, no one," he whimpered.

Don Paolo followed the trap until it disappeared around the

bend in the road. Outside the Girasole hotel a number of people were talking about the failure of the bank.

"As for Don Pasquale," Berenice was saying, "it's a well-deserved chastisement of heaven. He took a half-witted old woman as his second wife so as to be able to lay his hands on her money without having any children, and now he's lost the money, the children by his first wife are leaving home, and he's left with the old idiot."

Don Paolo was about to protest when someone took him by the arm. It was Bianchina.

"Come away," she said. "Don't get upset."

"How can your mother be so spiteful?" said the priest.

"Perhaps she feels it to be her duty because of me," Bianchina said. "Perhaps she feels it to be her duty as a good mother. In any event, that's what the poor thing believes herself to be."

"Good mothers, what a disastrous institution," the priest said. Then he added. "I'm sorry I didn't get on the trap and go back with Don Pasquale. I'm very worried about him."

"Poor old chap," said Bianchina. "But for the fact that he might misinterpret the gesture, I might try to catch him up and help him, and Cristina. But it's impossible to do so much as draw a breath here without being misunderstood. Listen, Don Paolo, you must take me away from here, please, I implore you, I can't go on living here."

"We'll discuss that another time," Don Paolo said. "Do you know the son of Don Luigi, the pharmacist?"

"Pompeo?" said Bianchina. "He's a friend of mine. I'm glad you're interested in him. I've already talked to him about you. If you'll come with me to the Villa delle Stagioni, I'll introduce him to you."

The Villa delle Stagioni was an old country house that had come down in the world and was now a farmhouse. Once upon a time it had been the vacation home of a baron who had subsequently died in Rome, riddled with debts.

On the way Bianchina said, "Alberto Colamartini, Cristina's brother, will probably also be at the villa."

"At Pietrasecca I heard some talk about the two of you," Don Paolo said.

"From Cristina?"

"No, you know how discreet she is."

"I should have preferred it if you had heard it from Cristina," the girl said. "She wouldn't have embroidered any gossip."

"But she too was opposed to the idea of your getting married," Don Paolo said.

"So was I," said Bianchina. "Alberto made the mistake of talking to his father without telling me first. Do you know I wrote to Don Pasquale on that occasion? Didn't he tell you? I told him I hadn't the slightest intention of getting married, but that if in a moment of weariness I ever resigned myself to the idea, I should put his son Alberto last on the list of young men to be made unhappy by me."

"Are you as fond of him as that?" said the priest.

"No," said Bianchina. "But he's too like me."

Meanwhile they had reached the perimeter wall of the villa. The two leaves of the main gate through which one entered the park had been taken from their hinges and were leaning at an angle against the wall. Stinging nettles and poppies grew freely along the main drive. An ivy-covered, Renaissance-style pavilion had been turned into a barn, and the peacock cage was being used as a hen coop. The villa consisted of two wings set at right angles. The ground floor of one wing housed horses and cows, and human beings inhabited the others. The unframed windows of the upper floors created the impression that the latter had either been abandoned or were used to store wheat. There were four empty niches on the facades between two balconies. On the walls, which were cracked and lined with damp, the words LONG LIVE CORPORATIONS WITHOUT BOSSES and LONG LIVE THE SECOND REVOLUTION had been painted in big red letters. In one corner a young man was playing alone with a leather ball.

"Alberto," Bianchina called out. "That's the famous Alberto," she said to the priest.

"Did you come down from Pietrasecca today?" Alberto asked Don Paolo. "How's Cristina?"

He had a boy's slim figure and immature eyes and voice; his face was open and yet stubborn at the same time.

"I'm worried about your father," Don Paolo said to him gravely. "You know about the failure of the bank in which he had all his money? The news may have struck him a fatal blow. I had to help him into his trap just now. I fear the worst may happen."

"The person you call my father threw me out," Alberto said. "He no longer considers me his son."

"If you had seen him just now," Don Paolo said, "I'm sure you would have forgotten all that. He was a poor old man who could no longer stand on his feet, a poor old man who had been struck a fatal blow."

"Won't you go to Pietrasecca at once?" Bianchina said. "I could get you a horse."

"If he were still alive when I got there, the mere sight of me might be fatal to him," Alberto said. "If I arrived too late my grandmother would throw me out. Have you met that terrifying old fury? I'm only sorry for Cristina."

Another young man arrived; he was about the same age as Alberto, but stronger and more robust, and he wore a T-shirt and shorts.

"This is Pompeo," Bianchina said.

"Bianchina has talked to us about you," Pompeo said.

"I think you're made to understand one another," Bianchina said.

"We are probably in agreement on essentials," said Don Paolo. "I'm referring not so much to political theories as to the use to be made of our lives. But it's the kind of agreement that is difficult to describe."

"Why?" said Pompeo.

"We are divided by a few superficial things," said Don Paolo. "In order to understand one another we should not be afraid of discarding commonplaces, symbols, labels."

"We are not afraid," said Pompeo.

"We have reached a point," Don Paolo went on, "at which a sincere Fascist should not be afraid of talking to a communist or an anarchist; and an intellectual should not be afraid of talking to a *cafone*."

"Are you perhaps saying that all divisions between men are artificial, and that struggles are useless?" Pompco asked.

"Certainly not," Don Paolo said. "But some divisions are artificial, deliberately created to conceal real conflicts. There are divided forces that ought to be united, and artificially united forces that ought to be divided. Many present divisions are based on verbal misunderstandings, and many unions are verbal only."

"Let us sit down," said Bianchina. "One thinks better sitting down."

Two wooden benches were fetched from somewhere on the ground floor and put against the wall. At that moment a young peasant arrived and let out the cows. They came out slowly, two by two, and went over to drink at a trough in a corner of the yard. They were thin, black and white, working cows, with big curved horns, and they drank slowly, looking askew at the persons sitting on the benches. The cowman shut the door of the shed and came and sat with the others.

Pompeo was saying, "There was a man who saved the country from ruin and pointed the way to regeneration. His words were plain and left no room for doubt. When he came into power we were surprised that his actions conflicted with his promises. We wondered whether he had betrayed us. Someone came to these parts a few weeks ago and told us what had happened. The man was a prisoner of the bank, he said. That's what he told us. But what did he mean? Is the man really chained up in a bank vault, or was that just a manner of speaking?"

"What do you think?" the cowman asked the priest.

"I cannot say positively whether it's true that the man of whom you speak is really imprisoned in a bank," said Don Paolo. "Some believe it. But in any case it's not a matter of one man only. What is certain, as anyone who keeps his eyes open can see for himself, is that the whole country is a prisoner of high finance."

"So what must be done?" said Bianchina.

"I too believe that a second revolution is necessary," Don Paolo said. "Our country must be freed from imprisonment by the bank. It will be a long and difficult enterprise and full of pitfalls, but the effort will be worthwhile."

Don Paolo spoke calmly and without emphasis, but with a firmness that left no doubt. Bianchina flung her arms around his neck.

"Whoever would have supposed we had a priest with us for the second revolution?" Alberto said with a laugh.

"Don Paolo is not a priest but a saint," Bianchina said. "Didn't I tell you?"

"In every revolution there have been priests who sided with the people," Pompeo said.

"I must tell you that I do not attach much importance to my priestly habit," Don Paolo said.

"It will be more prudent if you remain a priest," said Pompeo.

"Let us respect prudence," the priest said with a laugh.

"But what are we to do immediately?" the cowman asked.

"That is a matter that I should prefer to discuss with Pompeo alone," Don Paolo said.

The priest and the pharmacist's son went off on their own. They left the park, jumped a brook, and took a path flanked by tall hawthorn hedges.

"We belong to different generations, but to the same species of young man, recognizable by the fact that we take seriously the principles proclaimed by our fathers or schoolmasters or priests. Those principles are proclaimed as the foundations of society, but it is easy to see that the actual functioning of that society conflicts with or ignores them. The majority, the skeptics, adapt themselves, the others become revolutionaries."

"The skeptics," Pompeo said, "maintain that the discrepancy between doctrine and reality is an ineluctable fact of life. What is the answer?"

"It may be. But revolutions are also facts of life," Don Paolo said. "Everyone must make his choice."

"You're right," Pompeo said. "What matters is the use one makes of one's life."

The path continued along a row of almond trees between fields of burned stubble. It was very hot. There were some isolated clumps of ripe blackberries, and the two stopped to pick some. Farther on the path came to the highway, which at that time of day was crowded with donkeys, carts, and *cafoni* coming back from work.

"What are we to do?" Pompeo asked.

"Let us think about it together," Don Paolo said. "We'll discuss it again when we've thought about it."

"I'm delighted to have met a priest like you," Pompeo said. "I have friends in all these villages, and I'll introduce them to you."

"It seems to me," Don Paolo said, "that the troublesome illness that forced me to leave my diocese and come here is only now acquiring a meaning."

Before returning to Fossa the two friends separated to avoid being seen together.

The guttural voice of a sound film at the local theater filled the principal street of Fossa, which was crowded with boys, and followed the priest all the way to his room. He was tired but happy. Before undressing he packed his bag in preparation for his departure next morning. He put the papers he had received from Rome the day before in the fireplace and burned them without hesitation. No sooner had he taken his shoes off than he heard a rustle outside the door.

"Can I come in?"

It was Bianchina, cheerful and scented.

"Do you know that Pompeo's enthusiastic about you?" she said.

"I very much hope we shall be friends," Don Paolo said with a smile. "I'm grateful to you for having introduced him to me. To me it was an event."

"Really?" said Bianchina. "Love at first sight?" She looked at him with a smile. "The more I see of you, the more likable and strange I think you," she said.

"You shouldn't observe me too closely," Don Paolo said. "It frightens me and it might force me to do more pretending than is necessary."

"May I confess a suspicion of mine?" Bianchina said. "I'm not at all sure you're a real priest."

"What do you mean by a real priest?"

"A boring person who has the *Eternal Maxims* in the place where his head ought to be. In other words, a person like my uncle, the parish priest of Fossa, and a lot of others besides."

"You're right, I'm very different from that kind of priest," Don Paolo said. "Perhaps the biggest difference is that they believe in a very old God who lives above the clouds sitting on a golden throne, while I believe He's a youth in full possession of His faculties and continually going about the world."

"I prefer your God," Bianchina said with a laugh. "But can you guarantee that He too won't age eventually?"

"No, alas," he said. "How can there be a guarantee against such a disaster? All the young eventually grow old."

"Well, don't let's get depressed about it," said Bianchina. "Let's hope that the youth of the gods will last longer than ours. When are you sending me to Rome again?"

"This time it's my turn," said Don Paolo. "I'm taking the first train tomorrow morning. I've told your mother already."

"And you're leaving me here?" Bianchina protested, her eyes filling with tears.

"You'll stay here to help Pompeo," Don Paolo said. "Contacts with neighboring villages must be restored immediately. Perhaps the time for action will come sooner than we think. I'll leave you some money for expenses."

"Will you be coming back soon?" said Bianchina. "You won't forget me?"

"Stop asking silly questions," said Don Paolo. "You know very well that I often think about you."

"I'll set the alarm clock and come with you to the station," said Bianchina.

"You'll do nothing of the sort, for heaven's sake," said the priest.

"Why not? Are you ashamed of me?"

"It's the sort of thing married couples do, and it would be quite inappropriate in the case of a priest."

17

$\mathcal{I}$N THE TRAIN DON PAOLO quickly discovered how disagreeable it was to travel in disguise, surrounded by strangers who seemed to scrutinize him and seized every opportunity of striking up a conversation. He thought he had extricated himself from this by standing in the corridor with his face to the window, but hurriedly moved away at the first stop when he spotted familiar faces on the platform. He ended up huddling in a corner of the compartment, pulling his hat down over his eyes, and reading his breviary, holding it close to his face as if he were nearsighted. He read at random; psalms, litanies, lessons of martyrs and saints, checking the situation in the compartment after every stop. Fortunately the journey was not a long one.

His priestly clothing enabled him to make his way safe and sound through the close police surveillance at the Termini station. As an additional precaution he fell in with a group of foreign priests who got out of another train. When he reached the square outside he made straight for an underground public bathhouse.

"A bath," he said to the girl cashier.

The girl was called to the telephone and gave him his change without looking at him.

The corridor between the cubicles was long, low, and wet. The old woman attendant who made his cubicle ready for him looked at him with curiosity and said something that Don Paolo did not understand. He gave her a substantial tip. In his suitcase he had a jacket, a beret, and a tie, the minimum required for transforming himself into a layman. He took the bath seriously, for he needed it, and he lingered for a long time in the warm water. Before emerging from the cubicle he spent some time listening to the voices in the corridor, and as soon as he was sure that the old woman was cleaning the inside of another cubicle he made his exit unobserved. He was Pietro Spina again. He went back to the station to check the suitcase into storage, but how strange it felt to be walking in the street without a cassock. He felt everyone was looking at his legs. He started walking quickly, almost running, and several times he looked to make sure his trousers were properly buttoned. Eventually he jumped on a tram that took him to the Lateran quarter. The big sunbaked square between the basilica of San Giovanni and the Scala Santa was full of fairground swings and merry-go-rounds that were being dismantled. They had already been stripped of their nighttime attractions; carpenters were knocking down the timber framework, and tents, pasteboard, lamps, wooden horses, and tin swords were being piled onto trucks. Plaster trophies, a ghost ship painted on a stormy sea, and the fur of a Bengal tiger were lying on the ground.

Pietro crossed the untidy square and made for the cool shadow of the Scala Santa church. A number of women in black were climbing the stairs in the middle of the church on their knees. They stopped on every step, practically collapsed, sighed painfully, and said interminable prayers. Pietro stopped next to a marble group representing Pilate showing the scourged Christ to the people. On the pedestal were the words: HAEC EST HORA VESTRA ET POTESTAS TENEBRARUM. Pietro did not have long to wait. A man who looked like an unemployed worker approached and looked at him with curiosity.

"Excuse me," he said, "but are you the pilgrim from Assisi?"

"Yes," said Pietro. "And who are you?"

"I'm a friend of the driver."

"I have a message for you," said Pietro, handing him a letter.

"Do you know where to go this evening?"

"Yes," Pietro said. "I shall try to manage."

He went beyond the Porta San Giovanni and then continued along the Via Appia Nuova. Then he went down a side street and crossed a district that centered on some film studios and a new church. Beyond it was a huge expanse that was a domain of cats, stray dogs, and down-and-outs. It was cut up by ditches and trenches and also served as a dump for scrap iron, timber, tiles, pipes, and sheets of corrugated iron.

A few months earlier, fleeing from the police, he had taken refuge here in the hut of a former fellow villager of his named Mannaggia Lamorra. As a boy Lamorra had been a servant in the Spina household at Orta, and later he had emigrated in search of fortune. He had sold fizzy drinks in the La Boca quarter of Buenos Aires and worked as an unskilled laborer in a brickworks at St. André, near Marseilles, and after several years he had returned to Italy as poor as when he left it, which made him ashamed to go back to his village. He was now working as a laborer in a pozzolana quarry near Rome. Pietro had no difficulty in finding his wooden hut with its corrugated iron roof. Lamorra, cheerful and ready to oblige, came forward to meet him.

"Back again in these parts, sir?" he said.

"Yes, for a day or two," said Pietro. "Why aren't you at the quarry?"

"It was closed down," Lamorra said. "I shall have to find another job."

"Well, for a day or two you can work for me," Pietro said. He gave him an address, and said, "Go and find out if a bricklayer named Romeo is still living there; and find out if he's working, and if so where, but do so naturally, without arousing any suspicions."

Lamorra went off immediately, and Spina went into the hut, which was as hot as an oven. While waiting he dropped off to sleep.

Lamorra came back late and drunk, but with precise information. Meanwhile, Pietro had made two beds inside the hut, but

Lamorra, seized with sudden respect, refused to enter.

"It's a small hut," he said, "and how can I sleep by my master's side?"

"Don't bore me," Pietro said. "Here you're the master and I'm your guest."

"All the more reason why it's impossible," said Lamorra. "If destiny sends me my master as a guest, how can I possibly sleep beside him?" He looked back on the past without resentment. "Your father was a good man," he said. "When he was in a bad temper he'd beat me, but he was a good man. One Easter he gave me a suckling kid."

Pietro lay on a folding bed inside the hut and Lamorra lay on the ground near the door. The bed was swarming with lice and fleas. Pietro twisted and turned but did not complain, for fear of offending Lamorra. But the latter noticed it.

"There must be insects in the bed," he said. "If you take no notice of them they'll leave you alone."

"Good night," said Pietro.

Under the influence of the wine he had been drinking Lamorra began recalling the happiest times of his life.

"Once," he said, "your father gave me a Tuscan cigar. What a cigar. It was a Saturday night, and I smoked it on Sunday morning in the square outside the church while the women were coming out after high mass. They don't make cigars like that anymore."

Pietro dropped off to sleep while Lamorra went on recalling outstanding events in his long life.

"At Buenos Aires there's a sheet of water that's called Riachuelo," he said. "The Italians, who are called *gringos* and also *tanos*, live around it. Once upon a time there was a fine fat Negress there . . ."

Next morning Pietro got up early and waited at one side of the Porta San Giovanni. It was not long before Romeo appeared but, as he was with other workers, Pietro did not approach him, but followed at a distance. Workers arrived in crowds from all sides. Pietro was affected by the beauty of the scene, the beauty of Rome at dawn, when the streets were crowded with people going to work, talking little, and hurrying. Romeo went down the Via delle Mure Aureliane, left his companions at Porta Metronia, and went on alone along the Via della Ferratella. Pietro followed him, and whistled a song that Romeo used to sing on the island of Ustica when they were both deported there:

> Never a rose without a thorn,
> Never a woman without a kiss . . .

Romeo turned, pretended not to recognize him, and went on to a building site where he was foreman. Bricklayers and their mates were already waiting for him. The building on which they were engaged was still in the early stages. The wall came up to the bricklayers' chests, and it was now necessary to put up scaffolding. Romeo gave the necessary instructions, and when Pietro approached Romeo called out to him at the top of his voice, "Are you the owner of that terrace to be repaired?"

"Yes. I want to find out what it's going to cost."

The two left the toolshed to discuss the question. Pietro drew the plan of a terrace on a piece of paper, and then said, "I've arranged to meet Battipaglia this afternoon. But for the practical work in the Fucino region I need to find a trustworthy person, if possible a worker who comes from that part of the world and is still in contact with his home village. I want him to go back to it straightaway and to work in contact with me. It will be difficult for me to build up anything lasting without a working-class helper."

"You're asking for too much," said Romeo.

"He has got to be found," Pietro insisted. "The prospects in the Fucino are very favorable, but the people available to me are young and inexperienced. I can't do anything without some more trustworthy person. But it must be someone born in the area."

Romeo thought for a moment. "You're asking for too much," he repeated. Then he explained the situation. "The persecution of people from Apulia, the Abruzzi, or Sardinia who were among us has been ferocious. The police, as you know, nearly all come from the country, and you can't imagine their fury when they lay their hands on a subversive who is not a townsman but a countryman. If a townsman is for liberty, they certainly regard it as a grave crime, but if a workingman who is a former *cafone* is against the government it amounts to sacrilege. He's nearly always killed. If he manages to get out of prison alive he's a shadow of his former self, and even his fellow villagers are terrified and avoid him."

"What has become of Chelucci?" Pietro asked.

"They caught him again last month after the distribution of an antiwar leaflet, and now he's in Regina Coeli. He's nearly blind."

"What about Pozzi?"

"There are suspicions about him," Romeo said. "No one can explain why Chelucci was arrested and he was not, as the police found them together. But the police may have done it on purpose, to discredit and isolate him. How can one find out the truth? There are a number of cases resembling his, and they're the saddest."

"Are there no others from the Abruzzi?"

"There used to be Diproia before he married. As soon as he married he refused to have anything more to do with us. Now he goes to mass with his wife every Sunday morning. There was also a student named Luigi Murica, but he has completely vanished. I had several attempts made to find him, because he was an excellent young man, but we never managed to track him down."

"What about the seamstress, Annina?"

"She joined up with Murica."

"I know, that's why I asked."

"She may still be with him. You might try at the place where she used to live. If she has moved, they may know her new address. But what do you want her for? She's not from the Abruzzi."

"She may know where Murica is."

"Come back here tomorrow evening when we knock off," said Romeo. "I'll see what I can do on my own account."

Pietro walked away down the Via della Navicella and the Via Claudia, intending to make for the center of the city for the sake of seeing it again, but its beauty had already faded. No one was to be seen in the streets but men in uniform, civil servants, priests, and nuns. It was an entirely different place. But between ten and eleven o'clock, when the big parasites, the government bosses, the higher civil servants, the monsignors in their violet hose began to appear, he once more found Rome nauseating. He turned down the Via Labicana and made for the outskirts again, not before buying a tin of insecticide.

"What's it for?" Lamorra asked him.

Pietro explained.

"If you show the insects you think them so important," Lamorra said, "it'll turn their heads and they'll never go away."

"Would you be willing to go back to Orta?" Pietro asked him. "I'd give you a confidential little job."

"I'd go anywhere except Orta," Lamorra replied. "I'd go back to Orta only if I'd made money and could buy a house and land. But as it is . . ."

"But you wouldn't do anywhere else, you see," Pietro tried to explain. "If you went to Orta I'd bear all the expenses, of course. Think about it."

"I'm not going back to Orta," Lamorra said, putting an end to the discussion.

In the afternoon Pietro went to meet Battipaglia, the interregional secretary of the party. The appointment was in a little church on the Aventine.

When Pietro got there his comrade was there already, pretending to read a notice on the wall near the door. Pietro had not seen him for many years. He was rather bent and his hair had turned gray. Prison had aged him. To make him aware of his presence Pietro stopped for a moment beside him, standing right up against the wall to read the notice as if he were nearsighted. Then he went into the church. He had not been inside it before. Two rows of arches divided it into three. The arches rested on trunks of ancient columns of different sizes that rose from the floor without pedestals and with rough and differently decorated capitals. The stone floor was almost completely covered with memorial tablets. At the other end of the church the big altar looked like a simple stone tomb with a wooden crucifix, painted black, and four candlesticks. The church was half dark and deserted. There were only two women kneeling in front of the lamp lit at the altar of the

Sacrament. Pietro waited by the door, near the font. Battipaglia came in and walked slowly around the church. Eventually he came and talked to Pietro.

"I've had money waiting for you for a month," he said in an undertone. "I also have a new passport for you. How are you?"

"I've no use for the passport at present," Pietro said. "I'm not going abroad again."

"That's your business," said Battipaglia. "It's no affair of mine, as you know, it came straight from headquarters abroad. I'll send it to you through Fenicottero. What you do with it is entirely up to you. Who's the person you sent recently from Fossa with your news?"

"Her name's Bianchina, she's the daughter of a hotel keeper."

"Is she a comrade? How long has she been in the movement?"

"She's not a comrade, but she can be trusted. She doesn't know who I am or what the purpose of her trip was."

"Isn't that risky?"

"Even if she found out who I am she wouldn't give me away."

"That's your affair, it's no business of mine to lecture you. Is she your lover?"

"No."

"That's your business, it has nothing to do with me, as you know. The girl talked about a revolutionary priest said to be in your mountains, one Don Paolo, do you know him?"

"No," said Pietro.

"You ought to get hold of him, he might be useful. Your report has been forwarded to headquarters abroad."

The sacristan had come in through the little sacristy door and had lit two candles on the big altar. A priest in sacred vestments emerged from the sacristy, announced by the ringing of a bell. He stopped and prayed in front of the first step of the altar. The sound of footsteps outside the church door heralded the arrival of other worshipers. These were a number of nuns. They dipped their fingers in the holy water, made the sign of the cross, and hurried toward the altar.

"Were you able to do any work?" Battipaglia asked.

"It's difficult to do anything with the *cafoni*," said Pietro.

"They're more open to Gioacchino da Fiore than to Gramsci. Meridionalism is a bourgeois utopia. But I discussed all that in my report."

"Because they had no direct contact with you," Battipaglia said in an undertone, "headquarters abroad have asked me to press you for a reply to their request for comment on their latest political decision. As you know, it's a formality more than anything else."

"I've no head for formalities, as you know," said Pietro.

"Nobody of course believes you have the slightest hesitation about declaring your solidarity with the majority of the Russian Communist Party," Battipaglia said. "You're an old comrade, a rather strange one, but everyone has a high opinion of you."

"To tell you the truth," Pietro said, "I know nothing about the issue. If I find it so difficult to understand, I don't say my native region, but my native village, how do you expect me to have an opinion on Russian agricultural policy, to disapprove of some views and approve of others? It wouldn't be serious, would it?"

"Did Bianchina bring you the three reports?"

"Yes, but I haven't read them yet."

"When will you read them? Headquarters insist on having your reply as soon as possible."

"I don't know when I shall be able to read all that stuff," Pietro said. "I don't even know if I'm in a position to understand and form a genuine opinion about it. I've other things on my mind, I mean the situation here." Then, making an effort, he went on, "I don't want to pretend, I'll tell you the truth, I burned those papers. Bringing them with me would have meant taking a useless risk. And besides, frankly, they don't interest me."

"What you have done is very serious," Battipaglia said. "Do you realize that?"

"What it boils down to," Pietro said, "is that I do not feel able to form opinions on matters outside my experience. I cannot stoop to any kind of conformity, to approving or condemning things with my eyes shut."

"How dare you describe our condemnation of Bukharin and other traitors as conformity? Are you mad?"

"Always declaring yourself to be on the side of the majority is conformity," said Pietro. "Don't you think so? You backed Bukharin as long as he was with the majority, and you would still be backing him if the majority supported him now. How can we hope to destroy Fascist subservience if we abandon the critical spirit? Try to answer me that."

"Do you claim that Bukharin was not a traitor?"

"I genuinely don't know," said Pietro. "All I know is that now he's in the minority. I also know that it's for that reason alone that you dare oppose him. Answer my question if you can: would you be against him if the majority were for him?"

"Your cynicism is beginning to pass all bounds," said Battipaglia, barely restraining his indignation.

"You haven't answered my question. Give me an honest answer if you can."

"If it depended on me, I should expel you from the party immediately."

Battipaglia was trembling with indignation, but the place they were in imposed restraint. After a long silence he went away without saying good-bye. Pietro stayed where he was, leaning with his back against the font. The service continued. The faint light of the candles made the gold of the monstrance in the middle of the altar glitter and created a luminous halo around the priest's white hair. Then the service came to an end, and the small congregation moved toward the exit. When one of the nuns dipped her fingers in the holy water to make the sign of the cross she was struck by Pietro's appearance. She stopped beside him and looked at him for a moment. "Don't despair," she murmured with a smile.

"What do you want?" said Pietro.

"Courage," she repeated. "Refuse to despair."

"Who are you?" said Pietro. "What do you want of me?"

"Courage," the nun said. "The Lord tries no one beyond his strength. Can't you pray?"

"No."

"I shall pray for you. Do you believe in God?"

"No."

"I shall pray to Him for you. He is the Father of all, even of those who don't believe in Him."

The nun hurried away to rejoin her companions. After a while Pietro left the church too.

Evening had fallen. He had been intending to go to the movies, but gave up the idea. His fellow villager Lamorra was waiting for him outside his hut, where he had prepared something to eat. Pietro's appearance alarmed him.

"What's the matter with you?" he asked. "Has something serious happened?"

"Yes," said Pietro in a voice that discouraged further questions.

"Aren't you going to eat?"

"No."

That night Pietro did not sleep and Lamorra noticed it.

"May one ask what happened to you?" he asked. "Is it a disappointment in love?"

"Yes," said Pietro. "Leave me in peace."

"Has a woman let you down?"

"Yes."

"One shouldn't love too much," Lamorra said. "Your father was a passionate man too."

Next morning Pietro was late for his appointment with Romeo. His face was like an old man's and his eyes were swollen. The building site was deserted. Romeo was waiting for him behind the toolshed, and a boy was with him. He obviously knew nothing about the previous day's clash with Battipaglia.

"This is Fenicottero," Romeo said.

"Money and a Czechoslovak passport for you arrived from foreign headquarters a month ago," the boy said.

"How do you know it's a Czechoslovak passport?"

"I opened the envelope."

"That was wrong of you," Pietro said.

"We distributed the antiwar leaflet at San Lorenzo yesterday," the boy said to change the subject.

"What does the leaflet say?"

"I haven't had time to read it," the boy answered.

"You helped distributing leaflets?" Romeo asked.

"Yes, I did. There are few of us left, and we all have to do a bit of everything."

At this Romeo lost his temper.

"What?" he said. "Your job is liaison and you do propaganda too? Don't you know that every time the two things have been combined the whole thing has gone up in smoke?"

The boy was embarrassed and confused.

"What trade have you learned?" Romeo asked him.

"A bit of everything," the boy replied. "I don't have a real trade."

"That's the trouble," said the builder's foreman. "A man who doesn't have a proper trade can't do conspiratorial work. A builder who puts up scaffolding first of all puts up the spars and then connects them with the horizontals and then fixes them to the walls with crosspieces. A builder knows that a spar can't be used as a crosspiece. And it's like that in every trade. The conspiratorial trade has its rules too, and those who don't know them and don't respect them pay for it with years of imprisonment and sometimes with their lives."

Romeo's indignation was not yet exhausted. He too was now a partisan.

"I haven't the slightest desire to go back to prison because of you," he went on. "From today you will no longer do liaison work. Do you understand? Don't show yourself in this neighborhood again. If we meet you'll pretend not to know me."

The boy left with his tail between his legs.

Romeo gave Pietro the addresses of some people from the Abruzzi who had left the cells some years previously.

"You should be the best person to try to bring them back into the movement," he said. "But is it prudent? Decide for yourself."

"That's not the difficulty," Pietro said. He was going to say something else, but changed his mind. "Perhaps we'll discuss it another time," he said.

18

$\mathcal{P}$IETRO FOLLOWED UP the clues given him by Romeo and tracked down an old friend, a violinist named Uliva. They had not met for years, since they were both members of a communist students' cell, and all Pietro knew about him was that he too had spent several months in prison. After that, like so many others, he had kept away. He lived with his wife on the fourth floor of a house in the Via Panisperna in the Viminal quarter.

A young woman in a very obvious state of advanced pregnancy showed Pietro to his room. Her eyes were red and swollen as if she had been weeping the whole morning. Uliva received his old friend with indifference, showing neither pleasure nor surprise. He was a lean, skinny little hunchback, and the dirty black suit he was wearing gave him a sad, neglected appearance. Even after Pietro came in he remained lying on a couch, smoking, and spitting on the ground. The spittle was aimed at a washbasin but more often than not missed it, for yellow stains were to be seen all over the place, on the fringes of the rug, the desk, and the walls. The room was untidy, smelly, and in semidarkness.

"It's a long time since we saw each other," said Pietro. "I didn't expect to find you in this state."

Uliva replied with a short, ironic laugh. "Did you suppose I'd become a civil servant? Or an officer in the militia? Or a *commendatore*?"

"Is there no other choice?"

"I don't think so."

"It's sufficient to look around you," said Pietro. "Perhaps you're living too isolated a life. There are those who resist, who struggle."

"That's an illusion," said Uliva. "Do you remember our students' cell? Those who didn't die of hunger or in prison are even worse off."

"The worst thing that can happen to anyone is to surrender. One can accept the challenge; resist, struggle against it."

"For how long?"

"Ten years, twenty years, two hundred years, for all eternity. There's no life without struggle."

"Do you think that ventriloquism is struggle?" said Uliva. "What's the point of inflating yourself with empty phrases? I've lost my taste for that sort of thing, I tell you. After spending ten months in prison for shouting 'long live liberty' in the Piazza Venezia I spent some time sleeping in winter in public rooming houses and in summer under the bridges of the Tiber or the colonnades of the Esedra or on the steps of churches, with my jacket rolled up under my head as a pillow. Every now and then there was the nuisance of the night patrol coming and asking me who I was and what my job was and what I lived on. You should have seen them laugh when for lack of anything else I showed them my academic diplomas, my degrees from Santa Cecilia's academy of music. I actually tried going back and living in my native village in the province of Chieti, but I had to make a getaway at night. It was my relatives who imposed banishment on me. 'You're our ruin, our disgrace,' they said."

"All the same we mustn't capitulate," said Pietro. "We must remain united with the workers' cells."

"Don't talk to me about that," said Uliva. "I used to know some printers. They have all come to terms with the situation. The working masses have been either nationalized or brought to heel.

Even hunger has been bureaucratized. Official hunger entitles you to the dole and state soup; all that private hunger gives you is the right to throw yourself in the Tiber."

"Don't let yourself be taken in by appearances," said Pietro. "The strength of the dictatorship is in its muscles, not its heart."

"There you're right," said Uliva. "There's something corpse-like about it. For a long time it has no longer been a movement, not even a Vendéean movement, but merely a bureaucracy. But what does the opposition amount to? What are you? A bureaucracy in embryo. You too aspire to totalitarian power in the name of different ideas, which simply means in the name of different words and on behalf of different interests. If you win, which is a misfortune that will probably happen to you, we subjects will merely exchange one tyranny for another."

"You're living on figments of your imagination," said Pietro. "How can you condemn the future?"

"Our future is the past of other countries," Uliva replied. "All right, we shall have technical and economic changes, that I don't deny. Just as we now have state railways, state quinine, salt, matches, and tobacco, so we shall have state bread, shoes, shirts, and pants, and state potatoes and fresh peas. Will that be technical progress? Certainly, but it will merely serve as a basis for an obligatory official doctrine, a totalitarian orthodoxy that will use every possible means, from the movies to terrorism, to crush heresy and terrorize over individual thought. The present black inquisition will be succeeded by a red inquisition, the present censorship by a red censorship. The present deportations will be succeeded by red deportations, the preferred victims of which will be dissident revolutionaries. Just as the present bureaucracy identifies itself with patriotism and eliminates all its opponents, denouncing them as being in foreign pay, so will your future bureaucracy identify itself with labor and socialism and persecute everyone who goes on thinking with his own brain as a hired agent of the industrialists and landlords."

"Uliva, you're raving," Pietro exclaimed. "You have been one of us, you know us, you know that that is not our ideal."

"It's not your ideal," said Uliva, "but it's your destiny. There's no evading it."

"Destiny is an invention of the weak and the resigned," said Pietro.

Uliva made a gesture as if to indicate that further discussion was not worthwhile. But he added, "You're intelligent, but cowardly. You don't understand because you don't want to understand. You're afraid of the truth."

Pietro rose to leave. From the door he said to Uliva, who remained impassively on the couch, "There's nothing in my life that entitles you to insult me."

"Go away and don't come back," Uliva said. "I have nothing to say to an employee of the party."

Pietro had already opened the door to leave, but closed it and went back and sat at the foot of the couch on which Uliva was lying. "I shan't go away until you have explained to me why you have become like this," he said. "What happened to you that changed you to this extent? Was it prison, unemployment, hunger?"

"In my privations I studied and tried to find at least a promise of liberation," Uliva said. "I did not find it. For a long time I was tormented by the question of why all revolutions, all of them without exception, began as liberation movements and ended as tyrannies. Why has no revolution ever escaped that fate?"

"Even if that were true," Pietro said, "it would be necessary to draw a conclusion different from yours. All other revolutions have gone astray, one would have to say, but we shall make one that will remain faithful to itself."

"Illusions, illusions," said Uliva. "You haven't won yet, you are still a conspiratorial movement, and you're rotten already. The regenerative ardor that filled us when we were in the students' cell has already become an ideology, a tissue of fixed ideas, a spiderweb. That shows that there's no escape for you either. And, mind you, you're still only at the beginning of the descending parabola. Perhaps it's not your fault," Uliva went on, "but that of the mechanism in which you're caught up. To propagate itself every new idea is crystallized into formulas; to maintain itself it entrusts itself

to a carefully recruited body of interpreters, who may sometimes
actually be appropriately paid but in any event are subject to a
higher authority charged with resolving doubts and suppressing
deviations. Thus every new idea invariably ends up becoming a
fixed idea, immobile and out of date. When it becomes official
state doctrine there's no more escape. Under an orthodox totalitarian régime a carpenter or a farm laborer may perhaps manage
to settle down, eat, digest, produce a family in peace, and mind
his own business. But for an intellectual there's no way out. He
must either stoop and enter the dominant clergy or resign himself
to going hungry and being eliminated at the first opportunity."

Pietro had a fit of anger. He took Uliva by the lapels of his
jacket and shouted in his face, "But why must that be our destiny?
Why can there be no way out? Are we chickens shut up in a hen
coop? Why condemn a régime that doesn't yet exist and that we
want to create in the image of man?"

"Don't shout," Uliva calmly replied. "Don't play the propagandist here with me. You have understood very well what I have said,
but you pretend not to understand because you're afraid of the
consequences."

"Rubbish," said Pietro.

"Listen," said Uliva, "when we were in the students' cell I
watched you a great deal. I then discovered you were a revolutionary out of fear. You forced yourself to believe in progress, you
forced yourself to be an optimist, you forced yourself to believe in
the freedom of the will only because the opposite terrified you.
And you've remained the same."

Pietro made Uliva a small concession. "It's true," he said, "that
if I did not believe in the liberty of man, or at any rate in the possibility of the liberty of man, I should be afraid of life."

"I've ceased to believe in progress and I'm not afraid of life,"
said Uliva.

"How were you able to resign yourself? It's frightening," said
Pietro.

"I'm not in the least resigned," said Uliva. "I'm not afraid of
life, but I'm still less afraid of death. In the face of this pseudolife

stifled by pitiless laws the only weapon left to man's free choice is antilife, the destruction of life itself."

"I'm afraid I understand," said Pietro.

He had understood. An expression of great sadness appeared on his face. There was no point in going on with the discussion.

The young woman who had opened the door to Pietro came in to fetch something. Uliva waited for her to go out again and then went on, "I have a certain respect for you, in spite of everything. For many years I've seen you engaged in a kind of chivalrous contest with life or, if you prefer it, with the creator; the struggle of the created to overcome its own limitations. All that, and I say so without irony, is very fine, but it requires a naïveté that I lack."

"Man really exists only in struggle against his own limitations," said Pietro.

"You once told me about a secret dream of yours," said Uliva. "You expressed it in country terms. You wanted to turn the Fucino plain into a soviet and appoint Jesus president of the soviet. That would not be a bad idea at all if the son of the carpenter of Nazareth were still really living on this earth and could hold that office in person. But, if He were appointed and His absence duly noted, would you not be obliged to appoint a substitute? Now, we in this country know very well how the representatives of Jesus begin and how they end. Oh, how well we know it. The poor blacks newly converted by the missions do not yet know it, but we know it, and we cannot pretend that we do not know it. What became of your historicism, Pietro?"

"I gave it up," said Spina. "If Jesus ever lived, He is still alive now."

Uliva smiled. "You're incorrigible," he said. "You have a prodigious capacity for self-deception. I'm incapable of it."

Then he went on, "Listen to me. My father died in Pescara at the age of forty. He died of drink. He left me nothing but debts to pay off. One evening a few weeks before he died he sent for me and told me the story of his life, the story of his failure. He began by telling me about his father's, that is, my grandfather's death. 'I die poor and disappointed,' he told my father, 'but I place all my hopes in you; may you get from life what I failed to get.' When he felt his own end approaching, my father told me that he could only repeat what my grandfather had said to him. 'I too, my son, am dying poor and disappointed, but you are an artist, and I hope and pray that you may get from life all that I vainly hoped for.' So it goes on from generation to generation, illusions are passed on together with debts. I'm now thirty-five, and I've reached the same point as my grandfather and my father. I'm already a conscious failure, and my wife is expecting a baby. But I lack the folly to believe that the unborn child will get from life what I have failed to get. Either he'll die of hunger or he'll die in slavery, which is worse."

Pietro rose to leave. "I don't know whether I shall come back," he said. "But if you or your wife have need of me . . ."

"Don't bother," said Uliva. "We shan't be needing anyone."

In the Via Panisperna an uproar was being made by about fifty young men wearing students' caps who were carrying a big tri-color flag and a board with the words HURRAH FOR THE WAR. They had an escort of a few policemen, and shouted and yelled and called out to passersby and sang a new song that said: "We'll make hairbrushes of the Negus's beard." People at shop doors and windows looked on curiously and made no comment. In the Via dei Serpenti Pietro came across another party of students with a similar flag and a similar board, singing the same bootblacks' song and with a similar police escort. Among the throng hurrying home or going about their business Pietro recognized the uncertain footsteps of the unemployed, of those who had nowhere to go and ended up following in the students' wake.

Near the Colosseum Pietro stopped to watch some young Avanguardisti exercising with guns and machine guns. Boys of from fifteen to seventeen were being instructed in how the various parts of these weapons fitted together, how to strip and reassemble them, and how to pass from marching order to readiness for action. They were serious and attentive, like little men, and carried out the drill with great speed. Pietro's appearance attracted the attention of an old woman.

"Why are you weeping?" she said to him. "Are you feeling ill?"

Pietro nodded as if to say yes and took to his heels. He spent the whole afternoon aimlessly wandering about. He was obviously a soul in torment.

His appointment with Romeo was in a tavern in the Via degli Ernici in the Tiburtine quarter, next to the Acqua Marcia viaduct and the railway. The rust of the railway sidings and the smoke of the locomotives gave their color to the whole street, and the walls were impregnated with the smell of coal and heavy oil. The tavern was nearly empty when Pietro walked in. In one corner a *carabiniere* was eating spaghetti and meat sauce with a mournful and ferocious air, as if he were making a meal of an anarchist's guts. The floor was thickly covered with sawdust to receive the spittle. The only picture on the wall was of a majestic transatlantic liner crossing the ocean at night under a full moon with its cabins illuminated. Later porters and laborers turned up, ordered their half liters, and drank them, casting oblique glances at the liner so that the *carabiniere* should not notice them secretly embarking for America. Then they paid for their wine, disembarked, spat on the ground, and went off home in a bad temper.

Romeo turned up late, drank a quarter of a liter at the counter, coughed, and left again without approaching Pietro. Pietro went out after him and followed him at a distance, and had some difficulty in doing so because Romeo kept changing direction at every corner, obviously to make sure he was not being trailed. Eventually he slowed down in the Vicolo della Ranocchia and let Pietro catch up with him.

"Have you heard about the explosion in the Via Panisperna?" he asked.

Pietro had not.

"Uliva's flat was blown up, burying him and his wife and the tenants on the floor below. The press has been ordered to say nothing about it, but it happened in the middle of the city and the news spread in a flash. Uliva seems to have been preparing to blow up the church of Santa Maria degli Angeli in a few days' time during a service to be attended by the whole government. A fireman friend of ours who helped clear away the rubble told us that a plan of the church with a great many technical notes was found among Uliva's papers."

"I went to see him this morning," Pietro said. "I had the impression he was preparing a big funeral."

"If the concierge saw you going in, he'll certainly remember you," Romeo said. "You have a face that isn't easily forgotten. That's another reason for you to leave."

In the Piazzale Tiburtino a big crowd had gathered around groups of soldiers, militia, and *carabinieri*.

Pietro asked some bystanders what was happening.

"Mobilization is being announced tomorrow," someone said. "The new war in Africa begins tomorrow."

Tomorrow? There had been talk about it for some time, but just because there had been so much talk about it the idea had become improbable and strange. But now the improbable was going to happen, in fact it was already there, behind the scenes, and tomorrow it would make its entry on the stage.

"I forgot to tell you that that liaison lad has been arrested," Romeo said. "They'll certainly beat him to get him to talk. In these cases the wisest course is to expect the worst, so be on your guard. Here's the money that came for you a month ago, and the passport. We must avoid seeing each other for a few weeks."

"I've no more time to waste," Pietro said firmly. "I've been back in Italy for six months, I've done nothing yet, and I'm tired of waiting. I need a reliable colleague to work with me in the Marsica."

"An illegal organization is a web that's continually made and unmade," Romeo said. "You know that better than I do, and it's a web that costs blood and patience. Our organization in Rome has been smashed and rebuilt from the ground up several times. How much work is required to reestablish contacts, and what a short time they often last. I've seen many friends go to prison, and others have disappeared without a trace. Some we had to get rid of because they became suspect. But we have to stick to it."

"Very well," Pietro said. "I'll manage by myself."

"There's also something else," Romeo said with obvious embarrassment.

"What?"

"I've seen Battipaglia, the interregional organizer."

"What did he tell you?"

"He told me you might be expelled from the party."

"It doesn't depend on him."

"If that were to happen, I should be very sorry," Romeo said. "Do everything possible to avoid it. Don't be obstinate."

"Let them leave me in peace," said Pietro. "Don't let them ask me for the impossible. I can't sacrifice for the party's sake the reasons for which I joined it."

Romeo insisted. "Breaking with the party means abandoning the idea behind it."

"That's not true," Pietro said. "It would be like putting the Church before Christ."

"All right," Romeo said. "I know your way of thinking. But don't be obstinate."

The two firmly shook hands and went off in opposite directions.

19

BEFORE RETURNING TO the Marsica Pietro wanted to try again to find at least one experienced comrade to take back with him to help him. He wanted to avoid the risk of leaving Pompeo and his young friends to their own devices in the event of his being caught. So he told Lamorra that he would be staying in his hut for a few days longer. His former fellow villager took advantage of this to make a proposal of his own.

"I can't go back to Orta," he said. "I've already told you why. It's the only place in the world in which I refuse to set foot. But you're not going to Orta either. So why don't you take me with you? I'm sick and tired of digging pozzolana."

"What would you do with me?" Pietro asked.

"I'd do anything for you, even the humblest jobs," Lamorra said. "I'd carry your bags. Do you shave yourself? I'd take letters to your girl. And I'd hardly cost you anything. I'd eat your leftovers."

"You're crazy," Pietro said. "I can't stand servants."

Lamorra was disappointed. "Don't imagine I'd say this to anyone else," he said. "You're my master's son, and I don't say this to criticize you, but it seems to me that you're still a child."

"Don't waste time in idle chatter, but try to find the person I told you about," Pietro said.

Lamorra did not find Murica, but Annina, his girl, who had moved to a big council building in the Via della Lungaretta in Trastevere that exuded poverty and filth. Pietro went there immediately. He found the girl bent over her sewing machine in a small untidy room that was both workroom and bedroom.

"Romeo will have mentioned me to you," Pietro said. "I've come to ask for news of him."

The girl received her importunate visitor with obvious disappointment. She was still very young with an elfin-shaped face and regular features, and in spite of her hostile expression her eyes were beautiful. Pietro, embarrassed, stood by the door until she offered him a chair. When he sat beside her Annina looked at him with a smile veiled with sadness.

"Do you know there's a strange resemblance between you and the person you're looking for?" she said. "Even the arrogant way in which you call on people resembles his. Also he was born at Rocca dei Marsi, which is not far from where you were born, I think. He talked to me about it once."

"It's about five miles away," Pietro said. "Where is he now? I need to see him urgently."

"He often used to talk to me about you," Annina said. "He was sorry he did not know you personally. But the life of the cells was very isolated, it was difficult for comrades to get to know one another."

"How long is it since you saw him?"

"Nearly a year. Several people have come and asked for him."

"Might he be in prison?"

"No," the girl said with confidence. "He was picked up with others in the May Day roundup last year and was in prison for a couple of months. When he came out he swore he would kill himself rather than go back."

The sound of footsteps came from the stairs outside. A little girl came in, handed in a dress to be repaired, and went away again.

"Had you known him for a long time?" Pietro asked.

"Why reopen old wounds?" Annina replied.

"Forgive me," Pietro said. "I didn't ask out of curiosity. If you knew me better you would know that I deserve your confidence."

"I know that," Annina said.

She tidied up the table and fiddled with her sewing machine.

"We met in the cell about three years ago and liked each other immediately," the girl said, blushing. "It was not a flirtation, but a real love affair. I was still living at home at that time, and my mother kept scolding me for forgetting everything else and taking no interest in anything but him. He was my first young man, and to me he was son, brother, and lover all at the same time. He was very fond of me too."

The girl rose, and turned her back to her visitor to hide her tears. When she sat down again her eyes were red.

"I don't want to revive sad memories," Pietro said.

"It's not a matter of reviving forgotten memories, alas," said Annina, "but of a living, painful reality that is always before my eyes and dominates my life."

"Conspiratorial life is hard," Pietro said. "To hold out and not allow ourselves to be crushed we have to be pitiless."

"But our affair did not in the least diminish our activity in the cell," the girl said. "On the contrary, we were more active because of it. We organized outings and reading evenings, and sought out social novels to discuss and comment on. To give more time to the party we even renounced getting married, setting up a home, and having children."

"How did the idyll end?" Pietro asked. "Forgive me, but what most surprises me is that the break was so complete, both personal and political. I heard so much about you, and, if you allow me to say so, I always wanted to meet you. But the rules of conspiratorial life forbade it. You were talked about as a person in whom we could have complete confidence and actually with admiration. Everyone said you were a real comrade. And now? Don't you miss taking part in the struggle? I don't understand you. How can you resign yourself to ordinary life?"

Annina fell silent. Eventually she seemed to make up her

mind. "There are some things that it's difficult to talk about," she said. "But perhaps it's my duty to tell the story, and perhaps you are the best person to whom to tell it. You come from the same part of the world, you're like him, you probably think the same way as he does, and perhaps you have the same faults. Also you represent the party."

The girl had another fit of weeping and then, with difficulty, she began her story.

"When he was arrested last year," she said, "he was beaten a great deal, but what had a greater effect on him than the beating was the moral maltreatment, the slaps and the spitting. He came out of Regina Coeli upset and depressed. I attributed this to physical weakness, but with the passing of the weeks his fear of the police and the possibility of another arrest did not diminish. 'Rather than go back to prison I'll kill myself,' he kept telling me. The police had warned him to break off his old contacts and not to see me again, as I too was politically suspect. So when he was with me he was always ill at ease. The sound of a truck would make him grow pale. We no longer knew where to meet. He still loved me, he wanted to be with me a great deal, he was very jealous if he did not see me every day, but when he was with me he felt he was in danger, and as a result he almost hated me. The old carefree spontaneity had gone, and every meeting became a torment. 'The police may catch me at any moment,' he used to say. Also there were all sorts of physical effects; he had heart trouble, his digestion was irregular, and he had attacks of asthma. A policeman often came to see me to ask about him. He was from Apulia and had red hair and was particularly hateful, and he would come at the most improbable times, preferably at night when I was in bed. I soon realized that it was not so much Luigi as me that he was after, and several times I had to defend myself by force; and eventually I persuaded a girl cousin of mine to come and stay with me so that I should feel safer.

"On Christmas Day last year," Annina went on, "I had lunch with Luigi in a restaurant outside the Porta San Paolo. That day he was in an unusually calm, cheerful, almost carefree mood, just as in the old days. We hadn't been alone together for some time, so I asked him to come back with me to the small flat I then had in the Via del Governo Vecchio to spend the afternoon together. On the way we bought flowers, fruit, sweets, and a bottle of Marsala. He was helping me to arrange the flowers in a vase when there was a knock at the door, which we had locked. 'Who is it?' I called out. It was the police. Luigi started trembling, and to avoid collapsing he sat on a chair; he signaled to me not to open the door. But the knocking grew more and more insistent. 'I shan't go back to prison,' he muttered. 'I'll throw myself out of the window, but I shan't go back to prison.' Meanwhile the police had nearly broken down the door. Now, at that flat there was a small balcony from which it was easy to climb up on the roof, so I signed to Luigi to go and hide there. As soon as he disappeared I opened the door and two policemen came in, the man from Apulia and another, younger one whom I didn't know. It was no good denying it, they knew Luigi was with me, they had seen us coming back together. They looked under the bed and in the wardrobe. The man from Apulia said that if he wasn't in the room he must be on the roof. I barred the way to the balcony. 'Don't arrest him,' I said. 'Arrest me, but not him.' They tried to move me out of the way by force, but I fought them with my fists and kicked and bit. 'You won't arrest him,' I kept telling them. 'All right, but on one condition,' the policeman from Apulia replied. 'On any condition,' I said. I would have gladly given my life to save Luigi from prison, but the two policemen wanted something else. I don't know how long they stayed. I only remember much later hearing Luigi's voice behind the half-closed shutters of the balcony. 'Have they gone?' he said. He came into the room. 'What are you doing, are you asleep?' he said. He went over to the window and looked out to see whether the house was being watched. 'There's no one in the street,' he said with satisfaction. He picked up a biscuit from the table and ate it. He went to the door and listened, to make sure there was no one on the stairs. Then he came toward me. 'What are you doing, are you asleep?' he said again. I had a sheet over me, and he removed it. He saw that I was naked, and on the sheet he saw traces of the two men. He made a grimace of disgust. 'Whore,' he shouted at me, and spat on the bed and flung to the ground all the things that we had bought to celebrate Christmas. He upset the sewing machine, flung the bottle of Marsala at the big mirror and smashed it, and walked out, slamming the door behind him. I did nothing and I said nothing. What had happened had happened."

That was the end of Annina's story, and she fell silent. There was the sound of a man's footsteps outside the door.

Pietro sprang to his feet.

"If that's the policeman from Apulia," he said, "this time you'll hide and he'll have to settle accounts with me." Instead it was merely a postman, who handed in a parcel and went away again.

"That policeman," Annina said, "had the sense not to be seen again, and so had his colleague. Once or twice in the street I thought I saw them in the distance, but they slipped away immediately."

"What do you think has happened to Murica?" Pietro asked.

"He has probably gone back to his people at Rocca dei Marsi," Annina said.

"Haven't you ever thought of talking to him?"

"What for? What happened, happened."

"I'll go and talk to him."

"I couldn't live with him again," Annina said resolutely. "Not with him or with anyone else. The whole thing disgusts me now."

"Annina, thank you for giving me your confidence," said Pietro. "Perhaps it will not have been to no purpose. I hope to see you again."

20

$\mathcal{T}$HE CARRIAGE WAS CROWDED with young men who had been called up, and two gentlemen wearing the party emblem were talking about the war. The other travelers listened to them in silence.

"With the devices at our army's disposal, you'll see that the new war in Africa will be over in a few days," one of them said. "Our death ray will carbonize the enemy."

To illustrate how the hostile forces would be scattered, he blew hard into the palm of one hand as if to blow away some dust..

"Did you see in the newspaper that the men called up at Avezzano are to be blessed by the bishop today?" the other man said. "The death ray will of course also open the way to the missionaries."

Among the young men who had received their call-up papers was an old peasant with a mouth organ. His son was sitting with his head on the old man's shoulder and was fast asleep. "Give us a tune," his neighbors said, but the old man shook his head. Perhaps he didn't want to miss what the two gentlemen were saying about the war that was just going to begin and the mysterious death ray. The two gentlemen were armed with hunting guns, the cartridge cases on their belts were full, and they were going to the Fucino to shoot migrating quail.

"They arrived late this year," one of them said, "but this year they're fatter than last year."

"There's always a compensation," the other one said, and laughed.

Their neighbors, not wishing to seem stupid, started laughing too, though a little late.

Other young conscripts got in at every station. Nearly all smelled of grappa and the stable. Those who couldn't find a seat squatted on their bundles. Others took chunks of corn bread from their knapsacks and started eating. The old man with the mouth organ passed around a bottle of wine. "Give us a tune," his neighbor said again, but he shook his head, he didn't want to.

Don Paolo huddled in a corner. His worn, shapeless hat, his worn and threadbare cassock, made him look like a poor priest from a mountain parish. By many small signs he could tell the mountain villagers from those of the valleys and those who were coming down from the sheepfolds; they were poor people whose capacity for suffering and resignation had no real limits, and they were used to living in isolation, ignorance, mistrust, and sterile family feuds.

Whenever Don Paolo thought he recognized anyone from Orta he hid his face behind his breviary and pulled his hat down over his eyes. Even the landscape had put on uniform. The train, the stations, the telegraph poles, the walls, the trees, the public lavatories, the bell towers, the garden gates, the parapets of bridges bore inscriptions exalting the war.

He arrived at Fossa without incident. What with its multicolored adornment of orders for meetings, garlands, flags, and inscriptions on the walls in whitewash, paint, chalk, tar, and coal, the place was unrecognizable. The Girasole hotel seemed to have been turned into a mobilization center.

Berenice, untidy and disheveled, was dashing about in a state of great excitement. But she had time repeatedly to kiss Don Paolo's hand and bid him welcome.

"What good fortune to have you here with us on this glorious day," she said. "What good fortune."

"Where's Bianchina?" the priest asked. "Where can I find Pompeo, the pharmacist's son?"

But by this time Berenice was far away.

There was a continual coming and going of men and youths in the dining room and on the stairs. A group of men wearing the party emblem, already hoarse from talking too much, were sitting around a table, discussing the details of the spontaneous demonstration due to take place in the afternoon. The strictest precautions were to be taken to ensure the enthusiastic participation of the whole population of Fossa and the surrounding areas. Fossa must at all costs be prevented from making a bad impression.

"Must we send trucks as far as Pietrasecca?" someone asked.

"Of course, they must be sent everywhere," was the answer. "But *carabinieri* must go with the trucks so that people will see the necessity of coming here of their own accord."

At another table a number of landlords and merchants, big, strong, plump men carefully oiled and greased and presided over by the lawyer Zabaglia, had been furiously discussing for several hours past the menu for that evening's banquet. Zabaglione was so carried away that he did not notice Don Paolo's arrival. Serious disagreement had arisen on a matter of principle, and Zabaglione had ended up as usual by making it a matter of personal prestige. The issue was which was to be served first, white wine or red.

The committee for the reception of applications for voluntary enlistment was in session in Berenice's bedroom on the second floor. Those for whom there were no chairs were sitting or lying on the landlady's bed. The words HAPPY DREAMS were beautifully embroidered on the pillows. Over the head of the bed there was a chromolithograph representing a guardian angel caressing a dove. The owner of the clothes store in the town hall square facing the Girasole hotel had gone bankrupt and had had to close down, but the shop had reopened that morning. His wife, Gelsomina, was sitting behind the counter and there was a notice on the door saying, CREDITORS ARE ADVISED THAT THE PROPRIETOR OF THIS

ESTABLISHMENT HAS ENLISTED VOLUNTARILY. After looking through the list of volunteers Don Genesio, the clerk in the registrar's office, had exclaimed, "This will be a bankrupt's war."

This remark enjoyed an enormous success and was repeated to everyone who appeared on the scene. Don Luigi, the pharmacist, was looking everywhere for his son, but couldn't find him. He was desperate. Everyone else's sons were volunteering, and was his to be the exception? He too was in business and had promissory notes falling due. "Have you seen Pompeo?" he anxiously asked everyone he met. "If I find him and he doesn't volunteer I'll shoot him as sure as God's in His heaven."

Don Paolo too was anxiously looking for Pompeo, but for different reasons. Without saying anything to his father he went to look for him at the Villa delle Stagioni. It was silent and deserted. Near the cows the priest found Bianchina. She was alone, singing softly to herself, and playing with a rubber ball. She was delighted to see Don Paolo and flung her arms around his neck.

"Where's Pompeo?" he asked.

"He's gone to Rome," Bianchina said. "He was sent for."

"By whom?"

The girl didn't know. "It must be for the second revolution," she said.

"Where's Alberto?"

"At Pietrasecca, he's returned to the nest. His father's dead. He left me because he was jealous of Pompeo, and of you, and everyone."

"What's the cowman doing?"

"I don't know, he's engaged, he wants to get married."

"I have an urgent favor to ask you," Don Paolo said.

Bianchina made a curtsy and replied, *"Ecce ancilla Domini."*

"I want you to go to Rocca dei Marsi and find a certain Luigi Murica. All I want you to tell him is that an acquaintance of his from Rome would like to see him, and can he come? You mustn't say anything else to him even if he presses you."

"I'll go by bicycle," the girl said.

The bicycle was in a room in the villa reserved for sporting

equipment. Don Paolo watched her leaving in the direction of
Rocca and went back to the hotel.

As the time for the declaration of war on the radio approached
the crowd in the streets grew thicker. Motorcycles, cars, trucks
loaded with police, *carabinieri*, militiamen, and party and corporation officials arrived from everywhere. Donkeys, carts, bicycles,
and trucks arrived bringing *cafoni* from the valleys. Two brass
bands marched through the streets, playing the same anthem over
and over again ad nauseam. The bandsmen's uniforms were like
those of animal tamers at the circus or porters at grand hotels,
with magnificent gold braid and double rows of metal buttons on
their chests. Outside a barbershop there was a big placard showing
some Abyssinian women with breasts dangling almost to their
knees. A dense group of youths had formed in front of it, gazing at
it goggle-eyed and laughing.

At the bottom of the square, between the party premises and the
town hall arcade, a radio set had been hoisted, crowned by a trophy
of flags. It was from this that the voice proclaiming war would
emerge. As the poor people arrived they were herded beneath this
small object on which their collective destiny depended. The
women squatted on the ground, as in church or at market, and the
men sat on their knapsacks or donkey saddles. They had only a
vague idea of why they were gathered there and kept glancing surreptitiously at the metallic radio box. Finding themselves all together like that, they were ill at ease, sad, mistrustful.

The small square and the adjacent streets were packed, but the
influx from the surrounding countryside continued remorselessly.
The halt arrived from the quarries, the blind from the kilns, the
lame and the bent from the fields; the vine dressers came from the
hills with hands worn by sulfur and lime, and the inhabitants of
the mountains with legs bent by the labor of scything. Since their
neighbors had been willing to come, they had been willing to
come. Should the war bring misfortune, it would be misfortune for
all, in other words only half misfortune; but should it bring fortune
you had to try to make sure of your share of it. And so they had all
come. They had left the pressing of the grapes, the cleaning of the

barrels, the preparation of the seed, and had hurried to the local town by order. Eventually even the inhabitants of Pietrasecca arrived and were packed in next to the Girasole hotel. "Don't move from here," the village policeman advised the newcomers.

Signorina Patrignani, the Pietrasecca schoolmistress, kept explaining to those in her charge how they were to behave, when they were to shout and when they were to sing, but her voice was lost in the general hubbub. Magascià lost his temper. "Leave us in peace," he called out. "We're not children."

Don Paolo talked to Magascià and old Gerametta about what had been happening at Pietrasecca since his departure. Magascià told him the sad news of Don Pasquale Colamartini's death. "It was on the day he took you down to Fossa," he explained. "That evening he came back dead. The mare brought him right to the front door. On the way a number of people met him and greeted him, but no one realized he was dead or dying. He was sitting on the box slightly crookedly and with his head on his chest just as if he were asleep, and he was still holding the reins. Donna Cristina has asked me about you several times," Magascià went on. "She wanted to know when you were coming back. Alberto is at Pietrasecca, but he's no help to her."

The Pietrasecca men waited quietly for the ceremony to begin, but the women were more curious and impatient. Cesira suggested that they should go to church "before the machine starts talking," but Filomena and Teresa were against this, because they were unwilling to lose their places. But as the others went, they went too. Meanwhile the men passed around a bottle of wine.

"When is it going to speak?" Giacinto asked Don Paolo, pointing to the magic box.

"At any time now, I think," the priest said.

This piece of news was passed around and revived the general anxiety.

"It may speak at any moment," people said to one another. Only Cassarola the wise woman had been unwilling to get down from Magascià's cart. The women came back from church and tried to make her get down. "Come with us," they said. "Come and sit with us."

The wise woman did not reply.

"What do you want?" one woman asked her.

The old woman looked at her mistrustfully. "There's a yellow comet in the air," she finally announced. "There will be war and then there will be pestilence."

The other Pietrasecca women could not see the yellow comet, but they made the sign of the cross all the same.

"What saint should we pray to?" asked Cesira.

"Prayer's no use," the wise woman announced. "God reigns over the earth, the waters, and the sky, but the yellow comet comes from beyond the sky."

Sciatàp offered her the bottle of wine. She drank, and spat on the ground. Magascià climbed into the cart and whispered in her ear, "Tell me the truth, what do you really see?"

"A yellow comet," she replied. "A yellow comet with a long yellow tail." She turned to Don Paolo and said, "For you I see something else."

"What do you see?" the priest asked curiously.

She waited to make sure that no one else could hear, and then she said in an undertone, "Up on the mountain there's a white lamb, and a black wolf is looking at it."

Meanwhile some pale young ladies with baskets of tricolor rosettes were circulating among the submissive and anxious crowd. Don Paolo recognized them as Zabaglione's daughters. They came toward him and pinned a rosette on his breast. They were extraordinarily excited and out of breath.

"Oh, Father," they said, "what a marvelous day. What an unforgettable day."

The priest handed back the rosette. "I'm sorry," he said. "I can't."

A surge in the crowd caused by new arrivals who wanted a place from which they could see the loudspeaker carried the girls away.

The roar of a motorcycle drowned the general hum; the new arrival was Don Concettino Ragù, in the uniform of an officer of the militia. To avoid meeting him Don Paolo took refuge in his room. He took up a position behind the curtains of his window on the third floor. From this observation post the assembly around the loudspeaker looked like a gathering of pilgrims around an idol. Over the roofs he could see tall bell towers, the tops of which were crowded with boys like dovecotes packed with doves. Suddenly the bells started ringing clamorously. Party notables made their way through the throng and surrounded the destiny-laden loudspeaker with patriotic fetishes — tricolor flags, pennants, and a picture of the leader with exaggeratedly projecting lower jaw. Shouts of "Eia, eia," and other incomprehensible cries came from the group of notables while the rest of the throng remained silent.

The inevitable "mothers of the fallen" were ushered to the post of honor immediately beneath the loudspeaker. Their presence was obligatory. They were an assembly of poor little women who had worn mourning for fifteen years, had been awarded medals fifteen years before, and in exchange for a small allowance were condemned to be at the disposal of the warrant officer of the *carabinieri* whenever public ceremonies required their presence. Near the "mothers" and surrounding Don Angelo Girasole, the parish priest of Fossa, were the parish priests of neighboring villages: old, shy, good-natured priests, gloomy priests, athletic and impressive priests, and a canon who was as pink and white as a well-nourished wet nurse.

"What a lovely celebration," the canon exclaimed. "What a magnificent celebration."

A number of well-nourished landowners, heavily bearded men with fierce eyebrows and wearing sportsmen's velvet, were drawn up under the town hall arcade. The bells went on pealing loudly, with boys taking turns at the ropes. At one point members of the group of notables in the square signaled to them to stop, because the speech on the radio was about to begin, but the boys either didn't understand or pretended not to. Altogether there were about a dozen bells, the continuous ringing of which made a deafening din. Militiamen appeared at the top of the nearest bell tower and made the boys leave the ropes, but the other bells went on ringing, with the result that the first hoarse muttering that came from the loudspeaker went unnoticed. Then loud shouting arose from the group of notables and militiamen, a rhythmical impassioned invocation of the leader, "CHAY DOO! CHAY DOO! CHAY DOO! CHAY DOO!"

The invocation slowly spread, was taken up by women and boys, and then was repeated by the whole crowd, even by those farthest away as well as those at the windows, in an anguished, religious, rhythmical chorus. "CHAY DOO! CHAY DOO! CHAY DOO! CHAY DOO! CHAY DOO! CHAY DOO!" Those nearest the loudspeaker signaled to the crowd to be quiet so as to allow the speech to be heard, but the crowd massed in the adjacent streets continued to intone the redeeming invocation, went on crying aloud to the leader, the magus, the great wizard who held sway over the blood and future of them all. The shouting of the throng mingling with the continued pealing of the bells made the speech coming over the radio completely inaudible to the majority, and the repetition of those two syllables ended up losing all meaning and becoming a kind of exorcistic formula mingling with the sacred music of the bells.

At one point those nearest the loudspeaker indicated by signs that the broadcast was over.

"War has been declared," Zabaglione called out.

He indicated that he wanted to speak, but even his voice was lost in the clamor of the crowd that went on invoking grace and salvation. The spell was broken only by the loud roar of gasoline engines. The cars and motorcycles of the authorities began moving through the throng and going away in all directions. As soon as Don Paolo saw Don Concettino disappearing he abandoned his refuge and came down into the street. Zabaglione received him with open arms. "Did you see my daughters?" he exclaimed with pride. "Did you see them distributing rosettes? They were completely transfigured by patriotic ardor."

"They were as lovely as angels," said Don Paolo.

Zabaglione was deeply affected by this compliment.

Don Paolo added, "I have spoken about you to the bishop. I hope I may have helped you."

Zabaglione wanted to kiss him, and in spite of the priest's resistance he actually succeeded. "My dear friend," he said. "I have heard you talked of as a saint, but I didn't know that the Church had such obliging saints."

The lawyer took the priest's arm and led him to his house through the beflagged streets. "Hurrah, hurrah," he shouted to every group of people he met. His wife opened the door, pale and trembling.

"Kiss the Father's hand and leave us alone," Zabaglione said.

The lady bent and kissed the priest's hand, but before withdrawing she said to her husband, "The girls haven't come back yet."

Zabaglione raised his eyebrows. "Send the maid to look for them immediately," he ordered.

In the dining room Zabaglione offered Don Paolo a drink. "The Lord wanted to chastise me," he said. "Why did he give me daughters and not sons? At this hour they would already be in Africa. For lack of sons I have made my clients who are awaiting trial volunteer. Most of them will not be accepted, but the gesture remains."

The priest looked at him benevolently, as if to say that between friends one could talk more freely. Why, after all, had he come home with him? "The war will be a hard one," he began.

"It doesn't matter," said the lawyer. "At worst we shall always gain something. Don't you agree? Our country has grown greater after every war, and in particular after every defeat."

"After the broadcast you wanted to make a speech," the priest said.

"It was on the program, but the enthusiasm of the crowd made it impossible," said the lawyer. "In any case, I was only to have introduced the official speaker, one Concettino Ragù, who was to have spoken on 'The Revival of the Rural Masses and the Roman Tradition.'"

"The Roman tradition is a lot of nonsense in that context," said the priest with unusual frankness. "If the *cafoni* allow themselves to be mobilized for war, it is certainly not out of deference to a Roman tradition of which they know nothing."

His not having been chosen as the official speaker still rankled with the lawyer, so he was glad to have someone to whom he could unburden himself. "You're quite right," he said. "It's absurd to talk about the Roman tradition at the present time. Our tradition goes no farther back than the Bourbons and the Spaniards, against a background of Christian legends. Besides, even in Roman times there was no Roman influence here. The people here differed from the Latins in religion, language, alphabet, and customs."

"Do you think there is any opposition to the war among the *cafoni?*" Don Paolo asked.

"They don't have enough to eat, so how do you expect them to take an interest in politics?" said Zabaglione. "Politics is a luxury of the well fed. But there are some disloyal elements among the young."

Don Paolo quickly said good-bye and went back to the Villa delle Stagioni. When he was inside the perimeter wall he thought he saw a girl lying on the straw behind the peacock's cage, and he slowly approached. Too late he saw that it was not Bianchina, but one of Zabaglione's daughters in the company of a soldier. Warned by experience, when he saw two girls on intimate terms with two other soldiers on the other side of the small temple of Venus, he had no need to approach to realize that they were the lawyer's other two daughters. But the Villa delle Stagioni was deserted. Swallows were flying about in the big, empty courtyard, keeping close to the ground. They too were about to leave to spend the winter in Africa.

Don Paolo, disheartened and with his nerves on edge, went back to the town. There was great animation in the streets, particularly around the taverns.

Berenice had put a roast sucking pig for sale outside the hotel. It lay on a table, pierced by a spit from its tail to its neck. Through the rent in the belly you could see it was stuffed with rosemary, fennel, thyme, and sage. A small crowd had gathered around it but, apart from soldiers who had received their first pay since mobilization, customers were few. Some young *cafoni* gazed at it openmouthed, showing their fangs like hungry wolves. A sergeant in the militia had a big helping and was cutting it up with a new knife, one of those instruments with blade, punch, potato lifter, and scissors that aroused the admiration of the whole crowd.

Under the arcade of the town hall a booth had been erected offering enlarged and colored views of Abyssinia. You had to pay ten *centesimi* to see them. Who could not afford ten *centesimi*? Don Paolo paid up, got in line with the others, and filed past a series of apertures equipped with magnifying lenses. Putting one eye to the latter enabled one to see Abyssinian women with bare hairy legs and protruding breasts. The last picture showed the Empress of Abyssinia. The line of viewers moved much more slowly than Don Paolo would have liked, but there was no help for it. Some of those ahead remained absorbed for a long time in front of every picture, and a timid invitation to them to hurry attracted protests and jibes from the whole line. When at last he was able to get away from this artistic spectacle he had reached the limit of his patience. He wandered this way and that, feeling exhausted and discouraged. Twice he returned to the Villa delle Stagioni, and on both occasions he made out the white underwear of Zabaglione's daughters between the straw and the grass, but there was no trace of the cowman or the other young men. By now Bianchina should have returned from her search for Murica.

That was how the afternoon passed. Local high society gathered at Berenice's hotel for the celebratory dinner while the artisans, petite bourgeoisie, and *cafoni* of Fossa, as well as those from villages in the neighborhood who had stayed behind, gathered in a field next to the Buonumore bar on the banks of the stream. The host had put a great many benches outside for the occasion and was selling off black wine from Apulia at a reduced price. He had set up a big barrel under a poplar tree near the path that ran along the bank of the stream, and it was from this that he poured the wine, filling half bottles that young barmaids took to the improvised tables. Among others Don Paolo came across a party from Pietrasecca, including Magascià, Sciatàp, and others, many of them already drunk.

"Have you understood anything of what is going on?" the priest asked his acquaintances.

"What a thing to expect," said Sciatàp. "No one told us there was any need to understand."

"Things take their own course," said Magascià. "Like water in the river. What's the use of understanding?"

"If you fall in the river, do you let yourself be carried along by the stream?" the priest asked.

Magascià shrugged his shoulders. A man named Pasquandrea said the only thing that mattered was that soon it would be possible to emigrate again. Another, named Campobasso, said that horses and mules were sure to be requisitioned, but those who had only a donkey had nothing to fear, so he was all right. Sciatàp asked the priest whether the "death ray" could destroy seed in the ground. The others listened and drank, bewildered, stupefied, and silent.

"You'd do better to drink and not waste time asking us things we don't understand," Magascià said to the priest. "You see, at Pietrasecca a joke or a play on words lasts for many years, it's handed down from father to son and repeated an endless number of times, always in the same way. But here you hear so many novelties in a single day that you end up with a headache. What is there to understand?"

"Things take their own course whether you understand them or not," said Sciatàp.

Don Paolo saw Zabaglione approaching along the path beside the stream. He looked pale and distressed and took Don Paolo aside.

"Have you by any chance seen my daughters? I fear something may have happened to them," he said.

The lawyer was immediately recognized by many of the drinkers by whom he was surrounded. They offered him drinks and began shouting, "Speech, speech, we want a speech."

The crowd demanded a speech as they would have demanded a song or a tune or a mazurka, depending on the performer's specialty. Zabaglione refused, resisted, but ended up giving in. Some youths lifted him almost by force onto a table next to the barrel. He preened himself, smoothed his mustache, smoothed his hair, looked around the crowd, and smiled. His face was transfigured. He raised his arms toward the starry sky and began in his warm baritone voice, "Descendants of eternal Rome, O you my people."

The orator addressed the drunken artisans and *cafoni* as if they were an assembly of exiled kings, conjuring memories of ancient glory out of the fumes of wine.

"Tell me," he said, "who carried civilization and culture to the Mediterranean and to Africa?"

"We did," some voices answered.

"But the fruits were gathered by others," the orator declared.

"Tell me again, who carried civilization to the whole of Europe, as far as the misty shores of England, and built towns and cities where primitive savages pastured together with wild boars and deer?"

"We did," a number of voices answered.

"But the fruits were gathered by others. Tell me again, who discovered America?"

This time they all rose to their feet and shouted, "We did, we did, we did."

"But others enjoy it. Tell me again, who invented electricity, wireless telegraphy, all the other marvels of civilization?"

"We did," some voices replied.

"But others enjoy them. And lastly, tell me who emigrated to all the countries of the world to dig mines, build bridges, make roads, reclaim swamps?"

Once more they all rose to their feet and shouted, "We did, we did, we did."

"And there you have the explanation of all our ills. But, after centuries of humiliations and injustices, divine providence sent to our country a man who will recover everything that is ours by right, everything of which we have been robbed."

There were shouts of, "To Tunis, to Malta, to Nice."

Others shouted, "To New York, to America, to California."

One old man shouted, "To São Paulo, to the Avenida Paulista, to the Avenida Angelica."

Others shouted, "To Buenos Aires."

Sciatàp who was sitting near Don Paolo, was seized with wild excitement and tried to climb onto a small table, though he could hardly stand because of the wine he had drunk. He imposed silence on his neighbors and started shouting, "To New York, to Forty-second Street, to Forty-second Street, take my advice, I beg you, I implore you."

People were crowding around Zabaglione to get him to continue, but in the distance he had seen three girls arm in arm with three soldiers walking down the path along the stream. He jumped down from the table, forced his way through the throng, and went off in pursuit. After the orator's departure it was just as it is when a pleasing concert has come to an end and everyone repeats on his own account the tune that he liked best.

"In New York," Sciatàp was telling his neighbors, "on Mulberry Street, there's a shameless person who calls himself Mr. Charles Little-Bell, Ice and Coal. He must be the first to get his desserts. Everyone is entitled to his own opinion, of course, but my idea would be . . ."

Campobasso drew him aside and asked him, "What is there at Forty-second Street?"

"It's the entertainment quarter," said Sciatàp. "The entertainment quarter of the rich. There are beautiful women there, perfumed women."

He half closed his eyes and sniffed at that distant feminine perfume. He said no more because his son had arrived, comically arrayed in an ill-fitting uniform, with his sleeves folded over his wrists and his trousers falling down to his knees.

"Have a drink," his father said to him. His son drank. "Have another drink," his father ordered, and his son obeyed. "Now listen to me," his father said. "Don't forget what I'm telling you in front of everyone. If the government decides to send soldiers with the death ray to New York, step forward and volunteer. Tell the government that your father has been there and explained the layout to you. Well then, as soon as you disembark at Battery Place turn sharp right . . ."

His son laughed openmouthed, looked gratefully at his father, and nodded his head in agreement at everything he said.

Meanwhile a group of drunken *cafoni* had gathered around the barrel of wine and started singing an old emigrant's song:

> Thirty days in the steamship
> And we got to 'Merica . . .

At this point a row broke out because some soldiers left without paying. The waitresses shrieked and the landlord threatened them with a big kitchen knife.

"Get the money from the government," the soldiers shouted from a distance.

By now the barrel was nearly empty, but about a dozen *cafoni* went on singing the emigrant's song. Some of them were clinging to the barrel, holding tight, like men in a boat on a rough sea, and singing:

> We found neither straw nor hay
> We slept on the bare earth
> Like beasts of the field.

They sang out of tune, their voices were strident and tipsy, they prolonged phrases till their breath ran out and accompanied their singing with grotesque imitations of travelers embarking and leaving.

21

MAGASCIÀ WAS THE ONLY one to notice that Don Paolo was weeping.

Wearily the priest rose and walked slowly back into the town. By now it was dark. He wanted to go back to the hotel, to go up to his room and lie on his bed, but at the hotel entrance there was a group of laughing, guffawing people. He stood a little to one side, confused and undecided, until someone noticed him and called Berenice.

"Come to the dinner, come along," she said. "There are a number of gentlemen who want to meet you."

"Thank you, I've already eaten," Don Paolo said. "Is Bianchina at home?"

"She hasn't come back yet," Berenice replied. "I don't know where she is."

Don Paolo went away without knowing where he was going, but then he once more made for the Villa delle Stagioni. When he left the last houses behind, the darkness was complete. He stopped and walked on, not knowing what to do. He crossed the bridge over the stream and went down a path flanked by vegetable plots. Snatches of the emigrants' song reached him.

> And 'Merica is long and wide
> Surrounded by rivers and mountains

Near the perimeter wall of the villa he was suddenly attacked by a dog that leaped from a hedge. Fortunately a peasant came to his assistance. He was the cowman, Pompeo's friend.

"What are you doing in these parts at this time of day?" he asked in surprise.

"I'm looking for Pompeo," Don Paolo said.

"He's been called to Rome," said the cowman. "He hasn't come back yet."

"And where's Bianchina?" Don Paolo asked.

"I haven't see her," the cowman replied. "Good-bye, I must go."

"Haven't you got a moment for me?" Don Paolo said. "I should like to talk to you."

"I'm sorry," the cowman said. "My girl's waiting for me."

Slowly and reluctantly the priest turned back to the hotel. The streets of Fossa were almost deserted and were dimly lit. The flags, the trophies, the arches, the streamers created the impression of a carnival evening. Don Paolo was exhausted from walking, his feet were dragging, his cassock was dirty and dusty. But at the entrance to the hotel he hesitated again. The sound of voices and singing was still coming from the dining room. The last guests at the patriotic banquet were still there, and he could not go up to his room without going through the dining room. To avoid being greeted and talked to by those odious people he walked around the back of the hotel and tried the kitchen door. He found it at the bottom of a yard crammed full of boxes, vine cuttings, and piles of charcoal. The sound of dishwashing came from the kitchen.

The charcoal aroused the priest's interest. It was softwood charcoal. He picked up a few pieces and filled one of his pockets with them. Then he tiptoed back, forgetting his tiredness, and set out on a short reconnaissance of the neighboring streets. The street leading to the station was deserted, and no

sound came from the station, where a beggar with a dog was
sleeping in the waiting room. The last train had gone. Over the
ticket window Don Paolo wrote in charcoal: DOWN WITH THE
WAR and LONG LIVE LIBERTY. He crossed the small station
square and went back into the old part of the town, by way of a
dark and twisting alley that took him to the church of San
Giuseppe. The walls were cracked and unsuitable for charcoal
graffiti, but the three wide steps leading up to the church door
were smooth and polished. Excellent, Don Paolo said to himself. It was as if generations of Christians had day by day for centuries been keeping them clean in expectation of his arrival with
his bit of charcoal. He wrote in big block letters: LONG LIVE LIB-
ERTY and LONG LIVE PEACE. When he had finished he moved
away and looked back two or three times to admire his handi-
work. He was well satisfied. It really created an excellent impression at the foot of the church. In the lunette of the doorway
there was a picture of San Giuseppe with his flowering stick.
Don Paolo smiled, raised his hat to him, and went on with his
walk. At a bend in an alley he came across a drunk advancing in
zigzags. The man was taken aback, but then burst into idiotic
laughter and started following the priest, murmuring, "Wait a
minute, don't be in such a hurry, darling."

The priest hastened his stride but, as the drunk persisted in following him, he let the man catch up with him under a lamppost
and was ready to give him a couple of slaps. But the drunk realized his mistake, made a comic gesture of astonishment, and
began muttering apologies. "Oh, what a mistake," he said, "what
sacrilege I was about to commit."

Don Paolo went on with his walk and reached the tax office.
A government coat of arms was on the door and the windows
were solidly barred. Expensive and totally useless ornaments. But
the facade had been recently whitewashed. Had the men who
did this realized what they were doing? In any event, Don Paolo
carefully wrote in big letters on the white wall: LONG LIVE THE
INDEPENDENCE OF THE PEOPLES OF AFRICA and LONG LIVE
THE INTERNATIONAL.

More drunken voices reached him, and to avoid any more en-counters he went back to the hotel, using the back door, as the kitchen was now deserted. In his room he was surprised to find Pompeo, sitting on a chair and waiting for him.

"I came back from Rome by the last train this evening," he said. "As soon as I heard you were here I came to see you, I've been waiting for you, because I've got to talk to you."

"I've been looking for you too and have been waiting for you all day," Don Paolo said, and went on, "Pompeo, this infamous war has begun, the war of the bank against the poor, and what are we doing?"

Pompeo went pale. "No, Don Paolo, you're wrong," he said. "This is a war for the people and for socialism."

"Are you mad? How can you believe that?"

Pompeo described what had happened on his trip to Rome, where he had gone with a friend who, like him, believed in the second revolution. They had spent the evening with rich friends, and the conversation had naturally turned to the war. Pompeo had been greatly surprised to hear a banker who was one of the guests expressing reservations about the new war in Africa, which he con-sidered a very expensive political enterprise. Others who were present shared this feeling. So what was the reason for this war? the two young men had asked. The first answers had been uncertain and vague. No one dared mention a certain man's name, still less criticize him, but eventually the banker, after a great deal of cau-tious beating around the bush, had frankly expressed his opinion. He said that every war in modern times inevitably led to state so-cialism and the destruction of private property. That's good enough for me, Pompeo had replied. If that was the case, he would volunteer immediately to fight for the new social empire.

Don Paolo was about to reply, but hesitated. The hand in his pocket was still dirty with charcoal.

"The war will gain us fertile land for our unemployed," Pompeo went on. "They will be the free owners of that land." He took a piece of paper from his wallet and showed it to the priest. "I en-listed voluntarily today," he said.

"In that case we have nothing more to say to each other," Don Paolo muttered.

But Pompeo, after some hesitation, still had something important to say to him. "Promise me that you will do none of the things that we agreed on," he said.

Don Paolo did not reply immediately. Perhaps he did not want to lie.

"Promise me," Pompeo insisted.

"I promise you," Don Paolo said. He added, "Bon voyage. I sincerely hope you will return from the war safe and sound. Then we shall discuss things again."

Pompeo embraced him affectionately.

"I'll write to you from Africa," he said, and left.

Don Paolo washed the charcoal from his hand. The washbasin stank disgustingly of urine. He looked at himself in the dirty, tarnished mirror. He had aged greatly that day. His black clothing made him look dismal. While he was undressing he had a nasty coughing fit, and some light reddish foam appeared between his lips. He spat into the washstand. There was no doubt about it, it was blood. Slowly he lay down on the bed.

He was still lying there, dressed and awake, when he heard someone tiptoeing to the door and stopping and listening. "Come in," he said. It was Bianchina.

"I saw the light, that's why I came," she said. The girl was made up and smelled of grappa. "The declaration of war was celebrated at Rocca too," she said with a laugh. "Some friends of mine there insisted on entertaining me, of course. But that Murica of yours is an idiot. I went all over the place before I eventually found him on a vegetable plot where he was growing I don't know what. I did exactly as you said, and told him that a friend of his had sent me especially to tell him that he would like to talk to him, and that he would come and see him if he agreed. He didn't even thank me or offer me so much as a glass of water. He replied coldly that he didn't want to see anyone."

Don Paolo was breathing with difficulty and was afraid he might be going to have another coughing fit.

"Why don't you say anything?" Bianchina asked. "Why aren't you in bed yet? You haven't even taken off your shoes. What's the matter? Are you depressed?"

The priest nodded.

"Why are you depressed? Are you in debt? Are you in love?"

The coughing returned to shake him. His head fell onto his shoulder and from one side of his mouth a thin trickle of warm blood flowed onto his chin. He saw Bianchina grow pale, and she was on the point of hurrying to get assistance. But he managed to seize her by the hand and stop her. He smiled and muttered, "Don't be afraid, it's nothing. It's not the first time. It stops by itself."

Bianchina wetted some handkerchiefs in cold water and put them on his brow and his chest.

"The important thing is to keep calm," she kept telling him.

She took a dark blue veil from her waist and wrapped it around the electric lamp to dim the light. Every so often she renewed the cold compresses.

"I had an aunt who had this illness, so I know what to do," she said. "The important thing is not to be afraid. Leave everything to me."

Slowly, without his having to arouse himself or make an effort, she undressed him, put a sheet over him, and made him comfortable. Carefully she wiped away the traces of blood on his mouth and chin.

"You'll see, it won't be anything serious," she told him several times.

She forbade the patient to talk, and gave him a pencil and a sheet of paper in case he wanted to ask for anything.

"Now it's time to go to sleep," she said finally. "Good night."

She lay on a quilt stretched out on the floor beside the bed. But neither of them managed to go to sleep.

Later on the sick man said to her, "Did you celebrate the declaration of war?"

"Yes."

"Why?"

"I did what everyone else did. Does that displease you?"

"Yes."

"Go to sleep and don't worry about it," Bianchina said.

In the morning she went and told her mother about Don Paolo's illness, but came back to his room straightaway and told him that there was great excitement in the town because of some disgraceful antiwar slogans on a number of public buildings. They had been written in charcoal during the night. While Bianchina was cleaning the room she discovered some big black stains in the washbasin, as if a charcoal burner had been washing his hands.

"What's this?" she asked. But instead of waiting for a reply she quickly cleaned the washbasin. Then she went over to Don Paolo and said reproachfully, "You really are a baby. An incorrigible and reckless baby." But Don Paolo's appearance aroused her sympathy, for she immediately added, "But you're a nice person all the same."

"Bianchina," Don Paolo said, "how lucky it is that the human race includes women, it doesn't just consist of calculating males."

Bianchina thought for a moment. "Perhaps you say that out of pure calculation."

Don Paolo watched the girl scrubbing the floor. Her ankles were perfect. Her bosom was like a well-filled bread basket. The first time he saw her, her breasts were like little lemons; now they were like fine, ripe apples.

22

As soon as I'm fit enough to travel I'm going abroad," Don Paolo told Bianchina. "I can't go on living in this odious country."

"Find me a job and I'll come with you," the girl said.

The idea of meeting Bianchina abroad amused Don Paolo.

"If you go abroad," he said, "I'll tell you a secret that will make you laugh."

"Couldn't you tell me now?"

But Don Paolo was not to be persuaded.

Berenice looked after the priest in accordance with the advice of the Fossa municipal doctor. In particular, he told her to do everything possible to distract the patient from melancholy thoughts, a task that was conscientiously taken over by Bianchina. Because of the patient's condition the girl was obviously somewhat restricted in her choice of means; she had to renounce a whole series of forms of entertainment that Don Paolo would certainly have enjoyed, but at the expense of his health. But she was a bright and resourceful girl, and she recalled a number of harmless pastimes from her school days that distracted him from his

black mood. One of these was fly racing. At Bianchina's school
this had been practiced chiefly in class. The object was to catch
flies in flight, without hurting them and without being seen by
the sister in charge. A pin or small feather would be inserted into
the flies from the rear and then they would be lined up on the
bench and encouraged to engage in what was called a towing
race. Bianchina acquired quite a reputation at this, but when she
tried catching flies in flight now she sometimes damaged them.
Her excuse was that she was out of practice.

"You learn so many things at convent school, but later in life
when you need them you find you've forgotten them," she said.

The towing races took place on Don Paolo's bed. The black
leather binding of his breviary served as the track. Some flies started
out at once and made straight for the finish line, while others went
off at an angle and left the track or stopped after the first few steps.

"Those that won't go are the wives," Bianchina explained.
"They slow down to let their husbands win, the silly idiots."

Don Paolo discovered that, apart from the difference in scale,
fly racing, when watched at close quarters, was full of surprises
and distractions, just like ordinary horse or car racing. In spite of
Bianchina's precautions, echoes of the excitement produced in
the town by the charcoal antiwar slogans frequently reached the
sickroom.

"So many policemen have never been seen here before,"
Berenice said. "Anyone would think Fossa was a den of crooks."

Bianchina said nothing, or tried to change the subject.

Gelsomina, the clothes store owner's wife, who had taken her
husband's place now that he had volunteered, stood in the
doorway of the shop and stopped passersby. "Have you heard anything new?" she asked. "It must certainly have been a stranger."

Outside the hotel door there was a permanent group of people
talking about nothing else. What the bigwigs said was repeated
and commented on from one household to the next.

"It was such a delightful celebration, everyone was so happy,
and everything was so harmonious," Berenice said. "Who could
have had the idea of writing that nonsense on the walls?"

"What it amounts to is that envy is present among us too," said Don Luigi, the pharmacist. "Someone who cannot enlist and has no sons whom he could send to enlist relieved his feelings by doing this."

"Never a funeral without a jest, never a wedding without a sob," said Zabaglione. "Come, come, don't let us exaggerate."

"Night birds are birds of ill omen," Don Genesio proclaimed. "Appearances are never to be trusted."

"Quite right," said Berenice. "Fire is smoldering among the *cafoni*. We must be on our guard, you don't see fire in daylight, but at night it glows."

"*Cafoni?* Rubbish," said the pharmacist. "*Cafoni* can't read or write, and the antiwar slogans were written in block letters. *Cafoni*, my foot."

"It must be admitted that there are some young people who have lost their heads," said Zabaglione. "I'm not referring to anyone in particular, of course."

But Don Luigi caught the insinuation and retorted with venom, "For your information, my son has volunteered. The honor of a volunteer is unimpeachable. Apart from that, while we're on the subject, neither I nor my son have ever been socialists."

This was Zabaglione's Achilles' heel. The shaft went home.

"That repartee leaves me unaffected," he said, pale with anger. "Everyone knows that I gave up my ideas long ago. Who has never been a socialist? Even the head of the government was once a socialist."

"Why all the excitement?" Bianchina said. "Just because of a bit of charcoal on the wall? What a lot of fuss about nothing." In this case the girl's naïveté was genuine. "I really don't understand why people make such a fuss about a few words scrawled on a wall with charcoal," she said to Don Paolo.

Don Paolo, however, seemed pleased at the fuss, which showed no sign of abating, and he tried to explain the reason for it.

"The dictatorship is based on unanimity," he said. "It's sufficient for one person to say no and the spell is broken."

"Even if that person is a poor, lonely, sick man?" the girl said.

"Certainly."

"Even if he's a peaceful man who thinks in his own way and apart from that does no one any harm?"

"Certainly."

These thoughts saddened the girl, but they cheered Don Paolo.

"Under every dictatorship," he said, "one man, one perfectly ordinary little man who goes on thinking with his own brain is a threat to public order. Tons of printed paper spread the slogans of the régime; thousands of loudspeakers, hundreds of thousands of posters and freely distributed leaflets, whole armies of speakers in all the squares and at all the crossroads, thousands of priests in the pulpit repeat these slogans ad nauseam, to the point of collective stupefaction. But it's sufficient for one little man, just one ordinary little man to say no, and the whole of that formidable granite order is imperiled."

This frightened the girl, but the priest was cheerful again.

"And if they catch him and kill him?" the girl said.

"Killing a man who says no is a risky business," said the priest. "Even a corpse can go on whispering no, no, no, no with the tenacity and obstinacy that is peculiar to certain corpses. How can you silence a corpse? You may perhaps have heard of Giacomo Matteotti."

"I don't think so," Bianchina said. "Who's he?"

"A corpse that no one can silence," Don Paolo sighed.

Berenice burst into the room in a state of high excitement.

"At last, at last," she exclaimed.

"Have you won the lottery?" Bianchina asked.

"Pompeo knows who did the writing on the walls," Berenice said. "He's on his way to Avezzano to tell the authorities."

"How does he know?" the priest asked.

"He has just told the clothes store owner's wife himself."

Bianchina hurried to her room to fetch her hat and dashed to the station.

"Don't meddle in affairs that don't concern you," her mother shouted after her down the stairs. "Don't go on being our ruin."

But Bianchina was far away.

Don Paolo jumped out of bed to pack his bags and flee. He had had no fever for several days and his cough was better, but he could hardly stand. Besides, where was he to go? There was only one railway line, and if he took the train it would be easy to catch him. And if he went up into the mountains and spent a few days in the woods? In his condition that would be madness. So he unpacked and went back to bed. Everything considered, being arrested here in Fossa, in a place already in a state of ferment, might be more useful than being arrested at the station in Rome. Orta, his birthplace, was a few miles away. Don Benedetto was a few miles away. Classmates of his lived in every village in the neighborhood. News of his arrest would reach the *cafoni.* During the long nights of winter poor hungry people sitting around the hearth would remember his gesture.

Once more there was a protracted wait for Bianchina.

After a first quick check through his belongings to eliminate all traces of anything that might compromise others, he had plenty of time to repeat the process several times more. At every sound of wheels outside he dashed to the window, but his anxiety remained unassuaged. The time the girl took was incomprehensible. Avezzano was barely an hour away by train. Why were the police so slow?

Bianchina and Pompeo came back late that evening. The endless wait had left Don Paolo exhausted.

"We ate and drank," Bianchina told him, laughing. "We were just coming back when we passed a theater, and Mickey Mouse was on the program, so of course we went in."

"Is that all?"

"No, it isn't."

"Didn't Pompeo go to Avezzano to denounce someone?" the priest asked.

Bianchina smiled. "What an amazing memory you have," she said. "I'd forgotten all about it."

"Well, then, what happened?"

"By the time we got into the train Pompeo had told me that he knew for certain who did the writing on the walls. In the train we had an argument, we nearly tore each other's hair out. When we go out at Avezzano the chief of police was waiting to hear what Pompeo had to say, but by then he'd changed his mind."

"Whom did he denounce, then?"

"A cyclist coming down the road from Orta," Bianchina said. "Pompeo saw him in the distance, but wasn't close enough to identify him. I confirmed what he said. That night I myself saw a cyclist coming down the road from Orta."

Bianchina had told her mother the same story immediately after she got back.

"From Orta?" Berenice exclaimed. "So Gelsomina was right, it was a stranger."

Berenice hurried over to the clothes store.

"Gelsomì," she called out. "We were right. It was just as we said, it was a stranger, a man from Orta, who tried to compromise the people of Fossa."

The news spread through the shops and bars in a flash, and of course it turned out that many others had seen the cyclist from Orta that night. But he was not one of the men who came to Fossa regularly for the market; he was a stranger.

"The usual Mystery Man," the warrant officer of *carabinieri* exclaimed furiously.

Now that the danger was over, Don Paolo cheered up again. His spirit of adventure was revived.

"I'll take you abroad with me," he said to Bianchina, "and I'll tell you stories."

"Where will you take me?" the girl wanted to know. "To a mission station among unbelievers in the colonies?"

"Yes, among unbelievers, but in Paris or Zürich," Don Paolo replied.

23

NEXT DAY DON ANGELO Girasole, the parish priest of Fossa, appeared at his sister's hotel to renew his invitation to Don Paolo to visit the parish church. The strange priest could no longer extricate himself from a social duty that hitherto he had found various excuses to postpone.

Don Angelo was barely sixty, but looked much older. His hair was white, his face was lean and yellowish, and his back was bent. On the way he told Don Paolo that he was the oldest of ten brothers and sisters of whom the only survivors were Berenice and himself. His duties kept him busy from dawn to late at night. He had no one to help him, and the parish was big. Apart from masses, confessions, funerals, novenas and triduums, rosaries, and services of all sorts at which he had to officiate or attend, there were the new lay duties imposed by the state, the baptisms and marriages, and the illiterate mothers who came to him to ask him to read the letters sent them from America, there were the Children of Mary, the San Luigi Youth Club, and teaching the catechism at elementary schools, there were the children who had to be prepared for confirmation and for their first communion, and there were also the Congregation of Charity, the Confraternity, and the tertiaries of San Francesco.

"If I am to say my breviary and retire into myself a little and prepare myself for the death that I feel to be approaching, though so slowly, I have to take advantage of odd moments of leisure," he said.

Every evening he felt so tired that he could hardly stand. Yet sometimes, even in the worst season of the year, he would be awoken in the middle of the night to go to the bedside of someone who was dying. But he did not complain. On the contrary.

"A man of God must always be tired," he said. "For idle thoughts come in idle moments, and behind them the evil one is always on the watch."

In the little square outside the church a crowd of boys were kicking a football about. They stopped to let the two priests pass.

"Don't forget that catechism begins in a quarter of an hour," the parish priest reminded them.

On the steps of the church Don Angelo stopped for a moment to recover his breath.

"You will probably have heard of the sacrilege that took place here," he said to Don Paolo. "One night a stranger with a mask over his face came here, to the threshold of the church, and scrawled the most crazy things."

"By the way," Don Paolo said, "what do you think of this new war?"

A woman was waiting for the priest at the door of the church to arrange the date for a baptism.

"A poor country priest," said Don Angelo, "has a great deal to do and little time to think. For the rest," he added with a smile, "there are the Old Testament and the New, and the Pastor of the Church to guide us."

"I expressed myself badly," Don Paolo said.

The interior of the church seemed dark at first, but one's eyes quickly got used to it. Part of the uneven, disjointed stone floor was occupied by women, all dressed in black, who were praying and whispering among themselves, squatting in the Oriental manner as a sign of humility and familiarity with the house of

God. One old woman was crawling on her hands and knees toward the Chapel of the Blessed Sacrament with her face to the ground, licking the floor and leaving behind her on the old stones an irregular trail of saliva that looked like the silvery trail of a snail. A young man in soldier's uniform walked slowly by her side, looking awkward and embarrassed.

Don Angelo genuflected before the tabernacle, and Don Paolo followed suit. On the altar there was a picture of the body of Christ on the knees of His Mother, who was dressed in mourning. Christ looked like a *cafone* who had been killed in a quarrel and whose body was already decomposing; the wounds in the hands and feet and the deep rent in the breast looked as if they were in an advanced state of gangrene, and the red hair was probably full of dust and vermin. But His Mother looked like the widow of a rich merchant who had been overwhelmed by misfortune. Two paraffin tears shone on her handsome pale cheeks; her black eyes looked upward, as if to avoid seeing the son of whom she had had such high hopes but who could not possibly have come to a worse end; her finely embroidered veil covered her waved hair and came down halfway over her brow; a smart lace handkerchief was tied to the little finger of her right hand, and on the pedestal at her feet the woeful words VIDETE SI DOLOR VESTER EST SICUT DOLOR MEUS were carved in letters of gold.

The neighboring altar of San Rocco was adorned with the usual variety of polychrome votive gifts put there by those of the faithful who had been granted miracles. They varied according to the grace received: hands, feet, noses, ears, breasts, and other parts of the body were represented, some in natural size.

The soldier's mother had now completed her ordeal. "Please find out whether we can get the allowance at once," she said to Don Angelo. "Otherwise, how are we to live?"

"What allowance?"

"The mother of every conscript is entitled to four lire a day," the soldier said. "It says so in today's paper."

"To whom should we apply for it?" another woman came

and asked the parish priest. "The *podestà*? The town hall? The *carabinieri*?"

Another woman whose small boy was ill with erysipelas was waiting in the sacristy. She wanted permission to dip a small piece of cloth in the oil of the lamp that was burning at the side of the tabernacle so that she could lay it on her dying child's heart. Don Angelo gave her permission.

"Do you see? A country priest has little chance to think of the war," he said to Don Paolo. "Now we shall be having prayers for dependents' allowances, later there will be prayers for the safe homecoming of prisoners of war and prayers for the missing, and then there will be prayers for leave to be granted for those required to work on the land, and prayers for pensions, and prayers for orphaned children."

"Aren't there government offices to provide those things?"

"Yes, but the poor mistrust them and are generally rudely treated when they go to them, so they come and shed tears in the sacristy."

"Many years ago, in Rome, on the occasion of a jubilee, I met one Don Benedetto de Merulis who came from this part of the world. If I'm not mistaken, at that time he taught Greek and Latin at a diocesan school, I think. Is he still alive? Do you ever see him?"

"Come this way," Don Angelo said.

He wanted to show Don Paolo the parish treasure. He went to a cupboard that occupied the whole of one wall and with some difficulty opened its two enormous, inlaid wooden doors. He showed Don Paolo the jewelry and enamel work on the top shelves, the silver bust of a martyred saint in a special niche in the middle, and a large number of chasubles, dalmatics, and richly embroidered stoles hanging, as in a wardrobe, at the bottom.

The sacristan came in with two glasses of wine for the priests.

"You asked about Benedetto," Don Angelo said. "Yes, he's still alive. He is a very reckless man of God. For many years he lived an exemplary life, and in learning and virtue he was the master of us all. But now, on the brink of eternity, his contempt for the opinion of men and his excessive confidence in God prompt him to utterances that border on heresy."

"That is a risk that saints have often taken," Don Paolo remarked.

"It is not up to me to distinguish between virtue and indiscipline," said Don Angelo. "I cannot tell you how much I suffer on his account. When he was ordained I was still a seminarian, and I was full of admiration for his sober and dignified tranquillity, for the stainless purity of his private life. He insisted on celebrating his first mass in a prison chapel and his second in a hospital. You can imagine how shocked his relatives were, for a first mass is generally a social event."

"I hope you do not share the relatives' point of view," Don Paolo said.

"No," said Don Angelo, "but even at that time his brusque way of flying in the face of public opinion worried his superiors. For that reason they avoided entrusting him with a parish and directed him toward teaching. Study of the classics and the company of the young seemed to have a modifying effect on his character, but his relations with his superiors and the authorities did not improve. He had no feeling whatever for social conventions."

"I do not know to what divine commandment you are now referring," Don Paolo interrupted. Don Angelo went on as if he had not heard.

"Eventually he was suspended from teaching. I always tried to maintain my friendship for him in his solitude, but now I can really do so no longer."

"Is he so dangerous?" Don Paolo asked.

"Judge for yourself," Don Angelo replied. "Let me tell you the most recent incident. A man from Fossa, a parishioner of mine who worked for some days in his garden, told me that he had heard him say that the present Pope's real name was Pontius XI. At Rocca dei Marsi, where Don Benedetto now lives, this was widely repeated. In their naive ignorance and because of the respect they have for him many took what he said literally and believed it. That parishioner of mine was stricken with doubt and came here to the sacristy to ask me whether it were really true that the Church had fallen into the hands of a descendent of

Pontius Pilate, he who when he had to deal with any grave matter washed his hands of it."

"And what did you tell him?" Don Paolo said. "I'm interested."

The parish priest looked at his guest in surprise.

"Forgive me," Don Paolo said. "I expressed myself badly. You naturally believe that the Church does not wash its hands of those things."

The sacristan came in and told Don Angelo that the women were waiting in the church for the rosary and that the boys had started arriving for the first catechism class.

"Don Benedetto's case is now actually being investigated by the provincial committee for deportations," Don Angelo went on. "That is the pass he has come to. A former pupil of his who has a good deal of influence in the government party and I intervened on his behalf and went to see him. We wanted to suggest that he should sign a brief statement of loyalty to the present government and of acceptance of the present policy of the Church. That would have sufficed. He received us politely, but as soon as I started explaining that to avoid greater evils the Church often had to make the best of a bad business he interrupted me. 'The theory of the lesser evil may be acceptable for a party or a government, but not for a Church,' he said coldly. I tried to avoid getting involved in an abstract argument with him, because in the abstract the worst heresies always present themselves in seductive guise. So I replied, 'But do you realize what would happen if the Church openly condemned the present war? What persecutions would descend upon it, and what moral and material damage would result.' You will never imagine what Don Benedetto replied. 'My dear Don Angelo,' he said, 'can you imagine John the Baptist offering Herod a concordat to avoid having his head cut off? Can you imagine Jesus offering Pontius Pilate a concordat to avoid the crucifixion?'"

"That reply does not seem to me to be anti-Christian," Don Paolo said.

"But the Church is not an abstract society," Don Angelo said, raising his voice. "The Church is what it is. It has a history of nearly two thousand years behind it. She is no longer a young lady who can permit herself acts of foolhardiness and indiscretion. She is an old, a very old, lady full of dignity, respect, traditions, bound by rights and duties. It was of course founded by the crucified Jesus, but after him there came the apostles, followed by generations and generations of saints and popes. The Church is no longer a small, clandestine sect in the catacombs, but has a following of millions and millions of human beings who look to it for protection."

"Sending them to war is a fine way of protecting them," said Don Paolo, seeming to forget prudence for a moment. "In the time of Jesus," he went on, "the old synagogue was an old, a very old, lady with a long tradition of prophets, kings, lawgivers, and priests and a large following to protect. But Jesus did not treat it with much respect."

Don Angelo was still sitting in front of his glass of wine, which he had not yet touched. He closed his eyes, as if seized with a sudden dizziness, and remained like that for a few moments. There was a blue transparency and a slight nervous tremor in the eyebrows that surmounted his deepset eyes. "My God, my God, why do You frighten me?" he murmured.

The sacristan returned and told him that the women were still waiting for the rosary and that the catechism boys were kicking up an infernal din. The parish priest rose to his feet.

"Excuse me," he said, and followed the sacristan.

Don Paolo went back to his hotel.

Outside the town hall a noisy crowd had gathered. Two *cafoni* who had come to the local magistrate's court because of a lawsuit had been recognized as coming from Orta and attacked by a mob that appeared out of the blue with a most unlikely collection of weapons. The two unlucky scapegoats, who were of course quite unaware of why they were the objects of such hatred, had with difficulty been saved from lynching by a party of *carabinieri* and locked up in the police station. They continued to be the object of the most violent threats. The *carabinieri* appealed to the lawyer Zabaglia to try to calm the mob, but his most strenuous efforts failed. The excitement died down only when it was announced that the two unfortunates from Orta were to be officially declared to be under arrest and taken to prison on a charge of having aided and abetted the writing of seditious slogans on the walls of Fossa.

"Why only aiding and abetting?" someone objected.

"Because they're both illiterate," the warrant officer of *carabinieri* explained. "I appeal to your common sense."

The invitation to common sense, if the truth must be told, was not without its effect. The crowd calmed down and split up into groups. To enter the hotel Don Paolo had to force his way through a group of men and young mothers with babies in their arms who were arguing with Berenice.

"I'm leaving tomorrow," Don Paolo said to Berenice. "Where's your daughter? I want her to do me a favor."

Pietro immediately sent Bianchina to Rocca dei Marsi with a note to Don Benedetto, signed with his own initials, asking whether he could come and see him.

"Please don't keep me waiting twenty-four hours for an answer this time," he said to the girl.

"How old is this Don Benedetto?"

"Seventy-five."

"Don't worry, I'll be back right away," Bianchina said with a laugh. She jumped on her bicycle and was off in a flash.

Within an hour she was back with a note written in small, clear, regular, slightly tremulous handwriting:

> . . . *tibi*
> *non ante verso lene merum cado*
> *iamdudum apud me est; eripe te morae.* *

This was the first time Pietro had seen his former teacher's handwriting since he had left school many years before. It was like being confronted with a school task again, but it was an easy one and the invitation was cordial.

---

*"There has for a long time been in my house for you a cask of old wine not yet opened. Do not delay." Horace, Book III, Ode XXIX, to Maecenas.

24

*P*ERHAPS HE'LL BE LATE," Don Benedetto said to his sister. "Perhaps he won't come till after dark."

"Don't you think that having him here might be dangerous?" Marta said.

The way her brother looked at her made her correct herself immediately. "What I meant was that it might be unwise for him."

"By now he must be pretty expert in these matters," Don Benedetto said. "He has been doing nothing but hiding and getting away for years. In any event, you had better leave us alone," he went on. "He might want to tell me things it's wiser to confide to one person only."

"I shan't disturb you," Marta said. "But what I've been wanting to say is that he can't remain an outlaw for the whole of his life. Don't you think we ought to tell his grandmother? She and his uncle are rich, they might be able to get him a lawyer and have him pardoned by the government."

"I don't think Pietro would want to be pardoned."

"But there's no disgrace in a pardon. Why should he refuse one?"

"The point is I don't think he feels guilty. Only those who repent are pardoned."

"But he won't be able to live in the woods for the rest of his life," Marta repeated. "He must still be young. How old is he?"

"The same age as Nunzio, thirty-four or thirty-five."

"But ruining your whole life just for a political opinion isn't right, it isn't decent. You were his teacher, you ought to tell him that."

"I don't think he does it just for politics," Don Benedetto said. "He has seemed to me to have been picked for a hard life ever since he was a boy."

"But if he's persecuted it's because of his political opinions."

"Do you remember when he came to see us here immediately after taking final exams? It was the summer after the earthquake."

"Yes, he was wearing mourning, his parents had been killed."

"Well, I remembered the occasion a short time ago," Don Benedetto said. "He told me something in confidence that must have been very important for his future development. His parents' death had affected him deeply, as was natural enough, but something else happened in those terrible days after the earthquake, when we were all wandering about among the rubble and taking shelter where best we could, something that actually shattered him. I don't think I've ever mentioned it before, because Pietro himself asked me not to tell anyone. But now a long time has passed. Well," Don Benedetto went on, "he had the misfortune to see, without being seen, a monstrous incident that filled him with horror. He was the only witness, and he kept the secret. He didn't tell me exactly what it was, but it was obvious from what he said that the person concerned was a relative of someone from his immediate environment."

"Crimes have always happened," said Marta.

"The person concerned enjoyed universal respect and after the crime he went on living as before, honestly, so to speak, and enjoying general esteem. That was where the monstrosity of the thing lay."

"Can't you tell me what sort of crime it was?" said Marta.

"It was robbery with violence at the expense of an injured or dying man who was still half buried in the rubble," Don Benedetto said. "The criminal was not in need, the crime was committed at night, and, as I said, Pietro witnessed it by chance. He was fifteen at the time. He fainted out of sheer horror. When he told me about it some months later he was still trembling. The killer was a neighbor and acted in the certainty of not being discovered. He was what is called a decent, respectable man. Thinking about it now, I feel that Pietro's flight began at that time. At one time I used to think that he would end up in a monastery."

"Didn't you hear a noise?" Marta said. "Someone's knocking."

Marta hurriedly withdrew to her room. The expected guest was at the threshold. He was in lay clothing and without a hat, but a black garment he was carrying on his arm like a coat might have been the cassock he had taken off just previously. Pietro and Don Benedetto greeted each other and shook hands. Both were embarrassed by emotion.

"Did you come on foot?" Don Benedetto asked.

"I left the carriage down in the village," Pietro replied.

Don Benedetto pointed to a big armchair and sat beside him on a stool that was rather lower. As he was bent with age, this made him seem smaller than his former pupil. Pietro tried to react against the emotion of the scene and to appear perfectly at ease.

"Behold the lost lamb returning to the shepherd of its own accord," he said with a laugh.

Don Benedetto, who was looking with surprise at the young man's precociously aged face, failed to see the joke and shook his head. "It's not easy to tell which of us is the lost lamb," he said sadly.

"Many people talk about you in the villages around here," Pietro said. "What I've heard has been enough to convince me that you're the only person who keeps Christian honor alive in these parts."

"That is not at all my opinion," said Don Benedetto with bitterness in his voice, "and I assure you that that is not false modesty. The truth of the matter is that I know I'm useless. I have lost my teaching job, and I have no cure of souls. It's true that I have the reputation that you mention, but if someone comes here to tell me about some wrong he has suffered I don't know what to say to him. That's the situation, I'm useless. Making certain discoveries at my time of life is sad, believe me."

Pietro had tears in his eyes. In his hours of discouragement in banishment or exile the mere thought of Don Benedetto had been sufficient to restore his calm and confidence, and now the poor old man was reduced to this state. What was he to say to him that would not seem to be inspired by compassion?

"For the rest," Don Benedetto went on, "it is not those who say mass and profess themselves to be ministers of the Lord who are closest to Him in the intimacy of the spirit."

Hearing the old man talking of God as in the old days, Pietro suspected that there might be a grave misunderstanding in his mind that might falsify the whole meeting.

"I lost faith many years ago," he said quietly but distinctly.

The old man smiled and shook his head. "In cases such as yours that is a mere misunderstanding," he said. "It would not be the first time that the Lord has been forced to hide Himself and make use of an assumed name. As you know, He has never attached much importance to the names men have given Him; on the contrary, one of the first of His commandments is not to take His name in vain. And sacred history is full of examples of clandestine living. Have you ever considered the meaning of the flight into Egypt? And later, when He had grown up, did not Jesus several times have to hide himself to escape from the Pharisees?"

This religious apologia for the conspiratorial life brought back serenity to Pietro's face and gave it a childish cheerfulness.

"I have always felt the lack of that chapter in the *Imitation of Christ*," he said with a laugh.

Don Benedetto went on in the same sad tone with which he had begun. "I live here with my sister, between my garden and my books," he said. "For some time past my mail has obviously been tampered with, newspapers and books arrive late or get lost in transit. I pay no visits and receive few, and most of them are disagreeable. All the same, I'm well informed about many things, and they are demoralizing. In short, what should be given to God is given to Caesar and what should be left to Caesar is given to

God. It was to such a brood that the Baptist spoke the words: 'O generation of vipers, who have warned you to flee from the wrath to come?'"

Marta came in and said good evening to Pietro. She did so in a faint voice and with a frightened smile that seemed to have been prepared outside the door and then kept fixed with pins. She put a jug of red wine and two glasses on the table and hurried back to her room.

The old man continued, "There is an old story that ought to be brought to mind whenever belief in God is doubted. Perhaps you will remember that it is written somewhere that in a moment of great distress Elijah asked the Lord to let him die, and the Lord summoned him to a mountain. Elijah went there, but would he recognize the Lord? And there arose a great and mighty wind that struck the mountain and split the rocks, but the Lord was not in the wind. And after the wind the earth was shaken by an earthquake, but the Lord was not in the earthquake. And after the earthquake there arose a great fire, but the Lord was not in the fire. But afterward, in the silence, there was a still, small voice, like the whisper of branches moved by the evening breeze, and that still, small voice, it is written, was the Lord."

Meanwhile a breeze had arisen in the garden, and the leaves began to rustle. The garden door that led into the sitting room creaked and swung open.

"What is it?" Marta called out from the next room. Pietro shuddered. The old man put his hand on his shoulder and said with a laugh, "Don't be afraid, you have nothing to fear."

He rose and shut the door that had been opened by the evening breeze. After a short pause he went on, "I too in the depth of my affliction have asked, where then is the Lord and why has He abandoned us? The loudspeakers and the bells that announced the beginning of new butchery to the whole country were certainly not the voice of the Lord. Nor are the shelling and bombing of Abyssinian villages that are reported daily in the press. But if a poor man alone in a hostile village gets up at night and scrawls with a piece of charcoal or paints DOWN WITH THE WAR

on the walls the Lord is undoubtedly present. How is it possible
not to see that behind that unarmed man in his contempt for
danger, in his love of the so-called enemy, there is a direct reflection of the divine light? Thus, if simple workers are condemned
by the Special Tribunal for similar reasons, there's no doubt about
which side God is on."

Don Benedetto poured a little wine into a glass, raised it and
held it against the light to make sure it was clear, since it came
from a new barrel, and sipped it before filling the two glasses.

"I don't know if you can imagine what it is like to reach certain
conclusions at my age, on the brink of the tomb," he went on. "At
seventy-five it's still possible to change one's ideas, but not one's
habits. A retired life is the only kind that fits in with my character.
I lived in seclusion even when I was young. Revulsion from vul-
garity always kept me away from public life. On the other hand,
inaction irks me. I look around and don't see what I can do. With
the parish priests there's nothing I can do. Those who know me
personally now avoid me, are afraid of meeting me. The few
priests who have left the Church in the past fifty years in the Marsica diocese have done so because of scandalous breaches of
celibacy. That is sufficient to give you an idea of the spiritual state
of our clergy. If news spread in the diocese that a priest had abandoned the priesthood, the first thing that would naturally occur to
the minds of the faithful would be that another one had eloped
with his housemaid."

"I had to call on Don Angelo Girasole this afternoon," Pietro
said. "He gave me the impression of being a very decent man, a
good clerk in an administrative office."

"You're quite right," Don Benedetto said, "but Christianity is
not an administration."

"The others, those who believe they have historical vision, are
worse," said Pietro. "They believe, or pretend they believe, in a
man of providence."

"If they allow themselves to be deceived it is their own fault,"
Don Benedetto interrupted, livening up. "They were warned
about two thousand years ago. They were told that many would

come in the name of providence and seduce the people, that there would be talk of wars and rumors of wars. They were told that all this would come to pass, but that the end was not yet. They were told that nation would rise up against nation and kingdom against kingdom; that there would be famines and pestilences and earthquakes in divers places; but that all these things would not be the end, but the beginning. Christians were warned. We were told that many would be horrified and many would betray, and that if someone, whoever it might be, should say here is a man of providence, there is a man of providence, we must not believe him. We have been warned. False prophets and false saviors shall arise and shall show great signs and wonders and deceive many. We could not have asked for plainer warning. If many have forgotten it, it will not change anything of what will come to pass. The destiny of the man of providence has already been written. *Intrabit ut vulpis, regnabit ut leo, morietur ut canis.*"*

"What a fine language Latin is," said Pietro. "And what a difference there is between that honest old church Latin and the modern sibylline Latin of the encyclicals."

"What is lacking in our country, as you know, is not the critical spirit," Don Benedetto said. "What is lacking is faith. The critics are grumblers, violent men, dissatisfied men, in certain circumstances they may sometimes even be heroes. But they are not believers. What is the use of teaching new ways of talking or gesticulating to a nation of skeptics? Perhaps the terrible sufferings that lie ahead will make Italians more serious. Meanwhile, when I feel most disheartened, I tell myself I'm useless, a failure, but there's Pietro, there are his friends, the unknown members of underground groups. I confess to you that that is my only consolation."

Pietro was taken aback by the despondency in his former master's voice. "My dear Don Benedetto," he said, "we have not met for fifteen years, and after this perhaps we shall not meet again. You are an old man, my health is uncertain, the times are hard. It would be wrong to waste this short visit exchanging

---

*He will come in like a fox, reign like a lion, die like a dog.

compliments. The trust you have in me terrifies me. I genuinely believe I'm no better than my former classmates. My destiny has been more fortunate than theirs because I was helped by a whole series of misfortunes and cut the cord in good time. For the rest, you must forgive me for not sharing the optimism of that only consolation of yours."

"There's no salvation except putting one's life in jeopardy," Don Benedetto said. "But that is not for everyone. After his first meeting with you at Acquafredda, Nunzio, that poor soul in torment, came here and told me everything. He told me again about his position, which I already knew. Under a dictatorial régime how can one exercise a profession in which one depends on public offices and yet remain free? he asked me. What good fortune that at least Pietro is saved, he said."

"Saved?" said Pietro. "Is there a past participle of saving oneself? Alas, recently I have had plenty of occasions to consider what is undoubtedly the saddest aspect of the present degeneracy, because it concerns the future. My dear Don Benedetto, perhaps the future will resemble the present. We may be sowing contaminated seed."

Don Benedetto signaled to him to be silent. "There's someone at the door," he said in an undertone. "Come into the next room."

They rose and went into Marta's room. At that moment there was a knock at the door.

"Go and see who it is," Don Benedetto said to his sister. "Don't let anyone in. Never mind who it is, say you don't know whether I can see him. And please, before you open the door bring the wine and the two glasses in here."

There was another knock at the door, and Marta opened it. It was Don Piccirilli.

"Good evening," he said. "Am I disturbing you? I was told that Don Angelo Girasole was here with Don Benedetto, and I should like to see him too."

"You have been misinformed," Marta said. "Don Girasole is not here."

"Didn't a priest arrive here in a carriage from Fossa a short while ago?" Don Piccirilli said.

"No priest and no carriage have been seen here," Marta said. "You have been misinformed."

This conversation took place at the front door. Marta showed no inclination to let him in.

"I hope I'm not being troublesome," Don Piccirilli said, "but as I've come all this way I should like at least to say good evening to Don Benedetto."

"I don't know whether he can see you," Marta said. "He may be resting. I'll go and see."

In the next room she found her brother alone. Pointing to the window that gave on to the garden, he indicated that his first visitor had left. "Now we must try to keep Don Piccirilli here as long as possible," he said to his sister in an undertone. "Bring us some wine immediately!"

He went to meet the newly arrived guest.

"What are you doing standing there in the doorway?" he said reproachfully. "Come in, come in, don't stand on ceremony. You must tell me what you think of the wine from a new barrel."

25

MATALENA WAS PREPARING flour for bread making on the ground floor of the inn, and Don Paolo was keeping her company. At Pietrasecca bread was baked once a fortnight in a communal oven. It was a ritual with strict rules. The woman's head was wrapped in a cloth rather like a nun's veil and she was passing the flour through a sieve over an open bin. Thus she separated the white flour from the chaff and the best from the ordinary flour. The chaff went to the chickens and the pig; the ordinary flour was used for bread and the best for pasta. The woman's face and hands were covered with dust from the flour that rose from the rhythmical movement of the sieve. Chiarina, the goatherd's wife, was having difficulty in lighting the green wood under the pot in which potatoes were being cooked that were to be added to the flour to make the bread heavier and more lasting.

The sieving stopped when a strange young man, looking halfway between a *cafone* and a workman, came into the bar and asked for Don Paolo. He had a letter in his hand. He seemed rather surprised and embarrassed at the sight of Don Paolo, and was on the point of apologizing and going away again.

"Don Benedetto told me he was sending me to someone in whom I could have full confidence. To tell the truth, I didn't expect to find a priest here," he said.

"Never mind," said the priest. "Don Benedetto will have had his reasons." The youth handed over the letter of introduction. It consisted of these few words, written in Don Benedetto's fine, tremulous hand: "*Ecce homo*, my friend, here is a poor man who has need of you, and perhaps you also have need of him. Please listen to him to the end."

Don Paolo took the young man to his room and made him sit beside him.

"If you had come here as one goes to a priest," he said, "I should certainly have asked you to apply elsewhere. How long have you known Don Benedetto?"

"We belong to the same village," the young man said. "Every family at Rocca knows every other. Everyone knows everything, or nearly everything, about everyone else. When you see someone going out you know exactly where he's going, and when you see him coming back you know where he has been. My family has a vineyard near Don Benedetto's garden halfway up the hill above the village. We use water from his well to spray sulfur on the vines, and he borrows our stakes for his tomatoes, beans, and peas. My mother always consulted him about my education. His advice may not always have been good, but his intentions always were. He has always liked me, ever since I was a boy." After a pause he added, "He told me to tell you everything."

As he spoke the young man's personality became better defined. At first sight, particularly because of his plain, patched clothing, the earthy marks on his face and hands, and his untidy, ruffled hair, he created the impression of being half workman, half *cafone*, but on closer inspection he turned out to have extraordinarily lively and intelligent eyes, and his manners were controlled and polite. Also instead of using dialect he spoke very correct Italian with complete ease. After some hesitation he started telling his story.

"I was a delicate and sickly boy, and also I was an only son," he said. "So my mother decided that I should not work on the land. 'Our family has always worked the land, and we're still where we always were,' she said. 'For generations we have hoed, dug, sowed, and manured the land, and we're still poor. Let the boy study. He's not strong and he needs a less tough way of living.' My father didn't agree. 'Working the land is hard, but it's safe,' he said. 'Education is for the sons of gentlemen. We have no one to back us.' Our backing was Don Benedetto. 'Since the boy wants to study, let him,' he said. He helped my mother with his advice. As long as I was at grammar school my family could still regard itself as being prosperous. Apart from the vineyard, my father had two fields on which he grew wheat and vegetables and a shed with four cows. While I was a student the money orders my mother sent me to pay for my keep never arrived regularly, but they arrived. But during my three years at high school the family situation went from bad to worse, because of two bad harvests and an illness of my father's. On top of this were my heavy expenses. The result was that one of the two fields had to be sold to pay off my father's debts. Two cows died in an epidemic; the two that were left were sold at the fair, and the shed was let. 'No matter,' my mother said, 'When our son has passed his exams he'll be able to help us.' I passed the state exam three years ago and the following October I went to Rome, where I registered in the faculty of arts. Actually my mother didn't know where to find the money to keep me in Rome until I got my degree."

"Why did you choose the faculty of arts?" Don Paolo asked. "It's not the best from the point of view of earning a living."

"Don Benedetto said that was what I was best at. In Rome I led a life of severe privations. I lived in a small room without electric light. My midday meal consisted of white coffee and bread, and for dinner I had soup. I was permanently hungry. I was comically dressed and had no friends. The first time I tried to approach other students they laughed at me and made stupid jokes because of my provincial appearance. Two incidents of that kind were enough to make me completely unsociable. I often wept with rage and mortification in my little room. I resigned myself to a life of solitude. After the warm family atmosphere to which I was used

I was ill at ease in the noisy, vulgar, cynical students' world. Most of the students were interested in sport and politics, both of which offer frequent opportunities for rowdiness. One day I saw a typical piece of rowdiness from the streetcar. About a dozen students belonging to my faculty beat a young workman till the blood flowed. I can still see the scene in my mind's eye. The workman lay on the pavement with his head on one of the tracks while the students who had surrounded him went on kicking and hitting him with sticks. 'He didn't salute the flag,' they shouted. Some policemen arrived on the scene, congratulated the aggressors on their patriotic action, and arrested the injured man. A crowd had gathered, but no one protested. I was left alone in the stationary streetcar. What cowardice, I muttered to myself. Behind me I heard someone mutter, 'Yes, it's a real disgrace.' It was the conductor. We said good-bye to each other that day, but that was all. But as he was often on duty on the line that went down my street, we saw each other every so often and got into the habit of greeting each other like old acquaintances."

There was a long pause as if he had lost the thread. Then he went on, "I met him in the street one day when he was off duty. We shook hands and went into a tavern for a glass of wine. Each of us told the other about himself, and so we struck up a friendship. He asked me to his home, where I met other persons, nearly all of them young. There were five of them all together and they constituted a cell, and those meetings were cell meetings. All this was strange and new to me. Thanks to the conductor's introduction, I was admitted to the cell, and I regularly attended the weekly meetings. Those were my first personal contacts with townspeople. The other members of the cell were workers or artisans, and they liked me for being a student, and I enjoyed those meetings too. The purely human pleasure they gave me meant that I did not at first realize the gravity and significance of the step I had taken. At the meetings badly printed little newspapers and pamphlets were read in which tyranny was denounced and the revolution was proclaimed as a certain, inevitable, and not distant event that would establish fraternity and justice among men. It was a kind of secret and prohibited weekly dream in which we indulged, and it made us forget the wretchedness of our everyday lives. It was like a secret religious rite. There was no link between us apart from those meetings, and if by chance we met in the street we pretended not to know one another.

"When I went out one morning I was arrested by two policemen, taken to the central police station, and shut up in a room full of other policemen. After some formalities they started slapping my face and spitting at me, and that went on for an hour. Perhaps I might have put up better with a more violent beating, but the slapping and spitting were intolerable. When the door opened and the official who was to interrogate me appeared, my face and chest were literally dripping with spittle. The official railed at, or pretended to rail at, his subordinates, made me wash and dry myself, took me to his office, and assured me that he had studied my case with benevolence and understanding. He knew I lived in a small room, he knew the café where I had my midday bread and coffee and the inn where I went for my soup in the evening. He had detailed information about my family, and he knew about the difficulties that endangered the continuation of my studies. He could only guess the motives that had led me toward the revolutionary groups but, he said, that impulse could not in itself be regarded as reprehensible; on the contrary, in fact. He said youth was inherently magnanimous and idealistic, and it would be disastrous if it were otherwise. However, the police had the socially necessary but perhaps distasteful role of keeping a close watch on the magnanimous and idealistic impulses of the young."

"In short," Don Paolo interrupted, "he suggested that you should put yourself in the service of the police. And what did you reply?"

"I agreed."

Matalena appeared at the door and said, "Dinner's ready. Shall I set for two?"

"I'm not hungry this evening," the priest replied. He rose from his seat because he was tired and lay on the bed.

In a soft voice the young man continued, "I was given a hundred lire to pay the rent of my room, and in return I wrote a short report, like an academic essay, on how a cell works, what its members read and what they talk about. The official read it and praised it. 'It's very well written,' he said. I was proud that he was pleased with me, and I undertook to remain in contact with him in return for an allowance of five hundred lire a month. That enabled me to have soup at midday as well as in the evening and to go to the movies on Saturday nights. One day he also gave me a packet of cigarettes. Actually I had never smoked, but I learned to out of politeness."

"And what did you write in your next reports?" Don Paolo asked.

"They went on being very general, and he began to be dissatisfied with them," the young man said. "I always sent him a copy of the printed matter that was distributed in the cell, but that was not enough for him, probably because he received the same material from other sources. Eventually he advised me to leave that cell and join a more interesting one, and I had no difficulty in doing so. I told my friends that I wanted a transfer to a cell in which there were other intellectuals, and it was arranged immediately. In the new cell I met and struck up a friendship with a girl, a dressmaker. She was the first woman I had ever met. Very soon we were inseparable, and it was then that I began to have the first twinges of conscience. With her I began to have glimpses of a pure, honest, and decent way of living the possibility of which I had not previously imagined. At the same time an insuperable abyss opened up between my apparent and my secret life. Sometimes I managed to forget my secret. I worked for the cell with genuine enthusiasm, translated into Italian and typed out whole chapters of revolutionary novels that we received from abroad, stuck manifestos on the walls at night. But I was deceiving myself. When my new comrades admired my courage and my activity they reminded me that in reality I was betraying them. So I tried to get away from them. Also I told myself that I too had a right to live. No more money was being sent to me from home. When I was hungry and the rent was due I lost all restraint. I had no other resources. I regarded politics as absurd. What did all that stuff matter to me? I should certainly have preferred to live in peace, to have two or three meals a day, consigning both 'economic democracy' and 'the necessity of imperial expansion' to the devil. But that was impossible. I had no money to buy food or pay the rent. But that kind of cynicism collapsed when I was with my girl. We were very much in love. To me she did not represent a way of thinking, in fact she argued very little but kept silent and liked listening to others; to me she was a way of being, a way of living, a way of giving oneself in an unparalleled human and pure way. I could no longer think of life without her, because she was really more than a woman, she was a light and a flame, she was concrete proof of the possibility of living honestly, cleanly, unselfishly, seeking harmony with one's fellows with the whole of one's soul. It seemed to me that only after I met her had I become spiritually alive. But I did not blame my parents. They were good, honest people, but they were traditional. That girl did not follow rules, but her heart. She seemed to me to invent her life as she lived it. But in the face of her ingenuous confidence in me how could I not remember that I was deceiving and betraying her? Thus our love was poisoned at the roots. Being with her, though I loved her so much, was an insupportable pretense, a torment . . ."

"Why, when your relations with the police became morally reprehensible to you, did you not break with them?" Don Paolo asked.

"I tried to get away from them and cover my tracks several times," the young man said. "Once I moved, but they had no difficulty in tracking me down to my new address. For a time I tried to quiet my conscience by writing harmless, bogus reports that told them nothing. At that time I was beginning to receive a small monthly allowance from my mother again. I tried to deceive the police by telling them I had left the cell because my comrades no longer trusted me. But they had other informers who satisfied them of the opposite. Finally I became obsessed with the idea that my situation was irremediable. I felt condemned. There was nothing that I could do. It was my destiny."

The young man spoke with difficulty, almost struggling for breath. Don Paolo avoided looking him in the face.

"I don't want to make my behavior seem less ugly than it was," he went on. "I don't want to make my case more pitiful. This is a confession in which I want to show myself in all my repulsive nakedness. Well, then, the truth of the matter was this. Fear of being discovered was stronger in me than remorse. What was I to tell my girl if my deception were revealed? What would my friends say? That was the idea that haunted me. I feared for my threatened reputation, not for the wrong that I was doing. I saw the image of my fear all around me everywhere."

The young man paused. His throat was dry. There was a bottle of water and a glass on the table, but it did not occur to Don Paolo to ask him to help himself.

"I knew I was being trailed by the police who no longer trusted me," he went on. "I kept away from my friends to avoid having to denounce them. The police threatened me with arrest if I associated with suspects without informing them. I lived in terror of being arrested again. I tried to live in complete seclusion, with the result that every meeting with my girl was a torment. But in spite of that she was always patient, gentle, and affectionate with me. On Christmas Day last year we went together to a little eating place outside the walls . . ."

Don Paolo went on listening to a story every detail of which he already knew. The unusually cheerful lunch. The invitation to go home with the girl. The buying of flowers, fruit, sweets, and a bottle of Marsala. The arrival of the police and the escape onto the roof. The long wait on the roof. But the young man did not finish. He hid his face in his hands and burst into tears. After a while he resumed his story.

"I went home to Rocca dei Marsi. I told my parents that the doctors had insisted on my returning to my native climate. I spent the winter at home without seeing anyone. Sometimes I went to see Don Benedetto, who gave me books to read. In the spring I started working in the fields with my father, winnowing, pruning the vines, hoeing, and reaping. I went on working as long as I could stand on my feet, to the point of physical exhaustion. Immediately after dinner I went to bed, and in the morning, at dawn, it was I who woke my father. He looked at me with admiration.

He said, 'It's obvious that you come from a race of peasants; if you come from the land you cannot free yourself from it.' But if you come from the land and have lived in a town you're no longer a peasant and you're not a townsman either. Memory of the town, of my girl, of the cell, of the police, was a perpetually open wound, a wound that still bled and was beginning to putrefy and threatened to poison the rest of my life. My mother said town air had ruined me and put sadness in my blood. 'Let me work,' I said, 'perhaps work will make me better.' But in the fields my girl would often appear before me in my mind's eye. How could I forget her? Having glimpsed the possibility of another way of living, a clean, honest, and courageous way of living, having seen the possibility of open and frank communication and dreamed of a better humanity, how could I resign myself to village life? On the other hand, how could I undo the irremediable? In my solitary brooding, which left me not a moment's peace, I passed from fear of punishment to fear of nonpunishment. The idea that I was haunted by the wrong I had done only because of the continual risk of being found out began to frighten me. So I began to wonder whether, if better technique enabled one to betray one's friends with the certainty that one would never be found out, that would make it more supportable."

Don Paolo looked him in the face, in the eyes.

"I must confess," the young man went on, "that my religious faith has never been very strong. I have never believed very deeply. I was baptized, confirmed, and received Holy Communion like everyone else, but my faith in the reality of God was very vague and fitful. That was why I put up no resistance in Rome to accepting the so-called scientific theories that were propagated in the cells. These theories began to strike me as too comfortable. The idea that everything was matter, that the idea of right was inseparable from that of utility (even if it were social utility) and was backed only by the idea of punishment, became intolerable to me. Punishment by whom? The state, the party and public opinion? But supposing the state, the party, and public opinion were immoral? And then, if favorable circumstances or an appropriate technique made it possible to do evil with impunity, what was morality based on? So might technique be capable of destroying the distinction between right and wrong by eliminating the risk of punishment? The idea frightened me. I began to be seriously afraid of the absurd. I don't want to weary you with these digressions, which may seem abstract to you; nor do I want you to suppose that by moralizing I'm now trying to put myself in a more favorable light. No, those ideas became the very substance of my life. I no longer believed in God, but with all the strength of my mind I began to want Him to exist. I had an absolute need of Him to escape from the fear of chaos. A night came when I could no longer stand it, and I got up to go and knock at the door of a Capuchin monastery in our part of the world. On the way I met a monk whom I already knew, one Brother Gioacchino. I said to him, 'I want so much to believe in God and I can't imagine it, won't you please explain to me how it's done?' 'One mustn't be proud,' he replied, 'one mustn't claim the right to understand everything, one mustn't try, one must resign oneself, shut one's eyes, pray. Faith is a grace.' But I could not let myself go. I wanted to understand. I couldn't not try to understand. My whole being was in a state of extreme and painful tension. I couldn't resign myself. I wanted God by force. I needed Him."

The young man fell silent, as if exhausted.

"You must be thirsty," Don Paolo said. "Drink some water."

"Eventually I went to see Don Benedetto," the young man went on. "I went to see him, not because he was a priest, but because to me he'd always been a symbol of the upright man. He has known me since childhood, as I said. When I went to see him I told him that actually he did not know me yet, because he had no suspicion of what was hidden inside me. My confession lasted for five hours. I made a tremendous effort and told him everything, and in the end I was lying almost unconscious on the ground. I seriously believed I was dying. On that first occasion the words came out of me as if I were bringing up blood. When I had finished only a vague gleam of consciousness remained. I felt like an empty sack. Don Benedetto sent his sister Marta to tell my mother that I would be sleeping at his house that night, and that for the next few days I would be helping him working in his garden. We worked together for the next few days, and every now and then he stopped and talked to me. He taught me that nothing is irreparable while life lasts, and that no condemnation is ever final. He explained to me that, though evil must not of course be loved, nevertheless good is often born of it, and that perhaps I should never have become a man but for the infamies and errors through which I had passed. When at last he had finished with me and said I could go home I had no more fear and I seemed to have been reborn. I was struck by the air coming from the mountain. Never before had I breathed such fresh air in my village. Having stopped being afraid, I stopped brooding and started rediscovering the world. I started seeing the trees again, the children in the streets, the poor people laboring in the fields, the donkeys carrying their loads, the cows pulling the plow. I went on seeing Don Benedetto from time to time. Yesterday he sent for me and said, 'I should like to spare you the repetition of a painful experience, but there's a man near here to whom I want you to repeat your confession. He's someone in whom you can have complete confidence.' He gave me the necessary information, added some advice, and here I am."

By now it was dark, and the young man's exhausted voice faded away in the shadows. After a pause the other man's voice emerged from it.

"If I were a leader of a party or of a political group," Don Paolo said, "I would have to judge you according to the party rules. Every party has a morality of its own, codified in rules. Those rules are often very close to those with which moral feeling inspires everyone, though sometimes they are the exact opposite. But I'm not (or am no longer) a political leader. Here and now I'm an ordinary man, and if I am to judge another man I can be guided only by my conscience, respecting the very narrow limits within which one man has the right to judge another."

"I did not come here to ask for pardon or absolution," the young man said.

"Luigi Murica," the other man said quietly, "I want to tell you something that will show how much I now trust you. I'm not a priest. Don Paolo Spada is not my real name. My name is Pietro Spina."

Murica's eyes filled with tears.

Meanwhile Matalena of her own accord had set the table for two, and she now insisted on their coming down for dinner. "Convalescents mustn't miss meals," she said. "And if they have visitors the least they can do is to invite them."

She had put a clean tablecloth and a bottle of wine on the table. The two men dined in silence. The wine was the previous year's and the bread was a fortnight old. They dipped the bread in the wine. When they had finished Murica wanted to go straight back to Rocca, and Don Paolo went up to his room to fetch a coat to go with him for some of the way. Matalena did not conceal a certain amount of jealousy at this sudden friendship between a stranger and her priest.

"You talked for such a long time," she said to Murica. "Do you still have things to say to each other?"

"I confessed," the young man said.

When the two men parted in the road leading down to the valley Murica said, "Now I'm ready for anything."

"Good, we'll meet again soon," Don Paolo said.

The priest delayed returning to the inn. He sat on the grassy edge of the road, oppressed by many thoughts. Voices could be heard in the distance, shepherds calling to their flocks, the barking of dogs, the low bleating of sheep. A slight odor of thyme and wild rosemary rose from the damp earth. It was the time of day when the *cafoni* put their donkeys back in their sheds and went to sleep. Mothers called their children from the windows. It was a time favorable to humility. Man returned to the animal, the animal to the plant, the plant to the earth. The stream at the bottom of the valley was full of stars. Pietrasecca was submerged in shadow; all that could be seen was the cow head with its two big horns at the top of the inn.

26

*D*ON PAOLO MET CRISTINA on a visit to the cemetery. She was touched by the fact that he too had brought flowers to put on her father's grave. On the way back he accompanied her as far as her garden gate. The girl was looking thin and unwell; she wore a long, plain black dress loosely tied at the waist with a cloth belt.

"You must forgive me for what I said the last time we met," Don Paolo said. "I was presumptuous and rude."

"No, it was entirely my fault," Cristina replied.

They parted, promising to see each other again soon.

After the excitement caused by the declaration of war Pietrasecca had returned to normal. Women and old men ate their soup in silence in the doorways of their hovels without looking about them, and when they were spoken to they responded wearily. Some mothers were receiving a small allowance for sons who had been called up and prayed that it would last. Schoolboys engaged in battles with stones outside the inn, "Italians" on one side and "Africans" on the other. Sometimes, to the horror and indignation of the schoolmistress, the Africans won.

Apart from that, there was no point in worrying, because what was bound to happen was bound to happen. War had been bound to come, and it had come. If there was going to be a plague, there was no way of avoiding it.

Magascià's wife had been told in great confidence by Matalena that Don Paolo had confessed a young man who had come to see him from the valley. So he must have received permission. Therefore the woman came to implore him to confess her husband, who had not been reconciled to God for twenty-five years.

"He has no confidence in the priests in this part of the world," the woman said. "If you don't do him this grace, he'll die in sin and go to hell."

The priest had relapsed into a state of extreme weakness. He had caught a bad cold the day before, he had a headache and had not slept all night. So his reply to the woman was an absent-minded no, and he thought no more about it until old Magascià appeared in person in his room. Tall, bearded, and massive, with his hat in his hand, he filled up almost the whole of the doorway. His empty left sleeve hung from his shoulder and was inserted into his jacket pocket. Don Paolo was sitting in a chair near his bed and was going to say something, but the old man knelt at his feet, made the sign of the cross, kissed the floor, and with his face to the ground beat his breast three times. "*Mea culpa, mea culpa, mea culpa*," he muttered.

Without raising his head and lowering his voice still more, he went on mumbling incomprehensibly for some minutes; all that Don Paolo could hear was a sibilant sound accompanied by brief sighs. When this stopped the man remained prostrate on the ground, his huge form filling up half the room. His enormous frame made him look like a geological phenomenon, a fossilized antediluvian monster; his beard and hair were like wild vegetation; only the fear that his attitude expressed revealed him to be a man.

He remained prostrate and silent for some time. Then he raised his head and asked in a normal voice, "Have you given me absolution? May I go?"

"You may go," the priest replied.

Magascià rose and kissed his hand. "By the way," he said in an undertone before leaving, "I need advice on something I dare not mention to anyone else. Isn't murder pardoned after twenty-five years? If one is found out, does one have to go on trial just the same?"

"What murder?"

Magascià couldn't understand why the priest now simulated ignorance, but as he urgently wanted an answer to his question he repeated in his ear, "The murder of Don Giulio, the Lama notary."

"Oh, I see, I'd forgotten already," the priest said. "But I'm not a lawyer. I don't know the answer to your question."

The news that Don Paolo had received permission to hear confession spread like wildfire. All that Magascià said was, "He understands everything and forgives everything. Matalena's right, he's a saint."

"He's a saint who reads sinners' hearts," said Matalena.

People started coming along to find out for themselves, and very soon Don Paolo's room became public property, as it were, with people continually coming in and going out. Some wanted to arrange an appointment for their own confession. Children came up the stairs and stayed in the doorway without daring to approach the priest, who could not hide or defend himself. He rose, went to the window or the door, struggling like an animal caught in a trap.

Though he was feverish, he was on the point of taking flight, walking out, but was stopped at the door by the arrival of Mastrangelo, supported under the armpits by his wife Lidovina and his sister-in-law Marietta, because one of his legs was bandaged and he could hardly walk. As he could not kneel, the two women made him sit on a chair near the Father Confessor. They kissed his hand and left. Mastrangelo began to speak, putting his mouth to the priest's ear so that no one else should hear. His breath was foul, it stank of many years' wine drinking and made Don Paolo feel dizzy.

"My wife had eighteen children, but God took sixteen of them back," Mastrangelo said. "Two remain. There is flesh that is chastised from birth, and there's no help for it. My wife's sister Marietta has been chastised in a different way. She was poor, but healthy. Before her wedding day everything was ready, the banns had been put up, and Nicola, the bridegroom, came to see me and said there was a secret he must tell me. The war had chastised him, he said. He showed me what had happened. He was no longer a man. To save his life they had had to operate on him in the military hospital. The wretched man was alone in the world, he had no mother or sisters, he had no one to wash his shirt or make his bed or cook his soup, so it was natural that he should want to marry. Also he had a vineyard and a medal. If Magascià died, the salt and tobacco monopoly would go to him because of the medal. Magascià was already an old man then, and it was only reasonable to expect him to die soon; it isn't my brother-in-law's fault that he's still alive. Well then, Nicola and Marietta got married, and it was only after the wedding that Marietta discovered the misfortune. Nicola said to her, "Your brother-in-law Mastrangelo knew everything." Marietta sent for me immediately and started to weep. "You're the ruin of me," she said, "now I'll kill myself for shame." Nicola left us alone. Before going away he said, "Since God wished to chastise me I have no right to be jealous; but on condition that honor is saved and no one knows." Marietta has had six children, four of them still living. You may not know it, but making children is rather like drink. You swear that this glass is going to be the last, but then you get thirsty again and have another. I'll have this one and that will be that, you say, but who can control thirst? Sometimes it's the woman who's thirsty, sometimes it's the man, sometimes it's both. At first relations between the two sisters were very difficult, but in the course of time they settled down. We accepted it all with resignation, as God had sent it to us. Honor was satisfied, there was no scandal, no one suspected anything. But one day Nicola confessed to Don Cipriano, and Don Cipriano made him change his mind. He explained that the chastisements of God that we had already suffered were nothing in comparison to those we deserved and were yet to be inflicted on us, and that those that we did not suffer ourselves would be suffered by our children, who were the children of sin; and that those not suffered by our children would be suffered by their children, and so on unto the seventh generation. But, if God knows the truth, how can He go on chastising us? Haven't we suffered enough?"

The penitent fell silent and looked at the Father Confessor with staring, bloodshot eyes, awaiting his reply. The tipsy voices of some *morra* players floated up the stairs from the ground floor. On the windowpane two dusty, motionless flies were attached to one another, surprised by death in the act of union. Outside it was raining. Don Paolo shuddered. Mastrangelo seized his arm, shook it, wanting an answer. "Was Don Cipriano right?" he said. "Are Marietta's children and their children cursed already?"

"Cursed by whom?" said Don Paolo.

"Aren't they cursed by God?"

"God does not curse," Don Paolo said. "He has never cursed a living soul."

"Won't they be children of misfortune?"

"Perhaps they may be," Don Paolo said. "But like everyone else, neither more nor less."

Mastrangelo called Lidovina and Marietta, who came upstairs again and helped their man out, supporting him under the armpits and interrogating him with their eyes to find out the result of his confession.

Other penitents, men and women, were sitting on the stairs, waiting their turn to confess. An acute, pungent smell came floating up, as if these people relieved themselves in their pants and never washed. There was also another smell, a new and unusual one in an inn — the smell of incense. Matalena had hurried to get the keys of the church from Cristina and had taken a little incense from the supply in the sacristy. Don Paolo put on his coat and took refuge in the street. The penitents, disappointed and disheartened, watched him from the door.

"Wait, wait," Matalena told them. "He only wants a little fresh air. He won't be going far in this rain."

After about an hour he reappeared but, instead of coming back to the inn, he made for the Colamartini house.

Cristina opened the door. The girl seemed thinner and more unwell than before.

"We were just talking about you," she said.

She showed him into the big room in which the whole family was gathered, her grandmother, her aunt, and her mother.

"But you're wet through," Cristina exclaimed when she saw him in the light of the room. "And your teeth are chattering with cold."

She made him give her his coat so that she could hang it up to dry and made him sit by the fireplace.

"Stretch out your feet toward the fire," she said.

In the room there was the usual stuffy smell, modified by the odor of preserved fruit and aromatic wine. The three old women were silent. Don Paolo tried to avoid their eyes. Through a big window he could see the rain-drenched garden. The flowers had turned to seed, and the seeds had fallen to the ground. Cristina's aunt and mother rose and withdrew to the next room. Cristina murmured something into her grandmother's ear and followed them.

"Weren't you the last person to whom my son spoke before coming back from Fossa?" the old woman said to the priest. "What did he say?"

"He said, 'It's the end.' He didn't want me to go with him. It was in fact the end. That's all he said to me," the priest replied.

The old woman, who was dressed in black, was sitting on an armchair covered with old red velvet near a window that looked out onto the garden. She was small, shriveled, and wrinkled; she looked at the priest with glassy, inscrutable, abstracted eyes, and when she spoke she revealed her empty gums. The rain beat on the blurred windows.

"They left us alone because they want me to confess," the old woman said. "But I don't want to confess. Must I tell you the truth? I lack the repentance necessary for confession. Why should I repent?"

She held her hands crossed on her breast; they looked like old tools worn out by long, hard use. Her shriveled arms looked like two dry branches waiting to be broken off and thrown on the fire.

"Why should I repent?" she went on. "For eighty years I have cared about one thing only, a good thing, the only good thing, the reputation of my family. I have never thought of anything else, or cared about anything else, or done anything else. For eighty years. Am I to repent now?"

In her eyes, which suddenly opened wide, there appeared a hopeless anguish, a long-repressed fear, a dismay so fixed and irremediable, an expression of despair so primitive that Don Paolo was taken aback.

"Is it the end?" she asked. "Is it the end of everyone or only of the Colamartinis?"

"It's the end of all the landowners, I think," Don Paolo said.

When the old woman realized that the priest was looking her in the eyes, she closed them. The shape of her completely fleshless and almost hairless head recalled that of a sparrow. Such a fragile thing, but so tough, so stubborn, so tenacious, so pitiless, so durable that it had lasted for eighty years. Cristina had told her that if she did not repent and confess she would go to hell, and she had replied, "Very well, then, I shall go to hell." But, since an opportunity of consulting a priest had arisen, there was a detail on which she badly wanted information.

"How long do those who do not repent and go to hell have in the presence of God on the judgment throne? Do they at least have time enough to tell Him the truth?"

Don Paolo had to admit that he had no definite information on this subject, but he said common sense would seem to suggest a reply in the affirmative. "That is what is done at every decent tribunal," he said. That was sufficient for the old woman.

Cristina returned in time to accompany Don Paolo to the door, but before he left she wanted to show him a small room next to the kitchen in which there was a loom on which she worked in her rare moments of leisure during the day and until late at night.

"We do not know how we're going to manage," she said. "You know that we lost all our savings in the failure of the bank? We get nothing from our remaining land. The tenants don't pay the rent."

She had had the idea of earning something by weaving, but had changed her mind.

"Wool is expensive," she explained, "and nowadays no one wants handmade cloth any longer; it's a luxury. The few orders I've had so far have been from friends who gave them to me out of sympathy, I think."

"Have you given up the idea of taking the veil?" Don Paolo asked.

"How could I do it now?" she replied. "In this house I'm both the mistress and the maid, with three persons to look after. The most vigorous of the three, my grandmother, can't even dress herself."

"You do not realize how worried I am about you," said Don Paolo. "It distresses me that I'm not able to help you."

"Thank you," Cristina said with a slight smile veiled with sadness. "It will help me if you no longer bear me any ill feeling. Will you promise me that? Besides, believe me, material difficulties are the least of our worries. Spiritual troubles are much more painful. Some family matters I'd never heard of before are now the subject of continual arguments and disputes."

"And Alberto?" Don Paolo said.

"He has joined the militia," Cristina said. "He's certainly not cut out for military life, but it was the only thing that offered. If he does well, he'll at least be able to provide for himself."

Cristina showed the priest a piece of weaving she had finished the day before, a small red and white rug with graceful geometrical patterns that she had copied from an old one.

"Do you know that my brother Alberto greatly admires you?" she said. "He told me about your plot for the second revolution. Isn't it dangerous? Isn't it condemned by the Church?"

"In our time there are many ways of serving God," Don Paolo said with an evasive gesture.

"That is also Don Benedetto's view," Cristina said. "Do you know that he came here with Signorina Marta for the funeral? Alberto and I had a long talk with him. We asked his advice on certain family matters, and eventually, I don't remember how, the conversation turned to the question of obedience to civil authorities, and that led to Pietro Spina. 'You mustn't think badly of him,' he said. 'I know him, he was my pupil. Socialism is his way of serving God.'"

"Did he actually use those words?"

"Yes, I remember them distinctly. He also said of Spina, 'He was touched by God when he was a boy and was thrown by God Himself into the shadows in search of Him. I'm sure he is still obeying His voice.' In short, Don Benedetto talked to us about him as if he knew him very well. After what he said I felt very confused."

"I can well believe it," Don Paolo said. "But perhaps what he said was not to be taken literally."

The priest was about to leave when Cristina said she would like to confess to him at a time and place convenient to him.

"Oh, no," he replied, taken by surprise. Then he added in embarrassment, "Please don't take it amiss, but above all I lack the detachment desirable between penitent and confessor."

Cristina blushed. "You're right," she said. "It would be difficult for me too."

"I very much enjoy talking to you, but as an ordinary man," Don Paolo went on. "I too am going through a difficult period, and seeing you more often would help me."

"I don't have a single free moment all day long," Cristina said.

"Very well then, I shall come this evening after dinner," Don Paolo said. "I shall keep you company while you work at the loom."

"All right," said Cristina, a trifle hesitantly.

That evening the priest ate his dinner cheerfully and with a good appetite. Matalena too was radiant because of the afternoon's confessions. Her inn was becoming a sacred place. Two lamps were burning in front of the image of Our Lady of the Rosary.

"The carpenter will be coming later for the measurements," she told the priest. "The work will be at my expense, of course."

"What measurements?" Don Paolo asked, touching iron.

"The measurements for the confessional. Diocleziano's a good carpenter, but he has never made a confessional before. I'll put it in your room, where the small table is now. What do you think of the idea?"

"I think you're going out of your mind."

"You don't want to use a confessional? It's a pity, but as you wish. It was chiefly for the sake of the girls. I told them to wait until the confessional was ready. But if you prefer doing without . . ."

Matalena brought him an apple and a handful of walnuts.

"Just to let you know, those who lined up this afternoon will be coming back later," she said.

"What do they want?"

"You know very well, they want to confess. Now that you've started."

"I haven't the slightest desire to confess them."

"Shall I tell them to come back tomorrow? The trouble is that most of them work during the day."

"Just tell them never to come here again."

"Impossible. They'd say it was my fault, they'd blame me."

"You are not responsible for my actions."

"They'd say, 'Why others and not us?' They'd say, 'It's all Matalena's fault.' They'd never forgive me."

"Let them say what they like. I shall not confess them, that's certain."

"If that's the case, talk to them yourself when they come. Then they'll believe it's not my fault."

"I shall be out when they come."

"I'll make them wait till you come back."

"Matalena, listen to me," said the priest, raising his voice. "I shall not set foot in this house until they've gone."

This alarmed Matalena.

"If you don't want to, no one can force you to," she said. "I'll tell them you're tired tonight and that perhaps you'll change your mind in the morning."

The priest did not answer. But when she saw him pick up his hat and make ready to go out she was seized with remorse.

"It's raining," she said. "It's bad for you to go out in this weather. Stay here, I'll see about getting rid of them. I'll see you're not troubled. At most we'll talk about it again tomorrow. Where are you going in this weather?"

"Where I like," said the priest.

But when she saw him making for the Colamartini house all her anxieties vanished and she smiled with satisfaction. The spell was obviously working.

Don Paolo found the door half open and Cristina already at work at the loom, busily trying to untangle some warp cords that had gotten into a knot.

"Can I help you?" Don Paolo said.

"Do you know anything about it?"

"Try me."

The girl gave up her seat to him, as if it were a game.

"The trouble's in the register," the priest said with confidence as soon as he had tried the shed of the warp cords.

Cristina was left openmouthed with astonishment.

"You understand weaving?" she asked.

"I used to help my mother when I was a boy," he replied with a laugh. "She was an expert. She did it more for pleasure than for profit. I did it as a hobby too."

"Was it a loom like this?"

"Eventually my mother bought one exactly like this, but before that she had another of an older, bulkier, more complicated type. Have you ever seen one of them?"

"There's one up in the attic."

"In that case you'll know that with the old type of loom you had to have an assistant whom you told to pull up a new sequence of threads whenever that was required by the design. I was my mother's assistant, and I would not allow anyone else to take my place. While we worked my mother used to repeat the parables in the Bible to me as if they were fairy stories. When I come to think of it, if I have remained more or less a Christian, perhaps it's because of those fables."

"What are you saying?" Cristina interrupted, both shocked and amused.

"For once the truth slipped out of me," Don Paolo said seriously.

"And you worked at the new loom, even though your help was no longer required?"

"On the new loom my mother gave weaving lessons to a girl who was a friend of the family. I liked her, and for the sake of her company I took lessons too."

"So what it amounts to, if I may say so, is that you're backsliding in the same way again," Cristina exclaimed with a laugh.

Don Paolo laughed wholeheartedly too. Something had lit up in his face and eyes as if he had taken off a mask. One memory led to another, and he went on talking about his boyhood. While Cristina went on with her work he talked to her about the discoveries and surprises of his early reading, his first friendships, his first travels. There was no stopping the flow of his memories. Thus they spent the evening in a peaceful, affectionate atmosphere such as neither had experienced for a long time.

"Now it's time for me to go," Don Paolo said eventually. "You have been working hard all day and it's time you went to bed."

"Yes, you had better go," Cristina said. "Matalena might be jealous."

She shook hands with him at the door and said, "I shall see you again soon, I hope."

27

"AFTER ALL WE HAVE been through," Don Paolo said to Murica, "we can no longer talk of politics as others do. When you come to think of it, to us it has become something quite different."

"Wasn't it always like that?" said Murica. "Could purely political aims and calculations have caused either of us to join an underground movement that has not the slightest prospect of immediate success?"

Murica went ahead of the priest to make way for him between the brambles that lined the slippery path that led down to the bottom of the valley.

After a while he stopped and said, "I must tell you something that concerns you. In a short piece you wrote about two years ago you spoke of men painfully attaining consciousness of their own humanity. Romeo sent me a copy. It gave me food for a great deal of thought even then, but perhaps it's only now that I'm able fully to understand your meaning."

"That's something that can also happen to the writer," Don Paolo said. "There are infinite gradations of consciousness, just as there are of light."

The path led quickly to the stony streambed. A trickle of clear water wound its way between the rocks and boulders. The two walked one behind the other, and every so often they had to stop because the path was interrupted by holes. The jawbone of a donkey with the molars still attached was whitening in a ditch.

"When I come to think of it," Murica said, "it's obvious to me now that in the movement I was from the outset in the false position of a gambler who stakes much more than he possesses. But perhaps that's a more frequent occurrence than I assume."

"If you felt unready to face the risks, why didn't you leave after the first few meetings?"

"The fact of the matter is that that is an argument that was beyond me at the time," Murica said. "But I think about such things a great deal now, and I want to talk to you about the conclusions I have come to so that you can tell me whether you agree. Well, then, it seems to me that one can rebel against the existing order for two opposite reasons — if one is very strong or if one is very weak. By a strong man I mean someone superior to the bourgeois order, who rejects, despises, and fights it and wants to replace it by other values, by a more just society. That was not my position. I felt crushed by bourgeois society, I was at its margin, a provincial student, poor, shy, awkward, and lonely in a big city. I felt incapable of facing the thousand minor difficulties, the daily humiliations of life."

"In such case contact with a revolutionary movement can be a source of strength," said Don Paolo.

"No," Murica replied. "Since it's an underground movement, it offers the deceptive advantage of secrecy. The resentments of those who are offended and humiliated are offered satisfaction, but covert satisfaction. Their outward behavior remains unchanged. Their repudiation of legality remains internal, as in a dream, and for that very reason assumes extreme, reckless, and foolhardy forms. They conspire against the state, just as in a dream they may throttle their own father, whom they continue to obey and respect in the daytime."

"Until something happens that reveals their double life," Don Paolo said. "Then there's panic and terror."

After a few minutes' silence Don Paolo said, "When you were arrested, were you beaten?"

"I was slapped and they spat in my face," Murica said, "but from the first moment I was completely terrorized. Just imagine it, when they asked me for my particulars I couldn't remember the date of my birth, or my mother's maiden name. In short, my challenge to the law was disproportionate to my strength. I had staked more than I possessed."

For a short while the two walked on in silence along the path that flanked the stream, and then the valley widened and the road came close to the path.

"Let us stop here," said Murica. "If we go on they may see us from the road and recognize us."

"Do you have the feeling that you're still being watched?" Don Paolo asked.

"I don't know," Murica said. "Now that I feel strong it doesn't matter to me. I was thinking of you."

"Don't worry about me," Don Paolo said. "But you're perfectly right, after all we've been through we have no more reason to be afraid. It's the police who ought to be frightened of us."

Between the road and the stream there was a field with a sheepfold. This was the season when the flocks were brought down from the mountains to winter on the plain.

"When does Annina arrive?" Don Paolo asked.

"Perhaps tomorrow," Murica said. "She writes to me every day."

"She's a marvelous girl," Don Paolo said. "I'm certainly jealous of you."

"My father was in favor of our getting married immediately," Murica said.

Near the flock of sheep an aged shepherd was lighting a fire of twigs, a young man was blowing on it, and a boy was looking for dry branches. The old man's name was Bonifazio, and he told Don Paolo that he had dreamed about San Francesco. "He was smiling and wanted to give me a lira," he said.

"And did he?"

"No, he searched in his pockets, but they were empty."

Don Paolo laughed, and gave him a lira.

"Do you know the old story about the lake of Fucino?" Bonifazio said. "It's not a story to be found in books."

As Don Paolo didn't know the story, this was the shepherd's way of saying thank you for the lira.

"Well then, Jesus was going about looking for work as a carpenter," he said. "He traveled from place to place and eventually arrived in this part of the world. 'Have you any work for a poor carpenter?' He asked everywhere. 'What's your name? Have you a recommendation?' the employers asked Him. To all the jobless without recommendations whom He met on the road He said, 'Follow me.' And they all followed Him. 'Don't look back,' He told them, and no one looked back. When they were all on the mountain Jesus said, 'You can look back now.' In the place where land and houses had been there was a lake. Now the lake has been drained," Bonifazio went on, "and if the masters' wickedness goes on the land will sink beneath the waters again."

"Your story is certainly worth a lira," Don Paolo said with a smile.

"Next time I'll tell you another," said Bonifazio.

Don Paolo said good-bye to Murica and hurried back toward Pietrasecca. When he was halfway he came across a woman crawling along the roadside. She looked like a bag of rags and dust, a swaying, tottering bag. Don Paolo's first impression was that she was mad, but she explained that her son had gone to the war, and to get rid of an obscure premonition she had made a vow in a fit of religious fervor to go on her knees from Pietrasecca to Lama to obtain from Our Lady that the boy should come back safe and sound. The wretched woman had been on her way since morning, her voice was hoarse, her face unrecognizable, her sick, haunted eyes befuddled with dust and tears. She looked as if she were going to collapse at any moment. Don Paolo, not being convinced of the unbreakability of the vow, tried to persuade her to rise and walk, and he actually tried to lift her by her armpits and put her on her feet by force, but in vain, for she resisted with nails and teeth. Having made the vow, she must fulfill it or her son would be sure to die. She was astonished that the priest did not understand such a simple and well-known fact.

"What kind of priest are you?" she yelled at him.

Don Paolo left her to her fate and continued on his way. It had grown colder. The top of the mountain behind Pietrasecca was already white with snow. The village was plunged in the shadows mounting from the valley. Only the Colamartini house, which was a little higher up, was still lit by the sun. Cristina appeared at a window on the top floor, and her face was like a crystal receiving the rays of the setting sun. Don Paolo could see nothing of the whole village except that incandescent face.

As soon as the sun had disappeared it was freezing. Matalena was awaiting the return of her priest, sitting spinning in the doorway of the inn. "It will soon be snowing," she said, looking up into the sky.

Snow came two days later. Don Paolo awoke to find the landscape transformed. The snow had been falling all night and it went on falling steadily, silently, and thickly, like something expected and inevitable.

A few people turned up at Matalena's inn that evening to celebrate the first day of snow. Cristina arrived a little later too; suffering had made her eyes bigger, but she was no less beautiful because of that. Looking at her was a delight.

Don Paolo sat by the hearth, with *cafoni*, women, and children in a big circle all around him. On one side of the fire there was a dog and on the other Teresa's baby, who was to have been born blind but had been saved. The child was in a wicker basket on the ground like a cauliflower, and its face, reddened by the reflection of the fire, looked like an apple. Don Paolo was asked to tell stories, and Cristina specified sacred stories. In the end it was impossible to refuse, so he opened his breviary and looked up the *Index Festorum*. Then he started telling in his own way the story of the martyrdoms of which the breviary speaks.

The story was always different but always the same. There was a time of trials and tribulations. A dictatorship with a deified leader. A musty old Church, living on alms. An army of mercenaries that guaranteed the peaceful digestion of the rich. A population of slaves. Incessant preparation of new wars of plunder to maintain the prestige of the dictatorship. Meanwhile mysterious travelers arrived from abroad. They whispered of miracles in the east and announced the good tidings that liberation was at hand. The bolder spirits, the poor, the hungry, met in cellars to listen to them. The news spread. Some abandoned the old temples and embraced the new faith. Nobles left their palaces, centurions deserted. The police raided clandestine meetings and made arrests. Prisoners were tortured and handed over to the Special Tribunal. There were some who refused to burn incense to the state idols. They recognized no god other than the god that was alive in their souls. They faced torture with a smile on their lips. The young were thrown to wild beasts. The survivors remained loyal to the dead, to whom they devoted a secret cult. Times changed, ways of dressing, eating, working changed, languages changed, but at bottom it was always the same old story.

The heat of the fire made everyone drowsy. Those who were still awake listened, gazing at the fire. Cristina said, "In all times and in all societies the supreme act is to give oneself, to lose oneself in order to find oneself. One has only what one gives."

The fire went out, the customers said good night, and Don Paolo went up to his room. He picked up the notebook in which he had written the "Conversations with Cristina" he had begun during the early part of his stay at Pietrasecca, reread the first few pages, which were full of tenderness and affection for the girl, and then he reread and tore up the following pages, which had been dictated by disappointment and resentment. Several months had passed, and not for nothing, either for him or for Cristina. Before going to bed he added a few lines.

"Cristina," he wrote, "it's true that one has what one gives. But to whom and how is one to give?

"Our love, our readiness for sacrifice and self-abnegation are fruitful only if they are carried into relations with our fellows. Morality can live and flourish only in practical life. We are responsible also for others.

"If we apply our moral feelings to the evil that prevails all around us, we cannot remain inactive and console ourselves with the expectation of a life after death. The evil to be combated is not the sad abstraction that is called the devil; the evil is everything that prevents millions of people from becoming human. We too are directly responsible for this. . . .

"I believe that nowadays there is no other way of saving one's soul. He is saved who overcomes his individual, family, class selfishness and frees himself of the idea of resignation to the existing evil.

"My dear Cristina, one must not be obsessed with the idea of security, even the security of one's own virtue. Spiritual life is not compatible with security. To save oneself one has to take risks."

It went on snowing all night.

In the morning the priest was still asleep when Matalena called him. Outside the inn a small crowd of *cafoni* and boys were standing around Garibaldi, Sciatàp's donkey, on the rump of which was the body of a wolf that had been killed that morning on the mountain behind Pietrasecca. Its skin was gray, hairy, stained with blood and mud; its teeth were white and strong, and two bloody patches on the shoulder and flank showed where the bullets had entered. In accordance with custom, the dead wolf was shown from house to house so that alms might be given to those who had killed it.

Luigi Banduccia still had his gun on his shoulder and described what had happened. This was the fourth wolf he had killed. On the nape of the beast's neck he showed a love mark, the deep bite made by a she-wolf. Lovemaking by wolves is a serious matter. Banduccia could identify from a distance the different kinds of wolf howl: the howl of danger that the wolf utters when it is attacked with weapons; the howl of prey, which means that it has found an animal to tear to pieces and is summoning its companions, because wolves do not like eating alone; the howl of love, which means that it needs a female and is not ashamed to announce the fact.

Cristina's grandmother was unwilling to give anything for the dead wolf, but Cristina, who had had a special regard for wolves since childhood, tried hard to persuade her.

"Dead wolves don't bite," the old lady said.

That same day Magascià brought Don Paolo an urgent note that he said had been given to him by old Murica of Rocca dei Marsi. It was signed by Annina, who had just arrived at the Murica house, and it said that Luigi had been arrested. Don Paolo wanted to leave at once, but Magascià answered evasively; he was tired, and his donkey was not so young either.

"Very well then, I'll go on foot," the priest said. "A little fresh air will do me good."

"Is it so urgent?" Matalena said.

"It's a case of conscience," said the priest.

"Is it someone from your diocese?"

"Someone from my diocese and my parish."

Matalena had never seen the priest so agitated. He left with the briskness of a boy. He was perhaps surprised himself at his own energy. Fortunately the route was downhill.

28

THE RING OF MOUNTAINS that surrounded the Fucino basin was completely covered in snow; in places it had actually reached the lowest foothills. Don Paolo wore a black coat that came right down to his ankles and had a black woolen scarf around his neck. To rid himself of his ecclesiastical disguise all he had to do was to unbutton his coat and remove his scarf. But the most ingenious feature of his attire was the ordinary felt hat he had brought back from Rome that could equally well be adapted to ecclesiastical or lay purposes, depending on how it was shaped or worn.

The road, which acted as a boundary between a stony hillside planted with vines and an expanse of recently plowed fields, sloped gently downhill. When the snow finished he could walk more quickly. At a bend in the road he came to a trap waiting by the roadside.

"Don Paolo?" the driver asked him. "Get in, Annina sent me."

The priest got in, and they set off at a trot.

"I've been expecting you," the man said simply. "I've been expecting you for a couple of hours."

"I came on foot," Don Paolo said.

The man's beard was several days old, his shirt and suit were dirty and neglected, and he had a stricken appearance as if he were ill.

"Is there any news of Luigi Murica?" Don Paolo asked. "Is he still in prison?"

"He died yesterday."

"*Consummatum est*," Don Paolo said.

"The news does not seem to surprise you."

"No, in one way or another I feared it would happen."

There was a great calmness in the air, the calm of the countryside at the approach of winter.

"Were you friends?" Don Paolo asked.

"We were friends," the man replied. "One spent time willingly with him. He was a good man, and made others want to be good too. He also talked to us about the revolution. He told us that the beginning was being together without being afraid."

"We must stay together," Don Paolo said. "We must not allow ourselves to be divided."

"Luigi had written on a piece of paper: 'Truth and brotherhood will prevail among men instead of lies and hatred. Labor will prevail instead of money.' When they arrested him they found that piece of paper, and he didn't disown it. So in the yard of the militia barracks at Fossa they put a chamber pot on his head instead of a crown. That is the truth, they told him. They put a broom in his right hand instead of a scepter. That is fraternity, they told him. Then they wrapped him in a red carpet they picked up from the floor and blindfolded him, and the militiamen formed a ring around him and punched and kicked him backward and forward between themselves. That is the kingdom of labor, they told him. When he collapsed to the ground they trampled on him with their nailed boots. After this first stage of the legal proceedings against him he lived for a whole day."

"If we live like him, it will be as if he were not dead," Don Paolo said. "We must stay together and not be afraid."

The man nodded.

At the approach to Rocca he pointed out the Murica house in the middle of the fields. Don Paolo went to it along a grassy path. He took advantage of the short walk to laicize his appearance. The Murica house was a big, squat, single-story building, half dwelling, half stable. The windows were closed and shuttered and the front door was wide open, in accordance with the custom. People paying the obligatory visit were coming and going. Pietro went in hesitantly. No one took any notice of him. As soon as he crossed the threshold he found himself in a big room with a cobbled floor that normally served as a kitchen and storeroom for agricultural implements, but now it was full of people. Some women dressed in black and yellow were sitting on the floor near the fireplace, and some men were standing around the table, talking about land and harvests. Pietro spotted Annina at the far end of the room, sitting on a stool, alone, pale, and distraught, shivering with cold and fear among all these strangers. She was not weeping, for to weep she would have had to be alone or with people she knew. But as soon as she saw Pietro she broke down and sobbed. The dead man's parents came in from a neighboring room, dressed in black. His mother went to Annina, wiped away her tears, wrapped her in a big black shawl, and made her sit beside her on a bench near the hearth.

"Who's she?" the other women whispered to one another.

"She's the bride," someone replied, "the bride from town."

The father sat at the head of the table, together with the other men. Relatives arrived from a neighboring village. Some boys arrived. The mother, as is the custom, spoke in praise of her dead son. She described how she tried to save him, how she had sent him away to study, to save him from the fate that his weakness, his delicacy, his sensitivity had made her foresee. She had not saved him. The air of the city was not made for him, and the land had reclaimed him. He had started working on the land, helping his father. One might have supposed that he would soon tire of it and turn against it, because working on the land every day was a real chastisement of God. He had woken his father in the morning, harnessed the horse, chosen the seed, filled the barrels, and looked after the vegetable garden.

Every now and then the mother paused in her eulogy to poke the fire and add a dry branch to it. Marta, Don Benedetto's sister, and *cafoni* from the neighboring countryside arrived, and others rose and left. Old Murica stood at the head of the table, offering food and drink to the men around him.

"He helped me to sow, hoe, reap, thresh, and grind the corn of which this bread is made. Take it and eat, this is his bread."

Others arrived. The father poured out wine and said, "He helped me to prune, spray, hoe, and gather the grapes of the vineyard from which this wine came. Drink, for this is his wine."

The men ate and drank, and some dipped their bread in their wine.

Some beggars arrived. "Let them in," the mother said.

"They may have been sent to spy," someone murmured.

"Let them in. We must take the risk. Many, giving food and drink to beggars, have fed Jesus without knowing it."

"Eat and drink," the father said.

Finding himself in front of Pietro, he looked at him and said, "Where do you come from?"

"From Orta," he said.

"What is your name?"

Annina went up to the old man and whispered a name in his ear. He looked at the young man with pleasure and embraced him.

"When I was a young man I knew your father," he said to Pietro. "He bought a mare of mine at a fair. I heard about you from the son who has been taken from me. Sit here, between his mother and his bride; you too must eat and drink."

The men around the table ate and drank.

"Bread is made of many grains of corn," said Pietro, "so it means unity. Wine is made of many grapes, so it means unity too. Unity of similar, equal, useful things. Hence truth and fraternity, things that go well together."

"The bread and wine of Holy Communion," an older man said. "The wheat and the grapes that are trampled on. The body and the blood."

"It takes nine months to make bread," old Murica said.

"Nine months?" exclaimed the mother.

"What is sown in November and reaped and threshed in July." The old man counted the months. "November, December, January, February, March, April, May, June, July. Exactly nine months. It also takes nine months for the grapes to ripen, from March to November." He counted them, "March, April, May, June, July, August, September, October, November. That makes nine months too."

"Nine months?" his mother said. It had never struck her before. It took the same time to make a man. Luigi was born in April. Quietly she counted the months backward to herself, "April, March, February, January, December, November, October, September, August." Nine months from August to April.

More acquaintances arrived, and others left to make room for them. Marta said to the mother, "Do you remember when Luigi was a little boy and you were still young and went for walks on the hill carrying him in your arms? Don Benedetto used to say that you were like the vine and he the grape, that you were like the stalk and he the ear of corn."

Bianchina appeared in the doorway and Pietro went toward her. The girl was distraught and could hardly manage to speak.

"Pietro," she said.

"Why do you call me that?"

"Aren't you Pietro Spina?"

"Yes, I am."

"You must disappear as quickly as possible, you've been found out."

"How do you know?"

"Alberto Colamartini told me, he's in the militia now. They're going to Pietrasecca to pick you up tonight or tomorrow morning. You haven't a minute to lose."

Pietro consulted Annina. He took her advice and asked old Murica to lend him a horse for a few hours. The old man went to the stable and led a handsome colt, only just broken in, into the field.

"A little fresh air will do him good," he said and handed him over to Pietro.

"What can I do?" Bianchina asked.

"Do what Annina tells you," Pietro said. "I'm going to Pietra-secca, where I left some papers I prefer to burn. If there's time I'll come back here and go in the Pescasseroli direction, to Alfedana or Castel di Sangro. Don't worry about me. I'm not afraid. Forgive me for the deception. I'll send you news as soon as I can."

"It wasn't deception, it was only a secret," Bianchina said. Her eyes filled with tears.

29

THE COLT HAD NEITHER saddle nor bit, but merely a hempen halter around its neck. The moment it felt a man's weight on its back it whinnied and set off in a wild gallop across the fields. Pietro was taken by surprise. He had not ridden for many years, and to avoid being thrown he had to cling to the animal's mane and neck. But after the first furious dash it quieted down a little and allowed itself to be guided toward the Pietrasecca valley, trotting along a path parallel to the road. In spite of the steep slope, the colt negotiated the first stretch of the valley without pausing for breath. When it came to the snow on the road it slowed down.

Every so often Pietro looked back, but there was no sign of pursuit. The farther he got into the valley the more he was struck by its new aspect. A great deal of snow had already fallen, and the unbroken gray of the sky showed that there was more to come. The colt was panting, steaming, and foaming, but kept up a brisk steady pace. Pietro looked at the white walls of the chain of mountains. They had never looked so high and forbidding.

When Pietrasecca came into view he changed the shape of his felt hat and buttoned up his coat. His eyes were fixed on the mountain behind the village with its two unequal humps, like those of a dromedary. Between them there was a deep hollow known as the Goat's Saddle, which was the only way of crossing to the opposite slope. In summer it took four or five hours to reach the first house on the other side. But in winter? Apart from that, was there any other way of escape? Or, as an alternative, was there any way of hiding himself?

At Pietrasecca he tied the colt by the halter to a ring on the wall of the inn and was just going in when he heard someone hurrying toward him. It was Cristina. She looked so utterly dismayed that it frightened him.

"Alberto has told me," she managed to stammer out.

"Are you unwell, perhaps?"

"Please tell me the truth, are you Pietro Spina?"

"Yes, I am," he replied. "I ask your forgiveness."

Matalena emerged from the inn and interpreted in her own way the emotion by which both of them were obviously affected.

"Wait here for a moment," Pietro said to the girl. "I have something for you."

He hurried up to his room and took the notebook from the table drawer. On the cover he scribbled: "My dear Cristina, here you will find my defense, and something also that concerns you personally — something beyond the conventional fictions, the hidden truth, the truth of the heart. Pietro Spina."

He came down to the kitchen and handed the notebook to Cristina, who was waiting outside the door, looking livid and as if paralyzed. The girl hurried away, almost running, without saying anything. At that moment Sciatàp passed by. Pietro called him and asked him to take the colt back to old Murica at Rocca dei Marsi, for which he would pay him a day's wages in advance.

"Thank you," said Sciatàp.

In winter this was a totally unexpected windfall. Matalena was present at the scene, and she saw the man who to her was still Don Paolo going upstairs to his room again. Nothing had happened to arouse her suspicions. Cristina's display of emotion was in accordance with Cassarola's predictions. Matalena emerged smiling from the bar to go and buy some salt and, since she was in a good humor and in no hurry, she stayed and gossiped for a bit with Magascià's wife and some other women.

"How's Don Paolo?"

"He's very well. Now I'm sure he'll be staying the whole winter."

"When is he going to start taking confessions again?"

"It won't be long now. He's waiting for a definite answer from the Pope."

When she got back to the inn, still totally unaware of what was going on, she started cooking dinner. How long was it exactly since she'd seen the priest going up to his room? About an hour and a half, perhaps two hours. As soon as dinner was ready she went up to tell him. The room was dark and empty. Matalena turned on the light. There was some money on the table and a note of apology and thanks. She could not believe her eyes. What sort of joke was this? Had her priest gone mad? With her heart in tumult she went down into the garden, and recognized his footsteps in the snow. She followed them all the way to the stream, from where the trail led, not down toward the valley, but up toward the mountain. Matalena met the deaf-mute and asked him by signs whether he had seen the priest. He replied, also by signs, that he had seen him hurrying in the direction of the mountain. Magascià appeared on the scene and confirmed this incredible information. The priest had been dashing along like a madman. By now he must be a long way away.

"He has gone mad," Matalena exclaimed. "Why didn't you stop him?"

Without waiting for a reply she hurried back and went to the Colamartini house. She knocked several times, but there was no answer, so she went around to the back of the house and went in by a back door which she found open.

"Donna Cristina," she called up the stairs several times. But there was no reply.

Cristina was in her room, alone, in a state of extreme anguish. The sheets of Pietro Spina's notebook trembled between her hands.

"Our priest has gone mad," Matalena yelled, bursting into her room.

"Mad?" Cristina exclaimed.

"He left suddenly, and he's gone up toward the mountain," she went on. "Was it you by any chance who reduced him to that state?"

Cristina dashed to the window and looked out in the direction of the mountain. There was no sign of any human being on the white slope leading up to the Goat's Saddle. He must have taken the safer and longer route, the mule track that first followed the stream and then climbed in big zigzags to the pass.

"If he had only had his dinner," Matalena whimpered. "If he had only taken some warmer clothing. But he left it in the wardrobe in his room."

The course of the stream at the bottom of the valley was so hidden by boulders and shrubs that Cristina could not possibly see how far the fugitive had gone. The air was not clear either.

"It'll soon be dark," Matalena went on whimpering. "Even if he reaches the saddle he'll be caught in a blizzard."

Cristina was still standing at the window, gazing in the direction in which the fugitive must have gone. In his bad state of health, with his ignorance of the locality, without special clothing or food it was an adventure that might cost him his life. She seemed suddenly to make up her mind.

"Go," she said to Matalena.

As soon as she was alone she hid the diary under her pillow. From a wardrobe in the corridor she fetched some heavy clothing, a warm sweater, two scarves, a pair of thick woolen socks, and a pair of gloves and wrapped them up in a bundle. She went down to the kitchen, took a loaf of bread, a piece of cheese, and a bottle of wine and put them in the bundle. To avoid being seen or heard she took the big bundle and went out through the back door that Matalena had used. She made a small detour behind the church and the cemetery and slid about ten yards down a steep slope to the path that followed the stream and then started climbing beside it in the direction of its source. When she was sure that no

one from the village was following her or had seen her she started
to run. If she were to catch up with the fugitive there was no time
to lose. There were traces of footsteps in the snow, and as she hurried along she tried to guess which were his. They grew rarer and
rarer, but did not leave the side of the stream. This was a sure sign
that he had taken the mule track, the longer route to the Goat's
Saddle, instead of the shortcut up a steep slope about three hundred feet in height.

Even in summer tackling it was an enterprise best left to foolhardy boys and goats, and in winter it was almost impossible.
Cristina jumped the stream without hesitation and started
climbing it. She used hands and feet, clinging to branches,
bushes, and boulders that protruded from the snow. Several times
she stumbled and fell badly with her face in the snow and slipped
back. Luckily there was less snow where the slope was steepest,
because the wind had swept it away. But she sank in the deep
snow that was still soft between the rocks, and had to use all her
strength to struggle out of it. She was hampered by her skirt and
the bundle, but for different reasons she could rid herself of neither. In a place where a big projecting rock formed a kind of dry
cave she flung herself to the ground, exhausted and almost
breathless. Mist was mounting from the valley. Trails of gray
cotton wool filled the ravines, hid the houses, covered fields,
hedges, and walls. The earth had a shapeless, empty look, as if it
were uninhabited. Cristina rose and continued the ascent. Up
here the snow was harder and progress easier, but also it was easier
to slip. Sweat poured from her, and her hands, torn by the thorns
to which she had had to cling several times to avoid plunging into
the abyss, were bleeding. Her heart was hammering so much that
she had to hold her chest. When she reached the top of the slope
she found herself in a wide, nearly rectangular space known as
the Witches' Field. Beyond it the mountain continued sloping
gently upward. The snow all around was intact. Nobody had
passed that way. Going on toward the top, apart from being exhausting, was pointless. It would be more sensible to go around it,
so as to cut across the route taken by Spina. She went off in this

new direction. Soon she completely lost sight of the Pietrasecca valley. In front of her and all around her there was nothing but the white rumps and summits of other mountains. A freezing wind was blowing that cut her face. Twilight was approaching, and so was a blizzard. She reached the point where the hollow begins that divides the mountain into two humps, forming the Goat's Saddle. There was no trace of any human being on the snow. The ground was much cut up by boulders and landslides caused by floods and, with snow up to her waist, Cristina could not see very far. She went on climbing toward the saddle. Perhaps she thought that when she got there she would be able to see both slopes and spot Pietro more easily, or at any rate be seen by him. But a moment came when she could go no farther and let herself collapse in the snow.

So that he should not pass without noticing her, every so often she called out his name with all the strength of her lungs. She called him by his new name, his real name, "Pietro, Pietro."

If he had passed he would certainly have heard her. She brushed back her hair, cleared the snow from her face, her eyebrows, her ears, and her neck. And every so often she went on calling, "Pietro, Pietro."

Eventually a voice in the distance answered her, but it was not a human voice. It was like the howling of a dog, but it was sharper and more prolonged. Cristina probably recognized it. It was the howl of a wolf. The howl of prey. The summons to other wolves scattered around the mountain. The invitation to the feast. Through the driving snow and the darkness of approaching night Cristina saw a wild beast coming toward her, quickly appearing and disappearing in the dips and rises in the snow. She saw others appear in the distance. She knelt, closed her eyes, and made the sign of the cross.

THE SEED
BENEATH THE SNOW

I have placed in the hearts of men the
hospice of blind hopes.
— Aeschylus, *Prometheus Bound*

(Epigraph written by Ignazio Silone in his own handwriting to a typescript of the novel found in Zürich
by Maria Paynter)

To Darina

I

"PUT THE BRAKE ON, Venanzio, can't you hear the wheels creaking?"

"The brake is loose, madam; actually, madam, it's broken and doesn't grip any longer. This north wind smells of snow, madam."

"Mind the ditches, Venanzio, don't keep looking up at the sky."

The old Spina family carriage jerked and jolted its way painfully along the country lane that joins the villages of Colle and Orta. It was an unpaved track, and in the long months of winter was often impracticable, except for cattle and the peasants' two-wheeled carts, which in this part of the world are very high. The unfortunate Spina carriage, however, was of an antiquated type, now rare. The front wheels were smaller than the back ones, the body was divided into two, or *coupé,* as the French say, the black leather upholstery was torn and discolored, almost greenish, and there were white embroidered curtains on the windows. Venanzio, huddled on the box, looked more like a stableboy than a coachman. He was wrapped in an overcoat, and he had turned up the kid collar around the back of his neck and his ears and pulled his hat down over his eyes, so that all that was to be seen of his face was a pointed, mouselike nose and mouth and two long, thin gray mustaches. Every time the horses were brought up short or the wheels sank in a hole or rut, the carriage creaked and groaned in all its leather and metal joints as if it were about to fall to pieces. Inside it Donna Maria Vincenza Spina was bundled up in woolen rugs and shawls and supported on either side by two big cushions. The old lady's teeth chattered because of the icy draft that came in through the crevices in the doors and the seams that had come unstitched in the hood, and at every violent jolt she complained bitterly.

"At least mind the ditch, Venanzio," she implored him. "Now where are you going? Up that gravel heap? May heaven see us to the end of this. Mother of Sorrows, what a thing to be doing at my time of life."

"It's all right, it's perfectly all right, take it easy, madam. What time are we supposed to be there? Didn't we leave too early? Look up there, madam, over Forca it's snowing already, just look at it."

"Mind the ditch and don't keep gazing up in the air, Venanzio. Poor me, I thought I might be able to tell my beads on the way, but it's as much as I can do to refrain from imprecations."

"This is not a road for human beings but a mud-filled ditch, madam. How can I tell where the holes and the stones are? On the way back, after it's been snowing, it will be worse."

"Very well, Venanzio, if it isn't any use stop zigzagging, loosen the reins, and leave it to the horses, they're cleverer than we are in these things."

The road along which the unlucky carriage was struggling was covered with thick, clayey mud with deep ruts and puddles. It was flanked by two rows of dwarf, stumpy willows; their gnarled and twisted bare crowns looked like rusty old iron. Flocks of tiny sparrows flew from tree to tree, making no sound except for the slight flutter of their wings. The country all around was gray and desolate, as if covered with ashes. From a distant black haystack an invisible dog barked for a long time at the unusual vehicle. They came to a small open space with a drinking trough, and the road forked; to the left it climbed steeply between low, bare vineyards and skeleton-like small trees to halfway up a rocky hill and led to Orta, which lay in a narrow depression immediately beyond the hill; to the right it led straight down between two rows of tall poplars, between big fields that had been flooded for the past few days because of a stream that had burst its banks. When Donna Maria Vincenza realized that they were bearing right she told Venanzio to stop.

"What are you doing, Venanzio, where are you taking me?"

"Didn't madam say we were going to meet someone on the road to the old mill?"

He said "someone" nervously and diffidently.

"No, Venanzio, there are some things you mustn't meddle in. Now we're going to Orta, to see my son."

"Are we going to Don Bastiano's? Is he in the know?" Venanzio exclaimed, reassured.

Because of the slope the road up the hill was less muddy but no less difficult, for it had been recently relaid with big cobblestones, and the horses, particularly one of them that seemed to be lame, panted, sweated, and foamed. Venanzio stopped two or three times to let them recover their breath.

At one point a number of donkeys ridden by *cafoni* also coming from Colle emerged in single file onto the road from a shortcut that led upward between the vines. One after another they fell in behind the carriage. The men, most of them old, were wrapped in worn, muddy black cloaks, and they rocked slowly backward and forward in time with the motion of their weary beasts. The latter were brown, emaciated creatures, some so small that the feet of their riders nearly touched the ground.

"Hey, are you going to Orta too?" Venanzio called out.

"Yes, for the blessing of the animals. Do you think the weather will hold up? In the Forca valley it's snowing already," someone called out in reply.

"Yes, soon the snow will be coming down, and high time too," someone else said.

"What do you expect to be coming down? Flour? That's the sort of thing that long ago used to happen to the Jews."

"If it doesn't snow in January, when do you expect it to snow? Sant'Antonio doesn't feel the cold."

"Of course not, but the priest's an old man."

"And if it's very cold, sometimes even the holy water freezes. It wouldn't be the first time."

"Quite true, quite true, but it can always be warmed up again, it wouldn't be the first time either."

"A warmed-up blessing? A warmed-up grace? Oh dear, oh dear, these poor donkeys of ours, what harm have they done?"

Because of the lame horse, which Venanzio wanted to spare as much as possible, the carriage moved up the slope between the vines practically at a man's walking pace, and so it ended up being surrounded by *cafoni* on their little donkeys. They provided an unexpected, ragged, but polite escort for the invisible lady in the carriage. A loud murmur arose from its midst.

"Hey, Venanzio, is Donna Maria Vincenza sending her horses to the blessing? You could have spared yourself the trouble."

"Why? What an idea. Aren't horses animals too?" Venanzio protested.

"Who's denying it? But everyone knows that Sant'Antonio's blessing has always been especially for donkeys."

"That's true, but everyone knows that horses have never been excluded. There have always been a few horses at the blessing."

"And why shouldn't they be blessed? Aren't horses animals too?" another man called out.

"Who wants to keep them out? But horses don't need it. Donkeys are donkeys and horses are horses, that's an old story that everyone knows."

"But horses eat hay and bran with beans and donkeys eat straw. There *is* a difference, and everyone knows it."

"What you're saying is that at bottom all animals are animals, isn't that right?"

"But horses live and work for only about fifteen years, and donkeys, though they're not so strong, go on for twenty-five or thirty, almost double."

"Also if horses are ill the vet comes with his little black bag.

But donkeys are like poor human beings. All they get is straw and thrashings, and that's that."

"But though donkeys don't get bran or the vet, they have the special patronage of Sant'Antonio, which is a fine thing too."

"Mine would prefer bran, that's the way it's made, and you can't alter it."

"It's either one thing or the other, you can't have everything in this world."

"He who's born a donkey dies a donkey. Until you've changed that, you haven't changed anything. But can anything be changed?"

"If the blessing doesn't help the body, at least it helps the soul, that you can't deny."

"A donkey's soul? Ha, ha, ha!"

The lady drew aside the curtain of one window and looked out. "And what, may I ask, is the meaning of all this chitchat?" she said.

"Oh, Donna Maria Vincenza, our respects. Good evening to you, Donna Maria Vincenza, our greetings. On a road like this at your age, madam, what an ordeal."

Her pale, sad face disappeared into the carriage again, but after this none of the men dared to raise his voice. The north wind blew hard; on that stretch of road it blows day and night at all seasons, and the horses and donkeys found the going still slower and more difficult. At the last turn before the top of the hill a mule track branched off that served as a shortcut. The men took it, overcoming the animals' reluctance by kicking them in the flanks, using the halter as a whip and uttering gutteral cries of "ah, ah, ah." Only one of the men continued along the road.

"You're taking it easy," some of the men shouted back at him.

"My donkey couldn't manage it," he explained.

Previously he had remained silent and unnoticed among his comrades. In appearance he was no less poor than they, but was much taller, with a fine, sharp, clear-cut face. He went up to the carriage and spoke to Donna Maria Vincenza in a confidential tone.

"Donna Maria Vincenza," he said, "have you heard any more about that poor grandson of yours?"

"Is that you, Simone?" she replied. "Whenever I see you I hardly recognize you. Heavens, what a state you're reduced to."

"Has the body been found, at least?" Simone went on. "Has he been buried? I don't know if you trust me, Donna Maria Vincenza."

"If only I could trust my family as much," she replied without hesitation. "But what can an old woman of nearly eighty have to tell you? All she can say is: God's will be done."

Simone held the carriage door and said in an undertone: "But is there nothing, nothing we can do?"

"We can pray."

"Is nothing else left?"

"Yes, when we are alone in our homes we can weep."

"Donna Maria Vincenza, if you need me, call on me, even if it means going to prison . . ."

For about a hundred yards before the entrance to the village of Orta the road was lined with carts with their shafts in the air. Inside the village even the mud became tame and human. The little village street was lined with fetid stables and filthy hovels against which were piled heaps of dung, kitchen refuse, sweepings, broken plates, and other rubbish, while in the middle of the road, which was built like an inverted saddle, there was a black trickle of water carrying along decaying garbage. The square outside the church of Sant'Antonio was already packed with people and animals, and Donna Maria Vincenza drew the curtains of the carriage to conceal herself from the curiosity of the throng. She hesitated to show herself even when the carriage stopped on the opposite side of it, near her son's house. Her arrival was accompanied by a prolonged murmur from the crowd, which stopped when she put her head out of the window. Don Bastiano and his wife, Donna Maria Rosa, hurried to help their unexpected visitor to get out and climb the few steps up to the front door.

Don Bastiano did not conceal his irritation.

"You don't come and see us for years, Mother, even in summer, and now, in January, and with the road in the state it's in, this is the third time that you've turned up unexpectedly. What will people think?"

"I want to talk to you, my son, and I'm not interested in what people think."

"You could have sent for me and I could have come to see you without its being so conspicuous."

"I couldn't wait, my son. I'll tell you why."

"Very well, then, we'll see what crazy idea you're going to put to me this time. But first sit down and rest and get warm in front of the fire."

"Meanwhile go and have a look at the horses, my son, and tell Venanzio not to go too far away."

After taking off her mittens and removing her scarf and black woolen cape, Donna Maria Vincenza sat down slowly, as if her joints were painful, on a big wooden chair close to the fireplace. There was a sudden weariness about her movements, barely concealed by the abundance of her old-fashioned clothes. For a short time her rapid, painful breathing made her unable to speak.

"Why do you wear yourself out like this at your age, Mother, instead of taking things easy? Why do you do such things when there's no obligation?" whined her daughter-in-law. "Did you see the crowd that's come to watch the blessing?" she went on with a laugh. "It's all thanks to the priest."

Donna Maria Vincenza's chair was at one side of the fireplace; she had to move it back a little to save her skirt from the sparks coming from the wood crackling on the firedogs. The fireplace was huge, high, and black; the bottom was almost at floor level and the hood was big enough to accommodate about a dozen persons. The room was lit partly by a small window hardly wider than an arrow slit and partly by the intermittent reddish reflection of the fire. The old lady was in the shadow, an indistinct, dark shape against the smoke-blackened wall, an almost violet shape between the fireplace and the wall. The only living thing about her seemed to be the hands she held out toward the fire to warm: long, slender, fleshless hands, withered like old vine cuttings and trembling slightly. When one looked at them more closely one saw that they were slightly contracted; against the light one could see the pattern of the joints slightly deformed by arthritis and the

branching veins swollen by sclerosis. Only her wedding ring preserved its opacity and showed up like a dark shadow on the fourth
finger of her left hand.

When her daughter-in-law offered her a cup of something
warm and laughingly asked her to guess what it was she accepted
it reluctantly, and a moment or two later handed it back with a
gesture plainly indicating that there were certain matters on
which jokes were not permissible.

"What's this brew that you're offering me? A decoction of hay?"

"It's called tea, Mother. I had to buy some for important visitors. We entertain a lot of strangers, they're needed for everything,
contracts in particular. Certainly the taste is rather peculiar."

"You shouldn't invite them, Maria Rosa. Why should you ask
gypsies into the house?"

"Here, look at the box. It's by no means cheap."

"If you don't mind, Maria Rosa, I'd rather have half a glass of
wine and a little toast. And before he comes back, Maria Rosa, tell
me how Bastiano is doing. Did he get the contract?"

At this Donna Maria Rosa burst into tears.

"Must I tell you the truth?" she said between her sobs. "I
haven't the slightest idea. He hardly speaks a word to me all day
long, and he hardly even looks at me. Nearly every evening he
goes out without telling me where he's going, and he comes back
late, and sometimes he's so drunk that he can't manage the stairs
by himself. He loses his temper over nothing at all and smashes the
first thing he lays his hands on. Just imagine it, with plates and
glasses costing what they do now. I hardly ever go out of the house,
chiefly because I can't bear being sympathized with, because of
course there are always people who gloat over one's misfortunes."

"So he has started smashing things again?"

"And there are always people who gloat over one's misfortunes," her daughter-in-law sighed, wiping away her tears.

Donna Maria Vincenza broke the piece of toast and dipped it in
the glass of wine that her daughter-in-law brought her. It was a light,
sparkling wine and it shone like a ruby against the flames. Maria
Rosa was now sitting motionless in front of the fire; she was dressed

demurely in black, like a poor housewife on a working day. The
light of the fire threw into relief her swollen ankles, the tired, bony
hands resting on her knees, the high breast that protruded like a
shelf, and her full, flat face, which was of a brown, earthy color
rather like the skin of baked potatoes. She sat there in an attitude of
woeful resignation, her mouth half open and with the red, dark-
shadowed eyes of a person who does a great deal of weeping.

"There are always people who gloat over one's misfortunes,"
she repeated with a sigh, as if appealing for her mother-in-law's
aid and protection. But when she recognized her husband's footsteps on the stairs she hurriedly wiped her eyes and assumed an
expression of indifference.

"Your horses are going to rack and ruin," Don Bastiano said to his
mother. "That gray, what's its name, Belisario? Have you noticed the
nasty thing coming out under its jaw? And the other one . . ."

He stopped short and looked at his wife's red eyes.

"The other one?" Donna Maria Vincenza said to encourage
him to go on, but her son, standing in the middle of the room,
took no notice. The gray light coming through the narrow
window shone on his precociously gray hair and his strong, bent
shoulders, while the fire cast a red glow on the hollow features of
his ill-shaven face. You could see anger rising in the deep eye
sockets under his thick, bristling brows.

"Have you been crying?" he shouted at his wife. "Have you
been crying again? Have you been complaining again? How
many times have I told you that I can't stand the sight of you with
red eyes?"

"It isn't true, I haven't been crying, ask your mother," the
woman exclaimed, bursting into tears again and emphasizing her
denial with vigorous gesticulations. "It isn't true. I haven't been
crying."

"Get out of here," the man shouted, now completely beside
himself, pointing to the door. "Get out of here, for Christ's sake.
Do you hear me? Who am I talking to? The wall?"

He picked up a chair and was about to throw it, but his terrified wife vanished into the next room.

478 ❖ IGNAZIO SILONE

"Children, children," Donna Maria Vincenza murmured in agonized tones. "Children, children, is this what you've come to?"

"Listen, Mother, I can't stand the sight of her weeping. When I see her with her eyes swollen I lose my head and I'd be capable of killing her. As I was saying, Belisario has strangles under its jaw. Shall I turn the light on? It gets dark early in this room."

"Bastià, don't you remember when you were first married? You said Maria Rosa laughed too much. She's a fool, you used to say, she laughs at everything, she laughs at every fly. Don't you see the fire's dying down, Bastià? Put some wood on it. Heavens, how cold it is in this house, it's freezing."

He heaped the burning embers around the firedogs, added two beech logs, and opened up the fire to make it blaze. As he bent over the fireplace his eyes, reddened by alcohol, glistened as if they were bleeding.

"I forgot to tell you that I'm expecting some visitors," he said, standing erect again with difficulty. "Some acquaintances, local notables who want to watch the blessing from our balcony. If you don't want to meet them, as I expect you won't, you can stay here by the fire."

"Oh, don't be afraid, I shan't show myself, I shan't disgrace you."

"Mother, you know very well it isn't that. Far from it."

Donna Maria Vincenza gave her son an affectionate smile and made a gesture to draw him closer and indicate that she had something confidential she wanted to talk to him about, but he misunderstood the gesture and responded with an unexpected and totally disproportionate outburst.

"I won't listen to any more complaints," he shouted. "Once and for all, I can't and I won't stand any more women's whining around me."

But his mother's gentle and sorrowful expression brought him up short and he changed his tune.

"I wasn't of course referring to you," he added, quickly and apologetically.

"My poor son," said Donna Maria Vincenza, taking his hand. "It saddens me to see you more and more anxious and distressed.

How can you live without friends? How can you live among people whom you despise and mistrust?"

"You see, Mother, I'm in business, and you can't catch flies with vinegar," Don Bastiano replied with an evasive gesture.

"But not with soup either?"

"It's an art, if you like. Swallowing bitter and spitting sweet."

"You're well off, you're the biggest landlord in the district, and you have no children. Why can't you live in peace?"

Don Bastiano shook his head.

"If only I could," he said. "But if you go to the ball you have to join in the dance. If I withdrew now, they'd stab me in the back."

"Who would?"

"My friends. My so-called friends. It's a real war to the death."

"I don't understand."

"No, Mother, it's impossible for you to understand. The world has changed, you see. One's family name doesn't count anymore. Money still counts, but only on certain conditions. The authorities can ruin any landlord by the way they assess him for taxes. And then there are the contracts. I've explained to you before that public auctions have been abolished."

His mother interrupted him. "Why do you need contracts?" she asked him. "You have your vineyards."

"A good contract yields more than ten vineyards and isn't liable to damage by hail. If I leave the contracts to Calabasce, in a couple of years he'll have my vineyards too. Don't you see? I've no choice."

For a moment his mother seemed convinced. "A demijohn of wine always used to be sufficient to assure you of the support of Don Coriolano and other gasbags like him."

"But those people no longer rule the roost," Don Bastiano explained. "They're still kept on to make speeches, but the strings are pulled by new and evil people. You have the good fortune to be able to live your life apart from all that, Mother."

"You never wanted to have anything to do with politics either, my son. How many times did they want to make you mayor and you always refused? You wanted to remain free, you always said."

"But don't you see that nowadays no one is free? Even if I don't want to concern myself with politics, politics concerns itself with me. There's no way out. But enough of this, didn't you say there was something you wanted to talk to me about?"

"Yes, shut the door."

The sound of footsteps and voices came from the stairs. "Oh, Donna Maria Rosa, our respects. Is Don Bastiano at home? Have we come at an inconvenient moment?"

"Welcome, Don Coriolano, come in, I'll fetch my husband straightaway. Dreadful weather, isn't it?"

"I hope you'll forgive the liberty, Donna Maria Rosa, but I have brought two friends with me, political notables, two very agreeable gentlemen, on my word of honor."

"The honor of course is ours, Don Coriolano. This way, gentlemen, please. Come into the drawing room, the fire's alight and it's nice and warm. Terrible weather, isn't it?"

"Allow me, my dear lady, to present to you Don Marcantonio Cipolla and Signor De Paolis, the new trade union secretary."

"It's a pleasure to meet you, my dear lady, it's a pleasure and an honor. Please don't allow us to disturb you."

"The honor is ours. Won't you come in and sit down? The drawing room is heated, the pleasure is ours entirely. Appalling weather, isn't it? I'll bring you a drink immediately and fetch my husband."

"There's no hurry, my dear lady. We haven't got a train to catch, and we can drink even without him," the guests replied with a laugh.

Don Bastiano closed the door and sat next to his mother by the fire. For a moment they remained silent, sitting side by side and gazing at the flames. Meanwhile the wind must have started blowing even more violently, because puffs of smoke started coming down the chimney.

"Well, Mother, what's the latest?"

His mother beckoned to him to come still closer and murmured in his ear in a little trickle of a voice broken by emotion: "Bastià, it seems that that poor boy of ours is alive. Do you understand? He's alive."

"No," he replied dryly. "His remains were found on the mountain a few days ago. There wasn't much of them; he had been torn to pieces by wolves."

"That was what they first thought," Donna Maria Vincenza whispered. "But they soon found out that the remains were those of a girl belonging to the Colamartini family, a girl named Cristina. But he's alive. Do you understand? Alive."

Don Bastiano stayed motionless, staring at the fire; in his effort to control himself only his features contracted and became still harder. Then, while his mother watched him with an expression in which astonishment quickly gave way to terror, he rose, casually put a chair back in its place, rehung a frying pan on the wall, picked a cigar from a box, searched all his pockets for a match, and then, not finding one, bent over the fire and lit his cigar with an ember.

"I must go into the next room," he said to his mother in an unconcerned voice, as if he had suddenly remembered his guests. "Decorum must be observed," he added with a forced smile.

"Bastià, for heaven's sake don't leave me like this now, after what I've just told you," his mother implored, seizing him by the arm. "Come here, sit down beside me, so that we can talk without being overheard in the next room. Listen to me, my son, don't be pitiless, wipe that cruel expression from your face, stop looking like a damned soul. Are you listening to me? Well, someone from the place where that boy of ours was staying when he was discovered by the police came and told me that when he fled he didn't take the mountain route as everyone, including the authorities, believed, but hid in the valley, in a stable, and he's still there, and he's still alive. Apparently no one else knows apart from the two of us, and no one else must know. We must pretend to be resigned to his death; that, Holy Mother of God, is what we're reduced to, we have to pretend. Meanwhile the man says a safer hiding place must be found for him as quickly as possible. The man is a poor devil, and of course he wants to be compensated for the risk he's taking. Now, I can take care of the expense, but, as for the rest, I'm an old woman, and I've no experience of certain things, so you must help me a little. Are you listening to me?"

Don Bastiano, bent over the fire, seemed to be absorbed in drawing circles in the ashes with a bellows made of an old rifle barrel. His face, which had been contracted and hard, had slowly relaxed and resumed an unruffled expression.

"Bastià," his mother implored him, "have you been listening to me?"

"No, Mother, I haven't heard a single word," he replied, as if he had just awoken from sleep, and he assumed an apologetic smile. "Is that all? Have you nothing else to say to me? Now it's really time I went into the next room, because my guests will be expecting me. Won't you join us on the balcony to watch the blessing? I think it's just going to begin. There are more people than ever this year. Maria Rosa says it's entirely due to the parish priest."

He rose and made as if to go, but Donna Maria Vincenza again seized his arm and held him and, as his anger flared up and he made as if to shake her off, she began appealing to him again without letting him go.

"Don't go away like this, I implore you, my son," she said. "Even if you have no pity for that scapegrace, though he is your brother's son, your brother Ignazio, may he rest in peace, try at least to have some pity on your mother. I've come to the end of my tether, as you see. I can't describe my distress to you. I feel that my heart is breaking. Consider, my son, this could be the last time we shall talk to each other, so sit down, Bastià, sit beside me for a moment. Be patient with me even if I'm wrong. If you knew, my son, what it cost me to bring you up."

The old lady talked with difficulty, and every now and then she had to stop to recover her breath. Don Bastiano sighed deeply, sat down, and stretched his legs toward the embers to dry his muddy boots. A sudden peal of bells from the church opposite proclaimed the beginning of the blessing.

"Do you perhaps imagine that to save a grandson I'm willing to lose a son?" his mother went on, her eyes full of tears. "Last time, too, you tried to explain to me the new circumstances and the struggle you're involved in. You certainly didn't convince me, Bastià, but then it was a matter of fetching the body and giving it

Christian burial. But now he's alive. Do you hear me, my son? He's alive. Even if the arguments you used last time were right — and, forgive me, they were not — now they no longer apply. If you want to tell me that his joining the party of the workers was an act of madness, I agree with you completely. If you say that his going from country to country with false papers was dangerous folly, I agree with you completely. You see, Bastià, I admit you're right in everything. But you can't say I'm wrong, my son, if I add that in spite of all he is still one of us. No government law can change our blood. We are bound to one another in our bones, our arteries, our bowels. We are branches of the same tree. The tree was there, my son, before the government existed. We can certainly refuse to share the boy's faults, but we can't refuse to share his suffering."

In her exaggerated fear of being overheard in the next room the old lady grew more and more distressed and tearful. Her voice grew more and more anguished and less and less audible, and often deteriorated into a wheezing like that of an asthmatic. What she was trying to say was made plain only by the facial expression that accompanied and accentuated every word, giving it an agonized intensity.

"Bastià," she whispered, leaning toward her son, "Bastià, I really can't understand you."

He was sitting beside her, slightly in front of her, on a low stool, and she waited in vain for him to speak.

"Families," she went on patiently, as if she were talking to a child, "families exist above all to provide support in times of trouble. If life became permanently happy, it's easy to see that taverns and theaters and the bands that play in public squares would continue to exist. But families? I'm afraid they would vanish very quickly. Bastià, must I confess the truth to you? For the first time in my life, if I don't succeed in avoiding people in the street or in church and feel their eyes on me, I feel ashamed, more ashamed than you can imagine. Not, mind you, because a member of our family has caused a scandal by opposing the government. In most people's eyes, as you know, being against the government has never been dishonorable; at most it was foolish, but in any case, whether it was a misfortune or a crime, it was a matter for the individual and not his relatives. But the reason why I'm ashamed and hide myself from people is that we have done nothing to help him. I'm ashamed because when the news arrived of his death on the mountain we did not hurry to fetch him and bury him in the family tomb. To give him Christian burial in the family tomb by his father's and mother's side. Defying all danger and indifferent to any kind of fear or human respect. Bastià, are you listening to me? Well, if you are, I implore you to drop that deaf-mute expression. True, the Spinas have always been noted for their hard heads, their hard bones, their thick hides, but also for their heart. Offending one of them always meant facing the whole clan. All that's left of that in you, my son, is the hard head. Who changed your blood?"

In the light of the fire it was evident that the heads of Donna Maria Vincenza and Don Bastiano were made in the same mold. With its clean, delicate, fleshless features and skin adhering to the bone, the old lady's might have been worked in ivory; her son's was a faithful copy but in clay, a crudely enlarged copy, stronger and more hollowed and not yet completely finished, still a little rough edged.

"Are you afraid of the police?" his mother suddenly asked. "Are you afraid of prison? It wouldn't be the first time, you know, that members of our family have helped each other against the law. How did you get away with it during the war when they found out you had hidden half your wheat from the requisitioning board? Who saved you from prison that time when you broke a bottle of wine on poor Giacinto's head at a carnival party? Your brother Ignazio, the father of the boy whose life now leaves you indifferent, went to the *carabinieri* and pretended to have done it himself until the magistrate, who was a friend of the family's, cleared up the whole thing and arranged a settlement. Are you afraid of losing the new contract, perhaps?"

Donna Maria Vincenza waited in vain and with increasing anxiety for her son to respond, make a gesture, a grimace, any kind of sign. He was using a piece of wood to scrape the mud from his worn and down-at-the-heel boots; he did this casually and distractedly, as if he were alone, but his eyes were full of shadow. His mother looked at him in amazement and terror, and then started talking to him again with the desperation of one who feels the supreme ordeal of her life to be approaching.

"My son," she said, "you can't do less than a stranger. Do you remember Simone Ortiga? As soon as he heard the news he came to see me and offered to help; and just now, on the way here, he came up to my carriage and . . ."

"Simone the Weasel?" Don Bastiano exclaimed. "That's a fine example to hold up to me. Would you like to see me reduced to his state?"

All hope seemed to have vanished.

"Bastià," his mother murmured sorrowfully. "Bastià, my son, at least you must realize this. You are introducing into the family history a disgrace that, thank heaven, has never blackened it before. There have, alas, been crazy Spinas, violent Spinas, drunken Spinas, miserly Spinas. But you are the first to be a coward."

Of his mother's whole speech this was the first word that Don Bastiano showed he had heard. He grew suddenly pale, leaped to his feet, brought his clenched fists right up to her face, and, completely beside himself, shouted like a man possessed: "Be quiet, be quiet, will you be quiet? If you say another word, as sure as God's in His heaven I'll pick up your chair and throw it downstairs with you in it."

In response to his shouting Donna Maria Rosa appeared at the kitchen door, distraught with fear, but a furious glance from her husband caused her quickly to withdraw, shutting the door behind her. Footsteps and the voices of more guests arriving could be heard from the stairs.

"Good afternoon, Donna Maria Rosa, our respects. I hope we're not disturbing you."

"Welcome, Don Michele, Donna Sarafina, what a delightful surprise to have brought the young ladies too. Come in, come in, come into the drawing room, it's nice and warm there. What a gale, isn't it? Don't stand on ceremony, come in and make yourselves at home. I'll fetch my husband at once and bring you something to drink."

Don Bastiano strode up and down the room in a paroxysm of rage, picking up and smashing on the floor everything he could lay his hands on, the coffeepot, the coffee machine, the saltcellar, and some jars of preserved fruit his wife had left on the table. But he tried in vain to open a solidly constructed cupboard in which recently bought plates and glasses had been locked; eventually he collapsed on a small stool in a corner with his head against the wall, exhausted, out of breath and blue, almost purple in the face, with glazed eyes and hands trembling like an epileptic's. Donna Maria Vincenza looked at him in terror. In the semidarkness against the wall his head looked like a skull, not a bare, clean skull, but a drunken, unclean one, the frightening skull of a damned man. In repugnance and pity Donna Maria Vincenza closed her eyes. Don Bastiano's outburst of rage slowly subsided and left him panting, exhausted, depressed.

Some time elapsed before he remembered his mother and cast a furtive glance in the direction of the fireplace; she was motionless, with her hands in her lap, her white head resting against the back of the chair, and her eyes shut. The idea that she might be dead seemed suddenly to fill him with panic. Because of the darkness he could not make out from the corner in which he was sitting whether she was still breathing and moving her eyelids, but he dared not approach her.

He was still considering what to do when he heard his wife's footsteps on the stairs. He tiptoed out of the kitchen, went toward her, and took from her a big jug of wine that she was carrying. "I'll serve the guests," he said in such an agreeable tone that its very unexpectedness took the poor woman aback and moved her to tears. "Go and look after my mother," he said, "and if . . . anything should happen to her call me at once."

2

APART FROM A DENSE cloud of cigar smoke hanging in the air, the drawing room was empty when Don Bastiano walked in. The visitors had gone out onto the balcony over-looking the little square where the blessing of the animals had begun. The square was crowded; it was like a theater in which the play was the audience itself. Don Coriolano, Don Marcantonio, and De Paolis had assumed authoritative and protective attitudes at the threshold of the balcony, and to give himself importance Don Michele Canizza, the pharmacist, a bald little man, had joined them, coughing every now and then though he did not have a cold and equally unnecessarily continually taking a big watch from his pocket. Their appearance on the balcony resulted in some expressions of shock in the square, which were immedi-ately stifled by the timorous hush-hush of the crowd.

"Mourning doesn't last long in gentlemen's houses," someone called out.

"Your presence here reassures me," Don Michele muttered into Don Coriolano's ear. "You must excuse me if I express myself badly, but you will understand what I'm trying to say. Does this wind worry you?"

"I understand and respect your feelings. How is business?" Don Coriolano said, patting him on the shoulder.

"Must I confess it? I was uncertain whether or not to come," Don Michele went on in an undertone. "Business is bad, not because there's any shortage of sick people, on the contrary, in fact. On top of it I have two daughters to marry, so you can draw your own conclusions. Also I want to make it clear that this is the first time I've set foot in this house since the scandal. When I heard that you were here I said to my wife, Sarafì, I said, if a man like Don Coriolano can go there and take two notables with him, it means that it's all right. I don't know, *cavaliere*, if I've made myself clear."

"I understand you very well and, Don Michele, permit me to say that your sentiments do you honor."

"A thousand thanks. Sarafì, did you hear what Don Coriolano has just said to me? Nunziatè, Gemmì, did you hear? Such praise, *cavaliere*, goes straight to my heart. Above all, when one is in business and has two daughters to marry there's no place for idle curiosity."

The ladies were in the front row against the balcony railing, squatting on children's chairs and stools. It was obvious at first sight that the pharmacist's wife, Donna Sarafina, was a housemaid who had come up in the world; elated by the presence of so many strangers, she gave herself the airs of a grande dame in a box at the theater. "Michelì," she said to her husband in a tone of polite reproach, "why did you forget the opera glasses?" The two daughters, thin and ill-nourished brunettes in their homemade Sunday best, were the target of stupid jokes and flirtatiousness on the part of Don Marcantonio and De Paolis, and in the way they laughed and answered back and gesticulated they tried to seem as coquettish and emancipated as town girls. At one point general laughter broke out, no one knew exactly why, and Donna Sarafina declared that she had never heard anything so amusing in the whole of her life.

"Witticisms like that ought to be printed, upon my word," her husband said, wiping away the tears that had come into his eyes from laughing too much.

Donna Sarafina did not take her eyes off her daughters for a single moment. Her facial mimicry was too expressive not to be noticed by the others present, but was too complicated to be fully intelligible to outsiders. She was trying to show pleasure at the girls' success and at the same time trying to admonish them to be more reserved for the sake of that success. At opposite ends of the balcony two persons were sitting whose arrival Don Bastiano had missed: one was his sister-in-law Donna Filomena, a retired schoolmistress, a simple, thin, sallow little woman with shrewd and lively eyes who wore a black lace cap. She was sitting sideways, with her back to Donna Sarafina and her two daughters, her excuse being that she had a painful knee; the other was Calabasce's son, a dark, serious, and taciturn sixteen-year-old dressed like a little man.

"In our family, thanks be to heaven, respect for the authorities is complete," Donna Sarafina sighed, picking up the thread where her husband had left it after making sure that their host and hostess were not within earshot.

At this Donna Filomena, not being able to stand it any longer, said, not talking to anyone in particular but addressing the world at large: "Never mind, even sheep bite the unfortunate."

This remark took Donna Sarafina completely aback.

"Who was talking about sheep?" she exclaimed. "You haven't understood a word we were saying, Filomè. None of us, none of these gentlemen here, were talking about sheep."

This exchange of fireworks was interrupted by the appearance on the scene of Don Bastiano, who barely returned his guests' greetings and pretended to take an interest in the blessing. He looked pale and upset. His guests were embarrassed by the thought that he might have overheard what they had been saying, and they too fell silent and pretended to be taking an interest in what was going on in the square.

He went to the front of the balcony to show himself and enjoy the neighbors' envy, but when he spotted Simone in the throng he quickly withdrew.

"Don Bastià, Papa sends his apologies and says he'll be coming later," Calabasce's son said. "He's very sorry he couldn't come sooner."

"All right, all right," Bastiano replied absentmindedly.

"What? Did you invite him too?" Donna Filomena exclaimed with obvious disgust.

All around the square the balconies of houses were turned toward the church just as boxes in a theater are turned toward the stage. Don Coriolano greeted with expansive gestures the many spectators arrayed on the neighboring balconies, who recognized him, called out and waved to him and greeted him by name at the top of their voices. Times had changed, everyone knew he no longer had the authority he had had in the past, but he had accepted the new régime and now acted as intermediary between it and the poor, which was another reason why he was still the speaker most in demand for wedding breakfasts, baptisms, and funerals, and was the most sought-after godfather at the confirmation of one's children, though he was anticlerical and an atheist.

"On this day of all days you're not trying to compete with Sant' Antonio, are you?" Donna Filomena said to him disapprovingly.

Don Bastiano called the pharmacist aside for a moment. "Have you come to pay me the rent you owe me for your shop?" he asked him.

"What ingratitude," the pharmacist answered indignantly. "I expose myself to heaven knows what dangers in coming to your house and you show your thanks by insulting me."

"You haven't paid the rent for two years," Don Bastiano said. "And what dangers are you talking about?"

The old parish church was directly opposite the Spina house on the other side of the small, rectangular square. Two worn and blackened stone statues surveyed the square from the facade; two statues of unknown saints whose long cohabitation and familiarity with the *cafoni* had ended up creating a resemblance between them. The houses that huddled together around the square were tall and narrow, damp and muddy as if a river had been passing over them for centuries and had left a trail behind. The only exception was the new building that housed the schools and public offices, built in the heroic-funereal style that had become the fashion in recent years. Meanwhile in the big crowd that had gathered in the square it was at first difficult to distinguish *cafoni* from small landowners, carters from tradesmen, because all of them, in accordance with local custom, wore long, black, more or less heavy, more or less ragged, pilgrimlike cloaks. The women, for the most part dressed in dark rags, did nothing to diminish the gloomy uniformity of the assembly, which was confined within a border formed by a muddy track along which about a hundred small donkeys and mules, ridden by their masters and encouraged by the spectators' cries, were already filing past one behind another. The cold united and made visible the breath of men and animals, and from the whole agglomeration there arose a smell of damp, manured earth, earth taking its winter rest. Each animal that passed in front of the church was blessed by the aged parish priest in surplice and stole and with his holy water sprinkler. To get some shelter from the north wind, which blew into the square from a little side street and swirled against the church steps, the priest had abandoned his post at the edge of the track and sought refuge in the doorway of the church. The sacristan in his red cassock stood beside him with a pail of holy water, and farther back, better sheltered from the wind but visible to the throng, stood the papier-mâché statue of the saint, illuminated by the flickering of innumerable votive candles, all of different sizes. Old and young, as was the custom, rode without saddle or bit, with a simple hempen rope around the animal's head; some rode wearing their cloaks wrapped around their left shoulder, leaving their right arm free for the halter.

There was special applause for some donkeys that were decked out with colored ribbons on their head and tail and had bells around their neck, as had once upon a time been the general custom on this occasion. This cheap finery, borrowed for the day from the trousseaux of marriageable girls, failed to conceal the sorry state of the poor beasts, the abrasions and lacerations on the

back, the swollen shoulders, the distended or swollen and dangling belly, the cracks in the knees and shinbones, the hairless
tail, and the other indications of the daily life they shared with
their poverty-stricken masters. To most of the spectators, particularly the artisans and the young, the blessing ceremony came as a
welcome, noisy diversion that interrupted the lethargy of winter,
and they shouted jokes and jibes at the most pitiful animals and at
the usual two or three poor devils who in a gathering of this kind
become the object of collective derision. But here and there,
there were also groups of grave and silent peasants who kept their
eyes fixed on the arm of the officiating priest and the miraculous
statue of the saint. The latter, standing on a tall wooden pedestal,
was represented with a pale and pink young face set in a frame of
fair curly hair; he was dressed in a long brown sack and on his
shoulders there was a cloak of the same color. In his left hand he
bore a fiery flame (in memory of the fearful medieval plague
known as Sant'Antonio's Fire), and in his right a pilgrim's staff
surmounted by a bell.

In one corner of the square Venanzio was surrounded by a
group of landlords — big, powerfully built men in heavy cloaks
who were bombarding him with questions.

"The Spinas seem to be behaving very strangely nowadays,"
one of them said. "Aren't they in mourning?"

"Why isn't at least Donna Maria Vincenza in mourning?"
someone else wanted to know.

Venanzio was rescued by Simone, who took him to a deep
dark cave not far away that had been converted into a tavern. Simone was already drunk, and he reeled as he walked down the
steps. At the bottom of the cave a small lamp was burning in front
of Our Lady of Loreto.

"I'm sorry for your mistress's sake," he said to the groom, "but I
wouldn't set foot in that house."

"Apart from anything else, Don Bastiano is her son," Venanzio
said in embarrassment.

"I wouldn't set foot in the place," Simone repeated. "Filumè,
we're thirsty," he called out.

A shadow emerged from the darkness and approached with a heavy jug of wine; the shadow turned out to be a tall, thin woman with an abundant head of hair, wearing innumerable coral necklaces and big gold hoops in her ears.

"Once upon a time Don Bastiano and you were as thick as thieves," Venanzio said to Simone. "Then you each went your own wild way, he in one direction and you in another."

"Yes, once upon a time," Simone agreed, with a gesture indicating how long ago that had been. "Let us drink, Venà. The age of the masters is over and done with."

"Why did you let yourself get into this state?" Venanzio said. "And Bastiano, what changed him?"

"I don't know," Simone said. "Perhaps it was money. There's no pride left, Venà, so there are no more masters. Filumè," he called out, "bring us another jug, we want to drink to the disappearance of the masters."

"You've drunk too much already," Venanzio said. "How are you going to get back to Colle?"

"I shall sleep here with the landlady," Simone confided in his ear. "She has a huge bed over there behind the barrel; you may know it yourself. The bedroom's damp, but the landlady's as dry and hot as one of the devil's own braziers. Now drink, Venà, drink with me to the death of the masters."

"There'll always be masters," Venanzio said dejectedly.

"There was one left," Simone said, "but they killed him on the mountain. His pride was intolerable. And his relatives didn't dare to fetch the body and bury it in the family tomb. Perhaps they're right. Where there's no pride there are no relatives, but only bastards. Filumè, another jug," Simone called out.

But the landlady didn't answer; she must have been outside in the square. The two men rose to leave too, but before they did so Simone smashed the empty jug on the tabletop.

"Simò, no one will ever understand you," said Venanzio, who was upset. "Whatever you say, there'll always be masters."

"Then go and join them," Simone said contemptuously, giving him a shove and indicating the balcony of the Spina house.

Don Coriolano had taken advantage of a moment when his two colleagues seemed to be engaged in particularly lively conversation with the young Canizza ladies to draw Don Bastiano aside into a corner of the drawing room and have a word with him in confidence.

"This time you've really put your foot in it," he began in grave tones and with a gesture of consternation. "Since you've taken such poor advantage of my advice, on my word of honor I shall stop using my influence on your behalf. Don't interrupt me, Bastià, I'll tell you why straightaway. Well then, I suggested you should write a letter of congratulation and welcome to the new political secretary. Well, don't you realize how you've blotted your copy book? This time you've really gone too far."

"I wrote word for word what you told me to write, no more and no less," Don Bastiano said in annoyance. "Word for word."

"Rubbish. I saw the letter with my own eyes. Don't interrupt me. The secretary, bless him, knowing me to be your friend, sent for me urgently and showed it to me. Allow me to point out to you, my dear fellow, that you picked up the wrong end of the stick, and instead of offering him wholehearted congratulations, in your own name and that of your fellow citizens, you offered him, literally, wholehearted condolences, in your own name and that of your fellow citizens. I don't know if you realize the difference."

Don Bastiano looked at him mistrustfully, fearing that this might be one of the usual dodges to get money out of him. However that might be, he had other things on his mind, so he tried to cut the conversation short.

"If it's as you say," he muttered wearily, "it was sheer absence of mind. For some time past, God knows, I haven't managed to do anything right. If the priest sometimes errs at the altar, I'm entitled to make a mistake too."

But Don Coriolano was not willing to let him off so lightly.

"You will yourself admit," he went on, patiently and persuasively, "that on the occasion of an appointment, and times being what they are, to receive condolences instead of congratulations is sufficient to send cold shudders down one's spine. But that's not all. You must also take into account — and this, Bastià, is the really serious point — the fact that the new secretary believes in the evil eye. Yes, my friend, that is the gist of the matter. He frankly admitted in a confidential talk with me that he personally would not put his hand in the fire to testify to the existence of God; why should he, have *you* ever seen Him? he said. But, having had his experiences, the evil eye was one of the few things he found it impossible to doubt. So you can imagine his consternation when he received your letter. When he showed it to me he was literally pea green, and he smiled like someone who has inadvertently swallowed arsenic. Naturally, at the risk of compromising myself, I defended you with drawn sword. Come, come, I said, don't let's overdramatize things, it was a mere slip, an innocent blunder, I tried to explain. Do you know what he replied, Bastià? That's what makes it so serious, he said. If it had been done deliberately, it would have been equivalent to an act of opposition, and I could at once have taken appropriate measures. But against an involuntary act of ill omen nothing whatever could be done. How could one defend oneself against the invisible hand of destiny? We had a lengthy argument, and I must admit that as a speaker the new secretary isn't up to much — on my word of honor, I feel I could gobble him up like a ham roll — but as a logician he's hard to beat. It's sufficient to say, my friend, that he went to school with the Jesuits."

"So I shall have to write him a note of apology, shall I?" Don Bastiano, who was chiefly interested in the practical side of the matter, asked irritably.

"For heaven's sake don't make matters worse," Don Coriolano replied. "Suppose you committed another faux pas. Listen to me, Bastià, I spent a whole night thinking about your case, on my word of honor. The best thing for you to do would be to send him a small barrel of wine. Or rather, as he takes offense easily and I'm a friend of his, you could send it to my address, so that I could ask him in for a drink every now and then. It would have to be good wine, of course, otherwise it would be worse than nothing."

"But I don't draw wine from the fountain," Don Bastiano,

who had at last grasped the drift of the conversation, said with exasperation.

"Your ingratitude is equal to your irresponsibility," Don Coriolano concluded, his gorge rising. "You don't realize what I risk in coming to your house. I have my enemies too." And he turned his back on Don Bastiano and returned to the spectacle from the balcony.

Meanwhile the blessing of the animals dragged on. The *cafoni* must have decided that, if one blessing was beneficial, five or ten blessings must be proportionally more beneficial still, and so they tirelessly presented themselves to the priest and to Sant'Antonio over and over again, competing to see who could secure the most blessings, particularly in view of the fact (incredible but true) that they were free. But with the arrival of more and more donkeys and mules the congestion grew until eventually the track was completely blocked and no one could move either forward or back; the shouts, obscenities, and even curses that arose from all over the square completely failed to clear the blockage and set the pious merry-go-round in motion again. In the end even the sacristan lost patience, and this was a curious sight.

"In heaven's name," he shouted, "you're not proposing to keep me here all night, are you?"

And, passing from words to deeds, he was seen putting down his pail of holy water and dashing about in the throng, seizing by the halter donkeys and mules that in his opinion had been sufficiently blessed and trying to force them down a side road next to the church to make room for the latest arrivals. However, his authority outside the sacristy did not seem to be universally recognized, and the result of his intervention was a scuffle in which his red cassock was torn and two or three *cafoni* were knocked down. The one who emerged in the sorriest state was Simone, who had come hurrying along to try to reestablish peace among the *cafoni*. But, being very drunk, he had a bad fall and had to be picked up from under the hooves of a mule, semiconscious and with blood pouring from his head and face. Some men carried him toward Don Bastiano's house. But on the steps he opened his eyes and dragged his feet, refusing to go any farther. "No, not there," he insisted.

"But you've got to have your wounds washed," Venanzio tried to tell him.

"Very well then, at the fountain," he had the strength to reply, so he was carried to the fountain in a corner of the square and his head was held under the spout. Under the jet of water it looked like a beet, the skin of which had been gashed with a knife. A big pool of blood quickly formed around the fountain, and a gasp of pity and horror rose from the crowd of onlookers.

"Is he dead?" those farthest away asked. "Will he be crippled for life? Who is he?"

"Oh, his poor wife who'll see him being brought back on a stretcher," the women lamented. "His poor children. His poor family. How suddenly disaster strikes."

But soon afterward Simone, his head wrapped in a strip of shirt, was to be seen mounting his donkey again and making off, swaying from side to side as if he were going to fall to the ground again at any moment.

"What luck, what a miracle," some of the women were to be heard exclaiming. "Oh, it's Simone from Colle, Simone whom they call the Weasel, a man with the devil in his belly."

"Without Sant'Antonio's help he'd now be dead, that's certain," others said.

"Just look at him riding off like that. He looks just as if he were raised from the dead. Yes, it's Simone, a crazier man has never been seen."

Simone the Weasel stopped his donkey outside the church, not to thank the saint, but to have things out with the sacristan.

"Come out, if you've got the pluck, you lousy churchmouse, you scabby bat, you candle eater," he called out.

But some *cafoni* intervened and advised him, in view of the close proximity of Sant'Antonio, who was only two paces away, to postpone having things out with the sacristan to a more suitable occasion; and in spite of his drunkenness Simone ended up giving in, and he trotted off in the direction of Colle.

"In any other civilized country," Don Michele Canizza pointed out to his neighbors on the balcony, "an incident like that would have ended up at the pharmacy. But here, as you have seen with your own eyes, it ends up at the fountain. I don't say that in my own interests, of course, on the contrary, as you can well imagine."

"The important thing in my opinion," Donna Filomena interrupted, "is that wounds should heal. I don't see there's any need for bandages and poultices when cold water will do."

The pharmacist started as if he had been bitten by a viper, but left it to Don Coriolano to reply.

"The cold-water theory is subversive," Don Coriolano announced with a smile, rubbing his hands. "It's a threat, not just to the pharmaceutical industry, but to religion and the state."

"Excuse me," Donna Filomena insisted with a blush, "but you have not understood me correctly. I was only talking about cases in which bandages and poultices are completely superfluous."

"My dear lady, you as a churchwoman should be the first to point out to us that only the superfluous is necessary," Don Coriolano replied with the voluptuousness of a cat playing with a mouse. "History teaches us, Donna Filomè, that the more superfluous a thing is, the more noble and hence the more fundamental it is. Eloquence, for instance."

"Excuse me for interrupting, Don Coriolà, but you talk just like a book," Donna Sarafina exclaimed, "and it gives me great pleasure to listen to you, if you will permit me to say so."

The pharmacist pressed both the orator's hands warmly.

"Will you allow me a question?" De Paolis asked the former schoolmistress. "If you give preference to natural remedies, what becomes of grace?"

"Grace, you know as well as I do, can be anywhere, even in cold water," said Donna Filomena, who was annoyed that the course of the conversation had raised issues of such amplitude. "Actually, when you take into account the abundance of miraculous springs, you must admit that grace has a special predilection for cold water. With all due respect to eloquence, water was not invented by the government."

THE SEED BENEATH THE SNOW ❖ *499*

"But aqueducts and fountains were," the trade union official replied. "The rest is theology; that is, those who want to believe it, can."

"Since you mention theology," said Don Coriolano, gesticulating as if he were conducting an orchestra, "this would be an appropriate moment for Don Marcantonio to come out of his shell and tell us what he thinks. But briefly, I hope."

"What?" Nunziatella exclaimed, putting on a pout. "You're a theologian and haven't mentioned it to us all this time?"

Don Marcantonio had taken Don Bastiano aside, perhaps for the purpose of asking for a small loan, but had succeeded in expressing himself only in the most general terms, with vague allusions to a promissory note about to fall due and to his mother being in the most desperate straits, threatened with confiscation of her goods.

"But you certainly have a great many friends," Don Bastiano had said to him.

"In the sense that you have in mind, alas, I have none at all," he had replied.

His response to Don Coriolano's invitation was to blush to his ears. He was shriveled, bowlegged, and bespectacled, and, though he was over forty, he had preserved the way of dressing and the timid and humble manners of an impoverished student.

"But in that case, excuse my frankness, are you by any chance an unfrocked priest?" Gemmina asked him in alarm.

The girls' amazement and the embarrassment of the poor man, who could not put two words together, caused amusement on the balcony until Don Coriolano came to his colleague's rescue.

"Actually," he explained, "Don Marcantonio in his time graduated in agriculture but, wishing to improve his position and believing himself to have oratorical ability, a matter on which I am not yet in a position to form a definite opinion, last year he suddenly dropped his traveling professorship with its experimental potatoes, lettuces, and onions and went to Milan, where he learned German and attended the celebrated school of state mysticism, from which he returned a few weeks ago with a magnificent multicolored diploma that consecrates him as a government mystic.* So I must apologize for my inexact phraseology of a short time ago. He is not really a theologian, but a Passionist father of politics."

"Why should you apologize?" Don Marcantonio, who had at last found his tongue, interrupted. "Mysticism is of course nothing but theology's shortcut. It penetrates to the mysterious essence of the national soul, not by the arid paths of thought, but directly and, I would say, in a flash, *durch gefühlmässiges Erleben*,[†] to put it in the language of our transalpine masters."

The German phrase made a great impression. De Paolis had to have it repeated and explained three or four times.

"Actually we were talking about bandages and poultices and cold water," Donna Filomena pointed out, recovering herself. "What I was saying was that if a sick or injured man can do without bandages, why force them on him?"

"Then explain to me why people are forced to listen to public speakers," Don Michele replied angrily, losing his patience. "A distant relative of yours, Donna Filomè, whom we all know and who in any case is weak in the head, lost his job for refusing to attend a meeting. What I want to know is this. If listening to public speakers is obligatory, why shouldn't going to the pharmacy be obligatory too? Please note that I do not say this in my own interests, of course, quite the reverse in fact."

"Papa, don't keep interrupting all the time, let the *cavaliere* talk," exclaimed Nunziatella, losing her patience too.

Don Marcantonio coughed and blew his nose, while the others composed themselves to listen. He began with an embarrassed movement of his hand, like a novice schoolmaster giving his first lesson.

"Your error, Donna Filomè, and it is the most disastrous and pernicious error imaginable, is to take as your starting point the individual, if I may be permitted to call the devil by his right

---

*Under Fascism there was a "school of state mysticism" in Milan, where the language of the German ally was encouraged.
†Through the experience of feelings.

name. In an authoritarian state it should no longer be permissible to ask, as you did, whether an individual can do without poultices but, of course, whether bandages and poultices can do without the individual; just as public speaking exists, not for the benefit of those who listen to it, but the other way about, as is now taken for granted and sanctioned by appropriate police measures. In the same way schools do not exist for the benefit of pupils, but pupils for the benefit of schools. Railways are not there for the benefit of travelers, but travelers for the benefit of railways, *und so weiter und so weiter."* *

Don Marcantonio was now smiling the relieved artistic smile of the novice conjuror after his first few successes in publicly producing a rabbit out of an empty top hat, but Don Coriolano whispered a critical remark about him into De Paolis's ear.

"Don't you agree with him?" De Paolis asked, taking him aside.

"Whether he's right or wrong is beside the point," Don Coriolano explained. "He gets agitated and expresses himself badly, that's all."

The pharmacist wanted to congratulate Don Marcantonio, but Don Bastiano, who had been keeping his eye on him, got in first and with almost painful urgency forced him to be silent.

"I agree, I agree," he said, vigorously shaking both Don Marcantonio's hands.

De Paolis reacted mistrustfully to Don Bastiano's demonstration of assent, but Don Coriolano indicated by a gesture that he would take care of him.

"Instead of staying here, exposed to the wind and the indiscreet eyes of the *cafoni*, supposing we went back into the drawing room, wouldn't that be an idea?" Donna Sarafina suggested. "To avoid offending Donna Maria Rosa, apart from anything else, because I seem to see that she has the glasses ready."

The move indoors was watched attentively and commented on by the crowd in the square. Except for Calabasce's son, who

---

*And so on and so forth.

stayed to watch the blessing, the guests gathered around the drawing room table, polite, ceremonious, and finally reconciled and brought into harmony by the love of fine words.

Don Marcantonio had suddenly acquired such complete self-confidence that he did not stop gloating for a single moment, and every so often he rubbed his hands as if to congratulate himself on the honor of having made his own acquaintance. The little eyes behind his spectacles shone with emotion. In the close air of the drawing room you could tell that his jacket had been abundantly cleaned with gasoline, with the result that when he moved about he left a vague motorcycle smell behind him.

"A glass of wine?" Nunziatella asked him.

"Yes, how could I refuse? Tell me, how could I possibly refuse?"

He sampled the wine as if he were a connoisseur; he sipped and savored it as if it were nectar, and finally half closed his eyes and lightly licked his lips and then wiped them with the back of his hand.

"If you will permit me," De Paolis said, "I'll take off my tie and unbutton my collar. Rather democratic manners, it is true, but between ourselves, you understand."

"You have no need whatever to apologize," Don Marcantonio pointed out. "We must not forget that, though we are an authoritarian state, we are a people's state. I myself, when I receive *cafoni* in my office nowadays, shake them by the hand, smoke a pipe, though I prefer cigarettes, and spit on the ground, though I find spitting frankly disgusting. Obviously we must uncompromisingly oppose certain degenerate features of democracy, such as freedom of the press, elections, assemblies, and congresses and other diabolical British inventions that are offensive to our Latin dignity. But, apart from all that, it cannot be denied that democracy has its beneficial aspects. To put it in a nutshell, we bring about true democracy. In a mystical sense, of course."

Tears of emotion appeared in the pharmacist's eyes, but the prevailing harmony was suddenly and irremediably shattered by the unexpected arrival of a young woman. Her style of clothing and her elegance might have made her seem a foreigner, but her coloring, features, and facial expression left no doubt about her local origin. She seemed surprised at the large number of visitors she found in the drawing room and was on the point of apologizing and withdrawing, but she was prevented from doing so by Don Bastiano, who went forward to greet her and forced her to join the company. Apart from the pharmacist, who was immobilized by a threatening look from his wife, the other men greeted her with hurrahs and surrounded her, raising their filled glasses.

"Nunziatella, Gemmina, let us go back to the balcony," their mother exclaimed. "We came here for the blessing, thank heaven, not for a debauch."

Donna Filomena, after a half greeting to the newcomer and not without hesitation, ended up going out onto the balcony too.

"What an affront," Donna Sarafina protested. "The mistress of the house ought to have warned us."

"Did you see how she's made up?" said Nunziatella. "And what a funny little hat."

"A whitewashed house is an inn," her mother announced.

"What will she live on when that old man who's keeping her dies?"

"She'll beg for alms," said Gemmina with a grimace of satisfaction.

"No, it's not easy to understand Faustina," said Donna Filomena. "If she's not mad, she's a complete mystery."

"There's only one thing that surprises me, Filomè," said the pharmacist's wife. "You'll forgive me, won't you, for the words we exchanged just now? Let us not bear each other any ill will. I expressed myself badly, that's all, I assure you."

Donna Filomena pretended to smile. "Don't worry, words pass," she said.

"As I was saying, there's only one thing that surprises me. Our priest's a holy man, he goes without necessities for the sake of the poor, I admit. But why, if he's a real man of God, doesn't he send for Don Severino and insist on his breaking off his sinful relations with Faustina, who is not married to him and is thirty years younger?"

"Our priest, Sarafina, is a man of the old style. Perhaps he's a saint, I don't know, but at any rate he's a strange sort of saint," Donna Filomena replied. "He doesn't see things in the same way as we do."

A lively exchange followed.

"Don Severino isn't just anybody, he's the parish organist and takes part in every important service. As a churchman, he can't live in sin," Sarafina declared.

"But he's an old friend and schoolmate of the priest's," replied Filomena.

"He's a libertine, Filomè, and an unbeliever. Don't you remember the scandal he caused at the last census when he had himself put down as a believer in Bacchus?"

"What he put down was that he believed in Bach, who was a musician too, a great musician, according to what they say."

"But that didn't affect the scandal, Filomè, because when the results of the census for our borough were put up on the wall we had the shame of seeing it stated that we were all Christians except for a single worshiper of Bacchus."

"No one has ever seen Don Severino drunk, Sarafì, he's practically a teetotaler. Perhaps his only defect is pride."

"But he's also something else, Filomè, he's the parish organist; it's he who plays when we receive the Sacrament. The priest ought at least to get another organist."

"Don Severino plays the organ for nothing, Sarafì, as you know. Perhaps he does it for love of music, or perhaps out of friendship for the priest, it's difficult to say. But it's certain that no one in the village could take his place, and getting an organist from somewhere else would cost a fortune."

"But a scandal it is and a scandal it remains."

"The last time the committee of the Children of Mary went to the sacristy to complain to the priest about the organist's scandalous life, do you know what he told them, Sarafì? He said that no one but God could tell what united a man and a woman, whether it was sinful or not. That's what he told them. No one could tell, he said."

"That I can well imagine," Gemmina said with a laugh. Then she called out in the direction of the parlor: "Signor De Paolis."

"Michelino," his wife ordered, "come here, I want to talk to you."

"Signor Cipolla, Don Marcantonio," Nunziatella chirped.

There was no response from the drawing room.

"These men," Donna Filomena declared with a trace of satisfaction in her voice. "They come on to girls of good family, and five minutes later their minds are on something else."

"Quite right, they're just like flies," Donna Sarafina said bitterly. "How do flies behave in the garden? They fly this way and that, no flower is beautiful or perfumed enough for them, and they end up by taking pleasure, speaking with respect, on a bit of dung."

"*Cavalier* Cipolla, Signor De Paolis," the young ladies called out.

Their appeals were in vain. In the drawing room eloquence had abandoned the throne to beauty and was rendering it due homage. In their efforts to attract the young lady's attention each of the five men surrounding her looked more apelike than the rest. The most completely transfigured was Don Bastiano, but Donna Faustina's mind seemed to be elsewhere; she seemed disappointed at the absence of someone she had been hoping to see. In the ordinary sense of the word she was not beautiful, except for her figure, which was as slender and agile and fresh as an adolescent's. But her small, thin, almost feline face, all eyes and mouth, though not conventionally beautiful, was very attractive; her large eyes were moist with sensuousness, as it were, and this and her full, fleshy, camellia-colored mouth gave her an eager and ardent and at the same time sad expression.

"Gentlemen," she said, "I didn't come here to listen to your obscenities. I was passing behind the house when I saw Donna Maria Vincenza's carriage and, as it's years since I last talked to her, some of you know since when, I suddenly decided to come and wish her good afternoon. Why isn't she here with you, Bastià?"

"She's tired," Don Bastiano replied in embarrassment. "My wife's keeping her company next door in the kitchen, by the fire. We had better not disturb her."

This caused Don Coriolano to protest indignantly. "Don't

transplant these Arab customs among us," he declared with simulated exaggerated gravity. "I haven't seen Donna Maria Vincenza for about ten years, and the two comrades here present have not yet had the honor of meeting her. Thus today we have an opportunity that is not just rare, but also unique. My friends," he went on, turning to De Paolis and Don Marcantonio, "we as public speakers ought to light a candle in gratitude to Sant'Anna, who had the wisdom and prudence to cause Donna Maria Vincenza to be born a woman and not a man and, what's more, a woman of the Abruzzi, confined, that is to say, to her house; because I can guarantee that otherwise, with her candor and clarity of mind that come straight from the earthly paradise, she would have made life very difficult for us all. Furthermore, the blessed creature is as sure of God, as sure, I tell you, as we are of the things we see and touch, spaghetti or wine, for instance. Now, I am of the opinion that belief in God, if it is moderate, as sensible priests wisely recommend, apart from being an inexhaustible source of oratorical inspiration, is a highly important factor in the maintenance of public order, while if it is excessive, mark my words, it leads to anarchy."

Don Bastiano wanted to change the subject, but Don Coriolano's colleagues agreed with him, and the pharmacist congratulated him.

"Donna Maria Vincenza was a great friend of my mother's, as you know," Donna Faustina said, but she was unable to go on.

"Don't let us start being miserable again," Don Bastiano interrupted rudely when he noticed she had tears in her eyes. "Don't let's start lamenting again."

"I suggest," the pharmacist said in pacificatory tones, "that if Donna Maria Vincenza is too tired to come into the drawing room we should go and pay our respects to her around the fire for a few moments. That's only a suggestion, of course."

In spite of the lively objections of the master of the house, Donna Faustina was sent as an emissary into the kitchen. She went there timidly and hesitantly, but came back immediately, disappointed.

"They're praying," she said softly. "They're telling their beads. They didn't even look up when I went in."

"So much the better if they didn't see you," said the master of the house, reassured. "Sit down and have a glass of wine with us."

"The idea of those good souls praying for us miserable sinners should be an encouragement to us," Don Coriolano muttered into Donna Faustina's ear, caressing her shoulder.

"What a delightful perfume you have on your hair," De Paolis said with a sniff and a sigh. "What is it called?"

Donna Faustina had spent a few days in Rome and had come back with a new hairstyle, drawn up straight at the back with curls in front; she wore a tiny pillbox hat with a small feather, tilted forward.

"It suits you admirably, because now you look just like a little pony," Don Bastiano said, looking at her with awkward tenderness. "You know that for a long time breaking in young horses was a specialty of mine — leaping on their backs, holding on by the mane without a saddle, and away like the wind."

"The man who'll tame me, Bastià, has not yet been born."

"Yes, I know, there are horses that refuse to be ridden and prefer to pull a carriage."

"My carriage hasn't been built either, Bastià."

"That's something that nobody can deny," said the pharmacist. "Don Severino isn't even a carriage, at most he's a hearse."

Donna Faustina, furious, leaped to her feet. "And in comparison all of you are nothing but dung carts," she exclaimed.

The domestic kitten was transformed into a tigress.

Trembling with rage and with eyes flashing dangerously, she looked at the men one after the other, ready to scratch out the eyes of the first who dared to reply. But since everyone present preferred to retain his eyesight, she went off without saying goodbye, slamming the door behind her and without Don Bastiano's doing anything to detain her.

"If only I were a magician I might be able to understand her," he muttered.

A lively altercation between the pharmacist's wife and a group of youths under the balcony created a welcome diversion that rescued the gentlemen from their embarrassment.

"Sarafi, don't lower yourself by arguing with common people," her husband called out.

As the balcony railings bulged in what was known as the full-belly shape, chance willed it that the knees of the young Canizza ladies inadvertently ended up projecting too far, so much so as to give air and light to things that decorum required to be kept concealed. To prevent this golden opportunity of admiring the underwear of the pharmacist's daughters from being wasted, word must have passed right around the square, because a whole gang of youths, preferring this new spectacle to the blessing of the animals, had gathered under the balcony. As always happens in such cases, the strongest had secured the best places by pushing, shoving, and using their elbows, and four or five of them, with their hats tilted back, stared upward as if under a spell, forgetful of time and place, until Donna Sarafina noticed them and sounded the alarm.

"Disgusting ill-mannered pigs, you ought to be ashamed of yourselves," she yelled, leaning so far over the railing that she was in danger of plunging headlong to the ground. However, the prompt appearance of the master of the house and his guests nipped the incident in the bud. The youths moved away and vanished in the crowd, as at the exit of a movie, while the sacred merry-go-round approached its end. Donna Maria Vincenza's two horses were to be seen completing the last ritual circuits of the square. Old Belisario, whose gray coat was nearly white with age, was being ridden by a friend of Venanzio's, a former cavalryman, who, in order to show off and to the great admiration of the women, rode in the English way, raising and lowering himself in the saddle and leaning forward as if he were galloping. Venanzio was more modestly riding the second horse, which had the vice of nodding its head when it walked.

Don Bastiano took aside Don Coriolano, who followed him reluctantly. "Let's make peace," Bastiano proposed in a humble and conciliatory manner. "Will a demijohn do?"

The orator agreed, subject to a condition. "Yes, if it's the old wine," he said.

The two shook hands and laughed.

"Oh, look, look, there's poor old Plebiscito going by," Nunziatella exclaimed.

"Plebiscito?" De Paolis asked suspiciously.

"That's what they call the brown horse," Don Bastiano explained. "When it was young it was called Maltinto,* but when it developed the vice of walking like that, nodding, as if it were saying yes, yes, nothing but yes all the time, Don Severino renamed it Plebiscito. The curious thing is," Don Bastiano added with a smile, "is that now it answers only to its new name."

"Do they call it that to ridicule plebiscites or out of respect for them?" Don Coriolano asked suspiciously.

"Out of respect, of course, acceptance and respect," Don Bastiano assured him.

"You ought to suggest to your mother that when that horse dies she should present it to the nation," Donna Filomena suggested, laughing in her own way. "It would be very impressive if it were embalmed and exhibited in some school."

Venanzio came up to the kitchen to tell his mistress that the square was fairly clear and the carriage ready to go. Her son and daughter-in-law accompanied her down the stairs.

On the way they met a thickset man with heavy eyebrows and thick lips who greeted them ceremoniously and drew aside to let them pass. Donna Maria Vincenza looked him in the face without replying to his greeting.

"Go up, Calabà, I'll be back straightaway," Don Bastiano said to him.

Waiting outside the door with outstretched hands were three ragged, shriveled, and bent little old women who had heard of Donna Maria Vincenza's arrival and were waiting for her to beg for alms. One of them had two barefoot children clinging to her skirt, and Donna Maria Vincenza took her aside.

---

*Piebald.

"You're Maria Sabetta, aren't you?" she murmured in the woman's ear. "You need me, but today I need you even more. Have you some time to spare? Have you nothing to do for the next few hours? Well, Maria Sabetta, go to church and pray for me in front of the Host. You have suffered so much, Maria Sabetta, that the Lord will certainly listen to you. Tell Him one thing only. (Listen carefully to what I'm saying, Maria Sabetta, and don't go wrong.) Tell Him this: Maria Vincenza is not afraid (that He knows already), but she does not want to be tried beyond her strength."

"Since you ask me I shall do as you say," said the old beggar woman, kissing her hand. "But how can I appear before the Host and ask something for you? Suppose the Lord replies: presumptuous, shameless woman, how dare you plead for Donna Maria Vincenza?"

"Maria Sabetta, in the face of the Lord there is only one rank, that of suffering borne in a Christian manner. And you have suffered so much, Maria Sabetta, without ever despairing. Other women in your place would have gone mad. Go and pray for me."

Before getting into her carriage, while Venanzio was removing the blankets from the horses' backs, Donna Maria Vincenza said to her son: "Was that Calabasce whom we met on the stairs? The man who gave you the forged promissory notes? I'm surprised you've forgiven him."

"How little you know your son," he replied with a laugh. "Revenge is a dish that respectable people eat cold. Reacting to a wrong in hot blood is something to be left to *cafoni* and barbers."

Don Bastiano laughed, and his mother, who was now ensconced in the carriage, covered her eyes with her hand in horror to avoid seeing the grin on his face. Then, yielding to emotion, she drew him toward her and kissed him on one cheek. "My son," she murmured, "my poor son," and she could no longer restrain her tears.

The carriage moved off. The ceremony was over, the square was nearly empty, and the last spectators were drifting away. One after another the doors of the stables and sheds on the hillside opened and shut again. The poor donkeys, having received their blessing, went back into the earth. Just when the carriage was passing by, a group of boys behind the church had gathered around a cobbler who was using a carbon black brush in an attempt to eternalize on the wall the private parts of the pharmacist's daughters of which he had had a fleeting glimpse. The result of his efforts was two grotesque drawings with square heads and mouths like gratings, both exactly alike. ("They're sisters, you see," he explained to the boys.) The carriage left the village in the direction of Colle. The snow came to meet it like a thick gray veil hanging from the sky right down to ground level, and it moved slowly, carried along by the wind. The landscape was desolate.

"Madam, are we going home, or . . . ?" Venanzio asked, turning toward the inside of the carriage.

"We're going to the old mill. And hurry, because we're late," the old lady replied. She shut her eyes and made the sign of the cross.

3

IN THE DARKNESS OF THE room Pietro Spina's troubled breathing rose and fell and rose again like the wheezing of an old pair of bellows. On the bed beside him Donna Maria Vincenza pretended to be asleep, but every night she spent a long time listening to that new and painful wheezing that broke the silence of her house; and whenever sleepiness got the better of her and she was on the point of dropping off, the slightest irregularity in that breathing was sufficient to reawaken her and set her listening again.

"Why do you get up so early every morning, Grandmother? At half past four in winter it's still the middle of the night."

"I have to revive the fire, my son, and grind the coffee."

In the evening the remains of the fire were covered with ashes, and if one wanted to find some embers still glowing in the morning, one had to be up and about early.

"Couldn't the maid do it? She's young."

"Natalina generally does it, but I've always made the coffee for my children myself. Between ourselves, the young don't know how to make coffee nowadays. And besides, the older you get the

less you sleep, perhaps to prepare yourself for the day when you'll
stop sleeping once and for all."

At about six o'clock his grandmother went to mass, and Pietro
stayed in bed for a little while longer. He had to move about the
house as little as possible and never open a window or go near an
already open one. In any case, he told his grandmother, he did
not dislike staying in bed; the sheets had a pleasing odor of quince
and there was still a great weariness in his bones, the kind they
call pilgrims' weariness. The oil lamp that was used at night instead of electric light was on a high shelf, leaving the lower part of
the room, including the two beds, in darkness; it cast a feeble light
only on the old worm-eaten wooden ceiling and the sacred pictures hanging on the walls. Thus at night, in the big room, only
the saints were visible.

"Do they worry you?" Donna Maria Vincenza asked him on
one of the first evenings. "To be frank with you, without them perhaps I shouldn't be able to sleep at all."

Facing Pietro's bed there was a small picture in dim colors,
with red and blue figures and splashes of yellow, of the crucifixion
scene, and around it were printed the words of St. Paul: JUDEIS
QUIDEM SCANDALUM, GENTIBUS AUTEM STULTITIA.* In the long
hours that he lay awake that picture, in the uncertain light of the
oil lamp, grew immensely in size until it swallowed up the whole
room and Pietro himself came to form part of it.

A brood of mice that had found its way to the old beams of the
ceiling belonged to the same nocturnal world, and Pietro could
distinctly hear them gnawing; every so often they stopped and
scampered about, and then resumed their gnawing, hurriedly,
like men on piecework who have no time to waste. That stubborn, insistent, tireless gnawing engaged Pietro's thoughts a great
deal, and one day he mentioned it to his grandmother.

"It's characteristic of the aristocratic mentality of the authors of
classical antiquity," he said, "that they never mention mice."

---

* "[Christ crucified is] unto the Jews a stumbling block and unto the Greeks foolish-
ness." Corinthians 1:23, Authorized Version. (*Greeks* also means "Gentiles" here.)

"Never mention what?"

"Mice. And yet if it's true that the history of civilization has gone hand in hand with the development of towns, it cannot be doubted that ever since ancient times domestic life, particularly in the Mediterranean countries, must have been largely taken up with the struggle against mice. Despite the silence of classical authors on the subject, we have every right to assume that the wives of the Caesars and the priestesses of Delphi spent their evenings thinking out ways and means, whether chemical or mechanical, of getting rid of the hated race of little rodents. And with what result? I don't think one can deny that the ancient Greeks and Romans disappeared, leaving nothing but mice in the ruins of their buildings."

"You could say the same of flies," Donna Maria Vincenza pointed out.

At about half past six, when the old lady came back from church, she opened the shutters, suddenly letting in the daylight. The images of night faded and froze into their frames and the mice took refuge in their holes. Then with slow and silent footsteps the old lady went backward and forward several times between the bedroom and the kitchen, and put on a chair near the bed in which her grandson lay a bowl of warm wine and a jar of olive oil to wash and dress the abrasions he still had on his body. His long, thin, white bare trunk with its protruding ribs and hollow, sunken belly and the relics of innumerable cuts and bruises reminded her of paintings of early Christian boy martyrs in the parish church. But the earthen color of his prematurely aged face, with its hollow features and spectral, deepset eyes, was that of an entirely different person, and seemed to have been attached by mistake to a body that was not his.

"Now, my son, I can tell you something," she said to him with a smile. "On the evening of Sant'Antonio's day, when that man from Pietrasecca lifted you out of his cart, when I saw that Bedouin face of yours, I hesitated whether to take you into my carriage, fearing a hoax, fearing that you, my son, were someone else, a total stranger being planted on me."

"Perhaps I really am someone else, Grandmother."

"Oh, no. I told you it was only the hesitation of a moment. Every housewife recognizes the bread from her own kneading trough."

After carefully washing with warm wine the abrasions and scratches that her grandson had on various parts of his body, while keeping her eyes on his face in case there were sensitive places that still hurt, she dressed the scars with pieces of old cloth dipped in olive oil. The simplicity and grace of her gentle movements imparted to his poor body a feeling of tenderness of which he had lost all memory; her hand skimming lightly over his chest seemed to restore the normal beating of his tired heart, and if she tidied the hair on his brow his face relaxed and troublesome thoughts seemed to be chased away.

"My poor boy," the old lady could not help saying to him one morning, "how did you manage, with your delicate health, to stand up to all those dreadful hardships?"

"Well, Grandmother, you see, I'm the sort of person who has weak flesh and tough bones. An ordinary draft can be dangerous to me, but a shipwreck doesn't worry me at all."

This was an idea that appealed to Donna Maria Vincenza. "And do you know why?" she replied. "Perhaps the reason is this. The soul is attached, not to the flesh, but to the skeleton, and if the latter is made of good, solid bones it's difficult to separate the soul from the body. That's why some perpetual invalids live to be a hundred. You didn't succumb to your ordeals because you weren't completely on your own, your forefathers in your bones helped you to hold out. Just imagine them, generations of men who tilled the land, vine growers, farmers, and plowmen, sober, serious persons hardened by bad weather and physical exertion."

During the early stages of their life together the relations between Donna Maria Vincenza and her grandson were completely taken up with care for his health. She was careful to avoid not only any painful "explanations," but even the slightest reference to the scandal of which he had been the sad hero. As for the future, and the length of his stay at Colle, she said to him on the very first evening: "We'll talk about all that later. Don't worry about it now, my dear boy. The important thing is that you should get used to living again among human beings, I mean among Christians."

To the old lady "human being" and "Christian" were identical terms. "To be a human being it's not sufficient to walk on two feet; don't chickens do that?"

"Chickens don't talk," Pietro pointed out.

"But what about parrots? And gramophones? Don't they talk?"

"They don't have a conscience."

"There you are, you see, you agree with me."

The precautions adopted by Donna Maria Vincenza, with the aid and advice of the old groom and the maid, to prevent the news of her grandson's presence in the house from getting out were detailed and severe, and had led to a number of changes in the usual relations between the house and the world outside. The old Spina family home at Colle stood about a hundred yards above the village, and behind it was a big terraced vineyard; then came a flat expanse overgrown with brushwood and swept by the north wind, and beyond that again there was the desolate mountainside. The three-story house was solidly built entirely of bare stone, blackened by time, with massively thick walls and small windows on the ground floor with deep embrasures protected by solid iron bars. In front of the house there was a small cobbled courtyard with a disused well in the middle surmounted by a little roof, and beyond it there was a spacious yard with the stable, the chicken run, the hayloft, the dung heap, and the coachhouse. That was the realm of Donna Maria Vincenza. It was separated from the rest of the world by a boundary wall with only two entrances, a door with wrought-iron fittings at the front of the house and a big gate for carts and cattle on the yard side.

"The house, as perhaps you know," his grandmother told Pietro, "was built by Giambattista Spina, one of your most eccentric ancestors, about a hundred fifty years ago, at a time when, then too, there were brigands." She added with a smile: "Don't you think it's like a fortress built especially for the two of us?"

"Oh, things are much worse now," Pietro said, though he was uncertain whether to take his grandmother's naive words literally. "What's the use of barred windows against the police?"

"My dear boy, if you think that their throwing their weight about would be sufficient to make me open the door, you're very much mistaken. In my house I lay down the law."

To watch Donna Maria Vincenza going from room to room or climbing the stairs, gravely and slowly, with head erect and given additional presence by the wide petticoats that came down to her feet, was to penetrate the secret of her self-confidence. In spite of her age, everything about her bore the stamp of the woman of the mountains, the mistress of the house, the farmer's wife used to giving orders, used by her mere presence to exacting obedience from men and beasts; and her house was like her, it was old, solid, well worn, and clean. Two tiles were missing on the second floor, and others were dilapidated, but she was opposed to any restoration work.

"Those tiles are not to be found anymore, no matter where you look," she said. "To change them all just because a couple are missing would be really absurd. Besides, houses, like women, must accept old age and not pretend to be young when youth has passed."

Pietro was admitted to this room or that, depending on the time of day. The attic was the only place to which he was allowed free access at any time and, as he liked being alone, he spent a good deal of time there. It was full of broken or disused furniture, lampstands, mirrors, old guns, rusty swords arrayed on the walls, and other miscellaneous objects.

The enormous beams that supported the roof made the ceiling look like the keel of a ship, a childish pirate ship. Just as putting one's ear to certain shells can give one the illusion of hearing the echo of storms at sea, so did Pietro listen once more to the distant sounds of his life, the howling of the wind, the bleating of sheep, the barking of sheepdogs. Even as a boy, with his pockets full of nails, pieces of string, and licorice, he had liked hiding under that roof. Through the skylight he could watch clouds passing by and black birds of prey leaving the mountain skies and coming down toward the plain. Venanzio had told him that the carcass of a donkey had been lying near the mill for several days past; *cafoni* had competed for the best bits, and the rest had been left to the dogs and the birds. From the dark window of the attic he could also see a corner of the village square without being seen. In the evening a yellowish streetlamp lit up a space the size of a small stage on which at regular intervals there appeared two *carabinieri*, an occasional drunk, a *cafone* with his donkey, a young man with his girl. Every evening Pietro waited for the young man and his girl to appear in the yellowish light of the little stage, and as soon as they arrived he himself became the young man and took the girl for a walk, her arm in his. Farther away, where the slope of the hillside met the plain and the vineyards ceased, began the Fucino estate, cultivated with potatoes and wheat and beets. For several days past the huge basin had been covered by a gray roof of cloud. On the green, level, ashen plain surrounded by black and white mountains one could see the straight cut of long avenues and canals, the neat divisions imposed by man on land and water. It seemed a closed world, with all the valleys descending toward the plain, all the streams flowing and disappearing into a subterranean channel. In the winter landscape the neighboring villages halfway up between the mountain and the plain displayed their naked and tired old age, looking like black beehives in the purple shadow of the mountains, wretched beehives in a stony landscape almost devoid of flowers.

In the evening, when doors and windows were not just closed but bolted and barred, grandmother and grandson came down into the kitchen, which was a big, whitewashed, vaulted room with heavy, massive furniture, and sat side by side by the fire on an old bench with a high back. Donna Maria Vincenza was careful to refrain from making remarks if Pietro forgot to eat, stopped in the middle of a sentence, rose, and busied himself for a long time with the fire. But under the influence of his grandmother's calm composure his former good manners gradually returned. Before sitting down, at the beginning of every meal,

Donna Maria Vincenza said grace and made the sign of the cross. "You can sit down, please don't take any notice," she said to her grandson. But Pietro remained standing too.

"It's a serious problem," Donna Maria Vincenza admitted. "I assure you I've thought about it a great deal, but without finding a solution. Look, our soup is in the same tureen, and it's physically impossible that God should bless my part only. I'm sorry, my dear boy, but I don't see what can be done about it."

"Oh, now I see why there's sometimes too much salt in the soup," Pietro replied with a laugh.

On their first evenings together Donna Maria Vincenza brought Pietro up to date about the deaths, marriages, and births that had taken place in the neighboring families, the old ones that had disappeared and the new ones that had come into being, those that had gone up in the world and those that had come down. The neighborhood knew about every single family — what it was worth and its position, whether it was slowly rising or falling; even if attempts were sometimes made to create a pretense, the truth always emerged. Everything that happened, every marriage, every legacy, every purchase or sale, every misfortune, was discussed, commented on, and judged from the point of view of whether it helped the family concerned to rise or fall in the world. In recent times, what with wars and the earthquake, few families could be said to have remained in a static position; most had either risen or fallen. In the past decades relations among families had changed a great deal, and very strange things had happened. The stability of the family home lay behind everything. If the earth shook and houses collapsed, the result was not only loss of life and wealth; it also led to many other totally inexplicable phenomena. How many people Donna Maria Vincenza had seen coming up and then disappearing. Her world consisted above all of her relatives, and alliances and kinships made it a hierarchical world; the rest of the world consisted of the other families with their ramifications. Nothing else existed in this life. She had a prodigious memory for kinships, and she went back with ease through the generations to the most remote marriages, from

fathers, uncles, cousins to grandfathers and great-grandfathers, in
connection with land, mills, fulling mills, spinning mills, sandpits
and quarries, stables and sheepfolds, with the result that the
people, the livestock, the land of the region turned out to be
united by the same vicissitudes and involved in good and bad fortune together. Even hedges and stones ended up assuming a
family air, eventually coming to resemble the families to whom
they belonged.

"Every morning, as soon as he was dressed," she told Pietro,
"your grandfather, from whom you inherited the shape of your
head and the color of your eyes, had a small cup of coffee,
mounted his horse, and rode around his vineyards. When he
came back a piece of bread with a little ewe's milk cheese would
be waiting for him on the kitchen table, and he would eat it
without sitting down. Then he would go and see to the cows and
the horses. He used to say (and he too in his youth had had his es-
capades) that the best way to avoid excess was to work hard and in
your leisure moments listen to the grass growing."

Pietro listened to her without interrupting, sympathetically
and lost in reverie, and one evening his grandmother thought she
saw such filial devotion and childish wonder in his eyes that she
was moved to tears. She put her hand on his head and gently
made him rest it on her shoulder.

"It's as if at the end of my life the Lord has sent me one last
son," she said. "Now I see why He made me live so long."

"Do you believe it's actually possible to be reborn, Grandmother?"

"Possible? My dear boy, you know very well it's necessary. But
not of course in the style of the pious individuals who mistake id-
iocy for simplicity of heart and revert to second childhood, using
baby language and talking pussycats and cock-a-doodle-doos."

"But childishness in the other sense is of course illusory too."

"No, it isn't, my dear boy. Actually there are times when you
surprise me by seeming to be just like a child. Not because of your
appearance or (if you will excuse this rash judgment) in the moral
sense of innocence and confident abandonment to God. But now

I'd rather we talked about something else, because talking about these things may be painful to you, and I don't want you to suspect that I'm trying to examine you in any way. You're at home here."

"Let me tell you, Grandmother, what seems to you to be childish in me: it's the fact that I can't adjust well enough to ordinary life, with the weakness and parasitism that that implies."

"Well, my boy, your parasitism can't be so dreadful if you can talk about it so openly. What I was going to tell you, since you obviously want to know, was that there is often in your eyes and in the tone of your voice a note of surprise, of wonderment, I might almost say of amazement, that is not that of an adult. But now I want to tell you about a curious incident. Well, when I came out of church after mass this morning Don Gennaro was waiting for me and wanted to walk a little way with me. Don Gennaro is the brother of the parish priest of Orta, as you know; you must remember him, you must often have seen him in your house when you were a boy, because he married the only De Camillis daughter for the sake of the vineyards and above all the weaving factory. What was that poor woman's name? Oh, Donna Caritea, she was also a second cousin of your mother's on her father's side. And then of course they lost everything when the Catholic Bank for the Promotion of Agriculture failed and the poor woman died of a broken heart. Well then, as I was coming out of church Don Gennaro, who had pretended not to see me ever since the scandal about you broke out, was waiting for me. . . . Do you think our voices might be audible in the courtyard?"

Pietro, embarrassed, said nothing.

"Weren't you listening?" Donna Maria Vincenza asked him. "No, don't deny it," she went on with a laugh. "You're tired, and you were saying to yourself: how this old woman keeps rambling on."

"Grandmother, I can assure you I could repeat every word you said. But the fact of the matter is that while I was listening to you it struck me what a strange world I've landed in and how extraordinary it is that I should be here. Is this really my world?"

"I should like to know what you find so extraordinary about it, my dear boy. Have you forgotten that this is your home, that this is where your father was born? In my opinion it's just the other way about, it would be extraordinary if you were not here."

"No, I haven't forgotten anything. But to me these family stories sound like distant tales from a vanished world, the world that was buried in the earthquake. Forgive my frankness, but with you I can't pretend. While you were talking to me about my forefathers, the Spinas, the Presuttis, the De Angelises, and yours, the Camerinis, the De Dominicises, the De Camillises, or whatever their names are, I couldn't help thinking how extraordinary it was that such a world should still exist, or was I dreaming? What curious people these were, and what was I doing among them?"

Donna Maria Vincenza went pale and closed her eyes. "My poor boy," she said sadly after a long pause, "my poor boy, you talk as if you were a foundling, a person without a past, as if we had collected you from the foundling hospital, as if your father and mother and your forebears had left you nothing. I'm not talking about legacies or real estate, my dear boy, I'm talking about your soul. You talk as if we had bought it from Zingone Brothers or the Rinascente store. You talk to me as if I were a stranger."

"No, Grandmother, it's not that. Perhaps I expressed myself badly. Oh, how difficult it is to explain to you what I feel. Perhaps I can't explain even to myself the anguish I felt on the first evening I arrived here, the anguish that comes over me again and again, particularly when you are most loving and affectionate to me. Perhaps, I say to myself, perhaps it's the anguish of reliving the past, the anguish of repetition. Of course, Grandmother, it's good to be here with you, it's warm and comforting. But to me, you see, all that is the past, it's over and done with. Why should I conceal the truth from you? It no longer concerns me, it no longer concerns my life; at most it concerns my memory. Believe me, Grandmother, it's terribly painful to have to tell you this."

"My poor boy, that is how the dead would speak — if they spoke."

"It's possible to be dead to one's own family, one's own world, and to go on living. Sometimes it may be the only thing that enables one to go on living."

"Were you perhaps more comfortable in the stable in which you were hidden at Pietrasecca?"

"Oh, 'comfortable' certainly isn't the right word. And, to be accurate, it wasn't even a proper stable, though, apart from an incalculable but considerable number of mice, it provided a home for a donkey, a poor, wretched old donkey. Imagine a cave dug out of the rock with a stone wall in front and a single opening just wide enough to let the donkey in; you shut it by means of a door that was off its hinges, the place was perhaps about half the size of this room, but so low that I couldn't stand upright. Walls and floor were irregular because of the protuberances of the rock, and when the door was shut there was no window through which air and light could enter; and there was no drain or hole for the dung (which was quickly removed and piled next to the door once or twice a week). It could, if you like, be called a stable, but only out of courtesy to the donkey, who was in no way responsible for the conditions. In fact it was nothing but a stinking hole in the rock. You cannot imagine how grateful I am to you, Grandmother, for not having questioned me about my stay at Pietrasecca and why I went there and what I did there and the persons I met, because it would be extremely painful for me to tell you. Similarly it would be very painful for me to tell you the circumstances in which at the last moment, when I saw no way of escape from the pack of *sbirri** that was on my tracks, I found the door of that filthy hiding place. But one thing I can tell you. As soon as my eyes began to get used to the darkness and I slowly started making out the contents of the cave — a wooden manger against the wall, the old donkey lying on the ground between the straw and the dung, an old saddle, a halter and some harnesses hanging near the door, a pitchfork, a broken lamp lying in one corner, and a crumpled picture of Sant'Antonio the Abbot, patron saint of animals, stuck on the wall — I was filled with a sense of indescribable serenity, a profound sense of peace, such as I had never felt in my life before, and it drove all the anguish from my mind. In short, my being

---

*Pejorative term for policemen.

there seemed to me obviously natural and right. Here I am, I have arrived, *inveni portum*, I have reached harbor, I said to myself, so this was the supreme Reality, devoid of all illusory consolations, for which I had been searching."

"Now, my son, you're beginning to frighten me."

"But I now know that it was my situation before I found that hiding place that was frightening. In the state of extreme clarity that then established itself in my mind the whole of my past life at last assumed a meaning and revealed itself to me as having been a journey to that cave. When I thought back about my indolent school years, the earthquake, the flight from my family, my sterile and desolate years in exile, I saw my life as a successive casting off of the crude fictions that make life dear to most people, an emancipation from them. As I gradually found my way about in the dark and came across the poor primitive things in the place, the skinny old donkey, the thin little mice that lived there, I felt I had known it all for a long time, as if I had carried it about inside me for many years, perhaps too deep inside me for me to have been able to see it before. When I sat down on the ground beside the donkey, I couldn't help saying into his ear, and in a voice deeply affected by emotion, as you will readily understand: good evening, here I am. He didn't reply. . . ."

"He didn't? Now you really amaze me, my dear boy."

"But he turned toward me and, I assure you, Grandmother, he showed not the slightest surprise at seeing me there between the straw and the dung. On the contrary. Will you be offended if I say there are certain things you can't understand, Grandmother? Forgive me, and let us change the subject. But there's just one more thing I want to say. From my very first moment in that hole I lost all sense of time. Time exists, of course, for those with wants to satisfy and for those who are bored, but I was seeking for nothing (since I had arrived), and in any case I have never been bored. So for me time simply vanished. But when the owner of the stable and of the donkey, who had thus become my legitimate owner too, came to terms with you and accepted a sum of money from you — that is, when he actually sold me and put me on his cart and took me down to the valley hidden under a pile of sacks and rags to hand me over — my first strong feeling was of being reintegrated into time; and I started distinctly perceiving the passage of time, an extraordinary thing that had never happened to me before. To give you an idea of what I mean, let me explain that I was aware of the passing of time as one is normally aware of the flowing of a river; I don't mean that it passed in the uniform, artificial, abstract fashion of a clock, it was not at all like that. No, I was aware of real time passing as one is aware of the flowing of a real stream, that is, in a continually varying way, now slowly and now impetuously, depending on the slope and nature of the bed and the banks and on whether it encounters mills or fulling mills and whether there are women doing their washing and beating it on the bank. I had the distinct feeling that in relation to time the jolting little cart on which I was traveling was like an unsafe little boat on a river in flood flowing down from the mountain to the plain. Another surprise was that, when I peeped at the outside world through the gaping seams of the sacks that hid me, every single detail filled me with astonishment, though there was nothing whatever to be seen that was new to me. After we crossed the bridge at Fossa, for instance, a girl and a soldier walked close behind the cart for a good distance. The girl's eyes were red and tears rolled down her cheeks, and the soldier kept saying affectionately and resignedly: I've got to go back, there's nothing I can do about it, you knew that, didn't you? And the girl nodded submissively, yes, she knew, but she didn't stop crying for that reason; and the soldier, still walking, put his arm affectionately around her waist and repeated sadly that he had to go back because his leave was over, he couldn't help it, there was nothing that could be done about it, it was the law. They went on walking behind the cart like that for some time, the man and the woman side by side, carried along by the same irresistible stream. How extraordinary, I said to myself, what an extraordinary world, what extraordinary conventions, how can such a world continue to exist? The idea struck me that I might throw off the rags that hid me, jump down from the cart, politely take the soldier aside, and say to him: my

good man, believe me, you're the victim of a fixed idea. But we
had reached the Chapel of the Souls in Purgatory, you know, just
where the road begins to slope downward, and there was an eddy
in the stream that was carrying us along and we were suddenly
parted. The donkey that was pulling the cart took advantage of
the slope to start trotting, and the soldier left the road and took a
shortcut to the station through the fields. And so the girl was left
alone at the roadside, standing straight and motionless near a
heap of gravel; the stream had dumped her on the bank and left
her there, stranded. As soon as the road began to mount again
other people walked beside the cart for short distances. One of the
things that I remember is that at one point it had to leave the
roadway to avoid running over an old *cafone* who was bending
over in the middle of the road, almost on his knees, an old man
dressed in rags and spattered with mud, who was searching in
the mud for a lost coin. What a world, I said to myself, is there no
one who will say politely to the poor old fellow: man, that small
piece of metal you've lost, that accursed fetish . . ."

Donna Maria Vincenza, though she had been trying hard not
to lose the thread of her grandson's speech, had for some minutes
past been absorbed in silent prayer for the urgent intercession of a
personage who was in her own way also present in the kitchen,
though Pietro took no notice of her, that is to say, the Merciful
Mother of Jesus, whose sorrowful image was illuminated by an oil
lamp in a corner of the room. There are certain situations that do
not call for much explaining between mothers; a glance is sufficient. But the trouble is that nowadays a poor woman does not
know what kind of son she should wish for. Either they go in for
frivolity and vice, or they imperil their immortal souls for the sake
of money, or they are too serious and decide that the world is
wrongly organized. Is it their mothers' fault that they are no
longer able to reconcile them to domesticity? Alas, it has never
been easy to be a mother. The day when Jesus left home at the
age of twelve without saying why or where He was going and went
to the temple to argue with the learned doctors cannot have been
a happy one for Mary, particularly as there is nothing to discuss

with doctors, it's a waste of time. And if Pietro now expected that his grandmother might one day be willing to discuss ideas and other such inventions of the devil with him, he could cool his heels, because he would have a long time to wait. Donna Maria Vincenza had been a little girl with pigtails down her back when a celebrated Passionist father had come to the church at Colle to explain the *Syllabus Errorum* of Pius IX, and she still remembered as if it were yesterday and often repeated what the saintly man had said. "Wrong ideas," he had explained, "are the direct consequence of wrong feelings. So discussing errors and heresies is a waste of spirit. Moral behavior is the foundation stone of truth." After listening to one of these sermons Donna Maria Vincenza had found waiting for her at home a book called *The Betrothed,* by a certain Manzoni, which had been brought back from Rome as a present for her by Don Berardo Spina, her future husband, who was then a boy at grammar school. When she saw the word "novel" on the cover she unhesitatingly consigned the book to the flames. "You must have a very strange idea of me if you dare offer me a novel to read," she wrote to the young man.

"So is this world of such a nature," Pietro asked her, "that it's enough to return to it after an absence of a few weeks to find that it's totally absurd and unreal?"

"But my poor boy," Donna Maria Vincenza replied in consternation, "you forget that this world was created by God and survives thanks only to divine providence. How old are you now? Thirty-four? That's certainly a respectable age, you're what is called fully adult, but don't forget that God is even older than you and must have had good reasons for arranging things in the way that we see He has done."

After a moment's thought she added with a smile: "When you're His age, perhaps you'll understand."

In any event, it was now clear to the old lady that the frequent expression of wonder that she saw in her grandson's eyes did not come, as she had thought, from simplicity of heart; and she remembered something that Natalina, the maid, had said. With the intuition that the simple in spirit sometimes had, the girl had said something about Pietro that now seemed to her to hit the nail on the head.

"If I remember correctly," Donna Maria Vincenza went on, "it was on the second or third day after your arrival here that Natalina met you in the corridor on your way down from the attic, and you gave her such a fright that she collapsed in a faint."

"Yes, and smashed half a dozen plates she was carrying, I believe, which was the first tangible result of my presence in your house."

"Never mind that; the girl has always had a special talent for smashing dishes, and the things she can't smash, because they're unbreakable, she makes dents in. When she came around I asked her what had given her such a fright. Had she forgotten that you were here in the house with us? Do you know what she replied? (But perhaps I'm wrong to tell you.) What she thought she saw, she said, was a man risen from the dead."

One can get used to anything, even to men risen from the dead. On the evening of his arrival at Colle, Pietro had had only a fleeting glimpse of Natalina, and the vague impression that she left him with was of a submissive and intimidated domestic animal. Next day he had had a better opportunity of observing her from behind the curtains of a window while she was crossing the courtyard; she was carrying on her head, balanced on a circular mat, a basketful of wet sheets she had just washed and screwed up into snakelike shapes, and they dripped onto her cheeks, nose, and chin. He had looked at her with a certain amount of excitement. She had struck him at the time as small and not well proportioned, because of the shortness of her bust in relation to the rest of her body and also because of the fragility of her shoulders in comparison with the breadth of her hips; also there was a certain delicacy about her hands and arms in comparison with the thickness of her ankles and calves. Not the hardworking type but the childbearing type, he had decided at the time. Meanwhile a goat had come in through the open gate and, after a moment's hesitation, made straight for the horse trough. Natalina promptly put down her basket, ran over, and gave the animal such a violent kick in the stomach that it nearly fell to the ground. Bleating pitifully, it fled back to where it had come from. The girl, after looking all around to see whether anyone had noticed her, picked up the basket and went and hung the washing on the wire clothes-lines next to the stable. That evening Pietro had brought the conversation with his grandmother around to Natalina.

"She's an unbroken filly," Donna Maria Vincenza had said. "A filly that can't stand flies. She lost her mother in the earthquake, and her father died soon afterward, and that left her with no relatives at Colle except her Aunt Eufemia, you know, the last of the De Dominicises, a hysterical churchmouse who is everyone's aunt here and so is nobody's, with the result that I'm responsible for the girl's future, whether I like it or not. But I can't say a word to her and, what is worse, I can't get a word out of her."

"Is she pretty?" Pietro then asked with a blush.

"What? Can't you judge for yourself?"

"I mean, has she a young man? When she goes out after lunch on Sundays, where does she go? Do the young men run after her?"

"She never goes out except to run errands or to church. No doubt people say I keep her shut up, but actually she's a wild thing."

One Sunday afternoon Pietro could not open the door at the top of the stairs that led to the attic. He was on the point of turning back, but the fact that the door, which had no lock, had been barricaded from the inside, and that consequently somebody must have shut himself in the attic, aroused his curiosity. As it could not have been his grandmother, he tried to force his way in, and it was only with a great deal of difficulty that he managed to shift the things that had been put on the other side of the door; but as soon as there was enough room to put his hand inside he found it easier to move a box that was the principal obstacle, and his thinness enabled him to force his way through the opening as soon as it was a few inches wide. As he had expected, he found Natalina in the middle of the room; she was standing on two trunks placed one on top of the other. This improvised pedestal enabled her to rest her elbows on the edge of the skylight and look at the village in the distance, the Fucino basin, and the ring of high mountains that surrounded it. The girl was in her Sunday best; she wore a cotton cambric dress with a red and yellow floral design, a rather summery and scanty garment for the winter season, with a little straw hat decorated with small white flowers and cherries perched on top of her head. She was unaware of Pietro's arrival and went on looking at the view, with her head resting on one hand in the attitude in which angels are often depicted behind parapets of white clouds.

"Hello, good afternoon," Pietro called out. "Am I disturbing you?"

The startled girl grasped one of the window shutters to save herself from falling. "Oh, sir," she said, "how did you get in?"

"If I'm disturbing you, I'll go away," he replied.

"No, really, it's I who should go."

That was what she said, but she showed no sign of going.

"The attic isn't a drawing room, and there are no rules of precedence here," said Pietro. "But before I go, if I'm not being indiscreet, I should like you to tell me what you are doing up here all by yourself."

The girl was obviously rather embarrassed. "It's not that I don't trust you, but I'm shy of telling you," she said.

"In that case my apologies, and good-bye for now."

He was already on the stairs when Natalina called him back. "I'll tell you," she called out. "But it's a secret," she went on. "Do you promise you won't tell madam?"

"I swear it," Pietro said with simulated gravity.

When he too had climbed up onto the trunks the girl whispered in his ear: "I'm waiting for the train."

"The train?"

"Yes, the train. Are you surprised?"

Pietro was well aware that there was no railway at Colle; the nearest station was out of sight, three or four miles away. So he went on: "Are you waiting for a real train, with an engine and carriages and passengers?"

"Yes, of course, a real train. Are you surprised?"

"No, not in the least. Quite the contrary, in fact."

There was a grave and calm expression on the girl's pale face; only her eyes, her slightly dissimilar almond-shaped eyes, golden almond eyes, betrayed nervous tension when one looked at them closely. Her small nose and thin, narrow, lipless, rodentlike mouth went well with the little flowered hat. Pietro noticed an alarm clock on the attic windowsill.

"Is that to wake you if you go to sleep?"

"No, it's to announce the arrival of the train."

"Oh, I see. I'd have realized that myself if I weren't so stupid."

Sure enough, the alarm bell rang soon afterward.

"Here's the train," Natalina announced excitedly. "Stand back, stand back, let the passengers off the train first, please. As soon as I'm inside, please hand me my suitcase through the window. *Au revoir*, or rather good-bye. Ask your grandmother to forgive me. But if Aunt Eufemia dies, please send me a telegram. Because of the legacy, you see. I don't want my share to go to others."

"Quick, quick, it's time to get in."

"My ticket, good heavens, where's my ticket?"

"You can get it in the train, that is permissible under the regulations. Be quick, be quick," said Pietro, carried away by the childish make-believe.

"But I've already bought a ticket. I'm not going to pay twice, I'm not crazy."

"Don't you see the guard's getting impatient? Get in and then look for it."

Natalina produced a small piece of paper from her brassiere.

"Oh, there it is," she exclaimed in triumph. "Hand me up the suitcase, please. Thank you. Is it heavy? All my clothes are in it, of course. Where I'm going? I'm sorry, but I can't tell you. Have you a white handkerchief to wave when the train leaves? Yes? Thank you. Can you smell the lovely coal smell coming from the engine? It must be English coal."

"Safe journey and good luck. And take care, don't lean out of the window while the train is moving."

"Yes, I know. And I mustn't spit on the floor, but into my handkerchief."

"And don't use the toilet while the train is at a station."

"Yes, I know. And I mustn't pull the emergency handle without good reason. I know all about it. Good-bye, good-bye."

"Good-bye."

On the way down from the attic Pietro said: "Do you often go on these train trips?"

"Every Sunday," the girl replied.

That same evening Pietro, after long and painful hesitation, suddenly went to her room. She was barefoot and disheveled and nervously rummaging among a lot of underclothes that were lying all over the place, on the bed, the chairs, and in the wardrobe.

"Have you been doing your washing?" Pietro asked her with unusual agitation in his voice.

"No, I'm checking through my things again," Natalina replied. "One of my handkerchiefs is missing."

"You'll find it tomorrow morning," Pietro, who was anxious to change the subject, suggested.

"Why tomorrow morning?"

"You must have left it somewhere else today and you'll find it again tomorrow," said Pietro, hoping to dispose of the subject so as to be able to talk about something else. "Come, Natalina, there's no cause for despair. Wouldn't you rather talk to me?"

"But I've been looking for it for a year," Natalina replied with exasperation in her voice. "I've been looking for it every evening for a whole year. How can you say I'll find it tomorrow?"

"If that's the case, Natalina, why don't you forget about it? If you've been looking for it for a whole year."

Natalina looked at him with such loathing that Pietro was reduced to silence.

"It's one of my things," the girl exclaimed, beating herself on the breast. "What have my things to do with you?"

"For heaven's sake, Natalina, I was just talking," Pietro hastened to explain. "I didn't come here to quarrel with you. On the contrary. I'll give you a dozen handkerchiefs, if you'll allow me to."

"Do you know how much things cost?" the girl went on furiously.

If she says the word "things" again, I'll give up, Pietro said to himself.

"Things, sir . . ."

Pietro wiped the sweat from his brow and took his departure.

On the following Sunday afternoon Pietro met Natalina on the stairs and said to her: "Are you leaving again today with that heavy suitcase?"

"Yes, of course, with all my things. If you don't come to the station I'll have it handed up to me by a porter. I don't want to trouble you."

"So much the better. Safe journey."

"*Au revoir,* or rather good-bye. Write to me if my aunt dies."

"What aunt?"

"Aunt Eufemia. Because of my share of the legacy."

The fact of the matter was that at a certain distance the girl was not unattractive to him. But at close quarters he was put off, apart from her craziness, by an acute and persistent smell of perspiration, a slightly acid smell that on some days was compounded by the odor of poor-quality talcum powder of which she made abundant use, as well as by the salad smell that floated around her hair, which she anointed with olive oil and vinegar, with the result that whenever she stopped anywhere for some time she left behind her a slight effluvium of hors d'oeuvres that had gone off. Pietro had no difficulty in tolerating the smell of cows, donkeys, and sheep (which often actually gave him pleasure); but the smell of the human body could easily make him feel sick. "Perhaps that's another reason why I've always been a very bad socialist," he confessed to his grandmother. "Your true man of the left should have no nose, just as his counterpart on the right should have no ears." After this he no longer spent Sunday afternoons in the attic, but among the huge empty barrels in the cellar. Because of the bitter cold down there he had to muffle himself in extra woolen sweaters and scarves and heavy coats that hampered his movements and made them clumsy and awkward. The cellar attracted him because there was something secret and mysterious about it even when there was full daylight outside; and in the damp, greenish, nocturnal atmosphere that prevailed there the big empty barrels added a rhetorical adornment that stimulated his imagination. He spent whole days amusing himself with a piece of chalk, drawing unlikely allegorical figures on them, under which he wrote familiar names, such as TRADITION ACCORDING TO VENANZIO, THE GIRL WITH THE THINGS, AUNT EUFEMIA'S LEGACY, CHRISTIANITY ACCORDING TO GRANDMOTHERS. The hours passed silently; the river of time flowed far away and was hardly perceptible, just a vast, weak, distant murmur.

"You'll end up catching pneumonia," Donna Maria Vincenza warned him.

4

As soon as the old lady felt somewhat reassured about her grandson's health she gave him a room to himself next to her own. It was a big room that had been used as a drawing room and still retained from that time the now blackened and cracked gilt decoration around the ceiling and windows, a big mirror on the marble mantelpiece, and a huge glass chandelier; but since Donna Maria Vincenza had been left alone and had given up entertaining the drawing room had degenerated into a dressing room and had to support, among other things, the weight of three wardrobes full of clothes and linen, to which there was now added a divan that at night was converted into a bed.

A glass cabinet with two shelves contained the small colored figures of the manger scene, the naked Child on a small heap of straw, the humble, happy Mother, the devout San Giuseppe, the ass and the ox, the angels and shepherds, the goats and the rocks. On one wall there was a portrait of Don Saverio Spina, covered with a black veil. In one of the wardrobes Pietro discovered his uncle's cavalry captain's uniform, and he had the idea of wearing it and giving his grandmother a surprise. I'll give the poor old lady something to laugh at for once, he said to himself.

But as soon as he put it on he was assailed by doubt. The uniform would remind her of her son who died in Libya, and supposing she found the joke a painful one? He was still considering what to do when the door opened and Venanzio walked in. The old groom's amazement bore a comic resemblance to fright.

"Heavens above," he exclaimed. "For a moment I thought you were Don Saverio, God rest his soul."

But Pietro was furious at having been surprised in fancy dress. "Who sent for you?" he shouted. "And, even if I had, why did you come in without knocking?"

Venanzio, offended, walked out, shut the door behind him, and then knocked loudly, but Pietro kept him waiting before letting him in.

"Do you know how long I've been working in this house?" he said resentfully. "For forty-two years, sir. When I came here your grandfather, Don Berardo, God rest his soul, was on his horse near the well. 'Young man,' he said to me, 'are you the new stableboy? Well, if you do your duty by me, I'll do mine by you.' Oh, he was a real gentleman."

Pietro made a gesture of annoyance. "You told me that once before," he said. "And a few days ago you also told me that when I was a small boy you several times took me on your knee. No doubt you'll end up telling me you actually suckled me. But, even if you had, that wouldn't excuse you from knocking before coming into my room."

Venanzio was standing in the middle of the room, hat in hand, under the prismatic gleam and glitter of the fully lit chandelier, and all that light made him look even older, made his face and hands look darker, his clothes more wretched, his attitude humbler, meeker, and more offended. But a concealed, fleeting something in his eyes aroused Pietro's mistrust. And by this time he had had his fill of stories about the Spina family. To show his displeasure he abruptly turned his back on the man, and thus found himself looking at his own image in the mirror in the uniform of a

cavalry officer. The gray-green cloth, the chest that was inflated
like a concertina, and the shoulders that spread out like a Chinese
pagoda made him look like a comic and ridiculous stuffed
dummy. His dark coloring and ruffled hair almost suggested a colored soldier promoted to officer's rank on the battlefield for some
extravagant deed of arms. The uniform smelled strongly of cam-
phor, and he ended up seeing himself as a puppet, a grotesque, revolting, and also rather unreal camphorated puppet. Beside him in
the mirror was poor old Venanzio in all his simple, natural, servile
wretchedness; his boots were shapeless and muddy, his trousers
were turned up over his ankles and wound around his legs like the
cloth of an umbrella around the handle, and the sleeves of his
jacket were too short. He did not realize that Pietro was looking at
him; his hands were gnarled and scarred and blackened like old
agricultural implements, his thin neck was hollowed and stringy,
and his lined face was of the yellowish color of corn bread that had
gone stale and actually a little moldy; it was slightly greenish between the long gray thin mustaches and around the nostrils and
eyes and earholes. For forty-two years the poor devil had worked in
the Spina household, that is, since before Pietro was born. For
forty-two years he had worked there for twelve or fourteen hours a
day, including, in part, Sundays and holidays, because horses have
to be looked after seven days a week. How much dung, hay, straw,
earth those hands had shifted; how many sacks had been carried
on that poor old back in the course of forty-two years. To Pietro the
man's devotion, his attachment, his doglike fidelity were painful;
he suddenly turned to him and said in embarrassment: "Listen,
Venanzio, I was only talking. Venanzio, you know you can come
and see me whenever you like. By the way," he added, putting on
a friendly smile, "do you really think I resemble Uncle Saverio?"

Venanzio was touched by this change of tone and, to show that
he was thinking, he knitted his brows and half closed his eyes.
"Don Saverio was more solidly built," he decided. "Also he had a
fine pink complexion that pleased the ladies, as everyone knew.
But the eyes, nose, and chin are just the same. Also you're the
same height, I think. Oh, he was a real gentleman."

Pietro dropped the idea of presenting himself to his grand-mother dressed up like that.

Venanzio, who was still upset, indicated that he wanted to say something. "I didn't mean to disturb you," he stammered. "That, sir, would not be in accordance with my habits. As the saying is, the groom's place is in the stable and the master's is wherever he wants to be. But look, sir, I can't go on keeping silent about certain things that are happening now. Just imagine it, sir, today it was Lama. Today, I had to take your grandmother to Lama. We left immediately after lunch and came back half an hour ago. No, sir, there are certain things on which I can no longer keep silent."

"Why Lama? Is there a shrine there?"

"No, sir, it has nothing to do with pilgrimages, but it has to do with you. You look as if you don't understand. Well, then, to save you from the situation in which you find yourself Donna Maria Vincenza is seeking aid and advice right and left. Didn't you notice that I had to drive her to some village in the neighborhood practically every day last week? Today, at Lama, she made me stop at a lawyer's house. People who see us going here, there, and everywhere every day after years of quiet, retired life, are beginning to wonder. Few people are at work in winter, as you know, and when the carriage goes through a village everyone comes out into the street to look. Here at Colle, sir, I can't take two steps by myself without someone coming and asking what's happening to Donna Maria Vincenza, what fresh woe has befallen that unfortunate lady."

Pietro had noticed nothing. Since he had been given a room of his own he had spent less time with his grandmother. The frequent clip-clop of horses' hooves and the sound of the carriage in the courtyard had not of course escaped his notice, but it had never occurred to him that on each and every occasion it had been his grandmother who had been going out or coming back; and on the two or three occasions on which he had peeped from behind the curtains and seen her getting out of the carriage he had assumed she had been to church or had been paying a visit in Colle. But now he realized why she had been so tired on recent evenings and had apologized for not being in a state to keep him company in front of the fire.

"There's the danger, sir, and also there's the disgrace," said Venanzio, speaking with difficulty and obvious distress. "There's no danger of madam's letting slip the fact that you're living here. The danger I'm thinking of does not concern you, sir, but the family. Donna Maria Vincenza is not a child whom anyone can twist around his little finger. You ought to hear how cleverly she manages to talk about you, sir. I was present, for instance, the other day when she talked to Don Angelo Scarfò in the sacristy of the Church of the Holy Martyrs at Cavascura. If the unhappy wretch is dead, the Reverend Father said in that nasal voice of his and producing a hypocritical smile with his rubber dentures, all that is left to us is to pray for his soul. And if he is not dead? Donna Maria Vincenza said quite calmly. That is most improbable, the reverend gentleman declared. If the police have failed to find him it must mean that he's dead. Forgive me, but I do not follow that argument, Donna Maria Vincenza said with complete composure. If the police have failed to find him, it must mean that he's alive. My dear lady, he said, if you know more than I do, why not say so and tell me frankly where he is? If he's still alive, replied Donna Maria Vincenza, it means that the Lord in His infinite mercy wishes to grant him the opportunity to mend his ways and return to ordinary, decent life. But you will admit that if he is living in the mountains or wherever it may be under a false name that is hardly possible. That is why I have come to you, Father, she went on. We all know that you have excellent connections in the capital. Might it not be possible to obtain a pardon from the king? If expense were involved, Donna Maria Vincenza said finally, the family would not hold back."

Pietro was surprised and his curiosity was aroused. "A pardon from the king?" he interrupted. "What king?"

"Sir, how should I know?" Venanzio said, shrugging his shoulders. "I don't read the newspapers. Don Scarfò wrinkled his nose at that question, and I didn't hear his answer, because he got me out of the way by sending me to buy a stamp at the post office. In any case, that was not the last of our trips to neighboring villages. Since we went to Cavascura madam has been to Fossa, Orta, San Giovanni, and Rocca. Today it was Lama, and who knows where it will be tomorrow? Donna Maria Vincenza, such a proud lady to whom everyone has always respectfully bowed his head, now dashes here, there, and everywhere to beg for aid; and when she explains the object of her visit and mentions your name, she is invariably shown the door with a more or less pitying smile."

So far Venanzio had spoken with difficulty, with embarrassment, and obvious distress, avoiding Pietro's eyes or looking at the ground and twisting his hat in his hands as if he were wringing a towel. But suddenly, as if he had been moved by his own words, his manner changed, and he moved closer to Pietro, looking him in the eye with a grim expression on his face that suddenly revealed a hostility that had been too long repressed. Pietro maintained his composure as if he had not noticed the change; perhaps, in his usual way, he was only rather surprised.

"Have you anything else to say to me, Venanzio?" he asked casually.

"What about the honor of the house?" the groom shouted at him in a frenzy. "Don't you at least know what that is, for the love of Christ?"

Pietro coolly walked to the door, opened it, and with a good-humored smile indicated that the man could go. But he stayed motionless in the middle of the room, pale and distraught, with his hands and lips trembling slightly. Pietro's calm unconcern restored the distance that for a moment seemed to have been abolished between them. Venanzio started looking down again and gesticulating as if he wanted to explain or apologize, but agitation made the words stick in his throat.

"Heaven knows I did not wish to offend you," he at last managed to stammer out. "How should I dare? All my life and soul are bound up with your family."

"I'm not offended," Pietro replied. "I assure you I'm not so easily offended. Another day, if you like, Venanzio, we'll talk about honor, and I'll explain to you what I mean by it."

The door was still open, but the groom had no intention of leaving. He stayed by the door, grim, stubborn, and determined. "I haven't yet told you why I wanted to talk to you," he went on. "Well, later, or tomorrow," Pietro suggested. "Now I want to go to my grandmother in the next room."

"This is the time when Donna Maria Vincenza says the rosary," said the groom, who had no intention of leaving empty-handed. "Do as you wish, sir, but allow me to remind you that she does not like to be disturbed at prayer."

Pietro closed the door and asked Venanzio to sit down, while he took off his officer's uniform and put on his civilian clothes again.

"You are certainly wondering by what right I am interfering in family affairs, and perhaps you're assuming that I'm forgetting my place," Venanzio went on. "But if you could read my mind you would know what torment I went through, what a struggle I had with myself, before I made up my mind to speak. It hurts me, it kills me, to have to say these things to you; I almost think I'm going mad. The trouble, sir, is that the other relatives, including Don Bastiano, don't know you're here, and so have no suspicion of the dangers to which they, together with Donna Maria Vincenza, are exposed. So who is to speak if the servant does not do so? Sir, you must forgive me if I tell you that this situation cannot be allowed to go on. Oh, I don't say so for myself, you know that, or for the horses, what next? We have grown old in this house and we must serve it, and we serve it in good times and in bad. At her age, and with the love and affection she has for you and the anxiety that torments her night and day, there's no exaggeration in saying that the slightest strain might be the end of her. Suppose for a moment, sir, please, that one of these days (and may Our Lady of Mercy avert the evil omen), suppose for a moment that on returning from one of those outings I went to help her out of the carriage and found that the irreparable had happened. It seems to me that after such a long life a Christian lady like Donna Maria Vincenza at least has the right to close her eyes in her own bed, to die surrounded by her relatives, in the presence of the parish priest. Donna Maria Vincenza now herself feels that her strength is ebbing away. For the first time since I have known her I see that she is agitated, the prey of restlessness and anxiety. Since you have been here she, who was never afraid of anything, has been trembling over every trifle, has been in a state of perpetual alarm; not for herself, of course, but for you. In particular, because of you she's desperately afraid of dying. Today, when she ordered me to prepare the carriage to take her to Lama, I plucked up courage and took the liberty of pointing out that, to judge by her pallor, she seemed to be unwell and that therefore it would be wiser, if I might be permitted to express my humble opinion, to postpone the trip till tomorrow. But she replied that it was just because she felt unwell that she must go, because she had no time to lose. Every time we come back the first thing she does is of course to ask Natalina about you; and if the girl hesitates before replying (you know how absentminded she can be), she has a fright. And apart from Donna Maria Vincenza, I repeat, there's the family to think of.

"How many generations are needed for a family to acquire real honor and repute? A mere trifle can be enough to ruin it. Sir, you don't know the people in these parts, you grew up far away, you don't know that most of them are helpful, friendly, loyal to those on whom fortune smiles, and ungrateful, cowardly, odious, and treacherous as soon as contrary winds blow. When that happens you can no longer trust anyone. Let me tell you about a small incident, sir. Not more than an hour ago on the way back from Lama I had to stop the carriage near the Pilusi villa because one of the horses kept stumbling over a piece of harness that had worked loose. Giacinto the Hunchback, a servant of the Pilusis, happened to pass at that moment, and I asked him to oblige me by lending me a bit of rope to take the place of the broken harness. You won't believe me, sir, but he didn't even stop, and his own reply was to laugh at me. Don't take any notice, Donna Maria Vincenza said, you know very well the man's an idiot. On the contrary, I might have replied, hunchbacks are never idiots, and in any case Giacinto is not the only one who is beginning to laugh at us. I know these things, because people are frank with me and talk to me without beating about the bush. Up to a short time ago, before the scandal about you, sir, that miserable wretch would have felt it an honor to render a service to Signora Spina, and when he laughed it made my blood boil. I patched up the harness as best I could, and when we got going again I lost all restraint and told her what had been preying on my mind for a long time. I almost thought I was going out of my mind. Actually Donna Maria Vincenza let me speak without interrupting, and when I had finished she answered me gravely in a tone that permitted of no reply. Prudence, reputation, family, social position, public opinion, are certainly fine things, Venanzio, she said, but if a mother has a child in danger, he comes before them all. So it's no use talking to her, I said to myself, she'll never listen to reason. Everyone from whom she seeks advice or help tells her that nothing whatever can be done for you (assuming you are still alive), but it makes no difference. In vain they try to persuade her that if you were a thief or a murderer it would be easy to extricate you from your plight with the aid of famous lawyers or false evidence or complacent judges. But they say that yours is the most terrible of crimes, the only conceivable one for which there is no pardon, and that anyone unwise enough to dare to intervene on your behalf would not just fail to help you, but compromise himself. Donna Maria Vincenza has been told that over and over again by the relatives and friends to whom she has appealed. But she has other ideas, and anyone who knows her can be sure that so long as her strength holds out she will persist in going from pillar to post in the vain belief that in spite of everything she will find someone who will come to your aid. She has always been like that, it's her greatest virtue, I respect her greatly for it, but it's a luxury of another age."

Venanzio made a rather awkward gesture with his arms to indicate his sorrow, his desperation, his stubbornness. No one who saw him now would have taken him for a groom, but rather for a poor relation, a Spina who had gone down in the world, sunk to the *cafone* level, and was therefore more sensitive to public opinion. Apart from his long, lead-colored mustaches, his fleshless, sunburned face had now assumed the reddish color of old brass with deep, sooty lines in it, his ears had grown scarlet with agitation, and his eyelids flickered uninterruptedly in his dark, almost blue eye sockets. He obviously had clearly in mind a way of salvation that would save the Spina family from final disgrace and, if he hesitated to point it out, it was only because he hoped that Pietro would hit on it himself.

"Just during the past few days I remembered an incident in the earthquake that I don't think I've mentioned to you," he hurriedly went on when he thought Pietro was on the point of again showing him the door. "Sir, you unfortunately know through experience in your own home what a terrible catastrophe that was, and there's no need to remind you of it. It was, in short, a case of every man for himself. The parish priest of Fossa, for instance, though he was an ordained priest, jumped out of the window in his shirt and broke his leg, but he saved his life. You will remember that the earth started shaking early in the morning. Donna Maria Vincenza was on her way to church and was halfway down Vicole de Sant'Antonio. At that same moment I was crossing the square with a cartload of wood drawn by a pair of oxen. As soon as I realized it was an earthquake, and it didn't take long to do that, I stopped the cart and went and stood in front of the oxen, which lowed as if they were possessed by the devil. In less than half a minute about a hundred houses collapsed before my eyes. Many were apparently undamaged, but only the front remained. You won't have forgotten that the first shock was followed by two more that were just as violent. Well then, Donna Maria Vincenza was coming toward the square, where I and a great many other terrified people were already, but to get to us she still had quite a long way to go, about two hundred yards, perhaps, between two narrow rows of houses standing closely up against one another. As soon as I saw her, as you can well imagine, I instinctively started shouting: madam, hurry, hurry, hurry. Terrible shocks followed in quick succession. All along Vicolo de Sant' Antonio clouds of dust were bursting from windows and roofs because the interiors had already collapsed. The facades still stood, but might collapse at any moment and bury anyone who was still in the street. But Donna Maria Vincenza kept on walking toward the square at her usual calm, collected, regular pace. I was afraid that if she didn't hurry I might see her disappearing under a pile of rubble at any moment, so I shouted myself hoarse telling her to hurry. At last, when God willed it, she reached safety, and as soon as she was close to me she took me aside and said to me quietly: Venanzio, what manners are these? Why did you shout my name like that in the middle of the public square? Madam, I replied, the whole village is collapsing. I know, she replied, it's not very difficult to see that. But just because the earth has started behaving wildly, is that any reason why we should imitate it? Even then, you see, madam used arguments that were unanswerable even though they were unconvincing. That's why I have now taken the liberty of appealing to you. It's up to you, sir, if you will permit me to say so, to make a decision."

"There's no point in your going on, Venanzio," Pietro interrupted him. "If it helps to reassure you, let me tell you that I have never planned or intended to stay here for any length of time. If I'm here, it's because I was brought here, as you know. But during the next few days I shall go."

This was exactly what Venanzio wanted to hear, but on hearing it he turned a mental somersault and was suddenly seized with intense compassion for the young gentleman. "By Christ, by Our Lady, by all the saints," he started swearing, but Pietro walked out, leaving him standing there trembling, with his eyes full of tears and with beads of sweat on his face, as if he were in a high fever. Pietro went to Donna Maria Vincenza's room and found her bent over her desk and concentrating, like a little girl just learning to write. The reddish baize of the desk and the pink lampshade gave an almost youthful coloring to her face.

"Am I disturbing you?" Pietro asked.

"Stay, my dear boy, I've nearly finished. I haven't seen you all the afternoon."

"You were hardly likely to run into me at Lama."

"Oh, so Venanzio told you."

Donna Maria Vincenza stopped writing and remained

thoughtful for a moment. When she raised her head again all her tiredness, all her age, reappeared on her face.

"Our family pride seems to have taken refuge with that poor Venanzio," she said with a sad smile. "Do you know that today he dared make observations to me? As he seemed to be going on indefinitely, to get him to stop I had to remind him that I was the mistress and he was the groom. He stopped, but not before muttering that Don Berardo ought to come back to life at this moment. You can't imagine how much he's suffering. He used to go down to Colle on Sunday afternoons to play cards with friends and drink in some tavern. I discovered that he stayed here on the past two Sundays, and I asked him if he didn't feel well. After beating around the bush for some time he ended up admitting that he was ashamed. I asked him what he was ashamed of. Of the state to which we're reduced, he answered. Whom do you mean by we? I asked him, but he wouldn't explain."

"Basically he's quite right," Pietro said gravely. "A family is a community of living more than a community of blood. So I say quite seriously, and without trying to be paradoxical, that he's unquestionably more of a Spina than I am. He has always remained here, loyal, industrious, and sober, while I wandered from country to country like a soldier of fortune. Perhaps that's one reason why he hates me. Isn't it intolerable that an intruder should endanger the honor of 'his' family?"

"I note with pleasure that you're in a mood for joking," his grandmother said. "So far from being an intruder, you're the only surviving Spina."

Pietro changed his tone and went on in a firm voice. "Grandmother," he said, "I don't want you to continue your *via crucis** from one place to another for my sake. If there's one thing capable of inducing me to leave here immediately, without delay, without even saying good-bye to you, it's that."

Donna Maria Vincenza rose, went over to him, and said in a tone that admitted of no reply: "To do what my conscience and

*Way of the cross.

my heart require me to do I have no need of anyone's permission, not even yours. If you had a child who was on the point of drowning, you wouldn't ask his permission before jumping into the water. The trouble is that you have no children."

"Let us leave parables aside," Pietro answered impatiently. "Grandmother, listen to me. After all that has happened I don't want, do you hear me? I don't want" (and he struck the table with his fist and raised his voice) "anyone else to have to suffer on my account. I don't want other persons whom I love to sacrifice themselves for my sake."

The old lady's face contracted into a slightly ironic and painful smile.

"Oh, I recognize that voice," she exclaimed. "I recognize that way of banging the table. You men of the Spina family have lost the virtues of your fathers. You no longer know how to plow, or break in horses, or farm, or pray like they did. But deep inside you retain their way of shouting and acting when they grew arrogant. Do I have to tell you that I have never been impressed by that behavior?"

As it was winter, it had gotten dark almost instantaneously. Night had fallen without the intervention of twilight. Through the curtains Pietro saw lights being turned on in the village.

"If you knew, my dear boy, how tired I am," Donna Maria Vincenza went on after a long pause, stretching out with difficulty on her bed. "Tired, exhausted in every joint. Holy Mother of God, let me not be tried beyond my strength."

Pietro helped to make her comfortable and adjusted the pillows under her head. Later, when she had rested for a while, she went on: "In any case, my dear boy, let me assure you that what you call my *via crucis* is over. Even if I had the strength, I no longer know which way to turn. How was I to know that degeneration was so widespread? Persons whom I have known for generations and regarded as friends and decent, honest souls because I had never had need of them; so-called Christians who never miss mass on Sundays, who never miss a triduum or a novena, who go to confession and take Holy Communion more often than the precepts of the Church require; relatives, priests, people in authority have suddenly revealed themselves to me as petty, terrified creatures with minds totally dominated by a single permanent obsession, the desire to live a quiet life. I ask myself whether this is still a Christian country. It terrifies me, and I no longer feel at home in it. To me it's like a country in which there has been no rain for many seasons, in which drought has dried up even the roots of people's souls, turning it into a steppe, a desert. Alas, I did not know that the reclamation of the Fucino and the earthquake and wars had reduced us to such desolation."

Donna Maria Vincenza closed her eyes, but that did not stop the tears from flowing down her cheeks. Now that those eyes were shut Pietro could look closely at that dear, aged face. The distress that it reflected dismayed him deeply, and he was at a loss how to comfort her. The tears on her fleshless cheeks formed two little trickles that joined up in the wrinkles of her chin. Pietro suddenly discovered a strange resemblance between that face and the earth of which she had spoken just previously; the old, bony, parched, and dried-up earth. How many mothers' tears, what rivers of tears would be needed before that poor parched earth flowered and became fruitful again.

When Natalina came in to help the old lady to undress Pietro said good night and went back to his room.

Later that night, Donna Maria Vincenza awoke with a start. She stayed listening for a moment, then hurriedly put on a dressing gown and went to her grandson's room. He was packing a suitcase.

"Are you leaving?" she said.

"As you see, I'm packing a suitcase," Pietro replied in embarrassment.

"Then I'll have mine packed too."

"Why? Where do you want to go?" said Pietro.

"Wherever you're going. I'm coming with you."

"Listen, Grandmother, don't let us part in anger. I've got to leave here."

"You've misunderstood me, my dear boy. I'm not thinking of parting from you, I said I was coming with you. I'm not leaving you, you can be sure of that."

Then she added softly, almost involuntarily: "I have no reason to go on living except to be with you."

"But that would be madness," Pietro exclaimed.

"Oh, my dear boy, since when have you been against acts of madness?"

Pietro, convinced of the uselessness of going on with this argument, gave up packing his bag, went back to bed, and turned out the light.

5

"The spinas have always been a bit mad," said Aunt Eufemia. "Politically or nonpolitically, everyone knows that they've always had madness in their blood, and that's why fortune favored them and they became the first family in the neighborhood. When it wasn't politics it was money, when it wasn't the army it was women, or religion, or heaven knows what; people like that always have an excuse, and if they don't have an excuse they invent one. But let us be fair, it's not their fault if they're born mad. Just think it over carefully, Palmira, and you'll agree that it's not their fault."

"Yes, yes, but they've always thought themselves better than others," Donna Palmira replied. "That's the trouble. One should not think oneself better than others. Everyone has two hands and two hands only, Aunt Eufemia, and how can anyone think himself better than others?"

"It's sufficient to think of Don Berardo when he was young," Aunt Eufemia went on. "No one can deny that he was good hearted, but he was wilder than San Camillo before his conversion. Haven't you noticed that these anchovies are stale, Palmira?

The macaroni will taste bad. But madmen are like cats, the lucky creatures, they can jump from the roof without breaking their necks. And now, so it seems, we shall soon be seeing young Don Pietro Spina amnestied and pardoned and walking the streets of Colle and inciting the *cafoni* against the landlords; and that, Palmira, will be a wonderful sight to see."

"Aunt Eufemia, do you really think Don Coriolano could be behind that wicked action? People have been saying that he no longer counts for anything."

"I've heard that too, Palmira; they say that nowadays he's nothing but a trombone played by others. Others breathe into him and he produces the music. Why did you invite him?"

"My husband wants to find out what the situation is with the Spinas."

"And you're hoping to get him to talk by offering him macaroni with anchovies, Palmira?"

"I was thinking of asking you to make him pasta with eggs, because I know he likes it, and who doesn't?" Donna Palmira explained. "But I shouldn't have to remind a churchwoman like you, Aunt Eufemia, that it's Lent, and besides, the Lenten preacher is coming."

"Is it true, Palmira, that this year's preacher is a Piedmontese? What is a Piedmontese doing in our parish, I should like to know? As if there were any shortage of great preachers in our diocese."

"What I can't understand is this. How can the government at one moment be hunting a man down in order to shoot him and then suddenly decide to pardon him? I should like to think I was wrong, Aunt Eufemia, but it seems to me that that is an encouragement to wildness and a discouragement to decent people, people like us. You know that I've changed my place in church in order not to have to greet Donna Maria Vincenza. Now you'll see how the old woman raises her feathers again."

"It's no good looking for wool on a mule's back," Aunt Eufemia pointed out. "I've never had any illusions about Rome governments. What are you proposing to offer them after the macaroni?"

"Do you know that the *podestà* has again complained about

the things you say, Aunt Eufemia? If you simply can't help saying certain things, he says, at least you should lower your voice. That is, of course, if you really can't help saying them."

"Yes, I know, and I for my part have given him some friendly advice in return. I told him to put wax in his ears, you know, the special wax they sell at the pharmacy, to save him from hearing anything disagreeable. You must admit, Palmira, that his obscure threats are really absurd. If Christ had been afraid of mice He wouldn't be in church, I told him. And, Palmira, can you tell me where that wretched little pen pusher comes from? Who was his father? I ask everyone, but nobody knows. Perhaps his mother may have known, I don't want to be too pessimistic, perhaps she may have known."

"Oh, Aunt Eufemia, you'll end up compromising all of us with your euphemisms."

The sayings of Aunt Eufemia were commonly known at Colle as euphemisms. Many of them had already become proverbial. The freedom of her views conflicted with her appearances, for she looked like an ordinary churchmouse, a tall, lean, shriveled churchmouse invariably dressed in black, one of those poor, barren, and resigned old maids who for lack of a family of their own hang around the sacristy from morning till night, visit the dying, and weep at funerals. In fact she was the only survivor of the patrician De Dominicis family, which had held sway for several centuries in the neighborhood of Colle and Orta before the Spinas arose, or more specifically before the Spinas acquired church land put up for sale as a result of the repeal of the inalienable land law.* To avoid excommunication, good Christians, including the De Dominicises, did not bid at the auction, with the result that the Spinas, whose outlook was liberal and patriotic, acquired the lot very cheaply and so became the richest landowners in the district. The names of the earliest De Dominicises were still to be seen on the burial paving stones in the parish church of Orta, and those of the past century still dominated the Colle

*Under this law, church property was not subject to taxation.

cemetery in a monumental chapel built in the very middle of it; in expectation of the resurrection of the body they still lorded it over the impoverished dead. But among the living their authority had dwindled away and their very name was on the point of extinction. Aunt Eufemia was now the only survivor of the noble clan. She was not the aunt of anyone in particular, and thus for that very reason, strangely enough, she could be described as everybody's aunt without being unfair to anyone. Actually there was some foundation, human if not legal, for that universal claim, for her grandfather's will, in justification of a bequest to the poor of the locality, contained an explicit reference to an unspecified number of illegitimate children of his. At the time no one in Colle had laid claim to such paternity, but the inevitable approaching extinction of the legitimate De Dominicis line reminded the villagers of their interest in the matter. Particularly in view of the fact that it could be assumed that, with the fertility peculiar to bastards, these natural children had in the meantime increased and multiplied to such an extent that no family could be sure of being untainted by them. Thus Aunt Eufemia, though nominally she had no relatives, could now regard all the inhabitants of Colle as her nephews and nieces; and conversely, villagers who had no relatives could at least claim her. Moreover, she was no ordinary aunt, but one of distinguished lineage. But, as happens in the best families, relations between aunts and nephews and nieces were not always very cordial; on the contrary, they were sometimes rather stormy.

The greater part of the old De Dominicis house, which was built in the seventeenth century, largely collapsed in the 1915 earthquake, and all that remained of the facade was the big doorway, more than sixteen feet high, with the family coat of arms at the top of the arch and, poised precariously above it, a big balcony with an ornate wrought-iron railing. This noble, solitary, and windswept simulacrum was now covered with weeds and in spring by insolent clumps of red poppies. Of the rest of the building all that survived was a big room on the ground floor at the extreme north corner that had been used to store potatoes and two small second-floor rooms perched above it. Because one of these rooms had been used as the family chapel and, among other things, contained the remains of a relative of the De Dominicises who had lived in the first half of the eighteenth century and died in an odor of sanctity, some of the inhabitants of Colle proclaimed at the time that it was a miracle. These two rooms, restored, propped up by beams, and reroofed with tiles, looked rather like an abandoned dovecote, but now served as Aunt Eufemia's home. To gain access to it, in the absence of a staircase, Aunt Eufemia used a ladder that she raised like a drawbridge at night, as well as on bad days when the sirocco added the torment of migraine to the numerous personal reasons she had for hating her neighbors.

The news that she had pulled up her ladder would then go around Colle like a flash, warning everyone to keep their distance.

The old De Dominicis chapel now served also as a bedroom, but it still retained its sacred furnishings: an altar with relics, a crucifix, candles, a holy water stoup, and a prie-dieu. On the right of the altar there was an old picture symbolizing the exemplary death of the family saint; a white soul was to be seen painlessly detaching itself from a dead body and gently mounting toward the starry sky, escorted by a flock of small winged angels. On the other side of the altar there hung a more realistic picture with a profane subject, though to Aunt Eufemia it was no less sacred: it showed Queen Maria Sofia of Naples reviewing in martial but ladylike fashion the troops of the citadel of Gaeta during the famous siege. This picture was celebrated in Colle and the neighborhood, not for its artistic merits, but because of a strange and inexplicable phenomenon: with every year that passed Aunt Eufemia developed a more striking resemblance to Queen Maria Sofia. On the other walls of the chapel Aunt Eufemia displayed higgledy-piggledy all the most precious family relics she had managed to recover from the rubble left by the earthquake: portraits of ancestors, hunting trophies, medals and decorations, and collections of pipes. They might have struck a stranger as being banal, heterogeneous, and in any event out of place in a consecrated chapel, but

Aunt Eufemia had lost all sense of their origin, and to her they were saturated with melancholy, reminders of the world beyond, cult objects, and objects of meditation. It was therefore not surprising that in the midst of these relics she was able to collect her thoughts and pray with even more fervor than in the parish church, and it would be impossible to imagine a more appropriate place of worship than that chapel-bedroom for her special brand of religion. This was a touching combination of worship of her own family, the deposed dynasty of the Bourbons of Naples, a few old saints (few, it is true, but carefully selected), and the Crucified Savior. Like every good Italian, Aunt Eufemia was of course a Catholic, and a very earnest one, for she still abided by the *Syllabus*; in other words, she was more intransigent and papist than the Pope. She regretted the Inquisition and prayed ardently for its restoration, just as she refused to accept in her chapel the devotional objects continually devised and propagated by numerous Catholic congregations of recent origin, the Salesians, Josephites, and Don Brione's Little Work of Divine Providence, which were often in petty competition with one another and, not by chance, were of Piedmontese origin. Aunt Eufemia's religion remained southern like that of her forefathers, immune to the inflated piety of modern times; she directed her prayers to ancient, genuine, tried, and tested saints born between the Abruzzi and Calabria, and for preference she prayed in dialect, so that even if other saints listened in they would not be able to understand. With similar consistency she had always refused to pray for the usurping Piedmontese dynasty, the House of Savoy; on the contrary, she actually went on praying that its members should be visited by the well-deserved chastisement of God and the exterminating wrath of men. To her the annual national dynastic holidays were sad days of fasting and penitence. But she was not so politically naive as to believe in the possibility of a restoration of the Kingdom of Naples, just as she knew that nothing could now prevent the extinction of the De Dominicis family. So hers was a faith without hope, a desperate loyalty to a vanished world to which she felt bound by the bonds of birth and upbringing and even more by the memory of her father, the God-fearing, pious, unhappy Don Ferdinando De Dominicis, knight of the Bourbon Order of St. Januarius. At Colle many still remembered him with respect and compassion.

He died of a broken heart in the winter of 1895, a few days after returning from Naples, where in the church of the Bianchi allo Spirito Santo he had attended the funeral of ex-king Francis II, who had died in exile. In spite of everything the naive, loyal, pure-hearted gentleman from the Abruzzi had stubbornly continued to hope and to insist to his more pusillanimous friends that the final arbiter of history was divine providence and that the righteous had behind them the invincible host of angels as their strategic reserve. But at that funeral ceremony, at the sight of the empty catafalque and the black-clad officiants, when he heard the mournful notes of the *Miserere* and the *Requiem*, he realized that in spite of the preference of the gods the end of the Kingdom of Naples was irremediable. To his horror he recognized in that political disaster the same higher destiny that had already condemned the De Dominicis family, and it suddenly struck him that his whole life had been based on illusion. He died of grief, not so much at the descent in the social scale and the material losses that the new order imposed on him as at the blow to his faith. And the truth of the matter was of course that the trusting, gentle, naive Don Ferdinando had not the slightest personal responsibility for the destruction of his old political and family world. He had refused to believe in adverse destiny, had continued until old age to hope against hope, and if the impulses of a pure and honest heart could have changed the course of events, these certainly would have developed in a very different direction. It must not be forgotten that to save the Kingdom of Naples in that sad May of 1860 Don Ferdinando had sent to the Neapolitan court a confident and optimistic message assuring it of his unflinching loyalty. In spite of that, however, Garibaldi's excommunicated hordes had continued their march. But Don Ferdinando was unable to believe in the last triumph of an enterprise that lacked the blessing of the Holy See.

With equal confidence Don Ferdinando, the last of the De Dominicises, had set about ensuring the birth of a male heir. He was convinced that it was impossible that a family like his, which deserved so well of throne and altar, should die out, and when his first few years of marriage failed to produce a son he did not lose heart. Having exhausted the normal liturgical rites practiced in those circumstances, since the proverb says that God helps those who help themselves, he accompanied his docile consort on the most exhausting pilgrimages, spent nightlong vigils with her on the bare stone of remote shrines, took her to the best doctors, faithfully followed all the instructions given by wise women, and duly bathed in the sea as custom prescribed. But all these efforts, if it is permissible to say so, were as ineffective as the firing of blanks. The honorable, shy, and optimistic Don Ferdinando, with the encouragement and sympathy of the whole neighborhood behind him, went on hoping against hope. When he was well into his fifties and widowed for the third time, he made one last attempt to defy his sterile fate and married a woman thirty years his junior. It seemed that heaven at last relented at so much faith and granted the new marriage its well-merited grace. But there was a slight mistake, for, after a few months of exaggerated hope a little girl, the future Aunt Eufemia, was born, thus providing Don Ferdinando with a reward for his patient efforts, a reward that was certainly not to be despised but was nevertheless not the one he wanted. The courteous gentleman, supported by the intense interest and encouragement of the whole countryside, persisted in his efforts, but without further result.

From her earliest years, Eufemia showed obvious signs of her father's unsatisfied desire for a son, and as she grew up developed very visible black hair on her upper lip, male inflections in her voice, and male features in the musculature of her arms and chest and even in her aggressive and quarrelsome nature. However, several years of strict upbringing at a convent school made her more gentle and civilized and also pale, depressed, and peevish, as befitted a young lady of good family. But a crude joke of which she was the victim in her twentieth year (by that time she had lost her mother too and lived alone in the big house with an aged woman servant) had a disastrous impact on the rest of her life. She was denounced to the military authorities for failing to register for military service. No one ever discovered whether that stupid joke was a belated revenge by persons who nursed ancient grudges against the family and found it convenient to vent them on a defenseless young woman; or whether it was an idea thought up by the usual self-styled humorists, unemployed artisans, and pharmacy intellectuals who were then much more numerous in the provinces than they are today and were always ready to seize every opportunity for a practical joke, since laughing at others offered them a stupid consolation for their idle and empty lives. However that may be, the official procedure quietly took its course, and Signorina Eufemia herself and the few persons at Colle who, if they had heard of it in time, might have averted the distasteful incident came to know about it only at the last moment, when the military authorities had already ordered the suspect to be brought to the local headquarters by two *carabinieri* to be subjected to a medical examination. The indignant protests of the parish priest, the Spina family, and others were ineffective, because they were too late. All that was discovered for certain was that the ridiculous charge was chiefly based on the evidence of a half-witted youth, a man of straw put forward by the real instigators, who claimed to have seen Signorina Eufemia while she was changing her underclothes.

At that time, when those who failed to register for military service in southern Italy numbered tens of thousands, there was a more serious reason for suspicion in the eyes of the military authorities. According to a report by the political police, the allegation that the suspect was masquerading as a woman was stated to be perfectly plausible in view of the well-known legitimist views of the De Dominicis family, and, if it were confirmed by medical examination, it should be considered a deliberate refusal to serve the new state and take the oath of loyalty due to the new dynasty.

On the day of Signorina Eufemia's medical examination the whole population turned out in the main street of Colle in a noisy carnival spirit, while groups of young men sang conscripts' songs.

But when, after a long wait, Signorina Eufemia appeared between two *carabinieri*, ashen pale and wearing the dark blue
woolen cloak and velvet hat that survived from her school days,
the songs and jokes promptly gave way to a painful hush. Many
persons were ashamed and withdrew into their houses, and others
who stayed in the street almost involuntarily raised their hats as she
passed. Signorina Eufemia walked through the village without
looking at anyone, without speaking, without replying to greetings, as if she saw and heard nothing; she even ignored old Don
Berardo Spina's offer to take her and the two *carabinieri* to the
headquarters of the military district in his carriage, and she ignored the parish priest's sister, who wanted to put around her
neck as a protection against the Evil One a rosary that had been
brought back from a pilgrimage to the Holy Land and blessed on
the Holy Sepulchre, a rosary of thorn berries. She went on her
way, impassive and aloof, with the uncertain footsteps of a sleep-
walker and the weary resignation of a sacrificial victim.

No one saw her when she returned to Colle, because it was
late at night. And since no one had the slightest doubt about the
outcome of the medical examination, people talked about her less
and less in the days that followed, and only admiringly. The general impression, in short, was that she had faced her ordeal in the
worthiest possible manner and put her unknown denouncers to
shame. The cold, calm, silent indifference that she displayed revealed a strength of character with which no one had credited
her, a fearless strength of character sufficient to please her most
distant ancestors in the dust of their tombs. For some time her
outward behavior remained unchanged. She was seen, as usual,
walking along the brief stretch of street between her house and
the parish church, accompanied by her maid, when she attended
mass or vespers. In the street and in church she never looked at
anyone, did not reply to greetings, seemed to ignore the existence
of other people, but she looked grimmer and more tense as time
went on. But, as appeared later, this apparent apathy concealed a
fierce anger that was not to fade away for the rest of her life, an implacable anger that she struggled to keep down, perhaps because

she herself feared the streak of madness in it, and perhaps also because of the impossibility of finding an adequate outlet for it. The banks suddenly burst one evening when at the instigation of her aged servant some curious women went to see Signorina Eufemia for the pious purpose of relieving her gloomy and bitter loneliness, and also in the secret hope of hearing some intimate details about the medical examination. To save themselves from the outburst of rage that greeted their arrival they had to flee precipitously down the wide steps of the De Dominicis house. That evening lonely, funereal wails, cries of anger that had been too long repressed, obscure and sinister threats resounded through the terrified village. Henceforth such fits of rage and horrible cursing broke out whenever strange footsteps crossed the threshold of the De Dominicis house, whether they were those of the municipal clerk or a charcoal burner, a hungry beggar or a weary pilgrim, or merely a child playing hide-and-seek. But no one at Colle blamed Signorina Eufemia; everyone agreed that her behavior was completely justified by the excessive insult to which she had been subjected.

In the long run the very frequency of her outbursts made the people of Colle less afraid of them, and they ended up getting used to them, as to so many other evils. The young regarded them like other disagreeable aspects of life that were there before they were born — as an incomprehensible and irrevocable divine punishment for some unknown fault of their fathers. It seemed that there was no help for it until a Neapolitan Jesuit preacher succeeded in gaining her ear a few years after the earthquake and converting her, at any rate partially.

The preacher, according to the parish priest, succeeded in striking the right note with her. "My beloved daughter," he said, "though you can no longer prevail in pomp and pride as your ancestors did, thanks to religion you can still excel in humility. You could, my beloved daughter, become an example to all the parishioners of Colle. You, a De Dominicis, could and should dumbfound them with your humility." Aunt Eufemia was moved to the depths of her being by these pious suggestions. Thus new ways in addition to the old were opened up to her fury. In close accordance with the phases of the moon and the less regular appearances of the sirocco, her old misanthropical rages began alternating with long periods of painful, ostentatious, and impressive humility. Thus her conversion was both intermittent and lasting.

After this she took part every year in the barefoot procession on Good Friday, with a rope around her neck and her head covered with ashes, as at one time was done only by exceptional penitents, sinners who had been converted after years and years of public scandal; and this was considered all the more meritorious because of her patrician origin as well as her spinsterhood and her un-questioned virginity. There were actually people who came to Colle from neighboring villages on Good Friday to be edified by her extraordinary humility, and Aunt Eufemia was rightly proud of this. But envy pokes its nose in everywhere, and on one occa-sion during the procession of the dead Christ an envious church-woman had the nerve bitterly to denounce her behavior as not humble at all, but the very opposite. The result was an appalling scene that brought the procession to a halt. The sad psalms and mournful ejaculatories of the confraternities suddenly died away, and Aunt Eufemia appeared in the attire of her exceptional hu-mility, barefoot, with a rope around her neck, her head covered with ashes, her features distraught by the old fury. The silence of the interrupted procession was broken by her threatening wails, fearsome curses, and imperious invocation of the natural elements and the gods of the underworld, of earthquakes and thunderbolts, hurricanes and floods, poisonous snakes, wolves, scorpions, and mad dogs. It was terrible to hear, and the attention of the faithful was diverted from the Man-God being carried in procession in His glass coffin and Our Merciful Mother of Sorrows, who was present with the seven swords of her seven sorrows plunged in her thin aluminum heart. The priests, the crossbearers, the priors of the confraternities, the elders, the Sisters of the Good Death, the Children of Mary, the bearers of the sacred images, all sur-rounded Aunt Eufemia and, pale with horror, implored her to for-give yet another stupid insult, begged her to take pity on people most of whom were innocent, loudly appealed to her unparalleled humility, her admirable and incomparable humility. With great difficulty the procession eventually got going again, and it advanced through a crowd depressed and worried by this new outburst of cursing and the disasters that were bound to follow in its wake. The most influential members of the congregation surrounded Aunt Eufemia, who was silent but not placated, and while they walked went on praising her and entreating her to forgive and forget in order to avert the wrath to come. The ceremony with the sacred symbols went on, but it was no longer the procession of the Crucified Man-God, but that of the humble and terrible Aunt Eufemia.

In normal circumstances, however, she was full of respect for religion, full of zeal for its observances and liturgy, and cooperated graciously with the parish priest in various pious works. Taking advantage of a skill she had learned at school, she assumed the privilege of decorating the sacred statues in the parish church with colored paper flowers. There was no lack of real flowers in the fields and the few gardens at Colle, but everyone admitted that Aunt Eufemia's artificial flowers were much more beautiful and original. Her specialty, or rather her own invention, was a huge red flower of the shape and size of a big cabbage, a huge cabbage stripped of its leaves, with black, swollen, monstrous stamens, a flower such as had never been seen in nature, which the villagers therefore called Aunt Eufemia's heart. Placed over the tabernacle on the altar and surrounded by burning candles, it obscured the pink and anemic heart of Jesus painted on the tabernacle, with the result that the altar seemed to be dedicated to the heart of Aunt Eufemia, and it was toward the latter that the incense and singing of the kneeling congregation was directed.

In the past few years a marked improvement had taken place in the relations between Aunt Eufemia and the people of Colle following a discovery by a mason who was sent for to repair the floor in the De Dominicis chapel. Hidden in a corner was a mysterious vessel of the size and shape of a vat used for collecting grapes at vintage time. The mason was the first to spread the story that Aunt

Eufemia possessed a substantial treasure hidden somewhere in her home. This came as no surprise to the oldest villagers, not only because there was nothing left that could really surprise them, but also because they distinctly remembered having heard in their distant childhood of an ancient and priceless treasure buried between the walls of the De Dominicis house, and in fact they had been very surprised when no trace of it appeared in the rubble after the earthquake. Aunt Eufemia's ambiguous smile at timid references to the mysterious contents of the vessel that had come to light persuaded the last doubters. To avoid being outdone by their neighbors, the few Colle families that in the past had refrained from calling Signorina Eufemia "aunt" suddenly discovered old and forgotten kinships with her family; in most cases, however, these consisted of hypothetical acts of extramarital sinfulness carried out by their grandmothers and great-grandmothers with the arrogant forebears of the De Dominicis family.

It was after this that Signorina Eufemia became everyone's aunt. And it was clear to these strange nephews and nieces that there was only one way in which their irascible aunt could possibly defraud them of their precious legacy: that was, if she failed to leave a will and the treasure went to the hateful, greedy government. That, however, would be an incongruous gesture, inconsistent with their aunt's whole life, and an impious affront to the tradition of her forefathers, an atrocious insult to the sad memory of her unhappy father, the gentle, upright and disconsolate Don Ferdinando, knight of the Bourbon Order of St. Januarius, in whose sight his degenerate daughter would be too ashamed to appear after her death. Thus these strange nephews and nieces, though by nature and sad experience of life inclined to pessimism, in this single instance did not despair. Their cupidity did not drive them to the point of actually saying out loud that they hoped their aunt would die, for they feared the appalling consequences that would follow if it came to her ears. But, because death spares no one, they adhered strictly to the requirements of decorum and, as happens even in the best families, they secretly implored, entreated, prayed, and yearned that the sufferings in this vale of tears of their aristocratic and unfortunate aunt should cease and that she should join her beloved forefathers with all possible speed. For several years past tradesmen on the point of bankruptcy, peasants ruined by mortgages, girls without dowries had waited impatiently but confidently for that happy, sad event. Thus even the poor who elsewhere had no illusions left at least had that to look forward to in Colle.

So it was not surprising that among these heirs there were some who tried to make sure of their share by doing their best to get around their aunt on days when she was in a sociable mood by lavishing by no means disinterested attentions on her. Unfortunately it was the least indigent and most prosperous nephews and nieces, those who could have afforded to keep aloof, who were most assiduous in these selfish maneuvers and intrigues. In fact it was easier for them to exploit their gloomy, sorrowful, and chaste aunt's only weakness, her love of good cooking. At the convent school to which she had been sent to receive an aristocratic up-bringing her healthy countrywoman's instinct had saved her from learning the many strange and useless things that were taught there (music, poetry, painting in watercolors, etiquette, French, and other frivolities) and had concentrated, apart from her paper flowers, on the art of cooking. As a true artist, Aunt Eufemia was not greedy and had no interest in cooking for herself alone. In Colle the tradition survived that cooking was the task of the mistress of the house and not of the domestic staff, and even in houses in which a servant was employed the latter was admitted to the kitchen only as an assistant; and Aunt Eufemia sometimes yielded to the temptation of revealing to one or another of her nieces some of the secrets of the art she had learned at the convent. There were those who claimed to have seen her actually smiling in front of the oven. So, when moon and sirocco permitted, the best families of Colle competed in attracting Aunt Eufemia to their homes, particularly if important visitors were expected; and with the idea of the hidden treasure always present in their minds, they flattered her and paid her compliments on her expertise. But like all artists, fortunately for her, she was un-

grateful and temperamental, with the result that relations between her and the families that courted her most at Colle were
often the reverse of cordial.

"You know that you can always count on my husband and me,
Aunt Eufemia," Donna Palmira said. "You know that, thanks be to
God, we've never been like other people, and that to us respect is
respect. If it had depended on us, Aunt Eufemia, your life would
have been very different, very different indeed."

"Of course, Palmira, of course," Aunt Eufemia replied. "If pigs
could fly one could live by hunting, as everyone knows. But, if
you're expecting me to die in the immediate future, you're
making a grave mistake."

"Oh, Aunt Eufemia," Donna Palmira said, "with your euphemisms you're actually capable of taking away my appetite."

Aunt Eufemia was holding the plate of anchovies and looking
at them with distaste. As usual, she was dressed in black and had a
small black embroidered cap on her head; her hair, which was
still thick and which she frequently dyed a shiny black, was divided into two bands and drawn low over her temples, and she
had a black ribbon around her neck; she had the mauve-green
coloring peculiar to persons who can't stand flies but for whom
flies (creatures that bear no ill will) have a special predilection.

"Really, Palmira," said Aunt Eufemia, "for plain macaroni with
these anchovies I don't see there was the slightest need to send for
me. Is it true that the preacher is a Piedmontese?"

"I shouldn't have any need to remind a churchwoman like you,
Aunt Eufemia, that it's Lent, and it's not my fault," Palmira replied.

"You know very well, Palmira, that the preacher, if he is so
inclined, can give you a dispensation. Is it true that he's a
Piedmontese?"

"I shouldn't have any need to remind a churchwoman like
you, Aunt Eufemia, that a Lenten preacher has to set an example.
At home, or in his monastery, he can eat whatever he likes, but
when he is on mission he is under an obligation to show that he is
doing penance. He actually mentioned that he hoped that the
sauce would not be too pungent today."

"I really think, Palmira, that there was no need to send for me to cook for a man who wishes to do penance at the table. And if the Piedmontese actually wants to tell me how to make the sauce, Palmira, don't you think it would be an act of courtesy to ask him to make it himself? But you told me that you had also invited Don Coriolano because you wanted to get him to talk."

"Yes, Aunt Eufemia, Don Coriolano is coming too, but you can't give two lunches on the same day; you can't offer one guest Lenten food and another rich food on the same day; Aunt Eufemia, you know better than I do, you can't abstain from sin and commit it on the same day and on the same stove if the day is in Lent and the Lenten preacher is coming to lunch. Also you know better than I do that Don Coriolano did not come to Colle for our sake, but for Donna Maria Vincenza's. He went to Rome on her account, and now he has come back to give her the news, to tell her, as you heard before I did, that that scoundrel of a grandson of hers has been pardoned and can come back to his grandmother at Colle if he likes, or go to his uncle at Orta. Really, Aunt Eufemia, you must agree that it is not such good news to us that it deserves to be celebrated by an infringement of Lent. It seems to me, Aunt Eufemia, that the government encourages madness and discourages quiet, respectable people like us."

"Quite so, Palmira, but as you ought to know already, you can't expect tomatoes from stinging nettles. I've explained to you before that all the governments that have succeeded each other in Rome for the past seventy years have been illegitimate, but you have a hard head. Did you really expect to see Donna Maria Vincenza humiliated and cast down because of her grandson? She's an old lady, she must be nearing eighty by now, but she's a woman of the old type, it's sufficient to say that she's a Camerini, and she can still show you all how to thread a needle in the dark, Palmira. Yes, she's an old lady, but she's like a cat, she has nine lives. What are you proposing to give them after the macaroni, Palmira?"

"Oh, Aunt Eufemia, your euphemisms are really not comforting at all; they actually take one's appetite away, Aunt Eufemia."

6

*O*UTSIDE IT WAS SNOWING and a fierce north wind was blowing. In an adjoining room Don Coriolano and Father Gabriele, the Passionist preacher, were trying to warm their feet in front of a charcoal brazier. Don Coriolano had come back from Rome with a new plaid suit, a pair of bright yellow shoes, and a big dose of fresh optimism by which he seemed revitalized and rejuvenated; his carefully curled mustaches, his goatee beard, his brilliantined hair carefully parted in the middle, his pink cheeks, and his shining eyes completed the picture of a childishly excited and happy man. Facing him in the black cassock of the Passionists with its white emblem of the heart of Jesus crowned with thorns, the ecclesiastical orator made a lugubrious, insignificant impression, as if he were something to ward off the evil eye. Father Gabriele was a timid, bony, skinny little old man, probably sickly and certainly undernourished; his tiny flea's eyes jumped about the various sections of the breviary and closed during passages he knew by heart, giving him a corpselike appearance. Don Coriolano had tried to take advantage of the presence of the Passionist father to repeat his story of his trip to Rome. For several days he had had the illusion of being something more than a mere trombone blown by others, having been allowed to associate with the real performers in scenes played in places made sacred by newspaper reports and newsreel shots. To relive those sublime moments he had been talking about them for several days past to everyone he met, recalling every detail of what had happened, reproducing the gestures, the voices, the words, inflating his own success at every repetition, attributing brilliant repartees to himself followed by noisy laughter in the rooms and corridors of historic buildings.

"How sad it is, Father," he exclaimed, adopting a tone of deep distress, "how sad it is for a man like me to have to spend my life far from the places where historic pronouncements are made. Nothing ever happens in these lice-ridden villages, Father; poverty has made the peasants apathetic and resigned, crimes are rare and petty, there are no assassination attempts, no plots, no strikes. Tell me, Father, against whom am I to defend public order here if no one threatens it? Not even Cicero, Father, not even Demosthenes could show his mettle here. We have had only one enemy here, and we stupidly allowed him to escape. How sad, Reverend Father."

The Passionist preacher sat listening with a hermetic smile, with closed lips, the smile of a lady whose dentures are being repaired at the dentist's; and Don Coriolano ended up becoming irritated at a silence that might be ironic. He rose, snorted noisily, and started tramping up and down the room as if to warm his feet. On the sideboard there were the usual wedding boxes decorated with shells, a marble inkwell in the form of a restored Colosseum, and a saltcellar in the shape of a swan. "The usual trash," Don Coriolano said aloud. Behind the glass door there were some bottles of mineral water and alcoholic drinks named after saints; he tried to open it, but it was locked. "The usual revolting mistrust," he said. On the other wall, in a frame that imitated the branches of a tree, there was an enlarged colored photograph of a corporal with a medal on his chest; on either side of it, like trophies, were two sets of picture postcards, fan-shaped like a hand at cards. For lack of anything else to do, Don Coriolano used a pointed wooden matchstick from which he had removed the sulfur to rummage among the crevices in his teeth for relics of the past week's meals.

"Last night at Celano, Reverend Father," he confided to the priest's ear, "they served a roast chicken that had the purity, the freshness, the grace, I might say the innocence of a girl at her first communion. I don't know if you see what I mean, Reverend Father."

The preacher was shocked. He raised two amazed eyebrows toward the ceiling. "Have you forgotten that it's Lent?" he murmured.

"Forgotten?" Don Coriolano exclaimed indignantly. "What do you take us for, Reverend Father? Turks? Have the courtesy to lay aside your breviary for a moment and listen to me, Reverend Father. After the chicken and roast potatoes they served a pale green salad seasoned, I should rather say blessed, with fresh olive oil and very old, I might say classical, vinegar; a timid, bashful, spiritual, ascetic little salad, a conventual one in the real sense of the word. When that refreshing salad was brought to the table, Reverend Father, it was greeted with a general sigh of relief by all the guests, on my word of honor, Reverend Father. What a good job they didn't forget it was Lent, we all exclaimed."

The master of the house, Don Lazzaro Tarò, a tall, heavily built man with a big bushy beard that left only his eyes and nose exposed, arrived covered with snow and steaming like a drafthorse; and Don Coriolano embraced and kissed him with childish heartiness and helped him to shake the snow from his back.

Don Lazzaro took from the sideboard cupboard a bottle of Amaro Sant'Agostino, sniffed it, and filled three small glasses to the brim with the ease and precision of a pharmacist.

"When there's a flu epidemic it's excellent medicine," said Don Coriolano, examining the dark green liquid against the light.

"Is there a flu epidemic in these parts?" the preacher asked in some alarm.

"No, not yet," Don Coriolano assured him. "But there might be one. In fact it can be claimed with confidence that if there were nothing to drink there would be one already."

"Thank you, I don't drink," said the priest, with a polite but firm gesture.

Don Coriolano gave him a friendly pat on the shoulder and winked. "I understand, I understand," he said with a reassuring smile. "You must set a good example, an edifying example, an example of penitence. Oh, Reverend Father, if you only knew how well I understand. But we are among friends here, discreet friends, and you can drink as much as you like, you can even get drunk and we shan't tell anyone."

"Here you are among friends you can trust," said Lazzaro, winking too. "We are good Catholics, of course, but not to the extent of acting as informers to the bishop, thank heaven. And besides, have a look at the bottle, Reverend Father, it's almost consecrated stuff."

In fact next to the picture of the saint on the label were these words by a well-known anarchist writer who had been converted to Catholicism: DO YOU WANT TO BE HEALTHY? THEN DRINK AMARO SANT'AGOSTINO.

"Thank you, I don't drink," the preacher replied irritably.

Don Coriolano was upset by this and became dejected again.

"I see, you don't trust us," he said. "What is the subject of your sermon this evening?"

"Are you coming to church?"

"What a pleasure it would be if I could," Don Coriolano assured him. "But unfortunately the doctor forbids me to. You don't believe me? It's because of the smell of the candles. My doctor says it ruins the voice. Not in the sense that it silences me, of course, but he says that breathing candle-infested air weakens the voice and results in the abolition of all difference between sacred and political oratory. Whether he's right or wrong I don't know. But you'll agree that if I disobeyed him I should be taking an excessive risk. To a political speaker a masculine voice is what good legs are to a streetwalker or, if you prefer it, what flour is to spaghetti. The reason why I asked you what the subject of your sermon is to be, Reverend Father, is that Donna Maria Vincenza Spina told me that she wishes to postpone the signature of the appeal for her grandson's pardon until after this evening's service. Not that there's any doubt about it, but she says that she has always liked to subject important actions in her life to a certain amount of ritual, a certain amount of ceremonial formality; and one has to be patient with old ladies. That's also the reason why I'm having to stay overnight in this barbarous spot."

"Is it certain that her grandson isn't dead, then?" asked the preacher, closing his breviary. "Man's pardon often comes too late."

"He's abroad," Don Coriolano announced with the air of a man in possession of inside information. "Exceptionally, I'm authorized to reveal the secret. We have known for the past month that he has gone abroad again. Also Donna Maria Vincenza seems to have had news of him from France. But please don't press me to tell you more than that, because on my word of honor I cannot and must not."

Don Coriolano in fact knew many things, or rather, leaving modesty aside, knew everything, and always a month in advance, though his lips were always sealed. No news ever surprised him, and he had always known the news printed in the newspapers for at least a month. Actually he never wasted his time looking at the political columns, for it will be readily understood that he was bored by news that was at least a month old; and if he read the newspapers with a certain amount of assiduity, it was only for the sake of the court reports and the reviews of operatic performances, in which his favorite arts, those of eloquence and song, celebrated their greatest triumphs. Even the stop-press columns never told him anything new; they never contained anything but trash, stale news at least a month old that was hardly worthy of a glance, though he spared a smile of commiseration for the poor, credulous readers who were taken in by it, ha, ha, ha. Also, of course, the really important news did not appear in the newspapers at all, for it had to be kept from the man in the street. But, leaving modesty aside for a moment, Don Coriolano always knew everything, and he always knew it a month in advance, and what a pity it was that his lips were sealed. And, though everyone knew that he would be willing to risk his life for his friends, it was useless to press him, he could not and must not reveal what he knew even to his most trusted friends. Not that he mistrusted them, of course, but it was simply his duty; and there was genuine pain in his voice when he pleaded with them not to press him, and those big eyes of his, those big, bovine eyes that yielded so readily to emotion, glistened with real tears.

As an honest landlord Don Lazzaro could not conceal his anger and indignation at the government pardon that was threatening to restore the hated Spina family to favor. He strode up and down the room, making the windows and the sideboard rattle with his heavy footsteps, and he breathed heavily as if he were suffocating; it was obvious that the old bad blood between the Spina and Tarò families still affected him. Eventually he burst out: "Well, shall I tell you what I really think? I no longer understand anything. Why, I should like to know, should a troublemaking maniac like that be allowed to come back among peaceful folk like us? He obliged us by voluntarily going back into exile among a great many other stateless, godless scoundrels just like himself. What I say is, let him stay there, and don't let us hear any more about him. But what happens? It seems incredible, but the very same authorities who barely two months ago were rightly searching for him in order to kill him are now looking for him in order to pardon him. Perhaps it's because I'm a naive provincial, as you keep telling me, but I confess that I no longer understand anything."

"I understand your concern very well, Don Lazzaro," said the preacher, with an apologetic bow in the direction of Don Coriolano, "but pardoning a repentant rebel could be a wise and opportune gesture on the part of the authorities. It is not Christian to be pitiless, Don Lazzaro, and it is not even useful. It is my duty to tell you that. The Church itself . . ."

"What are you talking about?" Don Lazzaro interrupted angrily. "The horse does not change its pace to please the rider, Reverend Father. The Spinas have always been wild, and now of all times, just when they're on the point of ruin, we see the government hurrying to help them back on their feet. To me that seems scandalous."

"I understand what you are saying, Don Lazzaro," the preacher replied with a gesture and a smile that were an invitation to calm down. "I appreciate your honest concern. But you must not deny in principle the possibility of repentance. Our religion, our morality, Don Lazzaro, are based on grace, that's all I wish to remind you of. If the lost lamb . . ."

"I know that pious parable, Reverend Father," Don Lazzaro said furiously. "Excuse me if I raise my voice, Reverend Father, but the Spinas are not lambs, you obviously don't know them, they have never been lambs, believe me, they have never cropped the grass in the fields with the rest of the flock. Now, of course, they'll accept the pardon, they'll obviously accept it, because it will enable them to rise again, to replace their broken dishes and recane their broken chairs, that can be taken for granted. But they're not tame lambs, Reverend Father, that eat their fill, drink, and then go to sleep; they're not ordinary human beings who earn their living, put money aside, and live and let live. On the contrary, they have always thought themselves better than others, they have always been restless and discontented, that's the truth of the matter, they have always wanted the moon at midday and strawberries in winter. I don't know if I've made myself clear, Reverend Father, but it's that that makes it so shocking."

"I understand, Don Lazzaro," replied the preacher, assuming the implacable tone of the Lenten preacher, "but I repeat, you must not exclude grace, you must not deny the possibility introduced into the world by the Precious Blood of our Redeemer, you must not deny the possibility open to every human being who has gone astray to repent, to reform, to return to the right path, to find his way back to the fold. It is my duty to tell you this. Listen, Don Lazzaro, I repeat that you must not believe that sin is irremediable, that there is no brake on instinct, that nature is mindless. Most important of all, you must not believe that man is alone, at the mercy of his weakness. Above all, Don Lazzaro, you cannot totally ignore the Redemption and the New Testament, you cannot forget . . ."

"Certainly, Reverend Father, that would be the last straw,"

Don Lazzaro, who had lost patience, shouted. "I too am a good Christian, a real, old-fashioned Christian, I know by heart the creed, the Ten Commandments, the seven sacraments, the seven works of mercy, I go to mass nearly every Sunday and pay my tithes. I too believe every word the parish priest says about the life beyond. But by heaven, as against that, on matters that in no way concern you or your fraternity, Reverend Father, but do affect and concern me and my family, on those matters you must do me the courtesy of accepting what I say. You must avoid, at least here in my house, defending the family that is our enemy and contradicting every word I say. You must at least respect the old rules of hospitality, Reverend Father, you must at least pretend, for the sake of politeness if nothing else, to share my point of view, particularly as it will cost you nothing. I know in advance what you want to reply, Reverend Father, but I think you have talked enough for today, and about things you know nothing about. So save your breath for this evening's sermon and allow me to say something because, though I'm not a preacher on mission, I'm in my own home here, after all, and that at least is something you won't dare to cast doubt on."

Don Coriolano, who was enjoying the whole of this squabble enormously, interrupted. "By the way, Lazzaro, what time do we eat? You'll excuse me, won't you, but that's what we're here for, after all?"

The Passionist father rose to his feet. He was agitated and upset, and his face had darkened. He looked toward the door, but hesitated to go. The Adam's apple between the two vertical cords in his long thin neck was moving up and down like an unpleasant mouthful that was hard to swallow.

"Sit down again, Reverend Father, lunch isn't ready yet," said Don Lazzaro, taking him by the arm. "In the meantime let me give you an example, as fresh as a new-laid egg, to illustrate the strange mentality of Donna Maria Vincenza. Listen to me, Reverend Father, particularly as no one's appetite has ever been spoiled by keeping his mouth shut. Well, for several weeks we have been seeing her dashing here, there, and everywhere to seek aid on behalf of her grandson, who was believed to be a fugitive, until it became known that Don Coriolano here had left for Rome on a specific mission on her behalf. (Don Coriolano's an old friend of mine, Reverend Father, but you know the proverb: the only friends you can trust are those you have in your purse.) So Don Coriolano left, and while he was away, as was to be expected, Donna Maria Vincenza's anxiety increased from day to day. She was seen praying in church more frequently than usual, she paid a number of old women to pray for her in front of the Blessed Sacrament until late at night, and every morning she had a new candle lit in front of Our Lady of Perpetual Succor. Several times she sent her groom in the carriage to Fossa, thinking that Don Coriolano might be coming back early and wanting to know the outcome of his mission at the earliest possible moment. I know these things, because there are persons who come and report them to me and whom I pay for the purpose. Well, as you already know, Reverend Father, Don Coriolano came back yesterday evening with the text of the petition for a pardon in a pocket of his new suit together with the shocking assurance that it will be accepted by the government; you also know that all Donna Maria Vincenza has to do is to dip her pen in the inkpot and sign her revered name at the bottom of the petition. (At this point, Reverend Father, the prose ends and the poetry begins, and I must ask you to listen to me very attentively for a moment.) Well, then, at the precise moment when Signora Spina was assured of success her worry, her anxiety, her hurry vanished. Last night she put forward frivolous excuses for postponing the formality of the signature until this morning, this morning she put it off till this evening, and she isn't even going to sign it this evening; and not of course because she's undecided whether to sign or not, far from it, but simply because she wants to be asked, she isn't willing just to accept the pardon, she wants to grant it, and before granting it she wants to be adequately entreated."

"Well done, Lazzaro, well done," Don Coriolano exclaimed dryly and ironically. "I congratulate you on your eloquence, and particularly on your final shot, which hit the bull's-eye. But, by the way, what time do you think we shall be sitting down to the table?"

"If that's the case (and I have no reason to doubt what you say, Don Lazzaro) it is a grave sin of vanity on the lady's part," the preacher admitted with the obvious intention of making things up with the master of the house. "But perhaps the petition submitted to her," he added almost in an undertone, turning timidly to Don Coriolano, "contains humiliating phrases?"

"Not at all," Don Coriolano assured him with his hand on his heart. "At the first sight of it Donna Maria Vincenza was herself surprised at its ordinariness, if it is permissible to use the term. In any case the same text, *mutatis mutandis,* has been used before in similar cases, and it's actually a paltry thing, an insipid colored sweet, one of those laxative pills that you swallow, if not with pleasure, at any rate without disgust, and its purgative effects are felt only later in the depths of the organism. Disinfection without irritation is not only an excellent formula for laxatives, Reverend Father, it is also undoubtedly the wisest and most universal of political maxims. There was also a factor worthy of all respect that worked in favor of the Spina family. Let us not forget, comrades, I said and repeated to members of the hierarchy in the capital, let us not forget that Donna Maria Vincenza was the mother of Don Saverio Spina, the heroic officer who died as a volunteer in Cyrenaica."

"He died of despair because of an affair with a woman," Don Lazzaro interrupted. "Everyone knows that. He sought death in Africa because Donna Maria Vincenza refused to countenance his morbid passion for Faustina."

"The official version is different," Don Coriolano went on. "The state ignores gossip. It would be disastrous if the private motives behind acts of heroism had to be looked into. What I was going to say was that the only unusual feature of the petition was the preamble, which I drafted myself as follows: 'In the name of the heroic blood shed by my son Saverio on the arid and burning sands of the Sahara, O Head of the Government,' et cetera. We decided to ask the very minimum of Pietro Spina (for that, Reverend Father, is the name of the criminal who is to be pardoned), to avoid offending his diabolical pride; all we want of him, at any rate for the time being, is that he should state that he approves the step taken by his grandmother. The prodigal son who, tired of grazing pigs, returns humiliated to his family must not be received with a hard face. Chastisement, if need be, will come later, and it will be severe."

"I realize that politics come into this," Don Lazzaro said bitterly, "and also I'm very well aware that sheep are for wolves and politics for public speakers, but you can take it from me as a simple countryman that if you put a box of matches in dry straw, the barn is likely to go up in flames at any moment."

"Certainly, Lazzaro," Don Coriolano admitted with a smile, "but the fire brigade exists for the purpose of coping with such eventualities. What we want, Lazzaro, is no fires, and above all no firemen."

"I see where you're trying to lead me with your oratory," said Don Lazzaro, who was in a cold sweat, "but you can take it from me as a simple countryman that if I sow tares and vetch with my wheat in November, in the spring I'll have no choice but to reap wheat and tares together and use them as feed for the cattle. And then what shall I have to make my bread with?"

"Listen, Lazzaro," replied Don Coriolano, who was enjoying himself and rubbed his hands together in sheer pleasure, "I respect your simplicity of heart and your countryman's honesty, but you seem to me to be erring on the side of naïveté. No one is going deliberately to sow grass, tares, and vetch in your or your neighbor's field. We can leave that out of it, because it's the sort of thing that happens only in parables in the Bible. Instead I ask you to consider this. No one cultivates those wretched weeds; on the contrary, ever since cultivation of the soil began countrymen have done everything in their power to wipe them out, in spite of which they spontaneously reappear every spring and provide work and wages for thousands of women and boys whom the landlords have to employ to get rid of them. Don't you think, Lazzaro, that, if men had striven with equal obstinacy and perseverance to destroy wheat, beans, lentils, and tomatoes, those plants would long since have vanished from the face of the earth?"

"Weeds are much tougher, of course," Lazzaro agreed, "but as for their utility . . ."

"Have you never considered," Don Coriolano went on with the gesture of a matador transfixing the bull with his sword, "that agriculture itself exists only thanks to the weeds and other afflictions that affect the soil? There was no agriculture in the Garden of Eden. But your living as a farmer, Lazzaro, depends on weeds, drought, hail, phylloxera, and all the other calamities that you curse. And why do the state and oratory exist? You can't deny that they exist in exactly the same way as doctors exist thanks only to disease and the Church, with its preachers, exists only thanks to sin (please correct me if I'm wrong, Reverend Father)."

Don Coriolano stopped at this point with a smile of self-satisfaction on his face, and his smile remained suspended in midair, as if he did not wish to complete it until the preacher associated himself with his argument and congratulated him on it. But the latter, standing with bent head, looked at him over his glasses with the alarmed expression of a small child at the zoo. The orator was about to resume his demonstration of the absolute necessity of evil, in the absence of which virtue would be unable to shine forth in all its glory, when the angry voice of Aunt Eufemia was heard from the kitchen.

"Don Coriolano." (The voice rose.) "Don Coriolano." (The voice grew threatening.) "Don Coriolano."

At the same moment Donna Palmira appeared at the drawing room door in a state of great agitation. "Excuse me," she said imploringly, "but may I please ask you to be kind enough to keep quiet for a moment? Aunt Eufemia is just making the sauce, you see."

"Oh, is she making the sauce?" Don Coriolano said quietly and remorsefully.

Deep silence, like that of the congregation halfway through mass, descended on the drawing room.

7

THE NORTH WIND WHISTLED and howled against the windows, making the shutters tremble on their hinges. The wind had swept away most of the clouds, it had stopped snowing, and a cold, fitful, sickly sun was low on the horizon. The wind still raised clouds of floury snow from the heights above the village and drove them violently onto the streets and houses, and there was a furious waving of big gray flags of snow over the dark, almost purple alleyways. Every so often gusts of wind spread the intermittent, out-of-tune, and monotonous notes of a trumpet, the only discernible sign of life in the sad landscape. This was Mastro Anacleto, tailor and bandsman, who since yesterday had been practicing over and over again the aria from *La Traviata* that begins: "You do not know how much I suffered." Since the day before he had been breathing the notes of that sad aria into his brass trumpet with all the force of his lungs, and he had not yet succeeded in getting it right twice in succession. With an artist's patience he kept starting all over again: you do not know — you do not know how much I suffered — you do not know — you do not know; and the sound spread pertinaciously from his house over the rooftops and down the alleyways. As usual, about a dozen poor old men, or individuals who looked like poor old men, were sheltering from the wind behind the apse of the church, sitting on small stone seats almost at ground level. They were wrapped in black cloaks, motionless, and silent, and they were peacefully enjoying the little bit of sunshine, which was not at all warm but in February was better than nothing, and also the little bit of music, which, though it was monotonous and out of tune, cost nothing; and soon a good smell of fresh bread would reach them from the communal oven not far from the church.

Every now and again one of the old men would put his hand to the opening of the shirt on his chest and withdraw it, holding an invisible prey between thumb and forefinger. Few people were out and about. Some women carrying brass bowls on their heads passed silently by the church on their way back from the fountain. Later on a girl appeared dragging a goat behind her; the goat didn't want to come, and the girl was crying. Then a peasant passed, walking behind a small donkey loaded with two sacks of flour on his way back from the mill. Next Don Gennaro arrived, engaged in animated conversation with Don Luca, his brother, the parish priest of Orta. Not long before they had been seen in the distance at the gate of the Spina house.

One of the old men sitting behind the church rose to his feet and called out: "Hey, Don Gennaro, has it been signed yet?"

"Has what been signed?"

"Has Donna Maria Vincenza signed yet?"

"No, not yet," Don Gennaro replied. "She hasn't signed yet, but she certainly will tomorrow."

"She hasn't signed yet? Oh dear, oh dear, oh dear," the old men said laughing, as if awaking from their lethargy.

"The more you stroke a cat the more it sticks up its tail," one of them called out.

Everyone laughed again; they laughed painfully, as if they were coughing. Don Gennaro and his priestly brother disappeared behind the door of the sacristy. Simone the Weasel appeared, skipping along in an agile manner. He too, of course, came in search of news. The old men wrapped in their cloaks sitting on their little seats behind the church had difficulty in returning to their previous silence and immobility.

"He must be mad," one of them said, shaking his head. "Just imagine, he had plenty to eat and drink and a good bed. Would he have bothered about anything else if he hadn't been mad?"

"Perhaps he was mad when he left, but if he comes back now he must be even madder," said Simone the Weasel.

"If only the ship that brought me back from Argentina thirty years ago had been wrecked and sunk," another man said.

"My son has written to say that he wants to come back," said a third. "What an idea, I answered, just at a time when everyone would leave if only they could."

"But it's not the same thing. Your son left to escape from starving, but Donna Maria Vincenza's grandson lacked nothing."

"In other words, young Don Pietro left because he was crazy. It's easy to have crazy ideas when you're assured of bread and cheese and have a good bed."

"The rich often have ideas so fantastic that ordinary mortals can't begin to understand them."

"A horse has one way of thinking and a donkey has another. It has always been like that."

"A gentleman can afford to do anything, even if it's crazy, and then, if he changes his mind and doesn't like it, he can quietly go back home."

"If a *cafone* said half the things about the authorities that gentlemen say, he'd be jailed for life, that's certain."

"If a gentleman shoots a hare, he's a sportsman; if a *cafone* shoots a hare, he's a poacher."

"Game exists only for the gentry, that's an old story."

All this talk was not to the liking of Simone. "You're boring," he said.

"But why did he leave home? There was nothing to stop him from acting the madman here if he had wanted to."

"Yes, of course, if he had wanted to he could have acted the madman on behalf of the government here. Plenty of them are doing that already, and one more wouldn't have done any harm; and he would have been well paid into the bargain," Simone admitted contemptuously.

"But how can we tell? Perhaps he wanted to find out whether there's better bread than is made of wheat, better wine than is made of grapes, warmer flesh than women are made of. You never know."

"Ha, ha, ha, who knows what horrors he'll have found instead."

"But if he now accepts the government's pardon and wants to come back to Colle, it means he has found nothing better, that's certain."

"So you might as well stay where you are and save the train fare."

"He hasn't yet found a saddle for his back, that's the fact of the matter, he's an overage unbroken colt. If he had married . . ."

"A young horse can't stand flies; a single fly will send it off at a gallop."

"That's true, it's enough to think of Aunt Eufemia. At bottom it's the same story. And it's enough to think of Donna Faustina. And Simone here. How many scandals there have been during the past few years."

"It's an age of scandals."

"In any event, now he has been pardoned, and everything is returning to normal," Simone said, spitting on the ground. "You'll see that he too will end up as a government horse eating at the government manger. There's no point in wasting more words over it."

"Don't you think Donna Maria Vincenza's appeal for a pardon is a fake? In my opinion it's a stunt, thought up by that played-out old trombone Don Coriolano to make himself some money."

"Very likely, public speakers and *sbirri* and scribblers make a living by that sort of thing, that's an old story," Simone the Weasel concluded.

"St, st, st."

The wind had suddenly brought them a whiff of freshly baked bread, a good whiff of hot bread, and they seemed to see before their eyes the round four-pound loaves with a fine, crisp, golden crust and a soft, well-leavened inside. The very air seemed warmed by the odor. The poor old men promptly relapsed into silence and immobility, and one or two of them shut their eyes and actually smiled at the delicious smell and the little bit of sunshine; there wasn't very much of it, of course, but in winter it was better than nothing.

The smell of fresh bread and the sound of Anacleto's trumpet both came from a dark and squalid alleyway, encumbered with filth of every kind, which divided Colle vertically and mounted from the church halfway up the hill, where it reached the perimeter wall of the Spina house. Beyond the wall there was a vineyard from which the north wind was now sweeping the snow, uncovering the low, black vines that were twisted like frozen snakes; beyond the vineyard there was a row of skeleton-like fruit trees, and beyond that Donna Maria Vincenza's pink coral house with its ash-colored roof and windows. For some hours two persons had been working in the courtyard sweeping away the snow, Venanzio with a shovel and a wheelbarrow followed by Natalina with a broom. During the morning the girl had had to keep answering the bell and hurrying to the gate to deal with people who wanted to see Donna Maria Vincenza (some of them had actually come from Orta and Fossa). In accordance with orders, the girl let no one in.

"I'm sorry," she invariably replied, "I'm sorry you had to waste your breath coming all the way up here, but madam is not seeing anyone. No, she isn't ill, far from it, in fact, but she's tired, very tired. No, really, there's no point in insisting, people much more important than you have been ringing the bell all the morning and I didn't let them in, so I can't see why I should make an exception for you. I don't say that to offend you, of course, but simply to explain the position. You wanted to congratulate madam, did you say? Because of the signature? What signature? I assure you I know nothing whatever about it. On account of her grandson? What grandson do you mean? Yes, you had better go, you might have realized that sooner, but it doesn't matter. *Au revoir*, or rather good-bye, good-bye."

"You haven't got the manners of a real parlor maid, Natalina," Venanzio pointed out in some embarrassment.

"That's perfectly true, Venanzio, I can't deny it," Natalina admitted with a blush. "There is something ladylike about me, but I don't have the money to be a real lady."

All the shutters were closed and the house looked uninhabited. In an excess of caution Donna Maria Vincenza and her grandson had taken refuge in a room facing north on the third floor. Lunch, already cold and almost untouched, was still on the table in the middle of the room. On one side of the fireplace, in which a big log fire was burning, Donna Maria Vincenza lay as if in bed on a deep chaise longue with her head resting on cushions piled up behind her. She was wrapped in a long, heavy, red woolen blanket and seemed to be breathing with difficulty. Pietro squatted on the other side of the fireplace with his head and back resting against one of the posts. Both grandmother and grandson were obviously shattered, finished, exhausted, for they had just had things out, irreparably and once and for all. They might have been mourning, overwhelmed by some irremediable misfortune. They avoided each other's eyes, and for hours they had been silent, like persons who have been repeating the same arguments over and over again and know that it's useless to repeat them yet again. When Natalina came in to clear the table it was late afternoon. The girl started reeling off the names of the day's callers and describing the polite but firm manner in which she had prevented them from getting farther than the gate but, as Donna Maria Vincenza and Pietro paid her no attention, she stopped short in the middle of her story and left them alone. Later in the afternoon she brought her mistress a small cup of black coffee and the grandson a small bowl of nuts and a glass of wine. As soon as she entered the room she noticed a strong smell of burned wool and discovered that the edge of Pietro's jacket had been scorched. He rose and agreed to change his jacket without resistance. As the girl refused to allow him to squat on the edge of the fireplace again, he sat on a cushion near his grandmother. After a while, he rested his head on her lap as if he were tired. One of her white, cold hands, which held rosary beads, hung like an inanimate object next to the arm of the chaise longue. He took it and pressed it between his burning hands.

"My poor boy," Donna Maria Vincenza murmured in a tired and resigned voice. "What a hard fate you have chosen. What a grievous cross. Hitherto I at least had the illusion that one day you might free yourself from it. Now I no longer have even that hope."

"Do you think that a man should free himself from what you call his cross, Grandmother?"

"Oh, my dear boy, I know very well that pain can never be eliminated from birth and love and death. But the cross you bear you chose for yourself."

"Do you believe that there can be such a thing as complete freedom of choice about the kind of life one leads, Grandmother? I say that though I don't believe in fate."

He spoke slowly, pondering every word.

"Perhaps everyone," he went on, "depending on the material of which he is made, attracts to himself from his earliest years the decisive experiences that put their imprint on his soul, cause Peter to be Peter and not Paul. There are sorrows that draw to themselves all the strength of one's being, all one's vital energies, and they remain fixed and articulated inside us like the backbone in the body, the threads in a fabric. You can destroy the threads, but not without destroying the fabric."

"Can't the threads be used to weave a less gloomy fabric?"

"And become something different? But that's another way of dying. Don't imagine, Grandmother, that compared to the alternative that is offered me I live a life of self-sacrifice. Perhaps the most serious charge that can be made against the outlaw's way of life is that it's an easy, an only too easy and comfortable one. Apart from some material inconveniences and risks that should not be taken tragically, it's so easy for the outlaw to say no to everything, never to say anything but no. Actually I have never completely rid myself of the suspicion that my stubborn insistence on a life of illegality might be the result of my preference for comfort and security, and perhaps also of my laziness. An outlawed revolutionary, you see, is in the ideal state of a Christian in a monastery. He has burned the bridges with the enemy and the enemy's vulgar allurements, has declared open war on him, and lives according to his own law."

"O Lord," Donna Maria murmured with her eyes full of tears, "is it You or Your enemy who puts these ideas into the head of this poor boy of mine?"

8

"Lo, THE TIME OF AFFLICTIONS has come, Severino, the time of sorrow and bewilderment," said Donna Maria Vincenza. "Forgive me for receiving you in the kitchen, but at this time of day we are least likely to be disturbed here, and also it's less cold. For the past two days I haven't been able even to pray. You're a man, and you can't appreciate what that means to a poor soul like mine that needs prayer just as the body needs food. I feel as weak and exhausted as if I hadn't eaten for days. I feel there's a great void inside me, and in the middle of the void an acute pain such as I have never felt before, almost as if I had a knife right through me."

"My dear Maria Vincenza," Don Severino said, "I have always regarded you, I have always thought of you, as the only happy person I know. I can't tell you how painful it is to me to hear you talk like this."

"Happy? Oh, how ironic that word now sounds in connection with me. What with thinking about it continually, night and day, the distress I feel because of that poor boy of mine is turning into a monstrous, overwhelming reality, linking up with the sorrows of my whole lifetime, relegating memories of serene and happy times to the obscure corners of my mind, and giving a different color, a different imprint, a different meaning to the whole of my life. And I'm alone, alone and abandoned by everyone, like Our Lady of Sorrows in the Good Friday procession."

"But what about your relatives?" said Don Severino. "And all the people whom you have helped and protected?"

The old lady made a disconsolate gesture.

"That's the real revolution of our time, my dear Maria Vincenza, the disappearance of friendship," Don Severino went on. "It's the most terrible of all revolutions. The place of friendship has now been taken by so-called connections, which last just as long as they are convenient. The breaking of my friendship with Don Luca is more painful to me than any other loss I have suffered in my life, but I'm very much afraid that to him it doesn't matter one way or the other. That suspicion fills me with dread."

"Thank you, Severino, for having come to see me so promptly. It grieves me that at a time that is so sad for you I should be in distress myself. It's true, alas, that the heart is more important than blood and that, if I'd sent for you and confided my secret to you straightaway instead of turning to my relatives, your advice would have saved me from many false steps and humiliations."

Donna Maria Vincenza wore a white apron like an ordinary housewife with a black woolen shawl over her shoulders. Every so often while speaking she stopped and shut her eyes, holding the sides of her armchair as if she were dizzy and needed support. She rose slowly to her feet to make coffee for her guest. Don Severino De Sanctis, the organist of the church at Orta, was sitting on the other side of the fireplace, and he watched the old lady's every movement; he kept blinking, and his eyes were full of affection and concern. He was growing more and more worried, and two or three times he made a gesture as if to go to her aid, make her a sworn promise, or shout something compromising, but he did not know what to say. He might have been about sixty, and was dressed in the old-fashioned style that still prevailed in some places in the mountains: a long, light, tight-fitting dark blue overcoat with

frayed wrists and shiny elbows tightly enclosed his slender body
and shoulders, which were now a little bent; his thin neck, except
for his prominent Adam's apple, was invisible behind a high
winged collar, and his elastic-sided boots came up over his ankles.
A thin and mangy hunting dog lay curled up at his feet, asleep.

"You know my relatives, Severino, they're not at all bad people,"
Donna Maria Vincenza went on. "On the contrary, on minor occasions, in everyday matters, they're generally scrupulously honest and
decent. But when any risk is involved all of them without exception
let one down. There's not one of them that can be relied on."

"Sanctimoniousness and cowardice are now in fashion, my
dear Maria Vincenza, and they go well together. Combined with
mental reservations about one's good intentions, they are a better
preservative than alcohol," Don Severino went on, stretching out
his hands toward the fire. "My dog stinks, my dear Maria Vincenza, but it looks so happy by the fire that I haven't the courage
to put it out into the courtyard. Sanctimoniousness and cowardice, my dear Maria Vincenza, offer the soul the security enjoyed by a canned peach. We must resign ourselves; perhaps we're
the last specimens of a species destined to extinction."

"The last? Do you really think we're the last?" Donna Maria
Vincenza asked.

Don Severino, seized with sudden excitement, turned to her
and said in an undertone: "Could I talk to the boy? I've simply got
to talk to him. My life has suddenly become intolerable to me,
and if I too don't do something, my dear Maria Vincenza, I shall
go mad."

"What's the use of piling craziness on craziness, Severino?"
Donna Maria Vincenza replied. "All my life, as you know, I've disliked having politics discussed in my presence, and I've never mingled with the authorities. Why is it the Lord's will that at the very
end of my life I should have to associate with those scoundrels?"

"If only they were real scoundrels, complete scoundrels," Don
Severino exclaimed. "The trouble, my dear Maria Vincenza, is
that all of them are only half rascals, small and petty, lukewarm
rascals, of the kind that make God feel sick. For years and years,

my dear Maria Vincenza, I've been looking for a real, complete ruffian, and I haven't found one."

In his excitement Don Severino had raised his voice a little, and he fell silent at the sound of footsteps outside the door.

"But why should I have had to approach such people right at the end of my life?" Donna Maria Vincenza went on. "And is it my fault if, having no experience in these matters, I make stupid mistakes? I assure you, Severino, that when I sent that clown Don Coriolano to Rome I had nothing dishonorable in mind. I thought it legitimate to sell the wool to save the sheep, as the saying is. In our families mothers have often gotten their sons out of trouble. I believe that's why mothers stay alive after their children have grown up. Otherwise why should they? A grown-up son, even after he has married, is perfectly capable of momentarily re-turning to childhood and committing the wildest actions, some-times even seriously wild actions; and then his mother intervenes and tries to clear things up. Severino, I hope you won't mind my saying that your life would have been very different if your mother hadn't died in the earthquake."

Don Severino made a gesture and a disconsolate grimace to conceal his sudden agitation. "My misfortune was a different one," he murmured.

"And how was I to imagine," Donna Maria Vincenza went on, "that nowadays there can be remedies worse than the disease? I can't make head or tail of it all. Particularly, if I'm to tell you frankly what I think, because I can't think of Pietro as a scapegrace. Things would actually be easier if he were. But in fact he's the op-posite. To tell you the truth, I was in a state of trepidation before I saw him again. I was expecting to see, if not actually a gasoline bomber or a terrorist with a knife between his teeth, at least an ill-mannered, vulgarized human being. But the poor boy (and it's this that I can't understand) has remained exactly as he was at the age of fifteen. He still has the sensitivity, the shyness, the delicacy, even the modesty, that he had when he was a boy. But while at that time none of us, not even his mother, could see through him and we could not even guess whether a certain obstinate reserve was due to his delicate health or to a lack of intelligence, now he is as transparent, as open, as wide open, I might say, as a melon cut in half. He reminds me of a poor pilgrim carrying his bare soul in his hands. Just imagine a creature like that in politics, Severino. If only I could get him away from his fixed idea, his fanaticism. But I don't even dare to talk about it."

Don Severino had drawn still closer to the fire; his hands rested on a small black walking stick with an ivory handle and his chin rested on his hands. He gazed at the fire and smiled slightly at some vision in his mind. His wet ankleboots steamed in the warmth. His lively face, reddened by the reflection of the fire, contrasted strangely with his gray hair.

"Perhaps it's not a matter of political fanaticism," he plucked up courage to say. "Or, if I'm to judge by the little you've told me about him, perhaps it's so only in appearance. (As usual, Maria Vincenza, your coffee is excellent.) There's a kind of sadness, Maria Vincenza, a subtle kind of sadness that must not be confused with the more ordinary kind that's the result of remorse, disappointment, or suffering; there's a kind of intimate sadness and hopelessness that attaches itself for preference to chosen souls. Your son Saverio, if I'm not mistaken, suffered from that kind of sadness, it was his secret, and I remember well that throughout his life he tried in vain to shake it off. And besides, let us be frank, Maria Vincenza, if we calmly and thoroughly consider our lives, we see that there's little to be cheerful about, as you will agree. That kind of sadness has always been very prevalent among sensitive individuals in this part of the world. Once upon a time, to avoid suicide or madness, they entered monasteries. The question why monasteries no longer serve that purpose would be a serious theme for religious meditation."

"Might there not be a simpler, more immediate, more remediable reason for the secret sadness of which you speak, Severino? It seems to me," Donna Maria Vincenza said, "that it would be possible to live so peacefully and contentedly, if not always happily, if children stayed at home with their mothers, or at any rate did not go very far from home."

Don Severino made a gesture implying that she was talking about a mythical age, but Donna Maria Vincenza did not notice it and went on recalling the time when every evening, when work was over, she gathered the family around her and the servants around them, like a hen gathering its chicks under its wings. When they were all present she intoned the evening prayer and the others with bared heads chanted the responses; and when the prayer was over, if there had been a quarrel or any kind of misunderstanding or incident during the day, she would speak of it without beating around the bush and try to establish the facts, and she would allow no one, not even her husband, to go to bed until all misunderstandings and grudges had been cleared up.

"In that ancient way of life of ours there was obviously not very much scope for the devil," she went on. "So he did everything he could to separate what had been created to stay together, and now we see the disastrous consequences, one of which is the hopeless and inconsolable sadness of which you speak."

But Don Severino showed vigorous and repeated signs of disagreement, and he was so excited that when he jumped to his feet he banged his head hard against the mantelpiece. Donna Maria Vincenza anxiously tried to find out whether he had hurt himself, but Don Severino, red in the face and embarrassed by the absurdity of the incident, would not let her. He insisted that he had a hard head and indeed commiserated with the mantelpiece, and then hastened to express his disagreement.

"You forget, my dear Maria Vincenza," he said, "you forget that every scoundrel, or rather, to be accurate, every semi-scoundrel, every semi-demi-scoundrel, invariably justifies his depravity by concern for his family. On the other hand, you also know that families are often put into turmoil, not by the devil, but by Someone Else who Himself declared He had come into the world to divide what blood united, to separate son from father, daughter from mother, daughter-in-law from mother-in-law, and if there were five in a house He would set three against two and two against three. That was Someone who was very different from the devil, and was far from being evil, Maria Vincenza."

"Yes, you are quite right. Someone did say that, and the creatures He prefers and leads away are lost to normal family life. But how is it possible that I should now be reduced to such a state of confusion that I can no longer tell right from wrong? Though I think about it every day, actually I can't tell you whether that boy of mine is a saint or a damned soul, and I honestly don't know whether I'm doing good or evil with my complaints about him. That is what I'm reduced to."

"As you can well imagine, Maria Vincenza, I'm in an even greater state of perplexity. Perhaps the clandestine sects about which there is so much talk nowadays are the new remedies against despair."

The dog at Don Severino's feet began shuddering and complaining, sighing and squealing in its sleep.

"Is it ill?" Donna Maria Vincenza asked.

"No, it's dreaming," Don Severino whispered to avoid waking it.

"Won't you stay and have dinner with me?" Donna Maria Vincenza suggested. "Though it will have to be a very simple one."

"Thank you, Maria Vincenza, said Don Severino, "but I'm expected by Lazzaro Tarò, yes, by that boor. I go and see him once a year to collect the rent for a piece of land. I see that I'm already late."

Don Severino looked for his hat and his stick. Donna Maria Vincenza prepared to accompany him to the door, but noticed a strange hesitation on his part.

"Has your grandson heard about the dreadful death of Cristina Colamartini? It seems that her remains were found on the Pietrasecca mountain."

"I mentioned the unhappy girl only once," Donna Maria Vincenza said, "and he looked at me with such horror that it took my breath away."

Don Severino remained standing by the door.

"Before I go," he said finally, "there's something that weighs terribly on my mind that I want to talk to you about. As perhaps you know, Maria Vincenza, Faustina has been living in my house for some time."

Donna Maria Vincenza's face darkened at the mention of that

name, and to prevent Don Severino from noticing it she turned
her back on him and began putting some things away in a basket.

"Faustina wanted to come here with me today," Don Severino
went on in a voice trembling with emotion. "She wanted to accompany me. Actually it was she who suggested it. After the scene
with Don Luca she said to me: now we have no one left but
Donna Maria Vincenza. In fact she came with me from Orta to
Colle. But at the last moment, when she set eyes on your house,
her courage failed her and she went back alone and insisted on
my coming without her."

Donna Maria Vincenza carried the basket into the entrance
hall, and Don Severino followed. He was humble, embarrassed,
and agitated.

"I implore you to listen to me," he said. "You cannot imagine
what I would give to make you believe me. Faustina has never
ceased to love you, in fact to venerate you, and she wants me to
tell you that in any emergency, even the most dangerous, she will
always be at your disposal, like a daughter or, if that is presumptuous, like a servant. I know, Maria Vincenza, that you could
make her happy."

"Oh, Severino," Donna Maria Vincenza said, turning toward
him with tears in her eyes, "to heal one wound is it necessary to
reopen another?"

Don Severino put on his hat and left without saying good-bye,
dragging his sleepy dog behind him.

The gathering shadows mounted rapidly from the misty plain toward the snow-covered hills. They filled the ditches with pitch and
the alleyways of the village with soot and covered the roofs and vegetable patches with ashes. The air was damp and sad. The narrow
road that led from the Spina house down toward the church was
covered with wind-driven snow, and Mastro Eutimio was sitting on
a chair outside the door of his carpenter's shop with his little hat
perched boatwise across his head and his gnarled hands on his
knees. He had taken off his working clothes and put on a dark blue
suit, and before closing his shop he was taking the air in spite of the

cold and saying good evening to the passersby. A small fire of chippings and shavings was burning on the ground beside him, and the work he had finished that day was propped against the wall behind him. This was a massive oak cross, more than twelve feet high and painted black. When the Lenten sermons were over it was going to be carried in procession and erected on one of the peaks overlooking Colle, which was known to the people of the neighborhood as the Dead Donkey Mountain. The Lenten preacher intended it to be a solemn ceremony of repentance for the deplorable scandals of which the whole neighborhood had recently been the scene. The urgent necessity of the new cross had struck him on the day of his arrival at Colle, since a critical glance at the peaks in the area showed that one of them still lacked the symbol of the Redemption. Mastro Eutimio had finished the cross two weeks early.

This had exposed him to a rebuke from the parish priest, Don Marco. "Why the hurry?" he asked. "Where am I to put it in the meantime?"

"It must be given time to get acclimatized," Mastro Eutimio tried to explain, speaking politely but with confidence. "A cross, even if it's made of oak, is always a very delicate thing. You couldn't possibly take it up to the top of the mountain overnight. If it weren't made of wood, of course, it wouldn't be a matter on which it would be appropriate for a carpenter to instruct a priest."

"Very well, but where am I to put it in the meantime?" Don Marco replied irritably. "We have plenty of crosses in the parish already."

"Oh, did you think I wanted to hand it over right away? Nothing of the sort," Mastro Eutimio assured him. "I'll hand it over on the day for which it was ordered. Meanwhile I'll keep it here, leaning against the wall of the shop, with arms extended. It will be able to look at the mountain it's intended for, it will get to know the people passing by, and, if it likes, it will be able to watch me working. Wasn't He a carpenter in His youth? Might He not like the smell of wood and glue better than incense?"

"Do whatever you like," Don Marco replied, shrugging his shoulders, and off he went.

The little fire of chippings and shavings against the yellowed wall of the shop created an atmosphere of austere friendship, a family atmosphere, between the big black-painted cross and old Mastro Eutimio in his rough dark blue suit.

"Oh, Mastro Eutimio," Don Severino exclaimed, pointing to the cross with his stick from the middle of the road, "whom do you want to nail to that fearful gibbet?"

The carpenter raised his head, smiled, and blushed.

"If it depended on me, Don Severino, or, let us be frank and say, if it depended on us, if Pontius Pilate returned and summoned the district council and asked us in the name of the government who should be crucified, well, it's certain that this time that scoundrel Barabbas wouldn't get away with it."

"Excuse me, but I'm not so sure," replied Don Severino, suddenly growing serious. "Don't misunderstand me, I don't want to offend you, but frankly I have my doubts. Do you think your fellow villagers would find it easy to tell Christ from Barabbas?"

Don Severino's appearance, voice, and gestures were those of a man in a fever.

"Oh, Don Severino, I know very well you like joking," Mastro Eutimio said. "I know that you often like painting the devil on the wall in order to frighten us, but this time you're going too far. Are you being serious? It's like saying we can't distinguish bread from stones. It's true that we're poor people and not well educated, but we too were baptized, we too, so to speak, received discernment from the hand of the priest who marked our brows with the blessed salt. I don't mention the three churches we have in Colle, or the parish church that has existed for centuries, or the martyrs who are buried in them. But everything here, the animals, the air, the water, the earth, the wine, the ashes, the oil, and the dust of the streets, everything is Christian, so to speak. Oh, you're laughing, and I see you were only joking."

"No, I was not," Don Severino said, "and forgive me if your reply has not completely convinced me. Are you sure, Mastro Eutimio, that the choice of the people of Colle would be for Jesus and against Barabbas even if Barabbas arrived here on horseback in full uniform, with his breast covered with decorations, at the head of a legion of armed men, and was acclaimed by a host of liveried servants, scribes, and party notables and orators and priests, and if Jesus were shown to you between two policemen looking like an ordinary mortal, a fugitive, an outlaw, a stateless person without any kind of papers? It's a simple question, a question I often put to myself, but now I should like to hear your answer."

The fire of chippings and shavings had gone out, leaving nothing but a small pile of ashes, and the shades of evening had now reached the carpenter's shop. Mastro Eutimio scratched his chin, looked down at the ground, and remained thoughtful, while Don Severino watched him, smiling.

"Your question is actually its own answer, the most humiliating of answers," Mastro Eutimio finally confessed. "Excuse me, but can I come with you a little way? You mustn't leave me like this."

Mastro Eutimio closed his shop, and before walking away with Don Severino and the dog, cast an embarrassed glance at the cross.

"I ought to be going to Don Lazzaro Tarò's house," Don Severino said, "and actually I'm late already, but it will be a pleasure to go a little way with you, if it's no trouble to you. I don't feel well, I need a little fresh air."

They took a path that led out of the village, looking all around to see if anyone were watching them.

"My nerves are strangely on edge this evening," Don Severino said, "and a trifle is sufficient almost to make me weep like a child. Before I reached your shop, Mastro Eutimio, I was actually talking to the dog, telling it how wretched I felt, but don't suppose I'm excessively fond of animals. Actually they get on my nerves, and their aspect as degenerate human beings positively revolts me. But there are times when a human being feels the need to talk, to confide in someone, to have a witness, and then a dog or, if no animal is available, even a tree will do. But don't let me detain you; no doubt your wife is waiting for you on the doorstep and the soup is already on the table."

Mastro Eutimio smiled with two bright, gentle, boyish eyes, and bent down to stroke the dog. "I'm only a poor workman, an

uneducated carpenter," he said, "and when I was a boy my only
teacher was hunger, so I can't tell you how touched I am by what
you say. Don Severino, I don't think it was just chance that
guided your footsteps to my shop this evening. During the day,
while I was working on that cross that you saw, I several times had
a strange sense of anxiety that I could not explain; I felt that something wonderful was going to happen to me. I too sometimes find
myself talking to tables."

The two walked a little way in silence, almost in embarrassment, and Mastro Eutimio looked nervously all around, as if he
were afraid of being caught doing something unusual.

"If you knew," Don Severino said, "to what extent the contempt I publicly profess for scoundrels makes me feel the need of
the company of persons worthy of respect. But we've reached a
point at which two individuals, if they saw each other often
without being related or earning a living in the same way or at
least sharing a vice, would immediately arouse the suspicions of
neighbors and the authorities."

Mastro Eutimio again looked around nervously and suspiciously.

"Would you like to hear what I was telling the dog?" Don Severino said.

Mastro Eutimio replied with a courteous and humble gesture
as if to say: if you think I'm worthy of it.

"As a result of a public petition," Don Severino went on, "I
have been dismissed from the post of organist of the church at
Orta. Poor Don Luca himself came and told me so this morning.
I tried to cheer him up. Come, come, I said, it's not an irreparable
loss, either for the parish or for me. But the trouble is, he said, that
now we no longer have an excuse to see each other. Why not? I
asked. You can go on coming to see me as before. But in that case,
what am I to tell people? he pointed out. Exactly, what could he
tell people? He could perhaps say that he was calling on me out of
friendship, and perhaps the old men and women of the parish
would understand; but the boys, the girls, the devotees of San
Luigi Gonzaga, the Children of Mary, bless their innocent souls,
would say: friendship? What's that? And they would be shocked.

Poor Don Luca was certainly thinking of the terrible curse laid by Jesus on those who shock the innocent, and he must have feared for the salvation of their souls."

"They asked me for my signature too," Mastro Eutimio said. "People frequently call with a piece of paper asking for signatures. I'm sorry, I always tell them, but I'm only a carpenter."

"I wouldn't want you to get into any trouble on my account," said Don Severino. "Should they come back to you on my account, give them your signature."

"Talk more quietly," Mastro Eutimio murmured.

The two were overtaken by Don Nicolino, the clerk of the local magistrate's court. He had been hurrying, and was panting and sweating.

"What have you been telling this poor carpenter in such lugubrious tones, Severino?" he said with a grin. "Have you been ordering your coffin?"

The two stopped to allow the man to pass by.

"Don't let us detain you," Don Severino said, pointing to the way ahead.

"I'm not in a hurry. In fact I'm not going anywhere in particular," Don Nicolino replied.

"Don't let me detain you," Don Severino repeated with exaggerated politeness, again pointing to the way ahead.

Don Nicolino was taken aback. "Am I in the way?" he asked ironically. "I wouldn't have supposed that an organist and a carpenter had secrets. How's your girl, Severino? I don't want to boast," he added, stroking his chin, "but she'd be my type too."

"Go on with your walk, then," Don Severino interrupted him. "Good-bye."

Don Nicolino would have liked to express his resentment at this, but the two men turned their backs on him, and he was left stranded in the middle of the road.

"You see?" Mastro Eutimio murmured, upset and red in the face. "You see?"

9

ON SEVERINO, MASTRO Eutimio, and the dog walked back in silence. Outside the sacristy Don Severino heard the parish priest, Don Marco, calling him at the top of his voice. Don Marco, who was already in surplice and stole for the evening service, came halfway to meet him, and took him aside to talk to him without being overheard.

"Have you been to Donna Maria Vincenza's?" he asked in an undertone. "Did you see her? Did she tell you what gave her the crazy idea of refusing the government pardon for her grandson? Just imagine letting slip an opportunity like that. But it's not that that I'm worried about; I've too many troubles of my own to worry about those of other people. But you can't imagine the wicked slanders that Don Coriolano is spreading about the Lenten preacher. He accuses Father Gabriele of having instigated Donna Maria Vincenza's absurd, crazy, stupid decision. He's actually threatening to denounce him to the police authorities. Excuse me, Mastro Eutimio, can't you see that I want to talk to Don Severino? Couldn't you leave us alone?"

Candlelight from the windows of the sacristy shone on the

priest's head and made his eyes shine — his round, frightened, white rabbit's eyes that lacked eyebrows and were lined with red. His white surplice completed his clumsy resemblance to a big white rabbit outside its hutch. After some hesitation, Mastro Eutimio shook Don Severino's hand and took his departure.

"Do you see?" he murmured. "Do you see?"

"I'll come and see you later," Don Severino promised to console him. "Your Father Gabriele doesn't interest me," he added dryly, turning to the priest.

But the latter was not to be put off. "Promise me that if you meet Don Coriolano you'll talk to him and try to get him to see reason," he went on. "He knows the local families himself, but remind him that the Spinas have never needed anyone to encourage them in their acts of madness. Oh, Severino, how peacefully we could all live with a little mutual consideration, a little respect for the authorities, a little fear of God . . ."

"Ha, ha, ha," Don Severino exclaimed, breaking into an irreverent laugh. "What you want, Don Marco, strikes me as being too much like a recipe in a cookbook. Take a little olive oil, a little onion, a little parsley, a little tomato, and serve warm."

Don Marco's attention was abruptly diverted by the appearance of a strange-looking man who emerged from the shadow of the bell tower, approached slowly, and then stopped a few paces away.

"What, are you here again?" the priest shouted at him in evident revulsion and alarm. "What do you want? Who are you? Where do you come from?"

The unknown stranger's appearance was unusual even for a *cafone*. He was of indefinable age, tall, thin, strong, but clumsy and awkward looking; he was dressed in rags and tatters like a beggar who generally slept in a muddy ditch; he was hatless, and there was an alarming expression on his face. His gnarled, stiff head was surmounted by a thicket of tousled hair, he had a prickly ten-day-old beard, and there was a possessed look in his eyes, halfway between that of a holy hermit and a man possessed by the devil; he was barefoot, and his feet were black, huge, and ill proportioned.

"This man has been following me, watching me, circling

around me without saying a word ever since this morning," the priest explained to Don Severino without taking his eyes off him for a moment. "You'll agree that I have good reason to be worried. Do you know him, by any chance? Have you ever seen him at Orta? The *carabinieri* here have already stopped him and told him to go away and never again set foot in Colle. But here he is back again."

Don Severino went up to the man, looked at him, and said: "Who are you? What do you want? Do you need anything?"

But the stranger remained silent and motionless. The dog had been circling him, and when it wagged its tail and sniffed his feet the stranger stroked it and a strange grimace that might have been a smile appeared on his face.

"He must be hungry," Don Severino said, going back to the priest. "Or he has lost his memory. Or he's dumb."

"The *carabinieri* have already searched him," Don Marco said mistrustfully. "They even stripped him, but all they found on him was a piece of bread and a knife."

"Oh, a knife," said Don Severino in a voice of exaggerated concern. "An old knife? A well-sharpened knife? Poor Don Marco, may the Lord protect you."

"Are you trying to frighten me? The sergeant assured me that he confiscated the knife," Don Marco said, seizing Don Severino by the arm.

"He won't have had any difficulty in laying his hand on another one," said Don Severino. "Or a billhook, or a well-sharpened pruning hook, it's so easy. Don't you read the papers? Inexplicable crimes occur every day."

"But what can I do about it?" said the priest. "Shall I send for the *carabinieri* again?"

"Get yourself a knife and defend yourself, in heaven's name," Don Severino exclaimed in a harsh and provocative tone. "That's the only advice that one gentleman can give another. Let me go."

"You forget I'm a priest," said Don Marco, holding his arm.

"Can't one be both a priest and a gentleman?" Don Severino said.

602 ❖ IGNAZIO SILONE

"You forget that the *carabinieri* are responsible for the defense of unarmed civilians. What do we pay taxes for? For moonlight, perhaps? In short, there's nothing for it but to send for the *carabinieri* again."

Meanwhile a number of people had gathered to look at the unusual stranger: gaunt, yellowish *cafoni* with their hats worn sideways on their heads as a token of defiance; prematurely exhausted little women looking like black, greasy bundles; serious boys looking like little men; and a few old men wrapped in black cloaks. A small crowd showed the natural curiosity of the poor at the sight of someone poorer than themselves, and surrounded and questioned him. The little square was like a stage invaded by a ragged chorus.

"He must have come for the sermon," someone said. "He too must have his sins that need forgiveness, what's strange about that?"

"Hey, you, is your sin gluttony?" someone else called out. "Do you want to be forgiven for overeating?"

"He must have come to beg for alms outside the church after the sermon," someone else said. "Begging's a job like any other."

"Of course, of course, we can't all be bankers, it would be too boring," said a fourth man.

"Have you got your beggar's license?" asked Simone the Weasel. "You can't be a beggar anymore unless you have a license. And for every penny you take," he went on, "you have to give a receipt with a twopenny stamp. That's the law."

Two *carabinieri* arrived and made their way through the throng. They wasted no time on idle words but resolutely took hold of the stranger and set about taking him away with the naturalness of two road sweepers collecting rubbish. But the man resisted; he was like a firmly rooted tree, and the *carabinieri* managed only to shake him, just as a tree is shaken but not uprooted and taken away. As soon as the two *carabinieri* appeared the spectators scattered in all directions, like mice on the appearance of a cat. The unusual resistance put up by this unknown down-and-out created a frightening atmosphere of revolt in the little square. Many took refuge in the church, others made a dash for the nearest houses, doors and windows were hurriedly shut, and in the distance women were to be heard calling their husbands in loud and wailing tones, appealing to them to keep out of trouble and not get involved, to be careful not to compromise themselves or forget their children, those already born and those who were still to come. Don Severino and the priest took refuge in the sacristy. Don Marco, pale and sweating, said: "Do you think they'll maltreat him? Do you think they'll do him any harm?"

"Good gracious no, what an idea," Don Severino assured him. "You know very well how kind they always are. You'll see, Don Marco, they'll give him a wash and brush up, shave him, and comb his hair, and perhaps they'll even offer him coffee and biscuits."

"You know I didn't send for them so that they should beat him up. You yourself are my witness. I sent for them only so that they should send him away from Colle. Do you really think that they'll beat him up?"

Meanwhile in the now-deserted square the two *carabinieri* were sweating and working on the unlucky wretch with the patience, tenacity, and naturalness of two woodsmen. They kicked his shins hard with their hobnailed boots, and every so often they went back to shaking him to find out whether he was giving in yet. Eventually they got the better of him and managed to move him, and then dragged him away like an uprooted tree trunk. Doors and windows started opening again, people came out of church, and a small procession of curious sympathizers formed up behind the captive. The *carabinieri* with their prey and the procession behind them crossed the square and went down the alleyway that led to the *carabiniere* barracks, preceded by Don Severino's dog, which snarled and barked.

"But what harm has the wretch done?" Don Severino called out so as to be overheard by everyone. "Has he stolen anything? Has he killed anyone?"

"It's the usual suspect," Simone the Weasel explained at the top of his voice. "He's obviously too badly dressed and too poor, how could he possibly not be suspect?"

"Of course. Hey, you, why didn't you come in a carriage?"

604 ❖   IGNAZIO SILONE

someone called out to him. "Why didn't you come in a morning coat and top hat?"

One of the *carabinieri* turned and shouted angrily: "What do you people want? What are you, for instance, doing here, I should like to know?"

"Me?" Simone the Weasel replied. "Why ask me? Why pick on me?"

"Why are you following us? Why don't you go your own way?" the *carabiniere* repeated threateningly.

"For the poor there's no such thing as going out of the way," Simone answered.

"You're not really poor, you're just a fraud," the *carabiniere* answered, "and if you go on like this prison won't be out of your way."

"It's a way to which I'm no stranger. I was born down there at the corner."

"Flies prefer the naked and the ragged," an old man remarked.

"Crows nab worms," someone else said. "That's the courage of crows."

The small procession broke up, and only Don Severino's dog followed the prisoner and the two *carabinieri* all the way to the barracks.

10

*A*FTER VAINLY CALLING and looking for his dog Don Severino hurried to Don Lazzaro Tarò's house. Donna Palmira, pale, dark, in her Sunday best, and with an expression of bitter satisfaction on her face, received him at the top of the stairs.

"Welcome, Don Severino, you're as timely as grated cheese on macaroni. Poor Don Coriolano's in the next room, go and cheer him up."

"Cheese? If I were cheese, Donna Palmira, I'd be afraid of your fingernails."

"Oh, of course, you have a young lady of good family at home with velvety hands and painted nails. You act like a bear in its den, Don Severino, but it can't be so dull if there's a young she-bear there to entertain you."

Don Lazzaro came to meet his guest, making the floor tremble. "And he's quite right, of course, isn't he?" he said in that loud voice of his. "Good evening, Severì, how are you? Come in, and don't take any notice of envious old women. It's wrong of you to act as if you were living the life of a hermit in the desert, but for the rest, how well I understand you. The older a man gets and the weaker his teeth, the greater his need of tender flesh."

"Come into the kitchen, it's warmer there," Donna Palmira repeated. "And please say something kind to poor Don Coriolano, who's in despair after being let down by Donna Maria Vincenza."

"I can't stay, I'm afraid," Don Severino said. "I just came for the rent of that little bit of land of mine."

"Is it true you've lost the organist's job?" Donna Palmira asked. "We're very, very sorry."

"I was relieved of it as a result of a public petition," said Don Severino. "My scandalous conduct was considered incompatible with the post of parish organist. Among the signatures, incidentally, were yours."

"Who told you that?" Donna Palmira exclaimed indignantly. "Don Severino, you surprise me."

"It's true that Don Nicolino, the clerk of the court, came here with a sheet of paper," Don Lazzaro admitted. "How could we refuse him our signatures? It would have landed us in all sorts of trouble."

"Of course," Don Severino said. "What you did was quite right and quite natural."

The kitchen was dark, low, and wide. Hanging from parallel horizontal poles under the ceiling were hams, salami, sausages, cheeses, strings of onions, garlic, peppers, sorb apples, and mushrooms that had been put there to dry. Copper kettles, pots and pans, casseroles, grills, and coffeepots filled the whole wall facing the fire and reflected it. A rich and pungent smell came from the top of the stove. Don Coriolano lay on a big chair near the fire, with his legs and arms dangling; he was grim and distraught, with purple cheeks and eyes closed under his heavy brows. Accompanied by the master and mistress of the house, Don Severino stopped and watched him for a moment with pleasure and amusement. He then made him an exaggeratedly deep bow and addressed him with tongue-in-cheek solemnity: "*Cavaliere*, most influential of orators, my profound obeisance."

Don Lazzaro's big, bearded face split open and disintegrated

into a grotesque grimace, while Donna Palmira stuffed her handkerchief into her mouth to stifle her laughter and was seized with
a violent fit of coughing. Don Coriolano opened his eyes, but remained impassive; his thoughts were far away.

"Bewitching orator," Don Severino went on, repeating his
grotesque bows, "generous distributor of unwanted pardons, why
so downcast?"

Don Coriolano sluggishly raised his hand and made a gesture
as if to drive away a fly. He contracted his big lips into a fish
mouth and spat in the fire. "Have you any news of Don Marcantonio?" he said. "Hasn't he been seen at Colle? I know he's going
around gathering evidence against me."

A ragged fellow, Don Lazzaro's stableboy, appeared at the
door. "Jesus be praised," he said. "Is what they say true, sir?"

"What do you want to know?" Don Lazzaro growled at him.

"Whether it's true what they say."

"But what do they say?" Don Lazzaro growled again.

"About the signature? Is it true? Did she refuse it?"

"Everybody knows that, get the hell out of here. Is there anything else you want to know?"

"So it's true, then?" said the stableboy. "But it seems almost incredible."

"What's incredible?" asked Donna Palmira, who had gone to
fetch a chair from the next room.

"What they say."

"But what do they say?"

"About the signature. Did she really refuse it?"

"Get out," Don Lazzaro shouted. "Yes, it's true, it's true,
everyone knows it."

"So it is true, then?" said the stableboy. "But it seems impossible. Nothing so scandalous has ever happened before."

Don Coriolano undid the last button of his vest and the first of
his trousers; his pride was deeply wounded, and he felt sick and
disgusted. "To think that such a thing should happen to me," he
murmured as if he were dying. "To a man like me."

Donna Palmira poured oil on the fire. "*Cavaliere*, do you really want to know whose fault it is?" she asked him in a shrill and aggressive tone. "Shall I tell you frankly?"

"I'm not interested."

"Well, if you really want to know, I'll tell you. It's entirely your own fault. The fact of the matter is that you're too kind, too warmhearted. After an affront like that anyone else in your position would draw the consequences, but you . . . Forgive the indiscretion, but permit me to ask what action you propose to take against the Spinas."

Don Coriolano nodded to signify agreement and repeated a number of times in the sad and sorrowful tones of a man admitting a well-known but incurable defect or vice: "Yes, I was born too kind, too generous, too idealistic. But how can I help it? It's my nature."

Emotion took him by the throat. Don Severino seemed to have an inspiration. "I've heard it said," he suggested, sitting down with a friendly gesture at the orator's side, "I've heard it said that the Lenten preacher is not entirely unconnected with Donna Maria Vincenza's refusal, and that in the last resort the poor lady was not greatly at fault."

"Are you raving too, Severì?" Don Lazzaro rudely interrupted. "After all, it's perfectly straightforward. Who had to sign the appeal for a pardon, and who refused to sign it? Now let's see whether the authorities will impose an appropriate penalty."

"The Spinas have always thought themselves better than others," Donna Palmira repeated. "If their pride has now changed into madness, the time has come for the authorities to take appropriate action. Now we shall see once and for all whether there's any justice in this country."

"Certainly, Donna Palmira," said Don Severino with the hypocritical smile of a false judge, "but supposing it turned out that Signora Spina acted under the Lenten preacher's influence?"

"Father Gabriele is an outsider and doesn't interfere in family matters," replied Don Lazzaro, with the fury of a peasant whose cow someone is trying to steal.

"Father Gabriele is a holy man," Donna Palmira retorted. "In no circumstances would it occur to him to do anything displeasing to the authorities."

Don Coriolano raised one eyebrow halfway up his forehead. One of his eyes grew smaller and almost shut while the other opened wide and swelled enormously, looking like that of a maddened ox.

"I have the evidence here," he announced in hoarse, sibilant tones, putting his hand on his heart. "It's not just suspicion, I have the *corpus delicti* here, and no one will deprive me of it."

"Do you really have evidence?" Don Severino asked, half encouraging him and half incredulous. "That amuses me and arouses my curiosity, because you know my long-standing contempt for church people; all the same, it surprises me that a monk should have transgressed the fundamental virtue of Holy Mother Church, prudence, and should have left evidence of his intrigues."

The master and mistress of the house could not understand why Don Severino insisted so stubbornly on confusing the issue. Don Coriolano began anxiously searching for something in a secret pocket. He unbuttoned his jacket and his vest and inadvertently unbuttoned his shirt too, revealing a large amount of fat, hairy, and perspiring chest and the whole of his left breast with a purple nipple, which was swollen like that of a cow. "Pardon me," he muttered, covering it again with the modesty of a wet nurse. "Pardon me." He produced a crumpled, bluish letter.

"Do you know the excuse the old woman gave for not signing? None of you would ever guess. In the letter she sent to me she said literally: *I cannot sign because it would be against my conscience.* Do you see?" Don Coriolano shouted, rising to his feet and waving the letter in front of Don Lazzaro's nose. "The sudden, insuperable obstacle that caused the old woman to change her mind is called 'conscience.' Is there one of you who, closing his eyes while I repeat the word 'conscience,' does not immediately sniff the nauseating odor of candles?"

Don Coriolano looked around with the sarcastic smile of a public prosecutor who has routed the specious arguments of the defense with a decisive piece of evidence, and then sank back again into his armchair.

"Ah, now I too see the snake in the dark," Don Severino said seriously, trying hard to seem convinced.

Donna Palmira made the lively gesture of a hen that wants to try the mettle of a cock, but her husband rudely imposed silence on her and tried himself to express their joint indignation with Don Coriolano.

"I really can't understand you," Don Lazzaro said, "and I'm having to make a real effort to convince myself you're not joking. I'm only a simple countryman, a boor, a clodhopper, a member of the rural population, as the current phrase has it; and, as you keep telling me, I understand only simple, natural things, like the soil, the earth. But you know that I've always raised my hat to eloquence; you won't have forgotten that I sent for you to make the speech on the day I married Palmira, and that I asked you to speak at the funerals of my mother and my father-in-law, always paying you the proper fee; and I have always recommended you as a speaker to my relatives on days of joy and days of sorrow; and whenever I have had dealings with government offices it has always been you whom I asked for letters of recommendation. You are also aware that whenever you speak in the public square I always turn up surrounded by all my *cafoni*, and that I am always the first to applaud you whenever you pause for breath. But, by the Madonna, there are matters with which eloquence has nothing whatever to do. There are relationships, rivalries, and struggles between families in which eloquence, if it wishes at all costs to intervene, should at least be able to distinguish right from wrong and have regard for facts and not confuse them. And how is it possible because of a trivial phrase scribbled on a sheet of paper to turn things upside down, absolve Donna Maria Vincenza of her guilt and ascribe it to a stranger, an itinerant preacher?"

"A trivial phrase, you call it?" Don Coriolano shouted. "On my word of honor, Lazzaro, I'd say that you were used to drinking vinegar. So far from being a trivial phrase, I tell you, it's a grossly inflated one, an old, broken-winded warhorse of sacred oratory, an absurd, empty, nebulous invention of the priests. Let me make it plain, Lazzaro," he added, changing his tone, "that it's a word I profoundly respect in church, but which seems to me to be totally out of place in politics. At all events, in that letter the clerical origin of the old woman's refusal is plainly revealed. I will not accept instruction from you on that point, Lazzaro."

"Really," Don Lazzaro protested, clenching his huge fists, "really, now I understand you less than ever. Even granting that the word is so important, you can't seriously claim that Donna Maria Vincenza did not have a good education and is incapable of holding a pen in her hand. I can't understand your insistence that the old woman was incapable of thinking of and writing down that word by herself."

"It is precisely because Signora Spina had a good education that I insist on it," Don Coriolano replied irritably. "Left to herself, she would at most have invoked her pride, her honor, her convenience, her need of a quiet life, or some other nonsense of that sort. And besides, Lazzaro, you mustn't forget that I did not go to Rome on my own accord, for my own amusement, or to admire the ruins, but was expressly sent there by Donna Maria Vincenza; and if you're interested in the details, let me tell you in confidence that she reimbursed my traveling expenses, plus something extra. Now, Signora Spina is not a scatterbrained girl who changes her mind according to the direction of the wind or the state of her digestion. In spite of the ridiculous situation in which she put me, and forgetting family rivalries for the moment, Lazzaro, we cannot deny that she has always been a lady of unusual calm, composure, and steadiness of judgment. How, then, do you explain that up to two weeks ago, or rather three days ago, up to the evening when I returned from Rome, she was ready for any sacrifice for the sake of bringing her grandson back from abroad, and then suddenly refused to sign the appeal for pardon and put up such a strange, futile, stupid excuse? I should like to hear your countryman's explanation of that, Lazzaro."

Don Severino seemed to be enjoying the argument enormously, and he moved away a little to get a better view of the scene.

"I'll try," replied Don Lazzaro, panting and wiping away his perspiration like a clumsy peasant trying to tame a calf, "I'll try to accept your strange way of arguing for a moment. Out of regard for our old friendship and the requirements of hospitality, I'll admit for a moment that you're right. Did Donna Maria Vincenza allow herself to be influenced? Very well. So what? You have not, I hope, forgotten the fact that some time has elapsed since she came of age and became completely responsible for her actions. But if you insist that she allowed herself to be influenced and that others are responsible, I repeat: very well, who are they? Why pick on the Lenten preacher rather than anyone else? Could not the influence that caused her to change her mind at the last moment have come from some relative? Come, you know the Spinas, their vanity, their pride, you know they have always sought pretexts to evade their common duties. And now, by heaven, now that their pride has changed to raging madness, they actually dare reject the sacred hand of pardon. Our elders used to say that those who reject a pardon don't deserve it."

Don Severino was impatient to intervene. "Excuse my butting in, Coriolano," he said. "Excuse me if before you reply I put a small, but I hope not useless question to our host. Lazzaro, I understand your feelings, I fully appreciate your indignation as the head of a family, your anxiety not to permit the escape of a prey on whom you have patiently kept your eye for many years. But it seems to me that in your agitation you are shooting arrows from your bow that could easily turn against you. Do you really believe, Lazzaro, that Donna Maria Vincenza has relatives who are even more stiff necked than she and rather than act against their conscience are ready to sacrifice one of themselves, compromise the material interests of the whole clan, incur the anger of the authorities, and risk persecution by them? If you believe that, Lazzaro, then in your own interests I must put you on your guard. You think you are diminishing your rivals and thus striking them down, but in reality you are raising them up and putting them outside the range of your blows. Do you believe you're hastening the moment of your triumph over them? But on the pedestal on which you're putting them, my poor Lazzaro, they once and for all cease to be your competitors, all possible comparison between you vanishes, they come into conflict only with those who for opposite motives and ideals are nevertheless ready to incur the same sacrifices. Certainly, there's some risk, but what an unusual honor, what good fortune for mere provincials. All the same, Lazzaro, I don't believe that Donna Maria Vincenza's kin are worthy of such esteem, and I think that morally, and I say so without malice, they are more or less on the same level as you."

"Severì, I never knew you were a logician," Don Coriolano exclaimed in astonishment and, turning to the master of the house, went on: "You know better than I do, Lazzaro, that Donna Maria Vincenza's relatives are good Christians, excellent Christians, they're landlords just like the others. They'd put the Sacred Side of Jesus to boil in the pot together with the tears of Our Lady of Sorrows if they could make soup with it. What difference is there between Bastiano Spina and you, Lazzaro Tarò, apart from the beard, can you tell me that?"

The sound of animated voices floated up the stairs; a lively altercation was in progress between some *cafoni* who had come to beg the orator for letters of recommendation and the manservant, who had explicit orders not to let them in. But they refused to go away, they insisted on at least seeing the orator, and they kept repeating that they were not savages, they knew what was required by the rules of good society and had not come empty-handed.

Don Lazzaro and Donna Palmira had to go to the manservant's assistance.

"Severì," Don Coriolano muttered emotionally and confidentially into Don Severino's ear, "may I tell you something in fraternal confidence as from an orator to a musician? What honest scoundrels these landlords of ours are. In moments of bitterness I understand and appreciate your solitude. What good fortune to have been able to renounce making a career and to have music as a consolatory companion. But a solitary orator is, alas, inconceivable. To whom should I speak? To the cabbages, the tomatoes, the lettuces, the green and red peppers in the garden? And who would there be to applaud me? So at my age, apart from addressing meetings in the public square and writing letters of recommendation, at my age I still have to go here, there, and everywhere to speak at christenings, weddings, and funerals. You can't imagine what it means at my age, Severì, with my temperament, to have to speak in a cemetery during the rainy season in front of a pit with my feet in wet, slippery, wormy earth. It's true that people listen to me with pleasure and applaud me, but when the time comes to pay up they pull a face as if they were going to the barber's to have a tooth out, they haggle over the miserable fee, and look at me with contempt and envy as if I were a parasite, a bloodsucker, a sponger, and a drone. I ask myself what sins my fathers must have committed that I should have to pay for them among these dreadful people."

Don Coriolano fell silent for a moment, wiped his eyes that were swollen with tears, tidied his hair, and went on, lowering his voice: "As you could tell me, Severì, there are those clandestine sects. Agreed, but let's face the facts. What would I do among them? Are speeches made in them? Perhaps, but how big is the audience? It's not my fault if my eloquence is not of the catacomb type. Shall I tell you something? You remind me a little of Don Ignazio Spina, the father of the wretch who has now gone back to Paris. As perhaps you know, he and I were at school together in Naples, and we were very fond of each other. Oh, those were the days. You're more decent, more elegant than we were, you withdrew to drink the cup of human bitterness in your solitary garden, you renounced banal consolations, and over and above that, may the Lord be praised, you don't try to convert or save or redeem us, you don't act the hypocrite or the moralist, you're not like the priests who are comfortably off in the world and grow fat in it and bore us into the bargain by preaching detachment from the good things of life. I don't know if by any chance you had occasion to meet the Lenten preacher who has been sent to us in Colle this year. Have you had a good look at him? What a bird of ill omen he looks, doesn't he?"

Don Lazzaro and Donna Palmira, having gotten rid of the intruders, shut the front door and came back and sat by the fire. Don Lazzaro looked grimly at his two guests and muttered threats and expressions of contempt for those who lacked respect for other people's privacy. "People come here and behave as if it were a public place," he said to his wife, as if he were saying: He that hath ears to hear, let him hear.

Donna Palmira lent her ear to Don Coriolano's speech, waiting for an opportunity to interrupt the torrent of idle words and bring back the discussion to practical matters.

"Father Gabriele is a holy man," she said angrily, with the resentment of a housewife faced with a tradesman who insists on giving her short weight. "He's above all suspicion, I repeat. I haven't just met him by chance, as you have, but I've heard him preach, and I confessed to him last Saturday and, believe me, he's a real man of God, that's all I can tell you, he doesn't interfere in things that don't concern him. If only everyone were like him."

"But to me, if you'll allow me to say so, Donna Palmira, he seemed a complete humbug," Don Coriolano answered irritably. "He struck me as a hypocrite, a fraud, a falsely modest creep. Please note, Donna Palmira, that I have no particular prejudice against sacred eloquence, on the contrary. Catholicism is an allegory to which I raise my hat, a stupendous allegory constructed according to the most subtle rules of art. If I were married, Donna Palmira, I assure you that I would send my wife to mass every Sunday, because I'm the first to recognize that sacred eloquence fortifies the noble and delightful sense of fidelity in women and inspires them with the patience necessary to tolerate their husbands' inevitable infidelities. There is more that I can claim to my credit, Donna Palmira. No doubt you are aware of the fact that ever since the state made a concordat with the Holy See I have not failed on various occasions, including public speeches, to express my profound respect for Jesus and His Mother. In short, sacred and profane eloquence are now allied, the times are hard, one hand washes the other and both wash the face. So, Donna Palmira, when I met the Lenten preacher at lunch here yesterday, my first impression, since I am optimistic by nature, was favorable. My mistaken impression was that I was talking to a *capitone*,* you know, one of those that one cuts into finger-length pieces and cooks on a spit with a bay leaf between each piece. But after observing him better I discovered that he was indeed an underwater animal, but of an indigestible type, a snake. I observed with horror his black, pointed tongue while he ate; he's a real snake."

"We must ask the parish priest, Don Marco," Donna Palmira insisted stubbornly and angrily. "He'll be able to tell us whether Donna Maria Vincenza really talked to the preacher. The two may not have even seen each other, how do you know?"

"I have my information, and that's good enough for me," he replied irritably.

"Don't you trust Don Marco? He's one of us, he's a friend of yours."

"Yes, I know, he's a boiled fowl. He's good natured, mild, and inoffensive, I know; he's honest but ineffectual and he knows too well on which side his bread is buttered. In these cases friendship doesn't come into it. No, I don't trust him."

Don Lazzaro roused himself from his torpor, determined to lay all his cards on the table. "Let us stop this idle talk once and for all," he said, forcing himself to speak calmly and making a gesture as if he were driving away a wasp. "Let us consider the matter coolly and rationally, and work out the pros and cons like responsible adults. Perhaps we shall have the answer to the question of which side is right or wrong when we appear before the judgment seat of God, provided no lawyers or priests are present; but here on earth it's a matter of no importance. Even if I admit the preacher's responsibility for Donna Maria Vincenza's refusal, I take the liberty of asking you, *cavaliere*, what of it? Tell me frankly, what do you hope to get from him? Father Gabriele is an outsider, as you know, he's a Piedmontese. When Lent is over we shall probably never see him again in this part of the world, just as we have never seen previous Lenten preachers again. He belongs to the Passionist order, so he's not a priest, the name he uses is not his real name, he's a monk, he

---

*A species of large eel traditionally eaten in Italy on Christmas Eve.

owns nothing of his own, not even the sandals on his feet. If you were to accuse him it's only natural to assume that his superiors would defend him, and you know better than I do how powerful these monkish orders are in our country. In short, you'd be putting your foot in a hornet's nest that would leave you no peace for the rest of your life. Please let me finish, Severì, I'm not talking to you now, I'm talking to the *cavaliere*. Allow me to give you my ideas as they occur to me, for your sake and, I may add, for ours too, as from one friend to another. Listen to a man who has always stood by you. Leave that monk out of it and, if you have a score to settle and, as is your sacred right, want to get some benefit from it, you have only to take it out of the Spinas. They are still well off, they are already compromised and suspect in the eyes of the authorities, and they have many enemies, both in Colle and in Orta, on whose gratitude you can count. Am I to explain myself in still more concrete terms? Well, then, here we are among old friends whom we can trust completely and I know I can speak with the secrecy of the confessional. Well, Calabasce called here an hour ago, he came from Orta especially to see me. You know him, he's at daggers drawn with Don Bastiano Spina, and he asked me to tell you that if you now succeeded in delivering the coup de grâce to the Spinas, in striking a blow at them worthy of a great orator, he would be ready, as incidentally I should be too, to reward such an act of justice with a handsome present. By asking for contributions from other trusted friends it should be possible, I think, to get together a respectable sum of money. I don't know if I've managed to put across the idea. Why are you standing there like a stuffed dummy, Palmira? Can't you see our guests are thirsty?"

Don Coriolano's agitation did not escape Don Severino. Sitting with his elbows on his knees and resting his head in the palm of one hand, the orator's eyes were half closed, and his brow was knitted as if he were plunged in thought.

Don Severino had a sudden inspiration and nervously leaped to his feet. "Don't imagine, Lazzaro, that I want to spoil the effect of your speech," he said. "If I now take the liberty of adding a few naive ideas of my own, I can assure you that my purpose is solely

to fulfill the moral obligation of giving an old and trusted friend
who is faced with a decision a piece of advice that may, perhaps,
be mistaken but in any event is sincere and gratuitous. Thank you,
Donna Palmira, I don't drink, as you know. May I speak as if the
person most concerned were not present? Well then, I appeal to
your imagination. Don Coriolano is faced with the painful necessity of explaining the failure of his mission to Donna Maria Vincenza to the office in Rome that entrusted him with the delicate
task. Supposing he writes and says: 'Honorable Authorities, I'm
very sorry, but in the meantime Signora Spina (a lady on the
wrong side of eighty, an invalid with one foot in the grave) has now
changed her mind and no longer wants to sign the appeal for a
pardon for her nephew.' What will happen? Perhaps the police official who registers the letter on its arrival will shrug his shoulders
and mutter to himself: so much the worse for the grandson. That,
of course, is what might happen in the best of cases. But it's also
possible that the letter might end up under the bespectacled gaze
of the chief police official, who will curl up his nose, bang his fist
on the table, and shout: so that country clown, that ridiculous fairground magician, that crooked lawyer with the tragicomic name of
Coriolano was making a fool of us when he came here with a
cock-and-bull story? And it's easy to see that the next time Don
Coriolano goes to Rome no one will believe a word he says and
everyone will laugh in his face; and in the absence of any dam-
aging outcome to the Spina family he would not even get the
rather vulgar consolation promised by Calabasce. But in my
opinion a result entirely favorable to him would ensue if he reported to the authorities more or less in the following terms: 'It is
my duty to inform you, Honorable Authorities, that Signora Spina
was willing and anxious to sign the appeal for a pardon and was
completely confident that her émigré grandson would do the same
and would return home. However, the arbitrary intervention of a
Lenten preacher on mission to Colle here caused the pious lady to
believe that this action would be contrary to religion (I must point
out, Honorable Authorities, that the lady in question is an invalid
on the wrong side of eighty who expects to appear before the

throne of the Almighty at any moment), with the result that now, fearing the pains of hell, she no longer dares to sign.' I'm convinced (and I'm willing to wager any sum you like on it) that a letter in those terms would have the effect in Rome of a clap of thunder in a clear sky. The piece of paper would ascend in vertical flight from the hands of the *sbirro* to those of the minister; a telegram would be sent to Don Coriolano summoning him to the capital, he would become well known there, perhaps the journalists would take him up, and perhaps, God willing, the photographers would do the same. I note with pleasure that Don Coriolano is smiling and agrees. How could I have doubted it? And you too will now certainly have been convinced, Lazzaro. Just consider the situation a little. Destiny now offers our orator a rare opportunity to emerge from the mediocrity of provincial life and lift his eloquence to the national level. If he succeeds in becoming the hero of an incident in the relations between Church and state, he will have had the good fortune to mount one of the most noble of rhetorical steeds, a steed that could carry him a long way."

Don Coriolano smiled; he was lighthearted, boyish, cheerful again. "Severì," he said softly, "I already knew you were no fool, but how was I to suppose that music had made you so perspicacious? I congratulate you, and it makes me regret all the more that we never see you, or only once in a blue moon. Donna Palmira, this little wine of yours has a eucharistic flavor sufficient to raise the dead. Is it from a new barrel? There must be a great deal of Malmsey in it."

Don Lazzaro was bitterly chewing the cud and, though his wife signed to him not to give in, he preferred to drop the subject for the time being, contenting himself with glowering at Don Severino like a peasant whose watch has been made to disappear by a conjurer.

Assunta, the lame maid, was to be heard struggling up the stairs after coming back from church. "Praise be to Jesus," she said, appearing in the kitchen doorway. "Praise be to Mary. May I come in?"

"Come in, Assunta, is the sermon over already?" her mistress asked. "Is Father Gabriele's throat still bad?"

The poor lame woman was big breasted and big bottomed.

She had a black shawl over her head and her wrinkled little face was of the color of boiled potatoes. She advanced into the middle of the kitchen.

"It was even worse than yesterday evening, Donna Palmira," she whined. "Yes, it was a real torment. I had a good view of him, because I was sitting right under the pulpit. His mouth might have been full of broken glass, it was agony for him to speak. You did well not to come to church today, Donna Palmira, you must have been inspired by heaven. Do you know, everyone is saying things about you; no one talked about anything else in church, it never occurred to anyone to pray, apart from Aunt Eufemia, of course. She prayed very hard indeed. In short, everyone knows that Father Gabriele caught his inflammation of the throat, so to speak, in your house, eating macaroni with anchovies, and everyone is wondering what witches' brew you mixed with the sauce and what reason you had to do it, and saying you couldn't have committed a graver sin against the Holy Word."

"Was it I who did the cooking?" the mistress of the house exclaimed in fury. "You know very well that it wasn't, and you could have said so and told everyone, otherwise I don't know why I sent you to church."

"I did tell everyone who would listen to me," Assunta whimpered, "but you know no one likes arguing with Aunt Eufemia, so everyone says it's your fault. Everyone keeps saying that you don't offer a stranger, particularly a strange monk, and particularly during Lent, a hot sauce made with olive oil, anchovies, pepper, garlic, red peppers, and heaven knows what kind of witches' brew as well."

"Why did they send us that bird of ill omen if he can't stand our cooking?" exclaimed Don Coriolano, jumping to his feet. "A true orator is recognized above all at table. But, leaving that aside, Donna Palmira, I must admit quite between ourselves that it was only for obvious reasons of prestige and to avoid trouble with Aunt Eufemia that I behaved like a Spartan. That sauce was diabolically strong and would have burned the inside of a cow."

"I had to spend the whole night drinking water," Don Lazzaro admitted sadly.

*T*HE SOUND OF MORE footsteps came from the stairs, and Donna Palmira went to meet her guests in a very bad humor. There was a confused babble of voices.

"Good evening, Donna Palmira, our respects, is the bearded monster at home? And Don Coriolano? Oh, is he still alive?"

"Welcome, Don Marcantonio, Signor De Paolis, good evening, how nice to see you, what a delightful surprise, come in. Were you at the sermon?"

"They're coming," Don Coriolano murmured in Don Severino's ear. "They're my worst enemies. They're going around collecting evidence against me."

The new arrivals stamped their feet outside the kitchen door to shake the snow from their boots. Don Coriolano, strutting like a turkey cock, went forward ceremoniously to greet the two notables, who barely responded with a nod.

Don Marcantonio took the master of the house into a corner to confide to him the difficult situation he was in. His old mother had subjected herself to a life of hardship to enable him to finish his studies, had contracted debts and signed promissory notes that were now falling due, the bailiffs might be moving in and her furniture sold off any day now, and the poor old lady would die of a broken heart. Don Lazzaro pretended not to understand.

"I sympathize with and admire you," he said. "It is these misfortunes that strengthen a man's character. But now come over to the fire."

Don Coriolano for his part had taken Don Severino over to the window.

"I thank you, Severì, allow me to press both your hands, allow me to embrace you," he said. "Just now you talked to me like a brother. What am I saying? Like a mother. I swear to you that I shall never forget it. The advice you gave me with regard to Rome may be invaluable to me. What a shame you don't drink, Severì, because if you did we could have a drink together every now and then. You don't like wine? In the name of Our Lady of Sorrows, why not? Even the Church uses wine in the holy mass. Excuse me, but did you notice how those swine treated me just now? Did you hear how that ox Lazzaro dared to talk to me? And that scoundrel Calabasce, whom I several times saved from prison, doesn't come and have a confidential chat with me, but sends me a message as if I were a public prostitute. Are you feeling unwell by any chance, Severì? Wouldn't you like a glass of wine?"

Don Coriolano had been talking to him quietly, face to face, and as there was a strong whiff of undigested wine and spirits on his breath Don Severino had had a slight attack of dizziness.

"Thank you, thank you, it's over already," Don Severino said, forcing himself to smile and using one hand as a fan.

"Well, you won't believe me," Don Coriolano went on murmuring in a warm and friendly manner, "you have every reason not to believe me, but I swear to you that behind my tremendous effort to secure the return home to his grandmother of that outlawed boy, prestige was a powerful motive. Why should I deny it? Filthy lucre also played a part, I'm not ashamed to admit it. But underneath all that there was also the memory of my youthful friendship with the boy's father. By the way, I heard that you spent a long time with Donna Maria Vincenza this afternoon. Yes, the *carabinieri* keep me informed of everything. Won't you tell me what she said?"

Don Severino's face darkened. "Donna Maria Vincenza?" he said, pretending surprise. "She told me nothing, I assure you."

The maid came and told Don Severino that Don Gennaro, the brother of the parish priest of Orta, was walking up and down outside in the street; he had heard by chance that Don Severino was paying a call on Don Lazzaro, and took the liberty of asking him to come down for a moment, because he wanted to talk to him, it would only take half a minute, he said, and he needn't come down if it was inconvenient, there was no hurry about it really, but he hoped he would do so quickly, as it had started snowing again and he had a cough.

"Why doesn't the idiot come up?" Don Lazzaro protested in annoyance. "What sort of affront is this? Stay where you are, Severì, I'll go down and fetch him."

The master of the house disappeared down the stairs and soon reappeared, panting and dragging Don Gennaro behind him without saying anything, as if he were dragging a recalcitrant calf into its shed. Don Gennaro was a muffled-up, bent, skinny little man, and he looked around in bewilderment.

"Sit by the fire and warm yourself," Don Lazzaro said to him rudely. "And you could take off your gloves, don't you see they're wet? Palmira, give him a drink."

"Let him at least get his breath back," said his wife. "Don Gennarì, what sort of behavior is this? Why didn't you want to come up? Why be so unfriendly?"

Don Gennaro recovered his breath with difficulty; he was ceremonious, deferential, and ingenuous, and tried to gain the sympathy of those present by directing a disarming smile at everyone in turn.

"I really didn't want to disturb you," he said, "it's not my habit to call on people without being expected." On the shoulders of his worn overcoat he had a round sheepskin collar, a removable one, not attached to the collar of the overcoat. Both overcoat and detachable collar were wet through, but he refused to take them off, as he insisted he wasn't staying. He wanted to go to the Café Eritrea to watch the billiards; billiards was his sport and his passion, and sometimes he actually saw it in his dreams, he confessed with a blush. However, Don Lazzaro succeeded in removing the hood of his coat, revealing a head like a coconut, oval, dark, and covered with down.

"You wanted to talk to Severino?" Don Lazzaro asked. "Well, there he is, now you can talk to him. I hope our presence won't disturb you."

"No, of course not, on the contrary, what an idea," said poor Don Gennaro, getting flustered. "But at the moment I can't remember what it was about, I expect it was nothing at all, in fact I'm sure of it. Oh, yes, that's it, excuse my absentmindedness, I just wanted to wish him good evening. Will you be staying here long, Severì?"

This excuse made everybody laugh, except Don Lazzaro, who shook his head suspiciously and said, "I don't believe him."

"Good evening, good evening, Don Gennarì, how are you?" said Don Severino. "Were you in church for the sermon?"

Don Lazzaro added wood to the fire. The guests formed a wide semicircle around it, and their faces were reddened and hollowed by the light of the flames. The three notables avoided looking at one another.

"You may have heard about the plan to erect a big cross at the top of the Dead Donkey," said Don Gennaro, turning to the notables present and delighted at having found a subject of conversation. "Don't you think it not just a pious but a highly practical idea? People really feel the need of an expiatory act. The trouble, of course, is materialism. After the sermon this evening we had a little meeting of the preparatory committee; I blush to say so, but I'm the entirely unworthy chairman of that committee."

This piece of information filled Don Marcantonio with a delight that the others present at first failed to understand. With his short hair that stood up like a brush, his tortoiseshell-rimmed spectacles, his dark suit that was a little too big for him, and his abrupt gestures, he looked like an unfrocked priest; his reaction was unexpected and incomprehensible, and the company looked at him in surprise.

"Are you the chairman of the committee, Don Gennarì?" he exclaimed, taking his hands and shaking them warmly. "*Mensch, Herr Januar! Wie schicksalhaft ist unsere Begegnung!** I came to Colle especially to seek you out and offer you my official collaboration."

This statement alarmed and worried Don Gennaro. "Excuse me," he said. "Excuse me, but I'm afraid you've made a mistake or, as is more probable, I didn't make myself clear. The object of the religious ceremony planned for the end of the Lenten sermons is the Holy Cross of our Lord Jesus Christ. Politics doesn't come into it at all."

"On the contrary, I understood you perfectly well," Don Marcantonio said in the arrogant tones assumed by the timid when authority is vested in them. "You would have realized that yourself if you had allowed me to continue."

Don Coriolano directed at Don Marcantonio the compassionate smile of the master for the apprentice. "You're an enthusiast and a fanatic," he said to him, perhaps to bring matters to a head. "But those are dangerous qualities. Enthusiasm and fanaticism can lead to where they led young Pietro Spina."

"Isn't patriotism a passion?" Don Marcantonio interrupted.

"Yes, to the simpleminded," Don Coriolano replied with a forced smile. "But to political leaders it's an art, that is to say, a kind of loving with appropriate detachment, I might also say like the memory of young love."

It was like the beginning of a duel. The semicircle of red faces around the fire turned toward Don Marcantonio in eager expectation of his reply, but he said nothing. An ambiguous, indecipherable smile formed on his face. It was not a smile of embarrassment, but a defiant, crafty smile, unusual on that face, and it sent shudders down Don Coriolano's spine. Everyone felt that something serious was about to be revealed.

"The higher authorities have made their decision," he said.

---

*Well, Mr. January! What a fateful meeting!

"What has happened?" Don Gennaro asked in terror. "What has happened, for heaven's sake?"

"Give me a drink," Don Coriolano said. "Please, is there nothing to drink?"

Donna Palmira hastily opened a bottle as if she were wringing a chicken's neck, Don Lazzaro filled the glasses, and the men passed them around in silence. Don Marcantonio went on smiling enigmatically, relishing the curiosity, the embarrassment, the anxiety that was fed by his silence. Finally he rose, moved his chair, and stepped back a few paces, establishing the distance between himself and the rest of the company that marks off the speaker from the public, the actor from the audience, the authorities from the vulgar.

"I should not be averse," he began, "from accepting a platonic contest with Don Coriolano on the two opposite kinds of eloquence that we so brilliantly represent in this part of the world but for the regrettable fact that for disciplinary reasons I am prevented from doing so. It is extremely painful for me to have to tell you, Coriolà, that the matter at dispute between us (the details of which I shall refrain from mentioning in the presence of the uninitiated) has already been considered and settled by the higher authorities, whose decision it is that you are strictly excluded — that is the term employed 'ex-cluded' — from all future political ceremonies. You will see the announcement in the newspaper tomorrow or the day after. You cannot imagine how sorry I am."

Don Coriolano went livid and looked at those present one after the other, waiting for someone to deny this ridiculous piece of news.

"Excluded?" he repeated in stupefaction. "Excluded? At whose suggestion, may I ask?" he exclaimed. "And on what infamous denunciation is this based?"

"You are accused of being a pious fraud, in other words of pietism," Don Marcantonio explained. "Your complacency in relation to the Spinas was excessive at the very least."

"Heaven be praised," Don Lazzaro exclaimed with the spontaneity and fervor of a believer who has received a grace.

Donna Palmira had vanished into a neighboring room, and she came back with a lit candle that she put in front of a holy picture of Sant'Antonio on the mantelpiece. This completed poor Don Coriolano's humiliation. He turned imploringly to De Paolis, who responded with the absentminded gesture of someone who has not been following the conversation and does not know what it is all about; he then turned to Don Severino, who was openly and shamelessly grinning. Meanwhile Don Gennaro did not know what to do with his face; he tried to smile with the cheek turned to the new orator and to weep with the cheek turned to the old one. Don Coriolano, his head and hands in a cold sweat, collapsed onto a chair and clumsily undid the collar that was stifling him; with his glazed, bewildered eyes he was reduced to interrogating the floor, the fireplace, the cooking utensils hanging on the walls, and he was astonished that everything was still in its usual place.

"Excluded," he repeated mournfully. "A man like me, excluded."

Don Marcantonio was still standing, and he watched the scene with a cynical and shameless smile of triumph on his face; he was surprised at his own courage.

"Me, a pietist?" Don Coriolano hissed between his teeth. "But if it were necessary, I'd be perfectly capable of cutting my best friends' eyes out with a penknife."

"Nobody doubts that," Don Marcantonio admitted. "But you can't deny you went to Rome with Donna Maria Vincenza's money."

"Me a pietist," Don Coriolano repeated contemptuously. "But who made that ridiculous decision?"

"Who made it? Ha, ha, ha," Don Marcantonio said with a laugh. "*Vuolsi così colà dove si puote ciò che si vuole.*"*

Don Lazzaro rose, embraced him, kissed him on both cheeks, held him in both arms, and looked at him and again kissed him, leaving his whole face covered with saliva.

"You'll go a long way," he said emotionally. "Before you go

---

* "It is so wished in the place where whatever is wished can be done." Dante, *Inferno*, 3:59.

we'll have another little chat about those promissory notes of your mother's."

Don Gennaro tried to drag Don Severino away, but the latter insisted on remaining.

"The performance is beginning to amuse me," he said.

The semicircle around the fire broke up. Donna Palmira removed the glasses and the bottle and other fragile objects from the mantelpiece, because one knew how arguments between men began, but one never could tell how they were going to end, and glasses and plates cost a fortune nowadays. Don Coriolano collapsed on his chair, stunned, deathly pale, as lifeless as a straw dummy or a deflated bagpipe, while De Paolis seemed determined to know nothing whatever about it all. He was a trade union secretary, after all, and could not allow the welfare of the working classes to be compromised by misplaced sentimentality. So he carefully buttoned up his jacket and raised his eyes to heaven, heaven in this instance being the kitchen ceiling with a number of poles from which hams, salami, sausages, cheeses, and strings of onions, mushrooms, and red and green peppers were hanging; this was a pleasant surprise to him, and he smiled and spent a long time enjoying the heavenly spectacle, forgetful of time and place, in the attitude of Santa Teresa conversing with Jesus. Next to him, but still standing, Don Marcantonio was vigorously holding and shaking his own hands as if to congratulate himself on his deserved promotion and, as the secret was out without his having let it out deliberately, he became transfigured, gradually assuming the appearance appropriate to his new office. His chest expanded, his jaw protruded, and he was lavish with his protective smiles. The audience was small, but his mind was already on the multitudes who, though they did not yet know it, were waiting for him like clay waiting for the sculptor. Meanwhile the master and mistress of the house had disappeared and could be heard conferring in the next room. Don Severino, near the fireplace, was the only person present who was frankly enjoying himself, like a provincial at a performance of an old farce; to him its subject was far from new, for he had been present at similar performances ever since his boyhood, without their losing anything of their irresistible comic force. To Don Gennaro, on the other hand, the scene had been excessively dramatic and, though it had nothing whatever to do with him, thank heaven, in fact it left him basically indifferent, because whatever happened he wouldn't get a *centesimo* from it; nevertheless good manners caused him to assume a very serious air in harmony with the gravity of the occasion. The outgoing orator could interpret it as deep sympathy, and the incoming one as heartfelt congratulations.

"At any rate it's all the fault of materialism," he resolutely declared. "Severì, how much longer do you intend to stay here?"

Don Severino paid no notice to him. Don Marcantonio, impatient to relish his victory, took advantage of his success and proceeded to eulogize his predecessor as if he were already dead.

"The kind of lyric-celebratory eloquence that Don Coriolano has always practiced with such artistry," he declared, "is and will continue to be eminently suitable for weddings, christenings, confirmations, first communions, and funerals; it must be admitted, in fact, that for such occasions it cannot be bettered. But it is absurd in connection with scandals like that of Pietro Spina. That kind of eloquence no longer works, it no longer shakes audiences out of their lethargy; it's beautiful music that makes them dream, not act. It does not succeed in shaping and molding them into a collective whole, in arousing their deep ancestral instincts. Now that words alone have turned out to be insufficient to transform the minds and souls of our people, the time has come for our ancient art of eloquence to be associated with rites and ceremonies, spectacles and symbols. That, as you know, is my speciality. *Mein Steckenpferd, meine Herren, darauf reite ich.*"*

"But don't you realize," Don Severino exclaimed in simulated alarm, "that you're running the risk of plunging this peaceful country into a real revolution? As long as our ancient country has existed it has always been governed by words, and you now say that they are no longer sufficient? Was it not said of the political

---

*My hobbyhorse, gentlemen, on which I ride.

orator that words were his spear and his sword, his breastplate and his helmet? Did not Cicero by the device of words alone overcome difficulties in many ways similar to your own?"

"Don't forget that that distinguished colleague of ours was addressing senators," Don Marcantonio pointed out in a calm and confident manner. "He was addressing, not the plebs, not slaves, but patricians, and that is the essential point to remember. Certainly there are a few plain and simple words, a few ancient but not superannuated words, that are still sufficient to arouse slaves, just as a charge of dynamite can blow up a mountain; the sacrilegious words of Spartacus are an example. I do not wish to assert that we should not adapt some of those fiery phrases to our own purposes and in our own fashion; leaving modesty aside, we can do whatever we choose. Some of those disastrous phrases not only lose their virulence when introduced into our liturgy, but are actually transformed into a highly effective vaccine against the pernicious germs of social revolution and, moreover, add a salutary note of anguish to the national mysteries."

Don Severino was striding nervously up and down the room as if he had lost control of himself. "I do not deny," he said in an excited tone, "the invaluable contribution that priests, witch doctors, and talkers, each on their own account, have always made to the maintenance of public order in this highly civilized country. But what I wanted to say was this: hitherto their efforts have always been, if not conflicting, at least separate. Our classical culture, our classical way of convincing ourselves that we are progressive and civilized human beings has always benefited by that separation. I don't say this to discourage you, on the contrary, in fact, you can count on my sincerest sympathy. After all, I believe that what you are doing will turn out to be highly entertaining and therefore highly successful in a country such as ours. Amusements are rather rare in this part of the world, as you know. I don't imagine that your ceremonies will interest me in the long term but, if you will forgive my snobbishness, I should hate to miss the first performance. Will you remember me?"

"I certainly shall," Don Marcantonio graciously assured him. "Will you bring the delightful Donna Faustina with you? I don't know if you have noticed it, but young ladies have a special sensitivity in these matters."

Don Marcantonio kept a careful watch on his two comrades out of the corner of his eyes while he was holding forth. Don Coriolano seemed totally absent. His chin was resting on his chest, and the incipient bald patch on his bent head assumed the shape of a large tonsure. As the fire died down, his hands and face had assumed the yellowish color of a saffron risotto that had gone bad; and with his half-closed eyes he glowered at the ashes in the fireplace. De Paolis was still leaning with the back of his neck against the back of his chair, contemplating the ceiling; he had stopped counting the hams, the salami, and the sausages and had started making a rather more difficult inventory of the strings of onions, mushrooms, and peppers.

"In practice, what precisely will these new ceremonies consist of?" Don Gennaro plucked up courage to ask. "Are you proposing to arrange them in Colle? If I may be so bold as to make a suggestion, I think you should at least wait until after the end of Lent to avoid disturbing the religious functions."

"Your suggestion reveals a very acute intelligence, if I may say so," Don Marcantonio very courteously replied. "I don't say that to flatter you, it's just a fact. So don't worry, I'll wait till Lent is over. You have my authority to pass on that piece of information to your fellow citizens, you may tell them that at your suggestion I have decided to wait until Lent is over. And why should I not? Lent is a time of fasting, of sadness, of prayer, it's genuinely worthy of passing respect. I authorize you to pass on word for word to your fellow citizens what I am telling you; you can, if you like, also put it in writing. But now let us come down to practical matters. When have you decided to erect the new cross at the top of the Dead Donkey? At the end of Lent, did you say? *Oh, günstiges Schicksal! Oh, barmherizige Vorsehung!** That's as appropriate as a juniper leaf in

---

*Oh, fortunate destiny! Oh, merciful providence!

the beak of a roast thrush. My suggestion, Don Gennarì, is that your procession should be transformed into a solemn ceremony of state mysticism. I shall, of course, first have to apply for authorization to the higher authorities, and there will also be a great many details on which we shall have to reach agreement. Do you expect many people will take part?"

"But the world's so large, why do you want to begin in Colle of all places?" Don Gennaro asked in alarm.

"I have to start somewhere, Don Gennarì. It's all the same to me whether it's here or there."

"No, what I meant to say was that this is such a poor, backward, obscure little village."

"But it will become famous, Don Gennarì, that I promise you. Or don't you trust me? Just think, Don Gennarì, was Nazareth a metropolis, a celebrated watering place, the site of a famous university? The Pharisees, who knew everything, said contemptuously: can anything good come out of a place like that? And yet?"

Don Gennaro looked around vainly in search of aid. The others seemed to be enjoying his embarrassment.

"But this is a bad village," he went on with a sigh. "Present company excepted, of course, the people here are stubborn and averse to innovations. It's an ungrateful village."

"But that's just what I'm looking for. I want to begin at the point of most resistance," Don Marcantonio exclaimed. "If state mysticism catches on here, elsewhere it will go down swimmingly. And with your aid, Don Gennarì, I have no doubt that we shall succeed."

Don Gennaro was in torment but, as no one came to his aid, all he could do was to try to wash his hands of the matter.

"Excuse me," he said, "but why are you saying all this to me? I assure you I had no intention of coming to this house, I didn't come here looking for you, I just happened to be passing, and I just wanted to have a word with Severino before going to watch the billiards."

"But with whom am I to discuss the matter if not with you?

With the Lenten preacher? Didn't you ask me to wait till Lent was over?"

"Yes, but Father Gabriele is staying to the day of the ceremony, it's he who is going to bless the new cross."

"But didn't you say you were the chairman of the committee? Doesn't everything depend on you? Frankly, I much prefer dealing with a man who wears trousers; you can never tell what a man in a cassock is thinking."

"But excuse me, *cavaliere*, you certainly don't need an insignificant person like me to explain canon law to you. You know better than I do that laymen have little say in the Church. The conduct of Church affairs is restricted to consecrated hands; generally the sole purpose of lay committees is to raise money, and that's all."

"And you tell me that only now?" Don Marcantonio answered irritably. "Couldn't you have told me that a little sooner? Very well, then, I'll go and talk to the old crow. What sort of person is he? Is he dismal? Does he drink? By the way (even though you are a mere layman, this is something you ought to know), is the new cross to be of the traditional type? The reason I ask is that I want to propose an addition; it's an idea of mine, a highly original one."

"That's a matter entirely outside lay jurisdiction. I know nothing whatever about it," Don Gennaro insisted. Then he turned to Don Severino and said, imploringly: "Can't we go yet?"

"I came for the rent of a plot of land of mine," Don Severino whispered in his ear. "I'm staying till they pay up."

Don Coriolano had the greasy pallor of a corpse on the second day in a mortuary chapel. In a corner near the window De Paolis was talking to Don Marcantonio with both his hands on his heart, but Donna Palmira tried to restore the semicircle around the fireplace.

"We haven't yet wetted the new hat," she said, trying to seem completely at ease. "Will everyone please go back to his place? Don Marcantonio, Signor De Paolis, please go back to your places."

She went to fetch the usual greenish bottle of Amaro Sant'

Agostino from the next room, and Don Lazzaro started filling the glasses.

"Thank you, I don't drink," said Don Severino. "Could I have a glass of water?"

"Donna Palmira," Don Coriolano murmured gloomily, "don't you by any chance have a less revolting drink for me?"

"Would you prefer some San Pellegrino cordial? It's good for the heart."

Don Lazzaro rose and proposed a toast. He raised a big, meaty hand with a glass of the greenish liquor in it and began: "To our health and the greater glory of the new-style oratory. You know what the saying is in cases like this. The king is dead, long live the king. Or perhaps, as it's Lent, it would be better to say: when one Pope dies, they choose another. All honor to friendship."

Even Don Severino could not resist the temptation to speak; he rose, raised his long, slender, transparent hand holding a glass of water high in the air, and with an elegant gesture began: "Here's to friendship. And the better to honor it let me tell you about a curious incident that happened on a recent market day in Orta. A totally unexpected arrival that day was an old gypsy woman who sat down in the square and announced that she was a clairvoyant and that for the trivial sum of twenty *centesimi* she would reveal to every adult the most important secret of his or her life, at the same time insisting that her potential clients must keep the truths thus revealed strictly to themselves. As happens in such cases, at first only a few persons timidly accepted her invitation, but then their number rapidly increased to a quite unusual extent, and in the end a line actually formed that included a number of serious and responsible persons. It wasn't so much the small fee that attracted the crowd as the expression of convinced amazement assumed by those to whom the clairvoyant's secret was revealed. Each consultation lasted only a few seconds, the woman had no need to think hard to learn everyone's hidden secret, and everyone without exception responded to her brief murmured revelation with admiring gestures and exclamations. It's no exaggeration to say that the greater part of the population of the village, including landlords and shopkeepers, filed past the gypsy woman that day."

"She'll have told everyone an open secret," De Paolis interrupted.

"As we learned afterward," Don Severino concluded, "what she told everyone was: mistrust your best friend, he's betraying you; and no one had any difficulty in believing her."

"A bright idea," De Paolis admitted.

"I didn't know you were so ill mannered, Don Severì," Donna Palmira said. "Even if it's true, what need is there to say so? On my word of honor, you'd take away the appetite of a hungry wolf."

Don Marcantonio agreed. "One shouldn't carry sincerity too far," he declared.

"If my sense of smell doesn't deceive me," Don Gennaro interrupted in alarm, sniffing the air, "you're cooking meat, Donna Palmira. Excuse me, I've no desire to interfere in your affairs, but in Lent . . ."

"If you came here to spy, say so frankly," Don Lazzaro said threateningly. "What sort of manners is it to come into a house without being invited and then start sniffing the cooking pots?"

"Don't take any notice of him, Don Lazzaro," said De Paolis, with a grimace of contempt. "What do you expect of a priest's brother? Before making such a grave allegation, Don Gennarì, you might at least have found out what kind of meat it is. Might it not be Lenten meat?"

"Palmira, turn the light on," Don Lazzaro said to his wife. "Haven't you noticed we can hardly see anymore?"

"What sort of person is this Lenten preacher?" Don Marcantonio asked.

"Nothing out of the way," Don Coriolano said nastily. "A perfectly ordinary viper in vinegar, as you'll see for yourself."

"He's a holy man," Donna Palmira insisted.

"I have a brilliant and audacious plan," Don Marcantonio began, warming to his work. "I see the immediate future in rosy and hopeful colors. I'm convinced we are entering into a long period of warfare. The present little war in Abyssinia is merely the prelude to a series of conflicts that will lead inevitably to the restoration of the Roman Empire. Yes, I'm a believer in the theory of cycles, which says that everything recurs periodically. The time has now come for the Roman Empire to be reborn. Consequently, in the space of a few years we shall see a repetition of all the wars by which Rome built up her empire, the Italic wars, the Carthaginian wars, the war against Gaul, the Greek war, to name only the most important. That's the position. Don't ask me to explain, you wouldn't understand if I did explain. Besides, what explanation do you want? A wheel that has been turning of its own accord from the beginning of time doesn't start giving explanations to the parish organist of Orta."

"The ex–parish organist of Orta," Don Severino corrected him.

"How is the popular soul to be brought into harmony with its destiny?" Don Marcantonio went on. "*Das ist die Frage.** We can accept the challenge, relying on the certainty that the symbols of Roman power survive in the Italian soul (government laws require us to believe that, so it must be true); but they survive in a state of hibernation, beneath the later incrustations of Christianity. In other words, to reach the Roman symbols at the deep levels at which they lie sleeping, and to reawaken them together with the ancient virtues, we must pass by way of the Christian emblems. Well, now I'm beginning to fear I've told you only too much, and you yourselves will be able to understand the path to be followed by the new oratory."

"I say this, not to flatter you," Don Lazzaro declared in an eager and heartfelt manner, "but I swear to you by my wife's health that never in my life have I heard more remarkable ideas more impressively stated. They deserve to be handed down to posterity on parchment. Please, Palmira, haven't you noticed that the gentleman is thirsty?"

"Not a leaf moves unless God wills it," Don Gennaro announced. "That is my belief and I stick to it."

"Yes, Lazzaro, I have thought of writing a book," Don Marcan-

---

*This is the question.

tonio admitted with a blush. "Actually, so far I've only written the title, *The Lictor's Cross.** I hope the higher authorities will grant me the imprimatur."

"There could not be a more sublime and original title," De Paolis hastened to point out. "What I should like to know, Marcantò, is where you get such original ideas from. That title itself is as good as a poem. In fact, to save time you ought to publish the book immediately, even the cover alone."

"Will you accept a piece of free advice, Don Marcantonio?" Don Severino said coldly. "Well, then, beware of the cross, believe me, it's a rather dangerous object."

"What are you saying, Don Severì?" Donna Palmira protested indignantly. "How dare you talk so cynically about the Holy Cross of our Lord and Savior? You can make jokes about many things, if it gives you any particular pleasure, you can ridicule bigots and even priests, but the Holy Crucifix you must respect. Even if you are unable to venerate it as other good Christians do, at least you should take it seriously."

"He died for the sins of us all, Severì," Don Gennaro added, saddened as if by a recent bereavement. "For your sins too, Severì, as you seem to have forgotten. On your deathbed you will repent."

"The danger, in my opinion," said Don Severino, rising to his feet, "begins precisely when the crucifix is taken too seriously."

Don Lazzaro murmured in Don Marcantonio's ear, "Shall I send for the *carabinieri*? It would be a splendid coup."

"No, not yet," Don Marcantonio whispered back. "We mustn't be in too much of a hurry."

Don Severino, under the influence of growing excitement, went on: "When anyone asks us, Donna Palmira, not to die for the truth, which would be too much to expect, but to make a small sacrifice for it, to bear timid witness to it, or calls on us to perform some courageous act, make a small gesture of dignity and pride, our timorous, prudent, domesticated Christian morality invariably

---

*A reference to the Fascist emblem, derived from ancient Rome: a fasces, or bundle of rods crossed by an ax.

makes us answer: why should I? I'm not crazy. Here the most unheard-of outrages take place and, apart from the weak complaints
of the victims, no one protests. Every good Christian says: why
should I? I'm not crazy."

"It's all the fault of materialism," Don Gennaro, who was terrified, interrupted. "That's what you're trying to say."

"He ought to be locked up in a lunatic asylum," Donna
Palmira whispered into Don Marcantonio's ear. "That's where he
belongs."

"Hasn't he a family, relatives?"

"He never had a wife to tame him. He proposed to Donna
Maria Vincenza after she was widowed, but she turned him down
and he never got over it."

"Over the high altar in your parish church, Donna Palmira,"
Don Severino went on, in a state of greater exaltation than ever,
"there are some words that by themselves indicate the whole distance between Jesus and our conventional Christian ways.
OBLATUS EST QUIA IPSE VOLUIT. He sacrificed Himself because He
so wished. Thus, no one obliged Him, so to speak, nor, being
God, did He feel any compelling need to be written about in the
newspapers, nor was He tempted by the idea of becoming a
member of the town council of Jerusalem. What He did was completely gratuitous. Thus from the point of view of ordinary Christian common sense, Donna Palmira, His was an act of madness,
and note that the word 'madness' has been used by many saints in
connection with the cross. Is it a similar example that you propose
to hold up to the youth of our country, Don Marcantò?"

"Let me tell you, Severì," Don Gennaro, who was acutely un-
comfortable, suddenly announced, "let me tell you that I for my
part refuse to listen to you. I've often told you before that when
you start talking about religion I try to think about something else.
Not that there's any likelihood of my being converted by your
impiety, but simply because it's not a layman's business to talk
about religion. For my part, when I want to listen to a sermon, I
go to church."

"Don Severì," De Paolis interrupted, "as we're not all priests' brothers here, you may go on. To tell you the truth, I didn't know you were so good at sacred eloquence. Your argument amuses me a great deal. What the devil do you conclude from it?"

Donna Palmira, silent and terrified, was standing near the fireplace, watching the door and the window as if she were afraid that someone might be spying on them.

"I'm sorry," Don Severino said, "I don't know what's the matter with me this evening. Perhaps I am crazy."

"Did you say perhaps?" said Don Lazzaro. "Doubt's the name of the disease you're suffering from."

"In the end . . ." Don Severino would have liked to conclude, but he was brought up short by the look of hatred in Donna Palmira's eyes.

"In the end . . ." Don Marcantonio said, to encourage him to go on.

"You are mistaken," Don Severino went on, turning his back on the mistress of the house, "if you think you can use the crucifix for your purposes. According to the common sense recommended to us by the priests and the political authorities, Jesus would have been an ideal model for us if he had married, had many children, a mother-in-law and a father-in-law, sons-in-law and daughters-in-law and grandchildren, if he had expanded his carpenter's shop and by economizing on his workmen's pay had managed to outdo his competitors and had died at a ripe old age, troubled by gout, perhaps, but in any event with a comfortable nest egg in the bank. Instead of which —"

"It's all the fault of materialism," repeated Don Gennaro, taking advantage of the pause.

Don Severino was standing and leaning with one elbow on the mantelpiece, and he spoke with the passion of a man who is at last coming out with things he has been thinking about for years and refuses to be silenced.

"Why are you raving, Severì?" Don Lazzaro shouted at him. "What have you been drinking today? Be reasonable."

"Oh, no," Don Severino replied with a grimace of disgust. "Anything but reasonable. And for the very good reason that your common sense makes me sick. I don't know, *cavaliere*, if you have ever been into the church at Orta, which is dedicated to San Bartolomeo. Well, rather than renounce his faith that backward and primitive man preferred to be flayed alive. The statue of him in the little church in Orta shows him natural size, with the muscles of his whole body laid bare and bleeding and the skin hanging from his left forearm like a raincoat. I assure you it's not a pleasant sight to be permanently on view in a public place to which children are admitted; above all, it's not an edifying spectacle, an example, a model to be followed. San Bartolomeo did not let himself be skinned alive in order to pay his taxes or the interest on his mortgage; he faced his horrifying torture for the sake of the ridiculous, superfluous, intangible thing that's called truth. He didn't say to himself like a good churchgoer of the present day: who's making me do this? Why should I? He compromised his career in a senseless and scandalous manner."

Donna Palmira was shocked and breathless.

"Now you're really going too far," she protested, red with anger.

No one had ever heard Don Severino talk so much. He was transfigured. What was the matter with him? Don Lazzaro was on his knees, trying to revive the fire that had gone out by blowing on it, and he turned and cast him an ill-natured, resentful, furious glance. Puffs of smoke from under the chimney hood made the guests cough and brought tears to their eyes. Don Lazzaro breathed like a pair of bellows on the embers that refused to catch.

"You know, Don Severì," Donna Palmira exclaimed in an agitated, almost terrified voice, "you know I don't like interfering in men's discussions, but when the subject is religion it's a woman's duty to take notice, to prevent God and the saints from being offended beyond due measure. Often, of course, God causes horrible disasters to happen solely to punish them for impious talk. If you really have to talk like that, Don Severì, if you really can't help it, you ought at least to have the courtesy to do it in the open air or, if the weather's bad, in a house a long way away from mine."

This invitation seemed to make an impact on Don Severino.

"Actually, Donna Palmira," he said in some embarrassment, "I only wanted to give some gratuitous advice to Don Marcantonio, for whom I feel a great deal of sympathy for reasons I don't really understand. But I didn't imagine, Donna Palmira, that my blasphemies in any way endangered this old and robust Christian house of yours, which not even earthquakes and Don Lazzaro's sins have ever managed to shake."

"I thank you for your friendly advice," Don Marcantonio said in a polite and authoritative manner, "and I assure you that I appreciate the subtlety of your eloquence but, if you will forgive me for saying so, your fears are groundless. The question is not what thoughts or ideas might arise in the abstract from contemplation of the cross and the bones of the holy martyrs, but what kind of influence the crucifix and the relics of the Christian martyrs in practice exercise on the mass of the faithful. You yourself admitted a short time ago that in our country, which is permanently threatened by earthquakes and anarchy, the religion of the priests is one of the most effective forces for stability. And you cannot deny that the prudent domestic morality, the healthy fear of God and hell, the gentle resignation, the kneeling, the bending of the head, the kissing of the ground, the humble docility as of domesticated animals that so well justifies the designation of sheep by which bishops refer to the faithful and that of shepherd that they reserve for themselves, you cannot deny that all this is based, among other things, on devotion to the crucifix and the saints. And, to meet you halfway, Don Severì, let me add that it is based on the devotion in moderation that is recommended by reputable priests and is supervised by the *carabinieri*."

"But that is precisely why, *cavaliere*, I told you to leave the cross to the priests," Don Severino again insisted. "The priests have had agelong experience in the art of making the cross innocuous. But in spite of that, as you know, even those subtle experts do not always succeed in preventing ordinary Christians from taking the cross seriously and acting like madmen. To quote examples I should not have to go very far from Colle."

"No, not very far," Don Gennaro bitterly agreed. "To have all that money spent on your education by your family and then end up in that wicked manner instead of making your way in the world and establishing a position in life is not just scandalous, it's rank ingratitude, as every person of common sense is bound to admit."

"There's one thing I don't understand," Don Marcantonio admitted. "Has that maniac Pietro Spina, about whom there's much too much talk, got no ambition?"

"He's without ambition, but not without pride," said Don Severino.

"I don't understand," said Don Marcantonio. "What do you mean?"

"He's against the law," Don Lazzaro shouted, losing his patience. "Is that so difficult to understand?"

"We, the secular arm, are responsible, as you know, for dealing with our contemporary madmen," Don Marcantonio said with a protective smile. "Your fears do you honor, Don Severino, but they are superfluous."

"Persecution has never frightened the madmen of the cross," Don Severino replied. "Perhaps they actually welcome it, who knows?"

"The real trouble is materialism," Don Gennaro, as deaf and undaunted as a martyr under torture, repeated yet again.

"A highly effective weapon against those dangerous Christians," Don Severino went on, ignoring him, "used to be the monasteries, which at least took them out of circulation and made them innocuous. But for some time past there have been many signs that seem to show that monasteries no longer serve that purpose, and that the madmen of the cross who manage to keep out of prison and lunatic asylums take refuge in secret societies."

"In bad times," Don Marcantonio admitted, "mythomaniac knights, raving would-be saviors of the world, always arise and draw poor Sancho Panzas behind them. But that is a form of madness, Don Severì, that among us is disappearing."

"You're perfectly right," Donna Palmira agreed enthusiastically. "They're real lunatics, they think themselves better than others. But how can anyone believe himself to be better than others? You're quite right, they must be destroyed. You talk better than Don Coriolano."

"The struggle against those lunatics is, as you say, a struggle against pride," Don Lazzaro added. "The most irritating thing about them is their pride, their vanity, their continual talk of conscience and human dignity and respect. Anyone who thinks himself better than others must be destroyed, the hypocrites must be crushed."

Don Lazzaro repeated the word "crushed" three or four times, each time stamping his feet so violently that he made the walls shake.

"Oh, so here we are, all agreed at last," Don Severino exclaimed with ironic satisfaction. "But I don't share your optimism, Don Marcantonio, I don't believe you will ever succeed in completely uprooting that proud, rebellious plant. And even if you do, I don't believe you'll be able to destroy the seeds that are already germinating underground here and there. (Where? No one can tell, perhaps in places that no one suspects.) There will always be strange creatures who hunger not for food alone but for something else and who need a little self-respect to be able to put up with this dreary life."

"Severì, I appeal to you to turn off the tap now, the fields have been watered enough," said Don Coriolano, who was bored and tired. "If Lazzaro will permit me, I should like to take the liberty of asking whether he invited us to dinner this evening or to spiritual exercises."

"Assunta is setting the table," Donna Palmira announced.

The pitiful whining of a dog came floating up the staircase.

"Please don't make such a noise with the chairs, Assunta," Don Severino said. "Yes, it's my dog, I recognize it. Heaven knows where it has been hiding. Excuse me, friends, I must go."

"Won't you stay to dinner?" Donna Palmira said in feigned protest, though she was delighted to see him go. "After staying all this time, do you insist on going just when we're sitting down to eat?"

"Didn't you hear my dog, Donna Palmira? I really must go."

"If you're so fond of it, the dog can come up too. But I don't want to force you, of course."

"The truth is that I've no appetite," Don Severino said in embarrassment. "Actually, Donna Palmira, if you don't mind my mentioning it, I'm feeling slightly sick, or rather very sick. The fresh air on the walk back to Orta will do me good. Good-bye."

"Good-bye, good-bye, our respects to the beautiful Faustina," the notables called out.

Don Gennaro caught him up on the stairs.

"What is it?" Don Severino exclaimed, turning toward him angrily. "Don't you know that everything is over between me and your brother? Didn't he tell you? Didn't he warn you?"

"Don't talk to me like that," Don Gennaro said imploringly. "Let me explain."

"Your common sense stinks," Don Severino said contemptuously. "You call your cowardice religion."

"Luca's in bed, here in Colle, in my house, with a high fever and fits of delirium," Don Gennaro said with embarrassment. "And in his delirium he keeps calling you. That's why I came to look for you."

"Why didn't you tell me that before, you idiot?"

No sooner were they in the street than Don Gennaro said: "Let us go by way of the lower part of the village, Severì. Then no one will see you coming to my house. I don't want to arouse suspicions."

12

"THERE'S NO DOUBT ABOUT it," Pietro Spina said anxiously, "everything you tell me about him makes me more certain that he's my friend from Pietrasecca. Come over here, Venanzio, don't keep standing by the door, come and sit down. Now listen to me, Venanzio, you've got to help me to get that poor friend of mine released. In the stupid situation I'm in there's nothing I can do without your help, so let us think about what to do and do it immediately."

Pietro quickly gathered the sheets of paper that were scattered on the table, put them in a big envelope, put them away in a drawer, and locked it. It was the beginning of a "Letter to a Young European of the Twenty-Second Century, With Special Reference to the Young People of the Former Italian Nation."

"I'm afraid, sir, if I may say so, that you misunderstood me," replied Venanzio, his face suddenly darkening. "The man I saw being led away by two *carabinieri* could not possibly have been a friend of yours as you say. I think I've already told you that when he first appeared in the square he attracted the attention of many people precisely because of his wild appearance. He may be one of the usual vagabonds, he may have escaped from prison, or he may be one of those birds of ill omen that come from heaven knows where and appear on the eve of major disasters. In that case there's nothing whatever that can be done, even God Almighty can't fly in the face of destiny. A man of that kind passed through Colle on the day before the big earthquake, and many still remember him. You will of course do as you please, sir, but it is not my business nor is it to my liking to concern myself with such persons."

"That man is not a vagabond," Pietro said, forcing himself to speak calmly. "He's a poor *cafone*, only a bit poorer, a bit more wretched than others because he has been almost stone deaf from birth and has no family. In any event, Venanzio, I can assure you that I'm not afraid of birds of ill omen, down-and-outs, vagabonds, or men with no home and no land. In fact I can assure you that the few friends I have had so far have been of that type. It's a matter of great regret to me, Venanzio, that, despite my best intentions, every conversation we have had has degenerated into an argument, and that what I say so often shocks you. But now I don't want an argument, and as long as that friend of mine remains in prison I shall be unable to talk about anything but ways and means of getting him out. Don't look at me like that, Venanzio, please listen to me, don't be as stubborn as a mule. Well, then, if it's true that he was arrested only because he had no identity papers, it shouldn't be difficult to get him out. It will be sufficient, I'm sure, if someone from Colle says he knows him and is able to give definite information about him. You can rest assured that I'd go myself, Venanzio, but for the fact that it would be making them a present for which they are only too anxious and that my testimony on his behalf would harm rather than help him. But you would be running no risk whatever, Venanzio, and you would be doing a good deed."

"Really, sir, you must excuse me, I have never had anything to do with the *carabinieri*," Venanzio replied, frowning and looking grim. "You should know, sir, that I'm proud of the fact that never in my life have I been to the *carabiniere* barracks, either for good or for evil. And I don't see why now, at my time of life, I should start meddling in things that don't concern me. I can only repeat that I don't know the man who was arrested last night, I have no idea who he is, and what could I tell them about him?"

Thin rectangles of gray evening light filtered through the closed shutters of the two corner windows and crisscrossed and formed a grid pattern on the walls that suggested a big cage. Pietro took a step toward one of the windows to open it, but a quick and vigorous movement by the groom reminded him of the reasons why it was necessary to avoid opening the windows at certain times of the day. He shrugged his shoulders like a prisoner exasperated by vexatious prison regulations and started striding up and down the room in a state of great agitation. Every so often he cast an angry and contemptuous glance at the recalcitrant servant. Venanzio remained motionless; he was wet through, and was standing in a puddle formed by the melting of the snow he had brought in with him. His shapeless boots in the middle of the puddle looked like two enormous, muddy toads and, over and above the very visible traces of the work he had been doing in the stable, there was also something marshy, sticky, and moldy about the rest of him. He would never have dared appear in that state in Donna Maria Vincenza's presence, but he probably liked showing the youngest of the Spinas what work in the fields meant. Pietro, disgusted, impatient, and at a loss what to do, circled around him like a peasant around a mule that refuses to budge. Then he stopped and was about to speak, but at the last moment swallowed what he was going to say and tried a more conciliatory and persuasive approach.

"I've already explained to you," he began with difficulty, "I've already tried to explain to you, Venanzio, that that poor devil, that friend of mine, is a *cafone* from Pietrasecca. He may be twenty, he may be thirty, it's hard to tell. They call him Infante (as is the custom here) because he has been deaf from birth, but actually he's not completely deaf, and the only reason why he never learned to talk is that no one ever took the trouble to teach him. His mother died when he was a baby, his father left for America, during the first few years he seems sometimes to have written from

Philadelphia, and then there was no more news of him, and no one knows whether he's alive or dead. I was told this by the owner of the stable in which I was hidden at Pietrasecca. During my first few months there I never noticed him, I saw him once or twice in the street but didn't know about his deafness, and one evening when I was very depressed I followed him to his den to talk to him a little. I had never imagined, Venanzio, that in this country a human being could be in a plight worse than that of an animal. As the shed in which I hid was only a few yards from his den, chance willed it that he discovered my hiding place. He kept the secret, and often came to keep me company. I should never have imagined, Venanzio, that one could take such a liking to a person whom one hardly knew. I want to make it quite clear, Venanzio, that this had nothing to do with gratitude. Of course he might have betrayed me, denounced me, sold me in some way and, in view of his abject poverty, in a sense he would have been perfectly justified in doing so. Instead he helped me. But I assure you that my feeling for that poor man is not based on gratitude. It's a stronger, more disinterested feeling, something of the nature of kinship. I say that to give you some idea of what I feel about him, Venanzio, because you probably believe there's nothing stronger than links of blood. Well then, Venanzio, imagine that I had a brother who as the result of some foolish escapade had fallen into the hands of the police and was in prison, though innocent. Well, that is more or less Infante's position. There's a legal way of securing the poor man's release, and it's simple, honest, and in no way compromising. Let me repeat, Venanzio, I want you to go to the *carabiniere* barracks and tell them you're able to give definite information about the man who was arrested last night; you can tell them he's so-and-so from such-and-such and that you met him at a market, at Rocca dei Marsi, or Fossa or Orta, wherever you like, and that you bought a box of tomatoes from him for Donna Maria Vincenza."

"Donna Maria Vincenza sells tomatoes, she doesn't buy them; still less would she buy them from anyone from Pietrasecca where, as everyone knows, tomatoes don't ripen," Venanzio pointed out with a scornful grimace.

"Very well, say you bought a bag of lentils from him . . ."

"Lentils from Pietrasecca? Lentils are not grown in the mountains, but I'm not surprised you don't know that."

"Very well, Venanzio, then say you bought stakes from him for Donna Maria Vincenza's beans, tomatoes, vines, and fruit trees. I leave what you say you bought from him entirely to you. Tell them you didn't have enough money on you that day, so you still owe him some."

"But excuse me, sir, it isn't true, we don't owe him anything. Why should we owe him anything if we never actually bought anything from him?"

"Don't make me lose my patience, Venanzio, tell the *carabinieri* that he must have come to Colle to get the money my grandmother owed him. That would explain why he left home without provisions and without money. And take him fifty lire on my grandmother's behalf."

"I realize, sir, that all this would in a way be a made-up story, but suppose the man refuses to pay back the money when he leaves the barracks? Suppose he uses what I tell the *carabinieri* to claim that the money belongs to him, because it was owed him? Excuse me, but I'd be in a fine fix, wouldn't I, sir?"

"I didn't say anything about asking him to repay the fifty lire, Venanzio."

"Oh, so you want to give them to him? But sir, do you know what you have to do in the country to earn an amount like that? At least ten days' heavy labor. But I'm not surprised you don't know that."

"But Venanzio," Pietro exclaimed impatiently, "I think I'm entitled to do what I like with my own money."

"Certainly, sir, what next?" Venanzio replied, again assuming a surly and hostile manner. "But, if I may say so, sir, I don't think it's my business to go and testify in favor of a total stranger like that. I don't think it's wise for me to go and speak for a down-and-out who not only has no identity papers but also has no visible means of support; for even you, after all, can't say what he has lived on for the past few days or for what secret purposes he may

have come to our part of the world. I don't think you can exclude
the possibility, for instance, that he may have committed thefts on
the way."

"I don't exclude that possibility, Venanzio, and, to tell you the
truth, it doesn't interest me."

"In that case, if I may say so, sir, I don't think an honest man
should help that sort of person. I repeat, no one can convince me
that I have any sort of obligation toward an individual of that type."

"Nor did that poor beggar have any obligation toward me,"
Pietro replied, biting his lips in anger. "Nevertheless, I repeat,
apart from the owner of the stable, who later sold me to my grandmother like a fattened calf, throughout the time I was hidden at
Pietrasecca that man, of whom you now talk with contempt, was
the only person who knew of my hiding place, and he didn't give
me away. Certainly, Venanzio, you'll never have to hide from the
police, but you might possibly end up in a ditch with your cart
and oxen and be badly injured. I assume that in that dangerous
situation you'd shout for help and think it natural to be helped,
even by strangers."

"You're perfectly right," Venanzio replied with heavy sarcasm,
"and if such a disaster occurred (and may Sant'Antonio avert it)
those who came to my aid would certainly be quite right too. But
it would be very remarkable if they were strangers. Here everyone
knows everyone else, and when you meet someone in the street
you know where he's coming from and where he's going, and
even in the case of young children, whom a man of my age can't
possibly know individually, you can tell at a glance who their parents are. I've worked in this house for forty-two years, sir, I've
stayed here in good times and in bad, as you know, or ought to
know; and with God's will I hope to die here before infirmity
causes me to be thrown out or before a new master comes and
takes the Spinas' place. I have had opportunities for making myself independent, I assure you, and on several occasions there
were people who were willing to lend me the money to cross
the sea. But I stayed here even in the bad years when men left
Colle like bees swarming from a hive. Neither adventure nor

money has ever tempted me, sir. People know this, everyone knows everyone else here, and when misfortune strikes we help one another, for one thing because, as the saying is, today it's my turn, tomorrow it may be yours. Even those whom an unhappy fate sends far away from home, sir, as you know, rarely leave on their own, but go to places where they will meet people from the same village, names and faces whom they know. Many went to America, but did not mix with Americans; even there in a way they stayed at Colle. The few who sometimes venture among strangers on their own are nearly always lost souls and come to a bad end, as they deserve. Even here, when those from the same village go to the fair or to market, they stay together and eat at the same inns."

"I'm trying hard to understand you, Venanzio, to understand your farmyard-animal obstinacy," said Pietro, red with anger and having difficulty in repressing his exasperation. "But what am I to do to get you at least once to listen to me, not like a servant listening to his master, or like a peasant listening to a vagabond, but as one man listening to another or, if you prefer it, one Christian listening to another? I understand perfectly, Venanzio, that to hens the chicken run is the center of the universe, the safest place in which to grow fat, lay eggs, and hatch chicks, and that very likely to their little round eyes it seems to be the only honest and decent place and a shrine of morality. So I can understand that to you this being always together here among familiar people, this mutual aid in misfortunes when there's no way of doing without it, this willingness to help others on the condition or in the hope that you will be helped in return in case of need, can seem to be the most convenient and the least risky way of life. And, though you're not by any means a hen, I can also understand your making a virtue of necessity and priding yourself on a way of life that in the end is inspired by fear and self-interest. But what I want to know is whether, apart from that, you are capable of imagining (I say only imagining) a good deed free of all calculation, an honesty unconcerned with what people might say. I want to know whether you are capable of imagining a completely gratuitous generous act not tied to any idea of reward or repayment, even in the next world, but, on the contrary, connected with the threat of punishment, in short, a solidarity that is not that of the hen coop. I want an answer, not from your heart, but from your imagination."

"Of course, sir," Venanzio promptly replied. "I too know the story of the peasant who warmed at his breast the snake that was numbed with cold; it was in our reading book in the third grade at elementary school. Yes, sir, and I remember how that story ended."

"You may go," Pietro shouted in disgust. "And please don't set foot in my room again."

The pitiful whining of a dog came from the yard. Pietro turned his back on the groom, went over to a window, and tried to see between the slats of the closed shutters. Venanzio remained motionless in the middle of the room. He now looked just like an old beggar shivering after being pulled from a ditch full of dirty water; he shut his beady little eyes and gritted his teeth as if he were holding back tears. There was a yellow look about his face, halfway between the color of chalk and cork, there were greenish traces about his nose and ears, and his hair looked like a dirty wig.

"You're my master, of course," he muttered humbly, "there's no need to remind you of it. If you tell me to, I'll go wherever you like. What else do you expect?"

"Don't you understand I'm not your master?" Pietro shouted, giving vent to his anger. "I don't want to be anyone's master. But I assure you that if you were a sheep I'd sell you at the next market to avoid having to see you again, you repugnant creature."

Through the shutters Pietro saw a tall, grim-looking woman approaching the courtyard gate; her face was veiled, she was dressed completely in black, and she was an impressive sight. When she reached the gate she called Natalina, at first in an almost normal voice and then, as she lost patience, in long, loud, angry wails. After a few moments of silent consternation in the house, shrill cries from the maid were followed by a prolonged slithering sound and the noise of smashing dishes.

"It's Aunt, it's Aunt, it's Aunt," Natalina could be heard shrieking up the staircase.

With disheveled hair and without pausing for breath she hurried to find Donna Maria Vincenza, and said in a distraught voice: "Aunt's at the gate, madam."

"What aunt?"

"Aunt Eufemia, madam, she's waiting outside the gate."

"Don't get so agitated, Natalina, calm down. What was that noise just now? Have you broken more plates?"

"It's Aunt Eufemia, madam, Aunt Eufemia herself, she's waiting at the gate."

"What do you mean waiting, Natalina?"

"She's waiting for me to let her in, madam, she can't be left waiting."

"Then go and let her in, Natalina, and if she wants to talk to me show her into the drawing room."

The meeting between Signora Spina and the last of the De Dominicises was not without a certain embarrassed and pathetic solemnity, and also a certain absurdity.

"Please take a seat, Signorina De Dominicis," said Donna Maria Vincenza, pointing politely to an armchair. "Welcome."

Aunt Eufemia's black dress was hemmed with old lace and was moth-eaten in places, and her small black hat was adorned with a bunch of artificial violets; she did not seem to have noticed that her green stockings had slipped down her powerful shins. Slowly she took off her cinnamon-colored woolen gloves and gathered over her brow her veil with its little black and white dots, revealing a skinny face that was as yellow as tallow candles and two big watery eyes that were green and black like oysters.

"As perhaps you know, Signora Spina, we haven't talked to each other for about a hundred fifty years, if I'm not mistaken," Aunt Eufemia, who was shivering as if she were feverish, managed to stammer out.

"Really, Signorina De Dominicis," Donna Maria Vincenza replied with an affable smile, "I ask you to believe that in spite of appearances I'm not as old as that, and actually I doubt whether I shall ever reach that age. May I offer you a cup of coffee, Signorina De Dominicis? I should be genuinely dismayed, Signorina

De Dominicis, if you preferred the new fashionable drink, tea, as it is called, as I have none to offer you."

Aunt Eufemia was annoyed at being interrupted.

"What I meant was that for a hundred fifty years, if I'm not mistaken, Signora Spina, our families have not spoken to each other. Yes, I should be delighted to have a cup of coffee. As you know, Signora Spina, during my life I have with Christian humility drained to the dregs the bitter cup presented to me by destiny. But I have always refused to drink tea. Do you too, Signora Spina, believe it to be a beverage of Piedmontese origin?"

"Piedmontese or English, Signorina De Dominicis," Donna Maria Vincenza agreed out of politeness.

Aunt Eufemia made a grimace and gesture of disgust; she took a black lace handkerchief from the left cuff of her blouse and gravely spat into it.

"For a hundred fifty years, if I'm not mistaken," she repeated, having apparently lost the thread of what she was going to say, "for about a hundred fifty years, Signora Spina, if I'm not mistaken, our families have not spoken to each other."

"Perhaps they didn't have a great deal to say to each other, Signorina De Dominicis," Donna Maria Vincenza remarked to help her out. "Perhaps a hundred fifty years ago they took literally the admonition that after death we shall have to render an account of all the idle words we have spoken in this world. Our forefathers, Signorina De Dominicis, preferred deeds to words."

"Before coming to see you, Signora Spina, I went to the cemetery," Aunt Eufemia went on in a tone that excluded joking. "You will appreciate, Signora Spina, that I did not wish to take such an audacious step as setting foot in this house without consulting my forefathers. In a way I am now talking to you in their name. You will forgive me, Signora Spina, if my voice betrays a certain amount of emotion."

"Oh, Signorina De Dominicis, what a shame I don't play the lottery," Donna Maria Vincenza said in a tone of simulated reproach. "Perhaps if I did I should be able to get a lucky three from what you are saying."

"You will not be offended, I hope," Aunt Eufemia went on in more confident tones and with a display of amiability, "if I admit that my forefathers had certain doubts about your family's character. I know you were born a Camerini, but the sacrament of marriage made you a Spina. I must also admit that in the past there was no lack of charming madmen among the Spinas; but the truth is that side by side with their wild actions they knew only too well how to protect their interests. Perhaps my forefathers' mistrust was unjustified. However, it is in misfortune that a family's nobility is revealed; and in an age that is very hard on you and yours, Signora Spina, you have given the lie to the superstition that it is not granted to women to gain titles of nobility for their families. Your magnificent refusal of the offer of a pardon made to you by the Piedmontese dynasty . . ."

"Excuse me, Signorina De Dominicis, but do you take one or two pieces of sugar? Please leave the coffeepot on the table, Natalina, and leave us alone."

"No sugar, Signora Spina. If the coffee is good, I take it without sugar. Thank you. I was saying, Signora Spina, that that noble refusal of yours, if you will permit me a rather crude expression, has marked the final breach between your family and vulgar people. After a hundred fifty years of mutual hostility and mistrust, Signora Spina, allow the last of the De Dominicises . . ."

"Please, Natalina, don't pour the whole contents of the coffeepot in my lap; at least have some consideration for your aunt, who might want another cup. Look, Natalina, you'd do better to put the coffeepot on the table and leave us alone. Forgive me, Signorina De Dominicis, I'm so sorry to have interrupted you in the middle of your gracious remarks."

Meanwhile Pietro was striding from one room to the other on the top floor like a soul in purgatory. From the highest window in the attic he looked down at the irregular rooftops of the village three hundred feet below and tried to decide which of them was that of the *carabiniere* barracks. He recognized the public offices building, built in the heroic-funereal style of the most recent fashion, between the old part of the village, where a few hundred smoke-blackened, dilapidated hovels huddled around the church, and the part that was built after the earthquake, consisting of small, uniform, yellow one-story houses arranged in checkerboard fashion rather like beehives.

"Natalina, are the prisoners' cells on the upper floor or in the basement of the barracks?" Pietro asked the girl, whom he surprised eavesdropping outside the door of Donna Maria Vincenza's room.

"Really, sir," Natalina said with a blush, "it may seem strange to you, but I assure you that I've never yet been to prison."

"But at least you know who does the cooking now for the prisoners?"

"No, sir, I'm terribly sorry, but I haven't the slightest idea; I have all my meals here."

"But Natalina, you'll at least have heard whether there are other prisoners in the Colle prison. Haven't there been any arrests recently? I mean for theft, or assault, or being drunk and disorderly."

"Not among the few girls I know, sir. I'm sorry to have to admit it, but I assure you that there haven't been any arrests among my friends."

"Natalina, you don't know anything at all," Pietro exclaimed, losing patience. "Really, never in the whole of my life have I talked to such a stupid girl."

That evening at dinner he hardly touched his food and listened, bored and absentminded, to his grandmother's amusing account of Aunt Eufemia's visit. His excuse was that he had a bad headache, but his face, which up to the day before had expressed impassivity or detachment, now betrayed acute unhappiness. Donna Maria Vincenza avoided questioning him, pretended to believe in his headache, and after dinner asked him to join her in front of the fire, as he had done on the first few evenings after his arrival, perhaps hoping that he would unburden himself. But he drew his chair up to the hearth, leaned his head against a post, and remained silent, sad, weary, and distracted. His head cast a long, thin shadow on the smoke-blackened stone; his tobacco-colored face, with features that seemed to have been marked with a burned cork, seemed attached like a bas-relief to the dark stone, and the flames of the fire added a thin red outline to the profile. He created a very strange and contradictory impression, of a man in his own home and also of a wayfarer, almost an intruder.

Donna Maria Vincenza went about her little evening tasks. She added some oil to the lamp in front of the picture of Our Lady of Mercy, put some kindling on the fire, and drew a chair under the lamp and started mending linen. Her movements were very slow; she had the solidity, the good quality, the color, and perhaps actually the same age as the household objects; in short, it was evident that she had never been away from them and could move about among them with her eyes shut, repeating the familiar actions that mothers have carried out for thousands of years. She raised her eyes for a moment to the picture of Our Lady of Mercy in silent prayer, as if to say: O Blessed Virgin, it's not easy to be a mother. In the light of the fire her face had the transparency of old porcelain, and the same tiny cracks. Pietro remained silent, staring at the fire; heaven knows what he was thinking about. The dry firewood on the hearth burned up, leaving on the firedogs half a trunk of a beech tree that had failed to catch; the dampness boiled and bubbled on the gray and brown bark with its silvery streaks.

"Venanzio might have chopped it up," Pietro muttered. "Or he might at least have let it dry before putting it on the fire."

"He'll have put it there in order to dry it," Donna Maria Vincenza explained. After a short pause she went on: "I'm a little worried at his not having come back for dinner. Could something have happened to him? Forgive me for mentioning it, but after every talk he has with you he's very upset. You ought to be less hard on him, less demanding. He had a difficult and desolate youth, as perhaps you know; he's a child of the Madonna, as the saying is."

"A foundling?"

"Yes, hence his surname, Di Dio. And he has never resigned himself to that fact, though there are plenty of others in Colle. It's the bane of his life. Hence perhaps his devotion to our family, his fear of the unknown, his hatred and mistrust of tramps and vagabonds. Don't be hard on him. I remember once when there was an obscure quarrel between him and another servant, I've long since forgotten what it was about, your grandfather sacked both of them. The other man found himself another job without making a fuss about it, but Venanzio came back, went down on his knees, kissed the hem of my skirt, admitted he was in the wrong, and appealed to me to give him any other punishment, even the most severe, even to the extent of withholding his wages for a long time, if only we would take him back; and that in spite of the fact that at that time jobs were easy to find. But he was always afraid of the unknown."

Donna Maria Vincenza stopped, wetted the end of the cotton on her spool between her lips, held it up to the needle against the light, and threaded it; then she knotted the thread. In the yellowish light of the lamp there were straw-colored reflections in the pale gray hair wound around her head in two thin braids; and she bent over her work and sewed with such concentration that she might have been a girl doing needlework for the first time. Pietro let the conversation drop and remained thoughtfully gazing at the fire.

"I'm worried at Venanzio's being so late," Donna Maria Vincenza repeated after a time. "I haven't yet told you that he went to the *carabiniere* barracks to try to secure the release of that acquaintance of yours who was arrested yesterday. But he ought to be back by now. I hope it went off all right."

Pietro made a gesture of extreme surprise, and his eyes filled with tears.

"To think of having to have recourse to a third party to go to a friend's aid," he said. "Knowing him to be only two or three hundred yards away and not being able to see him, or go for a stroll with him, or invite him into the house."

Donna Maria Vincenza took Pietro by the hand and said: "You're as attached to him as that? Have you known him for long?"

"If you only knew," Pietro tried to explain. "The man's so poor."

"If I were poor, my dear boy, would you be a bit fond of me too? It may happen yet, you know."

"But Grandmother, what makes you think I'm not fond of you? But frankly, being fond of you seems to me to be just the same as being fond of myself, it's a form of selfishness. Also, to be perfectly frank with you, Grandmother, you'll never be poor, you couldn't be, however much you tried, and even if you were short of food and clothing, you'd be, let me see, what would you be like? You'd be like a queen doing spiritual exercises."

"From that point of view, my dear boy, you're not and couldn't be poor either."

"Yes, it's difficult to be genuinely poor. Did Venanzio tell you anything about the man they arrested in the square yesterday?"

"Yes, he told me what you told him. He's a deaf-mute, isn't he?"

"He can stammer a few half words his mother taught him, and the one that crops up most frequently is *tata*, which means 'father.' That's why they called him Infante."

"His father's in America?"

"He went to Philadelphia, and he stopped writing and never came back. No one knows whether he's alive or dead. His mother just had time to teach him to say tata in case her husband came back. Since her death the *cafoni* of Pietrasecca have used him as a communal donkey or mule; he's exploited and maltreated by everyone, and in a way he's everyone's slave. In return he's allowed to enter and leave everyone's house without knocking; they let him because, thanks to his deafness, he can't give away any secrets. He lives on leftovers, competing with the chickens, the dogs, and the pigs, and you can imagine what kitchen leftovers are like in *cafone* families: potato peelings, cabbage stalks, occasionally a bit of stale bread that has turned as hard as a stone. As he grew up he taught himself to make about a dozen harsh, shrill, guttural sounds, which he sometimes uses to try to express himself, rather like an animal. But he's not stupid and he's not evil; he lacks mind but he certainly doesn't lack soul. He's certainly not the noble savage either, the pure and ridiculous natural man of Rousseau-ish novels; oh dear, no. He's a perfectly ordinary *cafone*,

only a little poorer, a little more wretched than the others. But
how is one to be impartial about a man one likes? He came to see
me every evening in the dark and filthy stable in which I hid at
Pietrasecca. I waited for him every evening. When the whole village had gone to sleep I'd hear him crossing the alleyway, tripping
over something, stopping, turning back, removing the unhinged
door, and coming in. He would lie down on the straw between
me and the donkey, sometimes he'd mutter incomprehensible
monosyllables in my ear, perhaps he was trying to give me some
news, but generally he was silent. How can I give you an idea,
Grandmother, of the simple, silent, deep friendship that developed between us? Usually I was reminded of his presence only by
his slow, deep breathing, but there was an affinity, a community, a
fraternity between me and the other bodies and things in that cave
— Infante, the donkey, the mice, the manger, the straw, the
donkey's saddle, a broken lamp — the discovery of which filled
my mind with a new feeling that perhaps, Grandmother, I should
call peace. But in any event, Grandmother, don't conclude that
this was romantic exaltation at finding myself immersed in so-
called nature, because, like most people born and bred in the
country, I'm almost indifferent to nature. Nor do I think that that
spontaneous communion and recognition of myself in such petty
and humble objects can have been prompted by my ideas, my political beliefs; as a piece of evidence to the contrary, the owner of
that stable was a poor *cafone*, but his daily visits filled me with
horror and repugnance. I realized at once that the only reason why
he didn't hand me over to the police was that from the very first
moment when he learned my real name he realized that I represented an opportunity for substantial profit. Perhaps 'friendship' is
not the right word for the kind of relationship that developed between me and the other things in that hiding place; it would be
more correct to say I felt myself in company, in good, reliable company, that in short I had found companions. 'Company' was in fact
the first new word Infante learned from me. He could already say
pane, bread, which he pronounced 'paan'; and I explained to him
by gestures that two persons who ate the same bread became *cum-*

pane, companions, and that *cumpaani*, company, came from *cumpaani*. Next day Infante gave me another example of his intelligence and his complete harmony with my way of feeling by pointing out to me some mice that were scampering about in the straw looking for bread crumbs, and murmuring in my ear: *cumpaani*. After that he started offering a crust of bread to the donkey every day so that he too should be part of our company and we could truthfully call him a companion, as he well deserved. I ought to talk to you at length, Grandmother, about my stay in that stable, always with a view to making clear to you that it explains my present state of mind. Because when I left it I was, if not completely transformed, certainly stripped bare. It seems to me that previously I had not been myself, but had been playing a role, like an actor in the theater, equipping myself with the appropriate mask and speaking the required lines. All this life of ours now seems to me to be theatrical, conventional, a pretense."

"My dear boy," Donna Maria Vincenza said, "you're trying to frighten me."

"You'll agree, Grandmother, that if I had died, knowing nothing about this country except what is printed in books, I should not even have known that *cafoni* existed. And it's not as if there were only a few of them or they were of negligible importance, because in the end we all live on their labor. I should never have learned from books that Infante existed. I assure you, grandmother, that I dislike causing you pain and, if it were not repugnant to me to pretend with a person I love, I should gladly conceal from you what I now see. Looked at with the naked eye, as I now am able to see it, our country has the ephemeral and unsubstantial quality of a stage set; one night we shall have an earth tremor a little more violent than usual and next day the play will be over. There's little to be cheerful about. But the quiet, the peace, the intimacy, the well-being that I felt in that stable came to me from that humble and secure *cumpaani*. I spent hours listening to the donkey munching hay, and I couldn't help thinking that there were few human beings who preserved at the table such detachment and good manners. The rare signs of life from the outside world that reached me in that hole were of the same quality. At the top of a wall, near where the roof beam rested, I discovered an opening about a hand's breadth in size; if I sat astride the donkey it gave me an arrow-slit view of a dung heap and a few yards of snow-covered path. Sometimes a hairless old sheepdog with a spiked collar as a protection against wolves came along it, and occasionally a few chickens passed by. They came toward my hiding place, looked at the hole through which I was watching them, and perhaps they saw me, or rather they certainly did, but they kept the information to themselves. I could also see a small patch of empty, whitish sky across which a few rare sparrows sometimes flew; some of them perched on the dung heap and jumped about and picked in the dung; they were restless and hungry, as even the birds are in this part of the world. There was another opening, big enough to let a cat through, at ground level at the bottom of one of the walls, which I discovered when I moved a big stone that closed it from the inside. I got into the habit of opening it every morning to let in some fresh air in addition to the little that came through the chinks in the door; in fact, to get more benefit from it, I lay down and rested my head quite near it on a handful of straw I used as a cushion. There was no risk of my being spotted, because right outside there was a clod of earth that had accumulated against the stone that blocked the hole; without the stone it looked like a clod of earth that had been cut in two, and it prevented any passerby who noticed the hole from seeing through it. I stayed motionless for hours with that clod of earth only a few inches away in front of my eyes, and it was my only horizon. I had never looked so closely at the earth before. I had never thought that a clod of earth when observed at close quarters could be such a vivid, rich, immense reality, a whole universe, an intricate agglomeration of mountains, valleys, marshes, tunnels, with strange and mostly unknown inhabitants. That, in the real sense of the word, was my discovery of the earth. The strange thing was this. I was born here, in the country, and I have been to half the countries in Europe, and once I went all the way to Moscow, for a congress. How many fields and meadows have I seen? I must have seen thousands of hills and mountains, millions of trees, hundreds and hundreds of rivers, but I had never before seen the earth as I saw it then. Just imagine it, Grandmother, if police hadn't forced me to hide in a cave after living for several decades I should never have known what earth is. I must explain that the word 'earth' has now assumed a very precise meaning for me; what it means to me now is above all that clod of earth that I saw so closely, got to know so intimately, and lived with for some time. In short, the word 'earth' to me now is like the name of someone I know well. Perhaps you will already have realized it, Grandmother, but I want to make it perfectly clear that there was nothing in any way special about that clod of earth, it wasn't particularly rich or fertile, it was a perfectly ordinary clod of earth. What a moving experience it was one morning when I discovered that a wheat seed had germinated in it. At first I was afraid it was dead, but I gingerly used a bit of straw to move the earth around it and discovered a minute white shoot sprouting from it, a tender, living shoot of the shape and size of a tiny blade of grass. The whole of my being, the whole of my soul, Grandmother, concentrated around that small seedling. It worried me to death that I didn't know exactly what to do to give it the best chance of survival. I still don't know whether what I did was right or not, and I still worry about it. As a substitute for the protection provided by the stone that I had moved and to shelter it from the frost, I put a little earth on it, and every morning I melted some snow to water it; and I often breathed on it to give it some warmth. That clod of earth, with that small, weak treasure hidden inside it, alive though threatened by so many dangers, ended up acquiring in my sight the mystery, the familiarity, the sanctity of a maternal bosom. And since, for lack of anything else to drink, I too had to use the small amount of snow that I could gather through that opening, I tried to make sure it was as clean as possible, though there was always a slight flavor of wood and dung, a flavor of liquid earth, about it; and the result was that in a way that small seed and I lived on the same food; in a way we became real companions. I felt my life to be as fragile, as helplessly exposed, and endangered as that of that small, abandoned seed beneath the snow; and at the same time I felt my life to be as natural, as alive, as important as its own, in fact I felt it to be life itself; I mean, I felt it to be not an image, a fiction, a representation of life, but life itself in its humble, painful, and always endangered reality. And it's absolutely impossible, and it would be only too easy and comfortable to console oneself with the idea of immortality — the immortality of wheat — when one is trembling about the fate of a particular grain of wheat that one has gotten to know personally and with which one has lived. I'm sorry, Grandmother, my words are not simple enough, clear enough, plain enough for what I'm trying to tell you. Throughout that period, let me repeat, I suffered no particular physical or mental disturbance. Only my heart, I must admit, beat more strongly than usual. At times I could distinctly hear its deep, dull irregular beat against the weak thoracic cavity as if from a great distance though it was so close; it was rather like the sound of a miner's pick at the bottom of a shaft; and also (as a result of a strange and inexplicable but precise association in my mind) it was just like the hammer blows of the carpenter when he closed my father's coffin. Memory creates strange associations. You too were there, Grandmother, when Mastro Eutimio put the lid on the coffin in which my father had been lying for twenty-four hours and nailed it down. I remember it as if it were yesterday. It was twilight, and the funeral procession was waiting in the street. I was alone, locked in my little room, pressing my hands to my ears, and keeping my eyes shut to isolate myself, to avoid hearing the solemn chanting of the priests. But I distinctly heard the carpenter's hammer blows on the coffin lid, the short, irregular, muffled hammerings that seemed to be coming from a great distance. But I did not suppose they would endure so stubbornly in my mind, that they would be so ingrained in my blood, to the extent that whenever my heart is agitated and beats strongly I hear it distinctly all over again. Is it so difficult to bury one's father? I don't know if you've had the same experience, Grandmother."

"I've seen many coffins nailed down, my son," Donna Maria Vincenza replied. "I've seen many loved persons die, I've seen many graves opened up and filled in again."

"After the death of persons who are dear to us," Pietro went on, "life takes on a different color; there's a shadow over it, and even morning seems like evening. Perhaps grief at the death of Don Benedetto and of another person whom you know about, Grandmother, predisposed me to making friends with the creatures and things of my obscure refuge and to estranging me from the rest of the world. I actually believe that even being arrested would not have disturbed that frame of mind; and if I did remain hidden, it was only out of instinctive obedience to the old rule that forbids gentlemen to hand themselves over spontaneously to their pursuers in order not to facilitate their disgusting job. Several times during the early days of my concealment, when the valley of Pietrasecca was infested with police, militia, and *carabinieri*, I had the idea of emerging from my hiding place and saying to them: may I ask, gentlemen, whom you are looking for? May I ask why you are sniffing and searching like hunting dogs under every bush, inside every cave, behind every rock? Oh, you're looking for me? You want to take me with you? You want to take *me* with *you*? But don't you see, you fools, that I don't belong to you, that I belong to a different species? Don't you know that even if you load me with chains you will never have me in your grasp? As you are so stupid, let me explain. I'm not one of those whose kingdom is of this world, you see, that is my secret and that of my friends. But please don't misunderstand me, I don't mean that our kingdom is in the heavens; that we magnanimously leave to the priests and the sparrows. No, our kingdom is underground. That is what I would have said to the stupid men who were hunting for me, but for the fact that even in those early days I would have found it very difficult indeed to part from the companions I found in that stable. But it was only later, in the cart that took me back to the valley on the river of time again, that I realized how much they had entered into my life. I must confess, Grandmother, that when I wake at night I often find myself wondering what Infante is doing now, whether he found any leftovers to eat last night or has learned a few more words, or still remembers what I taught him, and what Susanna is doing."

"Susanna?" Donna Maria Vincenza exclaimed in surprise.

"Yes, I've already told you she was there too," Pietro said. "Why are you so surprised?"

"A woman?"

"Yes, I mean no. The donkey I've mentioned so often is a female and her name is Susanna; I thought I'd mentioned it. Speaking dispassionately, there's nothing special about Susanna. She's a perfectly ordinary female donkey, thin, almost skeleton-like, deformed by hard work and with many abrasions and bare patches on her back and legs. But she's not without her qualities; she's taciturn, patient, resigned, and unemotional; yes, very unemotional indeed, and completely without the ridiculous ambitions by which the poor are often corrupted. You will have appreciated, Grandmother, that my affection for Susanna is not of the vague and insipid 'animal lovers' type. I took a liking to the poor beast only because for some time we ate the same food and slept on the same straw; and, I may add, we did this for a long time without quarreling and without her getting on my nerves. There's an expression in Susanna's eyes . . . Grandmother, have you ever looked a donkey in the eyes?"

"I may have done, my dear boy, I don't remember."

"In that case you haven't, because otherwise you'd certainly remember. Grandmother, if donkeys could speak . . ."

"Believe me, my dear boy, they wouldn't and couldn't say anything superhuman. They'd ask for good straw and clean water."

"Well, that may be. Even if they didn't go beyond those two or three words, at least they'd be referring to concrete, visible, tangible things. What an immense benefit it would be to our old, baroque civilization if we could only start all over again from the beginning, from bare straw and clean water, and grope our way forward from there, subjecting the big words in current use to severe scrutiny one by one."

"My dear boy, no one has any need to consult anyone or anything to understand what justice, honor, and loyalty are and, so far as I'm concerned, the devil can take the rest. Meanwhile I don't understand why Venanzio hasn't come back. Perhaps he has ended up in some tavern without realizing that we're waiting up for him."

As the wait grew protracted, Pietro persuaded his grandmother to go to bed and leave him to wait for Venanzio alone.

To pass the time he went into a neighboring room that was still called Don Berardo's room thirty years after his death and started rummaging among the old books about agriculture and the lives of the saints; literature was represented only by the *Divine Comedy*, Tasso's *Jerusalem Delivered*, and Silvio Pellico's *My Prisons*; there were also Muratori's and Botta's histories. There was no sign of any book on teaching deaf-mutes to speak. Pietro had already complained bitterly about this to his grandmother.

"In short, your library lacks the essentials," he said to her one day without beating around the bush.

"We've never had any deaf-mutes in the family," Donna Maria Vincenza apologized.

"Oh, the family, always and only the family," Pietro replied irritably.

He started looking through *Blackbeard's Almanac* and read with curiosity the meteorological, agricultural, dynastic, and terrestrial prognostications for the year. But, as no earthquake was foreseen for the Rome region, he ended up deciding that the almanac was stupid and reactionary. He yawned, his head grew heavy with sleep, and he rested his chin on his chest. He turned out the light and opened the window, perhaps counting on the cold night air to keep him awake; the window, like all the others on the ground floor, was protected by a solid grille. He climbed up onto the windowsill in order to be able to see a little farther, but his horizon was still restricted by the perimeter wall; beyond it the twisted and skeletonlike branches of the trees looked like barbed wire. Though the sky was overcast, the snow caused the courtyard to be suffused with gentle light; the objects under the snow had lost their materiality and had become pure shapes, rectangles, squares, triangles, pyramids around the cylindrical well. The gate was a black rectangle. Beyond it was the world. Pietro concentrated on his hearing, on trying to hear what he could not see. Outside the gate he once more heard the flowing of the ancient river of time, and the murmur of its waters brought him the querulous barking of some watchdogs. He listened to it for a long time with his brow against one of the iron bars. The courtyard in front of him was like a small island, the perimeter wall like a dike, the bars on the window were like those of a prison. He looked in the direction of the gate, which must suddenly have seemed very close, incredibly close, to him. He jumped down from the windowsill, shut the window, and walked quickly to the front door. It was solidly barricaded; apart from a heavy lock and a big chain, it was solidly bolted and barred. But it was easy to open from the inside. Pietro decided to leave. He tiptoed upstairs to his room, took from the wardrobe a heavy coat, a scarf, woolen gloves, and a pair of boots, and set about writing a note of farewell to his grandmother.

But at that very moment she called him from the next room. He hesitated, but when she called him for a third or fourth time he had no alternative but to put the woolen garments down on a chair and go to her room to see if she needed anything. The room was lit by an oil lamp placed on a shelf. She was lying on her back with her hands joined as if in prayer. St. François de Sales's *Introduction to the Devout Life* lay open on the bedside table.

"Hasn't Venanzio come back yet?" she asked. "And you're not in bed yet? Midnight struck a few minutes ago, my son. Oh, I feel I've been asleep for hours. I dreamed about you, my dear boy, and I was just coming to your room to tell you about it when I heard your footsteps. What a strange, sad, exhausting dream. I awoke with a start a few minutes ago. Sit down at the foot of the bed for a moment, my dear boy, and perhaps I'll get over it and be able to tell you about it. Well, I dreamed I was a she-donkey, not a metaphorical but a real one with four legs, a very ordinary beast of burden and an old one at that. In the end there was nothing strange about that, after all. But I had to carry you on my back, to help you try to find your father. I would be false modesty to say you weren't heavy, my dear boy; you must certainly have weighed at least a hundred twenty-five pounds; and it was a very difficult route that we took, through valleys, over mountains and hills, along rapid streams and strange rivers, through dark and frightening woods. Never in my life have I had to do anything so exhausting, and I assure you that my back and my knees are still aching, though I know very well it was only a dream. So perhaps it wasn't a dream. I can't complain of you as a rider, and I can't even say you beat me too much; but whenever I slowed down you jabbed me in the side with your heels and shouted at me to gee-up, gee-up, as it is the custom to do with donkeys. Well, what I had to do was to take you back to your father, and I had been told in a vague sort of way that he had taken refuge in a shrine. Heaven knows why, because though your father was a good Christian, he always preferred the smell of tobacco to that of candles. So I took you first to San Domenico di Cocullo, but he wasn't there. From there we went to Our Lady of Libera at Pratola, and then to San Giovanni da Capestrano. Going up some of those hills, my dear boy, I thought I'd never get my breath back. At every shrine I put you down at the door, went into the church, and looked for your father among the pilgrims in the sanctuaries, the confessionals, the side chapels, behind the high altar, in the sacristy, and in the guest quarters, and the strangest thing was that no one seemed surprised to see a donkey walking around the church."

"Donkeys are perfectly at home in churches," Pietro pointed out. "There's a donkey in every manger scene, in every flight into Egypt."

"To all those I met on the way I said: my good people, have you by any chance seen this boy's father pass by? Good donkey, they invariably replied, we are truly sorry, but we have not seen him. And so we continued our quest from one shrine to the next. From Capestrano I took you to San Gabriele dell'Addolorata; and then, leaving the mountains behind and making our way along the seashore, we finally reached the Santa Casa di Loreto, where he, your father, was waiting under the big gateway. He was very pale and, to tell you the truth, he didn't seem to be in a good mood, no, he didn't look a happy man at all. As soon as he sees us, I said to myself, as soon as he recognizes us he'll burst into tears of joy, and it will be just as in the parable of the prodigal son. I turned my head toward you to invite you to get off my back and run to your father's arms. But you were no longer there, there was no sign of you anywhere in the square or on the steps of the shrine. You had vanished. Now, my son, you must tell me why you made me go all that way and then ran away without saying a word to me. Was that a good thing to do?"

"It was a dream, Grandmother," said Pietro.

"Oh, excuse me, I'm obviously still half asleep, I haven't got over the fright yet."

At that moment they heard the gate creak. From behind the shutters Pietro saw the shadow of a man crossing the courtyard, raising his head for a moment in the direction of Donna Maria Vincenza's room, hesitating for a moment, and then turning to the left and disappearing into the house.

"It's Venanzio," Donna Maria Vincenza said. "I recognize his footsteps. Thank heaven nothing has happened to him."

"But why doesn't he come up?" Pietro asked. "He ought to realize that I, that we have been waiting for him."

"He'll be hungry and tired. But if you like you can go down to his room. There's no need to go outside and walk around the house; you can get to it by way of the inside staircase on the other side of the grain loft."

13

PIETRO WENT DOWN A spiral staircase to a dark corridor; Venanzio's room was at the end of it. He was sitting on the edge of the bed, eating cold soup from a big soup plate resting on his knees. There was also a piece of yellowish dried salt cod, seasoned with olive oil, pepper, and vinegar, in a pan on the chair beside him. The ground-floor room was big, dismal, cold, and damp, and the tiled floor was worn and uneven. In one corner there was a pile of casks, a sulfur sprayer, a wheelbarrow, and some stakes; apart from the bed, it looked like a storeroom. When Pietro walked in Venanzio put his soup plate on the floor. He was covered with mud from head to foot, his clothes clung to his body, his long mustaches drooped like rat tails, and he looked exhausted, depressed, and bad tempered.

"Did they let him go?" Pietro asked him anxiously.

"Next time, believe me, sir, I'd rather drive a couple of oxen up Monte Marsicano," he replied furiously. "I'd rather walk all the way to the Shrine of the Holy Trinity."

"If you think that would be sufficient to save your soul, you should certainly do so, Venanzio, but that wasn't what I asked you."

"Yes, yes, your friend's out, they released him, and that of course is all you care about."

He said "your friend" with heavy sarcasm.

"Do you suppose by any chance that the *carabinieri* wanted to keep him in prison and feed him for the rest of his life?" he went on. "Everyone of course likes the idea of being a state pensioner, but that privilege is not for *cafoni*, it's reserved for those who have lived a life of ease and when they reach old age are exhausted by never having done anything. Besides, the sergeant told me that even if I hadn't gone there and made a statement they would have released that deaf vagabond at latest tomorrow or the day after, because he had managed to explain to them by means of gestures and mumbling that he came from Pietrasecca and that his name was Fante or something of the sort; and in any case they arrested him chiefly because the parish priest had panicked and insisted on their doing so."

Pietro interrupted.

"Where is he now? Did they take him back to Pietrasecca?"

"I'll be coming to that in a minute, sir, please be patient for a moment. In the meantime let me tell you that the release didn't go as smoothly as you led me to expect; in fact I found myself in bad trouble. As I said, the *carabinieri* already knew who the man was and had no doubt about his identity, but they needed a signature before they could let him go because, it seems, that is what the law requires. The sergeant explained that they need a signature for everything they do, a signed document to put in the Files. And, as Pietrasecca is a village separate from the town that is the headquarters of the local authority and has no administrative offices of its own, they were waiting for a signature from the local authority in Lama, which is responsible for Pietrasecca; any signature on a piece of paper stating that so-and-so was really born and consequently existed would do, that was all that was wanted, it was just for the Files. The sergeant had written to the local authority this morning and, barring unforeseen circumstances, the signature would arrive at latest tomorrow or the day after, the requirements of the official records would have been satisfied, and the arrest, having become superfluous, would have come to an end."

"To tell you the truth, Venanzio, at this moment I'm not very interested in the *carabiniere* Files. Did you see Infante? Did he show signs of maltreatment, of having been knocked about?"

"I've never been interested in Files either, sir, you can take it from me. I've always minded my own business, as you know, or ought to know. But the sergeant talked to me about his Files, you should have seen him, sir, he showed as much respect when talking about them as Aunt Eufemia shows when she worships in front of the Blessed Sacrament, but he was only leading up to an act of duplicity like that of a man who pats you on the back with the hand in which he holds a knife. Well, Venanzio, he said, I'll write out an identification statement, I'll put down on a piece of paper what you've just told me about the man, you'll sign your name underneath it, and he'll be released at once."

"Well, to cut matters short, you signed and he was released. Thank you."

"No, I picked up my hat. Good-bye, Mr. Sergeant, I said, and walked quickly toward the exit. When he saw his prey escaping the sergeant ran after me, shut the door, and put a man to guard it. Then he tried to persuade me that I'd misunderstood him, though actually I'd understood him very well indeed. He tried to persuade me that what he asked me to do was the most innocent thing in the world, a mere formality. What the devil, Venanzio, he said to me, you've counted up to thirty, so you can count up to thirty-one, talk is all very well, I'm not saying I don't believe what you say, but words vanish into thin air while the Files remain. Be reasonable, Venanzio, he went on, your signature is essential, not to me, if it were only for me things would be quite different, but it's essential for the Files, there's no joking with the Files. Then he took a sheet of paper and started writing. That caused the blood to rush to my head. I grabbed his arm and made him put the pen down. For the love of God and the salvation of our souls, Mr. Sergeant, I said to him, spare yourself the trouble, I won't sign. Don't suppose, Mr. Sergeant, I told him, that you're dealing with an ignorant *cafone*, I went to school, and I know very well what a signature means and how many people's lives have been ruined just because of a mere signature. When he heard me talk like that he looked discouraged, he seemed unable to grasp the fact that he had failed to take me in, and it seemed to him to be impossible that an honest citizen should leave the *carabiniere* barracks without having been put in the Files. But he stubbornly refused to accept defeat and started talking to me again in a half-appealing, half-threatening way, while I recited the *Mea Culpa* and thought to myself that this was a well-merited punishment that had befallen me for having gotten mixed up with other people's affairs. All my life I had minded my own business, and why, now of all times, should I have fallen into this trap?

"Well, Venanzio, are you going to sign? the sergeant said at the end of his tirade. For the love of God, Mr. Sergeant, I replied, at least have respect for my gray hairs, I've lived honestly all my life, Mr. Sergeant, and why should I compromise myself now? Venanzio, he said, giving up hope, I didn't know you were so stupid. Certainly, Mr. Sergeant, I hastened to reply, it must be very boring for an intelligent person such as yourself to waste your time talking to a person as stupid as me, so I hope you'll let me go."

"In short, Venanzio, I suppose you ended up signing since, as you said, Infante was released. Did they take him back to Pietrasecca?"

"No, sir, far worse was to follow. When the sergeant was finally convinced that there was no chance of his taking me in, his whole attitude changed. So you won't sign, Venanzio? he said. Very well, you'll stay here as long as I choose. You'll regret it, he added with a contemptuous smile, I'll stick you in the Files just the same. The Files are not to be trifled with, you see, Venanzio. I'll make a written report of what you said and add that you made specious excuses for refusing to sign it. Your refusal will be vouched for by my signature and that of the *carabiniere* on duty and will remain in the Files for the rest of your life and for a long time afterward, you can be sure of that, because the Files are not to be trifled with, Venanzio. Sir, I didn't have to think about the meaning of those words, I realized I was lost, lost irreparably. So my worst presentiments, for which you laughed at me, had come true. I could not have been more dismayed if at that moment the earth had opened in front of my feet and I had plunged into the abyss. The honest efforts of a whole lifetime had turned out to be in vain. When the first dismay was over I started weeping like a child; what else could I do? A big lump in my throat prevented me from saying a word of protest or in self-defense, and even if I had been able to speak, what would have been the use? Meanwhile the sergeant went on writing with a diabolical little smile on his lips; he wrote slowly, lingering with pleasure over every one of his damned words. After every sentence he put down the pen and put a lit cigarette to his lips; then he breathed out deeply and watched the cloud of blue smoke dissolving in the air. Every so often he'd put a question to me, he wanted to know my personal particulars. What's your name? Venanzio Di Dio? he said. Who was your father? I can't hear you, he shouted, speak up. Who was your father? I answered him more loudly, but he insisted that he couldn't hear. He made me repeat every answer four or five times, louder each time, on the pretext that he couldn't hear me. Even the man on duty at the door could hear my answers and laughed, and even people in the street stopped to listen. How long did my martyrdom last? I was sitting on a bench with my hat in my hands, my whole body was covered in sweat, and my head seemed about to burst. Beside me there was a barred window, and facing me was a wall with portraits of the king and queen. Eventually the sergeant looked at his watch, rose, and said to the man on duty: I'm going to get something to eat, keep an eye on this fellow. It had grown dark by now, and when I thought of myself sitting on that bench, alone and helpless in that hostile room, I realized the full extent of my unhappiness and my sad destiny. This new misfortune seemed both natural and incomprehensible."

"I'm sorry to have interrupted your dinner," Pietro said. "Can't you go on with the story and eat at the same time?"

"I'm not hungry," Venanzio replied.

Telling his story was both an ordeal and a relief to the poor

man. For a long time to come it would be impossible for him to
think about anything else.

"After an hour or an hour and a half the sergeant came back,"
he went on. "He had a toothpick between his teeth and he
switched on the light; he was humming a tune, and seemed to
have had more to drink than to eat. He signed his name at the
bottom of the sheet of paper he had left on his desk, and sent for
the man on duty and made him sign too. Then he put the sheet of
paper in a box, looking at me with a grin on his face. I realized at
once that that was the accursed File. There was no need for him
to tell me. Eventually he told me I could go. No, wait, he said,
you still have to pay the deaf-mute the money you owe him. I saw
the wretch coming out through a trapdoor that led underground;
he was reduced to a state like the *ecce homo*, he was limping, one
of his eyes was swollen, and his beard had run wild, and I handed
him the fifty-lire note that Donna Maria Vincenza gave me."

"Wasn't he surprised?"

"No. He glanced at it casually, as if it were a picture postcard.
Perhaps he had never seen such a large sum of money in his life
and didn't realize what it was; or perhaps he thought he was entitled to it, that it was a wage paid to people under arrest, there was
no way of telling. Now clear out, both of you, the sergeant said
rudely. When we were outside I realized how late it was. I walked
for a few yards with the fellow, showed him the shortcut to Orta,
and told him to go, with God's blessing, and never show himself
in these parts again. But he hesitated, and then started following
me. It was late, as I said, but there were still people about, one or
two women who had stayed in church after the sermon and the
usual drunks near the taverns. I really didn't want to be seen in
the company of that down-and-out stranger in the state he was in,
and I didn't want to be asked whether I too had been arrested, and
how and why. You can't imagine how malicious the poor can be,
sir. So come along, I said to the wretch, I'll go a little way with
you, and I took him by the arm. We took the shortcut below Don
Lazzaro's house, and that got us out of the village very quickly. At
the bottom of the hill we left the mule track, where we sank up to

our knees in the snow, and took the road. After we had gone a good way I signed to the man to go on by himself. Go, I told him, go with God's blessing, and may you never again have the bad idea of coming back to this part of the world. But while I was hurrying toward Colle I heard footsteps behind me, and when I turned to look there he was, following me. At that I admit I lost my patience. Do you want to be my ruin? I shouted at him. Aren't you satisfied with having compromised me in the *carabiniere* Files? Why are you following me? Am I your father, by any chance? Go, I told him, go your own way. But it was useless, because he couldn't hear. His only answer was an incomprehensible mumble. Just then it started snowing heavily again. So there we were, standing in the middle of the road in the snow, looking at each other and unable to make ourselves understood to each other though chance had thrown us together, just as sometimes at market you see a goat and a donkey both tied to the same stake. It was obvious that the poor devil, in the state he was in, half lame because of the beating he had gotten, would have had to keep walking all night to get to Pietrasecca in that weather and on that road, that is, in the best of cases, if his strength held out. It then struck me that it would be a good idea (though I must confess that it was chiefly for the sake of getting rid of him) if I found him a shelter for the night somewhere near where we were. So I told him to come with me and took him by the arm so that he should understand my meaning. We left the road and cut across the fields for a few hundred yards until we reached the canal that leads to the mill; then we followed the row of poplars and took good care not to fall in the water, and came to the old Spina barn, which is still called that though Don Bastiano, your uncle, sold it thirty years ago to Simone the Weasel, who still lives there. You don't know who Simone is? He's a strange man; anyone who didn't know him would never imagine him. From being well off he reduced himself out of pride to a state worse than that of a *cafone*, and I couldn't say which is the greater, his kindness of heart or his wildness. At one time he was a great friend of your uncle Don Bastiano, though it would be impossible to imagine two more different characters. When the news spread that the police and *carabinieri* were looking for you in the Pietrasecca area, he didn't wait to be told twice, but went there immediately. We learned later that he was stopped at once and cross-examined by the police. I came here to hunt, he explained, to hunt wolves, and he produced a sawed-off shotgun. But he didn't have a license. Wolves don't have licenses either, he said in self-defense, but that was not accepted; they confiscated the gun and imposed a fine that he certainly won't have paid.

"Well, in the situation I was in," Venanzio went on, "the only person to whom I could turn and be certain that he would help me was Simone. When we got to the barn I called him at the top of my voice and knocked hard at the door, but there was no response except from the dog. It barked at us like a damned soul and flung itself angrily at the door, which fortunately was shut. But there was no sign of Simone. I had just decided to go and leave the deaf-mute there when I saw a shadow moving along the canal bank along which we had come. I could tell from the way he was lurching that it was Simone, because as usual he had had a great deal to drink; and, as he was hurrying, perhaps because he was alarmed at the barking of his dog, he tumbled several times into the snow. It must have been the luck that favors drunks rather than familiarity with the place that saved him from falling into the water. Each time he got up he incited the dog to attack us. Bite them, eat them alive, Leone, he shouted. He recognized me only when he was a few yards away, and he recognized the deaf-mute too, having seen him when he was arrested. He already knew about my cross-examination at the barracks, of course, having heard about it at the two or three taverns at which he had spent the evening. He had also heard that I had been arrested, and the result was that when he saw me in the deaf-mute's company at that time of night and at that out-of-the-way spot he was delighted with us, thinking we had both escaped from prison, and he started embracing and kissing and congratulating me. Simone has always been like that, unfortunately. I don't mean he's a bad man; on the contrary, he certainly has a kind heart and, when he's sober, he's a

man of uncommon strength and courage. But he has never been
able to look after his own affairs, with the result that things have
gone from bad to worse for him; he lost the mill and the vineyards
he used to own and for some years he has been reduced to living
like an animal. So I was longing to say good night and come
home and leave the deaf-mute with him, but Simone couldn't get
out of his head the idea that we had escaped from prison, and he
insisted that it would be dangerous for me to go back to the place
where the police would look for me first. While he was searching
his pockets for the latchkey he silenced the dog, which was still
barking, informing it that we were doubly sacred, as guests and as
persons fleeing from the *carabinieri*; and he started singing into
the deaf-mute's ear a prohibited old song the refrain of which is:
'Oh the day will come, will come, will come . . .'

"Several times I tried to explain to Simone, at the cost of dis-
appointing him, that actually we had not escaped from prison, but
he refused to believe me. You're shrewd, he told me, but you can't
tell a story. Venanzio, he said to me, still hunting for his key, to tell
you the truth, I never expected this from a rabbit like you. I don't
say this to offend you, he went on, but to encourage you. If you go
on like this, he also said to me, you'll end up becoming a man. In
the end he found the key and started looking for the keyhole.
Have you noticed, he said to me, that in the dark the key gets
bigger and bigger and the keyhole gets smaller and smaller and
sometimes mysteriously disappears altogether? And he went on
talking nonsense of the same kind while I stood there wanting
frantically to get away and come home. Be careful, Venanzio, he
said to me, if you try to escape I'll set Leone on you. So I had to resign myself to listening to his nonsensical talk and waiting for him
to fall asleep once he was inside. So I started lighting matches to
help him to find the keyhole, but he was not in the same hurry.
Have you noticed, Venanzio, he said, that when there's light there
are suddenly two keyholes instead of one? And how is a poor man
to tell which is the right one? Eventually, with God's help, the
door opened and he went in and lit an oil lamp. He very ceremoniously introduced us to the dog Leone and made us squat on his

bed in a corner of the big room. He also introduced us to his donkey, which goes by the name of Cherubino; it was lying on its straw at the other end of the room, and he wished it good night. Simone's straw mattress, with a few ragged blankets, was in the middle of the room, and next to it there was a bottle of wine on two trestles. My room's really on the second floor, he explained, but I dislike solitude. Lie down and turn out the lamp, I said to him, it's sufficient to look at you to see how tired you are; I'll go up to the hayloft and throw down straw for the deaf-mute's bed and mine. But Simone insisted on filling a jug of wine and offering it to us. I'm poor, he said, but I know and respect the laws of hospitality. They are the only laws worthy of respect, he added, and in a civilized country there should be no others. Then he insisted on offering us bread and cheese. We could live so well, he murmured into the deaf-mute's ear, if we could only manage to hang the police. Of course, he added, after thinking it over, we might shoot quite a number of them and cut the throat of a great many others; and he accompanied these words with the gesture of a housewife cutting a chicken's throat and the chicken's guttural cry. But the important thing, he went on, would be to destroy their seed forever, so it might be sufficient to castrate them. Just imagine how well we could live then, deaf-mute. Listening to that nonsense made me more frantic than ever to get away and come back here so as to be able to rest my poor weary head at last. But there was one extraordinary moment when the deaf-mute, perhaps under the influence of the wine, suddenly started laughing. And talking. First of all he laughed, and then, pointing to the bread we had in our hands, he said clearly and distinctly in an ordinary voice, just like ours: *companions*. We could hardly believe our ears. What, so you're not dumb? we shouted at him. Have you been pretending all this time? Have you been pulling our leg? He laughed, and repeated: *companions*. Then he wanted to give bread to the dog and the donkey, and he pointed to all five of us, and laughed and repeated: *companions*. In fact it was the only word he could say properly. What's the matter with you, sir? Do you feel unwell?"

"No, it's only a slight cold, Venanzio, don't take any notice, it's of no importance."

"Meanwhile time was passing and I couldn't wait to get away and come home. At a certain point I blurted out without meaning to: heaven knows how worried Donna Maria Vincenza will be. At that Simone sat up, raised his eyebrows, and said: do you really think, Venanzio, that Signora Spina will be worried if you don't come back and she doesn't know where you are? Of course she will be, I replied, I'm surprised you should ask me that question, I've worked in her house for forty-two years and I've always come back, every night. And supposing the *carabinieri* lay their hands on you again? Simone said, and he offered to go and wait for Donna Maria Vincenza when she came out of church in the morning to tell her that I was in a safe place and that she needn't worry. But I haven't escaped from prison, I said to Simone, losing my patience. I've already told you that and I repeat it, I wasn't arrested. I've always minded my own business, as everyone knows, and that's how I hope it will continue in the future. So I had to explain to him all over again why and how it came about that I had gone to see him at that unusual hour, solely to ask him to put up the deaf-mute until next morning. If that's the case you can go, Simone said to me in disgust. I didn't wait for him to repeat it. As I passed by the bakery on the way home I saw in the distance two *carabinieri* walking along our perimeter wall; they were probably on their usual night round. But they never used to come as far as this. At any rate, because they were coming in my direction, at the first corner I came to I took a side alley and hid in the dark under the stairs, I think it was of Anacleto the Tailor's house. Why did I hide? I immediately asked myself. Whom or what was I afraid of? What crime had I committed? What, in short, had been happening to me in the past few hours? When I heard the footsteps of the *carabinieri* coming closer and closer, coming down the alley and turning in my direction, toward my hiding place, I stopped being able to think at all. I stayed there, huddled in my black cloak and with my hat, which was black too, pulled down over my eyes, and it would have been difficult to make me out in the dark.

But suppose the *carabinieri* had a dog with them, as they sometimes do? I suddenly said to myself. Suppose Anacleto's chickens suddenly start squawking and fluttering? And suppose they discover me in this suspicious situation, what plausible explanation can I give? When they passed within a yard or two of me I shut my eyes and held my breath and pressed my fists against my chest to try to stop the violent beating of my heart. I stayed like that even when their footsteps died away; I was tired, humiliated, disgusted with myself and with life. This is what happens, I said to myself, to those who don't mind their own business, who chase after a toad and fall in the ditch."

"Venanzio," Pietro said to him, taking his hand in a friendly way, "I think you're wrong to regret having done a good deed, but we'll talk about that another time. Now it's late, and before we go to bed I only want to tell you that there's no need to worry too much at your name being in the *carabinieri's* Files. Believe me, it won't be long before all that wastepaper is burned. Good night, Venanzio, sleep well, and dream about bonfires of Files."

14

ᴇARLY NEXT MORNING Pietro went to the attic and
climbed up to the highest window with the aid of a ladder to
try and make out in the distance the barn where Infante had spent
the night. He had difficulty in finding it, because he looked for it
too far away. He had been there a number of times in his boyhood,
when his uncle Bastiano still had his stable there and, as often happens with youthful memories, he remembered the distance as
having been greater than it really was. A cold north wind had
cleared the night mists from the Fucino plain. The big, gray-green
basin looked empty, silent, and dead, and it was shut in by a complete, uniform lid of stratus cloud at the height of the surrounding
peaks; it was like a huge basket that had been put upside down, or
an enormous mousetrap. When Pietro was on the point of giving
up and leaving his observation post in disappointment, he spotted
right beneath the village what he had been looking for in vain in
the distance. Just where the hillside leveled off and the vertical
lines of the vineyards met the horizontal lines of the vegetable
plots, his eyes fell on a row of poplars on a canal bank; by following
the line of the trees he found the squat, rustic building that now

served as Simone the Weasel's home. There was no sign of life near it, and Infante must certainly have left. A thin column of bluish smoke emerged from the top of the building, which, seen in the distance and from above, seemed to be planted on top of the row of poplars; and, as the wind imparted a wavelike motion to the treetops, the house looked like a ship about to weigh anchor.

"Are you predicting the future, sir?" Natalina asked him with a laugh. "Shall we have the chicken pest again this year?"

The girl had in her hands a new wire mousetrap containing a tiny gray mouse that had been caught during the night and was still alive.

"What are you going to do with that poor little creature, Natalina?" Pietro exclaimed.

"I'm going to drown it in the trough behind the stable, sir, as usual."

Pietro came down the ladder quickly, two rungs at a time.

"Mice caught in church suffer a worse fate," Natalina went on with a smile. "Donna Carolina, the priest's sister, sprinkles gasoline on them and burns them alive. Boys gather outside the sacristy every morning and enjoy the spectacle enormously (what a pity you can't go, sir). Actually on some Sundays at mass what with the stink of burned mice it's hard to smell the incense. I don't say the mice don't deserve it, good gracious no, but in my opinion, sir, it's better and simpler to drown them, particularly with gasoline at its present price. But Donna Carolina says that to rid the church of mice an example must be set, and she says that the mice must smell the horrible torment that awaits them in advance, while they are still alive. But in spite of that it can't be claimed that there are any fewer of them in church. On the contrary, in the women's confessionals nowadays you can hear the disgusting creatures scampering about and gnawing away even in broad daylight."

"Natalina," said Pietro, who could no longer suppress his indignation, "your way of talking is not just mean, it's hateful."

At that moment the bell rang, and Natalina put the trap on the floor and hurried to open the gate. Later, when she came back to the attic, she found the trap empty. She went angrily in search of Pietro, who had vanished too. He had taken refuge in a storeroom on the third floor, where there were some shelves with piles of fruit, pears, apples, almonds, walnuts, apricots, and bottles containing olives and jam. For several days he had been coming to this room to write undisturbed. Surrounded by these delightful smells, he had started planning an *Apologia for Deafness*. Without false modesty, he reread the proposed contents page with a great deal of pleasure. *Introduction:* "In the Country of Loudspeakers Blessed Are the Deaf." *Chapter 2:* "The True Art of Being Deaf." *Chapter 3:* "On the Best Means of Spreading Deafness among the Italians." But Natalina discovered his hiding place and burst in like a fury.

"Where's the mouse, sir?" she shrieked angrily.

"Oh, has it gone without leaving an address?" he asked with an ironic smile.

"Where is it?" she repeated still more shrilly.

"What a sentimental girl you are," Pietro replied in the same tone. "Did you grow so fond of it in such a short time?"

"Where is it?" Natalina cried.

But Venanzio appeared and imposed silence.

"Have you gone mad?" he said to the girl. "Don't you know that madam has a visitor, and you shriek like that?"

Donna Maria Vincenza had only just come back from mass when she was told of an unexpected visit by the parish priest.

"Why didn't you let me know through the sacristan that you wanted to speak to me?" she said without concealing her surprise. "I would have gone to the sacristy immediately after mass."

"If I'm not disturbing you," Don Marco said apologetically, "I thought we could talk more confidentially here. In my house I don't have a moment's peace even at night. The sacristy is like a station waiting room, there's always someone coming in or going out, and some people come only because the place is heated."

On the table there was a brass coffeepot, a porcelain milk jug, and a cup for Donna Maria Vincenza's breakfast. She asked the priest to sit by the fire and sat opposite him to listen to what he had to say.

"How is Donna Carolina?" she asked, to break the silence as much as anything else.

Without her cape and veil she looked poorly dressed. Age had not spoiled the lines of her face, but seen at close quarters it expressed a sadness that made a deep impression on Don Marco. In spite of her weariness, she held her head high, leaning against the back of her chair, which was upholstered with a piece of old tapestry, and her head seemed to have undergone the same wear by time as the faded roses of the fabric. Don Marco had not been in the Spina house for many years, and he looked around stealthily, surprised and disturbed at the austerity that had obviously taken the place of the abundance that had prevailed when he was a poor seminarian; at that time it had teemed with the life of a big landowner's family, with many children, bailiffs, laborers, and servants. He could not overcome his obvious uneasiness. In his faded, almost greenish cassock in the half light of the morning he looked like a long bundle of firewood put to dry by the fire, a bundle topped by a white plaster head with two round, dark glass eyes that had been inserted into deep eye sockets. His hat had imprinted a permanent ring on his head, a kind of halo marked by beads of cold sweat and embroidered with black arteries. Just when Donna Maria Vincenza seemed to have made up her mind to ask him the reason for this unusual visit the priest, in order to gain time, started talking, slowly and quietly, in a grave and plaintive voice, swallowing half his words since, as is well known, it is not essential that words of comfort be heard; the important thing being that they be spoken. His speech, once under way, went ahead of its own accord and flowed like oil. The phrases that he used were those he had been repeating more than once a day for several decades, and anyone who wished could work out how many times he had used them; he knew them by heart, and could have repeated them while shaving or playing chess, that is, while thinking about something else, provided only that the physical possibility of opening and shutting his mouth was left to him. They were sacred words, and it is not essential that sacred words be thought or heard; to be efficacious it is sufficient that they be pronounced.

"These are bad times, Donna Maria Vincenza, and we must have patience and rely on God's help. You have had patience for eighty years, and now, when the blessed day is approaching when you should gather the rich fruits, are you beginning to become impatient? Try to have a little more patience, Donna Maria Vincenza, try with the help of Jesus and the Blessed Virgin to be patient for a little while longer. Grit your teeth. In view of your advanced age it cannot be for long."

His talk was like a sedative offered to a dying man; it did not save him from death, but it relieved the pain. Don Marco had a cold, and the warmth of the room started to make him sneeze. He turned his head to one side to avoid giving the cold to Donna Maria Vincenza and sat with his body twisted like a man with a stiff neck, and this gave him an excuse not to look her in the face. Without pausing he went on from the theme of Christian patience to that of preparation for a good death. During the night he had been called to the bedside of two persons who were gravely ill.

"I had to go, of course, I had to go straight away, a priest can't say he's tired or has a cold. There's some pneumonia about again, the illness that takes the old to the grave," he went on. "Today it's my turn, tomorrow it'll be yours, no one can escape the goddess with the scythe. An old *cafone*, Graziano Pallanera, perhaps you may remember his name (yes, it was he who killed the baker's wife, the very same man), has been in the throes of death for several days, but can't manage to die. It's not surprising, the wretch hasn't set foot in church for forty years, Donna Maria Vincenza, and he must have a great many devils in his body. A priest does his best to drive them out, of course, but perhaps there are places that his blessing doesn't reach. Oh, these are bad times, Donna Maria Vincenza," he sighed, "and we must rely on God's help and have patience."

Several buttons of the priest's cassock were undone at the level of his chest, and every so often he put his hairy hand through the opening and, with an effort, as if he were extracting some internal organ, produced a watch as big as an onion, which he put to his ear and then restored to its deep hiding place without even looking at it.

"Perhaps you came for alms?" Donna Maria Vincenza asked him, showing signs of impatience. "Are you in need of money for some good cause?"

"Oh, no, I didn't come for that," the priest replied, flushing. "In fact I must apologize to you for not yet being in a position to settle that little debt."

Donna Maria Vincenza glanced at her coffee, which was getting cold, and the priest plunged into a lament about the poor attendance at catechism and the way the women chattered during church services. The Lenten preacher, who was a monk and a Piedmontese into the bargain, had warned him that he would mention the matter in his report to Monsignore, and the parish would cut a poor figure as a result. Don Marco had tried to persuade the preacher that if he stayed here a little longer he too would turn a deaf ear; one must be patient, he had pointed out with a smile, it had always been like that. It wasn't a matter of turning a deaf ear, the preacher had replied coldly; one should not resign oneself to the congregation's behaving in church as they did in the public square. As a priest, Don Marco had replied, I am bound to agree with you, what else do you expect? But what I meant to say was that as a local man, Father, I can assure you that if you stayed here for ten years or so, you too would turn a deaf ear, you can take it from me. You have to be patient, I told him, it has always been like that. However that may be, the preacher insisted, I shall mention the matter in my report to Monsignore. And so it had come about that every day without exception, instead of the black coffee that he had given up for reasons of economy, providence now supplied the poor parish priest of Colle with a dose of gall.

He breathed with difficulty. The air passing through his nostrils, which were yellowed with tobacco, made a hissing sound rather like that made by old mice in dry wood.

"How is your sister?" Donna Maria Vincenza asked. "Please give her my kind regards."

Donna Maria Vincenza made as if to rise as she said this, but Don Marco either did not notice, or pretended not to; he removed the handkerchief from his nose and made an expansive gesture of desperate resignation.

"My sister Carolina would be quite all right," he said, with his neck still twisted, "she would be quite all right, Signora Maria Vincenza, but for the fact that she has gotten into her head the absurd idea of completely ridding the church of mice. Just imagine it, Signora Maria Vincenza. I keep telling her there have always been mice in the church, I repeat it ad nauseam. Be patient, Carolina, there have always been mice in church ever since the remote and glorious times of the holy martyrs. The catacombs certainly swarmed with them; perhaps it was actually they that dug them in accordance with a preordained plan of divine providence, and perhaps the apostles took possession of them only later, when they had completed the job; in fact, if one observes them closely today, they look like huge mouse holes. Don't misunderstand me, Donna Maria Vincenza, I have no desire to undertake the defense of mice, I merely confine myself to the banal and irrefutable statement that they have always been there. Can one conceive of a Catholic place of worship without mice? I ask myself. One must have patience. Of course, if they multiply beyond all measure and actually threaten to take over sacred places and drive away the faithful, action to reduce their number becomes necessary, though it's an illusion to suppose that it's possible to eliminate them completely. Let me make myself clear, I'm the first to admit that there are beginning to be too many mice in our church at Colle. They have installed themselves in the confessionals, and there are pious women who because of them no longer dare approach the sacrament of penance. In his sermon last night Father Gabriele took these women to task. What? he said to them, are you more afraid of mice than of remaining in mortal sin? Do you realize what everlasting torments would be awaiting you in hell if you died suddenly tonight? he went on. Of course, Signora Maria Vincenza, from the religious point of view he was a thousand times right, and as a priest I cannot possibly contradict him. But let us stick to the facts. It's obvious that the mice in my parish are now exceeding their natural rights, and if there are women who dislike feeling them jumping about in their clothing while they are reciting the *Mea Culpa* and the Act of Contrition, the legitimacy of their desire that an attempt should be made by appropriate means to eliminate the little beasts, at least from the confessionals, must be admitted. In the end the church is a big one and there's room for everyone. My sister Carolina goes to the opposite extreme: she would like actually to exterminate the mice, wipe them out completely, destroy their seed, just imagine it, Signora Maria Vincenza. My advice as a priest and as her brother has no effect on her. I tell her over and over again, I tell her ad nauseam, that her ambition is utopian. Listen to me, Carolina, I say, perhaps it's actually a heresy, perhaps it's actually Manichaeism, Carolina. But on this point Carolina is inaccessible to the arguments of theology and the promptings of common sense, with the result that she is ruining her life. If she fails in her purpose (and how could she possibly succeed?) she will end up dying of a broken heart. What makes her do it? I ask myself."

Donna Maria Vincenza had difficulty in suppressing a yawn, and cast a glance full of regret and annoyance at her breakfast, which was now cold.

"Don Marco," she said wearily, "I don't want you to sacrifice to me your time, which is so valuable to the parish."

The priest shook his head.

"Forgive me, Donna Maria Vincenza, but I didn't come here to pay a courtesy visit, you know that that is not one of my habits," he blurted out.

He paused, ill at ease and afraid of having said too much, while Donna Maria Vincenza waited for him to go on and explain himself.

"No one can hear us," she said to encourage him.

"Well, Donna Maria Vincenza," he went on, speaking with difficulty and putting one hand on his breast, "I am too simple a man. My father, as you will remember, was a poor peasant, my mother used to mend chairs, and I was able to become a priest thanks to a grant provided by the Spina family; so I would not dare beat about the bush or play the diplomat with a lady like you. You also know, Donna Maria Vincenza, that I have never liked interfering in other people's affairs, my place has always been in church. Every family has its troubles, one must bear them patiently; my only object is the salvation of the souls for which I am responsible before God. If I have never excessively concerned myself with you, Donna Maria Vincenza, it's for a very simple reason: a shepherd who from morning till night has to chase after sheep that tend to stray from the flock has no time left for the few that always remain faithfully in the fold."

"Oh, so you came, or were sent, to see me today to guide me back to the right path," Donna Maria Vincenza helped him to say with a resigned smile. "Well, let us hear what you have to say."

"Spare me your irony, Signora Maria Vincenza, and please forget my human unworthiness, my origin, my parentage. Please think of me only as your parish priest. I assure you that at this moment I have no aim other than the peace of your soul."

He put so much sincerity and feeling into these words that Donna Maria Vincenza was touched by them and hastened to say: "I should never permit myself, Don Marco, to judge a consecrated priest by his birth. In matters of religion I am just as much a parishioner of yours as the humblest peasant woman."

Don Marco had to make a painful effort to go on. "There are not only the commandments of God and the precepts of the Church, Donna Maria Vincenza. There are also the counsels of prudence that a shepherd owes his flock, the prudence that is given first place among the cardinal virtues in the catechism and helps to avoid scandals and keep consciences at peace."

"God alone knows, Don Marco, whether I have ever sought the limelight, tried to have myself talked about, to attract the attention of the authorities and the crowd. But now, Don Marco, there are Christians to whom the cross itself is a scandal to be avoided."

"I know, Donna Maria Vincenza, that recently you have had to face terrible trials and, what is worse, that you have had to face them alone. But it is my duty as a priest to tell you that it is useless to struggle against the world. The world, Donna Maria Vincenza, is irretrievably what it is. The Church itself, with its glorious saints, popes, preachers, confessors, martyrs, and hermits, has not been able to change it in two thousand years of struggle, and it has remained evil. One must leave to Caesar that which is Caesar's."

"Believe me, Don Marco, I am not interested in the world and, so far as I am concerned, I willingly leave it to the devil, who is its worthy overlord. Oh, Don Marco, I'm only a poor mother in distress about a son, and I neither feel nor hear anything else. Please don't attribute to me intentions that I do not have. A mother must certainly be prudent, but there are also times when she must be brave. Forgive me for reminding you of it, Don Marco, but had you not had a brave mother you would not have become a priest."

The priest shut his eyes and had a shivering fit.

"But for love of her children a mother does not have to follow them everywhere, even into acts of madness," he muttered.

"She can leave them alone in times of joy, Don Marco, and in certain circumstances she must, I agree, but she cannot abandon them in times of trouble."

"We are living in hard times, dangerous times, Donna Maria Vincenza, and we must have patience. You know that I do not like interfering in other people's affairs, and as a priest my concern is only with the salvation of souls. But even the Church, in spite of some apparent advantages, is now having a more difficult time than ever, and it should be the duty of every good Christian at least not to increase its difficulties. Do you know that they are now trying to put the responsibility for your refusal upon the Lenten preacher and me?"

"It's some time, Don Marco, since I passed the age of six."

"You will agree, Donna Maria Vincenza, that that argument is not sufficient to close the mouths of the wicked. More than that is needed."

"That is true, Don Marco, but the croaking of toads has never reached up to heaven. In heaven there is God."

"True, Donna Maria Vincenza, but it must not be forgotten that the Church is down here on earth. And here below among men it must complete the mission given to it by the Divine

Savior. Now, you are not ignorant of the wickedness of the times through which we are passing, Donna Maria Vincenza."

"I don't read the newspapers."

"It's not just a question of petty news items, but of major events that have totally transformed the conditions of our ministry."

"What events are you talking about, Don Marco? So far as I know, the last important event for every Christian was the crucifixion. Has anything happened by any chance that has canceled out or in any way diminished the sacrifice of our Redeemer?"

The priest knitted his heavy, yellowish brows, the expression on his big plaster face disintegrated, and he burst out laughing. Then he suddenly grew serious. He seemed moved, and was unable to go on. He rose hurriedly to take his departure. "I shall ask Father Gabriele to come and continue this conversation if he wants to," he called out from the door.

In the courtyard he was surrounded by a number of old beggar women who were waiting to be given the weekly alms provided by Donna Maria Vincenza.

"How is the lady?" they whined. "Does she know what has happened to that wretched grandson of hers? Oh, Don Marco, what times, what troubles."

"She's better off than we are," Don Marco answered hurriedly. "In any event, she's better off than I am."

But the poor women went on muttering words of sympathy for the old lady; they made a hum as if it were a long litany.

"How can a mother be all right if her son's in danger?"

"Oh, what afflictions a mother has to bear; a mother's life is suffering as long as she lives."

"What's the use of money if a woman can't even help her son? Poor or rich, giving birth is always painful."

"Children are our cross; in one way or another they're always our cross, even though they don't want to be."

"Even Jesus made His Mother suffer; He certainly didn't do it on purpose, but how much He made her suffer."

Don Marco hurried down the hill like a maniac, looking neither to the right nor to the left. But in the square, between the church and the government offices, he failed to avoid Don Nicolino, the clerk of the court, who had heard about his visit to the Spina house and had been lying in wait for him for half an hour in the hope of picking up some news. As the court was sitting that day, the new public building, which was as sad and whitewashed as a sepulchre, was surrounded by a crowd, and there was a subdued murmur, like that at a hospital during an epidemic. On days when the court sat most of the shops were shut; the artisans, the tailors, the shoemakers, the carpenters, and the barbers came to enjoy the lawyers' speeches. The clerk of the court took the priest aside.

"Well, Don Marco, did you manage to exorcise the ghosts in that house?" he asked with a grin. "But seriously, Don Marco, there's a rumor that for some time past the Spina house has been haunted at night. There's even someone who claims to have recognized Don Saverio, God rest his soul, leaning out the attic window and walking around the whole house on the edge of the roof with a lamp in his hand."

Don Nicolino's face was rather like an owl's; his thin mustaches drooped in the Chinese style and were stained yellow by nicotine, and while he spoke he smiled and half shut his eyes as if he wanted to conceal his pleasure and enjoy it for himself alone.

"Oh yes, Don Nicolino, you don't know how close you are to the truth," the priest sadly admitted. "The spirit I found there was really frightening, even to a priest. But it is not of a kind to be exorcised."

"A purebred dog can catch rabies just like any other, Don Marco," said Don Nicolino, rubbing his hands and laughing in that special way of his. "And it must be dealt with just as if it were a mongrel."

"Listen, Don Nicolino," said the priest, trying to put as much persuasiveness as he could into his voice, "you weren't born in these parts. You've been here for many years, but you came from elsewhere, and there are some things you can't understand as we do. You can't understand Donna Maria Vincenza. But at least there's one thing that anyone can understand. She's an old lady, an old lady approaching eighty, and she's a mother, yes, a real mother, and she deserves to be allowed to die in peace. Forgive me, Don Nicolino, if I interfere in matters that don't concern me, but I'm talking to you now, not as a priest, but as a local man."

"Don Marco, you know very well that no one wants to prevent your precious protegée from dying in peace, and I don't see why you're now trying to make out that she's being victimized," Don Nicolino exclaimed indignantly. "What I say is that the sooner she departs to the next world and leaves us in peace the better. But for the rest of the time she spends with us here below we'll see to it that she's taken down a few pegs. You may rest assured, Don Marco, that we shall be having some amusing little scenes, ha, ha, ha!"

The priest took Don Nicolino by the arm and answered in a very grave tone: "I think I know what you're referring to, Don Nicolino. The magistrate referred to it vaguely yesterday. Excuse me if I interfere in matters that don't concern me, but permit me to ask: if new scandals arise, who will benefit from them?"

"Ah," said the clerk of the court, adding an equivocal tone to his usual smile, "ah, now I can understand certain suspicions about you. You owe the old woman money, don't you? Is she blackmailing you? Well, we'll talk about it again another day, Don Marco, now I've got to go in, for the court is about to sit."

The priest held him by one arm. He was dismayed and upset, and managed with difficulty to stammer out: "Listen, Don Nicolino, just now I was speaking purely as a priest, but as a layman I'm in complete agreement with you, what else do you expect? In fact, to be frank with you, I'd go much farther than you, much farther. Believe me, Don Nicolino, I should be extremely upset if I had not made my meaning perfectly clear."

Don Nicolino burst out laughing. "Your sonnet would be perfect if it didn't have a line too many, Don Marco," he said with an air of mistrust.

The priest was left openmouthed. Don Nicolino gazed at him for a few moments and then disappeared through the big door of the government building with a grin on his face. The crowd of

shopkeepers and artisans who had been waiting for the various offices to open and the court to sit drifted in small groups, silently
and with bared heads, into the white mausoleum. The usual *cafoni*, wrapped in their long black cloaks, remained sitting on the
stone benches on either side of the entrance, sheltered from the
north wind; they were silent, indifferent, and resigned, like beggars at the gate of a paupers' cemetery. They were the few who
had lost interest in eloquence.

"Good health to your Worship," some of them said to the
priest. "How did you find Donna Maria Vincenza?"

"She's better off than we are," Don Marco replied wearily. "In
any case, she's better off than I am, believe me."

"Will she be giving evidence tomorrow in the Lazzaretti
brothers' case?" Simone the Weasel asked. "It's disgraceful that
she should have been subpoenaed."

The priest went off in alarm without replying. The case in
which the Lazzaretti brothers were suing each other arose out of a
garden-variety stabbing fray of which Donna Maria Vincenza had
been an involuntary witness one morning on her way to early
mass. When the examining magistrate called to take a statement
from her, she told him she had recognized neither of the contest-
ants and was in no position to say which had provoked the other
or struck the first blow. As she obviously could not have hoped either by force or by persuasion to separate the two men, who were
crazed with hatred, she had continued on her way and had told
some men who were unloading firewood outside the sacristy
about what was happening. So she had no information to give and
did not want to have anything to do with the case.

"If you are unaware of it," she concluded, "you can consult your
records, and you will find that in the course of my long life I have
never had anything to do with so-called justice; and there's really no
reason why I should be subjected to such a grave humiliation now,
when I'm on the brink of eternity. I know that all that is wanted of
me in this case is to make a straightforward statement in court, but
even that is repugnant to me. In our family we have always settled
quarrels and conflicts of interest quite simply among ourselves, and

on complicated issues we have sought the opinion of persons of confidence. I have never believed in the justice of public offices and clerks, and besides, it's sufficient to look about you to see doubtful individuals going about in cars and on horseback whom people talk about in whispers as criminals who ought to be in jail but whom official justice leaves, or has to leave, in peace."

The examining magistrate, who was a man of the world, laughed wholeheartedly and assured her that she would not be troubled again, particularly as she had nothing to contribute about the quarrel itself. But since then things had happened that had resulted in extinguishing official goodwill toward her, and she had been subpoenaed on the eve of the hearing. Everyone in Colle was talking about it.

"It's an act of gross discourtesy, of sheer boorishness," Simone the Weasel declared. "What heroes they are to want to take it out of an old lady."

"Hunters prefer doves to crows, they're tastier," one old man remarked.

"Once upon a time a lady was a person who didn't have to render account to anyone," someone else said, "but now everyone has to render account, there are no more ladies and gentlemen."

"As it's impossible for us all to become ladies and gentlemen," Simone the Weasel pointed out, "we shall all become *cafoni* and we shall all be lousy. That'll be a fine form of equality."

"There'll always be generals and privates," an old man said. "There'll always be those who command and those who obey."

"But the point is," said Simone, "that the generals will be lousy too, so in a way they'll be *cafoni* too. That will be a splendid kind of equality."

"Donna Maria Vincenza is the last lady in this part of the world," said somebody else. "There may still be some rich women in the future, perhaps, but real ladies are finished, they're not born any longer."

"But even if they are rich, they'll be lousy too," Simone the Weasel insisted. "That's what equality means."

"But who'll give alms then?" someone else wanted to know.

"Public officials, of course," Simone explained. "They'll do everything, it's inevitable. And they'll be lousy too, of course."

"As long as there are those who command and those who obey nothing will be changed," an old man insisted. "Everything will be just as it was before. As long as there's carrion there'll be crows."

"Yes, everything will be basically as it was before," Simone the Weasel agreed. "Of course the world won't change. But there'll be more lice around. No living person will be without them, we'll all be just like *cafoni*, and that will create a semblance of equality. But everything will be just as it was before."

"When we're dead we all stink alike," said a *cafone* who had not yet spoken. "That's the real equality."

Simone saw the Spina groom passing in the distance.

"Hey, Venanzio," he called out, "Venà," and ran to catch up with him. The two stopped and talked for a while. Poor Venanzio seemed to have aged a great deal, and looked around him in alarm.

"Tomorrow I've got to take Donna Maria Vincenza to court," he said with tears in his eyes. "Just imagine Donna Maria Vincenza's name in the court records, what a humiliation for the family. Oh, if only Don Berardo could come back to life now."

"But what does Bastiano think about it?" Simone asked indignantly. "Why does he allow his mother to be maltreated in this way? Has he no blood in his veins?"

"There's that matter of the contract that's still hanging in the balance, and there's his battle with Calabasce. He can't see or listen to anything else."

"But suppose she refused to appear, what could they do? Would they dare send the *carabinieri* for her?"

"Up to yesterday she was determined not to go, but now she has resigned herself to it as a penance imposed by God. She's tired, very tired, and doesn't want any more scandals."

"If there's anything I can do, let me know, do you remember? Even if it involves risk," Simone said.

"She doesn't want anything like that. I don't know, but perhaps she also has other reasons for being cautious. She doesn't want to attract attention to the family."

Donna Palmira was watching the two men talking from be-hind the shutters of her window; Venanzio noticed this and made off without saying good-bye.

Next morning in the courtyard of her house Donna Maria Vincenza's departure for the local town was such a sad spectacle that it suggested there had been a great bereavement in the family. She delayed coming down long after the carriage was ready, but finally appeared, dressed demurely in black and car-rying a prayer book in her hand.

"Take the road by the old cemetery," she quietly told Ve-nanzio. "I don't want to go through Colle."

The groom's eyes were red and he was too upset to be able to speak, but he nodded.

"Natalina," she said, turning to the girl, "let me remind you once more not to let anyone into the house during my absence."

Natalina was sobbing like a little girl and promised to light a lamp in front of Our Lady of Perpetual Succor and to pray to her at about the time her mistress would be appearing in court.

The morning passed without incident, except for a lively squabble at the gate between Natalina and Donna Faustina, who turned up totally unexpectedly. When the bell rang Natalina, who was busy with her cleaning, appeared at the window and, after a moment's surprise, signaled to this unusual visitor to go away, as there was no point in waiting, because the gate would re-main shut. But Donna Faustina stayed where she was, making au-thoritative movements of her head to indicate that the maid should come down and open the gate immediately, as she insisted on being admitted. But when she saw Natalina shutting the window and returning to her domestic tasks she was no longer able to control herself and angrily pulled the bell again, where-upon Natalina dashed downstairs as if she were possessed by a devil, dragging her broom behind her.

"What do you want?" she exclaimed furiously. "I've already told you I can't let you in. Aren't you ashamed to come to this house again?"

"As you can well imagine, I didn't come here to talk to you," the visitor replied disdainfully. "Please tell Donna Maria Vincenza that I have something important to tell her."

"We don't want to be told anything by you."

"I don't think there's any need to remind you that you're only the maid and what I have to tell your mistress doesn't concern you."

"And I don't think I have any need to remind you of what you are. My maiden modesty prevents me from using the exact word."

"Your dirty mind certainly makes you attribute all sorts of nasty things to me, but that doesn't interest me. Now please open the gate and tell your mistress I'm here."

"If my mistress hadn't asked me to avoid any kind of incident, at any rate today, I'd wipe the makeup off your face with this broom because of what you've just said, you can be sure of that."

"I wouldn't in the least mind scratching out those bleary eyes of yours and putting them on a plate, like the picture of Santa Lucia in church. But I've talked to you long enough now, so run along and tell your mistress I'm here."

"You can thank heaven she's not at home, otherwise she'd have told you what she thinks of you to your face."

"I can forgive Donna Maria Vincenza that and other things too, but that doesn't apply to her maid, you can rest assured of that."

"Oh, so you came here to assure us of your forgiveness? You really are brazen."

"When is your mistress coming back?"

"I don't know. She has gone to court."

"I'll wait for her," Donna Faustina said resolutely.

And she sat down on one of the stone posts that stood on either side of the outside gate. But when Natalina went back into the house and looked out a window she saw her get up and slowly walk away, wiping her eyes with a handkerchief.

"Who was that beautiful young woman, Natalina?" asked Pietro, who had watched the scene from behind the shutters. "Why didn't you let her in?"

"To call her by her right name she's a tart, of a kind of which there are very few, thank heaven, in our part of the world."

"What's her name? Does she come from these parts?"

But Natalina had gone back to her cleaning and didn't answer.

At the entrance to Orta outside the public wash place, which was crowded with women washing and beating clothes, Donna Faustina met Donna Maria Vincenza's carriage coming back unexpectedly early. The girl waved vigorously to Venanzio, wanting him to slow down and stop, but produced the opposite effect, because he whipped up the horses and made them trot. For a moment Donna Faustina was left stranded in the middle of the road like a rejected beggar; then, stung by the scornful laughter of the women at the wash place, she hurried off in the direction of Colle without even noticing Donna Filomena, Don Bastiano's schoolmistress sister-in-law, who came toward her to speak to her.

"In the old days," one of the washerwomen called out, "women like that were burned in the public square."

"In the old days," said Donna Filomena, "washerwomen went barefoot and didn't go to school when they were children. But nowadays they are taught at school that there are no such things as witches and witchcraft."

"But there are still such things as scandals," one of the women said.

The other women stopped washing and beating clothes and joined in the altercation.

"If the sons and daughters of the gentry turn their backs on the old ways, what are the poor to think?"

"Why did young Pietro Spina reject the pardon?"

"Why did Donna Faustina leave her aunt Lucia's house and go and live with an old gentleman without the sacrament of matrimony?"

"And why did she drive poor Don Saverio Spina to death?"

"Perhaps you're right," Donna Filomena said. "But the point is that no one entrusted us with the task of judging our neighbors."

"And if earthquakes, fires, and floods happen?" the oldest of the washerwomen complained. "Alas, this is indeed the age of scandals."

"Perhaps you're right," Donna Filomena said. "But isn't denouncing the sins of others in the street a scandal too?"

Meanwhile Donna Maria Vincenza's carriage had reached the courtyard of the Spina house. Natalina hurried to help the old lady to get out and anxiously interrogated Venanzio with her eyes to find out what had happened.

"It couldn't possibly have had a happier ending, heaven be thanked," Venanzio called out, laughing like a child and making the sign of the cross.

Not for a long time had the poor man laughed so wholeheartedly. Donna Maria Vincenza was delighted too, and she sent urgently for her grandson, asking him to come to her room.

"The Lord first wanted to frighten me," she told him with a smile, "but at the last moment He got me out of it. Listen to me, my dear boy, the whole thing was like a fairy tale. Well, I arrived there punctually, but I was so tired that I could hardly stand. They made Venanzio wait in the corridor and put me in a room reserved for witnesses with a number of *cafoni* from Colle who were involved in the same case; actually the poor people were very embarrassed at seeing me seated on the same bench. One of them was Simone Ortiga, who is known as Simone the Weasel. He explained to me that he had applied to give evidence on the remote causes of the dispute, though in fact they were so remote that they had nothing whatever to do with it. But actually he had gone there to help me, in case I needed him, he said. I don't know, my dear boy, whether you have heard of the man; he's an honest fellow reduced to despair by lack of faith. To me the whole scene seemed completely unreal, and I thought it was going to vanish into thin air at any moment. But I pretended to be resigned, and I actually tried to smile to make my fellow villagers less painfully embarrassed. I told them they could rest assured that I had gone there reluctantly and that it wasn't their fault; and, after all, we came from the same parish and had breathed the same air since we were born. Eventually a man with a big round face that was pitted with little holes like a spaghetti strainer came in with a lot of papers in his hand, and he ordered us all to rise, and then he began reading out a roll call of the witnesses in alphabetical order, which is the only form of order still respected in this country. Eventually he called out: Signora Spinelli Maria Vincenza. Nobody answered. Isn't Signora Spinelli here? the Spaghetti Strainer repeated. Aren't you Signora Spinelli? he went on, addressing himself to me. Everyone burst out laughing. No, I quietly replied. I can assure you, my dear sir, that never in my life have I been Signora Spinelli. The others burst out laughing again. Simone the Weasel chimed in and said: Signora Spinelli is someone else. Who doesn't know Signora Spinelli? In that case what are you doing here? the Spaghetti Strainer asked me. What seemed to upset him most was the laughter of the *cafoni*, so, wishing to show his authority, he said to me: I invite you to take your departure as quickly as possible. As you can well imagine, I didn't wait to be asked twice. If you say so, I have no alternative, I replied. Outside in the square Venanzio was giving the horses bran and beans, but he immediately realized that there was no time to lose, and helped me, or rather practically pushed me into the carriage, and he made the horses canter to get me out of the danger zone as quickly as possible. Even Plebiscito, the sick horse, seemed suddenly to have acquired wings. When I think about it quietly now, the whole thing seems to me to be like a parable. The Lord obviously first wished to mortify my pride, He wanted to frighten me, but at the last moment He took pity on me and saved me."

"Really," Pietro remarked, laughing too, "I don't want to contradict you, Grandmother, but a mistake in a name can be explained without any direct supernatural intervention."

"The Spina family is too well known for confusion to be possible," the old lady said with confidence.

"Forgive me, Grandmother, it's not incumbent on me to lecture you on these matters, but don't you think one should be cautious about involving God in our petty affairs?"

"It isn't we who involve Him," Donna Maria Vincenza replied, almost resentfully. "It's He who involves Himself with us. He can't be ordered to stay in the sacristy as if He were an ordinary priest."

"If God is so fond of intervening in the affairs of this world,"

Pietro pointed out in semiserious tones, "you must admit that there would be other things He could do that would be much more worthy of Him: a nice big earthquake in Latium, for instance, with the Viminal and Vatican City as its epicenter, would not be an enterprise that would bring discredit on Him; and I can think of others of the same kind."

"The things that are important in the eyes of men are perhaps not at all important in the eyes of God," Donna Maria Vincenza pointed out after thinking over the matter. "How can we tell? I had the same argument this morning with Simone the Weasel while we were sitting on the same bench in that room in the court building. Why, he asked me, breathing in my face with that breath of his that smells of wine, why doesn't the Lord make up His mind once and for all and cause our rulers to have a fatal accident? I tried to explain to him that in His eyes heads of government don't even exist. Perhaps in His eyes they are mere creations of the human imagination, and hence He leaves to men the task of getting rid of them, if they are capable of it. And the police? Simone insisted, don't they really exist? And judges?"

"I've no need to tell you, Grandmother, how much your way of seeing things pleases and amuses me," Pietro admitted. "But if on reflection I don't find it completely convincing, it's because when I read the diocesan bulletin and look at the items listed under the heading GRACES RECEIVED, the obvious conclusion seems to be that the supreme realities of life in the eyes of the Almighty are above all little items such as a widow finding a lost pair of scissors, a baby suffering only minor bruises after being dropped by its nurse, or a letter arriving from someone of whom there has been no news for several years."

"Forgive me, my dear boy," replied Donna Maria Vincenza, who was rather disappointed, "but your incomprehension surprises me. It seems to me to be natural enough that petty incidents such as those you have just mentioned should strike journalists as commonplace, ridiculous, and unworthy of being reported, since, as is well known, even when newspapers don't adorn themselves with untruths they thrive on a fictitious and fatuous though rowdy and glittering kind of life. It's intelligible, in short, that newspapers should ignore the finding of a pair of scissors or the arrival of a letter while they devote a great deal of space to an ambassadors' conference or a speech from the throne. But no one can claim that the Almighty bases His infallible judgments on the superficial and venal judgment of the newspapers. Actually I think it irreverent to suppose that He even reads the newspapers; they are so badly written that he certainly doesn't miss much."

"Oh, Grandmother," Pietro exclaimed, his eyes shining with emotion, "why didn't my mother, when she was alive, send me to have lessons with you instead of sending me off to boarding school?"

"Well, you're here now, my dear boy," Donna Maria Vincenza replied with satisfaction. "You came rather late, it's true, you kept me waiting for so many years, but you came in the end. To exchange one kindness for another, let me tell you that I too always wanted a son like you, a rather crazy son like you, with the kind of craziness that basically I like so much. But now you must excuse me, I must go and rest, because this morning's scare has made me very tired."

Donna Maria Vincenza spent the rest of the day resting in bed, and Pietro took refuge in his den to write an essay "On Things That Get Lost and Are Found Again, On Dropped Babies, And on Letters That Arrive at Last."

He was in a very good mood after dinner that evening, and he went down to talk to Venanzio in his room.

"Last night," the groom told him, "I dreamed that the *carabiniere* record office was on fire. It was dreadful. All the furniture and the papers were reduced to ashes, everything, absolutely everything was burned up, except for that accursed sheet of paper on which my name was written. It danced in the flames like a salamander," Venanzio said dejectedly.

"There was also something else that might interest you that I forgot to tell you," he went on. "I met Simone the Weasel. Well, that deaf-mute from Pietrasecca, that friend of yours, is staying with him. Yes, he's still there where I left him. The two get on splendidly together, just like bread and cheese. The proverb is perfectly true, the one that says that God first makes us and then matches us."

At breakfast time next morning Pietro was not in his room or anywhere else in the house. On his bed that had not been slept in he had left a short note of farewell to his grandmother.

15

I'M SORRY, *CAVALIERE*," said Mastro Eutimio, "but I assure you that what you ask is beyond my abilities. I don't know if they've already told you that I'm a simple, humble carpenter, a rather old-fashioned one."

Mastro Eutimio smiled graciously and apologetically, as if to counter any possible suggestion that his refusal implied any discourtesy; he confessed to being rather old-fashioned in the resigned tones of someone admitting to an infirmity that has become chronic and calls for some consideration.

"Please don't misunderstand me, it's not a matter of ill will," he hastened to add. "But the fact of the matter is that with the best will in the world I would not know how to set about carrying out your order. I'm a rather old-fashioned carpenter, and I can do only the few things I learned when I was a boy, the usual, simple, practical things."

Mastro Eutimio, standing in the doorway of his shop, was trying to persuade Don Marcantonio of his inability to make the additions and modifications to the cross he had already completed on behalf of the parish that would be required if it were to be adapted to the rituals of the new eloquence. Over his usual suit Mastro Eutimio wore a greenish overall of crude material and cut, and he looked like the trunk of an old fruit tree that had been treated with copper sulfate, a tree that, though it was full of years, was still fruitful and well protected against seasonal diseases; at the top of the old trunk his bright eyes stood out like two springtime shoots. But his short head of hair and week-old beard were also reminiscent of two fields of stubble — in many respects two hard and meager mountain fields; he had a red pencil over one ear and half a cigar over the other.

Beside him Don Marcantonio preened himself on rubber heels that made him look taller. He listened to the carpenter in silence, with a little smile of authoritative compassion.

"I'm very sorry indeed, sir, but I simply cannot do it," Mastro Eutimio repeated, handing back to Don Marcantonio in a polite and agreeable manner a sheet of paper with a sketch of a lictor's cross on it. "Every living creature does the best it can, and it's useless to ask a vine to produce wax or bees to produce wine."

Between the shop and the street there was a small space where Mastro Eutimio worked when weather permitted; that morning he had cleared it of a great deal of snow that had fallen during the night and piled the snow into three heaps by the roadside.

At one side of the door the big, heavy oak cross that had been treated with pitch was leaning against the gray wall and extending its great arms. Though it completely dominated the small, one-story house, it did not create the impression of overwhelming or crushing it, but rather of supporting it. On the other side of the door a new kneading trough that had just been finished and still smelled of pinewood and only needed varnishing was standing on two trestles. It was an ordinary kneading trough, with a cupboard with two drawers underneath; on one drawer there was a rough design of a crescent moon and on the other a shining sun.

"With your permission," the carpenter said, pointing to the work that awaited him, and he bent down to light a small fire of shavings and kindling underneath his pan of linseed oil. Squatting on his heels, he fed the flames and warmed his hands with rapid, boyish movements. Don Marcantonio, leaning against the doorpost, looked at his watch every now and then, and yawned.

"The Lenten preacher will at last be ready to see me in a quarter of an hour," he said. "He apologized for the delay a short time ago on the ground that he has so many penitents to confess. What next, I told him, I don't want to confess. At most I might listen to your confession if you have anything on your conscience, Reverend Father, I told him. Ha, ha, ha, *es wird lustig sein.*"*

He took from a small pouch a tiny brush and comb with which he carefully tidied the small mustaches that formed a short, thick tuft of hair on his upper lip.

"By the way, Mastro Eutimio," he went on in a patronizing manner, "I asked your expert opinion on the wood for the patriotic cross that I visualize because we too are democratic in our own way, in fact we are the only true democrats. But, as you can well imagine, your opinion has and can have no importance, otherwise we should be back where we were before. That's why I was telling you that your cross as it is, is of no use, its simplicity is ridiculous, it's no use for my purpose, and in any case, *so oder so,*† it's going to be modified, either by you or by someone else, *und Schluss.*"‡

Mastro Eutimio was now preparing the kneading trough for varnishing. He quickly smoothed out some hollows and cracks with putty, sandpapered it, and then rubbed a pumice stone dipped in olive oil over some rough places left by the plane. He walked around it, looked at it against the light, knelt in front of it, rose, passed his hand across it, looked at it again from a distance, and his light, clean, precise, caressing movements were imbued with an elegance and self-confidence that no one would have attributed to a man of his age who, when not engaged in his trade, was rather shy, slow, and clumsy.

"Will you permit me a question?" he suddenly asked. "If you put a bundle of rods at the top or, what comes to the same thing,

---

*It will be hilarious.
†One way or another.
‡And that's that.

if you have a bundle of rods carved on it and fix a big ax at the top as shown in your sketch, where will our Lord rest his head?"

"You forget that Jesus is no longer on the cross," Don Marcantonio replied in surprise. "The Church itself teaches that."

"In these parts there are people who believe He is still on the cross, still dying," Mastro Eutimio said gravely. "There are people who believe He never died and was never resurrected, that He is still on earth, still dying. And that would explain many things."

"You forget," said Don Marcantonio, annoyed and ill at ease, "that in any case He's not on your cross, whether dying or dead. That's for sure, *und Schluss.*"

"How can you be sure of that?" Mastro Eutimio said, offended and upset. After a moment's reflection he went on: "If that were the case, so far as I'm concerned, one might as well burn it."

The two men turned to the big oak cross that was leaning against the wall and looked at it in silence, Mastro Eutimio humbly and confidently and Don Marcantonio in a strange state of embarrassment. Some women were returning from the fountain with basins balanced on a pad on their heads; as they passed the carpenter's shop they piously crossed themselves and greeted the carpenter.

"Jesus be praised," they said to him.

"Jesus be praised," Mastro Eutimio replied.

"Now I must go," Don Marcantonio said irritably. "You know I have an appointment."

From behind their half-closed windows several women had been watching what passed between the orator and the carpenter without being seen themselves; they had seen the carpenter's painful efforts to evade an obscure threat and the orator's cynical indifference in insisting on it. This inauspicious piece of news passed from door to door and reached Maria Antonia, the carpenter's wife, who was busy with the housework. Her neighbors already knew that the poor woman had been oppressed all morning by a terrible sense of foreboding as the result of a dream. So the bad news, far from surprising her, came as a confirmation of her fears. Panting and frantically raising her arms to heaven, she dashed along the alleyways of the village toward the carpenter's shop, accompanied by the compassionate sighs of the women of the neighborhood. But when she arrived in her husband's presence, perhaps mistaking his surprise for dismay, her strength almost failed her, and she had to lean against the shop door to prevent herself from collapsing.

"Oh, poor us, poor us," she complained. "I knew something dreadful was going to happen."

Mastro Eutimio tried to calm her, to reassure her, to comfort her. "Nothing serious has happened, really it hasn't, believe me, Maria Antonia," he kept repeating affectionately.

But his wife, alas, was no longer a child who could be twisted around one's little finger.

"Oh, Eutì, you think I can't be told the truth?" she moaned in sorrowful tones. "The whole village can be told the truth, but not your wife?"

The poor woman was white and haggard and sweating, and she trembled as if she had a quartan fever.

"Oh, poor us," she went on lamenting, "what harm have we done? Eutì," she said bitterly, changing her tone to one of recrimination, "how many times have I told you to mind your own business? You laughed at my fears, but now everyone will be laughing at us."

Mastro Eutimio went on patiently trying to soothe and comfort her and make her see reason; he did not like public displays of moaning and whining.

"If you must weep and moan," he said to her gently, "if you really can't help it, why don't you go home? In the end that's what a home is for."

He could not explain this sudden dismay since, when he thought about it coolly, his conversation with the orator had taken place at a polite and courteous level. But when his wife asked him outright whether or not it was true that the notable had been to see him and had asked him things and had ended up leaving dissatisfied, he grew confused and passed one hand over his eyes as if his sight were failing.

"I don't know, I don't know," the poor man muttered, and he had to lean against the cross to save himself from falling.

Many women, without being seen themselves, were watching the painful scene between husband and wife from behind their half-closed windows; none knew exactly what had happened to the two unfortunates, but details didn't matter.

"Hello, how are you, Mastro Eutimio?" Don Severino exclaimed cordially, suddenly appearing outside the door.

The carpenter looked at him in embarrassment and went pale; he was at a loss for an answer, and made a vague, uncertain gesture with his hand.

"What's the matter, my friend, why are you so upset?" the organist asked anxiously. "Is this your wife? How do you do, Maria Antonia, I'm a friend of your husband's."

There was no reply to this greeting. Don Severino's slender form, topped by a little round hat and covered in a long dark blue overcoat, moved forward hesitantly and then stopped.

"The fact is that we have our business to mind, Don Severino," Maria Antonia replied coldly. "You must excuse us, but we're not interested in other people's business."

Don Severino looked at the carpenter, searching for a plausible explanation for this strange speech; but Mastro Eutimio seemed a changed man; he was frightened, perplexed, and hesitant, not knowing which way to turn to avoid his friend's eyes and those of his wife; he pretended to be extremely busy, made incoherent gestures, picked up tools, and put them back again without rhyme or reason.

"I didn't come to discuss my affairs with your husband, I assure you, Maria Antonia, that is not in my nature," Don Severino said with visible distress to the woman who had planted herself rudely in front of him. "As on other occasions, I simply wanted to pass the time of day with him and have a little chat about nothing in particular."

"Yes, Don Severino, but my husband is not a chatterbox, he's a carpenter. I don't know if you realize the difference," the woman replied with the simulated patience, not devoid of irony, of someone who finds herself in the position of having to explain the obvious. "If you needed a table or a window, there would be no objection to your coming here. But, as it is, you know yourself how suspicious the authorities are. The fact of the matter is that we must look after our own business."

The woman turned to her husband for confirmation.

"I'm only a humble carpenter," Mastro Eutimio said docilely, looking down to the ground with a sad smile that implored indulgence. "As you know, Don Severino, I'm only a poor, rather old-fashioned carpenter. And, what is more, I have a family."

He said the word "family" in a timorous little trickle of a voice, as if he were revealing a secret, an infirmity.

"We are not persons of independent means," the woman said bitterly and resentfully. "We can't permit ourselves irresponsible actions."

Don Severino walked away. He went back slowly in the direction of Orta from which he had come shortly before. He was paler and more round shouldered than usual as he walked leaning on his black walking stick, and after a time he noticed that someone was hurrying to catch up with him; it was Venanzio, the Spina groom.

"Donna Maria Vincenza would like to talk to you," he said, out of breath because of his hurry. "Something new has happened, something serious."

"I'm sorry," Don Severino muttered, walking on without looking at him. "I'm in a hurry to get back to Orta, I don't want to see anyone."

"I think Donna Maria Vincenza wants to talk to you urgently," Venanzio insisted. "I'll take you back to Orta in the carriage afterward, if you like."

"You may tell your mistress that there's another matter of urgency," Don Severino replied in a changed voice. "You may tell her that it's time to stop treating Donna Faustina without due respect."

Venanzio, with his hat in his hand and his eyes swollen with tears, went on walking beside him for a while, but then stopped and stood looking at him as he walked away, hoping at any moment to see him turn and come back in a friendlier frame of mind. But Don Severino walked on unsteadily, like a man who is very tired or ill, and eventually disappeared around a bend.

Venanzio, dismayed and disheartened, turned and slowly retraced his steps.

Outside the sacristy a knife grinder, surrounded by an audience of silent youths, was whistling and working his wheel with his feet, causing sparks to fly. The oily smell of the mice that had been burned that morning still hung in the air. Venanzio made a wide detour to avoid being seen by the usual little group of notables in the middle of the square. Even to those who did not know them, the way they laughed, gesticulated, coughed, and swung their walking sticks made it obvious from a distance that they were authoritative and optimistic individuals. The little square itself was like a stage set. The government building, the emblems that adorned the walls, the speaker's balcony, the church with its big door rich with carvings and decorations constituted the wings, while the ruins of the old De Dominicis house provided the backdrop. In the middle of the stage there was a raised platform for the band on festive occasions; a big arc lamp was suspended over it. The auditorium was in front; the first row consisted of landlords' houses with balconies and windows facing the square, and behind it, huddled together on the hillside, were the dwellings of the poor, hovels, stables, sheds, pigsties, hen coops piled on top of one another and joined by dark alleyways, steps, balconies, roofs, and arches. Don Marco, with one lachrymose eye on his breviary and the other uneasily directed toward the square, had been standing behind the shutters of the sacristy for an hour, waiting for them to go so that he could leave himself.

"Have you noticed," Don Nicolino said to the magistrate, "that the priest keeps his shutters closed even in daylight?"

Don Gennaro had narrowly escaped being caught in the street looking for Don Severino, to whom he was to have given secret information about the progress of Don Luca's illness. But he had spotted the danger in time and had hurriedly taken refuge in the Café Eritrea.

Don Nicolino took Don Sebastiano, the magistrate, aside for a moment. "Be careful," he whispered to him. "Watch your step, your turn is coming."

"What can anyone have against me?" asked Don Sebastiano, panic-stricken.

"Be careful," the other man repeated. "I can't say any more, but I know what I'm talking about."

"These reverend gentlemen think they can play passing the buck with me," Don Marcantonio angrily told his colleagues. "The Lenten preacher insists that he was sent here solely to preach and that relations with the civil authorities are therefore a matter for the parish priest. But Don Marco claims that the initiative for putting up the new cross came from the Lenten preacher, who is also to lead the procession; the logical consequence of which is that he, the parish priest, is not responsible for the ceremony. So I shall have to waste more precious time applying to the bishop to get him to solve the question of competence as quickly as possible."

"It's obvious, *cavaliere*, that you come from agriculture," Don Nicolino said to him maliciously. "Don't you know that in the Catholic Church settling a question of competence may take decades, if not centuries?"

Those present burst into a long and loud guffaw, which was abruptly cut short when a sign from the clerk of the court indicated that the new orator must be treated with proper respect.

"Priests are as cunning as foxes," Don Lazzaro remarked. "In my opinion the new eloquence should waste no time on them. You'd have much more to gain from striking down the Spina family. I don't know if I've made myself plain, Don Marcantonio, but we could have a little chat about it in private."

"So far as I know, Don Lazzaro, cunning has never saved foxes from the furrier," said Don Marcantonio with a gesture of complete self-assurance.

This time the comrades' laughter was a tribute to the new eloquence. Those present congratulated the orator.

"I haven't heard so much wit for weeks," Don Nicolino admitted in an adulatory tone.

"There may be something worse against the Lenten preacher,"
Don Sebastiano, the magistrate, hinted with an air of mystery.

He was a corpulent, crude, and jovial man; his mouth, which
protruded rather like a watering can, and the big violet bags under
his eyes made him seem a sociable, sentimental, greedy person.
He had only to adjust his epicurean mask to an expression of seriousness or sadness for the comic effect to become irresistible; and
he was therefore much sought after at funerals, weddings, confis-
cations of bankrupts' goods, and public ceremonies in general by
colleagues who wished to take protective measures against tears.
Don Tito, head guard of the parish, nodded and confirmed the
magistrate's suspicions.

"Yes, there is something worse," he said.

Don Tito wore a uniform just like those worn by generals on
ceremonial occasions in the golden age of uniforms before 1914;
and the ornateness of his hairstyle, eyebrows, mustaches, lips, and
belly were in harmony with the style of his uniform, though his
stature and his shoulders, which were rather gaunt and weedy, recalled his workman origin. His duties were actually those of an ordinary municipal guard, and the fact that he was called head
guard was mainly due to his uniform. When Don Saverio Spina
went to Rome on one occasion, the municipal council of Colle
had entrusted him with the task of buying a uniform for the newly
appointed guard and at the same time asked him to do so as eco-
nomically as possible; and he picked up for a song from a dealer
in old clothes and theatrical accessories a uniform that greatly appealed to him, though it appealed rather less to the notables of
Colle because of the excessive authority it would confer on an ordinary municipal guard. But because of the modest price as well
as the dignity that would accrue to the local authority the purchase after endless discussions was eventually ratified. No sooner
had Don Tito put it on than he became acutely aware of the dis-
proportion between the splendor of that uniform and the mediocrity of his rank, and he claimed that the municipality should face
up to the expense of buying him another, more suitable one. But
as it was cheaper to promote him, he was appointed head guard

with the pay of an ordinary one. More blackmail followed, and for a time Don Tito's extravagant uniform became a nightmare to the people of Colle. In the course of time he usurped a number of completely preposterous functions in addition to his legitimate duties as municipal guard; but even the humble duties of that office carried out by a man wearing that uniform assumed a much more far-reaching significance. Even the authority of the *carabinieri* failed to act as a check or brake on his abuses of power for, being strangers to the locality, they needed him for information and advice.

His concurrence with the suspicions expressed by the magistrate in regard to the Lenten preacher derived its importance from the fact that he was the head of the Denunciation, Suspicions, and Rumors Department, which was an organization of his own invention covering the whole local authority area.

Simone the Weasel, freshly shaved, hatless, and wearing a military cloak that barely came down to his knees, suddenly appeared as from the wings of a theater on the stage of the small square. With a quite unusual, light, tripping, rhythmical gait he flitted around the group of government party dignitaries, sniffing at them curiously.

"What have you got to be so cheerful about, Weasel?" said Don Tito, who because of his official functions was always ready to interrogate.

"It's spring," Simone replied with a laugh.

"You feel it's spring in this bitter cold? Ha, ha, ha! And with all this snow? Ha, ha, ha, Simò, wine has affected your brain. Sometimes it starts like that, you know."

"Can't you see anything down there?" Simone asked, pointing to the hills and fields in the distance that were covered with snow.

Several voices answered: "All we can see is country covered with snow."

"You can't see anything beneath the snow?"

"Ha, ha, ha! While there's snow on the ground how can you see what's beneath it?"

The chorus was amused.

"If you saw what I see you wouldn't laugh so stupidly," Simone told them pityingly.

"Be careful, Weasel, what you say and to whom you say it," the head guard advised him, frowning severely.

"*Cavaliere*, you ought to show Weasel the new cross," Don Nicolino said to the orator as if to change the subject, but in the secret hope of extracting more malicious pleasure from what would follow. "It would give you a first impression of the impact it will make on the public."

The orator showed Simone a sheet of paper with the sketch and, to avoid any misunderstanding, explained it to him.

"This, at the top of the cross, will be a big hatchet or ax," he explained. "A big ax."

"A real ax?" said Simone, suddenly extremely interested. "An iron ax? Real iron? Well, I don't think it will be left at the top of that beam in the open air for a single night. A good, solid, real iron ax?"

"That's another problem, one for the *carabinieri*," Don Marcantonio pointed out. "All that interests me are the feelings it will arouse, or rather rearouse, in people's souls."

"It will make a great impression," Simone sincerely admitted. "Everyone will wonder: is it real iron? As it's a state instrument, won't it by any chance be just painted wood? Or wood covered in tin? Some will rush to Mastro Eutimio's to find out; others, simulating religious fervor, will want to touch or tap it."*

"You haven't understood at all," interrupted Don Tito, whose only desire was to use the opportunity to ingratiate himself with the new government speaker. "Your expectations, Weasel, are not of course totally mistaken, but the new eloquence is not interested in petty, vulgar details of that kind."

"To put it in a nutshell," said the magistrate, who was similarly impatient to demonstrate his agreement with the new eloquence, "the question at issue is that of devising a symbol capable of arousing patriotic feelings side by side with religious feelings."

---

*The Italian equivalent of "touch wood" is "touch iron."

"From that point of view," Simone said frankly, "permit me to point out that the ideal of the ax on the cross seems to me to be mistaken. To arouse the feelings of the good Christians of this part of the world something entirely different would be needed, you can take it from me. Will you allow me, in accordance with my gentlemanly code, to offer you a brilliant idea, free, gratis, and for nothing? Well then, do away with the ax and put in its place, done perhaps on beaten iron, a colored picture of a big plateful of spaghetti with tomato sauce."

He jumped away just in time to avoid an angry kick aimed at him by Don Marcantonio, but he was caught on the wing by the head guard, who grabbed the edge of his cloak. In the slight struggle that ensued a pin securing the upturned collar around his neck gave way, and for some moments the buttonless cloak opened down to the level of his stomach, revealing a shirtless body, skinny and black like that of a mummy. The chorus of notables reacted to this unexpected spectacle with a murmur of astonishment and disgust. Don Tito let him go and called after him: "Sheer off, you wretch, your bones can be counted just like an old donkey's."

"But, Tito, don't you know what the donkey said?" Simone shouted from a safe distance. "One day it said to the pig: you may be fatter than I am, but you'll end up with your throat slit."

"What do you mean?" Don Tito shouted at him. "What exactly do you mean?"

"He that hath ears to hear, let him hear."

"I don't know how you put up with that *cafone*'s continual jibes," Don Marcantonio complained to his colleagues. "Shove him inside."

"It wouldn't be the first time," said the clerk of the court, who had greatly enjoyed the scene. "But what's the use? You have to let him out again."

"Besides, Simone isn't a *cafone*," Don Sebastiano pointed out. "He's not a *cafone*, he's a rebel, don't let's confuse things. He deliberately reduced himself to a state worse than that of a *cafone*, it's really scandalous, but in the end he's of gentle birth, he's an Ortiga. You can't treat him like a *cafone*."

"This indulgence on your part is very suspect," Don Marcantonio announced coldly. "We're living in a pitiless age."

The clerk of the court and the magistrate went pale.

"We don't want to be misunderstood," they both said almost simultaneously.

"Some day or other the scandal will cease and I'll put that wild individual in his place," said the head guard. "I've an old score to settle with him, you know what I'm referring to. Did you notice," he added, "Don Severino talking to Mastro Eutimio and the Spina coachman a short time ago?"

But Don Marcantonio was interested in something else.

"How much did Don Severino lose when he was sacked as the parish organist of Colle?" he wanted to know. "How long will he be able to manage without a job?"

"He has never been paid," said Don Tito. "It's a poor parish."

This aroused Don Marcantonio's indignation.

"So Don Severino has private means?" he said with disgust. "There's one of the many cases in which economic independence encourages license of thought."

"Pietro Spina is another example of that," the magistrate added to rehabilitate himself.

"There's no genuine and certain civic spirit," Don Marcantonio announced, "where there is not total dependence, including economic dependence, on the state."

"Are we all to end up as state employees?" Don Lazzaro asked anxiously.

"All of us," the orator replied.

"Including landowners?"

"Certainly."

"And the *cafoni*?"

"Of course."

"And we're all to be equal?"

"No. Some will be given state employment as landlords and others state employment as laborers. Those who rebel will lose all employment."

"There's the case of Don Bastiano," Don Lazzaro insinuated.

"That's a matter for further consideration," Don Marcantonio announced in a grave and authoritative manner.

Simone went down a filthy little alleyway behind the square and slipped quietly into a low, dark grocer's shop. It was so dark in the poky little place that he did not at first make out the old woman dressed in black whose shop it was; she was sitting in a corner silently praying, or perhaps weeping. He began helping himself.

"Well, Simò," she said, after watching him for a moment or two, "do you think you're at home here?"

"Oh, Maria Luisa," he said apologetically, "I didn't want to disturb you, that's all. How are you, Maria Luisa? Have you had any news from America, from your husband?"

"When are you going to pay me, Simò, for what you've just taken, I should like to know? What pleasure can there be in robbing an old woman?"

"Note it all down in your big book, Maria Luisa, and oblige me by not mentioning the matter again. It's monotonous, and I don't like monotony. It simply means that I'll pay you when I can."

"And why did you help yourself to a packet of sugar, Simò? Are you giving a party, by any chance?"

"It's impossible to hide anything from a woman like you, Maria Luisa. Don't tell anybody, it's a secret, but today is Cherubino's birthday."

"Who's Cherubino? One of your illegitimate children?"

"Yes, Maria Luisa, he's my donkey. He gets older every year too, poor chap."

"Are you going to stay crazy for ever, Simò?" said Maria Luisa. "Aren't you ever going to learn sense?"

Simone hurried back to his barn like a housewife returning late from market. When he reached the path along the canal bank he looked all around to see whether anyone was following him or whether there were any suspicious footsteps in the snow; he was as mistrustful as a wild animal returning to its den. The snow came up to his knees and made the going hard. The canal was frozen over. All that was to be seen were the light footprints of nocturnal animals. Outside the barn door Leone wagged his tail and barked with pleasure. Simone closed the door behind him and shouted in the direction of the trapdoor that led to the second floor: "Anything new?"

"No, nothing," a clear voice answered. "And in the village?"

"Nothing but the usual vermin in the square." Then he added cheerfully: "There's a treat for lunch today. Coffee with sugar."

A long, childish squeal of delight came down through the trapdoor, together with a question: "But where did you get the money from? Did you win the lottery again?"

"You stay up there for the time being," Simone answered. "I'll call you when you can come down."

Pietro went on with the lesson he had been giving Infante during Simone's absence. They sat facing each other on two big straw-filled sacks that they used as beds at night; both were covered with rags to keep out the cold, and they were so close that their knees nearly touched. The interrupted lesson was resumed. Pietro looked Infante in the eyes in a way that was both gentle and firm, showed him a bottle of wine, and said *vi-no*, carefully articulating the two syllables. He repeated this three or four times until Infante with a great effort managed to say *i-no*. Pietro patiently repeated *vi-no*, emphasising the V; after a number of failures Infante eventually succeeded in pronouncing the initial consonant, but with a sound closer to an F than to a V. *Fi-no*, he said. Pietro nodded appreciatively and laughed.

"You ought to be ashamed of yourself," he said, "you pronounce Italian just like a German."

Infante, who could not have understood a single word of this, laughed too. The two men sitting facing each other seemed to be practically of the same height, but the deaf-mute was more solidly built. Both had had their heads shaved by Simone, who among other things had once been a sheepshearer. Their thoroughgoing haircuts, the gray winter light, and the motionlessness of their bodies overloaded with rags accentuated the anxious expression on the faces of both men, their state of extreme and barely contained tension that was ready to explode into cries and gestures at any moment. The emotion in Pietro's eyes was that of a man

raised from the dead who had found something that in his previous life he had sought for in vain; his emotion gave him an un-
canny look, as if he had had an almost inhuman experience; his
earthy coloring was like that of a disinterred statue, and his thin,
gray lips made him look as if he had eaten earth and still had the
taste in his mouth. Infante's eyes were the predominant feature of
his face too, though for different reasons. His deafness had enlarged his eyes, in which the energy that his ears were deprived of
was concentrated. The whole world passed through those eyes;
and in the past few days his world had been suddenly enlarged
and enriched through Pietro's teaching, by the acquisition of
new words, each corresponding to a definite thing, new relations
among words and new and hitherto unimagined ideas; and, what
is more, the whole of his poor, primitive old world had been cap-
sized by Simone's hospitality and the sudden, inexplicable, and
unaccountable reappearance of Pietro, that strange gentleman
who was wanted by the police. Infante must have had a great
propensity to believe in miracles; otherwise Pietro's reappearance,
being in such sharp contrast to the world with which he was familiar, would have struck him as utterly fantastic. In fact, however, he was moved, but by no means surprised. In addition to the
old, hard, hostile world of Pietrasecca he had by chance discovered another, absurd, marvelous, friendly world, which was natural too, since it existed, though it was of another and totally
different nature; a strange world, a strange way of living, not based
on money, profit, violence, fear, or services rendered that had to
be repaid, but on what his eyes saw, on personal liking, and a kind
of liking that was totally unprecedented in his experience, being
completely gratuitous and disinterested; a new world, superficially similar to the world he knew, only turned upside down. But
since it existed, he did not seem to be surprised by it; and, as he
liked it, he observed and enjoyed it. His whole head expressed
that intense enjoyment. It was emaciated by hunger, with two big,
useless, prominent ears, his face roasted by the sun, with numerous old scars that were calcified with mud and more recent
bruises, abrasions, and swellings on the chin, the jaws, and the

brow; it was not a face that knew how to laugh, and the necessity of expressing his new and unexpected happiness resulted merely in grotesque grimaces. Pietro watched him gravely and fondly, as if he were in charge of a newborn infant. Sitting on their two straw mattresses, they were in the most sheltered corner of the barn, though the snow and the wind came in freely through two big, shutterless windows. It was as cold as if they were in the open air. In the dark and when a gale was blowing, the straw beds on which they spent the night ceased to be beds and became prickly bushes or ditches, or hills, or rocky mountains, or rafts on a stormy sea. In the morning the hair that was beginning to grow again after their drastic haircuts bristled like the spines of a porcupine, their joints ached, and their feet were swollen.

"As there are no shutters on the windows, of course the bad weather comes in," Simone explained. "But for the same reason it goes out again in just the same way. You'll see I'm right when the spring comes, Pietro."

16

THE BARN WAS BIG AND spacious, and had obviously
been built by the Spinas to keep hay and straw for a large
number of animals, though all it contained now was straw for
one donkey. The roof timbers groaned and creaked in the wind
like the keel of a ship in a storm. Innumerable spiderwebs, as big
as sheets, billowed and survived the gusts. A number of holes in
the bare stone walls must have been used to support beams while
the barn was being built and now accentuated its state of neglect.
To reach the ground floor you had to use a ladder, through the
same trapdoor from which straw for the bed and fodder for the
donkey was brought down.

The wind did not come in at ground level, but the cobbled
floor was damp, and even that part of it not used by the donkey was
covered with a layer of brown mud. The three men had to wear
their overcoats all day, just as if they were in the open air. They
made a fire between some big, blackened stones in the corner;
there was also a tripod on which a pot and a saucepan could be put
for heating water and cooking. Pietro liked lighting the fire,
helping with the cooking, peeling potatoes, peeling, cutting up,

and chopping onions, and soaking and frying the dried salt cod. But his favorite dishes were those for which he had envied poor children when he was a boy: *panunta*, for instance, which consisted of thick slices of toast rubbed with sliced garlic and copiously seasoned with olive oil. The sharpness of the garlic went perfectly with the blandness of the olive oil, and whenever Pietro ate it he felt tears coming into his eyes, and to avoid seeming ridiculous he blamed the garlic.

"When I was a child I was convinced that the blessed in Paradise lived on *panunta*," he confessed to Simone with a blush.

For a change they sometimes had *panzanella*. All that was needed for this was a few drops of olive oil, some salt, and a few crushed basil leaves. The olive oil that Simone acquired "on credit" from Maria Luisa was of a greenish yellowy color and had a slightly bitter flavor, incidentally just like the milk, the water, the wine, the fruit, the bread, and the whole of the rest of the region.

"But to appreciate it you must not have a depraved heart," Simone remarked.

"When I came from Rome by the night train last year," Pietro agreed, "I realized I was approaching this part of the world by the slightly bitter flavor in the air."

The three men were, so to speak, joined at table by the donkey and the dog, who completed the company. With his big, heavy, thoughtful head, Cherubino's contribution was his calm, his patience, and his dignity; without ostentation and also without shame he stretched out beside the table with all his infirmities, his swollen belly, his back worn by the saddle, his knees grazed by falls. On his back there was the dark line in the shape of a cross that is frequent among donkeys and makes them look like poor Christians.

"Alas, Cherubì, you used to carry three hundredweights, but those times are past," Simone said to him. "That's not a rebuke, I don't grudge you the little straw that you eat. You've carried enough loads in your time."

Cherubino let him talk. Leone too suffered from the cold; he sneezed, coughed, and had a running nose and eyes, but he didn't complain either. When Simone and the dog looked each other in the eyes the mutual sympathy between them almost became visible.

"He knows everything," Simone confided to Pietro in an undertone.

"What do you mean, everything?"

"Everything about us. He has guessed every detail. Ever since the night you arrived here he has had a way of looking at me that leaves not the slightest doubt. Besides, he's to be trusted. Mind you, he doesn't have a dog's usual servile fidelity to its master; if he had, I'd despise him for it. But Leone and I have been through all sorts of things together, and we have ended up understanding and appreciating each other."

Among other things, Leone could laugh when he felt like it; he raised his upper lip and bared his teeth. This always delighted Simone, who showed his pleasure by affectionately calling him a bastard, a pig, and a son of a cow, which he would never dare do to the donkey.

"The donkey too is kindhearted, but he's serious and perhaps a bit sulky," he explained. "He's still a *cafone*, he has no sense of humor. But think of the loads the poor devil has carried in his time."

Infante did not have cheerful blood in his veins either; on top of the sadness natural to a *cafone*, he was dominated by the melancholy and mistrustfulness of the deaf, by the impossibility of understanding the jokes and the play with words indulged in by the others, though fortunately Pietro's presence reassured him that the jokes were not at his expense. But he too tried to contribute to the cheerfulness of the company; he was able to move his ears like a hare and, as Pietro burst out laughing the first time he did this, he did it again whenever he noticed that his comrades were downcast; and whenever he did this they laughed to avoid offending him. Thus his poor, big ears were at least useful for something. Another and different source of good cheer was the small cask of wine that occupied a prominent position on two low wooden trestles almost in the middle of the room. It was a light, clear, fruity wine that encouraged long, friendly conversation. Though Simone was the reverse of abstemious, the cask was still nearly full when Pietro arrived, and this did not fail to surprise him.

"To drink you need company," Simone explained. "It's well known that traitors and priests' sons like drinking in secret. In taverns the wine generally isn't worth very much, but who goes to a tavern for the sake of the wine? The only advantage of going there is that you're never alone. And even if many of the customers are vile, degraded, and stupid, the fact that they're there is better than nothing."

But now Simone had company in his home, and in their honor he started drinking first thing in the morning, to rinse his teeth, as he said, to clear his sight and his voice, and to be able to wish his friends good morning with a clear conscience. And he emptied the last jug before stretching out on his straw mattress in the evening, after wishing his guests good night and happy dreams, to dispel his troubles, as he put it, and drive out any vile suspicions or feelings that might surreptitiously have introduced themselves into his body in the course of the day. But as time passed this drinking became a ceremonial matter more than anything else, a mere act of propitiation. He ended up preferring conversation with Pietro to drinking, asking him questions and listening to him talking about the countries he had been to and the way other people lived; and with the passing of the days they went on telling stories and exchanging confidences into the small hours. Eventually he drank less even at meals, after he himself suggested a system of taking turns as being the only decent one in good company. This system required a permanent effort at eloquence.

"Refresh your heart, it's your turn," he said to the deaf-mute. "Refresh your mind, Pietro, it's a sincere wine. Pietro, your dilatoriness surprises me. Pass the jug, decadent youth, and let an old man teach you how to drink."

To entertain them he demonstrated drinking in various spectacular ways, pouring it down his throat from the jug, or straight from a bottle, or drop by drop, or in huge gulps, or like a patriotic or a sacred orator, or an infant at the breast, for instance, or like a chicken, a cow, or a pilgrim, as well as in a number of other ways, to the great amusement of his guests. But all this was more bark than bite, as with every day that passed he took greater care to keep his mind clear, because he took greater and greater pleasure in talking and listening to Pietro, and the trouble then was that a whole evening seemed to last only a few minutes. Between one drink and the next he smoked a filthy old pipe with a broken stem tied up with string, and when he spoke he took it out of his mouth and spat on the ground. Pietro tried to avoid hurting Infante's feelings by not leaving him out, not letting him feel disadvantaged as a deaf-mute, and he was greatly relieved to note that, like a bird making its nest in the straw, Infante began adapting himself to the rest of the company and started looking after the donkey and the dog, getting firewood, going to the stream with a pail to fetch water, washing and hanging out to dry the small amount of underwear with which Simone had supplied him.

"If I'm not mistaken, Infante must still have in his pocket the fifty lire that Venanzio gave him," Pietro said to Simone one day. "Perhaps you might be able to buy him something useful with the money."

He should never have said that. Simone was surprised and hurt.

"Is he in need of anything?" he asked.

"Even if one has all the essentials," Pietro explained, "there's always something useful one can buy."

"But what is he short of?" Simone asked indignantly. "I'm sorry, I haven't noticed. Tell me, what is he short of?"

"Really, I didn't want to offend you, Simone," Pietro said apologetically. "He's not short of anything, let's change the subject."

"To be perfectly frank with you, Pietro, this is something I should never have expected of you," Simone went on. "Is that what you think of me? Certainly I'm poor, but I look after my guests. If I have no money, I manage all the same. That's my business."

"I'm sorry, Simone, I apologize," said Pietro. "Now that I come to think of it, I agree that Infante is not short of anything."

"Money only exists to be spent, of course, but you forget that this is not a hotel but a private residence," Simone went on resentfully. "That's the whole point. You forget that you're not paying me for board and lodging. I certainly regret that the place isn't overcomfortable."

"If I attached such importance to comfort, Simone, I should have stayed where I was, or gone back to it," Pietro interrupted. "You know very well that that was not in my mind."

"Very well, you expressed yourself badly," Simone said in a conciliatory tone. "If you're short of anything in the future, or if you notice that Infante is short of anything, please tell me."

"We're not short of anything at the moment," Pietro insisted. "We really couldn't be better off than we are here."

Pietro was not a very demanding guest. Simone put him to the test immediately after his arrival. "We eat what there is," he said. "Often there's nothing, so then we eat nothing."

"Fasting's good for the figure," Pietro answered with a laugh.

There were no glasses at the table; one had to drink from the jug. What would Pietro make of that?

"No doubt at your grandmother's you had a different wine glass for every kind of wine and a different liqueur glass for every kind of liqueur," said Simone. "But here you'll have to manage."

"While we're about it," Pietro suggested enthusiastically, "why don't we give up the jug? We could drink straight from the tap."

"That would be going too far," Simone had to say.

Every morning Simone had a bath, in summer in the canal and in winter in the snow that he piled up for the purpose behind the barn. This custom of his was well known by now to all the people of the neighborhood, and nothing contributed more to his reputation for wildness and eccentricity. As evidence of his diabolical nature some pious women insisted that they had seen flames and smoke emerging from the heap of snow when he laid his thin, dark body on it.

In spite of Pietro's adaptability, Simone did not dare offer such a crude way of having a bath to his guests, and nothing else was available. But improvements are always possible even in the best-organized households, and he made holes in the bottom of an empty gasoline can with a nail and hung it from a piece of rope, thus creating a practical and economical shower. He hung a cowbell that was lying idly in an old toolbox from another rope and used it to interrupt the lessons that Pietro gave Infante and summon them to the table. Cherubino the donkey was the only guest who remained indifferent to these innovations.

"Is it indifference or snobbishness?" Pietro kept asking.

"I've been watching him for about fifteen years and I still don't understand him," Simone replied.

"Perhaps it's ancient, innate superiority," Pietro suggested. "If it were a pose he would give himself away, even if only for a moment."

"In that case it's a good thing that there should be one of us who so thoroughly and consistently reminds us of contempt of the world and its pomps and vanities."

One day, for the second time since he took up residence in the barn, Pietro found a chicken on the table, a magnificent creature of the Paduan variety, plump, long limbed, and with a tuft of feathers on its head. He looked with astonishment at this "bourgeois" victim on the poor table. Its neck was extended, its feathers were ruffled and stuck together, its wattles hung loosely under its beak, and its eyes were closed as if it were horrified at the prospect of being eaten in a stable.

"Chicken again?" he asked suspiciously.

"It's Sunday," Simone replied. "A day of rest has to be sanctified in one way or another."

"If I'm not being indiscreet," Pietro went on timidly, "where is your chicken run?"

"Over there, just behind the house," Simone announced convincingly. "There's a vegetable garden and a chicken run. Haven't you ever heard the noise?"

Simone went outside to dump the feathers in the refuse pit, and a prolonged, hoarse, guttural cock-a-doodle-doo came from behind the barn, though it was too well done to seem completely natural. Only Simone's accomplice Leone pretended to believe it was genuine, and he barked, whimpered, and scratched at the door.

"By the way," Pietro asked during the meal, "may I ask why they nicknamed you Weasel?"

"Just the usual slander," Simone replied evasively. "We all have nicknames here — the Spinas are called hardheads, as you know — and in the end I got to prefer the nickname to my real name."

"And what would that be?" Pietro asked.

"Ortiga, if I remember correctly."

"Ortiga? A boy named Remo Ortiga slept in my dormitory during my first year at boarding school; later he died in the earthquake, as his mother did too, if I'm not mistaken. He had a fine voice, he was best at Gregorian chant."

Simone had a sudden reaction that Pietro missed.

"Oh, so you knew Remo?"

"Of course," Pietro replied. "It was a small school, and we came from the same part of the world, though not from the same village. Was he a relative of yours?"

"He was my son."

But perhaps this was something of which he did not want to be reminded, because he went on immediately: "Drink, Pietro, it has been your turn for the past half hour, refresh your heart. Your slowness in drinking is beginning to revolt me. And you drink too, Infante, refresh your guts, if you please. Look at me, this is the way to drink, learn from a poor father."

There was only one practicable path to Simone's home in winter, along the embankment between the canal and the fields; Leone sounded the alarm if anyone approached, and one could see from a distance who it was. Simone took special precautions to prevent surprise at night. There were sluice gates at intervals by means of which the water for irrigating the fields in summer was regulated, and at these points there were plank bridges that anyone using the path had to cross. Simone, helped by the deaf-mute, removed the planks every evening, thus preventing access. It was hard work, but it was satisfying all the same.

"At nighttime it's just as if we were in a castle," Simone explained to Pietro with evident pride. "We are defended by a number of drawbridges."

While he was putting back the heavy planks one morning Simone discovered some recent footprints on the snowy embankment. Someone had been there during the night and must have stopped at the first ditch, since the path stopped there; Simone could tell from the footprints in the snow that the stranger, after testing out the ground, had gone down into the field but had realized the impossibility of going any farther when he reached the first fence and had then turned back. He reluctantly told Pietro of his discovery, and together they decided to take precautions.

"If it was a so-called friend," Simone said, "he'll probably come back in the daytime. But whoever it is, and false friends are the worst, at the first alarm you and Infante will go upstairs, pull up the ladder behind you, and close the trapdoor. There's no other way up, it's not so easy to clamber up the wall with nails and teeth, and bringing another ladder here will take time. And in the meantime you can be quite sure that Leone and I will not be just standing about idly, looking on, and applauding."

But no one turned up all day long. Whenever there was a gust of wind stronger than usual or a dog barked Simone hurried to the door to see if anyone was approaching, but no one appeared. Perhaps the uncertainty got on his nerves, and in the evening he put on his military cloak, repeated his instructions to Pietro, and went to the village, where he sniffed about in a simulated casual manner. Outside the Flag Inn he was challenged to a game of cards by the shoemaker Nazzareno the Pegleg, half drunk.

"Weasel, I've heard you gambled your cloak and shirt and lost them just like San Camillo," the man called out in mocking tones, "but I see with pleasure that you still have your trousers. Come and wager them on a game of cards."

"And if you lose, Pegleg, how will you manage without your trousers?" Simone replied pityingly. "You'll get rheumatism in your wooden leg."

The tipsy voices of other drinkers emerged from the dark and smoky cavern of the inn.

"Hey, Weasel, what's up with you? Why don't we see you anymore? Have you fallen in love again, Weasel? Where do you spend your evenings nowadays, we should like to know?"

"In church, my dearly beloved brothers and sisters," Simone answered from the middle of the street, imitating the voice of a preacher. "In church, doing penance."

This reply produced a burst of laughter and a number of jibes, ha, ha, ha.

"Well, Weasel, keep your secret, but come in. If you've lost your cloak and shirt and don't want to wager your trousers, Weasel, wager your donkey," another voice called out. "What's the use of that animal to you?"

"Oh, Damià," replied Simone, still in the middle of the street, "Cherubino's the only friend I can trust."

"Well then, Weasel, be off," the one-legged shoemaker said disdainfully, leaning against the doorpost to prevent himself from falling. "For some time past you've been no good for anything."

"Let him go," a raucous woman's voice called out from inside the inn. "One devil can't seduce another, everyone knows that."

"Well said, Matalè," Simone called out with a laugh as he went away. "My devil was already a canon when yours were still in their swaddling clothes."

A group of young *cafoni* wrapped in tattered old cloaks were standing in the middle of the square and smoking, waiting for the women to come out of church; they had all contributed to buying a single cigarette and were taking it in turns to smoke it, one puff each; the last one carefully put the stub in his hatband, since it could still be used on another occasion. When they caught sight of Simone some of them started imitating the clucking of chickens.

"If you need someone to feel whether you're going to lay an egg, you'd better ask your mother, fine gentlemen, because I washed my hands this morning," Simone told them.

A good smell of mutton being cooked on a spit caused Simone to change direction. While he was holding his nose in the air and sniffing in the hope of tracking down the source of the delightful scent, he ran into Venanzio, who was slowly coming up the hill. Signora Spina's groom signed to him, indicating that he wanted to talk to him, but not there, to avoid arousing suspicion. The two walked in silence to where the alleyway led out into the vineyards.

"To come and see you at night nowadays you need wings," Venanzio finally announced.

"Oh, so it was you, was it?" Simone replied, reassured. "And what, may I ask, did you want at that time of night?"

"I was bringing you a basket full of good things," Venanzio went on, searching in his face for an expression of greed. "Not for you, of course, I meant not for you only, you understand."

"I don't understand."

"My mistress told me to take a basket full of victuals for you and your guests to your house without being seen. Perhaps you understand me now."

"No, not yet."

"I'm sorry, but I can't explain myself more clearly."

"Whose idea was it? Your mistress's? That seems to me to be almost impossible. Yes, she's rich, but in spite of that she's a lady, and she has always reciprocated the respect I have for her and that we both deserve. How could she imagine that I would receive guests in my house without offering them everything they require?"

"Now you're exaggerating. My mistress doesn't doubt your generosity, but she also knows that you're poor. Now, in the long run, having two guests in the house . . ."

"I may lack means, but not ideas," Simone answered haughtily.

He at once demonstrated the truth of this statement by cleanly blowing his nose with two fingers. Then he turned his back on Venanzio and made for home. His way of walking, slightly bent and almost skipping, his long thin legs, his gray-green cloak that did not come down to his knees made him look like a huge grasshopper. A few leaps and he was back at the barn, where he found Pietro radiant; the deaf-mute had learned the useful and honest word *letame*, dung, and with it the beautiful word *letizia*, happiness, that derives from it. This was the first abstract term that Infante had learned and understood. Pietro had hesitated for a long time before teaching it to him, fearing that this first abstraction might introduce an evil germ into his mind. But he had the

pleasure of observing immediately that Infante understood and
used the word *letizia* with its meaning strictly limited to the effects of *letame*, exactly as Pietro had taught him. The primary
meaning of *letizia* is a naturally manured field; the smell, and also
the vapor, that rises from a heap of dung is *letizia*; the natural,
humble, and certainly pleasurable action of a donkey ridding itself of its feces is *letizia* too. During the evening meal, after
noticing Simone's boots, which were dirtied with dung, like
Cherubino's hooves and shins, the deaf-mute thought for a little
while and then said, laughing in that way of his: *company letizia.*

Pietro found this very moving. Infante's pronunciation was
painful, guttural, and shrill, but it was distinct. Pietro was always
deeply affected by it, as if he had put his whole life behind that
difficult speech. Later Infante disappeared for a few minutes, and
when he came back he laughed and said *letizia.* Simone could
not conceal his concern.

"At this rate he'll end up as a public speaker," he said with a
frown.

When Pietro cleaned the dust and cobwebs from the inside of
the two leaves of the big door he discovered that a great many
names were written on them, in pencil, in chalk, and sometimes
scratched with the point of a knife, followed by cryptic phrases,
figures, and conventional signs.

"That's part of my accounting system," Simone explained
shyly and modestly. "Haven't I told you about the little business I
run? If I don't talk about it, it's actually for reasons of discretion,
but I have no secrets from you. Haven't you ever heard of the
everlasting pill? Oh, I see, there has always been a conspiracy of
silence about it in good families. Well, don't let your imagination
run away with you; if it becomes available in the next few days, I'll
show it to you. There's nothing special about it to look at, it's just
a small white ball the size of a pigeon egg, but when you swallow
it it acts like a foreign body and causes powerful intestinal con-
tractions and thus, if I may refer to it without actually mentioning
it, it brings about the desired result. I don't know what it's made
of, a pharmacist once told me it must be antimony, but heaven

knows whether that's correct or not. Its great advantage is that it emerges intact. After a wash in cold water it's ready for use again. In short, it really is Columbus's egg. It has been in use, without exaggeration, for at least a century, and it will probably outlast all of us. Please forgive me, talking about eternity makes one sentimental and one tends to lapse into overemphasis. But, believe me, it gives me no small satisfaction when I consider how many governments have succeeded each other in the course of a hundred years. At any rate, the everlasting pill is all that remains of what my father left me, the only thing I wouldn't give up for all the money in the world. I say so in no spirit of boastfulness, but if some part of the population of Colle is devoted to me and comes at any rate intermittently under my influence, the credit is due not so much to any merit of mine as to that pill. The meager income I get from it (as you can well imagine, use of the pill is not gratuitous, but it is cheap) has never permitted me to take a seaside holiday, but it has helped me through some grim and desperate quarters of an hour. Also it enables me to get credit, and credit is the soul of trade. But what makes me value it most, I think, is, alas, all the trouble it has gotten me into. As perhaps you may remember, once upon a time there was a pharmacist here, but after about ten years he had to put up his shutters for lack of customers. Not that the village enjoys perfect health, but for serious illnesses the good people here prefer to have recourse to the saints; for others they use the leeches supplied by Aristodemo the Barber; and to purge themselves most of them have always used my pill, which is cheap, old, and local. I'm not a blind praiser of the past, but it can't be denied that there used to be more tolerance. The old eloquence was as fraudulent as all eloquence is, but it at least allowed you to live. A famous case was brought against me by the pharmacists of the area for practicing medicine without authority, and the lawyer Zabaglione's fees cost me an eye out of my head, but I won. A golden age for my pill followed. But a few years ago the new orator, Don Coriolano, egged on and bribed by the pharmacists of neighboring villages and without even the formality of another trial, announced in the public square that the purging of citizens was a basic function of the state, if not the most basic of all its functions, that the government could not surrender it at any price, and that my pill, besides violating the sacred principles of hygiene, morality, and religion, was a threat to public order. I was therefore ordered to hand over the antimony pill to Don Tito, the head guard, within twenty-four hours. As you can well imagine, I refused, appealing to the liberal principles enshrined in the constitution. The result was that I was put under arrest for several days, and in my absence the head guard started trying to track down the pill. But how do you confiscate something that for most of the time is inside people's intestines? How can you hope to catch it just at the moment when it emerges? Don Tito made the mistake of not foreseeing this, and as a result he covered himself with ridicule. He was led astray by false denunciations and was seen going about the village streets in his pompous general's uniform, generally early in the morning and after meals, descending like a thunderbolt into the bosom of suspect families in the hope of finding the *corpus delicti*. You can imagine the reception he was given. Some squalid incidents occurred that out of respect for decency I shall not now recall. The whole village, all the *cafoni* of the neighborhood, were shaken out of their age-old apathy and swept by waves of hilarity, the echo of which even reached me in the stinking underground cell in which I was confined as a modest martyr to the freedom of trade. The scandal could not of course be allowed to last too long and it was in fact brought to an end in a correct and dignified manner in complete harmony with tradition. To save the prestige of his uniform, Don Tito announced in the square one morning that the pill had been confiscated, and he showed the curious something that resembled it; it may have been a dove egg or a small billiard ball. But, as you will have guessed, the everlasting pill had not been confiscated. Everyone in the village was well aware of the fact as, indeed, Don Tito himself must have been. But what mattered to him was not so much the destruction of the pill as the prestige of his uniform, and he was therefore more than satisfied by the formal announcement of its confiscation, accompanied by a formal document to that effect, signed by me without batting an eyelid and duly put in the Files. Since then a tacit agreement has arisen between me and the authorities: the pill can go on being used, but officially it no longer exists, and it must of course never be mentioned."

Meanwhile Infante was sitting on the straw near the donkey, trying to teach him the words *letame* and *letizia*; he repeated them slowly, one syllable at a time, steadily looking the donkey in the eyes. Cherubino listened with obvious interest, but failed to repeat the two important words; perhaps he considered them unnecessary, or perhaps he thought that talking in general was of no use to him. To Infante this complete silence was excessive, and he lost patience and wanted Pietro to come and help him. But Pietro, fascinated by Simone's revelations, took no notice of him.

"I must confess with pride that I have always respected the agreement," Simone went on. "But Don Tito, in spite of his uniform, has remained a hot-blooded, excitable peasant. He has to pretend, he tries his hardest, but he suffers acutely. Every now and then, especially if he meets me when he's tipsy, he gets nasty and provokes and threatens me. It's as if the pill had stuck in his throat and he can neither spit it out nor swallow it. With both the legal fiction and reality on my side I have an insuperable advantage, which is another reason why I don't allow myself to be intimidated; on the contrary, I enjoy teasing the ridiculous fellow, pinpricking him. I bow respectfully and praise the unparalleled astuteness, the flair as a sleuth, the lynxlike sharpness of vision that he so convincingly demonstrated on the occasion of that famous confiscation, and I lament the cruel fate that deprived me when I most needed it of what would have been a source of revenue in my old age. If others are present at our skirmishes, it is not unusual for volunteers to imitate my serious voice and gestures and associate themselves with the compliments I pay him. He puts on a sickly smile on these occasions, he can't help it, he turns green, gets frantic, foams at the mouth like a mad dog, but he can't speak. But certain clues lead me to suppose that he still has hopes of confiscating the pill. To him it's a matter of faith. That humble, elusive pill that continues to emerge from one intestinal tract and enter another shows the limits of his authority. The illusory consolation of his uniform seems to be effective only on an empty stomach, that is, early in the morning, when he spends a long time contemplating his image in a big barber's mirror that covers half the wall of his Denunciations, Suspicions, and Rumors office. But as soon as he starts drinking, and he drinks every evening, the consequences are disastrous, for he resumes contact with naked reality. If he ever makes another attempt to lay his hands on the pill, he'll have to make sure of success in advance, because he can't risk another downfall."

This story left Pietro full of wonder and admiration. "There you are," he confessed shamefacedly, "you can be born in a place, you can spend twenty years in it, you can believe you know everything about it, and yet you can be ignorant of the most elementary facts. If chance hadn't brought us together, I should probably never have heard this moving story."

"I don't think it was chance that brought us together, Pietro," Simone said thoughtfully. "Perhaps it was fate, or perhaps it was God. I don't know, there are things I don't understand. If you hadn't appeared, my life would have had no meaning. But now let's stop prattling like a couple of silly women. Drink, Pietro, refresh your soul, please don't make me angry, it's your turn. And you drink too, Infante, warm those ears of yours. And now, inexperienced youths, watch carefully and learn how to drink, learn from an unscrupulous old businessman."

The days passed quickly. Never in his life had Simone spent so much time indoors, not even before the earthquake, when he had a comfortable house and a family; but that was in another life that he did not like recalling; it was painful to reopen old wounds. Those distant years were like stones on his heart; moving them was more of a pain than a relief.

"By the way," he always interrupted if the conversation came around to that time, as if he were about to point out something important, though what he was actually doing was changing the subject. "I'm becoming a domesticated animal," he used to repeat with a laugh. "I'm becoming a confirmed bachelor." One evening he brought back and hung in the middle of the ground-floor room an old oil lamp that cast a greenish light and hissed like a cat when it arches its back to intimidate an enemy. The lamp added a spectacular element to the primitive simplicity of the barn that aroused the enthusiasm of Leone and Infante, while Cherubino yet again did not bother to conceal his indifference.

"Where did you buy that museum piece?" Pietro asked curiously.

"I won it in a lottery," Simone explained modestly and evasively. "You'll find it useful if you want to read or write in the evening. I'm sorry I couldn't find anything better."

From Simone's barn Pietro could see the whole village of Colle up on the hillside; seen from the plain it looked a different place, a heap of black houses, one on top of another, with no gaps in between.

"The question that arises is how they manage to breathe," Pietro said.

"Those inside the place don't ask that question," Simone replied. "But those who leave it can't stand it any longer."

"It's not worse than other places," Pietro admitted.

"No, not worse, perhaps only more unfortunate," said Simone. "When the earthquake demolished the roofs it exposed things that generally remain hidden. Those who could, left."

"Not all who remained were corrupt."

"Yes, the real scoundrels are few," said Simone. "Most of them are half honest. The most pitiful cases are the decent people who have to pretend to be vulgar in self-defense. The only one who doesn't have to pretend is Donna Maria Vincenza."

"That's not because she's well off. I don't believe she would be any different if she were poor."

"If she were poor, she'd now be with us here."

"That would be marvelous," Pietro exclaimed. Then he added: "My grandmother has faith. Those who converse daily with God and the saints don't attach importance to life's troubles."

"Forgive me if I'm indiscreet," Simone said, "but how old were you when you stopped believing in God?"

Pietro remained thoughtful for a while. "I don't know," he answered. "I'm not sure that I've ever really stopped believing in Him." Then he asked in his turn: "Forgive me, but what about you?"

"I turned my back on Him once and for all after the earthquake," Simone replied without hesitation. Then he added with a laugh: "But sometimes I have the feeling that He's running after me. For lack of other certainties, I believe in friendship."

The presence of his guests revived Simone's memories of forgotten, distant friends, generally from the time of his early youth or his emigration to Brazil and Argentina. Were they still alive? Where were they now? Had they adapted themselves, debased themselves, submitted? Simone was himself surprised at the clarity, precision, and freshness of memories that suddenly returned to him, at the ease with which faces, ways of speaking, names of persons and places, and even trivial circumstances, things that had been buried and forgotten for so many years, returned to his mind.

"It must be the wine," he apologized. "There are wines that numb the mind and make you forget and others that refresh you and make you remember."

In the evening, when Infante lay down to sleep, Pietro went and sat with Simone, and the conversation invariably ended by coming around to some forgotten friend.

"Oh, Pietro, if you had only known Bartolomeo, the dyer from Celano, or rather if he had only known you. Forgive me for talking to you like this, Pietro, but his misfortune was that he never met a man like you. When he died at Santa Fe, in Argentina, he was living with a family from Andalusia, an enormous family, a real tribe. As the doctor had to put down something on the death certificate, he gave the cause of death as typhus, but I was the only one who knew that he died of despair. I suppose you must have been three or four years old at the time."

"Why was he in despair?" Pietro asked.

"Some fellow villagers of his told me that when he was in his teens he ran away from a monastery."

"Didn't he have a family?"

"He left a wife and seven children at Celano."

Though both tried to avoid it, in the course of their reminiscences the name of Don Bastiano Spina cropped up one day in connection with the purchase of the barn in which Simone had been reduced to living for several years past.

"I know that at one time you were inseparable," Pietro said.

"I don't know," Simone replied in embarrassment. Then he went on reluctantly: "He was the biggest disappointment of my life. Drink, Pietro, it's your turn, away with sadness, I no longer have anything to grumble about."

"According to my grandmother," Pietro went on, "my uncle Bastiano's ruin began on the day when the two of you quarreled."

"It wasn't a quarrel," Simone said, speaking with obvious difficulty. "The time came when Bastiano discovered women. And some time afterward he discovered money. To him it was a real disease, like typhus or meningitis. He became arrogant, rude, and deceitful, and he had violent quarrels with his brothers and his mother. I tried not to lose sight of him even after a piece of disgraceful behavior, a deception he practiced on me; I was willing to forgive him, because I was fond of him. So I went to see him, sought him out, asked him to come and see me. But he kept out of my way, and eventually, when he found out that I had discovered the trick he had played on me, he wrote me a letter. Do you realize how low he had sunk? Instead of coming and talking to me he wrote me a letter. I didn't even touch it, of course. Salvatore the Postman came one day and said: excuse me, but here's a letter from Bastiano. From that moment he was dead so far as I was concerned. I showed the postman the rubbish dump behind the house where I was living at the time and told him to put it there. And, I may add, I've never opened a letter since."

"But supposing a real friend wrote to you?"

"Anyone who has anything to say to me can come and see me. I can tell from his voice whether he's speaking the truth. Salvatore

the Postman understands my attitude in the matter and ever since
then, if he has a letter for me, he doesn't even call me, but dumps
it in the refuse pit behind the house."

"But suppose a friend writes to you from a long way away?
Suppose someone writes from America?"

"He can come and see me, and as a friend he'll always be welcome. If what he has to say to me isn't important, there's no need
for him to write."

"You're quite right, I'd certainly come and see you all the way
from America. That is, if I had something important to say to you."

"How would you know what is important to me? But you
should come in any case," Simone said.

"Yes, I would come in any case."

"And why did you mention America? Are you thinking of
leaving here? Are you short of anything?"

"No, I'm short of nothing, I'm living like a lord here."

Infante was fast asleep beside them, curled up on his straw
mattress like a wild animal in its den, covered by Simone's military cloak and other odds and ends; at one point when he rolled
over two strong, hairy legs were revealed, two huge feet with some
old, deep, black scars. Pietro rose and covered him again.

"Why don't you talk to me about your party friends?" Simone
suddenly asked. "I don't understand how you were able to leave
them, or why they let you go away and finish up in this wilderness.
It would be a different matter if you had gone back to your home
discouraged and tired of grazing pigs."

"I left no real friends in the party," Pietro replied in embarrassment. "Relations between comrades are rather like those in the
army. You come into contact with persons of every sort, more by
chance than by choice. In the party I must have met several thousand persons, and there were perhaps several dozen whom I got to
know more closely; but in the course of fifteen years there was no
one whom I got to know as well as I know you and Infante. Sometimes I thought it was my fault, but others had the same experience. The fact of the matter is that in the party friendship is
looked at askance, I might almost say regarded with suspicion;

and rightly, I may add, since in the party it implies cronyism and intrigue. Few understand friendship in the true sense of the word; most despise it as showing a hankering for private life. They call it petit bourgeois."

"But how is it possible to take part in a joint struggle and face risks if the man beside you isn't a friend?" Simone asked incredulously.

"Isn't that what happens in war?" Pietro replied.

But there was a note of sadness in his voice.

After a long silence Simone rose to prepare his bed for the night, and murmured: "I didn't think the rot had gone as far as that."

Their mattresses were laid out on a layer of straw and dried shoots and covered with a woolen blanket; but as this was not heavy enough to keep out the cold, the three men put their day-time clothes on top. Pietro was always the last to go to sleep; lying on his back with his hands behind his head, he spent a long time listening to the distant sounds of animals, the wind, the earth, the night. Every so often there were gaps, long silences, pauses of total calm, when even the sheepdogs were silent. The poor, exhausted donkeys slept in their stables, the sheep in their pens, the chickens in their coops, the hares in their holes, the frogs in their ponds. But in a beam just behind Pietro's head there was a small woodworm that did not sleep or rest but kept gnawing away at the bottom of its hole, from which every now and again a tiny grain of sawdust fell on Pietro's brow. Pietro could distinctly hear the insect's gnawing, and ended up hearing nothing else. The night, the huge, dark night was full of it and it completely dominated the sleeping earth. It was like the secret ticking of the clockwork of a time bomb; there was so much patience in it that it was difficult to guess when it might blow up. Pietro hurriedly rose, dressed, and to protect himself against the bitter cold put his woolen blanket around his shoulders. Then he went over to a corner of the room, took some sheets of paper, tiptoed to the table, lit the old oil lamp, and began to write. To avoid waking his companions he covered the lamp with a piece of cloth and sheltered it with his body. He wrote, at first hesitantly, but then it began to flow, and he seemed to forget time and place. He wrote a line, crossed it out, rewrote it, and then crossed it out again, and then rewrote it a third time. The scratching of the nib on the yellow paper sounded like the gnawing of a rodent. Wrapped in the green blanket and sitting bent over the little table that was covered with sheets of paper filled with his writing, he was rather like a solitary mouse gnawing away at small pieces of paper.

"Whom are you writing to so passionately? Your sweetheart?" Simone murmured with a smile.

Pietro was startled, and turned around. Simone was standing behind him, his tall, thin body covered down to his knees with a red woolen blanket and his bare, gnarled feet on the slippery floor. Pietro showed him the heading he had written on the first page: "Letter to a Young European of the Twenty-Second Century."

Simone sat down on a stool facing him. "Do you think a letter can last for two hundred years?" he asked with some concern.

"Yes, it can last even longer. It doesn't depend on the paper or the ink, of course, but on the words. They must be pure and sincere. That kind are incorruptible."

"But suppose the police come and tear it up?"

"There are some words that were spoken softly thousands of years ago and still survive, though the police didn't like them."

But Simone was in favor of taking precautions, and he had an idea. "When you've finished writing," he suggested, "we'll put the letter in a metal box or tube and have it built into the wall of some house that is under construction. I know a bricklayer who'll certainly do it if I ask him. There'll undoubtedly be another earthquake in this part of the world within the next two hundred years, and they'll find your message in the ruins."

"'Our' message," said Pietro, showing him the last page, on which the ink was still wet. It began with these words: "At that time Simone known as the Weasel liked to say: 'One could live so well among friends.'"

At this Simone could not conceal his emotion. "I'm an old man, Pietro, old in age and in body," he said. "But sometimes I feel I've never lived at all. If I died now, Pietro, they ought to take me to the cemetery in a white coffin, as they do with children under seven."

A strong, bitterly cold wind had risen, and it shook the shutters and caused part of the eaves to bang against the roof.

"Luckily Infante can't hear," Pietro said.

Leone had joined the two friends. With his moist, black nose and sitting on his haunches, he listened to them and seemed to be moved too.

"There are moments of peace that cause troubled and wasted years to be forgotten," Pietro said. "But now let's go back to bed. With those bare feet of yours you'll catch your death."

"No, let's stay awake," Simone begged him, though he was shivering. "We may never again be in the mood we're in tonight."

Pietro began to read him what he had written under the chapter heading: "To the Youth of the Former Italian Nation": *At that time Simone known as the Weasel liked to say: One could live so well among friends, without the police.*

17

INFANTE, WHO HAD GONE to fetch a pail of water, came hurrying back with the pail empty, panting, upset, and alarmed. He pointed in the direction of the road, clearly trying to indicate with his agitated mumble that something dreadful had appeared, that a very definite danger was imminent. *Tup, tup, tup,* he kept repeating. Simone promptly bolted the door and the ground-floor windows while Pietro offered Infante a glass of water, as one does to calm frightened children. Infante spilled half of it, and Pietro signed to him to hurry upstairs and stay there quietly. Infante disappeared with the speed of a terrified monkey.

"Go up too, Pietro," said Simone, working away at barricading the door with iron spikes. "Go up too, for heaven's sake," he insisted. "What are you waiting for?"

"It will be better if I stay down here with you," Pietro tried to persuade him. "Listen to me, Simò, don't you think it would be far better not to barricade the door? If the police find me here, we can say I've just arrived, that I just came in a few minutes ago to get warm, or to ask you for a piece of bread, or something. We can say you don't know who I am and that you have never seen me in your life before. It will be far better if you don't bolt the door."

"What's the point of making agreements and then forgetting them at the critical moment, which is what you're doing, Pietro," Simone interrupted irritably. "Please go up too."

"But why should all three of us be caught if they're looking only for me? Why do them that favor?"

"The one they're looking for might be me. Leaving modesty aside, Pietro, and without wanting to boast, I deserve a little attention too. If you go up, perhaps they'll take me only and won't realize that anyone else is here. Please go up and don't make me angry."

"But suppose they're looking for me, which is more probable? If I'm hiding when they find me, won't it be obvious that you're an accomplice, and that Infante is too?"

Simone made an angry, weary gesture. The door was barricaded, the windows were shut, and the two men stayed listening in the dark. The silence was complete.

"Another possibility," Pietro suggested after a long pause, "is that Infante had a vision, you know what he's like."

They went up to the loft to question him, to try to find out — more by gestures than by speech — whether what he had seen had been *carabinieri*, men in uniforms with rifles, whether there had been two, four, or six of them, whether they had been coming toward the barn along the canal, or had stopped, or were lying in wait or were hiding in a ditch; or whether he had seen a wild animal, a wolf or a bear, a monster or a devil. Infante responded to all these questions with unambiguous gestures of denial; and he kept saying to Pietro, as if he at least were bound to understand: *tup, tup, tup,* and imitated the movements of a man on horseback. But neither Pietro nor Simone could make head or tail of all this. Infante then cautiously went over to one of the big windows and with excited gestures pointed to the mountain in the distance behind which Pietrasecca lay; a big, rounded, snow-covered peak with a yellow outline against the gray sky. Pietro and Simone looked at it and racked their brains, but were baffled. The wind was dragging heavy cartloads of clouds over the valley of Pietrasecca and piling them up on the mountain; some seemed full of dung, others of straw.

"Oh," Pietro suddenly guessed, "Sciatàp."

Infante immediately and repeatedly confirmed this. Of course *tup, tup, tup,* couldn't possibly have been anything else; it shouldn't have been so hard to guess. Of course he had meant Sciatàp, the owner of the stable in which Pietro had been hidden for several weeks before being handed over to his grandmother.

Pietro explained to Simone that Infante had been terrified at the idea that he might have to go back to Pietrasecca, and his terror would not have been unjustified. Every *cafone* there treated him as if he were his own property, a kind of public donkey.

But, quite apart from that, Sciatàp's new appearance at Colle seemed suspicious to Simone too. Pietrasecca was only about twelve miles from Colle, but the two villages belonged to different worlds; there had never been any direct administrative connection between the two places, there had been no intermarriages, and there were no other personal links between them. People from Pietrasecca never came to the small weekly market at Colle, not even on the summer religious feast days; moreover, today was not a market day or any other occasion, but an ordinary day in Lent. Sciatàp knew no one at Colle. He had set foot in the place probably for the first time in his life when he called at the Spina house toward the middle of January and told Donna Maria Vincenza that her grandson was alive and that she could have him back by handing over a sum of money. That had been a good stroke of business from Sciatàp's point of view. Actually he had already helped himself to the money that Pietro had on him, but Donna Maria Vincenza was not to know that, and, even if she had, for the sake of getting her grandson back she would have paid up just the same. So what could he be wanting now? Why had he come back to Colle? Simone hurriedly put on his hat and his cloak, hid something in his pocket, and went off to find him.

"Damià," he asked the first acquaintance he met, "did you by any chance see a stranger passing by a short time ago, a man from the mountains, of my age, more or less, on a horse or a donkey?"

"Do you mean a *cafone* on a horse? He went up the hill half an hour ago."

Simone hurried after him and stopped breathlessly outside Mastro Eutimio's shop. "Did you by any chance see a stranger on a horse passing by a short time ago, a stranger who looked as if he came from the mountains?"

"Yes, he passed a short time ago, I expect he was going to the Spina house. But look, there he is, coming back already. Where is he from, I wonder?"

A man wrapped in a faded and threadbare old cloak was coming down from the hill on a small bay horse. His face was hidden by a big, black, neglected growth of beard, his eyes glowered, and he wore his hat tilted over one ear as if he needed to show that he was afraid of no one.

"You're riding that horse as if it were a donkey," Simone called out to him, going forward to meet him in a distinctly provocative manner. "It's obvious that you're a *cafone*, and if you didn't win that horse in a lottery you certainly bought it with money you didn't come by honestly."

Sciatàp stopped the horse. He looked suspiciously and in wide-eyed astonishment — at close quarters you could see that his eyes were reddened — at this strange man who looked like the most abject down-and-out but addressed him with upper-class assurance and arrogance.

"If you want to quarrel, Simone, if you really can't help it, why do you have to do it right outside my shop?" Mastro Eutimio implored him.

"Can't you see that that horse is swallowing the bit?" Simone went on in the same provocative manner. "You'll ruin the poor beast if you go on pulling like that, you bumpkin. But how long have you had it, I should like to know? What money did you buy it with?"

Sciatàp decided to behave as if he were faced with a crackpot, and he gave Simone an exaggeratedly forced smile of pity. To gain time and demonstrate his nonchalance he produced from under his cloak a broken pipe that was crusted black from long use; he slowly filled it and lit it with two wax matches.

Then, between one puff and the next, he turned to Mastro Eutimio and said: "Can you please tell me, master carpenter, where
to find the government orator in this parish? I assume you must
have at least one."

"We're all orators here," Simone interrupted more provocatively than ever. "Here in the hills it's not like up in the mountains, you can take it from me. And we have no need of spies from
outside here, because we have only too many of our own, thank
heaven, though that's nothing to boast about."

"I assure you I haven't the slightest idea what you're talking
about," Sciatàp interrupted irritably.

"Stranger, you'd better be on your way," Mastro Eutimio politely advised him in his most persuasive manner. "I don't understand what gave you the idea of stopping right in front of my shop.
Good-bye to you and good luck."

Sciatàp shrugged his shoulders and trotted off on his horse in
the direction of the square. Curious onlookers, the usual boys and
artisans from the various shops, gathered to look at the stranger.

"Hey, uncle, what have you got to sell? What do you want to
buy?" they called out.

Sciatàp had lost his self-assurance and did not know which
way to turn to find out what he wanted. There, opposite the
church, there was a new white building, with a balcony for
speakers on the second floor, in the new style that had been
adopted for public offices. But suppose it wasn't? To gain time
and consider his next move he dismounted and tied his horse to
a metal ring fixed into the sacristy wall and tied a nose bag full of
bran around the horse's head like a muzzle, and stood and
watched it while it ate; then he tidied its mane with ostentatious
affection and patted it on the rump, perhaps to show onlookers
that he knew how to handle horses. His horse had what looked
like a ram's head, a thick mane, and fleshy, projecting shoulders,
its back was hollow like a hare's belly, and the whole of its
hindquarters was rather weak. Off his horse Sciatàp immediately
regained his thickset *cafone* appearance, and with his short legs
and big chest and shoulders he bore a strange resemblance to his

horse; he also looked uncertain, suspicious, timid, and a brag-
gart. Aunt Eufemia suddenly appeared, crossing the square and
making straight for the church for the evening devotions. Her
face was covered with a black veil, and she looked meek and
melancholy. Sciatàp could not have hoped to hit on a more reliable person to ask for information.

"Excuse me, madam," he said, approaching her and clumsily
raising his hat, "excuse me, but can you oblige me by telling me
where I can find the house or office of the government orator? I
assume that you have one, of course."

"I can tell you, all right," Aunt Eufemia replied with feigned
politeness. "Go to hell, you certainly know the way, go straight
there, and you'll find exactly what you want."

Sciatàp was left gaping with astonishment and with his hat in
his hand while the pious lady disappeared into the church.

"What a place I've landed in," he muttered in discouragement.
"What sort of people are these?"

He walked a few yards in the direction of the government
building and heard someone calling him by name at the top of his
voice from some distance away. "Wait, Sciatàp, I want to talk to
you, I want to do you the honor of having a drink with you."

It was the strange individual who had behaved so provocatively
to him for no apparent reason outside the carpenter's shop not
long before. The man actually knew his name. When Sciatàp
trotted off Simone had wanted to run after him in order not to
lose him from sight, but Venanzio, greatly distressed and in a state
of much greater alarm and agitation than usual, had been coming
down the hill and had called him. Donna Maria Vincenza's
groom had hastily and confusedly told him that Sciatàp had again
been to the Spina house, that Donna Maria Vincenza had refused to be blackmailed into handing over the new and crazy sum
for which he had asked, and that he had threatened to tell the authorities the whole story and thus earn the considerable price that
he said was on Pietro's head.

Simone had got rid of Venanzio as quickly as he could and
came chasing after the man from Pietrasecca.

"Come along, Sciatàp, come with me," he said to him in a dry and authoritative manner.

Sciatàp thought he recognized him.

"Am I mistaken, or are you the so-called hunter of wolves whom the militia arrested at Pietrasecca some time ago?"

"You have a good memory," Simone replied.

Sciatàp followed him curiously and mistrustfully down a steep alleyway and through a low doorway with a branch of mistletoe over it, looking all around as if he feared an ambush. They went down five or six steps to a dark, damp, and smelly room with a few crude tables for customers and in one corner an unmade bed with some rolled-up mattresses. The landlady, a ragged old woman with a two- or three-year-old baby on her lap that was as brown and thin as a long crusty loaf, was squatting by the fireplace. The two men sat at a table without removing their cloaks. At that time of day the place was deserted. The old woman brought a jug of wine and two glasses. Simone made a vigorous gesture indicating that she should make herself scarce, but she hesitated.

"If you want to quarrel, Simò, why did you come here?" she whined. "Aren't there other taverns in Colle? Please, I appeal to you, you know what glasses cost nowadays."

"Go and get some fresh air," Simone told her. "Haven't you noticed how this friend of mine stinks?"

The old woman took a stool and went and sat outside in the street with the baby in her arms. The baby started to cry, perhaps because of the cold. Simone filled his own glass and emptied it in a single swallow. Sciatàp's glass remained empty. Sciatàp looked all around; he was suspicious and uncertain. The room was low and as oppressive as a cave. What little light there was came in through the door. On the wall there was a picture of San Rocco, protector against pestilence, with long fair hair, white breeches, and yellow coat. The tables were old, chipped, and unsteady, marked with innumerable dark and indelible stains left by the glasses of many generations of drinkers. Simone again helped himself to wine and laughed. A black cock with a red crest was painted on the jug.

"But what is it you want?" Sciatàp asked him irritably. "Why are you wasting my time? Who are you, I should like to know?"

"We're not here to talk about me, Sciatàp," Simone quietly replied. Looking him straight in the eyes he went on: "The man you want to denounce is someone else."

"What do you know about that? And even if it were so, what has it to do with you? Is it your business?"

"If it's not my business, whose is it?" Simone replied in astonishment.

"Do you belong to his party, then?"

"It's much more than that," Simone replied. "Colle's like Pietrasecca, we have no parties."

"Are you a relative of his? Though, to look at you, that seems impossible."

"It's much more than that, I repeat. There's no relative for whom I'd be so willing to risk my life or liberty as I am for that young man. You'd do well to remember that for your own sake."

"My dear fellow," Sciatàp said with a grotesque grimace of contempt, "you're barking at the moon, let me go."

Simone suddenly grew grim and threatening. "Don't try and be witty, you fat louse," he said, "unless you want to offer salt cod to someone who's already thirsty."

Sciatàp took out his pipe and with an air of exaggerated nonchalance began carefully cleaning the stem with a stalk of millet. Simone, with his elbows on the table and his chin in one hand, studied him for a short while, then filled his own glass and drank again. Outside the door the baby would not stop crying; it filled the whole alley with its lamentations.

After some time Sciatàp winked at Simone and said: "There's no denying that you're singing a pretty tune. But at least you ought to tell me how much the old woman paid you for coming and singing it to me."

Simone burst out laughing as if he had heard a tremendous joke, and his sudden hilarity caused him to spray the wine he still had in his mouth in Sciatàp's face. His laughter was so genuine and convincing that Sciatàp did not insist.

"But who are you, then?" he repeated impatiently. "Why are you wasting my time? Why do you interfere in other people's business, I should like to know?"

"Out of friendship," Simone replied frankly.

This time it was Sciatàp's turn to split his sides with laughter; he laughed so interminably that it brought tears to his eyes and almost took his breath away. Two or three times the laughter seemed to be coming to an end, but perhaps because he could not get that extraordinary reply out of his head he started guffawing all over again. For a short while Simone stayed looking at him in astonishment, but the sight of that poor sad tramp shaken by laughter was so comic that in the end he began laughing too. The landlady's shrill voice floated from the street.

"Have you been telling him one of your tall stories, Simò?" she called out.

The two men were sitting facing each other. Both looked as if they were the same age, about fifty, but Sciatàp was smaller and more thickset, with a big, heavy head and a face contracted into a grimace that at first sight suggested an almost animal-like cunning but was too deliberate not to reveal the signs of a strong dose of concealed cowardice; he was breathing with difficulty, and his breath stank of undigested wine and garlic and shreds of tobacco between his teeth. He took a wrinkled little apple from a pocket and started slowly peeling it with a knife with a bone handle and a well-sharpened blade about nine inches long.

"That's a fine knife you have there," Simone said in a flattering tone.

"In wolf country every dog of course wears a spiked collar," Sciatàp replied.

With a feint at the man's face and a well-aimed blow at his hand Simone made him drop the knife on the table. He grabbed it and threw it under the bed at the other end of the room. Sciatàp flung himself at him in a fury, but Simone was ready for him and butted him in the stomach with his head and sent him reeling back, causing him to strike his back and head hard against the wall. For a moment he was half stunned, and Simone, with the patience of a tamer faced with a rebellious animal, waited for him to recover.

"For heaven's sake remember my glasses," the old woman shrieked from outside in the street. "What did I tell you, Simò? Aren't there any other taverns in Colle? If you wanted to quarrel, why didn't you go somewhere else? Oh, Simò, you're the ruin of me."

"Be quiet, " Simone told her. "Don't worry, if there's any damage, my friend here will pay for it."

The old woman quieted down; even the baby had stopped crying and watched the scene from the doorway with a smile. The two men took off their cloaks and threw them on the bed, and Simone pushed the chairs and the table aside and put the jug and the glasses in a place of safety on the mantelpiece. The fight then started all over again. In the dark it was like a battle between two wild animals. Sciatàp, grim and furious, struck out blindly with slow and heavy movements, panting and with his head bent forward, stung by Simone's taunts. Simone leaped about on the tables and chairs like a crazy monkey, avoiding his blows and bewildering him with feints. But Simone did not succeed in avoiding one powerful onslaught on his neck with a chair, and this caused him to change his tactics. Many blows on both sides either missed or glanced off their target until Simone jumped in to close quarters. A number of blows to the head that might have been delivered with a cudgel made his opponent dizzy, and this time Simone did not allow him time to recover. He grabbed him by the chest and bumped him like a bag of bones on the table and against the doorpost, and then dumped him in a sitting position on the trunk. Sciatàp sat down facing him and started feeling his bones. Everything seemed in order, or almost. The most painful blow he had received was on one ear. There were some marks and bruises on his face, and he might have lost a tooth or two, because he was spitting blood, but his eyes seemed to be all right. Simone rose and put the jug and the glasses back on the table, to indicate that so far as he was concerned the fight was over. He poured out a glass of wine for Sciatàp and one for himself, and waited for Sciatàp to recover his breath sufficiently to be able to speak. But he had to wait for some time.

"Drink, Sciatàp," he said eventually, forcing himself to smile. "And listen to me, because I want to talk to you seriously."

Sciatàp spat on the ground and raised his glass to drink. Simone touched his glass with his own. "Your health," he said with a laugh. But Sciatàp still looked dazed and grim. The two men drank. Simone refilled Sciatàp's glass several times.

"This wine's not bad, but we have better at Colle," Simone assured him in confidential tones. "If you ever come here again, you must promise to come and see me, I'll give you a bottle of my wine, it has a bouquet of cloves that's enough to make your mustache curl."

Simone refilled his own glass, the old woman brought another jug, and the two went on drinking.

"Forgive me for not yet having introduced myself," said Simone, "I'm known as Simone the Weasel."

Sciatàp, stung by a sudden timorous curiosity, scrutinized him. "Oh, you like chickens, don't you?"

"The usual slander. The usual envy," Simone replied modestly. "Besides, let's be frank, who doesn't?"

"Your health," Sciatàp, dazed but reconciled, eventually replied.

"There's one thing I don't understand," Simone began as soon as he decided that Sciatàp had come around sufficiently. "During the past month you have bought yourself a horse, shoes, a watch with a gold chain, and perhaps other things too. Permit me to ask you whether that is not enough. You could now live in peace and enjoy that unexpected gift from heaven, so why be greedy and risk losing it all? I really don't understand you, Sciatàp. Good heavens, a practical man like you ought to try to be reasonable. Why am I making you this speech? Look, Sciatàp, I'm very sorry, but if you don't change your ideas the situation between us two will unfortunately be as follows: either I do you in, or you do me in. It grieves me to have to say so, but a third alternative simply doesn't exist. And even in the very improbable event of the worst happening to me, you, as you can well imagine, would go to prison. Sciatàp, I know from bitter experience what looking at the world through iron bars is like after one has reached a certain age. In any event, you'd no longer be able to enjoy the horse, the shoes, the watch with the gold chain, and the rest of it. I'm very surprised that a man like you, Sciatàp, a practical man, should not realize these simple things."

"There's another thing that I don't understand," Sciatàp replied, making a very obvious effort to be reasonable. "To judge from your ideas, your manners, the way you speak, you're probably not a real *cafone*, but it's also obvious that you're not living in the lap of luxury either. It's sufficient to look at you to see that you're a poor devil living from hand to mouth. Why do you take so much to heart something that concerns the gentry?"

"It's not for the sake of money, Sciatàp, I assure you."

"And I assure you that it's not just greed, or covetousness, as you say, on my part either. Certainly, with all due respect to San Francesco di Assisi, every one of us likes money. Don't you, for instance, like it, Simone? I frankly admit that I like it, that I like it very much indeed, and that I find it very useful. But, apart from money, there can also be something else, something less useful but more enjoyable, even to a *cafone*. Why don't you see what a heavenly pleasure it is to a poor *cafone* like me to have a unique opportunity of frightening members of the gentry, dominating them, seeing them grow pale without being able to send for the *carabinieri*, without being able to defend themselves or have me arrested?"

"I too have had a hard life, Sciatàp, but yours is not a reason."

"Perhaps you haven't been through what I've been through. In my wretched life I've never been able to make both ends meet. I've grown old eating my bread in sorrow, I've followed horses to pick up the dung; those are things that can be mentioned, but I've also done other things. When I gave up the struggle to work for myself, I worked for others, I ate my bread seasoned with contempt. I didn't change masters often, because I realized quite early in life that it wasn't worth the trouble. In Pietrasecca the master's name was Co-lamartini; in New York the name was Don Carlo Campanella, which he changed to Mr. Charles Little-Bell, Ice and Coal, but it was the same thing; in Rosario it was Don Edmundo Esposito y Rodriguez y Alvarez. 'Esposito'* because of his noble but unknown parents, 'Rodriguez' because of his wife, 'Alvarez' in memory of the latter's first husband. What? Did you know that bloodsucker? Were you in Rosario too? In that case I can spare myself the details. Well, as you know, they call me Sciatàp. Did they tell you what that means in American? 'Shut up,' it means, that's what it means, 'shut up.' That's what Mr. Charles Little-Bell said to me on every possible occasion whenever I tried to open my mouth, and I must admit that it's the only American word that has stuck in my mind. And since it stuck to me and became my nickname it accompanied me for the rest of my life, and in a way everyone who ever speaks to me tells me to shut up even before I've opened my mouth. Don Edmundo used to say: *Cállate, hombre*, which in Argentinian means the same thing. I admit that not all bosses are exactly the same in this. Don Pasquale Colamartini, the boss at Pietrasecca, for instance, may he rest in peace, was a real gentleman and never rudely told me to shut up, but whenever I went to see him, even before I opened my mouth, he would say to me with his kindest smile: have you come to complain again? And then I would say nothing. (Thank you, Simone, but you must drink too.) Now, I'm not a Jeremiah, a malcontent, a grouser, I know very well that it was God who created differences, worms and grasshoppers, donkeys and horses, and even in dreams I've never supposed that the world could be different from what it is. But there's one thing I've often dreamed of, and dreams help one to go to sleep, and what I've dreamed of is a master who would call me by my real name and say to me: come and speak your mind and open your heart, tell me everything that's on your mind. But that one evening I should find in my stable a gentleman, an outlawed gentleman hunted by the police but still a gentleman, one of the cursed breed that live riotously on the sufferings of the poor, a gentleman reduced to the

---

*"Esposito" (exposed) is a surname often given to foundlings, from the southern Italian practice of leaving unwanted babies at the *ruota* (wheel, rotating surface) in the outer wall of a Catholic institution.

point of begging for my hospitality, not even in my house but in my
stable next to my old ass, that was something that by far surpassed
my powers of imagination. And when I think it over now in cold
blood, it's clear to me that the finger of God was involved. You
don't believe in God? Oh Simone, you're wrong. Only the Heavenly Father in His infinite cunning could have organized the intricate combination of circumstances that led a gentleman to my
shed like a mouse into a trap to compensate me for the innumerable humiliations I had suffered. I could do what I liked with him,
strip him bare, put him in a sack and drop him in the stream, sell
him by weight at so much a pound, stick pins into him, skin him,
make him drink castor oil, cut off his ears, or — what counts more
with me — force him to be silent and make him listen to me, Sciatàp. I don't know if you can imagine a more unexpected, a more
miraculous situation. You don't believe in miracles? You're wrong.
I couldn't believe my eyes and ears. When I awoke at night and
thought about it I began to doubt. I told myself I must have been
dreaming. I got up and hurried to the shed to check that he, young
Don Pietro Spina, was really there, lying in the straw next to the ass.
Yes, there he was, at my mercy. When I went back to the house I
often went down on my knees in front of the crucifix and said:
I thank Thee, O Lord, with my face to the ground I thank Thee for
having given me this immense joy at the end of my wretched life.
You have already cast in my teeth the fact that I relieved my prisoner of the money he had on him. That money came in very
handy, and to whom would it not have come in handy? But to me
the supreme satisfaction was being able to help myself to it without
his being able to deny it to me. Can you imagine a more marvelous
situation? A gentleman falls into your hands, he has money in his
pocket, you take it from him, and he lets you. Meanwhile the police were hunting for him all over the valley, they searched for him
everywhere, they sniffed behind every bush and promised a handsome reward to anyone who handed him over, alive or dead; but I
didn't hand him over, because if I had done so I should have lost
him forever, I should no longer have had him at my mercy. So I
jealously guarded him, using a thousand cunning dodges to ward

off the risk of the police finding him. If I eventually decided to apply to his relatives, his uncle and his grandmother, it wasn't only for the sake of getting more money, though it was bound to come in handy (and to whom would it not have come in handy?), but because, to tell you the truth, the pleasure I derived from having young Signor Don Pietro Spina as my prisoner turned out in the long run to be rather meager. I don't know whether the young gentleman has been half-witted or crazy from birth, but the fact remains that even in the wretched conditions to which he was reduced he managed to act the gentleman with me. There he was behaving like a little king, surrounded by dung. The loss of his money, for instance, left him completely cold, he was much more interested in the donkey and in a deaf-mute who constantly visited him than he was in me, he never listened to me and, what was worse, never gave me an opportunity to tell him to shut up, *sciatàp*, because he never talked to me, and I often caught him smiling at the angels, as we say in our part of the world of those who smile to themselves and talk to invisible companions. I was told that his grandmother, Donna Maria Vincenza Spina, was an admirable lady (I made my inquiries before calling on her), and that gave me redoubled pleasure. If she had been nasty, mean, arrogant, what I did might have seemed to be directed against all that, but the fact of the matter was that I needed to relieve my feelings against the gentry as a breed, I needed to see a lady trembling and in distress, begging and imploring me, suffering in front of me, Sciatàp, because of her grandson. Donna Maria Vincenza gave me money, as you know, and I took it, because it was useful to me (and to whom would it not have been useful?) but on no account did I think of relinquishing the power over young Spina that providence had put in my hands. And if I ended up arranging the young man's transfer from my stable to the house of his fathers, it was because I thought it would increase my power over the whole family, binding them to me, Sciatàp, by a great and lasting secret."

"You're quite right, Sciatàp," Simone said, "the rich and the poor are almost like two different breeds, one would have to be blind not to see it. But there are also men who have plenty to eat but are unable to tolerate others being hungry; men who are ashamed of being well off when the majority are poor and cannot resign themselves to the oppression, the sufferings, the humiliation of other human beings."

"I see where you're trying to lead me. But what is the phrase? Hold your horses."

"I'm not trying to say, Sciatàp, that a few good men with a thirst for justice are sufficient to establish the Kingdom of Heaven in this vale of tears if the saints were incapable of it, if San Gioacchino, San Francesco, San Celestino were incapable of it. No, Sciatàp, I mean something else. Meanwhile drink and refresh your mind. Those men are repudiated by polite society and the Church excommunicates them, and that's very understandable. The police harry them as enemies of public order, and that's quite normal. But that *cafoni* too, Sciatàp, the poor and the down-and-out, should despise and hate them, maltreat and betray them, and vent on them their resentment at the humiliations they have suffered, and that by so doing they should aid and abet and complete the work of the police — does that seem right to you, Sciatàp?"

"What you are saying, in a nutshell, is that out of respect for their fantasies those members of the gentry should not be confused with others. But tell me, do a person's ideas change his status? Aren't ideas, any kind of ideas, themselves a luxury? Of course they are, and I'm surprised that you haven't realized that they're just a luxury for gentlemen."

"Including ideas that are opposed to the privileges of the gentry, Sciatàp?"

"Yes, those too, it seems obvious to me. They're a luxury, an ornament, a pastime for the gentry."

"But if that's the case, Sciatàp, and perhaps it's as you say, even we, even you and I, can become gentlemen; and we can do so straightaway, whenever we feel like it, it obviously depends only on us."

"How? Excuse me if you make me laugh."

"By adopting those ideas, that is to say, the luxury, the pastime, the ornament, the superfluity which, as you say, really characterizes the gentry and distinguishes a gentleman not only from *cafoni* but also from other prosperous people."

"But how can we concern ourselves with the superfluous, lay our hands on it, enjoy it with a heart at rest if we're short of the bare necessities?"

"Sciatàp, have you never met on mountain paths, or on pilgrimages, or in the fields strange men covered in rags, dust, and sweat and obviously hungry into the bargain who are short of necessities, but by their bearing, the look in their eyes, their smile, and their sadness are real kings?"

"Maybe, maybe," Sciatàp replied uncertainly, "but do you think . . ."

Other persons came down the steps into the tavern. They greeted Simone and Sciatàp, sat down at the tables, ordered wine. Simone and Sciatàp left.

"In any case," Simone said when they were outside in the street, "I've heard that that ex-prisoner of yours, that Pietro Spina, is back again in France, as free as a bird on the wing, and that it's not worth worrying about him."

"And that deaf-mute? Has he gone abroad too?" Sciatàp answered with a wink.

"What deaf-mute?"

In the square Sciatàp's attention was suddenly distracted by a disagreeable discovery. "Who took that blanket?" he shouted threateningly.

He had left a new woolen blanket on the horse's back.

"Where's that blanket?" he repeated. "In the middle of the square, in broad daylight," he went on shouting angrily. "Can no one have seen the thief?"

He looked around at the few idlers who were hanging about the square and seemed to be concentrating on watching the birds flying about in the sky.

"Sciatàp," Simone said, "try not to be surprised, try not to add ridicule to injury, thank Sant'Antonio that the horse is still there. After all," he added dryly, "you didn't exactly inherit it from your father."

As Sciatàp went on making a scene, Simone went off, suddenly disgusted at having made the acquaintance of such a vulgar individual. "The only thieves worthy of respect," he said by way of farewell, "are those who understand how to be robbed themselves."

In the alley of the Flag Inn he saw Don Tito, the head guard, approaching. He was chasing a one-armed beggar. Simone stood aside. "Hey, hey, where are you going?" Don Tito shouted after the man. "You ask me for alms and then rush off to squander it on drink?"

The one-armed beggar stopped under the mistletoe over the tavern door and waited for the head guard to catch up with him so that he could answer him without shouting. "How much did you give me?" he asked.

"It's not a question of the amount," Don Tito tried to explain.

"How much did you give me?" the man repeated coldly.

"Twenty *centesimi*, but I told you, it's not a question of the amount."

The beggar still had the coin in his hand, and he handed it back. "Did you imagine you'd bought my soul for twenty *centesimi?*" he said.

Don Tito pocketed the money and went off muttering. Simone had watched the whole scene with bated breath, and he went up to the beggar with his eyes shining with emotion. "You cannot imagine, my dear sir, how much I like you," he said with feeling.

The beggar, who was just entering the inn, turned and smiled. "But this is so sudden," he said. "Love at first sight, obviously."

Simone blushed. "If I had a daughter," he went on, "I'd offer her to you in marriage."

"Couldn't you oblige me with a match?" the man said with a laugh.

"I'm afraid I haven't any with me," Simone said with obvious regret. "But I've got something better for you."

And he offered the man the knife that Sciatàp had forgotten.

When one pressed the button the blade sprang out; a very practical knife for a one-armed man.

"In another age, in another country, I should have given you a sword," Simone declared.

"A knife is less conspicuous," the beggar replied, "and it's better for cutting bread. One shouldn't be too conspicuous."

He took half a long loaf from an inside pocket, held it between his chest and the stump of his arm, and cut off a chunk, which he offered to Simone.

"It was given to me just now by the women at the communal oven and it's well risen, it's still warm, do you notice the lovely smell?"

"Couldn't you spare me another two slices?" Simone quietly asked. "For two friends of mine, two excellent comrades."

"If they're poor you can have the lot, I've already eaten today," said the beggar.

"They're not poor," Simone quietly explained. "On the contrary, one of them is actually rich. But — how am I to explain it — he too prefers living on charity."

So Simone went back to the barn with three chunks of bread, and he didn't seem so much to walk as to fly, for he positively skimmed over the snow with his light, dancing footsteps.

"Take it and eat," he said, beaming with delight at his two friends, "a marvelous beggar gave it to us."

The three chunks of bread were turned into five, to enable the donkey and the dog to have their share.

"Couldn't we ask him to stay with us here?" Pietro suggested.

But Simone had a different idea. "That beggar's way of laughing and talking reminded me of Mastro Raffaele of Goriano," he said. "Haven't you ever been to Goriano? As soon as the weather's better and the Forca climb isn't too difficult we simply must go and see Mastro Raffaele. He'll be rather surprised to see us again, but he'll certainly be delighted. At one time he lived at the entrance to the village, on the right. Haven't I ever told you about him? It seems almost impossible. You'll like him very much, he's a mason, a master builder, a gentleman, an honest, solid, decent, straightforward man. Try to imagine in one and the same person a man of the old days and a child, an incorruptible old-style adolescent. Before and after meals and before he begins work and after he stops he always makes the sign of the cross; when bigots do that it gets on my nerves and makes me want to scream, but you should see him do it, it's simple, natural, and wonderful. That kind of person is getting rarer and rarer and, when it has completely disappeared, what will the world be like that's so depressing already?"

"It won't disappear," Pietro answered confidently. "When it's destroyed in one place it's reborn somewhere else, you'll see."

Simone smiled and agreed. "No, it won't disappear," he repeated.

"Hasn't Mastro Raffaele ever written to you?" Pietro asked.

"Written?" Simone exclaimed indignantly.

Pietro felt ashamed of himself and apologized.

"When I was twenty," Simone said, "I was going to marry a sister of his. But can one marry a woman only because one likes her brother?"

Meanwhile Infante had been on guard at one of the big upstairs windows, half hidden under the straw. Suddenly his shrill, guttural, angry voice indicated the reappearance of Sciatàp.

"*Tup, tup, tup,*" he shouted. Simone and Pietro came hurrying along and saw Sciatàp on his horse descending the gentle slope in the direction of Orta. The track wound its way between vineyards and was flanked by slender fruit trees.

"He can't have understood anything of the adventure that has passed him by," Pietro said. "But why is Sciatàp going toward Orta? It's at least three miles farther to Pietrasecca that way."

"He'll have asked someone the shortest way," Simone suggested, "and of course everyone will have competed to tell him the longest."

Infante kept his eyes fixed on Sciatàp, and when he finally disappeared behind the hill he made an amusing and unexpected childish gesture: he put his head out the window and spat and, as if he were pronouncing a curse, added a word that he had learned that day. *Simony, simony,* he said. Pietro had taught him that "simony" was the exact opposite of "Simone." Following the same criterion, and with little regard for the ordinary sense of the two words, he had taught him the day before that "*fante,*" foot soldier, was the opposite of *Infante.* This series of opposites had been inaugurated three days before by Simone, who had tried to teach Infante to pronounce "Pietro" correctly. What the deaf-mute no doubt involuntarily made of it was *pietra,* stone, and Simone had accepted this, though he had used a stone to show that it was hard, dirty, cold, bruising, sterile, and inanimate, quite different and in fact the exact opposite of Pietro. All this must have stimulated Infante's imagination and encouraged his natural inclination to understand words in the broadest sense, because soon afterward he was heard muttering *Pietro* as a term of endearment to the dog and the donkey, and it was clear that to him that name, besides indicating his friend, meant many other inexpressible things. But what terrible consequences resulted from a slight change in the position of the lips. A simple A was sufficient to reverse the apparently stable and immutable meaning of the word "Pietro" and indicate such hostile, crude, and insensitive things as stones, rocks, landslides in the mountains, and even the Pietrasecca he hated. The two words "pietro" and "*pietra,*" so alike and yet so irreconcilable, continued to occupy the deaf-mute's mind next day. He repeated them on every possible occasion, but for preference to the dog and the donkey, changing the expression of his face in accordance with their conflicting meanings. Leone wagged his tail and barked with pleasure, but Cherubino remained unmoved; to judge from his expression, he did not seem to attach much importance to the deaf-mute's revelations. In spite of this Pietro was convinced that teaching by antonyms was far better than teaching by synonyms. He thought about this, and discussed it with Simone. As soon as Infante seemed to have recovered from the excitement of learning the resemblance and difference between "Pietro" and "*pietra*" he was taught that other pair of opposites: "Infante" and "*fante.*" The deaf-mute already knew what "Infante" meant, but if it had not been Pietro who kept repeating it to him he would perhaps never have believed that that familiar word, which was all his own and had been his from birth and belonged to no one else among all the people he knew, could by merely being deprived of its first syllable reveal within itself his mortal enemy, *fante*, foot soldier (a man in uniform, a militiaman, a *carabiniere*, a man who had handcuffs and put one in prison). In fact it took him a long time to show that he was sufficiently persuaded of this to pronounce and repeat the word. One difficulty arose from the fact that Pietro could not show him a *fante* as Simone had shown him a stone a few days before, and Pietro had to remedy this by doing some playacting, making his jacket look like a uniform and his hat like a lamp or a fez and using pieces of wood for a rifle and a saber and marching with his chest stuck out as the military do, repeating *fante, fante, fante*. Infante eventually showed that he understood, but a greater difficulty arose from his bad habit of frequently dropping the initial vowel when saying his own name. Pietro had recourse to the most alarming gestures and grimaces to get him to see the extreme importance of avoiding confusion between "*fante*" and "Infante," which were so similar on the lips but meant different and conflicting things. He was evidently disturbed by this discovery, for how many times had he not said *fante* or '*nfante* instead of *Infante* to indicate himself.

For the whole of the rest of the day he forgot his domestic tasks and kept explaining and repeating to the dog and the donkey the essential and irreconcilable difference between "Infante" and "*fante*," which he explained to them in his own way with serious and amusing gestures and mumblings. This made Leone bark and wag his tail with delight, but Cherubino's profound apathy was totally unaffected. In fact he listened to Infante with infinite patience and without the slightest irony, actually creating the impression of taking seriously and not casting the slightest doubt on the correctness of the deaf-mute's explanation, though he never thought it opportune to express the slightest agreement or give him the smallest encouragement. When Infante could stand it no longer he did not conceal his annoyance at this coldness. *Pietra*, he shouted at Cherubino, and put out his tongue at the animal.

This behavior did not escape the notice of Simone, who was greatly concerned that harmony should prevail among his guests; and as he thought that Pietro to some extent shared Infante's indignation and annoyance, he took him aside and spoke to him.

"Pietro," he said, "you mustn't imagine that the donkey's behavior indicates hostility toward our friend. I should be most upset if you suspected anything of the sort. Perhaps there's a kind of radical stoicism in Cherubino, a rejection and repudiation of any kind of eloquence. Who knows? The possibility cannot be ruled out."

"I agree with you completely," Pietro replied with genuine concern, "and you can rest assured that I should never complain about a donkey's silence, for one thing because of the liking and admiration I have always had for donkeys and, indeed, for silence in general. But the problem is Infante. As you know, he's still a child and it gives him a great deal of pleasure to feel that he's appreciated. Leone, after all, does show him appreciation, even though he's only an animal. Don't you think we might try to make Cherubino do the same? It might be sufficient to teach him some simple movements of the ears or lips to enable him to express his feelings."

"No," said Simone with obvious regret, "I don't think it's worth the trouble. I've known him for many years, and I'm very sorry, but I don't believe there's any way of persuading him to show greater expansiveness toward Infante or anyone else. Actually I wouldn't know how to tell him or even how to begin to try."

"Forgive me for using such a crude term, but do you think he's completely stupid?"

"To tell you the naked and brutal truth," Simone replied, "Cherubino couldn't tell the difference between a violin and a cooking pot. I'm dreadfully sorry, but that's the situation. But he has a good heart, that he has. Would he have stayed with me otherwise?"

"And that's what matters, Simò. When you come to think of it, there's only too much intelligence in the world, and it's not a better place as a result. So, if you agree, I shall try to explain to Infante that Cherubino's behavior is the result of reticence rather than indifference."

"That's the correct word for it," Simone agreed.

He was delighted at having disposed of a painful misunderstanding between his guests.

"Let us drink," he said. "Infante, you begin the round, gladden your heart. Now it's your turn, Pietro, refresh your eyes. Have you finished already? Oh, degenerate youth, look at me, see how I drink, learn from a poor old man."

Pietro then taught Infante the next pair of opposites, "Simone" and "simony." Infante learned easily how to pronounce "Simone," and he already knew who Simone was. To represent its opposite, the hateful and contemptible sin of simony, Pietro had to have recourse to gestures and portrayals of evil, avarice, treachery, and cruelty to animals and men, and Infante showed signs of understanding pretty quickly. Thus in a few days the deaf-mute's world with its two hemispheres, one of friendliness and the other of hostility, was immensely enriched. Later, while Simone and Infante were removing the planks to prevent access by the path along the canal bank, Venanzio arrived in a state of intense excitement of the kind to which he had only too often succumbed recently. The poor groom seemed to have aged greatly.

"That rogue Sciatàp, that scoundrel, went straight from here to Orta," he said. "The ruffian has not yet made his denunciation, he seems to be saving it for the new government orator, Don Marcantonio, who is expected for a dinner party at Orta this evening. That shameless dog, that gallows bird, not content with what he has had already, went to see Don Bastiano to try and blackmail him too, and then, I don't know how, he got hold of that other hellhound whose name is Calabasce. Don Severino (oh, Simò, the breed of gentlemen is not completely extinct yet in this world) came hurrying along to warn Donna Maria Vincenza, fearing that Don Pietro might still be in the house. The police will certainly be on the trail this very evening after the denunciation. Donna Maria Vincenza has sent me to ask you whether you think he'll still be safe with you."

"Tell her not to worry, that's all I can say at the moment. And don't weep, Venanzio, you're a man, after all."

"You know what Donna Maria Vincenza is like; can't you give me something more definite to tell her?"

"Tell her not to worry. She knows me, and tell her she can rely on me."

With Infante's aid, Simone hurriedly removed the planks and went to consult Pietro on what was to be done.

"The state of alarm you're in amuses me," Pietro said to him jestingly. "Calm down, if you can, and listen to me. You know very well that whatever happens they'll never have me; they never can. Even if they catch me and lock me up, for instance, even if they treat me with their usual brutality, you know very well that they will never have me. So why get excited? Come, don't let's make ourselves ridiculous."

"If you talk to me in those terms, Pietro, you certainly won't get a weakling's reply from me. So leave me out of it. But what about Infante? Haven't you thought of him?"

"Do you think they'll separate us if we're arrested together?"

"Now you make me laugh, Pietro. You don't seem to know the difference between a prison and a family hotel. Haven't you ever been in prison? I don't want to offend you, but forgive me, that's the impression you create."

"There's only one thing I have to say: I'm tired of competing with the police at their own level. Nothing horrifies me more than the idea of behaving like a character in a detective story."

"Perhaps you're right, but please respect my point of view if I say there's one thing we can't agree to, Pietro, that is, handing ourselves over to them on a plate. That's all I mean."

Simone put the halter around the donkey's neck and a blanket on his back instead of a saddle.

"Are you going out?" Pietro asked in surprise. "Where are you going?"

"To Orta."

"Listen, it's not worth the trouble of dirtying your hands with that wretched *cafone* from Pietrasecca. Listen, there's something I want to tell you."

But Simone was already outside the door, and he mounted the

donkey and trotted off. The night had fallen, cold and dark. Pietro stayed in the doorway, watching Simone going away. Simone and the donkey, looking black and spectral, kept appearing and disappearing in the indistinct whiteness between the bare, skeleton-like, twisted trees. There was not a living soul on the narrow, muddy, rough road to Orta; it was actually a track rather than a road. Suddenly behind Simone's back there was the clatter and din of a motorcycle approaching with powerful headlights. Simone jumped down from Cherubino, put him across the middle of the road, and signed vigorously to the motorcyclist to stop.

"Are you the new government orator?" he shouted to the stranger, who wore a leather jacket and whose face was half hidden by a pair of big goggles. "Get off, I've got to talk to you."

Simone seemed to have made up his mind to settle accounts immediately.

"I'm the trade union secretary," the man replied, putting his feet to the ground. "I'm De Paolis, the representative of the workers. Don Marcantonio has been delayed at Fossa, he'll be coming this way in about half an hour. Who are you? What do you want?"

"I'm the sacristan of the parish of Orta," Simone replied. "Everyone knows that."

"Well, then, you'll be able to talk to Don Marcantonio at Calabasce's house at Orta," the man said, starting up his engine again. "He's presiding at a dinner there this evening."

18

THE NOISY ARRIVAL of a motorcycle outside the Calabasce house, where the other guests were already showing signs of impatience, made them believe that Don Marcantonio had arrived. The host and hostess solicitously and obsequiously hurried downstairs to greet him.

"Come in, come in, what a pleasure, what an honor, you're as welcome as the Holy Spirit."

The mistake was soon cleared up.

"What, he's not with you? Has anything happened to him?" Signora Maria Peppina exclaimed in alarm. "Why is he so late? The food is getting cold."

"Don Marcantonio sends his apologies," De Paolis said, taking off his leather jacket. "He'll be coming later, in time for the coffee and liqueurs. He's been delayed at Fossa; affairs of state, you understand."

Calabasce accepted the situation, though reluctantly. "All right, all right, so long as he does come," he said.

But his wife stamped her feet and wouldn't listen to reason. If she had known about it in the morning, she wouldn't have spent

S T E E R F O R T H   P R E S S

Post Office Box 70

South Royalton, VT 05068

STEER
FORTH
PRESS

Founded in 1993, Steerforth Press is committed to publishing serious works of prose, both fiction and nonfiction. Our interests as publishers fall into no particular category or field and our only tests of a book's worth are whether it has been written well, is intended to engage the full attention of the reader, and has something new or important to say. Steerforth's books should be available at your bookstore, and most booksellers will special order any book not in stock. If you would like to know about other Steerforth books or forthcoming titles, please return this card and we will send you our catalogs at no charge. You may also visit our website at *www.steerforth.com.*

Name

Street Address or Post Office Box

City   State   Zip

In which book did you find this card?

nearly so much money on her shopping, that was why she was so angry, that was all. Calabasce was a short, thickset, violent boor and would have been completely unremarkable but for the fact that his nostrils and jaw gave him a certain distinction. His nostrils were as large as those of a bull, and in a diocesan competition in his youth they were recognized as the biggest in the district, with the result that he was given a prize and the title of Bull Nostrils. But when he made money he renounced the title.

"I'm the victim, as usual," De Paolis complained. "I shall have to eat for two. But am I not the representative of the starving masses?"

He pinched the mistress of the house while saying this but, as her husband noticed, he apologized immediately. "My usual absence of mind," he said. Maria Peppina laughed and vanished into the kitchen. She was a curvaceous little pink and white countrywoman, much younger than her husband, with a wasp waist, black arched eyebrows, bright eyes, a coral necklace, a small tortoiseshell comb in her thick, jet black hair, and gold hoop earrings; in fact she was a typical rustic Venus, but in spite of it by no means stupid. Calabasce was as proud of her as he was of his cows, though the latter had cost him more money.

"Don't hang about, come into the dining room" Calabasce said to De Paolis, pushing and edging him away from the kitchen door.

Calabasce, in his Sunday best, was dressed in the American style, with wide trousers, a double-breasted plaid jacket with padded shoulders and a split at the back, and shoes that squeaked.

The authorities, after a great many agonizing changes of mind, had at last given him the contract for building the new bridge, thus turning down Don Bastiano Spina in spite of the latter's ferocious battle and the endless humiliations to which he had abased himself. The result was that in the next few months the local labor force would come under the control of Bull Nostrils, who would end up pocketing some tens of millions of lire. But the moral importance of the event far exceeded that of the mere profit, substantial though this was. So far as the Spinas were concerned, it was the beginning of the end. The news made a deep impression throughout the area and, though dislike of Calabasce was general, no one whom he invited dared refuse the invitation to the dinner he gave to celebrate his victory. The table was set for about fifteen, and they had been waiting for dinner to be served for more than an hour; they were standing about in the limited space available between the table and the wall, yawning, pale, and exhausted, some leaning against the furniture and others at the window. Calabasce had insisted on their being punctual, and now? What a letdown.

"If I'd known this was going to happen, I should have had my dinner at midday," Don Michele, the pharmacist, murmured in an undertone.

One by one the ladies had ended up in the kitchen, where it was nice and warm and there was such a lovely smell. In their husbands' absence the conversation turned to laxatives, and, as usual, some were in favor of magnesia, while others wouldn't hear of anything but syrup of figs. Each of the women tried hard to persuade the rest, they all raised their voices and quoted irrefutable evidence, and eventually the confusion was complete and no one could hear what anyone else was saying. The conflict was insoluble; arguing was useless, it was an emotional issue more than anything else, and even their grandmothers had been divided into two irreconcilable parties on the subject. In the hope of restoring peace and harmony among her guests Maria Peppina, with the warmhearted optimism of a healthy countrywoman, suggested a compromise: she praised the gentle but effective merits of stewed prunes; you wouldn't really believe it, but all the same. But she earned herself nothing but compassionate smiles. Bless her innocence, everyone knew that prunes were effective, if at all, only for little girls. In the dining room. De Paolis's funereal jokes were received with yawns and indifference. Before his arrival there had been a rather sour argument about whether or not to open the window to let in some fresh air, because the room was stuffy as the result of the presence of two braziers and a great deal of cigar smoke. The argument led to nothing, though everyone said his piece in order to vent his ill humor, and everyone ended up at sixes and sevens.

"I'd rather die of suffocation than of cold," said Don Michele, the pharmacist.

"Then you could have stayed at home," several of his fellow guests pointed out.

"What do you mean by that?" he replied.

Meanwhile the windows remained shut. The magistrate Don Achille Verdura had turned up, though he was ill. But what sacrifices will a man not make for the sake of friendship? Actually he was in a rather delicate situation, because he owed his appointment to Don Bastiano and Don Coriolano. He was the father of a family and had to be careful to avert all possible suspicion; *mors tua vita mea*, after all, that was the law of life. He would have turned up even if he had been dying, for duty takes precedence over everything. The poor man had a severe attack of jaundice, he was yellower than any Chinese had ever been, saffron yellow; his small, black, swallow-tailed beard and his hair in a long bob, pitch black and shiny with brilliantine, formed a marvelous contrast to that color of pure gold. He looked like the idol of a hairdressers' religion. To cure the jaundice and avoid all complications his doctor had advised him to make at least one speech a week, an idea to which Don Achille was not at all opposed in principle, because he was never at a loss for words; on the contrary, in fact. But because of certain indiscretions his position was politically rather delicate. An old friend, a bigwig in Rome to whom he had secretly turned for advice and protection, had advised him to speak as little as possible. "The less you speak, the less you'll compromise yourself," he had said. To Don Achille death would have been preferable.

Don Michele, who had quickly found out what was on the menu, said to him with an obvious touch of sarcasm: "Don't you think it will be bad for you to interrupt your diet?"

"I have written permission from the doctor," the magistrate assured him, and smiled for the first time that evening, displaying two rows of teeth that seemed to be afflicted with jaundice too, for they were of a fine yellow color shading into gold like ripe corn.

In any case, the other guests were in a position no more comfortable than that of Don Achille. They too had all more or less enjoyed the support and patronage of or owed their jobs to Don Bastiano and Don Coriolano, with the result that in varying degrees they were all rather suspect. Don Coriolano's plight, since no one asked him to dine any longer, was apparently the worst. In theatrical terms, what had happened to him was equivalent to being transferred from center stage to the gallery. His only remaining pleasures were secret. Like a young mother who has lost her newborn baby and for the sake of her health has to breast-feed someone else's child, Don Coriolano, partly to earn his living but even more to give vent to his irrepressible oratorical urge, now devoted himself to writing speeches for others to read or learn by heart and declaim. For the most part his clients were *podestàs*, government officials, parish priests, and, it seemed, one or two hucksters at fairs. His vanity suffered, but the necessity of putting aside his own personality in order to identify himself with that of his clients gave him a kind of satisfaction he had not previously known. In short, he had become the secret dramatist of the whole area. Unfortunately the very same persons who applied to him for speeches, orations, exhortations, homilies, and panegyrics and preened themselves in his plumage avoided him if they came across him in public; they went out of their way and pretended not to recognize him in order to avoid compromising themselves. The result was that he had not yet succeeded in finding suitable premises for the "School of Choice Language for Use on Solemn Occasions in Life" that he wanted to found for the benefit of ambitious youth.

In Calabasce's eyes what outweighed everything else was the heavy blow inflicted on Don Bastiano, and satisfaction exuded from his every pore. But he could not afford to rest on his laurels, for his enemy had suffered a defeat but was not yet crushed; he must be allowed no breathing space but isolated, mortified, provoked, and exasperated. Every false move must be taken advantage of to bring about his ruin. The dinner was a first warning to

local opinion. He had gotten together the few people who mattered in the Orta area — the magistrate, the pharmacist, the trade
union secretary, a priest, some employees of welfare organizations, a couple of teachers — giving priority to those who had
hitherto been known as friends of Don Bastiano. In the circumstances even some of those who otherwise would have felt
ashamed to climb the stairs of his house had had to accept the invitation. The fact that Don Marcantonio was going to be late was
a cold douche. Suppose he didn't come? A dinner at which there
was no link among the guests apart from the fact that they were all
in the shadow of the same suspicion was not a very cheerful occasion. Everyone looked with distaste at his neighbor, as if the
latter's presence aggravated his own position. Everyone seemed to
be saying: good heavens, what people I've fallen among.

The lady of the house could not understand why the atmosphere was so gloomy. Could hunger depress these people to such
an extent? The guests belonged to the various categories of village
notables, they were used to showing off and throwing their weight
about and patronizing the *cafoni*, so why did they now look like a
group of extras behind the scenes, a group of players threatened
with the sack? If only the meal could begin; so many things were
forgotten when one sat down to eat. The priest Don Piccirilli
walked backward and forward and around the table with the tired
and listless gait of a corpulent, flat-footed penguin; Santa Teresa
de Avila, his patron saint, had written: "To suffer, to suffer and not
to die," and now he felt the full impact of that saying. A thin, bespectacled schoolmaster with a face that was all eyes and mouth
had put on the black suit he used for first communion days; no
one spoke to him and no one looked at him, and he stood by a
window and spent his time lighting and extinguishing a cigarette
lighter. The oldest of those present, Don Filippino, a quiet, dim,
insignificant little man who was noted for his beautiful handwriting and was also known as Swash-Letter because of his artistic
signature, was troubled by persistent hiccups. They had first affected him in the street on the way here, and when he arrived he
had asked for a bottle of water, after which he stood in the corner

and sipped it, but all in vain. At regular intervals the hiccups
made him start back as if an invisible hand had given him a blow
on the chin. What made matters worse was that every hiccup gave
everyone else present a kind of simultaneous electric shock. It was
a trivial, commonplace, and absurd complaint, and extremely disagreeable in the long run. Poor Don Filippino had already drunk
two pints of water to no effect; he was ashen pale, he sweated with
anxiety, his eyes popped out of his head because of the effort he
was making, and everyone commiserated with him, for all that
useless water in his stomach was usurping the place of the meal
that was still to come. It was just as well that the government orator had not yet arrived, because what a pitiful figure he would
make. Maria Peppina tried to help him by patting him on the back,
as mothers do with babies; she told him to look up at the ceiling
and try to think of something else, because that was the only
remedy.

"Don't lose heart, Don Filippì," she kept saying to him
cheerily. "Don't let it get you down and it'll go away by itself."

"That's not at all certain," Don Michele gravely pointed out.
"Oh, no, that's not certain by any means. There have actually
been cases in which it has proved fatal."

"It's a perfectly everyday occurrence," Maria Peppina protested,
maternally wiping away the perspiration from Don Filippino's
brow with a napkin from the table. "The important thing is to
think about something else."

"Certainly," Don Michele agreed. "But every now and then
there's a fatal case. If I say so, you can take it from me. Look, Filippì, I don't say that to frighten you, but you're not a boy any
longer, and you can be told the truth."

The waiting continued. To keep themselves in countenance
and to try to get away from Don Filippino's hiccuping, two of the
guests began reading, or pretending to read, the newspaper, and
they looked like rabbits nibbling at a cabbage. On one wall there
was a portrait of a man on horseback, and on a small shelf in front
of it Calabasce had put an oil lamp for the occasion; every so
often he looked up at it as if to invoke divine mercy. De Paolis on

the other hand behaved as if he were the master of the house and kept going into and coming out of the kitchen and announcing, releasing mouthfuls of smoke as he did so: "Just a little longer, my friends, and very soon now there'll be something to nibble."

"How comes it that that lout is so sure of himself?" the pharmacist whispered in the magistrate's ear. "Hasn't he got anything to be afraid of? Weren't he and the man who's in disgrace as thick as thieves?"

"Oh, he's all right, he's got good backing, the lucky fellow," Don Achille whispered into Don Michele's ear with a gesture of resigned and impotent envy. "About ten years ago, you see, he killed a socialist worker in a quarrel at Bussi."

"If only we too had killed a socialist instead of wasting the family money and sweating away at the university for that stupid degree," Don Michele said with a sigh. "But we never thought of it."

"It was a grave oversight," Don Achille agreed. "But now we're old, and it's too late."

"It's never too late," Don Michele insisted. "For an act of heroism it's never too late. But frankly, who is there to shoot? There's no political struggle here, we live in a ridiculously backward village. We had one lunatic, but we let him get away."

"Would you have been capable of shooting him?"

Sciatàp, filthy, grim, and embarrassed, appeared in the doorway of the dining room.

"Has the orator arrived yet? How much longer am I to wait?" he said to Calabasce in the tones of ones whose patience is exhausted.

The appearance of this unknown *cafone* caused astonishment and revulsion among the guests.

"Be patient, can't you see for yourself that Don Marcantonio hasn't arrived yet?" said the master of the house, trying to guide him downstairs again. "I'll call you as soon as he arrives, but now go and wait in the street."

"But do you realize that it'll take me several hours on horseback to get home?" Sciatàp insisted at the top of his voice. "In heaven's name have a little consideration."

"What is it? What's it all about?" said De Paolis, intervening in an authoritative manner.

"I want to make a denunciation," Sciatàp said hesitantly and timidly.

"A denunciation of whom? Explain yourself."

"It's a matter of putting justice on the heels of an enemy of the government, a pretty important enemy. But first of all I want to have a clear understanding."

"What's his name? Speak up, man."

"First of all I want to know definitely whether there's a price on his head, and if so how much, and whether it's payable in cash, and if not how it's payable. I've got to look after my own interests like everyone else."

"But who is the man? How can I tell you whether there's a price on his head without knowing who he is? Come out with it, man."

"I'm only going to talk to a properly qualified person. Who are you? Clear agreements make good friends. Even the priest doesn't say mass for nothing."

"If you want to talk to Don Marcantonio you'll have to wait," De Paolis said irritably. "I'm the trade union secretary, but if you don't trust me . . ."

Calabasce accompanied Sciatàp back down the stairs and, as the latter complained of the cold outside in the street — not so much for himself, because he was used to every kind of discomfort, as for the horse, whose blanket had been stolen — he took both of them to his stable a few yards away and actually offered him fodder for the animal.

"I'll come and fetch you when the orator arrives. He won't be long now," he said. "You did well not to talk in public, good man."

Calabasce went back into the house and found the guests at the table. Everyone had in front of him a small bowl of soup in which little stars and letters of the alphabet were floating about. This had been Maria Peppina's idea; it was a polite tribute to culture.

"Culture is a good thing only if it is accompanied by the fear of God," Don Piccirilli announced.

Thus the conversation reverted to the usual topic, and everyone said his piece or agreed with the views expressed by others in order to avoid any suspicion of holding something back.

"It seems that young Don Pietro Spina was always at the top of his class, and what good did that do him?" said Don Filippino.

"There's one thing I don't understand," said Donna Sarafina. "If he didn't want to make a career in the world, why did he let his family make such sacrifices for the sake of his education? He could at least have saved them the money."

"The Spinas have always thought themselves better than others," Maria Peppina said resentfully. "That's the fact of the matter. They've always been high and mighty."

"In short," said Calabasce, "the roast wasn't good enough for young Don Pietro Spina, he wanted sweet-smelling herbs to flavor it, but all he got was hemlock. Ha, ha, ha!"

"He laughed at his own witticism and looked around at his guests one by one, obliging them to laugh too. "I shouldn't like to be in Don Bastiano's shoes," he added with a guffaw. Then he went around the table serving wine from a big jug containing four or five liters.

"This little wine doesn't taste so strong," he explained to his guests, "but it goes to your head just the same. Don't worry, you'll notice it later."

The place on the host's right was occupied by the magistrate's wife, Donna Teodolinda, a kindly and self-possessed lady, good looking, pink, fat, and freshly shaven, with the result that she looked like a tuna fish. On his left was Donna Sarafina, the pharmacist's wife, prim and proper and behaving like a perfect lady, with a polite and subtly allusive smile on her face; her double chin was like a turkey's wattles. Two other women, wives of office workers, sat at the center of the table. One was a faded and affected blonde who seemed to have relapsed into an attitude of profound melancholy and incomprehension, and the other a brunette who still looked girlish with her curly hair, big, red, fleshy lips, full cheeks, and lively little squirrel eyes; she was the only one who seemed to be on good terms with Maria Peppina. The conversation languished, in spite of a general desire to keep it going. Don Filippino's hiccups had stopped on Sciatàp's appearance and the others had not noticed it. The silence became painful. Not only the men, but even the women said nothing. They responded to De Paolis's continual provocations and equivocal questions with smiles and chirps, without falling into the trap. Before leaving home their husbands had obviously made them swear by the lives of their innocent children not to open their mouths the whole evening, for the whole future of the family depended on it. It was easy for De Paolis to make jokes, the lucky fellow, for he was protected by his homicidal past.

A handsome fish was served with mayonnaise. Calabasce drew the attention of his fellow diners to the exceptionally delicate flavor of the sauce, but Maria Peppina had no desire to deck herself in borrowed plumes and revealed the secret. "The cripple made it," she explained. The guests from Orta knew what she meant, but it had to be explained to the others. There was an old stonemason in the village whose legs had been paralyzed for many years, and one of his arms was affected by a violent tremor. The poor fellow lived on charity, and when well-off families had important guests they took advantage of his trembling to make him beat the eggs for zabaglione and mayonnaise. Heaven knows how many eggs the poor fellow beat at Christmas and Easter; his trembling arm had, so to speak, become public property. The guests were also told that he lived in a kind of stinking pigsty, and that to give him a chance of breathing some fresh air in the spring Don Michele used to have him carried on a chair to his garden; the poor devil enjoyed this, and the trembling of his arm kept the sparrows away just as if he were a scarecrow.

"So it's an ill wind that does nobody good," remarked Don Piccirilli, who had not heard the story before.

"Other people's ill wind, of course," added De Paolis, bursting out laughing.

But only Calabasce followed suit. Don Achille started shuddering, and his wife affectionately wiped the perspiration from his brow and murmured words of encouragement in his ear. After this silence returned. De Paolis looked around irritably. Near him the

Misunderstood One was listlessly pecking at her food, the Squirrel was nibbling and winking at the lady of the house, farther along the Penguin was guzzling, the Rabbits were nibbling, the Golden Idol was chewing the cud like a he-goat, and the Tuna Fish was opening and shutting her mouth. Calabasce kept looking at his watch and muttering in an undertone as in a dream: "If all goes well, tomorrow Don Bastiano will wake up in the clink."

"I'm extremely surprised," De Paolis eventually exclaimed, addressing himself challengingly to the company at large, "I'm extremely surprised to see that an incident of a certain importance such as the success of our friend Calabasce here should leave you all so quiet and depressed."

"But suppose we are overcome by emotion?" Don Achille retorted.

After a moment's panic everyone's eyes settled anxiously on the magistrate. Because of his providential attack of jaundice Don Achille was the only person present who could say what he liked without running the risk of blushing or going pale. His deepset yellowish eyes now sparkled like a couple of fried eggs. De Paolis had a past that nobody could deny, far from it, but he was no match for Don Achille Verdura in an argument. Good gracious no, murder and eloquence being quite different things, after all. Were it not for a pretty dubious past as a pacifist and humanitarian speaker in his younger days, he would have been much more by now than a modest magistrate in a rural area; it was not quickness of wit that he lacked.

The murmur of agreement that followed Don Achille's happy intervention was submerged in the applause that greeted the appearance of the cook with a big trayful of steaming sparrows that had been roasted on two spits. The diners, noses in air, sniffed eagerly at the fragrance; oh, what a heavenly sight. The birds' thin little breasts were wrapped in pink slices of bacon, their small black beaks were stuck in their breastbones, their wings were folded back with a bay leaf in between, and their little claws, the ends of which had been cut off, were crossed as if in prayer and held another little bit of bay leaf. Oh, what tasty innocence. Between each bird and

its neighbor a small piece of toast lay like a soft cushion. No
sooner were they on the table than they flew, just as if they had
been alive, from dish to plates and from plates to greedy mouths
so that it was a delight to see, and palates confirmed the expectation of noses and eyes. Quick, the birds were thirsty, light
sparkling wine was urgently called for, but the maid was slow to
produce it, she was dallying in the cellar. What could the old
woman be doing? She had gone downstairs ages before. Why
hadn't she come back yet?

"Anyone who goes to the cellar without taking a swig is a liar,"
Maria Peppina, who had been in service before she was married,
said suspiciously.

As soon as the old woman reappeared with the jug her mistress
ordered her to approach, told her to take a deep, deep breath with
her mouth wide open, and then said to her threateningly: "Stand
like an angel."

"In front of all these ladies and gentlemen?" the old woman
complained.

"Do as I say immediately. Stand like an angel."

"I'm so tired," the servant lamented. "All these stairs, from
morning to night."

"Are you going to do as I say or not?" the mistress scolded her.

Standing like an angel meant standing with one leg raised and
keeping one's balance without holding on to anything in the position in which angels are represented in churches; it was an old device practiced in respectable households to find out whether the
domestic staff engaged in secret tippling. No sooner did Maria
Peppina's maid attempt it than she lost her balance. Alas, imitating angels is not easy. Meanwhile, the first flock of sparrows
had flown away and a second flock, hot and fragrant, was placed
on the table.

From the street an imperious voice, made hoarse by the closed
windows, called out several times: "Come down, Sciatàp, come
down, Sciatàp, I want to talk to you."

At the same time the sound of heavy knocking on the door
came echoing up the stairs.

Calabasce hurried to the window in alarm and saw some shadowy forms outside the front door that seemed to be those of a man and a donkey. After a short pause the man again shouted threateningly in the direction of the open window: "Come down, Sciatàp, come down."

Calabasce fetched a lantern and hurried downstairs.

"Who are you?" he asked the stranger mistrustfully and angrily, only half opening the front door. "Why are you shouting like that outside my house?"

"Tell your friend from Pietrasecca to come down," the man ordered him sharply. "I've something interesting for his ear alone."

"Oh, you're Simone from Colle, aren't you?" Calabasce answered in surprise, coming forward and raising the lantern toward his face. "Good evening. What are you doing so far from home at this time of night?"

"I'm looking for Sciatàp from Pietrasecca," Simone repeated grimly. "I've a small account to settle with that great friend of yours. Send him down."

"He's not a friend of mine," Calabasce replied. "I hardly know the man, and I'm surprised that you should talk to me like that. He dropped in here a short time ago, and I expect that by this time he's up in the mountains on his horse. I'm sorry, but you're too late, you've missed him. Good night. Please excuse me if I don't ask you in, but there's a family party upstairs, you know, the usual boring relatives."

Calabasce accompanied Simone, who dragged the donkey behind him, down the alleyway as far as the square and then went back to the house, rubbing his hands with satisfaction.

Meanwhile the second flock of sparrows, their little bellies warm with bacon and soft, golden cushions of hot toast, had flown away too, leaving behind a pungent smell of mountain shrubs and herbs, and a green salad was being served.

Don Filippino leaned over toward Don Achille to express his admiration. "Don Achì," he murmured into his ear, "you must satisfy my curiosity. Excuse my asking, but do you believe what you said just now?"

"What do you mean by believe?"

"If I'm not being indiscreet, I should like to know whether you really believe what you said."

"Now you make me angry. What has belief to do with it? Was it well said, or was it not?"

There was a sound of footsteps hurrying up the stairs and Don Marcantonio appeared in the dining room, but in such a state that made him almost unrecognizable. He was hatless and was covered from head to foot in mud, as if he had emerged from a ditch full of slime; the color of his shoes and trousers was completely concealed by gray mudstains, and on his hands and on part of his head and on one ear the gray was tinged with red. But the expression on his face showed that he was not in pain, and his erect stance by the door made it evident that he was uninjured. There was a glowering look on his face, however, that gave the diners cold shudders.

Calabasce was taken completely aback. "How did you get into this state?" he exclaimed, going forward to greet him.

"How did you get here?" said De Paolis. "We didn't hear your motorcycle."

"I left it at the last bend before Orta," Don Marcantonio said, recovering his breath. "I left it there in a ditch, and for the time being it can stay there, particularly as it's state property. Meanwhile, ladies and gentlemen, you can light a candle to Sant' Antonio, because it was a miracle I got away with it. Don Achille Verdura, you've lost the opportunity of making a fine funeral oration. Someone had the kind thought of laying a tree trunk across the road at the bend just before Orta so that I should run into it. It wasn't there, De Paolis, when you went that way a short time ago? I'm not surprised. Instead of searching for the mote in our neighbor's eye we should notice the beam right in front of our noses. That tree trunk didn't look as if it had grown there or been put across the road for fun. It was waiting for me there, waiting patiently. The mute, friendly patience of trees. It was waiting for me right on the bend, especially to give me a surprise. You can light a candle to Sant'Antonio, ladies and gentlemen, in gratitude for the fact that I was going slowly, otherwise . . . Calabà, tomorrow morning you can go there with an ax and chop me a good sliver of that historic tree trunk; I want to keep it on my desk as a talisman, for remembrance. Do what you like with the rest of the trunk. As I was personally involved, modesty prevents me from giving you specific instructions, so do what you like with it but, just as a suggestion, you might have it put in church as a votive offering, or displayed in the local party office in memory of this baptism of fire of the new eloquence. Unfortunately, as you can see, it was more like a baptism of mud, but that was just a manner of speaking; where should we all end up, I'd like to know, if everything was always called by its right name? And, in any case, what is eloquence for? And now, ladies and gentlemen, I shall be very grateful if you will spare me your fraternal congratulations on my narrow escape. And I shall be even more grateful to the beautiful Maria Peppina if she will take me to her room and enable me to wash and lend me a change of clothing until mine is clean and dry again. I'll be back directly."

The master and mistress of the house solicitously escorted Don Marcantonio to a neighboring room. The new government orator's unexpected appearance in that sorry state and his cynical and mocking remarks left a painful sense of uneasiness in the dining room. The future looked grim again. Husbands and wives exchanged glances of apprehension and alarm. Some plucked up enough courage to go on eating. Cheese and a great deal of fruit that had not yet been touched were still on the table. If refraining from eating served any purpose, well, it might have been different, but as it served no purpose whatever, it was better to face what destiny had in store with a full belly. Others rose and betrayed their nervousness by pacing up and down the room. The pharmacist and De Paolis confabulated in undertones in a corner.

"Do you suppose Don Marcantonio has suspicions about me too?" Don Michele asked dejectedly. "That would be monstrous."

"Of course," De Paolis replied in surprise. "Why shouldn't he? What next?"

"But I've never given him any reason to suspect me."

"If you had, you wouldn't just be suspect, you'd be guilty."

"Do you think the others are suspect too?"

"Of course. What a question. Don't forget that every citizen is suspect. Otherwise what would become of equality in the face of the law? I'm surprised to hear you talking in such a primitive way, Don Michè."

Don Marcantonio's reappearance, flanked by the host and hostess, promptly reestablished unity among the guests, who once more assumed the smiling, self-assured, and loyal attitude that the delicate circumstances called for.

"Please sit down everyone, coffee will be served in a moment," Maria Peppina announced.

Don Marcantonio, cleaned up and washed with violet-scented soap, looked rather grotesque in a brown corduroy hunting suit that was broad in the shoulders and short in the legs. From a small leather pouch especially made for the purpose he extracted a small comb and brush with which he trained the forelock on his brow and the short thick moustache he had under his nose.

"I went to a number of villages today," he began, taking a seat at the table. "I was continuing my search for a carpenter able to make the new kind of lictor's cross that I've designed as a symbol of the new eloquence. You may not believe me, but I haven't found one yet. So far no one has criticized my idea, far from it. Every carpenter to whom I spoke in fact praised it. But when it came to the crunch they all refused, they all said they couldn't do the job, they'd never tried such a thing in their lives, they had not been taught how to do it. As a matter of fact, it's no longer so urgent. The Lenten sermons in the parish of Colle have been suspended by the bishop on the grounds of the preacher's indisposition, and so the procession for the setting up of the new cross has been postponed."

Don Marcantonio was so transfigured by his new office that to those who had not seen him for some months he was hardly recognizable. His face was now a chalky white, like that of a bust in a cemetery, his eyes were fierce, his jaw projected like a horseshoe and looked detachable; and he kept touching the little mustache he had under his nose that was shaped like a butterfly, a little black butterfly between his mouth and his nostrils, and the lock of hair on his brow as if to make sure they were still in position. Every time he found that indeed they were, his satisfaction was obvious.

"Don't get disheartened," De Paolis said to him, slapping him on the back in friendly fashion. "As you know, the great martyrs encountered all sorts of setbacks at the beginning of their careers, but everything turned out all right in the end."

Calabasce was in a frenzy of impatience to tell Don Marcantonio that Sciatàp was waiting to see him. A decisive blow at the Spina family would suit the new eloquence as well as grated cheese suits macaroni, but he did not dare to interrupt the orator either while he was declaiming or while he was meditating. Nor did he want to raise the subject in the presence of his guests, for if trust is good, mistrust is better. And how can one be sure that one's optimistic and powerful friend who uses his influence on one's behalf today, one's influential friend whom one applauds so violently at meetings that one nearly wears the skin off one's hands, how can one be sure that he will not be dismissed from his post tomorrow? It is a terrible thing to become an accomplice without realizing it. Even the ladies seemed to realize the delicacy of the situation; sitting on their chairs as if they were at the photographer's at the anxious moment when he says "smile, please," they gazed fixedly at the orator, the exorcist of the moment. They smiled at him, tried to move him, subjugate him, soften his heart, they looked at him with an intensity that was both seductive and maternal, with a tigerish coquettishness and desperation, aware that their married happiness and the future of their children might depend on their smiles. The others present, schoolmasters and office workers, formed a separate group; they were tired, motionless, dispirited, like shipwrecked men in a flimsy boat. Any movement might be dangerous, and there was no point in shouting, for who was listening? If the others are rescued, I shall be rescued too, they might have been saying to themselves. But the new orator seemed determined to protract the agony and say nothing to relieve their anxiety; he looked at them stealthily, one by one, with the glassy, impenetrable eyes of a stuffed owl.

"He laughs best who laughs last," he announced derisively.

This sarcastic remark reinforced the glacial atmosphere in the dining room. Maria Peppina served coffee in tiny china cups from a big copper coffeepot. The master of the house at last managed to seize the opportunity to take Don Marcantonio into a neighboring room and tell him about the highly important denunciation that a *cafone* from Pietrasecca wanted to make to him, like winning the lottery for the new eloquence; fortune must be seized by the forelock. But during their brief absence the door leading from the staircase was flung wide open and Sciatàp appeared in a furious rage at having had to wait so long. Few among those present could understand this filthy *cafone's* persistence.

"What is this lout doing here?" Don Michele exclaimed in disgust. "Let's throw him downstairs."

"So the orator's here?" Sciatàp shouted, glowering ferociously. "And you leave me down in the stable?"

To pacify him Maria Peppina smiled and wanted to offer him a glass of wine, but De Paolis was quicker; he picked up a bottle, filled a glass, and offered it to Sciatàp, wishing him good health. The label on the bottle was that of a well-known Tuscan wine, and De Paolis showed it to the *cafone*; actually the bottle contained vinegar, and had been left on the table after being used to dress the salad; it was very strong vinegar, a real stomach turner. The guests and Calabasce, who came back into the room at that moment with Don Marcantonio, noticed it at once, but said nothing in order not to spoil the joke, being curious to see how Sciatàp would react to the first sip. Sciatàp, in all good faith, and perhaps also to show the orator that he did not bear a grudge at having been kept waiting for so long as well as to demonstrate that he knew how to behave in society, raised his glass, wished the company good health, and tasted the liquid. After the first sip he remained uncertain for a moment, and then, without batting an eyelid, he slowly and impassively emptied the glass. What a shame, the joke had not come off; those present exchanged embarrassed glances.

"Did you like it?" De Paolis asked him with a laugh.

With incredible calm and indifference Sciatàp looked him in the face without replying.

"Would you like another glass?" De Paolis asked.

"If you offer me one," Sciatàp replied simply. "Why not?"

The second glass was as full of vinegar as the first, but he drank it slowly and imperturbably, slowly and without bravado, just as if it were a glass of water. His lips turned pale, almost white, but not a wrinkle on his face betrayed the slightest unpleasant sensation.

"Thank you," he said, returning the glass and wiping his mouth with the back of his hand.

"Are you offended?" asked De Paolis, annoyed at the failure of his joke.

"Offended?" Sciatàp replied. "Why?"

"Laugh, in heaven's name," Calabasce shouted at him. "Can't you take a joke?"

The others also revolted against his sad, stubborn, loutish insensitivity.

"It was a joke," several people explained, happy to have found a diversion. "Come, come, it was a joke, come, a harmless joke, nothing to be angry about. One must know how to behave in society. It's not the first time that a joke like that has been played on someone."

To save the situation Maria Peppina, smiling, offered Sciatàp a cup of coffee; she herself put sugar in it and stirred it, as one does with a child. But Sciatàp coldly and politely refused it. He was positively unrecognizable.

"Thank you," he said, "I've already had something."

"Well, if you came here to talk to me, out with it," said Don Marcantonio, who had grown tired of these civilities.

The host and hostess and their guests moved to the other end of the dining room to leave them undisturbed. This diversion was by no means unwelcome to the guests. You never could tell, it might be a providential lightning rod. There could be no better lightning rod than a *cafone*. Don Marcantonio arrogantly and authoritatively began the interrogation.

"How did you find our Pietro Spina's hiding place?" he asked. "I advise you to speak the truth, so get on with it."

Sciatàp, solid and earthy, stood in front of him with his worn, patched cloak over his arm and his hat in his hand. Instead of replying, he seemed absorbed in contemplation of the table, which was still covered with the remains of the meal. The fatigue and disappointments of the day had rid him of all his proud and greedy pretensions and brought him back to the hard, humble, painful reality of his life as a *cafone*. He looked like a beggar.

"How did you find out where Pietro Spina was hiding?" the orator repeated, irritably and impatiently.

"It came to me in a dream," Sciatàp murmured, speaking close to Don Marcantonio's ear.

"So you won't tell me?" the latter went on. "Are you afraid of compromising someone? An accomplice? Well, for the time being I'm not in the least interested in how you managed to find out where he's hiding. Tell me where he is, and be quick about it."

"It came to me in a dream," Sciatàp repeated in his ear, as if he were telling him a great secret, "and he said to me, 'I'm in New York, I'm quite well off there, I live in Mulberry Street,' he told me, 'I'm running a fine shop selling fruit and macaroni, and I'm doing quite well.'"

"Calabà," Don Marcantonio called out furiously, "don't you realize that this *cafone*'s an idiot? What sort of people are you bringing me?"

Sciatàp vanished hurriedly down the staircase, but Calabasce went after him and caught up with him outside in the alleyway as he went off, dragging his restive horse behind him. The alley was dark, narrow, sunken, and full of dung. The three bodies occupied the whole of its width and constituted a single black mass that advanced with difficulty. Calabasce clung to Sciatàp like a dog to its prey, and Sciatàp kicked the shins of the horse that was dragging them both along.

"You cowardly, double-crossing wretch, you think you're going to get away with it as cheaply as this?" said Calabasce in threatening tones, gripping him by the arm. "Well, listen to me, if you don't

bring up the toad you've got in your stomach, in heaven's name I'll
cut it out of you with this knife that's generally used on pigs."

Sciatàp went on without replying, and Calabasce followed
him, fuming with rage and mingling bloodthirsty threats with extravagant promises.

"Sciatàp, stop, be sensible for a moment, don't you realize that
I want to help you? Why did you change your mind? Have you
gone crazy? You've already got a horse, Sciatàp, you could have a
carriage too. I don't understand you, Sciatàp. Look, Sciatàp, if you
don't turn back, as sure as God's in His heaven I'll cut your throat.
Do you see this knife, do you see it?"

At a bend in the alleyway a yellowish streetlamp threw a spectral light on a few yards of old wall from which the plaster had
dropped off and on a man with a donkey, both motionless.

"Calabà," said Simone, detaching himself from the wall and
coming forward determinedly, "take my advice, if you don't want
to catch a bad cold leave that man alone and go straight back
home."

Sciatàp took advantage of this to free himself from Calabasce's
grasp.

"Simone," Calabasce said, suddenly docile, "I have some personal business to settle with this *cafone*, some urgent personal
business. Go on your way and leave us to discuss the matter."

"For your information, Calabà," Simone replied, grabbing
him by his coat collar and pushing him against the wall, "for your
information, that business also interests me. And, if you really
want to know, that pocketknife you have in your hand doesn't im-
press me in the least. It's actually ridiculous."

"Simò," said Calabasce, trying to free himself, "I repeat that I
don't want to pick a quarrel with you. So go your way, go back to
Colle. What are you doing here?"

"Calabà," Simone said to him threateningly, pushing him
vigorously against the wall two or three times, "you know me, so
you must be very well aware that when it comes to blows I don't
like being two to one. So to encourage you I'm now going to
send away this poor Sciatàp, and we shall be able to continue

our conversation at ease between ourselves, here or somewhere else, as you prefer. I say that just to encourage you."

Sciatàp moved the horse and the donkey a few paces away to clear the arena. "Go for him, Simò, go for him," Sciatàp egged him on, "crush the louse." And he began listening in case anyone was approaching.

"Let me go," Calabasce begged in a tone of impotent rage.

"Off with you, go back to your kind, go back to your pigsty," Simone said, detaching him from the wall and giving him a shove in the direction of his house that sent him sprawling.

Calabasce rose, dripping mud, and went off toward his house, muttering unintelligible threats. Meanwhile Sciatàp drank from a fountain that was close by, holding his mouth open under the tap for a considerable time; that accursed vinegar was obviously burning his stomach. Then he mounted his horse and went off without speaking a word. Simone mounted his donkey, lit his pipe, and in the maze of the alleyways of Orta tried to find out in which direction Colle lay. When he passed the Spina house he recognized Don Bastiano, alone, motionless, wrapped in a black cloak, and bareheaded in spite of the cold, on the balcony over-looking the outside steps. Simone ignored him and went on his way, and did not even turn or make the donkey slow down when he heard a man's heavy footsteps behind him.

"Simone, stop, I want to talk to you," a voice said behind him. "Stop, Simò," the voice repeated anxiously, "for God's sake stop."

"Don't waste your time, Bastià," Simone replied without turning.

"I want to talk to you, it's not about you or me."

"Write me a letter if you have something to tell me."

"Do you read letters now?"

"No," Simone replied, making his donkey trot, "never, since that time."

19

As he left the village Simone passed Don Severino's house and was surprised to see light filtering through the slats of the shutters. Had Don Severino not stayed at Colle with Donna Maria Vincenza? He looked around cautiously, dismounted, and tied the donkey to a ring fixed in the wall; then he changed his mind, untied the Cherubino, went around to the back of the house, and tied him to a tree in the garden so that he could not be seen from the road.

"Good evening," he said softly to the woman who opened the door. But just as he was about to walk in the door was slammed violently, nearly hitting him in the face, as if it had been struck suddenly by a gust of wind. Simone shrugged his shoulders and went away; then he went back and knocked again, this time more firmly. A ground-floor window was opened.

"Who is it?" a woman called out angrily.

"Good evening," Simone said again, turning toward the window. "If Don Severino hasn't gone to bed yet, and if I'm not disturbing him, I should like to speak to him. My name is Simone," he added quietly. "They call me Simone the Weasel."

The door was opened immediately.

"So you're Simone?" said Donna Faustina in surprised and friendly tones. "Come in, forgive me, how could I tell it was you?"

She switched on the light in the hall.

"Don Severino hasn't come back from Colle yet," she went on politely and anxiously, "but he may be coming at any moment. Has anything serious happened? Please, Simone, don't stand there in the doorway, come in, they might see you."

She led the way into a big ground-floor room and turned on all the lights. Half the room was filled by a grand piano; in one corner a fire was burning in the grate and on either side of the fireplace there were two big, low armchairs. One wall was covered with shelves full of books; the others were adorned with an old pink tapestry with a faded gold flower design. A soft red and black carpet covered the floor from wall to wall.

"Please come in, Simone," Donna Faustina repeated with a charming smile. "You must forgive me, but how could I tell it was you? Severino will be delighted to find you here, I'm sure, he has often talked to me about you recently. He has a high opinion of you; as a matter of fact, he envies you."

Simone blushed. "Really?" he said, embarrassed. "I don't understand."

He was still standing rather awkwardly by the door; perhaps he was afraid of soiling the carpet with his muddy boots. In the well-lit and well-warmed room he really looked like a down-and-out. A piece of twine tied tightly around his waist held up his trousers and kept the flaps of his buttonless jacket together; his frayed sleeves were too short, and his collar was turned up and secured at the neck with a safety pin. He look all around him with curiosity.

"It's very nice here, Donna Faustina," he said on his best behavior, "and it's lovely and warm. But at my place, I don't say so to boast, there's more air, much more air."

"Have you got a big house?" Donna Faustina asked. "Whereabouts do you live? Forgive me, you'd never believe we're from the same village."

"At my place there's never any need to blow on the fire to

make it blaze up," Simone said with obvious pride. "The wind does it. In fact, when I light the fire, I have to be careful that the wind doesn't spread it to the whole house."

"Oh," Donna Faustina exclaimed in admiration, "is your house so big that the wind actually lives there too?"

"Not only the wind," said Simone, losing all restraint. "There are also the rain and the snow in winter, and in summer there's the sun in the daytime and the moon and the stars at night."

"It must be wonderful," Donna Faustina repeated, carried away with enthusiasm. "It must be marvelous."

"But here you're more sheltered," Simone went on graciously, in order not to offend the rules of hospitality. "And it's certainly better here for a girl."

Donna Faustina went out through the garden gate to cover the donkey with a woolen blanket, a beautiful homewoven red and black blanket. Simone was surprised and greatly touched by this unexpected gesture.

"But Donna Faustina, there's no need to do that," he barely had time to say. "You put blankets on horses, not donkeys. A donkey has a tough hide."

But Donna Faustina was already outside in the garden, and Simone watched the scene through the open door; he was taken aback and deeply moved, like someone who can hardly believe his eyes.

"Now he looks just like a cardinal," he said gravely to the young woman when she came back into the room. "Donna Faustina, I don't know if you realize what you have done."

"I realize it now, seeing the pleasure I have given you," the girl replied with a laugh.

The two looked at the donkey who was so unusually and luxuriously arrayed. Actually he did not seem to be in the least impressed, but kept his head dangling beside the tree with the greatest possible indifference.

"Donna Faustina, please don't take offense," said Simone. "Please don't misunderstand the animal's indifference. He's not stupid, I assure you, and he's not ungrateful. You're a girl, and I don't know if you can understand what I'm saying, but luxury has never meant anything to him, he never took the slightest interest in it even when he was young. How can I explain it to you?"

Donna Faustina seemed tremendously amused.

"Of course, of course," she hastened to say, "I never expected anything else from your donkey, Simone. Have you had him for a long time?"

"Donna Faustina," Simone said, "I don't want you to form exaggerated ideas about me, I don't want to adorn myself with peacock feathers. Cherubino, for that is my donkey's name, has been like that ever since he was young, and the truth of the matter is that in the many years of our life together it was not he who learned from me, but I who learned from him. I hope, Donna Faustina, you are taking what I say literally, and that you don't think I'm joking."

Donna Faustina suddenly grew serious.

"Simone," she said, "you mustn't expect me to understand immediately and completely everything that you're telling me. But I can assure you of one thing — I'll think about it seriously, and perhaps I shall end up getting myself a donkey too. Or do you think it's too late? Please answer me frankly, Simone."

"For any other girl it would be too late," Simone replied after considering the matter. "But not for you. I'm not saying that to flatter you."

"Thank you," Donna Faustina replied with a blush. "But please, Simone," she went on affectionately, "please don't go on standing there between the door and the window but come and sit by the fire. Severino won't be long now. You'll see how delighted he'll be when he finds you here."

Donna Faustina bent over the fire, added more wood to it, and then put a small copper coffeepot near the embers. Simone, now completely captivated and at ease, sat and watched her. There was a nimbleness, a gentleness, a grace about the girl's movements that seemed to enchant him. She must have been nearly thirty by now, an age at which *cafone* women were already old, and donkeys were old too; but Donna Faustina still seemed to him to be a girl. She had already done her thick, luxuriant hair for the night, and it was magnificent; her complexion was still soft and fresh, and there was something immature about her big, bright eyes, in which there was a trace of exaltation or even feverishness, and about her painted lips. She put a small table with two cups and a sugar bowl between the two armchairs and sat on a cushion on the ground near the visitor's feet. Simone's huge, dilapidated, muddy boots, which were laced with packing string, were now close to Donna Faustina's little snakeskin shoes.

"I must often have seen you in the street without knowing it was you," she said after a long silence. "If I hadn't been stupid, I should have recognized you," she added with a gesture of apology.

"Actually we're distant relations," Simone said with a smile. "Your aunt Lucia's first husband, who died in the earthquake, was my brother. But you had only just been born, I expect."

"Don Enicandro?" the girl exclaimed.

"You remember him?"

"A terrifying memory," she said to herself.

Simone was too absorbed in his memories to notice the girl's surprise and emotion.

She rose to light a candle on the piano and turn out the ceiling lights, which were too bright. In the semidarkness Simone's poverty disappeared and his hidden qualities emerged: his thin, sensitive, regular features, his well-shaped, straight nose and intelligent eyes, his charming, ironic smile. Donna Faustina looked at him admiringly.

"If I hadn't been so stupid I should certainly have recognized you," she repeated, as if asking to be forgiven.

"One would never have supposed that we lived in the same little village for so many years," he said with a smile.

"Actually," she went on to explain the situation, "I haven't belonged to these people for a long time now. I went on living here, but as an outlaw."

"I too, as you know, Donna Faustina," Simone hastened to say, "I too am in a way a deserter from the ranks of the respectable. I don't say that to compare myself with you or to boast, but I've been outlawed by respectable families for many years now."

"We both ran away, that's true," Donna Faustina agreed with satisfaction. "But the difference is that you went in one direction and I in another. That's why we never met until today. Hardly anyone would say we lived in the same village, particularly such a small one. We might never have met but for this evening's chance."

"No, it wasn't chance," Simone said seriously and politely. "When two outlaws meet, Donna Faustina, it's never chance, even if it seems to be."

Donna Faustina immediately agreed, and laughed with pleasure.

"That's perfectly true," she said. "When two outlaws meet. You must excuse me for being so stupid, Simone," she said shamefacedly. "How could I talk of chance in connection with a person like you?"

Simone was seized with sudden pity. "It's difficult for women to run away, to escape," he said sadly. "Because of their skirts, Donna Faustina. Trousers are much more convenient for escaping in."

"What matters is escaping," Donna Faustina replied. "Whether one does it in one way rather than another is of no importance."

"In the state to which this country is reduced, perhaps the important thing is to lose oneself," said Simone. "But basically it's the same thing, it's a question of words. What I meant to say, Donna Faustina, alas and alas, is that it's difficult for women to lose themselves, for them it's far more painful, because of the scandal, the gossip, and so on and so forth. Don Timoteo, for instance, the parish priest at Cerchio, was no sort of weakling when he was young. I knew him well, he was a lively young man; I don't know whether you've ever had occasion to have any dealings with him, Donna Faustina. But now he's as spineless as so many of them are, he's just a capon. The last time I spoke to him I asked him whether it was the Bible that had reduced him to that state. No, not the Bible, but the cassock, he explained. In a cassock, Simone, I have to watch my step, you see, it's impossible to speak or act as my heart dictates, the scandal would be too great, he said. He may be right. What can you expect of a man in a skirt?"

"One shouldn't be afraid of scandal," Donna Faustina said.

Whenever Simone had had occasion to observe Donna Faustina in the past she had struck him as being proud, irritable, highly strung, and frightened. No one so calumniated and yet so proud had ever been seen in that part of the world. On the day when she returned to Colle to fetch her luggage and other personal belongings from the Spina house she was nearly stoned by the women of the village; the two-horse trap on which she had loaded her things was stopped and surrounded in the square by a crowd of screaming, threatening, disheveled women, and she had to use her whip to clear a way for herself. Simone had actually been struck in the face by her whip, though he was hurrying to her aid. He had also been present at a similar scene at the entrance to the church when the memorial service for Don Saverio Spina was held. A number of pious women had blocked the way when she tried to go in. Simone had seen her walking away, distraught and in tears. Fearing she might do something desperate, he had hurried after her with a view to accompanying her back to Orta, but when she noticed she was being followed she panicked and started running, so he let her go.

He looked at her now and could not conceal his astonishment. Could this girl, with her childlike smile, her clear, frank, honest eyes, be the creature whose incredible love affair with Don Saverio Spina had been the talk of the whole countryside and who now lived in an open, illicit relationship with old Don Severino? Simone looked at her and smiled incredulously.

"Everyone saves himself as best he can," he said eventually. "We've reached a state in which he saves himself who can, and as best he can."

"Don't you think everything is predestined?" Donna Faustina said. "When the earthquake happened and the house started shaking I was in the bathroom. The house collapsed, and I don't know how I got there, but the next thing I knew was that I was in the garden in my nightdress, with my toothbrush still in my hand."

"It's very difficult to find out how we react in moments of danger, when there's no time to think," Simone said. "We choose our course of action in a flash. But haven't you ever wondered, Faustina, why at those moments we don't all choose the same escape hatch?"

"Do we choose or are we chosen?"

"Perhaps it's the same thing," said Simone. "Perhaps real freedom is complete loyalty to oneself."

"How is one to discover one's real self in good time?"

"It's impossible, and it would even be absurd to know it in advance," said Simone. "Sometimes one begins to get a glimmering as one goes on one's way; and how could it be otherwise? How could one realize the meaning of one's actions before carrying them out?"

"Then how are we to ensure loyalty to ourselves? Can destiny be retroactive?"

"In my opinion destiny boils down to this," Simone said. "Our most genuine actions can be nothing but our own. Destiny reveals itself to us gradually as we undo the knots in our own tangle. I believe that the more loyal we are to ourselves the plainer our destiny becomes to us."

After a few moments' reflection Simone went on: "Perhaps it would be more exact to talk of destination rather than destiny."

"Does that also presuppose an addressee? Who can our addressee be?"

"For the time being that's illegible," said Simone with a smile. "It may also be unknown to the post office."

"Simone," Donna Faustina said, "thank you for so patiently explaining your ideas on these things to me. I too think about things, but I never get very far. Perhaps because I'm still wrestling with some dreadful, inexplicable old things."

"For a woman, of course, everything is more complicated," Simone said.

"That contempt for women is unworthy of you," Donna Faustina said with a trace of irritation in her voice. "Would you advise a woman to sacrifice her loyalty to herself for a quiet life? Is the destination of women simply other people, like that of cats? Why baptize us, then?"

"Forgive me," said Simone, "I wasn't talking about women in general, but about you. Besides, being blinded by pity, I'm always a very bad adviser of other people. My sister-in-law Lucia . . ."

"I'd rather we didn't talk about her," Donna Faustina interrupted.

"Why?" Simone asked in surprise.

Donna Faustina did not reply.

"As you wish," said Simone.

Donna Faustina rose to remove the coffeepot from the fire.

"For the past quarter of an hour I've been thinking whether or not I should tell you about a certain incident," she suddenly said. "It was a serious incident of which I was the only witness when I was a child, and I've never told a living soul about it."

"If it's painful to tell the story," said Simone, "I wouldn't want . . ."

"Up to a quarter of an hour ago I didn't know it concerned you in any way," Donna Faustina went on. "Didn't you say you were the brother of Don Enicandro Ortiga? Do you know how he died?"

"In the earthquake, as everyone knows," Simone said in surprise.

"Do you remember the circumstances?" Donna Faustina went on. "Were you at Colle at the time?"

"I certainly was," said Simone. "I didn't do anything immediately about Enicandro, because barely an hour after the biggest shock I met my sister-in-law wandering about in the ruins, crazed with terror. She told me that the house had collapsed and that her husband must certainly be dead. But five days later, on my way back after burying my wife and son, I met Bastiano, who was looking for me to tell me that moans were coming from the ruins of my brother's house, and that it might be Enicandro. To tell the truth, he also said that there were members of his own family whom he still had to dig out, but that I was to send for him if I needed a hand."

"The moans had been going on for two days," Donna Faustina interrupted, "and there was no doubt that it was Uncle Enicandro. I called him, and he answered. But I was only seven at the time, and all I could do was to weep in front of the pile of rubble under which he was buried. I implored the passersby for help, but everyone had his own pile of rubble."

"Enicandro answered me too as soon as I got to the spot," Simone went on. "His voice was so weak that I thought he must be dying. Having learned by the experiences of the past few days, I realized at once that the thing to do was not to try to get him out straightaway, but first of all to make an opening to enable a little light to get to him, as well as food or drink. It was evening, and I didn't want to waste time looking for help. I was tired, and some wounds I received when my own house collapsed were still bleeding, but I went desperately to work. I've done some tough jobs in my life, but that was the toughest. It wasn't just hard work with arms and hands, but a struggle involving my whole being. I fought my way like an animal, like a wild beast, under beams, sheets of corrugated iron, furniture, blocks of masonry, which I lifted and moved with a supreme effort of my whole body. I should never have thought myself capable of such effort, and I don't know why my heart didn't burst and why my spine and neck and knees didn't break. And it was impossible to take a breather. Enicandro's voice grew closer and more distinct. Courage, I shouted to him, it won't be long now, it won't be long now, it won't be long now.

"At one point I had the distinct impression that his voice was coming from a kneading trough that was there among a lot of other rubbish," Simone went on. "I opened it, but there was nothing in it but a little flour and yeast. I moved it, uncovering a bit of wall with an intact stovepipe. My sister-in-law had had the stove put in the cellar to heat the water on washing day. My brother had fallen under it and found some space and air under the hood of the stove. I couldn't see him, but I could talk to him freely. He said he was injured, but not seriously. He said that perhaps he had a broken leg, and perhaps also a broken shoulder. The vent of the stove was too narrow for an adult body to pass, and removing the rubble to get him out would have taken several more hours, even with the aid of two or three men; also it would have been dangerous to try it in the dark. I explained this to him and begged him to be patient. Meanwhile I told him I would go and fetch some food and drink, which I would pass to him through the stovepipe. I also said I'd tell his wife, and that we'd take it in turns to keep him company during the night. I trust you, he said. His voice was tired, but calm and confident. I also remember that just at that moment it started snowing again. It may have been barely five o'clock in the afternoon, but at that time of year it was dark already."

"Before you went away, didn't you put a big table there to protect the opening where the stove was?" Donna Faustina asked.

"Yes, now I remember," Simone agreed. "I put the lid of the kneading trough obliquely over it, like a roof, so as to protect the pipe without preventing the air from coming in. As there was no telling where the road was during those first few days, people and animals walked over the ruins, and I wanted to prevent anyone from stumbling into the hole."

"Do you remember a little girl being there, a little girl of about seven or eight?" Donna Faustina asked. "Do you remember telling her to stay there on guard until you came back?"

"Certainly, now I remember, she was a pretty little thing," Simone agreed. "She was there when I arrived, and it was she who took me to the place where Enicandro's voice was most audible."

"Go on," said Donna Faustina. "How do you think he died?"

"While I was fetching him something to eat and drink," Simone went on, "there was another shock, and stones and pieces of masonry fell into the vent of the stove and killed him. When I got back there was no answer when I called him."

Donna Faustina shook her head, but hesitated to go on.

"Yes, there was another small shock," she said eventually, "but it didn't displace any rubble. To kill Don Enicandro someone had deliberately to lift the piece of wood that you used to cover the vent of the stove and to drop pieces of masonry through it with his or her own hands."

"But who could have committed a crime as vile as that?" Simone exclaimed. "To kill an injured man, kill him without being seen, kill him while he couldn't even move?"

Donna Faustina hesitated, but then said: "Did you tell anyone that your brother would soon be rescued?"

"A number of people had seen me digging and looking for him in the rubble," Simone said. "How can I remember their names after all these years?"

"Didn't you tell his wife?" Donna Faustina went on.

"Of course," Simone said. "I found her and told her immediately."

"She arrived soon after you went," Donna Faustina said. "She was already resigned to being a widow. During the previous days she had wept uninterruptedly, and her grief seemed genuine and exemplary, and she actually wore mourning. Where and how she managed to lay her hands on a black dress during those days of gypsylike existence I never discovered, but she found one. I may say that black suited her rather well. She also tried to arrange a requiem mass for her dead husband, but the priest advised her to await the recovery of the body. I had been living with her for about a year, ever since my mother's death. I was very fond of her, and she looked after me and treated me very affectionately; and my two uncles always got on so well that there was a very happy atmosphere in the house. After the earthquake, in the hut in which we took temporary refuge, my aunt always kept me with her and was careful to protect me from premature knowledge of the coarse, crude, and foul happenings that were taking place all around us. Thus, one morning when Donna Clorinda Tatò, who was living in the same hut with her two daughters, began panicking about the imminent end of the world, or rather about the end of the world that she believed had already begun, and started confessing her sins at the top of her voice, my aunt sent me away immediately on the pretext that I needed some fresh air, and it was actually then that I went to the ruins of her house and heard Uncle Enicandro moaning. My aunt refused to believe me. You dreamed it, she said, you imagined it. My persistence irritated her, and I couldn't persuade her to come with me and see for herself. This incredulity of hers upset and amazed me, particularly as she forbade me to mention it to anyone else on the bogus pretext that the dead should be left in peace. In spite of that, whenever I managed to get away for a moment I went to the ruins of the house to enable my uncle to hear at least one friendly voice and to prevent him from dying abandoned by everyone. My persistence ended up attracting the attention of quite a number of people, and so the news spread that Don Enicandro was still alive. Eventually you arrived one evening. You were not yet Simone the Weasel, but perhaps you didn't often go to your brother's house, because I didn't remember ever having seen you; or your appearance may have been affected by the ordeals of those few days. But your desperate efforts to find a way through the rubble remained permanently in my mind. You were like a lion fighting against death. When you told my aunt that her husband could certainly be saved, she hurried to the spot and found me there, and without even asking me what I was doing she slapped me hard twice and told me to go straight back to the hut. I went away weeping, but I didn't go very far. I stopped a few yards away on the church steps, and started thinking about ways of getting back at my aunt. If she doesn't find me in the hut and waits for me in the rain all night she'll certainly have a terrible fright and she'll be sorry she was so unkind to me, I said to myself. I turned and watched her from where I was standing. So, to my everlasting sorrow, I saw the most horrifying of murders. I didn't miss a detail."

Donna Faustina could not go on. She rested her head on Simone's shoulder and burst into tears. Simone shuddered; then he put his hand on her head and stroked her hair, as if she were a little girl. The two remained like that for some time, without speaking.

"Your brow and hands are burning," Simone said eventually. "Poor girl, still, after all these years."

"What should I have done?" Donna Faustina went on. "Should I have told the other relatives?"

"It would have been useless."

"Should I have denounced her to the *carabinieri?*"

"It would have been useless. There are sorrows that are not driven away by making a fuss."

"There are sorrows that are not driven away at all," said Donna Faustina. "Was I wrong to tell you?"

"Oh, no," Simone said. "Now you've created a new kind of

kinship between us. And Enicandro's death no longer seems to me to have been premature. Just think, if I'd rescued him, he'd have been the husband of his own widow."

Donna Faustina rose and poured the coffee.

"Severino regrets not having known you better," she said, handing him a cup. "I assure you that's not just a compliment, Simone. I'm convinced you would have done him a lot of good."

"I'm afraid I've become too plebeian for him, too aggressive, too common," he said. "It's difficult to make friends with me. And forgive me, but perhaps for me Don Severino is too refined, too cold, too sophisticated, too well mannered, or whatever it is."

"That may be, but those things are only appearances. Basically you, we, belong to the same species, I'm convinced of it. A species that's now tending to disappear."

"Your coffee's excellent, I congratulate you, it's a good sign. You're right, Faustina, these are bad times for people like us. But perhaps we shouldn't give up hope," he went on with a laugh. "There will always be madmen."

"Always?" Faustina asked anxiously.

"Madmen," Simone announced with quiet optimism, "are like the birds of the air and the lilies of the field. No one breeds or cultivates them. And yet."

"Aren't you mistaken?" Faustina said doubtfully and anxiously. "Aren't you saying that just to comfort me? Severino talks to me about these things; he says that a new invention to degrade mankind is made every day."

"I know, I know," Simone said with a reassuring smile. "But the essential thing to remember is that madness cannot be eliminated from mankind. If it's driven from the streets it takes refuge in monasteries; if it's driven from monasteries it takes refuge in schools, or barracks, or at any rate somewhere. Believe me, there will always be madmen," he concluded with a laugh.

Faustina seemed reassured, and smiled. "I haven't heard anything so pleasing for years," she said.

A mouse was to be heard scampering about and scratching behind the piano. A log collapsed and the fire smoked. Simone went down on his knees to rearrange it with his bare hands, without using the tongs.

"It's a very old house, so it's full of mice," Donna Faustina said apologetically. "Haven't you got a cat you could give us, Simone?"

"I'm afraid not," Simone said, "but I could give you a great many more mice. There are all sorts of very interesting different strains in my house."

Faustina laughed aloud. "For some time past the mice have been concentrating furiously on Severino's manuscripts," she complained. "There's no way of protecting them."

"Does Don Severino write?" Simone asked. "What does he write?"

"Yes, he has been writing for many years," Faustina said. "It's a way of relieving his feelings. He keeps a diary that he calls *The Story of My Despair*. I shall be forced to buy a trap to protect it," she concluded.

"A trap?" Simone interrupted in alarm. "Please have second thoughts, Faustina; Pietro would be most upset."

"Pietro?" Faustina repeated.

There was a long pause full of that name, and Simone almost regretted having mentioned it.

Faustina's voice now came from quite a different place. "I heard," she murmured, looking at the fire, "that when the news spread that the police were hunting him in the Pietrasecca area you immediately hurried there to help him."

"Who told you that?" Simone asked in some confusion.

"How much I should like to have gone with you," Faustina went on, and blushed.

"It was a silly idea," Simone said with embarrassment. "I went at night, and in some places the snow came up to my waist. I had too much confidence in my sense of direction, and plunged blindly ahead. The police mistook my footprints for Pietro's, and that was the only positive result of the trip. When they caught me I told them I was hunting wolves."

"How much I should have liked to have gone with you," Faustina repeated.

"Wouldn't you have been afraid of the wolves?" Simone asked in jesting tones.

But the girl took him seriously. "It's better to be torn to pieces by wolves than to be gnawed by pigs for the whole of one's life," she said.

Simone was touched by these words and made a move as if to hug her; but he stopped himself, and to conceal his emotion he rose and added a log to the fire.

Faustina suddenly said to him: "Did you ever meet Cristina, the Colamartini girl? It seems she was very beautiful. Does Pietro ever talk to you about her?"

"No, never. It's a kind of grief that's difficult to talk about."

There was a long silence.

"Simone, I want to confess another secret to you, a secret that's entirely mine and I've never told anyone; and, though it concerns Pietro, he has never had the slightest suspicion of it," Faustina said. "He was the great flame of my life. It began when I was barely fifteen. Even before I knew what love was, I was completely captivated by him. If I had been less in love with him, perhaps I might have been able to show it. But it was too strong, too absolute. I couldn't think about anything else, and I couldn't confide in anyone. That was the beginning of my long solitude."

"At fifteen," Simone said with compassion.

"There's no solitude more complete than the solitude that comes from the impossibility of expressing one's feelings," Faustina went on. "The break with the outside world becomes an abyss; there's no comfort or distraction."

"At fifteen," Simone repeated. "Nature is often brutal to the creatures it loves best. A lovely girl like you. For the same reason that it's forbidden to hunt young game that's unable to defend itself, passion ought to spare adolescence, give it time."

"Simone," Faustina interrupted, "I regret nothing. Pietro was several years older than I, and you could see in his eyes that he would have a strange destiny. Very soon he went away, but nothing could stop my thinking about him. He was my secret companion throughout those years of desperation. I never expected to see him again; after all this time I can't even imagine what he looks like now, but in moments of distress I drew strength from him and his example."

"I ask your forgiveness, Faustina, for the question I'm now going to ask you," Simone said. "In any other situation or state of mind it would sound like a stupid indiscretion, but now, after all that we have told each other, perhaps it's my duty to ask it."

"Whatever you say to me, Simone, can only be honest and friendly."

"Are you really fond of Don Severino?"

"Yes, Simone."

"Have you never considered the advisability of getting married to him?"

"No, Simone, never. I'm fond of Severino just as henceforth, if you will allow me to say so, I shall always be fond of you, but not otherwise."

"Bless you," Simone exclaimed, much moved. "I didn't imagine that destiny had chosen you to such an extent."

But the girl's mind was already elsewhere. "I understand nothing about politics and, as a matter of fact, I'm not even inter-ested in it," she said after a long silence. "I understand how one can risk one's life for a person. But for an idea? If I had lived at the time of the catacombs, perhaps I too might have sacrificed my life for Jesus. But for Christianity? What a shame, Simone," she went on, lowering her voice, "that a man like Pietro should lose himself in politics."

"I too, Faustina, was afraid of him before fortune brought him to my house," Simone said with a smile. "To talk about it, it sounds like a myth, and if it had happened to me on Christmas Eve I might have believed it was a grace from heaven. But I found him in my house just like an absurd present that turns up one morning under the hood of the fireplace; in those circumstances the only acceptable explanation is a miracle. I assure you, Faustina, that he has nothing to do with politics; I mean with struggles and plots and intrigues for power. The secret dream of a servant is that one day he will give the orders, and Pietro is the opposite of a servant. He too ran away, it is true, he too wanted to lose or, as you call it, save himself. He too had to run away. Like you, like Don Severino, if I may presume to say so, like me and others who did so, each in his own way. But he chose the way that leads farthest and discovered the poor, or rather the raw material of which the poor are made, that is, earth and dung."

"Oh, it's easy to say that. Who doesn't know the poor?" Donna Faustina exclaimed. "The earth swarms with them, like worms."

Simone did not agree. "I spend time with them every day, in the street and at the tavern, I know so many of them, and in appearance I'm exactly like them. When Pietro began to talk to me about the *cafoni* I couldn't help smiling, I was reminded of the clumsy blunderings of young humanitarians who go to the people. But then I realized that in his case it was entirely different. For he has been underground, Faustina, and has seen the world from inside, and that way of seeing it has stayed with him. No, Faustina, I assure you he's not an intellectual, a logician, a hairsplitter. He's still a boy from this part of the world, a country boy, rather absent-minded and rather absurd, and you wouldn't even say he'd been to a university. Destiny willed that he should go underground and see everything from inside, and consequently he's not taken in by appearances. He sees that the things that the world worships and adores are worth nothing, and so he despises them; and he sees that the things that the world scorns and abhors are the only true and real things. But how am I to explain these things to you, Faustina, how am I to enable you to see them in their true light?"

"Oh, tell me about them, tell me, tell me about them," Faustina begged him with tears in her eyes.

Simone smiled, filled his pipe, and lit it with a brand from the fire. Faustina put another coffeepot full of coffee on the hearth. Simone spent the rest of the night talking.

20

"WON'T YOU GIVE ME the reins? You look a bit tired," Faustina said to him. "And stop calling me Donna Faustina, otherwise I'll call you Don Pietro."

"I'm not tired, but annoyed," Pietro replied. "All this running away, don't you see, Faustina."

"But this time you had to. A little later, and you'd have fallen into the trap."

"Why had to? Why couldn't the others run away and hide once in a while?"

"What others?"

"The *sbirri* and their friends."

"You forget that they're the stronger."

"The stronger? Oh, Faustina, you mustn't be taken in by appearances. Why do you think they're the stronger? Because they have uniforms, perhaps?"

"And besides, if they ran away and you ran after them, you'd be the *sbirro*. I don't see that that would be any improvement."

"Who told you that I'd run after them? What makes you suppose I'd do anything so nasty? If only they would run away, I assure you, Faustina, that I wouldn't run after them."

"Well, if you wouldn't, Simone or someone else certainly would. That's the rule, Pietro, we've got to put up with it, we didn't invent the game. One is either a hare or a hound."

"And if one refuses to play?"

"One puts oneself outside the rules and has to run for it, in other words, be a hare. Take care, Pietro, or you'll have us in the ditch."

"Don't worry, this is what they call a parish doctor's horse; a child could drive it. What you were just saying, Faustina, is by no means foolish, but it's a dilemma that I don't accept."

"Unfortunately reality is not based on our likes and dislikes. It's older than we are."

"Reality?" Pietro asked curiously. "What the devil's that?"

Faustina argued with him, but in the end she obviously approved of his irrationality.

The light, nimble gig with seats for two on two tall and slender wheels seemed an ideal vehicle for that rough and muddy track; and the horse (Belisario, one of Donna Maria Vincenza's) picked its way skillfully, following its instinct rather than Pietro's inexpert hands. The two passengers wore heavy fur coats with collars turned up to their ears, which protected them from the bitter cold and also made them almost unrecognizable. The woman was distinguished from the man only by the green scarf that she wore around her head like a turban, while Pietro wore a fur cap pulled down over his forehead. He kept looking from side to side — everything interested him, every tree, every house, everyone they passed — and several times he cordially greeted some stranger, whether man or woman, bowing and waving his hand. This made Faustina nervous.

"Look, Pietro," she said eventually, "it would be better not to attract attention."

"Do you think that greeting people attracts attention?"

"If a man in a carriage, dressed like a gentleman and accompanied by a lady, greets a *cafone* on foot before the *cafone* greets him, you ought to be capable of realizing that it attracts attention."

"Strange," he said. "Why?"

"Because it's not the usual thing. You've forgotten the customs of this country."

"Oh, you attach so much importance to the customs of this country? Forgive me."

The road followed the dried-up bed of a stream; it was a vast expanse of yellow mud with small elongated piles of white stones that were as porous as dog bones. On the opposite bank there was a row of bare trees, blue larches alternating with silvery poplars. Women in black, kneeling on the bank where a trickle of water ran, were washing and beating clothes and putting them in a heap beside them, and singing a slow song with long, detached cadences, as in church; the song was sad, and like a litany.

"When do you think Simone and Infante will catch up with us?" Pietro asked after a long silence.

"It depends on the donkey," Faustina replied. "Sometime tomorrow, I expect; I've never been this way before."

"And how will they manage to find us?"

"Acquaviva can't be such a big place, and we can wait for them at the entrance to the village, or go and meet them."

The road went on between two hills that were planted with vines, with some trees between the vines. Pietro recognized the trees though they were bare and skeleton-like; they bore red cherries, brown pears, gray almonds, and he also knew the taste of the fruit. The Spina estate, the realm of Donna Maria Vincenza, extended as far as this.

In one of the vineyards there was a hut where Pietro in his boyhood had sometimes gone with his friends for an Easter Monday picnic. The hut, which generally served as a storeroom for agricultural implements and a shelter for the rural guard, was surrounded and nearly covered with rose plants.

"You came here with us once," Pietro said to Faustina. "Uncle Saverio brought us in the carriage."

"Do you still remember it?"

"You wore a beautiful blue dress and had white ribbons in your braids."

"I wore it in your honor."

"Uncle Saverio gave you a white rose that you pinned on your breast."

"I asked you for it. I should like to have that rose, I said to you."

"Yes, but Uncle was quicker. I was greatly put out."

"You didn't say a single word to me during the whole outing. You went on talking to the other boys about nothing but books."

"I was rather stupid," Pietro admitted.

No trace of the hut remained; many trees had been cut down, and the place was the sadder for it, as if it were in mourning. The gig went through a village just when bread was being taken from the oven, and Pietro could not resist the smell.

"Being shut up indoors the whole time isn't good for one," he cheerfully admitted. "Shall we buy a loaf?"

"If you're hungry, we have the provisions your grandmother gave us," Faustina said.

But it wasn't that for which Pietro was hungry. Women were standing at the doors of their houses, gossiping and spinning; and in the square men were idly standing about.

"Who knows what they're waiting for?" he said.

Men had been waiting there when he was a child, and they seemed to have been waiting ever since. How much longer would the poor devils have to wait? In the middle of the square there was a wooden cross on a tall pedestal with an iron cock at the top; its beak was open as if it were about to crow, but how much longer would it have to wait?

"Perhaps it has crowed so much that it has lost its voice," Faustina suggested.

At the other end of the village the road started winding its way uphill. The brown, horizontal lines of the plain gave way to gray, vertical lines, and one could see at once that they had been traced from bottom to top by peasants bending over the stony earth, almost on their knees. The road went on climbing, and the horse had to slow down and walk, panting and sweating. The ground began to be snow covered, the banks at the roadside began to be like little mountains, the hills flattened out and turned into fields, distances expanded. The eye took in the whole great circle of peaks, stretching for some sixty miles around the vast Fucino plain; huge, bare, barren, snow-covered limestone masses, the highest and most distant steep and rocky, the others rounded: Monte Ventrino, Monte Sirente, Monte Velino, Monte Cicca, Monte Pietrascritta, Monte Turchio, Monte Parasano. The sky rested on the grayish white ring of mountains; that day it looked like a heavy yellow awning with red streaks. Those mountains had been the limits of Pietro's childish world; Donna Maria Vincenza had never been beyond them. They had been driving for several hours, and the journey seemed to be only just beginning. In a hollow between two dreary heights the gig passed through a village that had been destroyed in the earthquake and abandoned by the few surviving inhabitants.

Among the shapeless piles of stones and the remains of walls some houses still looked intact, but trees unexpectedly emerged from windows and forced their way through roofs. A rat was nonchalantly taking the air on the windowsill of an elegant balcony overlooking the road, and Faustina shuddered at the sight of it. But Pietro smiled, raised his hat, greeted it cordially and respectfully like an old acquaintance. Immediately afterward they rounded a bend and came to a big wooden cross fixed into a granite mound; Jesus, with His hands and feet firmly nailed to it so that He could not escape, was covered in blood and dying in an agony that was terrible to see. Faustina shuddered again, while Pietro once more smiled, raised his hat, and greeted Him.

"He's not dead yet," he said.

"What a country," Faustina murmured to herself, horrified, covering her face with her hands. "Where are you taking me?"

"It's our country, Faustina, the country of our souls," Pietro said, putting his hand affectionately on her shoulder. "Don't you recognize it?"

Pietro was born and bred in the foothills, amid the vines and the almonds, as indeed Faustina was too. In all his life he had rarely been in the mountains, because of both natural laziness and indifference to so-called nature; his hardest ascents had been made in comfortable cable cars abroad. But this landscape, through which he was now passing for the first time in his life, aroused a deep feeling in him that took him by the throat, and if he had been alone he would certainly have wept. He could hardly believe his eyes, and he looked about him as if he were afraid that it was a mirage. "My country," he muttered, and he looked at it, recognizing every detail with eyes that were astonished and veiled with tears.

"Look, Faustina, those stone walls enclose the sheepfolds that are used during the summer." He explained that the flocks were now wintering in the south, in Apulia. "Do you see that rock? That's where the shepherds make their straw hut, and hang the blessed image of San Panfilo at the entrance; and outside the hut they milk the ewes, make a fire, boil the milk, and make wicker baskets for the cheese. Under that dry wall in summer there's probably a small spring, and the ground all around is soft and damp and covered with tender grass. Do you see? But they have to be careful, because the water is too cold for the sheep — if they drank it they'd get asthma — so they have to be taken down to the valley to drink at some stream that's exposed to the sun."

"How do you know all this?" Faustina asked.

It certainly was not a cheerful landscape; the mountains looked dismal even in summer, and how the sheep managed to get enough to eat was a mystery. The soil was poor, stony, and dry, in summer the scarce vegetation grew yellow between the boulders as if it were being burned by an underground fire, and caves and holes swallowed up all the rainwater. It was not for nothing that in days gone by the area had been populated by hermits. But these sheep could not settle down anywhere else, this was where they were born and where they belonged; in winter they had to be taken south to Apulia, but in summer they were brought back here.

"Hard little seeds of rosemary and thyme must now be sprouting for them beneath the snow," said Pietro. "I don't know if you have ever seen them."

"What? Beneath the snow?" Faustina interrupted.

"Without having ever seen this landscape, these peaks, this

life," Pietro said, "how often I dreamed about them during my nights in exile."

Faustina forced herself to smile at the desolate landscape because he told her it was his, the rediscovered landscape of his soul. She tried to make him forget her initial horror of it, and discovered on more thorough inspection that it wasn't frightening at all, though perhaps it was a bit bare, harsh, and inhospitable. The road went on climbing, the snow grew whiter and deeper, the air sharper and more biting. A brisk wind arose and echoed in the depths of the mountains.

The gig reached the last village on the Fucino slope, an agglomeration of black shacks and smoky caverns under the tutelage of a pointed bell tower. There was a strong smell of goat as they made their way between the hovels, and two or three earth-colored little donkeys were to be seen, as well as some thin, spectral women clothed in black who looked at them with hostility and suspicion. In spite of the snow, one could tell from the conformation of the ground that at this point cultivation stopped; the earth was rocky, cut up into humps, crags, ravines; there were no more trees, only a few black bushes dotted about; the mountains, barren and white with snow, were piled on top of one another, the buttresses consolidated into a massive ridge. When the gig reached the top of the pass Pietro looked back with the air of one who is crossing a frontier.

"There's somebody waiting for you over there who wants to talk to you," said Faustina, growing pale and suddenly pulling the reins.

A man on horseback emerged from a corner formed by three abandoned black hovels by the roadside and came toward them.

"Who is it?" Pietro asked curiously.

He handed over the reins to Faustina, jumped down, and went toward the man, who dismounted too. He was tall, strong, elderly, and slightly bent, and looked like a rich farmer.

"Don't you recognize me?" he asked, controlling his feelings.

"Uncle Bastiano?" Pietro exclaimed in surprise, stopping a few yards away from him. "Well, it's not easy to recognize you, you really have gone downhill, poor man."

Uncle and nephew hesitated to greet each other.

"No, I haven't gone downhill," Don Bastiano replied, greatly upset. "I stayed where I was born, there's no denying that."

"You stayed and fought that little scoundrel Calabasce," Pietro went on, "and gradually you became just like him."

"Who else was there?" Don Bastiano said resentfully. "Was it my fault if no one else was in my way?"

"If there was no one else, anyone else in your place would have wrestled with God."

"Oh, so you still believe in Him?"

"Or with the devil."

"You believe in the devil?"

"Or you might have wrestled with the government, for instance."

"Politics have never interested me; idle talk bores me."

"Then you could have quarreled with yourself."

The horse, as motionless as a wall, was between uncle and nephew, and Don Bastiano leaned with his forearms on the animal's rump so as to be able to talk quietly.

"As a matter of fact, for about twenty years I have been struggling with myself," he said. "And with you. You can't imagine how much you have been troubling me in recent years."

"You struggled hard, but it didn't help," Pietro said. "Calabasce beat you."

"It's not over yet," Don Bastiano replied. "I'm not buried yet. But that doesn't concern or interest you. I came here for quite a different reason. I have something definite and very painful to confess to you."

"There's no need to," Pietro interrupted. "Apart from everything, I know what it's about."

"You can't possibly know what it's about. You can't even imagine it."

Don Bastiano took an old, worn leather wallet from an inside pocket of his jacket and held it with trembling hands.

"Please, Uncle," said Pietro, "I implore you to leave that wretched wallet alone. Please don't tell me that wretched old story. I know it already."

"You can't possibly," Don Bastiano said, almost stammering in his agitation. "You can't even imagine it; and I've got to tell it to you, I've got to rid myself of it once and for all, I've got to spit out the poison that has been rotting my guts for so many years."

"Listen to me," Pietro said bluntly. "I'll help you to tell the damned story. I too, though in a different way, have been afflicted with it for many years and have even suffered remorse . . ."

"Remorse? You?" Don Bastiano interrupted.

"Come," said Pietro, noticing that Bastiano was able to stand only by holding on to the horse's mane.

The two went and sat on the doorstep of one of the uninhabited houses, and Pietro tied the horse to a ring fixed in the wall.

"Was it the third or fourth evening after the earthquake?" Pietro said to his uncle.

"You were little more than a child," Don Bastiano replied, shaking his head. "You couldn't know, you couldn't remember."

"It must have been on the fourth day after the earthquake," Pietro went on. "I was fourteen, little more than a child, as you just said. I had spent the whole day shifting the rubble under which my mother was buried."

"I helped you that morning, I don't know if you remember."

"Venanzio was there too, and so was Grandmother for a few minutes."

"Until they came and told us that Saverio was calling for help under the ruins of his house, where he was only slightly injured."

"Toward the end of that afternoon," Pietro went on, "just when I was going to give up, I found my mother's body; but in spite of all my efforts I couldn't move it because of a heavy iron sheet that was lying across her knees. I told you that, late that evening, when I went back to the sleeping quarters you had rigged up in your garden. As I couldn't go to sleep, I told you that while I was trying to extricate my mother's body a big wallet had slipped from her apron."

"You remember all that?" Don Bastiano muttered, shuddering.

"I remember every word of our conversation, every gesture," Pietro went on. "A child's memory is terrifying. I asked you why my mother had happened to have such a large sum of money on her on that day of all days. You said that perhaps she had been going to take it to the bank that morning. In any event, I said to you, it seemed to me to be appalling to be worrying about the smallness or largeness of the sum of money she might have had on her even before her body had been removed from the rubble."

"Then you fell asleep, exhausted," Don Bastiano murmured. "I turned out the oil lamp and lay down on the straw too."

"Soon afterward I opened my eyes," Pietro went on, "and saw a man outlined against the entrance of the shelter, and he stayed there for some moments as if he were listening. The sight gave me a terrible fright, I didn't know precisely why. I wanted to cry out, but couldn't, it was as if a heavy hand were clutching me by the throat. As soon as you went away I leaped to my feet and followed you. The sky was cloudy that night, but the visibility was quite good because of the snow and the three or four fires that were kept burning at the highest points in the village to prevent wolves from coming down from the mountain. So there was no difficulty in following you at a distance."

"At one point I had the feeling that I was being followed."

"Was it in the bakery alley? I tripped over an empty gasoline can and luckily fell into a ditch, where you couldn't see me when you looked around."

"I thought it was a dog."

"When it was obvious to me where you were going and I saw you searching in the ruins where my mother's body lay, I must admit that it wasn't horror at your wicked greed that filled me, but a panic fear that you might notice I was watching."

"What an accursed night," Don Bastiano murmured.

"Next day I was aware of no longer being the same," Pietro said. "Growing up takes a whole lifetime, but to grow old a single night like that is enough."

With trembling hands Don Bastiano held out the wallet, but Pietro took no notice and let it drop to the ground.

"Accursed money," said Pietro, "accursed enemy."

He picked up the wallet, cautiously, with the revulsion he

would have felt for a viper's nest, and took out the banknotes. Then he took a box of matches from his pocket and started burning them, slowly, three or four at a time, taking care that not a shred was left. Don Bastiano started at the sight as if he had been stabbed; his hands gripped the stone seat and his face contracted into a painful grimace. But Pietro calmly and systematically went on with his work of destruction, holding three or four banknotes in one hand and a lit match in the other. The notes shriveled and quickly turned to ashes, and eventually there was a small heap of black ashes on the ground. Old Don Bastiano was breathing stertorously, as if he had undergone a severe operation.

"Accursed money," said Pietro, "accursed enemy."

He rose and scattered the ashes with a vigorous kick.

"You look tired and depressed," Faustina said to him when he returned to the gig. "Did you quarrel?"

"Let's go," Pietro answered. "We're late."

"Bastiano has always been a poor soul in torment," Faustina said. "He could have used a friend, but everyone quarrels with him. Was I wrong to make him come here?"

"No, on the contrary, thank you."

The opposite slope opened on to a huge valley contained between two high mountains with deep lateral valleys. The horse was covered with foam and was panting and snorting, and they were still only halfway; and there was no knowing whether poor Belisario would make it. The breath from his dilated nostrils was like that coming from a boiling coffee machine. The road zigzagged steeply downward. The mountain, treeless and uninhabited, was cut up by deep ravines and brief level spaces; in places huge boulders were perched precariously right above the road. There was a rapid procession of clouds across the gray sky; when one looked at them they seemed to be motionless and the whole mountain and the valley below seemed to be moving.

"At this rate we'll be in Dalmatia by tomorrow morning," Pietro said.

"Dalmatia?" Faustina said in alarm.

"Perhaps even farther," Pietro insisted.

"What do you mean, farther?"

"I mean the mountain, and we with it," he explained.

No light or other sign of human habitation was to be seen in the valley; only in the distance, halfway up the mountainside, could the lights of some villages be descried, looking like small bunches of luminous grapes; but it would take several hours to get there. Pietro was suddenly overcome with fatigue; perhaps because of the sharp changes of altitude, and perhaps also because of the emotion of his meeting with his uncle, his heart started beating irregularly. Faustina noticed, took the reins from his hands and told him to close his eyes. But the gig kept jolting and, as is usual with that kind of vehicle, the seat had no back on which to rest one's head or even one's back; dropping off to sleep would have meant the risk of falling beneath the wheels. Pietro slipped down and curled up on the footboard with the back of his neck against the seat, but it was impossible to sleep. The only visible reality in front of him was the horse's hindquarters, and that heavy, opaque, monstrous thing ended up becoming a reality in itself, a pure autonomous animal reality consisting of two huge buttocks, a black tail that never stopped moving, and a dark anal orifice.

"What's the matter? Are you having nightmares?" Faustina asked. Her voice surprised him; it was like balm to his heart.

He hid his face in a corner of her coat, and she rested her hand on his head and stroked it. But her courage did not go beyond that shy gesture, as if it had already exceeded the extreme limit.

"Try to go to sleep," she suggested, allowing him more of her coat. "We may still have a long way to go."

He closed his eyes. A delicious scent of spring herbs emanated from Faustina. Gradually a steadily growing roar filled the valley, perhaps from a torrent that ran along the bottom. The whole valley seemed to be in motion in that roar, and the jolting gig was like a small boat tossing on dark waters. Much later, when Pietro opened his eyes again, there was a house with a lamp by the roadside, and a hundred yards farther along there was the entrance to a big village. Their first reaction was relief at this "landfall," at having arrived after the stress of the journey; but this was succeeded by embarrassment at the equivocal situation that awaited them, a matter that neither had dared to mention on the way. To both it seemed too late to discuss it now, so they avoided even looking at each other.

In the principal street of the deserted and silent village two *carabinieri* walked toward them with the mournful gait of prison wardens on their rounds.

"Is there a decent hotel here?" Pietro asked them.

"There's only one, in the corner of the square over there," one of them replied.

"It's more an inn than a hotel," said the other one, after taking a look at the lady in the gig.

After some noisy and protracted knocking at the inn door a man's voice answered from inside. Before the man himself appeared, a huge electric lightbulb over the top of the door was switched on, illuminating the two travelers and a sign saying VICTORY HOTEL, FORMERLY COMMERCIAL HOTEL. Pietro noticed Faustina's extreme pallor.

"Don't worry, Faustina," he barely had time to murmur.

While the landlord talkatively and obsequiously took charge of the horse and gig, a disheveled, sleepy woman took the bags and led the new arrivals up a dark and stinking staircase to the only available room, on the third floor; she led the way hurriedly and the two followed hesitantly behind her.

"Haven't you got another room free?" Pietro insisted. "We'd pay for it, of course."

"No," the woman replied, yawning. "What do you want another room for? Are the children with you?"

The two did not reply.

"I can put a mattress on the floor for the children," the woman went on while she uncovered the bed. "I slept on the floor when I was a girl."

"We'd pay whatever was necessary," Pietro repeated.

"Good night, sleep well," the woman said after putting towels on the washstand, and she left, closing the door behind her. A moment later she reappeared. "I forgot to tell you," she said, "that the lavatory's in the courtyard at the other end of the alley; if the dog barks, don't take any notice, it has never bitten anyone yet."

The room contained a huge double bed, as big as a parade ground, a ceremonial piece of furniture of a size that must have dated from the matriarchal age. It was flanked on either side, as if by two sentry boxes, by the usual smelly night tables; a look was sufficient to make one realize that opening them for a moment would fill the whole room with the smell of ammonia. Faustina stood by the window, looking out at the street. Pietro sat down, exhausted. On all four walls of the room the faded wallpaper repeated over and over again a hunting scene consisting of a tree, a bird, a dog, a sportsman with a gun, so that whichever way you looked your eyes met the dog, the tree, the sportsman with the gun, and the bird waiting to be shot; and if you shut your eyes and opened them again they were still there. At the head of the bed there hung a picture of the black Madonna of Loreto, a holy water stoup, and an olive branch. Pietro turned toward Faustina; he was extremely embarrassed, sought for something to say but could not find it, and then said simply: "You must forgive me, Faustina, for not having spared you this extremely tiresome and ambiguous situation. Believe me, I'm extremely upset."

"It's not your fault, Pietro," she replied without turning, "and there's no need to apologize. It was circumstances, as we know very well."

"Faustina," he went on after a long silence, "if circumstances thought they were playing a joke on us, it's now our turn to laugh at them; I'm sure you will help me."

"How, Pietro?" she asked, turning and facing him.

"No one can force us to behave like characters in a trashy novel, Faustina. For the simple reason that we are not characters in a trashy novel. If we simply remain ourselves we can laugh at circumstances. From the practical point of view, the only difficulty is eliminated by the preference I have had for some time for sleeping on the floor. Don't look so incredulous, Faustina, if you don't believe me you can ask Simone tomorrow; there were no beds in his barn, and I have never in my life slept better than I slept there. So now I'm taking one of the pillows and a blanket and am going to settle down on the floor here. Good night, Faustina."

"But, Pietro, sleeping on the floor has always been my ideal," Faustina replied indignantly. "I'm strong, I've never been ill in my life, you can ask anyone, and you saw for yourself that the drive here didn't worry me in the least; or have you the nerve to deny it? So don't be obstinate, Pietro, go to bed, and I'll settle down here on the floor."

"Faustina," Pietro said with all the firmness of which he was capable, "let me inform you that it's no use trying to bully me. You're my guest, moreover you're a woman (yes, let us try not to think about it, but you're a woman, after all, and you can't deny it), so you will go to bed without making any more fuss and I shall stretch out here on the floor where, I assure you, I shall be very comfortable indeed, as I'm used to it. Good night, Faustina, and let's say no more about it."

"Pietro, if you think you can get the better of me by confronting me with a fait accompli, you're very much mistaken," Faustina replied. "You haven't the faintest idea what I'm made of, you poor fellow. So I'm taking a pillow and a blanket and I'm going to make myself comfortable on the floor in this corner, as you see, and you can do what you like, though in view of your exhaustion the most sensible thing to do would be to go to bed. Good night, Pietro."

The floor consisted of reddish tiles with blue and yellow stripes, undulating as if a river had been passing over it for many years. Pietro's long, thin, arched body, wrapped in a gray woolen blanket on the tiles, assumed the shape of the keel of a boat drawn up on the beach; he coughed, and his violent and irregular coughing resembled the explosive noises made by a motorcycle engine that refuses to start up. Faustina lay near the door with her cheek on her open hand, and after a short while she seemed to have gone to sleep; her body, motionless under a dark blue, almost black, blanket, had the shape and composure of the dead as represented on the granite floors of old churches. All night long (it was now March) two cats on the roof next door did not for a single minute stop calling and imploring and appealing to each other in the most distressful tones.

21

NEXT MORNING PIETRO woke up just when Faustina
had finished washing her face in a small enamel basin
after pouring water from a chipped jug. His surprise almost took
his breath away. He looked around in amazement at not being in
Simone's barn. While the girl, standing in front of a small mirror,
tidied the fragrant river of her chestnut hair with graceful and precise gestures, all her beauty revealed itself, like that of certain
flowers in the morning: the slender fullness of her breast, the perfect articulation of her slim shoulders, the olive brown skin of one
shoulder divided by the blue ribbon of her chemise. She noticed
in the mirror that Pietro had opened his eyes and was looking at
her in bewilderment.

"Oh, good morning, did you sleep well?" she said.

"What are you doing here?" he asked.

But his curiosity yielded immediately to admiration. In the
morning light Faustina struck him as even more beautiful than
before; and, as he was still lying on the floor, she seemed taller,
more graceful, fresher, and more willowy than ever; she was an
enchanting, shady palm tree. Oh, to be able to climb it and gather

the hidden fruits that were sweeter than any sweet thing, to taste and enjoy them slowly, stretched out in her warm shade.

Pietro gathered his strength to face the effort of getting up and dressing. First of all he put on his hat and knotted his tie, and then he lay back and rested. The worst task facing him was putting on his shoes; to do that he would have to get up. The mere idea was absurd. After putting them on he had a rest, and when he had tied the laces he sat down and rested again.

"I've never understood, Faustina," he said, "I've never managed to understand why you have to take off your shoes every evening if you have to put them on again in the morning. It's not the effort that gets me down, Faustina, of course, but the superfluity, the absurdity of the whole thing."

"Your forefathers probably wore *ciocie*,* Pietro," Faustina announced after thinking over the matter.

"All our forefathers wore *ciocie*, Faustina, all of them without exception. It was the Spaniards who brought us shoes. Tell me, Faustina, what are those suspicious-looking suitcases in the corner over there?"

"The two big leather ones are yours. Didn't you know?"

"Mine? You make me laugh. I haven't had a suitcase since I left school. A few handkerchiefs and a spare pair of socks have always been enough for me; I wash the shirt I have on my back myself and dry it overnight. Why drag heavy and suspicious-looking luggage around with me?"

"Donna Maria Vincenza gave them to Severino for you, don't you remember, Pietro? I told you yesterday. Is your memory always so bad in the morning? Severino told me your grandmother worked for a whole month to fit you out properly again. She even wanted to embroider P. S. on your things, but then she realized it might be inadvisable."

"P. S.? For Public Safety, or even *post scriptum*, what an idea. How could a person as sensible as my grandmother think of such

---

*A kind of footwear formerly customary in parts of southern Italy, consisting of a sole and a length of cloth bound around the foot and leg.

a thing? Well, let's have a look at the bridegroom's outfit. Have you the keys of the suitcases?"

"The keys?"

Faustina did not have them, Don Severino had forgotten to give them to her. Pietro was triumphant.

"There you see the advantages of traveling with suitcases," he remarked.

While Pietro was washing Faustina wanted to go down to the kitchen to order breakfast.

"What would you like?"

"Some nice, sweet dates or a fresh coconut," he replied absent-mindedly. But he immediately realized that what he had said was stupid, and he blushed and apologized. "I had a slight attack of cannibalism," he explained. "Forgive me, Faustina, it's a thing that can happen to anyone. Please order me some black coffee."

Faustina couldn't make head or tail of what Pietro had said, and she was a little worried when she went down to the kitchen to order the coffee.

The landlady was overflowing with affability, she was all sugar and honey in the morning, and she received Faustina with great amiability and informed her immediately, obviously to demonstrate what a reliable person she was, that she was known as Sora Olimpia and that she had just had a glass of magnesia; her digestion was so delicate that she could not take other laxatives. This was merely an opening move to encourage Faustina to confide in her.

"You quarreled last night, didn't you?" she went on with an understanding smile. "You must forgive me, I don't like being indiscreet, but while the maid was sweeping outside your room this morning she happened to put her eye to the keyhole and noticed that the gentleman was sleeping on the floor. You have nothing whatever to be ashamed of, my dear lady, such things happen in the best of families, and in any case it's obvious that you haven't been married for long. Oh, it's always very difficult at first. My husband and I quarreled regularly every night. Bride-grooms are always intolerably conceited, and what makes it worse is that they're so inexperienced they'd try the patience even of a saint. Would you like me to give you some practical advice, my dear lady?"

"For heaven's sake, no," Faustina had the strength to exclaim.

The landlord too had a good-natured air before breakfast; he was jovial, familiar, and attentive. If you wanted anything you only had to ask, Sor Quintino was always at your service. He met Pietro on the stairs and could not refrain from commiserating with him on having spent the night on the cold, hard floor.

"There's no need to explain, no harm was done, it doesn't worry me in the slightest, you get used to seeing the most extraordinary things when you run a hotel," he said. "When my wife was dusting the stairs this morning she happened to put her eye to the keyhole, and so she noticed that you were sleeping on the floor. At first she was frightened and thought, saving everyone present, that you were dead. She sent for me, but I reassured her. It's a shame to sleep on the floor when you have a wife as pretty as yours, but don't lose heart, my friend, it's always difficult at first. The best advice I can give you is to persevere. It's well known that women embark on marriage with the most amazing demands, equaled only by their crass ignorance. Even a hermit would lose patience with them. You have no children yet? That's bad, my friend, bad. If I can give you any practical advice . . . forgive me, I have no desire to offend you."

In the ground-floor room that was also used as a bar Faustina and Pietro silently sipped their black coffee as if it were hemlock.

"Forgive me," Sora Olimpia asked, stopping her sweeping for a moment, "but was it the *commendatore* who gave you our address?"

"How did you guess that?" Pietro replied with the most confidential smile he could muster.

"How is the *commendatore*? Is he well?"

"Very well indeed," Pietro assured her vaguely. "He's as impressive, as optimistic, as eloquent as every true *commendatore* is."

"And his gout?" the landlady asked solicitously. "Has he had any more attacks?"

"Oh, yes, the gout, indeed he has," Pietro admitted, sighing sadly and making a gesture implying submission to destiny. "But who does not have gout? In a sense, it's one of the inevitable consequences of optimism, and in this country most people prefer it to typhus."

"True," said Sora Olimpia, taking a seat beside her guests. "We must be patient. If you have figs you have to put up with the skin," she went on. "In August, when the *commendatore* comes here with his lady, we always give him the room you have now; we've actually gotten into the habit of calling it the *commendatore*'s room."

"Oh, what an honor," Pietro exclaimed, raising his hat.

"The *commendatore* spends his summer vacation at Acquaviva, he comes here every year from Rome," the landlady went on. "In a way he's the protector of the village. Strictly between ourselves, for several years past he has promised to make Acquaviva a vacation resort, but there are the usual difficulties. He says our present altitude is insufficient; twenty-five hundred feet for a vacation resort is ridiculous, it's nothing at all, what village is not twenty-five hundred feet high? he keeps telling us. So he has undertaken to persuade the government to increase our allowance of altitude, but there are obstacles to be overcome. When you consider the fact that there are completely unimportant places as high as six thousand or ten thousand feet that don't know what to do with it, it's really not fair that we should be permanently stuck at twenty-five hundred, because, after all, we pay taxes too, and what taxes. So the *commendatore* undertook to persuade the government to increase our allowance at least to thirty-five or thirty-six hundred feet, to enable Acquaviva to become a health resort and give business here a boost. Of course, the *commendatore* keeps telling us that to persuade the government to make the tourist authorities grant us a higher altitude it's absolutely essential to oil the wheels; he says he must oil the wheels, oil the wheels, and keep on oiling the wheels. He says that the state is a delicate piece of machinery that needs constant oiling. We're not well off, but we do the best we can. We send a ham, a cheese, and a salami sausage to Rome every year. It's not to pester them, but when he comes here with his wife in the summer we put them up for nothing. He always tells us that for the sake of the cause we must keep our mouths shut and not breathe a word to a soul, but as you're friends of his."

"I know all about it," Pietro murmured with an air of mystery.

"Oh, so the *commendatore* told you?" said Sora Olimpia, passing from occupational amiability to conspiratorial fellowship.

"Yes, he asked me to give him a hand in bringing that magnificent project of his to a successful conclusion," said Pietro in the tones of one who has already said too much.

"I see," Sora Olimpia hastened to reassure him in an undertone, with the air and gestures of an accomplice. "I'm only too aware of the difficulties. But now, alas, the whole thing has been shelved, as I have no need to tell you, for the *commendatore* will certainly have told you himself. The war has been our ruin. It seems that the government was just on the point of deciding to change our altitude and give us forty-two hundred feet, a very decent allocation, that is to say, it would have made us and we should have been well and truly in the saddle, when the new war in Africa broke out. The *commendatore* explained to us that there's a moratorium on altitudes for the duration of the war, which is displeasing but very understandable, with a war on there's little one can say."

"In spite of the war," Pietro suggested flatteringly, "the chill in the air this morning is that of an altitude much greater than twenty-four hundred feet. You can't complain."

"But it's no good to us," Sora Olimpia said sadly. "In the absence of recognition by the government it's a wasted chill."

"Do not give up hope," Pietro announced with a confident and authoritative gesture. "Look, Sora Olimpia, I am not authorized to say more, at any rate not for the time being. But I know that a woman like you can take a hint. All I can say is: do not give up hope."

To avoid yielding to sudden emotion Sora Olimpia had to lean against the table.

"Did you perhaps come here," she plucked up courage to ask in a thin little trickle of a voice, "did they perhaps send you here to increase our altitude? In the next few days?"

"I've said too much already," Pietro interrupted.

A ray of sunshine came in through the window and shone on Sora Olimpia's face, which bore the marks of deep feeling; her tawny hair turned out to have been horribly dyed. She looked imploringly at Faustina, as if to remind her that there should be no secrets between women.

"Your hair is beautiful, Sora Olimpia," Pietro went on in the tones of a connoisseur, "but I don't want any of it in the soup. Spinach and hair are the only vegetables I can't stand."

Faustina and Pietro were just on the point of going out when the landlady presented them with the two obligatory forms to be filled in by new arrivals and submitted later to the *carabinieri*.

"The usual formalities," she said. "And also so that we may have the honor of knowing with whom we are dealing."

"When we come back," Pietro said distractedly. "In the meantime please ask your husband to look after the horse."

"Let's go for a walk," Faustina suggested when they were in the street. "Let's find somewhere where we can talk in peace."

Outside the inn there was a small rectangular square. It was full of shops with bombastic signs imitating those to be seen in towns: HAIRDRESSING SALON, HAT EMPORIUM, PRIZEWINNING PASTA MADE HERE, NATIONAL FASCIST PARTY, NATIONAL ORGANIZATION FOR RECREATIONAL ACTIVITIES, NATIONAL ASSOCIATION OF ARTISANS. In one corner, over a door leading to a cellar, there was a single word in black on the whitewashed wall. WINE, it said (also BEER). This was enough to persuade Pietro.

"We must go and have a glass of wine there this evening," he said to Faustina. "You drink, don't you?"

"If it gives you pleasure," she replied.

Snow was piled against the houses in the short space between the doors; the area in the middle of the square where vehicles passed was full of slush; trickles of yellowish water carried bits of ice and animal dung and other refuse into side puddles. Pietro stood rooted to the spot; he was absorbed in admiration of a strange monument on a tall, thin marble pedestal in the middle of the square.

"A beet," he exclaimed at the top of his voice with tears in his eyes. "Look, Faustina, isn't it wonderful? They have erected a monument to the beet here."

Tradesmen and apprentices came hurrying from the shops to gape at the two strangers.

"As a citizen of the Fucino basin in which beets abound and as a Marsican," he announced, addressing the bystanders in mildly emphatic tones, "I am especially grateful to you for having honored this humble but useful plant. Sugar is extracted from it, as you know."

Among those present was a distinguished gentleman, perhaps a local dignitary, to whom it seemed sacrilegious that the populace should be given something to laugh at as the result of a simple mistake. But Pietro's serious appearance, the genuine feeling and total lack of irony in what he said, and above all the quality of his fur coat, as well as the presence of a beautiful young woman who protectively put her arm in his, must have persuaded him that it was merely a mistake and that there was therefore no need to call the *carabinieri*. So with the smile of a benevolent guide he explained to Pietro that he was in fact admiring the bust of a local benefactor. It was the snow that had temporarily given it a shape halfway between that of a pear and a turnip, and if he went closer he would be able to read the benefactor's name on the pedestal.

Faustina politely thanked the stranger for this valuable information and dragged Pietro away; he was disappointed and upset.

"I don't want to criticize you, Pietro," Faustina said to him, "but it would be a good idea if you consulted me next time before making a public speech."

"Are you afraid of compromising yourself?"

"I say that for your sake; you create the impression of being, how shall I put it? Slightly disoriented."

"Seriously, Faustina, we shall become good friends if you overcome the temptation to treat me as a wet nurse treats her baby. I could be your father, after all."

"Oh, Pietro, how can you talk such nonsense? You know very well that you're only four or five years older than I am."

"What has age to do with it? The important thing about a father is his appearance."

Acquaviva was a big agricultural and bureaucratic center on top of a watermelon-shaped hill that rose like an island in the middle of the valley. It was buffeted by winds from all quarters of the compass. It was built on a fishbone pattern, with a main street that extended from one end of the hill to the other representing the backbone and side streets running off it.

"Let us go and meet Cherubino," Pietro said, suddenly remembering. "He won't be long now."

"We could wait for them at some quiet spot where we could talk in peace," Faustina suggested.

The main street was lined with white public buildings with facades in the neocolonial style, and some handsome patrician houses, now uninhabited, bolted and barred, and shored up to prevent them from collapsing.

"As you see, Faustina, we are reduced to orthopedics," Pietro said at the top of his voice, like a schoolmaster on an educational outing.

Landlords, office workers, artisans, and shopkeepers lived on the main street and *cafoni* on the side streets. Halfway along the main street there was a huge church, dating perhaps from the fourteenth or fifteenth century but obviously restored, enlarged, and disfigured by each succeeding generation of worshipers. Above the door there was a niche with the statue of a saint in the act of giving a blessing; the niche was decorated like a baldachin, with drapery, tassels, fringes, and plump little angels on stucco clouds. Pietro was seized with pity for the saint who was obliged to remain night and day in his niche; his skinny hand raised in the act of blessing reminded him of a child putting up his hand at school when he wants the teacher's permission to leave the room.

"At my school," Pietro told Faustina, "the smallest room was for decency's sake referred to as the *licet*; the school provided a classical education, you see."

The poor old man in his niche looked very pale and exhausted from having waited so long.

"Run along, then," Pietro called out to him with a benevolent smile. "Run along, quickly."

And, as people did not understand what was happening and came rushing up to see, Faustina took Pietro's arm and hurried him away, taking the first turn they came to. It was not so much a street as a sequence of puddles, with fetid slum dwellings on either side, dilapidated walls, small black hovels that looked like rubbish dumps, and women in the doorways who looked like dark specters. Hardly anyone was about except for an occasional bent and silent *cafone* with an unshaven, bony face, walking with the slow, lethargic gait of peasants in winter. They were pale, sad, hostile people and looked like refugees, though they had lived on that hill for a thousand years and it was they who had built the church, the patrician houses, and the main street.

"It's a Christian ghetto," Pietro explained to reassure Faustina, who was horrified. "But don't be afraid, these people are unfortunately resigned."

On the doorstep of one hovel a mother was drying her little girl's tears and saying: "Don't cry, darling, what's the good of crying?" But she was crying herself, and no one wiped way her tears or told her not to cry. Faustina clung to Pietro's arm. At one point the alley widened into a muddy open space with a little fountain and a drinking trough. Some small donkeys tied together in charge of a boy had plunged their black, thick lips into the cold water and looked at each other at close quarters with big, sad eyes. How much more hunger and thirst, how many more heavy loads and beatings were still to come their way? The lane gave on to the valley, and led down to it by a steep, neglected track between two prickly hedges. In some places the track was still covered with snow; an icy brook leaped and scurried down along one side of it; one could see the water dashing along and foaming and hear its murmur through the ice, in which twigs, stones, clods of dung and scraps of hay and straw were imprisoned and preserved. Faustina and Pietro had to hold hands to save themselves from falling. Eventually they reached a small, flat open space outside a tiny church that was evidently no longer used. Through a shutterless window they could see a poor, wooden altar, and on it a colored plaster statue of San Martino giving away his cloak. Huge spiderwebs filled the corners of the ceiling, and a great deal of yellow dust, the result of generations of woodworms, lay at the foot of the altar. The branch of a cherry tree entered the church through a window, showing the way to the wind, the snow, and the rain; when the cherries were ripe it would be a pretty sight. On a yellow wall there was a faded fresco, and it was still possible to make out a faint green outline representing two skeletons playing a flute and a lyre with the inscription: THE BONES OF THE HUMBLE SHALL REJOICE.

"The bones?" Faustina said with a shudder. "Why only the bones?"

"Perhaps," Pietro suggested to cheer her, "perhaps it doesn't mean a temporary and superficial rejoicing, only of the skin and the muscles, or only of the eyes and ears, but a rejoicing of the whole being, a lasting, deep joy that will make even the bones rejoice. One day, Faustina, if I ever again become the editor of a working-class newspaper, I'll have a motto on the front page saying: PROLETARIANS AND CAFONI OF ALL COUNTRIES, UNITE: THE BONES OF THE HUMBLE SHALL REJOICE."

Faustina and Pietro sat on the doorstep of the church, which was free of snow and dry, as it faced south; but drops of water followed one another along the branches of the cherry tree and dripped one by one, shining for a moment, onto the wall behind Faustina's back. From this vantage point they could see a long stretch of road, and they would be able to see their friends from Colle approaching; they would be able to go and meet them and agree about what to do before entering the village. This slope of the hill on which Acquaviva was built seemed to be completely covered with vineyards divided up into irregular squares and rectangles and separated from one another by low dry walls and rows of almond and cherry trees. It was warm where they were sitting, and Faustina took off the scarf she had had around her neck, thus revealing the perfect curve of her throat, the delicate shell of her ear, the pure line of her chin. After a long silence she said:

"Pietro, do you think you'll be able to stand living for any length of time in a place like this?"

There was a great deal of anxiety in the question; and Pietro thought before replying.

"A village," he said finally, "isn't the houses, the streets, the shops, but the people who live in it. The most beautiful village is where one's best friends live, that's where one's real home is. In that sense you're perfectly right, to us Acquaviva is still a steppe and a desert. But let's wait for Simone. He knows one or two people here whom he talks about with great respect; we'll meet them, and then we'll see."

"Pietro," Faustina said again, "even if we make friends with some decent *cafone* or artisan, do you think you'll be able to put up with a place like this?"

Pietro disliked the way in which Faustina said "a place like this," so he hesitated to reply.

"Perhaps I expressed myself badly," he explained. "What I meant was that with you and Simone I could easily live in hell itself."

Faustina blushed. She shared his attitude in the matter, but it didn't square with the practical difficulties.

"When we get back to the inn," she pointed out, "we shall have to fill in the form that has to be submitted to the *carabinieri*, and we may be asked for some sort of identity papers. I'm afraid there may be complications."

"Don't worry about that nonsense, Faustina," Pietro said with a laugh. "Apart from the verbal reference supplied by the *commendatore*, I have in my pocket the papers of Simone Ortiga, respected agriculturalist and well-known chicken breeder, which, I assure you, will be more than sufficient. Simone is twenty years older than I am, but it isn't age that counts in these matters, it's appearance, and you can't deny that our profiles are exactly alike. Not to mention our characters; in that respect we're twins. Simone is bringing more papers with him, and there'll be a choice. Let me assure you, Faustina, that no underground worker has ever suffered from lack of stamped documents. In my former party we actually had trouble for a time because we had too many. I once

spent a month in prison at Marseilles because an indiscreet policeman found three passports on me, all with my photograph but
in three different names, and I had to admit that that was two too
many. Moderation is advisable even in the use of false papers.
Moderation does not exclude keeping alert, and I shall try, here
and elsewhere, not to arouse the suspicions of the police unless it
is absolutely unavoidable. For that I rely on their natural obtuse-
ness and my own wits. And, Faustina, let me tell you that I've
never believed in danger; in one way or another I've always managed to extricate myself."

"Can one love someone without trembling for his safety?"
Faustina asked.

"Of course not," Pietro replied. "But there's no point in exaggerating dangers. Try to imagine how easy life is for a person who
believed he was dying, was resigned to death, spent weeks in a
kind of tomb, as it were, is still believed by many to be dead, but
instead has come back and walks about among men and talks to
them. Think of the ease and self-confidence of a man who has
risen from the dead. Everything that life now offers or shows me,
this poor gray stone, that pallid sun that heralds the spring, that
graceful reddish branch on the hillside, above all your lovely and
loving presence, is an extra, a gift, an entirely gratuitous grace.
The extent to which the sense of death can revive the sense of life
is incredible, Faustina. No living being can appreciate his good
fortune if he has never been close to death or on intimate terms
with it. I now feel that life is clearer, simpler, calmer; life itself
being a kind of happiness, I can renounce happiness without its
being a sacrifice."

"Don't you think, Pietro," Faustina murmured, avoiding his
eyes, "that personal attachment is necessary to enable one to live?
Is there such a thing as happiness in the void?"

"I don't want you to think I'm purer than I really am," Pietro
replied. "I'm not an ascetic. Oh, no, I'm anything but an ascetic.
When I awoke this morning and saw you . . . Faustina, do you
think our friends will be long now?"

"My dear, I don't know. When you saw me this morning . . .

Look, when I think it over," Faustina went on, making an effort, "when I think it over, Pietro, it seems to me that the only real thing in my life was the memory that, as an adolescent, I kept of you. It was a mere memory of something that was never expressed, while the life I lived in reality was an adaptation to a succession of fictions and, in the case of the less depressing experiences, a sublimation of the commonplace. When I think about it, it doesn't seem to me to have been living at all. For me the past has the uncertainty, the unsubstantiality, the unreality of a dream, or the memory of something in a book. The first cigarette I smoked when I was fourteen was of course disgusting, and made me feel sick, but with goodwill and the aid of time and a mirror I learned how to do it, and now it has become a so-called necessity to me. All I remember of the first time I was kissed was the man's bad breath that smelled of alcohol and his prickly mustache. But what a lot of poetry has been written about the first kiss. Most girls, to avoid seeming inferior to others, end up substituting fine phrases for the disgusting memory and thinking of the first kiss as an enchanting experience in Armida's garden. At every stage in my life I have had to submit to fictions and pretend pleasures and admirations I did not feel. To me the day of my first communion, from five in the morning till evening, was a day of exhausting torment; the white dress, the crowd, the music in church, the lunch, the presents were the principal events. I went up to the altar with a splitting headache and I had to concentrate all my little remaining strength to avoid collapsing. But the prayer book said I was to remember it as the most beautiful day in my life. Some years later at school the sister ecstatically read us Dante's *Paradiso*. Pietro, you'll think me sacrilegious if I shamelessly admit that I preferred Pinocchio. But I pretended to admire the *Paradiso* to avoid seeming stupid."

"I preferred the story of Bertoldo to the *Paradiso*," Pietro admitted with a laugh.

"But later, when I was very ill," Faustina went on, "Donna Maria Vincenza read me the *Paradiso* and, perhaps because I was very fond of her, or perhaps because I was very weak, I thought it sublime. In the course of the years I accepted many other opinions; I wasn't able to remake the world from top to bottom. The rose is the queen of the garden, the lion is the king of the jungle, the eagle is the queen of the Alps, Italy is the garden of Europe, woman is the angel of the family, all the most brilliant inventions have been made by Italians, honor once lost cannot be regained. Amen. In view of my goodwill in the matter and my acquired capacity for simulation, I had the sacred right to hope that I would end up like any girl of good family as the wife of an honest and thrifty husband who after three months of marriage would deceive me with the maid; but let us shut one eye, pretend not to notice, the honor of the family and the future of the children far outweigh the importance of such trivialities. If I have been spared that worthy goal, it was through no merit or fault of my own. Pietro, I haven't yet had the courage to talk to you about certain misfortunes that happened to me, and perhaps I never shall, because to do so I should need the permission of someone who is dead. Having been the heroine of a matrimonial scandal, I was automatically excluded from the career of respectable married woman and mother of a family and had to accept the fiction of being a free woman or, as our chivalrous people politely put it, a kept woman; providential fictions, I hasten to add, because they resolve the problem once and for all. You know from the beginning the part you are expected to play, how you are expected to dress and get yourself up, how to laugh and how to walk, and what are your rights and duties. This is truly a classical country, Pietro, the play is still performed by the same four or five characters as before the time of Christ and in accordance with the same old rules."

"Please, Faustina," Pietro interrupted, "don't feel obliged to tell me anything you don't want to."

"I've been waiting all my life for an opportunity to talk to you about these things. No, I have never been alone. I had the good fortune to find a real gentleman as my fellow performer and stage colleague in the comedy of my life. I very much hope, Pietro, that you'll have an opportunity of meeting Severino, because I'm sure you'll like him. In short, given the times we live in, I shouldn't complain. But sometimes I have the feeling that I've never lived, that I'm still a larva, clinging with torn hands to the gate beyond which life begins, condemned to looking beyond it without ever being able to pass that threshold. Sometimes I feel that my strength is failing, that my blood is slowly ebbing away, that I'm going to pieces. Heavens, if only before I died it were granted me to be able to stop the playacting, escape from the nightmare, drop the fictitious, and pass that threshold, go beyond it and live. I'd accept any penance, prison, lunatic asylum, convent, eternal damnation; but first I want to go beyond it. Forgive me, Pietro, if I create the impression of being crazy. At other times I tell myself, I repeat, that the trouble is only my lack of resignation, that this is human life, that it has always been like this and cannot be otherwise, and that one must put up with it. Our forefathers played this comedy for thousands of years and were patient, so why should I not be patient too? Unfortunately I'm still young, perhaps that's why it's so difficult; but youth will pass and resignation will come, and then the stillness of death. What's the use of always wondering who I am and what is the meaning of this life? I repeat that to myself, I try to convince myself, to hypnotize myself into believing it. But my mind protests, it refuses to accept it, and I'm back again where I started from."

"Solitude is the only thing that's really intolerable," Pietro said. "If one loves, what does anything else matter?"

"But if the object of one's love is in one's imagination, there's no difference between it and madness."

A peasant woman appeared with a goat and looked at them in surprise; she turned around several times to look at them again.

"We must seem two refugees, two fugitives," Faustina said.

"Two escapees," said Pietro.

"Pietro, isn't that man with the donkey down there Simone?" Faustina asked.

"No," Pietro replied immediately, "he doesn't walk like that; and that donkey isn't Cherubino, Cherubino looks quite different."

"Can you tell the difference at this distance?"

"Yes, I think I could even with my eyes shut. But now it's

midday already; can't you hear the bell? It must be the town hall clock; they'll be expecting us for lunch at the inn."

Pietro and Faustina counted the strokes. Improbably, the town hall clock struck twenty-six times.

"It can't be a clock," said Faustina.

"What else could it be?"

"There's no such thing as twenty-six o'clock."

"Perhaps our *commendatore* introduced it to Acquaviva," Pietro suggested. "A *commendatore* can do anything if he sets his mind to it."

"Yes, it must have been the *commendatore*," Faustina gravely admitted.

Meanwhile a warm breath of sirocco had arisen and the earth began to breathe. The snow began to melt on the highest slopes, and patches of yellow grass appeared. Melting snow formed a rivulet on the path they took to get back to the top of the hill. It was as if innumerable transparent snakes coalesced with each other, separated and multiplied, assumed the color of things, became liquid earth, liquid stone, liquid wood. The trunks and branches of the trees shone with crystal-clear water.

"It'll soon be spring," Faustina said quietly.

There was sudden hope in her voice. Pietro picked a blade of new grass from a snowy clump of earth and ceremoniously offered it to her as if it were a rose, though it was an ordinary, pale green blade of grass.

"Oh, how deliciously it smells," she said with a laugh, putting it in her buttonhole. "It has a lovely earthy smell."

"Let's go back this way," Pietro suggested. "It will get us back quicker."

"Have you been in this part of the world before?" Faustina asked. "How do you know the shortcuts?"

"Oh, I'm like a mountain hare, I can tell the way by the scent."

The shortcut was steep and stony. Pietro went ahead, and when he turned around after a short while he saw that the girl's cheeks were pearly with tears.

"Are you all right? Would you like to rest?" he asked solicitously.

"My dear, I was thinking that all the sorrow of my life was a preparation for the joy of today," she answered with feeling. "I wish that God, who is seeing and listening to us now, would become visible for a moment so that I could fling myself on my knees and kiss His feet."

He bent over her and embraced and kissed her.

"You have a strange fragrance," said Pietro, putting his face close to her hair. "An ancient fragrance, the fragrance of which the sacred books speak, the fragrance of Christian girls disinterred after centuries and found uncorrupted."

"What are you saying, Pietro? A graveyard smell? A corpselike smell?"

"No, on the contrary. A smell of nard, violets, lemon."

"A smell of death?"

"No, of resurrection, of spring."

"It must be the water here, and this air; but why are you smiling like that?"

"A distant memory of you has just occurred to me. In the chapel at our school there was a picture by Patini representing the glory of the Sacrament. One of the angels surrounding the Host bore a striking resemblance to you. I mentioned this at home, and they told me that the painter actually used your face as his model for the picture."

"I must have been about ten at the time," Faustina said with a laugh. "Patini came to our house several times."

"After that, of course, I could no longer take my eyes off you in chapel. The other boys ended up noticing it and made fun of me."

"So I was already a cause of scandal?"

"No, of worship. Perhaps, if I hadn't seen you among the angels every day, I might have had the courage to confess to you . . ."

"You still have time."

Again he embraced and kissed her tenderly.

"We must hurry," she said.

The shortcut brought them out onto the main road in a few minutes. At the first shop Faustina bought bread and honey to make *crostini,* a specialty of hers. The street was now very busy.

The wives of office workers were on the lookout at doors and windows, ready to finish cooking the pasta as soon as they spotted their husbands in the distance.

"What's happening outside our inn?" Pietro asked in alarm.

Outside the Victory (formerly Commercial) Hotel two *carabinieri* were waiting, together with a number of other individuals who began talking to one another in a by no means reassuring way when they spotted the two strangers.

"They seem to me to be waiting for us," Faustina murmured, gripping Pietro's arm. "Don't you see how they're looking at us? Run for it, Pietro, quick."

"It would be too late in any case," Pietro said. "If we keep our heads, perhaps we may be able to brazen it out."

"Pietro, I shan't allow anyone to touch you," said Faustina, who was pale and agitated. "I'll scratch out the eyes of the first person who approaches you."

However, a few yards away from the inn an unexpected performance awaited them. The two *carabinieri* stiffened to attention and brought their hands to the peak of their hats in a smart military salute, while the others present respectfully raised their hats. Pietro was so taken aback that he hardly returned this greeting.

"Drama is certainly pursuing us," he whispered. "Go in quickly, Faustina, let's go and eat."

"Have you the faintest idea what this is all about?" Faustina whispered, responding to the salutations of those present with exaggerated bows and smiles.

Sor Quintino, wearing a chef's white hat, came bustling in; he was deferential, anxious to please, and also embarrassed.

"I've set for you in the private room," he said. "What can I offer you?"

"Anything you like so long as it isn't spaghetti," Pietro replied.

Sor Quintino had to apologize for a most regrettable incident.

"A most unfortunate thing happened to the maid while doing your room," he said in an abashed tone. "I'm terribly upset about it, and I implore you to forgive the wretched woman, who is the mother of many children, all young. What happened was that the poor woman carelessly dropped your suitcases on the floor, with the result that they opened."

"The suitcases were on the floor," Pietro pointed out.

"To sweep the floor she had to put them on the dressing table," the landlord said.

"There is no dressing table in our room," Faustina interrupted.

"No dressing table? Oh, madam, you must forgive me, I'll remedy that immediately. I'll send one up from my room at once, a dressing table with a mirror. You must forgive me for not having done so before, but I must say in self-defense that we didn't know whom we had the honor of putting up. When the *carabinieri* came to inquire an hour ago I had to tell them that the lady and gentleman had gone out for a walk and had not yet filled in the form, though I was able to assure them that they were friends of the *commendatore*. Just at that moment the maid came down in floods of tears and told us about the unfortunate accident that had happened to her. To sweep the floor of your room the poor woman, as I was saying, had to put the suitcases on the bed and, as was to be feared, they fell to the ground and opened. To see for myself what damage had been done by that unhappy woman (though I implore you to forgive her, I swear it won't happen again), I hurried to your room and indeed found the suitcases still open on the floor. Shall I tell you the truth, Captain? At the sight of your silver medals, the uniforms, the diplomas, the certificates, the many photographs, particularly the one of the martial scene in which you are riding your horse at the head of your squadron, as well as others in which you are wearing the colonial helmet, I dashed downstairs four steps at a time and told the *carabinieri* and my wife and everyone else who was present that providence had sent a hero to our house. Does the lady feel unwell?"

Pietro was just in time to catch Faustina and put her on a chair to prevent her from collapsing in a faint.

"It's nothing, it's the sirocco," Sor Quintino said with a knowledgeable smile.

He called his wife to come to Faustina's assistance.

With her head resting on Pietro's shoulder as he sat beside her,

Faustina remained deathly pale and as if inanimate for some time; she did not answer his anxious and affectionate questions and appeals, and showed no sign of having heard them. Her pulse was almost imperceptible, and when she at last opened her eyes again they were terror-stricken. With Sora Olimpia's help Pietro lifted her and took her to their room. The landlady was prodigal with lamentations and kindness and maternal advice.

"Fainting like this is nothing to worry about, my dear lady," she said with a smile. "It's a healthy sign. When I was expecting my first, I felt faint whenever there was a sirocco."

The suitcases were still open in the middle of the room. Instead of Pietro's underwear, the uniforms, equipment, and other reminders of the military life of Captain Saverio Spina were revealed. The locks had evidently been systematically picked. Lying on the bed with her hair loosened over the pillows and her arms motionless by her side, Faustina's whole person revealed a death-like dismay and a childish delicacy, charm, and frailty.

"Won't you help me put her to bed?" Sora Olimpia said to Pietro.

But he muttered an unintelligible excuse and left the room. To avoid inquisitive questioning by the customers who were lunching downstairs, he hesitated for some moments, uncertain what to do, and ended up sitting on the staircase like a boy told to wait outside during a doctor's visit. He rose when he thought he could go back into the room without being indiscreet, but just when he was turning the handle of the door Sora Olimpia came and said: "Madam asks you to leave her alone."

Pietro left the inn and wandered about the main street like a soul in torment. He walked up and down the same part of the street ten times in succession, and then spent a long time gazing into a shop window as if in a trance. When he noticed that the goods on display were gravestones and funeral wreaths he had a moment of terror and hurried back to the hotel as if fearing a disaster. The expression on his face silenced even Sora Olimpia. He went up the stairs two at a time and stopped for a moment outside the door to recover his breath. He found Faustina in bed, her back and head supported by a mountain of pillows. She was pale, aged, distraught; her features were hollow and her big eyes looked dead, almost glassy. On the night table there was a bottle of water, a small glass with two round syrupy-looking objects, perhaps cherries in alcohol, and some medicine bottles containing sedatives.

"How do you feel?" Pietro asked in a voice stifled by emotion. "Are you better?"

Faustina tried to smile, but her eyes filled with tears. "Was it this morning, Pietro," she said, "that we sat together outside that little church dedicated to St. Martin? Yes, of course, it was today, actually only three or four hours ago. To me years seem to have passed since then. What we said to each other this morning, sitting on the doorstep of that little church, was beautiful," she went on. "It was a beautiful dream. But in a few days' time, after too much brooding about it, I shan't know whether we were really there together or whether it was something I once read many years ago in some forbidden book."

"As soon as you're well enough to get up, Faustina, we'll go for that walk again," said Pietro. "Soon it will be spring, and the violets will be out under the hedges along those paths."

"As soon as I can get up, Pietro, without wasting a moment, I must go back to Orta," Faustina said.

The girl's face, changed by suffering, displayed an inflexible determination. Pietro approached her, but she was imprisoned in her grief and did not seem to see or hear him. Her staring eyes were turned toward him and did not avoid his; but they did not seem to see him, and perhaps it was not him that she saw, but a ghost. With her hand she made a gesture of infinite weariness. The emotion flooding Pietro was revealed only by the great effort he made to contain it; to hide his tears he went over to the window and pretended to take an interest in the goings-on in the street. The monument in the middle of the square had been freed from its covering of snow, and instead of the handsome turnip that had been before there was now a bearded and mustached bust suitable for display in the window of a barbershop. Some sweepers with big wooden shovels were clearing the streets. The roofs of the houses steamed, and the eaves poured water from the melting snow on to the pavement. Women dressed in black crossed the square, carrying little black prayer books with red-bordered pages.

"Pietro," Faustina called out.

He turned, went over to the bed, and timidly took her hand.

"You had no lunch, Pietro," she said reproachfully. "You mustn't neglect yourself so much, you're a real baby."

He could no longer master his anguish. "Look, Faustina, what matters is not living together, though it would be marvelous; the important, the essential thing, whether we're together or separated, Faustina, is caring for each other. There are men and women who spend thirty or forty years of their lives together, who live chained to each other from morning to night like galley slaves, at the table, in bed, when they go for walks or go to the movies, who are inseparable but inside are strangers to each other or, what is worse, enemies. But what you told me about your life this morning, Faustina, entered my soul and will stay there as long as I live. What would I not give, Faustina, to free you from that obsessive despair of yours. If you think you'll feel calmer, safer, less unhappy at Orta, you must of course go there as soon as you can. Simone will be arriving today, and he'll be able to go with you. There's no need to go back the hard way across the mountain; you can take the train to Fossa, and from there a carriage to Orta."

"Pietro," Faustina interrupted him, "do you think your grandmother will ever know we spent a night together at a hotel? Do you think anything can be done to prevent her from ever knowing?"

Faustina had another attack of dizziness; she shut her eyes, breathed with difficulty, and gripped the sides of the bed as if to prevent herself from plunging into an abyss. Pietro was at a loss; he did not know what to do to help her, what medicine to offer her, whether to send for a doctor. He sat by the bedside, took her hand, caressed it, and said again: "Courage, darling, go as soon as you can, you can go tomorrow if you like."

"Now I feel better," Faustina said at last, drying her brow, which was wet with perspiration. "At times I feel that my skull is being filled with hot water, boiling water, and that the lobes of my brain are dancing about like gnocchi in a cooking pot. Our kind of gnocchi, made of flour and potatoes. It wasn't for nothing that when I was a child my mother always told me that my head was full of potatoes. Pietro, have you ever had the feeling that time suddenly stands still? For a few seconds the world seems black and funereal; if it lasted a little longer it would inevitably be the end of the world. And, Pietro, have you noticed that after each of those dreadful stoppages time goes backward before it resumes its forward march again? I think it really does go backward, it's like at the movies when the projector is put into reverse and you see a tower blown up by a mine, for instance, being miraculously restored, every stone flying back to its place. To me there's nothing more frightening, Pietro."

"Faustina, can't I give you anything for your headache?"

"There's nothing that's any good against the real headache, Pietro, at any rate my kind of headache. There's a secret I ought to tell you, Pietro, so that you should understand, but I dare not tell you; I've never told anyone. But you're the only person to whom I can tell a secret of that kind. Sit down and listen. When I was thirteen or fourteen, I took part for the first time in spiritual exercises at the end of Lent with about fifteen other girls of roughly the same age under the direction of a Capuchin friar. You know what such spiritual exercises consist of, I don't think there's any difference between those for men and those for women. For five days we pledged ourselves to complete silence, listened to three sermons a day, read the devotional books we were told to read, and applied ourselves to meditation, to an examination of conscience on the lines laid down for us. The theme chosen for our exercises that year was the Passion of Our Lord, His sufferings on the cross. The Capuchin father talked to us so vividly about those sufferings that some of us were so terrified that we felt ill. He told us that we could relieve those sufferings by remaining or becoming virtuous, humble, and honest, and ourselves assuming part of the agony of the crucified Jesus. I knew I was neither virtuous nor humble, and at that age I already knew myself well enough to have no illusions about my possible improvement. But I wanted at all costs to relieve Our Lord's physical suffering, and it was intolerable to me to think that, though I could have helped Him, I had done nothing to do so. So when the exercises were over I spent a whole night on my knees in my little room, praying to Jesus and weeping and imploring Him to give me His crown of thorns, to take it at any rate sometimes from His innocent holy brow and put it on mine. Oh, Pietro, I'm positive, I'm sure, that that prayer of mine was answered. That's why I have those inhuman headaches that have afflicted me ever since, and that's why sedatives are useless. Sometimes I can distinctly feel the thorns going right through my skull. And how can I complain? For I asked for them myself."

Her sad eyes suddenly revealed the depths of her sadness; she closed them and scarcely felt Pietro's caress.

"I don't know whether it's from this moment that I love you or whether I've done so for centuries," he said tenderly, bending over her. "My love," he went on, "I now know that I can never leave you again. I could never again live in the desert of your absence."

22

ID YOU SEE HER?" Pietro asked. "How is she? Did she give you a message for me?"

Simone grabbed the landlord's arm and told him to bring wine and not water. "And bring something to eat," he said. "Get your wife to help you, if she isn't too dirty."

"How is Faustina? Is she better?" Pietro asked. "Did she give you a message for me?"

Simone poured out some wine.

"Drink, deaf-mute, wake up your ears," he said. "And you drink too, Pietro, I've a great deal to tell you."

Infante, leaning with his big head against the wall, was looking at Pietro, whom he had found again; he was delighted at having done so, and didn't bother about the wine. As Pietro waited for an answer, Simone was obliged to drink alone.

"Why didn't you come before? Did you have any difficulties? I expected you every day," said Pietro.

"The everlasting pill," Simone finally said with a sigh, completing the phrase with a gesture indicating it was all over.

"Oh, everything comes to an end," Pietro remarked, "even eternity. Did Don Tito get it?" he asked curiously.

"No, rather than that I should have cut his throat," said Simone. "Aunt Eufemia asked me for it and didn't give it back."

"Was she one of your clients?"

"When she felt she was dying she sent a pious woman to ask me for it," Simone replied. "I didn't honestly think I could refuse. Just imagine it, she and the pill were the oldest things in Colle."

"And she didn't give it back?"

"It was still inside her when she died."

The memory filled Simone with consternation, and Pietro adjusted his face accordingly; even Infante, though understanding nothing, did the same.

"She was found dead yesterday morning, but she must have died on the day you left," Simone said. "She pulled up her ladder that day and hadn't been seen since. The hungry meowing of her many cats first suggested that she might have died."

"And what about that famous fortune of hers? The ancient treasure that she was going to leave? Are all her nephews and nieces rich now?"

"The inventory of her possessions took place yesterday afternoon," Simone went on. "You can imagine how tense and excited her nephews and nieces were, in fact all of us. Two or three thousand persons must have gathered in the square in front of the ruins of the old De Dominicis house, but they made enough noise for fifty thousand. Even the small windows of the bell tower were crowded, and good families didn't mind mingling with the *cafoni*. Your grandmother's maid Natalina was beside herself with excitement. Perhaps I'll be leaving tomorrow, she kept telling everyone, *au revoir* or rather good-bye, good-bye. Before I arrived on the scene (I'd been busy all day getting ready to leave) it seems there was some shouting and arguing about choosing a committee of elders to attend the reading of the will, if there was one, and the taking of the inventory. The crowd of poorer nephews feared the usual abuse of power by the authorities and the richer nephews. When I turned up I was told that the crowd had insisted that I be put on the committee. Hundreds of arms pushed me toward the ladder, and up I went. The body, surrounded by candles and wreaths, had been placed on a table in the middle of the chapel.

The terrible Aunt Eufemia looked angry even in death; her hands and face had the dark, dry color of a liver sausage. I had never been in the chapel before; it was a curious mixture of junk shop and miraculous shrine. The air was unbreathable; the place smelled like a sewer. Thin, starving cats bit people's calves and sank their teeth in the candlesticks and chair legs. When I arrived the will hadn't yet been found. Don Sebastiano, the magistrate, was rubbing his hands with glee. There'll be a lovely lawsuit, he kept saying, a lovely suit between the nephews and nieces and the state that will last for at least a century. Don Nicolino had nearly finished drawing up an inventory of the furniture, pictures, and domestic utensils. Meanwhile the famous, legendary vats, the mysterious containers about which our old folk never tired of speculating on winter nights, had been discovered behind a red velvet curtain. The tension took our breath away. The vats, which were like those we use for the wine harvest but stronger and with double hoops, were at last uncovered. When the first moment of general stupefaction was over, I was the only person who burst out laughing; I was told later that it was audible all the way to Mastro Eutimio's carpenter's shop a couple of hundred yards away. The nephews and nieces responded to this unexpected, high-pitched, unseemly cackle with a terrified shudder, because their first thought was that Aunt Eufemia had been resurrected and that it was she who was laughing. The faces of the notables and the elders standing around the three uncovered vats were masks expressing stunned consternation and bewilderment, while I could not control my laughter, which turned into an uninterrupted, derisive guffaw. The disgusted and horrified masks turned toward me and looked at me as if I had gone out of my mind, and a threatening murmur arose from the impatient crowd of nephews and nieces in the square. I was forgetting to tell you, Pietro, that the vats were full of, how shall I put it? the leftovers of Aunt Eufemia's digestive processes for many years past."

"What?" Pietro exclaimed, jumping to his feet. "Have I understood you correctly?"

"You have," said Simone.

"What an amazing woman," said Pietro after thinking about it for some time. "The virulence of her mind fully equaled her contempt for hygiene."

"Those poor nephews and nieces," said Simone. "They've lost even that hope."

"What stupidity, what recklessness on the part of the authorities to allow those vats to be uncovered in the presence of a public committee," said Pietro.

"Don Marcantonio had in fact suggested that they should be sealed and preserved as cult objects in a patriotic shrine at some suitable spot," Simone said, "but the notables convinced him that that would cause a revolution in Colle."

"I'm sorry you left Colle at such an exceptional time because of me," Pietro said.

"Don't talk nonsense, but drink," Simone interrupted him. "If I'm here, it's for selfish reasons. What is there left for me to do in Colle now? The pill was my only remaining link with tradition."

To avoid involving Simone and Infante in case he were arrested, Pietro remained at the Victory (formerly Commercial) Hotel. After the incident with the suitcases there was no alternative to the unpleasant one of assuming his dead uncle's identity. "Spina, Captain Saverio, born at Colle dei Marsi of Berardo and Maria Vincenza, married, no children, traveling for pleasure," was written in the register. Before she left Faustina had warned Sora Olimpia that Pietro must not be worried in any way.

"He's suffering from great nervous exhaustion," she confided in her ear. "The doctor has insisted that he must stay away from his family and his usual environment for some time, and said that if possible he must live among simple country folk."

Sor Quintino and the regular customers of the inn immediately concluded that this nervous exhaustion was a consequence of the captain's heroic life, with the result that every strange action or word of his, so far from being criticized or laughed at, was admired as evidence of patriotic virtue. Don Saverio had no need of this encouragement to behave in his own way. He even gave up worrying about the *carabiniere* sergeant after Sor Quintino told him that the latter was under investigation by his superiors and was not yet completely convinced that the presence of Captain Spina at Acquaviva was not in some way connected with the investigation. Don Saverio was careful to say nothing to diminish the sergeant's anxieties, and responded to his greetings with inquisitorial coldness. His rare appearances in the private bar always caused a sensation among the usual customers, who were conventional and timid bureaucrats. He exercised the fascination of a man who has nothing to fear, is immune from criticism, and can say whatever he likes, being protected by his past. Oh, military valor, how convenient it can be. Generally he was sad, aloof, with his mind on other things, and he did not sit at the table with the others or join in the conversation. One evening when the *podestà* made some polite remark to him he rudely replied: "Let me tell you that my kingdom is not of your world."

"Oh, of what world is it then?" the *podestà* asked in astonishment.

"Not yours," Don Saverio replied dryly. His outspokenness explained the uneasiness caused by his mere appearance but, as he was basically not ill natured, he would often add something to try to reassure them.

"Don't let me disturb you," he might say. "Please don't be frightened, the danger is not imminent."

A picture of a personage who was all jaw and neck and had the eyes of a man possessed hung on the wall facing the place where he usually sat. It was framed in red, white, and green, and underneath it there was a placard with the words: BEFORE EVERY DINNER PARTY DRINK AN AMARO SANT'AGOSTINO. During the first few evenings Don Saverio got to know all the regulars. Those who were not national or local government employees were all called professors. One professor gave mandolin lessons, another taught bicycle riding, a third was the local champion at the game of *bocce*, and the others occupied similar academic chairs. The most important character was the *podestà*, who had the reputation of being a cultivated and scholarly person; instead of saying "rain," for instance, he said "Jupiter Pluvius." He was the lion of the village, with a physique to match. He had a huge head, a red nose, big, drooping lips like those of a camel, and protruding eyebrows over his yellowish eyes.

"The *podestà* is a gentleman of the old school," Sor Quintino confided to Don Saverio. "He eats cheese with a knife and fork even when he's alone and there's nobody there to see."

What the *podestà* chiefly resented about Captain Spina was his dislike of pasta, because it seemed to conflict with his deeply rooted belief in the connection between spaghetti with tomato sauce and the Italian character.

"When I was living in Rome," he used to say (reminiscences of his life in the capital as a young man were his hobbyhorse), "I generally took my meals at a restaurant to which a celebrated demagogue, a longhaired, bearded agitator who was a well-known speaker for the communists at that time, used to go. I must confess that the natural repugnance I felt for that individual vanished when I noticed the voluptuous mental and physical pleasure and the subtle technique with which he introduced enormous forkfuls of spaghetti with tomato sauce into his big, voracious mouth. I confess that I couldn't resist the impulse to rise and approach him and say to him in a voice charged with emotion: sir, I see now that you are not a stranger to the sense of national unity. Sir, he replied politely, political theories may divide us, but pasta unites us. Several years later, when it was announced in the newspapers that he had abjured his humanitarian heresies and joined the movement of national regeneration, many were astonished. But I, well remembering his great love for spaghetti with tomato sauce, was not. So, when a friend of mine returned some time ago from abroad, where for professional reasons that are of no interest to you he had to associate with political émigrés, the first thing I asked him was what those wretches ate. Many were hungry, he told me, but the few who could do so naturally stuffed themselves with spaghetti. Well, I told him, if that's the case there's no cause for despair, they're not yet completely lost to their country."

"But a hero can of course permit himself that, and indeed other things," Sor Quintino pointed out.

"Nothing will convince me," said the *podestà*, "that the captain's nervous exhaustion is not the result of his absurd abstention from eating pasta."

The hero's asceticism became a frequent subject of conversation among the notables.

"A hero is always inhuman," announced the professor of cycling, a former anarchist who had refused to serve in the Tripoli war.

"What's he like with women?" the professor of *bocce* asked.

This question revived hopes, like an appeal after a conviction.

Such a conversation would of course have been out of the question in the captain's presence, since in spite of his youth his presence was intimidating. But one day two schoolmistresses who occasionally took their meals in the private room agreed to act as bait to draw him out and try to tame him. They were fascinated more than anything else by his melancholy. What was the cause of it? An unhappy love affair?

Don Saverio seemed to swallow the bait. Signora Sofia, who taught the top grades at elementary school, was a large, florid woman with long, black, heavy eyelashes that were twisted like mustaches. Big, round shoulders were visible through her transparent blouse; her shoulder straps cut into them deeply, making two pink hams per shoulder, or four hams altogether. What a sight for a hungry soldier just back from the colonies. She laughed and spoke with her mouth in her plate, making her soup bubble like a seal under water, but her strong, monumental, cylindrical legs were lined with dark varicose veins like ivy growing on marble columns, and Don Saverio did not like seeing the emblem of the Republican Party* on them. So he shifted his attention to her colleague, Signorina Santafede, who was paler, taller, and more angular but, the times being what they were, was by no means to be despised; she was a handsome bell tower on nervy little white columns. One evening Sor Quintino, egged on by the *podestà*, plucked up courage and put the captain at the ladies' table; if this failed to work, he could always blame the waitress. However, it worked.

---

*The emblem of the Italian Republican Party is an ivy leaf.

"What is your Christian name, may I ask, Signorina Santafede?" Don Saverio asked.

"Faustina," the girl replied, adjusting one of her curls. "Do you like it?"

Don Saverio finished his meal quickly, said good night, and disappeared. His flight filled the whole company with astonishment and dismay. Such a difficult hero had never been seen before.

Among the regulars in the private bar the individual to whom Don Saverio took the greatest dislike was a young architect, a lout with heavily padded shoulders and a vest adorned with sporting badges. His head, which was all neck and jaw, seemed to have been modeled on that of the anthropoid whose picture was on the wall. His father had been converted to anarchism in America and had given him the name of Spartaco, after the leader of the Roman slave revolt, but to adapt himself to the new times he had abbreviated it to Sparta, to the amusement of local people to whom "Sparta" sounded like a woman's name. On one of the first few days after his arrival Don Saverio found him drinking a glass of rum and smoking a cigarette.

"What do you think of the imitation-antique patina that they're now putting on new public buildings, Captain?" the architect asked him. "The same critics who up to yesterday attacked me on the ground that those buildings looked like whited sepulchres now criticize me for making them too dark; they call them catafalques for funeral masses."

Don Saverio had indeed noticed during the past few days a painter's scaffold halfway up the white wall of the *carabiniere* barracks. The man was spraying large patches of umber on it and smearing greenish moss under the windows.

"Color's not sufficient," Don Saverio replied. "You ought to know that the universally admitted beauty of ancient monuments is not so much the result of the patina of time as of the fact that they are ruins. Even in regard to Greek statues critics and public are united in valuing most highly those without a head or an arm. Have you ever seen a complete miniature reconstruction of the Roman Forum? Wasn't it just like any square in Washington or

Berlin? The fact of the matter is that public buildings are always more or less ugly, not to say horrible, so long as they're new and in good condition."

"But excuse me," the architect interrupted, "do you consider the Quirinal and Piazza Venezia ugly?"

"When they are ruins, and the Romans take their girls for picnics in them, they'll certainly be far, far more beautiful," the captain said with confidence.

The architect looked around in alarm, and the *podestà* laughed sharply, blowing rhythmically through his nose like a piston. So far from arousing suspicions about the captain, this ostentatious freedom of thought confirmed his untouchability.

"Someone came and asked for you while you were out, Captain," Sor Quintino told Don Saverio. "A strange gentleman. He said he'd come back later."

"A *commendatore* type?" the captain asked.

"I should say rather a gentleman who has gone down in the world," said Sor Quintino. "A retired colonel, perhaps."

"I'm going up to have a rest," said Don Saverio. "Call me if he comes back."

The unexpected visitor turned out to be Don Severino. While wandering around Acquaviva he had been spotted by Simone on the latter's way back from the fields with some peasants, a mattock on his shoulder.

"I shouldn't have recognized you," said Don Severino. "But it's lucky I met you before seeing Pietro. We've got to talk things over."

"Did Faustina send you?" Simone asked. "Come with me, I'll take you to a friend's house."

They entered a tumbledown house at the bottom of the alley and found themselves in a big, dark room that was both kitchen and bedroom. In a corner there was a little woman of indefinable age, though she was very old, with a naked baby of only a few months on her lap. She rose and hastened to fetch chairs; even after the two visitors were seated she went on fetching chairs and made Severino rise to offer him a cleaner one. Then she went away again and came back with a kind of armchair borrowed from a neighbor and made Don Severino rise again and sit in it.

"No, Faustina didn't send me," Don Severino said to Simone. "She doesn't know I'm here, but I came here because of her. I don't know what passed between her and Pietro, but I do know that she's now living only on the memory of the two days she spent here. If she doesn't come back, it's because of a nightmare by which she's obsessed, and I'm wondering if it isn't our duty to help her."

Simone remained thoughtful for a time, then filled his pipe and lit it. "Pietro can't talk to me about anything else either," he said at last. "But, frankly, I don't know whether we ought to help them. Put obstacles in their way, certainly not, but help them? Believe me, Severino, I'm not at all sure that it would be good for them."

"Faustina's an exceptional, amazing girl."

"I completely agree," said Simone. "She's the most admirable woman I've ever met."

"A real love affair is worth more than any politics."

"Why do you mention politics?" Simone asked. "Do you by any chance consider Pietro a politician?"

"Real love is worth more than any ideology."

"I agree," said Simone, "but that's not the case with Pietro. He has the good fortune to be an outlaw, a man in jeopardy, and he's that in the simplest, most spontaneous, most natural way possible. One might almost say he was born with that vocation. Can you see him as a settled family man?"

Don Severino blushed and made an awkward gesture.

"You and I have grown old alone, Simone," he said. "But Pietro and Faustina are young. Before I met you just now I watched a boy and a girl talking under a tree in the garden behind the church. It was obvious from their appearance that they were repeating the words that men and women have said to each other millions and millions, thousands of millions of times since the world began: I love you; do you love me? Our future in this country isn't cheerful, we agree about that, I believe, but so long as men and woman say to each other: I love you; do you love me? perhaps there's hope."

"There's the grain that's put aside as seed corn, and the grain that is taken to the mill and consumed." After a pause Simone went on, "What does Faustina think about it?"

"She's convinced that meeting Pietro has at last given a meaning to her life, but at the same time the idea of seeing him again fills her with panic. She says Donna Maria Vincenza will curse her, and that she'll bring him misfortune. I'm sure of it, she says, you'll see, I'm sure I'll bring him misfortune."

"Poor, dear, adorable, unhappy girl," Simone murmured.

In the alleyway outside the door some children were playing with Infante; they made him behave like a wild man of the woods, they had blackened his face and hands and made him sing. Infante was extraordinarily docile that day, and his singing sounded like the growling of a bear. Then the children formed a ring around him and counted; the one who lost had to leave the ring and keep the bear company inside it.

"I put the question to Pietro," Simone said. "I asked him whether, if the government pardon that he refused a month ago were offered him again, now that he had met Faustina, he would again reject it. Of course, he replied immediately. Afterward he was thoughtful, and we sat down at the table in silence. When we had finished I again asked him whether he would reject it. Probably, he said. Let me make it quite clear, Severino, I'm absolutely convinced that in the end he would again reject it; but that 'probably,' that shadow of doubt on the part of a man like him, frightened me."

"I'm going back to Orta," Don Severino muttered. "I shan't mention this conversation to Faustina. So far as Pietro is concerned, do what you think best."

23

*O*NE MORNING THE authorities in Acquaviva were abruptly
shaken out of their lethargy by what at first sight might have
seemed a trivial incident. During the night someone had added a
big question mark to the slogan THE STATE IS EVERYTHING,
which stood out in big block capitals on the facade of the town
hall. A painter was hurriedly sent for to wipe out that insidious
manifestation of doubt; the notables hurried to the *podestà's* office, and endless discussions began on who could have done it
and why. An echo of all this quickly reached the entrance to the
hotel.

"Is it serious?" Sora Olimpia asked her husband.

"Very."

"Perhaps it was only a joke."

"The *podestà* said it was an expression of sacrilegious doubt."

"What a bad impression it will make on the captain."

But her husband, having recognized the sound of Don
Saverio's footsteps on the stairs, signed to her to be silent.

"Off again today to healthy work in the fields?" he asked him
deferentially.

"Yes."

"May it do you a great deal of good."

Simone was on the hillside already. "How is Pietro making out?" he asked Cesidio.

"I've never had a more willing lad. But it's a pity that he's often so gloomy."

Simone's donkey was loaded with manure, he shouted to it to get moving, and off they went. Cesidio stopped spraying the vines for a moment and looked up to see in which direction a flock of birds flying over Acquaviva was going. A good sign, he said to himself, reassured. He had reached the end of the row and stood out on the skyline; his gesture appropriated a small piece of sky and spread some fine verdigris dust into the blue.

At the other end of the vineyard Pietro filled his sulfur sprayer, put it on his back like a knapsack, and went on with his spraying. He advanced between the vines slowly, carefully, and assuredly, turning this way and that, spraying the tender, bluish shoots, moving as if he talked to every plant, communicating his pleasure and also his sadness to each one of them. His movements bore witness to a long-standing familiarity with vines. Behind him the grass-green row turned emerald green, and in his blue-striped working clothes and with his light blue shoes and hands he looked like a small perambulating tree looking for somewhere to put down roots; when he smiled the tree seemed to flower.

In the course of a few days the sirocco had awakened winter to spring, the fields were populated with peasants, and men as busy as bees were to be seen everywhere. The drainage channels between the rows of vines steamed in the spring sunshine, and the peasants working there seemed to be surrounded by little clouds like the blessed in Paradise; but it was an agricultural paradise that lived in fear of the phylloxera blight, a small landowners' paradise split up into watertight compartments. A man climbed the hill with a small black lamb over his shoulder; it had been born during the night and looked all around as if it already knew everything. The sky was as green as a field of young grass, but numbers of little clouds gathered on the mountains that formed the horizon like sacks full of wheat in a rich granary. Rivers of light and of warm air flowed up and down the valley and crisscrossed on every slope.

At the top of the hill Simone spread manure with a fork, and a large area of gray earth was already dotted with brown all around him. He advanced slowly; his body seemed taller, slimmer, lighter than it really was; he moved on the hill as if it were a globe. Every so often he stopped, but not out of tiredness, and put two fingers in his mouth to produce a long, high-pitched whistle, and Pietro replied from halfway up the slope with childish gestures. But some suspicious and resentful peasants wanted to know who these strangers were who actually managed to be cheerful while at work.

The almond trees were already in blossom, as usual earlier than all the other trees, and the whole hillside was white and pink with them. The elders say they have blossomed early every year, even at the cost of losing flowers and fruit at the first frost, as often happens, ever since Mary put the infant Jesus between the branches of an almond tree to hide Him from Herod's police. Pietro had not heard this story, which was told him by an old beggar woman whom he met by the roadside; and now he was moved and affected whenever he saw an almond tree.

A gray-green mosaic of small fields filled the bottom of the valley. In the green rectangles and squares boys and women were busily hoeing to let air into the compacted soil and free the tender wheat from weeds; in the gray parts men with mattocks, plows, and animals were busy sowing corn, peas, chickpeas, and lentils, clearing ditches, and mending banks and hedges.

At midday women appeared on the paths carrying baskets of food on their heads, and wherever they arrived work stopped. Cesidio's daughter Carmela brought a whole loaf stuffed with fried salt cod and a small cask of wine. After calling the two men, she put the basket under a cherry tree near the grassy edge of the vineyard. She was a rough, almost wild creature, serious, perhaps too serious, of indefinable age and uncertain beauty, though to talk of beauty in such cases is frivolous. Pietro was the first to arrive.

"Last night we stayed rather too late at your house, you must excuse us," he said, wiping the sweat from his brow with the edge of his jacket.

The girl turned her back on him without replying.

"Have you anything against me? Against us?" Pietro asked.

Carmela forced herself to reply. "If you really want to know, you frighten me," she said. "Who are you? Do you want our ruin?"

"Are you afraid of us?" replied Pietro, taken aback.

"You strike me as crazy, both of you," the girl went on.

Pietro wanted to laugh, but couldn't. "Perhaps you're right," he said. "Sometimes I wonder myself."

The previous day Carmela and Pietro had worked together in the vegetable garden, putting seeds in holes made with a dibber, bending over the soil, almost on their knees. The girl had sharply asked him to stop calling her signorina.

"It's not the custom with peasants' daughters," she said. "You ought to know that if it's true you were born in the country."

Her young man was in the army in Abyssinia, and they would get married when he came back; she had promised to wait and be faithful to him, though she expected him to come back crippled.

"And he won't be the first," she said resignedly.

"There are some who come back safe and sound," Pietro replied in astonishment. "It's a small war, a wicked war against a badly armed enemy; fortunately most of them will come back safe and sound."

"Of course," the girl replied irritably, "but that's no reason why my young man should not be among those who come back crippled. I've never seen or heard of anyone who was more unfortunate than we are."

Cesidio's house, where the friends met in the evening, was a dark, damp cave. Carmela never opened her mouth in her mother's presence or, if she did speak, it was only in monosyllables and rudely. She was capable of spending a whole evening resting her head on one shoulder and staring at the fire, avoiding turning in the direction in which her mother was sitting.

When looked at closely her head, with her reddish brown hair wrapped around it like the successive layers of an onion, her freckled and already wrinkled face, and her narrow pointed lips resembled a fruit that had frozen and withered before ripening. To get her to do anything she had to be asked by her father, though her mother did not yet seem to be resigned to this insubordination. From the outset she had been openly hostile to Pietro and Simone, whom she took to be typical of her father's tavern friends, the usual drinkers and card players who kept him away from home on winter evenings, false friends who took money from him, leaving the family in need; but then she realized that these new acquaintances were strange types, different from the others, and perhaps more dangerous. She took no more notice of Infante than she would have taken of a goat, and why Pietro and Simone kept him with them was beyond her comprehension; he was a half-witted relative, perhaps. Nor could she understand Pietro's natural but unusual politeness to everyone, even including her mother. On the first evening, when Pietro arrived with a bottle of wine and a bunch of flowers he had picked in the fields, Carmela thought it was a joke, and was particularly rude to him for that reason; when he spoke to her, to show him that she was no longer a child and knew the real facts of life, she replied sharply and boorishly, more like a loutish youth than a woman. But when she saw that abruptness and bad manners made no impression on him she gave that up too, though she went on treating him mistrustfully. This upset him greatly and nearly made him weep, and he discussed it with Simone.

"There are ditches dug by centuries of poverty," Simone said.

"But I thought I'd jumped the ditch," Pietro complained. "I thought I was on their side."

He did not accept this situation. He could not resign himself to being excluded both from Faustina's love and from the community of the poor, so he tried to talk to the girl whenever he could do so without being importunate. She had been initiated into life's troubles at an early stage.

"Boys can at least go out and spend their time in the street," she said, without concealing her envy. "As soon as they have a few *centesimi* in their pocket they go to the tavern and play cards; and nowadays the government takes an interest in the lucky fellows, and there's drill and training and entertainment for them every evening, and Sundays as well. But a girl has to stay at home. While she's still a toddler she discovers what a dreadful thing it is to have a mortgage, not to be able to afford the rent for your land and have no money to pay a hundred-lire promissory note that's falling due; she knows all about animal diseases, she's used to turnip soup without salt and to there being no bread in the bread bin and Mother spending her time weeping alone in front of the empty fireplace. Sending her to bed early isn't any use. And when Father comes home from the tavern and hasn't had his dinner, he's not a bad man, on the contrary, he's a good one, but he's hungry, and he got drunk on an empty stomach and he shouts, swears, curses, and quarrels with Mother and breaks what little dishware there's still left to break; and the little girl who has been sent to bed keeps her eyes shut and pretends to be asleep, but she hears it all, and learns words she will never forget, and bites the sheet to stop herself from crying out.

"From her earliest years," Carmela told him, "she learns that life is painful both for children and for grown-ups, one would have to be blind not to see it, and there's nothing to be gained either from prolonging childhood or from growing up quickly, because there's nothing to hope for. If one doesn't put up with it, the consequences are even worse. Who doesn't know the horrible story of what happens to girls who don't resign themselves? Who doesn't know how they end up?"

Carmela laid a white napkin on the dry ground, and on it she put a loaf of bread, a knife, and two forks. The two men took their places beside it, and Cesidio cut the bread and shared out the salt cod.

"Eat and drink," he said. "Aren't you going to join us?" he asked the girl. She did not reply, but stood waiting silently for the two men to finish. Pietro praised the oil that went with the salt cod and the sparkling wine, which he drank by holding the small cask in the air and pouring it straight into his mouth, as Simone had taught him. Cesidio looked on and laughed.

"In the space of a few days you've changed your skin and you look at least thirty years younger," he said. "I don't understand how you managed it."

"It must be the air in your vineyard," Pietro said, blushing.

In the past few days Pietro's face had in fact finally lost the earthy, precociously aged coloring that he had himself given it two years before by treating it with a solution of tincture of iodine in order to make himself less recognizable to the police, and he had regained his natural pale, fresh coloring.

This worried Cesidio. "Now I shan't be able to send you around anymore," he said. "Anyone who looks you in the face will be able to see what you're thinking, and you can imagine the consequences."

"Will you two hurry up?" Carmela brusquely interrupted. "At two o'clock I've got to go to the mill."

Her father took no notice of her; he was lying on the ground, leaning on one elbow, eating slowly, and talking about past times and distant places.

"While I was using the sulfur spray," he said, "I remembered an old friend of mine who lives at Popoli, Battista the Dyer, there's a great deal I could tell you about him. He's not a dyer, but his forefathers were, and that's what they still call the family. I met him at São Paulo in Brazil about thirty years ago, two years before I met Simone. We worked on the same *fazenda*, and I liked him straightaway. He was a good fellow but wouldn't stand any nonsense. When we came back to the Motherland, as the phrase goes, we went on seeing each other, but more and more rarely. I married, he married, other things cropped up, you know how it is. But now I'd like to see him again, I don't know why. Yes," Cesidio suddenly decided, "I'll go and give him a surprise next market day."

"May he not have changed?" Pietro asked.

"Battista? I don't think so," Cesidio replied after considering the matter. "Perhaps he drinks; he was very fond of wine even then. And frankly, who isn't? Drink, Pietro, that cask has got to be finished today."

Cesidio was a powerfully built man; his hands and face were

earth colored, chapped, and scarred, the very visible bones of his head were well proportioned and strong, his eyes were deepset and his gray hair was cut very short. But for his two eyes, which were like those of a faithful dog, he might have been taken for a brutish peasant. Our Lady was tattooed in blue on his right arm in memory of a pilgrimage he had made many years before to the shrine of Loreto.

"I've drunk enough," said Pietro.

"It's lucky there's wine," said Cesidio, offering Pietro a piece of cod. "It's one of the last defenses. When you come to think of it, drink and laziness are the only ways we have left of getting back at the world. Public speakers like haranguing us, and if I'm drunk I'm not carried away by their eloquence. And they can't prohibit wine, because they like it themselves and the landlords have to sell it. As a matter of fact my reputation as a drunkard is so well established and officially recognized that for some time past I've been drinking less, and I should be able to go on enjoying the advantages of drunkenness even if I became a teetotaler. In a way I'm the communal drunk here, and I prefer telling you that myself, Pietro, before you hear it from others. The *podestà* has exempted me from attending public meetings ever since the memorable occasion on which some questions I asked after a speech of his caused hilarity that was considered dangerous. In fact I hadn't been drinking at all, as was obvious to everyone, but the *podestà*, being at a loss what to do, found it convenient to ignore my questions and told the head guard to take me away because of my obvious state of intoxication. Ever since then I've enjoyed the privilege of living on the margins of public oratory. Listen to this. When a party of conscripts left for the war in Abyssinia, they were escorted to the station by a kind of procession. Because of my status as the communal drunk I was under no obligation to go, but I wanted to, because one of the conscripts was Carmela's young man, and he's a good lad. Before he left he put his head out the window of his compartment and asked me jokingly what I would like him to bring me back from Africa, would I like a monkey or a banana tree or would I prefer a little slave girl perhaps, and in reply I called out what I wanted most, which was that his hands not be soiled with blood (and everyone understood). This caused a bit of a panic among the crowd and the passengers in the train, until the *podestà* burst out laughing and called out: it's Cesidio, the usual drunk. That caused general laughter and a sigh of relief. As you can well imagine, I soon had imitators, though none of them was as lucky as I've been, because Acquaviva is a small place, and there's no room for more than one recognized and licensed drunk. In favorable circumstances others are tolerated, shall we say, and some, who can't afford it, occasionally pretend. In short, to me it's a real privilege, and because of it I've been given the nickname of Don Quart Jug, as you may already have heard. But in some instances relatives are not so understanding, and it's obvious why. Nowadays you depend on public offices for every breath you draw, for every step you take you need a stamped document, and if they don't like the shape of your nose they turn you down."

"It was your fault that Uncle Achille was not appointed road keeper," Carmela interrupted. "And that Aunt Maria was refused her allowance. You can't deny that, can you?"

"That is what we are reduced to," Cesidio concluded.

"If you go to Popoli, I'll come with you," said Pietro. "There's an old friend of mine in that part of the world whom I'd like to look up too. I heard he was arrested, but he may since have been released."

"Will you hurry up," Carmela exclaimed irritably.

"To avoid attracting attention," Cesidio said, "it will be best to get there early with the people going to market."

"If you're not doing anything wrong, why the need to avoid attracting attention?" Carmela interrupted suspiciously.

"It's just because we're not doing anything wrong that we have to be careful," her father replied. "That's the very reason."

"If you want to be inconspicuous it must mean you think you're doing wrong, mustn't it?" Carmela insisted.

His daughter's obduracy caused Cesidio to make an angry gesture. "You're too stupid," he said. "You're just like your mother."

The girl flushed scarlet, picked up the basket, flung the napkin and the knives and forks into it, and went off, after calling out: "You'll have us all sent to prison."

"You see the respect with which my family treats me," said Cesidio. "You're lucky still being a bachelor." Then he added: "I don't want to be indiscreet, but your dolefulness saddens me. Yes, I know, it's hard for a young man to give up love. Why don't you try drinking a little more? Love's a fine thing, of course, but it enslaves, while wine sets you free."

"Isn't it a form of escape?" replied Pietro. "To me it seems a form of escape."

"Of course it is," Cesidio admitted. "But if we're to remain free there's nothing left to us but running away. Don't you think that you too are running away?"

There was unusual excitement at the hotel when Pietro got back; the usual small group of notables had gathered around the *carabiniere* sergeant and were discussing with him a repetition of the strange question-mark phenomenon. In the past few hours more question marks had actually been reported on cottages in the country, which had been adorned with patriotic slogans during the previous year when an important member of the government had passed through in a car.

"Three question marks have appeared on the facade of the old mill," the architect announced indignantly. "The slogan now reads: BELIEVE? OBEY? FIGHT? and the usual loafers are standing about and looking at it and nudging one another."

But the greatest outrage had been perpetrated on the war memorial. The question mark added to the words THEY DIED FOR THEIR COUNTRY was considered to be the basest sacrilege.

"To judge by the writing," the *carabiniere* sergeant remarked, "one would say it was the scrawling of a semiliterate."

"Perhaps it's a joke," Sora Olimpia, who suffered at seeing her customers so depressed, dared to suggest. "Don't you think it might be a joke?"

The only response to this was angry looks.

"Here comes the captain," said the sergeant. "I don't think we can conceal the outrage from him any longer."

"What a disgrace, what a bad impression we shall make," Sor Quintino lamented, advancing to report the deplorable phenomenon.

"What do you think about it?" the architect asked Don Saverio point blank.

"You use question marks yourself, if I'm not mistaken," he replied, looking at him severely.

The architect went pale.

"However," the captain went on, addressing the others present, "I must point out that your faith cannot be very solidly based if it can be shaken by mere punctuation marks."

"It must have been done by a drunk," the sergeant hastened to say in extenuation of their collective responsibility.

Pietro went to his room intending at last to write to Faustina; in his mind he had been talking to her for a good part of the day, and he had decided to unburden himself to her with total frankness. But he couldn't get out of his mind the *carabiniere* sergeant's reference to a drunk. He ended up leaving the hotel and going back to Cesidio's.

When he arrived he found that Pasquale the Cooper was there. Pasquale's house was bigger and more respectable than Cesidio's, but he couldn't entertain his friends there because of his wife. On the first evening when Simone, Pietro, and Infante had gone there his wife had wandered around the house trembling with anxiety like someone who fears a disaster.

"Who are these strangers?" she ended up asking her husband. "Why don't they stay in their own home? Don't they have a home?"

"They're friends," old Pasquale tried to explain, "friends of my youth."

"Your youth is over and done with," the woman replied "The time for folly is dead and gone, and you ought to know it."

Pasquale tried to defend himself. "One's soul to God, one's taxes to the government, and one's heart to one's friends," he said. "I can't give up my friends at my time of life."

But his wife refused to be comforted. Whenever Simone and Pietro went there the poor woman grew frantic with anxiety and wandered around the house listening intently. She was scraggy, doleful, and disheveled, and now she had a new cause for worry on top of all her old ones, which included her husband, her daughter-in-law, and her son, who was in America and hardly ever wrote. She also had to look after the goat and the pig and the kneading trough and the fire, besides going to church, and there was a promissory note that was about to fall due, and all these things left little time for anything else. There ought to be thirty hours a day, she said. No, she didn't complain about her husband, except that he had grown old without learning sense. In her presence the poor man was reduced to communicating by signs. To say "Eh?" Simone would raise his eyebrows, and to express agreement Pasquale would lower and raise his eyelids. But this method of communication did not escape his wife's notice, and it redoubled her alarm.

"What are you talking about?" she asked. "Can't you tell me what you're talking about? Pasquà," she announced, "you'll be the ruin of your family. Who are these strangers?" she asked again. "Is it true that one of them's a captain? Why doesn't he associate with his own kind and leave poor people in peace? I don't want madmen in the house."

"They're friends," poor Pasquale repeated, "friends of my youth."

"Why do you need them?" his wife insisted.

"They're friends," Pasquale pleaded.

"One's no company, two's good company, three or more and the devil's at the door," said his daughter-in-law.

She was a prolific young woman. She had filled the house with children in a very few years. In the children's bed she put two at the head and two at the foot; in her own bed she had one at the head and two at the foot; and in their grandparents' big bed she had one at the head and one at the foot, in between Grandpa and Grandma. The children's father was in America, in Philadelphia, where he had been for about ten years, but he had several times returned home for short periods, given his wife a baby each time, and left again.

"If you work out how much the trip costs, you'll have an idea how expensive each of these children was," Pasquale complained.

That evening he told his wife he was going to the tavern, but he walked a little way, looked all around without seeming to, and ended up in Cesidio's house.

"There are one or two bugs on the road," he said to Cesidio, screwing up his nose.

"You've got to be careful," Pietro agreed.

His trade as a cooper enabled Pasquale to go from market to market. He left early in the morning loaded with tubs, pails, sieves, and wooden spoons and came back in the evening. Pietro lent him his horse.

Taking advantage of markets, fairs, and religious holidays, Simone too had found some old friends in the valley among those who had not adapted themselves, and through them he met others of the same kind, though not many, unfortunately, most of them having become demoralized. At most he found three or four in each village. Two old friends who met had such woeful stories to tell. But what a pleasure it was to be able to talk face to face to someone with whom one was not bound by ties of kinship or business interests or other commercial motives, to be able to unburden oneself freely to someone one could trust.

"Friendship between men," Simone confessed to Pietro, "can be more delightful than the love of women, but it has to be more discreet."

So he invented pretexts to go and see people. After the usual greetings and expressions of surprise such as: good heavens, fancy seeing you, wonders will never cease, you don't look a day older, on the contrary, and similar banalities, he would say that he had just happened to be passing that way for some reason or other. Because of his reputation as an eccentric, the more far-fetched his excuses were, the more plausible they sounded. They would sit down and have a glass of wine, and the conversation would inevitably turn to memories of old times, to the hard, painful, hazardous, but warm, intense, and free life they had once led. Words were hardly necessary; the flicker of an eyelid would be sufficient to show whether a friendship was dying or was already dead. When they were alone, when it seemed that there was nothing else to say, it sometimes happened that they would begin to exchange confidences, like survivors of a shipwreck who met again. Voices lost their intonation, gestures ceased, complaint would be inadequate, ambiguities were avoided and hints would have been suspect, not for reasons of prudence, but because they would be superfluous, and for heaven's sake let's not talk politics. It's too early for that, perhaps talking politics will be something for our grandsons.

"You too ought to go about a bit," Simone said to Pietro. "Fresh air would do you good."

The new wheat was already as high as a man's hand, and the whole countryside was crisscrossed by old friends seeking each other out, visiting, and returning visits. There were not many of them, and they came and went a few at a time, in spite of which there were those who wondered who these strangers were who kept going here, there, and everywhere, did not buy or sell, and went into a house and stayed there till late at night.

Neighbors sent their children to spy. Front doors in that part of the world are shut only at night, and children keep going in and coming out of all of them, just as cats do. Even those who can't stand up yet but still crawl on all fours creep into neighboring houses like snails, clamber up the stairs, bring up their mothers' milk, piddle, and so on, and so forth.

"Now they're eating soup," children came back and told their mothers.

"But who are these people, why did they come?"

"Now she's just come up from the cellar with a jug of wine," children ran and told their mothers.

"But where do these people come from, what do they talk like, are they relatives? Don't be so stupid, ask the children of the house."

"They're not relatives," the children came back and told their mothers.

"Are they selling or buying anything?"

"No, they're not buying or selling anything; now they're eating soup."

"Are they road keepers? Do they have some government job?"

"No, they haven't got a job; now they're eating salad."

"But what are they talking about?"

"About old times in Argentina and Brazil."

"And what are they saying?"

"They're not saying anything now, they're just drinking in silence."

"But who are they? Don't be so stupid, ask the children of the house."

"They say they're their father's friends."

Every woman went to see her neighbor.

"Have you heard the latest?"

"Yes, my little boy has just told me."

"And do you believe it?"

"Oh, no, I'm not as stupid as that."

In the past two or three weeks the whole countryside seemed to Pietro to have changed; it was like warm dough that was beginning to rise. Winter had gone, and the shy and gentle cooing of doves announced the arrival of spring. The fig trees put out their first new leaves, and the young wheat tinged the air with green, and did the same to the boys and young women busy hoeing to get rid of the weeds, as well as the donkeys tied to the willow trees near the ditches and the carts making their way along the edge of the fields. To reach many of these mountain villages one has to go on foot, one has to earn it, sweating profusely like the pilgrims of old, one has to climb long, steep slopes, drop down again and then climb once more; one has to prove one's strength, in fact. These are mountains not for tourists, but for hermits; not for cows, but for goats and snakes; arid, deserted mountains, with little grass and poverty-stricken people. In many places if one stamps one's feet the earth creaks like worm-eaten wood or the auditorium of an old theater; it is ancient earth, rumbling with tremors. As one gains height or loses it the landscape expands, contracts, or disappears, changing continually but never losing its harsh, gloomy quality. At every fountain or stream Simone bent down and drank, as if he were expecting to cross a desert. Infante lapped up the water with his tongue, as dogs do. When they reached a village on a public holiday, the friends they sought were easy to find, for everyone would be in the square. If it were cold, the men would be standing about with their hands in their pockets on the sunny side; if the sun were hot, they moved around slowly with the shade; in the evening they were to be found in the taverns. When there was a religious service of any importance without a sermon they waited outside the church for their wives, their sisters, and their girls; if the waiting was protracted, every now and then they would send a small boy inside to see what was happening.

"Go and see whether the priest is getting a move on," they would say.

Pietro greatly enjoyed these expeditions with Simone, or Cesidio, or Pasquale, this going to villages to look up old acquaintances or forgotten friends. These encounters gave him a sense of peace and happiness and pleasure; he walked with a lightness of foot as if he were carried along by a new and unaccustomed rapture, by wings that had been atrophied. He had to stop himself from running or turning somersaults. He was like a prisoner who has broken his bonds. When they passed through inhabited places he assumed a childish gravity; he walked on the pavement, taking care not to lose his balance, not to step on the line between one paving stone and the next, and counting his footsteps. But sometimes when he came back from these excursions he would be tired and depressed in the evening. Sometimes it turned out that a former acquaintance, someone he had known in the old days of the peasants' leagues, had died, or was in prison, or his whereabouts were unknown; he might be abroad or living as a fugitive in another province under a false name, and even his family didn't know, or dared not say, where he was; or perhaps the man he found was unrecognizable, bent with labor, stupefied by poverty, hardships, persecution, loneliness, terrified by incomprehensible fears; perhaps he had relapsed into the lethargy and apathy of age-old servitude and become inaccessible even to the simple words of friendship with which Pietro approached him.

"I haven't come to talk to you or to discuss anything dangerous," he would say. "On the contrary, I assure you, I was just passing and remembered you and the old days when we knew each other, and I wanted to see how you are, that's all."

A peasant of Introdacqua whom Pietro had met two or three times about fifteen years before and of whom he had kept a pleasant memory had died the previous month. His old mother, a doleful, spectral figure in black clothing whom Pietro found in the silent house, took him aside and muttered in his ear: "Are you the man who was to come, the man whom my poor son was waiting for? Oh, why didn't you come at least a month ago? If you only knew how hard that poor son of mine worked and how much he suffered, and what bitter tears he shed in secret."

The dead man's brother asked him to accompany him to the tavern, bought him a drink, invited others whom he met in the street to join them, and paid for their drinks too. His wife called out angrily from the window of their house: "Are you trying to ruin yourself like your brother did? Why do you waste your money at the tavern while your children go barefoot and have nothing to eat?"

"You can't make a better use of your money than buying drinks for your friends," her husband replied with a laugh. "Come and drink," he went on, turning to the people around him.

Pietro accepted a glass of wine and, when the tavern filled with people, tried to leave. But the dead man's brother would not let him go and said to him in the presence of everyone: "Aren't you he who was to come whom my brother, God rest his soul, was waiting for? Tell us what you would have said to him."

Pietro drank another glass of wine and, after a long silence, said to the men who were crowding the tavern and were waiting for him to speak: "I tell you to be proud."

The ragged *cafoni* were astonished.

"What?" several exclaimed.

"Be proud," he repeated. "I tell you to be proud."

Pietro walked out; those present were too taken aback to try to stop him. Just as he was leaving the village two men in uniform overtook him and asked to see his papers and, as these were in order, allowed him to go on. Partly elated by this incident and partly blushing for his relapse into oratory, he told Simone about it, and Simone could not conceal that it worried him.

"One of these days it will end badly," was all he said.

One day on the road to Pettorano a tramp told him about an aged convict, a native of the place, who after serving his term asked to remain in the prison as a sweeper, as he lacked the strength to go back to the life of a *cafone*. The man whom Pietro went to see at Pettorano lived in a hovel in the old part of the village behind the church of San Dionisio. The windows were shutterless, the floor unpaved, and there were basins here and there to collect the water that dripped from the roof. The man was tall, as many are in the mountains in that part of the world, and he looked like a huge skeleton clothed in rags; the blackness of chronic hunger showed in the sockets of his eyes. He listened to Pietro without showing any particular signs of recognizing him, as if he were a messenger from another world. Eventually he said: "Take it from me, young man, the real enemy of man is damp. In this house it actually goes on raining long after it has stopped outside. How do you explain damp in houses in a waterless country? Thank you for calling, but you could have spared yourself the trouble."

"I'll come again," Pietro said. "I'll bring some friends with me."

"Spare yourself the trouble," the old man repeated.

24

*H*E SEEMS NOT TO be thinking about that girl any longer," Cesidio said to Simone. "It's just as well."

Simone shook his head. "No, it's still an open wound," he said. "But there are days when it hurts less than others."

Whenever he had been away for the day the first thing Pietro asked when he came back to Acquaviva was always about Infante. During the week Infante, with Simone, would work as a casual laborer for some peasant or do some heavy job for Pasquale the Cooper. On holidays or market days, when he was often left alone, Infante would roam around the fields, climb like a goat up steep stony places where there had been landslides, hide for hours behind prickly bushes, wander about aimlessly, be attracted by some trivial thing, or lose his way, guided more by his feet than by memory. Pietro had several times been greatly worried when he did not come back, fearing he might have had an accident or been arrested. Also there was no end to his squabbles with the boys of Acquaviva. In spite of Pietro's efforts, he still looked like a dirty, violent, and timid savage. At Pietrasecca he had been used to accepting good and bad weather alike with the indifference of a tree, but now when it rained he remembered Pietro's advice and walked under the eaves, where he thought he was better sheltered, though he got wetter than ever; and when the sun shone and he had nothing to do he would lie on his back, no matter where, waving his arms and legs about in the dust of the road just like a beetle that has fallen on its back. Pietro worried about him; no father was ever as anxious about his child as he was about Infante.

"We must do everything possible to ensure that nothing happens to him if we two are arrested, as may happen any day, so please help me with your advice," he said to Simone.

"Do you want to make him your heir?" Simone replied with a laugh. "Do you want to turn him into a landlord? Is that your way of showing how much you care for him?"

"I'm not in a mood for joking," said Pietro, his face darkening. "He's my chief worry now. You know that in a way I met him underground; perhaps it was the most important thing that has ever happened to me. In Sciatàp's stable he gave me a name and a face for poverty, and you know how much I owe the poor; it's no exaggeration to say I owe them everything. After all, Simone, but for them I might have ended up as a *commendatore*. You laugh, but there's nothing to laugh at. Now I've got to do everything I can to ensure that if we are arrested Infante does not relapse to the state of a beast of burden in which he was kept at Pietrasecca. Fear that that might happen to him is a completely new feeling to me, and I can't bear it."

Infante lived with Simone in the poorest part of Acquaviva in an abandoned hovel that Cesidio had found for them. One reached it by way of an alley as narrow and deep as a crevasse, where the sun hardly penetrated. To enter one had to climb some disconnected steps; apart from two poor beds and something for Leone, the dog, to sleep on, the room was bare. Leone seemed very unhappy; he moaned inwardly, his eyes were always watering, and he certainly regretted the good old days at Colle, where everyone had lived happily together day and night. The fire was lit between some bricks in the middle of the room, and the smoke went out the window. Under the influence of Infante's

presence, and to make himself more intelligible to him, Pietro
had gotten into the habit without realizing it of not conjugating
verbs and using only the few dozen words that were known to the
deaf-mute. Infante eat, Simone wait go work, Pasquale not come,
Faustina go. Come back? Come back. Sometimes this made Simone laugh, but Pietro blushed, and then decided that it was far
better to use the present tense only, for it repeated the past and an-
ticipated the future, an almost magical operation. "Faustina go"
was much stronger and more effective than "Faustina has gone,"
and also more exact.

The words that Infante had just learned were still warm from
birth, still raw and alive; it was sufficient for him to say *sun*, and
everything all around them was light; he only had to repeat *bread*,
wine, *happiness* to create those things.

Pietro had given his friends a large part of the underwear provided by his grandmother; and, as Infante did not understand the
difference between day and nightshirts, and as the latter took his
fancy, he started showing himself off on the street in a nightshirt
with embroidered neck and wrists. When a girl saw him and
mocked him and then ran away he chased her, raging like a fury,
to the door of her house, from which her father emerged to defend her, and if Pasquale the Cooper had not happened to be
passing there might have been a dangerous quarrel.

Pietro did not regret having rescued Infante from his servitude
at Pietrasecca, but with every day that passed he became more
aware of the difficulty of adapting him to social life among
strangers. An ideal environment like Simone's home at Colle
would not be found again. What troubled Pietro most was his
failure to get him to accept the minimum of discipline and physical decency that were essential if he were to become tolerable to
others. After he began worrying about his future he discovered an
obstinacy in him that drove him to distraction. He was irritated by
Infante's preference for sitting on the ground rather than on a
chair and for blowing his nose forgetting that he had a handkerchief in his pocket. But then he grew angry with himself for at-
taching importance to such trivialities. Pietro's incomprehensible

outbursts of ill humor filled Infante with fear and dismay, and he gazed at him on these occasions like a dog that has been unjustly beaten; and when he thought that Pietro had gotten over it he wagged his ears to make him laugh.

Simone was skeptical about the prospects of his being accepted into the family of some friend, because Cesidio and Pasquale the Cooper, who might have been able to do so, counted for little in their own homes; but by and large he was less worried than Pietro.

"Friendship must not become a form of enslavement," he said. "On the contrary, it should make us freer and lighter. Friends shouldn't crush us, be a burden to us, shackle us, like women or a family. The best thing about our band of friends is that all of us are more or less living in jeopardy; our skin has already been sold and we don't have to worry about the buyer. I'm surprised at having to remind you of these things, Pietro."

But Simone could not conceal a growing anxiety about Pietro.

"You ought to leave the inn," he suggested abruptly one evening. "I don't understand why they haven't yet found out who you are."

"They were taken in by my uncle's papers," Pietro tried to explain. "What's strange about that? They're not false papers."

Actually when Pietro was with the distinguished clientele of the inn he was like a man from another world; his closeness to the other customers was fictitious, fictitious as the superimposition of two pictures of different worlds. He had no need to dissimulate, and everyone had given up trying to understand him, though they did not regard him as mad in the ordinary sense. In any case he could no longer dissimulate; there was a singular clarity in his eyes, he was like an open book.

"Don't trust Sparta," the *podestà* advised him. "He's a traitor."

"I'm not afraid of him," the captain assured him.

"He's collecting gossip to use against me," the *podestà* said, "and he might try it on you."

"But aren't you doing the same to him?"

"I'm authorized to do so, it's actually my duty."

The *podestà* described a painful experience he had had at the Prezza station the day before: he had seen a handcuffed *cafone* being taken away by two *carabinieri*. The memory nearly took away his appetite.

"It's a pretty frequent sight at our stations, I know," he went on. "But, I don't know why, as soon as I set eyes on the man I felt sure he was a subversive. He was a peasant, about forty years old, and he had the bewildered look of an animal of some extinct species, a man from another age, almost a museum specimen. The *podestà* of Prezza who happened to be at the station told me that the night before the wretch had uttered seditious cries against the war in Abyssinia. A lady waiting for the train beside me said he looked like a rat in a trap."

Don Saverio pricked up his ears on hearing this, but he confined himself to saying: "It's a human species that's difficult to eradicate."

"They are wretched survivors from another age," the *podestà* said with contempt. "You can rest assured that the young men of today are immune to that kind of malcontent."

"There are hens that hatch basilisks without realizing it," said Don Saverio. "Many heretics, as you know, have come from Jesuit schools. Do you see those children who have just come out of school? Who can guarantee that in twenty years' time one of them won't arouse the country?"

A crowd of children came running past the inn. The *podestà* looked at them with sudden suspicion.

"Nonsense," he said. "In any case, who cares? In twenty years' time I'll be on pension."

At Pietro's suggestion Cesidio took a bag of onions and went off straightaway to Prezza to make discreet inquiries. The poor, dark village under the steep mountainside seemed oppressed by a secret menace: the few inns were empty and people in the streets walked hurriedly, silently, and mistrustfully, keeping close to the wall. In the course of the past few days the place had been afflicted by a series of misfortuncs and seemed to be attracting the anger of the authorities. The last and most serious had become known that morning. A government speaker who had arrived the day before had been accommodated in the best and cleanest room available, but during the night he had been attacked and reduced to a pitiful state by tens of thousands of fleas; as it was spring, no one could understand where they came from. The speaker had left early in the morning, half blinded and unrecognizable, uttering obscure threats.

Cesidio with his sack on his back climbed the steep and stony alleyways and called on two or three families he knew on the pretext of offering his onions for sale. "If we needed onions, we'd buy them at the market," they told him sharply, and he could get no more out of them. But one family took half his onions in exchange for beans. When this transaction had been completed Cesidio tried talking to them about the weather, about seeds, about sulfur spraying, but there was no response; he asked for a glass of water, and they gave it to him without speaking. In one peasant's house only the wife was there; her husband was out. The woman was sitting near the empty fireplace with two children clinging to her skirts.

"Where's Nicandro?" Cesidio asked, putting his sack of onions and beans on the ground.

"He's out," his wife replied without turning her head.

"Will he be long?"

"I don't know."

"I can wait for him."

"I don't think so."

"Oh," said Cesidio.

The woman was dressed in black, her little face was wrinkled like that of a fetus, and her eyes were red as if she had been weeping a great deal. The children clung to her neck, trembling like frightened little animals, and one of them cried out in fright.

"I'm a friend of Nicandro's," Cesidio plucked up courage to say. "I'm very sorry. If there's anything I can do to help . . ."

"Friends have been his ruin," the woman interrupted, rising to her feet and looking him in the face with hatred in her eyes.

"Who will feed these children when there's no more bread? It's time to hoe a field of ours that's sown with corn, but who will hoe it now that he's not here? Jesus?"

"Perhaps, why not?" said Cesidio, quietly and sorrowfully. "In any event, I owed your husband some beans and onions, I don't know if you knew. I came to give them back. I'm very sorry he isn't here."

Cesidio left the sack on the ground and took his departure.

The village was huddled on a rocky slope. To reach the fields one picked one's way among rubble, rocks, brushwood, parched and prickly bushes, one went through vineyards, and still farther down, in the direction of the Pratola basin, one came to fields of beans and corn, and poplars, willows, and fruit trees became more and more numerous; still farther down, past fields of vegetables and wetlands, one came to vast fields of wheat. Every morning the poor villagers left the dark dens carved out of the mountainside and made their way down to the plain like a procession of ants in search of food. Winter had left white sheets of snow on the surrounding peaks, Monte Prezza, Monte San Cosimo, the Morrone mountains; but the long, arid lower slopes, some rounded, some steep, were already covered with gray and brown blankets, and the plain was an irregular carpet of every shade of green. For several days past the tender young corn plants had been putting out three or four tender leaves, and the time had come to feed them, hoeing the earth with a mattock.

Hoeing with a mattock is hard work for women, and only the most robust would attempt it. Maria Catarina, Nicandro's wife, had barely finished two rows and already her strength was failing her. She was not used to work in the fields, she had never done anything but the lightest jobs; her father was a carpenter, her mother a seamstress, and besides, she was now very weak. Her eyes, tired by lack of sleep and tears, could not stand the reflection of the sun on the ground, and her back, though she was used to work at the kneading trough and doing the washing, seemed about to break whenever she used the mattock. She was so weak that her knees bent at every step. And several times instead of turning the earth she destroyed little corn plants, not so much because of inexperience or lack of skill but simply from exhaustion and because her mind was elsewhere. Not for a moment could she get out of her head the thought of her husband in prison, probably being reviled and tortured. Suddenly she could not go on, but dropped the mattock and sat on the ground under a tree, hiding her face in her hands and weeping. She broke out into a cold sweat, as if she were covered with melted snow.

The neighboring fields were deserted, for there the hoeing had been finished. Her long, narrow field, which was about a quarter of an acre in extent, was surrounded by willow trees and separated from the road by a small stream. There were few passersby; an occasional peasant with a donkey carrying manure and an occasional woman on her way to the mill. But a *cafone* dressed in ash-colored rags, looking like one of the tramps who came from distant parts, jumped the ditch and came striding toward her. He was tall and strong and had a mattock on his shoulder. To the woman sitting on the ground he must have seemed a giant. He came bounding along between the rows of corn rather like a bear, and his vagabond look frightened her, though perhaps he was only using the field as a shortcut.

Maria Catarina was squatting in the light shade of the willow tree and pretended not to look at the approaching stranger; the shadow of the leaves fell on her face and dress and made her look like a heap of leaves. When the man was a few yards from her he stopped, smiled, and made an awkward gesture of greeting with one hand. His appearance at close quarters was really alarming; no one at Prezza looked so wild. But his gestures were those of a reliable domestic animal. He flung his worn and greasy hat on the ground, took up his mattock, and began hoeing from the place where the woman had stopped.

"Hey, my good man," she called out in surprise, "you've made a mistake, I didn't send for you."

He took no notice, but went on hoeing, bent over the soil, advancing quickly and powerfully, handling the mattock as if he didn't feel the weight.

"Hey, my good man," Maria Catarina called out more loudly, "you've made a mistake, I tell you, please don't go on, I can't afford to pay you."

He took no notice, but went on as if he did not feel fatigue, without raising his head or looking back, and, depending on whether he was working to the right or left of the plants, turned his head now one way and now the other as if he were talking to them, as if he were confiding a secret to each one of them, first in one ear and then in the other, with a smile.

"Hey, my good man," Maria Catarina called out still more loudly, "listen, for heaven's sake stop, don't go on, I've no money to pay you."

She plucked up courage, rose, and ran after him. He didn't even turn, but went on hoeing, bent over the soil, as steadily and naturally as an ox pulling a light plow, while she followed behind him and kept saying: "Hey, my good man, please stop, for heaven's sake stop." But she might have been talking to him in some unknown tongue, for he went on without taking any notice of her, with the unshakable calm and confidence of a peasant working his own land. For several days past unusual disasters had been happening in the neighborhood, and Maria Catarina was suddenly seized with panic. She started fleeing across the field, jumped the stream, and with her heart in tumult started hurrying up to Prezza, seeking refuge from some imminent peril. Every now and then she looked back to see if the man were pursuing her. The few people she met on the way recognized her and looked at her with horror and pity as a wretched victim of destiny. Who knew what fresh disaster had now befallen her? She reached the village breathless and exhausted, and hurried to take refuge with her mother-in-law, the only person left to help her. Her mother-in-law was very old and hardly ever went out of doors, but that morning, when she heard that Maria Catarina, though she was not used to working in the fields, had gone to weed the cornfield, she felt a great pity for her and asked a neighbor to lend her a piece of white bread and an egg, and she was keeping these as a treat for her that evening. But now Maria

Catarina suddenly appeared in her house in a state of frenzied
despair and flung herself weeping into her arms. The two poor
women spent the day in tears and prayers, for they had no one to
turn to for advice. But toward evening the old woman suddenly
made up her mind and decided to go and see for herself what
strange things had been happening in her son's field.

"You stay here, my dear, and shut the door," she said to her
daughter-in-law. "If anyone knocks, don't open."

"But supposing something happens to you?" her daughter-in-
law complained. "You can see for yourself, Mother, that destiny
has turned against us."

"Don't fear, my dear girl. Destiny can't reduce us to a state
worse than we're in already. And the devil doesn't like women of
my age."

The old woman took her beads, made the sign of the cross,
and slowly found her way down the track leading to the plain.
Small children loaded like little donkeys with knapsacks, casks,
and bags came climbing up the hill; solitary women came
walking along the edge of the road flanking the stream, bearing
heavy weights on their heads, their free hands knitting away at
socks in order to save time. Everyone was astonished to see the
poor old woman in her widow's weeds going down to the fields
at that time of day, and some actually dared to ask her whether
some fresh misfortune had befallen her. But she went straight
on with her rosary beads in her hand, responding to greetings
with slight movements of her head like a pilgrim on the way to a
shrine.

Three times she had to stop and sit by the wayside to recover
her breath, but as soon as she saw anyone approaching in the distance she rose and went on again. The air was warm as on a
summer evening, and the rustling of the leaves in the poplars was
refreshing. A rat crossed the roadside stream, its sharp, mustached
little face on the surface of the water. When she reached her son's
field the stranger had just finished the last row. He stood erect,
spent a moment or two looking at the work he had done, and
smiled. Then he bent down, picked up his hat, and put his mat-

tock on one shoulder; he also picked up the mattock that had been left there by the woman he had met that morning, and he made his way slowly toward the road. He was strong, but he walked as if he were tired. When he reached the brook he bent down and drank. The old woman was now by his side. He smiled at her and handed her the second mattock.

"And what now?" she said to him. "You've finished the hoeing, and that's fine, but my daughter-in-law told you over and over again that she can't afford to pay you. What are we to do? If there's a good harvest, my son will send you your day's pay. Where do you come from? What's your name?"

The man seemed not to understand and looked at her thoughtfully.

"You've done the work and that's fine," the old woman went on rather confusedly. "But my daughter-in-law's an unfortunate woman, you can take it from me, she can't afford to pay you at once, I'm very sorry. What's your name?"

The man understood at last. "Money?" he said, and laughed. "Money? Oh, no money," he stammered in a strange voice, shaking his head and hands in a gesture of refusal.

Then with a slight, awkward gesture he said good-bye and went off in the direction opposite to that of the village, striding along beside the stream and the row of poplars. His mattock was on his shoulder and his jacket was folded over his arm, and now he walked with body erect, like a gentleman. He had dropped all trace of weariness or servility. The whole thing was strange and inconceivable and certainly not natural, and the old woman stood there watching him. Suddenly she thought she understood, and she leaned against a poplar to prevent herself from falling. Her lined face was covered with tears of joy, illuminated and transfigured by a happiness she had never known before.

"Rejoice, my soul," she eventually managed to murmur, clasping her hands to her breast, "and again rejoice, because today you have seen the Lord."

How did she manage to get back to Prezza so quickly? Where did she get the strength from?

Kneeling by the fireplace at her mother-in-law's side, Maria Catarina wept tears of joy and shame.

"How can I believe myself to be a Christian," she said, "if He appears to me and I don't even recognize Him? What was the use of baptism, the catechism, confirmation, Holy Communion?"

"He was in His shirtsleeves and had His jacket over His arm," said the old woman. "But it was only when He was surprised at my mentioning payment that I noticed His silk shirt. That regal underwear beneath His ragged clothing, that voice, that smile, those words, that astonishment when He said: Money? Oh, no money! Oh, my daughter, how shall I describe it?"

No *cafone* had ever worn silk underwear, of course. In that part of the world even landowners and public speakers didn't aspire to such luxury. In the course of her life Maria Catarina's mother, who was a seamstress, must have sewn thousands of shirts, including shirts for local notables, but never had she sewn a silk shirt. Girls belonging to well-off families had silk wedding dresses, which they wore on one day only and then kept for the rest of their lives; the cloak of Our Lady of Libera was silk, and so was the parish priest's chasuble. Silk was ritual material.

"If it is He, Mother," Maria Catarina suddenly said, "if it is He who is now in this part of the world, it would have been a good thing if you had taken this egg to Him."

"Oh, my daughter," the old woman replied, "He could, if He wanted to, by a simple blessing change all the stones of Monte Prezza, Monte San Cosimo, and the Morrone mountains into eggs."

"If it's He, Mother," Maria Catarina went on in an undertone, "He could also set Nicandro free. He could do anything."

"Not everything, my daughter," the old woman said with a sigh. "Perhaps the poor stones in the road, the stones that everyone tramples on and the carts wear away, are closer and more obedient to His heart than evil men. Jesus, my daughter, cannot command His crucifiers."

The incredible news of the stranger who had hoed the field of corn and wouldn't hear of payment flew from mouth to mouth and caused amazement everywhere. Nothing of the sort had ever happened before, either there or elsewhere, in the memory of the oldest inhabitants.

There was a cobbler in Prezza who was well known throughout the countryside for never being surprised at anything. Just imagine it, he had been to Marseilles and Philadelphia, he had been all over the world, and so-called novelties merely made him laugh; he was also very emancipated, and did not believe in the fables of the priests, and if he sang the *Gloria* in church on Sunday it was only because he had a good voice. Well, even this cobbler was left speechless with amazement at the story of a stranger who had hoed a whole field of corn and wouldn't hear of payment.

"I never heard of such a thing in my life," he finally admitted, "not even in Philadelphia."

The devout were no less agitated and alarmed. They all of course believed, or believed they believed, or pretended they believed what is stated in the catechism, including the Real Presence of Jesus in church, in the tabernacle, in the guise of the Host and the wine, but believing Him to be alive and visible in the fields of beans and corn only a mile or so from the village was quite a different matter. Maria Catarina and her aged mother-in-law shut themselves up in the house, wouldn't talk to anyone, didn't want the house to become a public place or what had happened to be turned into an event to be talked about, a mere curiosity.

"I assure you that Jesus is not in the least interesting," the old woman repeated. "He is not in the least peculiar."

Even among themselves the two women avoided talking too often about the great event in their lives.

"We must be very careful, my daughter," the old woman said. "An immense gift was bestowed on us, a blessing sufficient to last us for the rest of our lives. But we must be very careful. A blessing is so easily wasted. We must talk about it very little and think about it always in the depths of our souls."

Maria Catarina hurried to the prison to tell her husband the great news.

"The Lord, Nicà, has hoed our land."

"What lord, Catarì?"

"There's only one, Nicà, only one real one. And He hoed our land."

"He? He Himself?"

The neighbors naturally tried every possible pretext to insinuate themselves into the house, like cats, and one or two succeeded. But as soon as they tried to bring the conversation around to Him, the old woman interrupted. "Those who want Jesus should pray to Him," she said.

"But tell me what He said to you, dearie."

"But, dearie, you ought to know that He's not an orator, good heavens no."

"There's one thing you must tell me, dearie, you simply must. When you saw Him, was He cheerful or sad? That's all I want to know, dearie, I swear it."

"He was sad, dearie. Even His smile was sad. And now go, dearie, and don't tell anyone what I've just told you."

The good woman left and hurried down the street. "He was sad, very sad," she said, running from door to door.

"I'm not in the least surprised," said a hermit who lived in an abandoned stable in the country outside Prezza to those who reported this to him. "If every intelligent person is sad, how much more so must be a God who knows everything. To Him who knows everything there can be little to be cheerful about."

Some cafoni went to consult him. He spent his time either cultivating his garden or reading, and he did not like wasting time on idle talk, though sometimes out of pity for the poor people's ignorance he relented.

"Oh," he said, "you're surprised that He looked like a beggar? What did you expect? Did you expect Him to look like a banker in a top hat, frock coat, and yellow gloves?"

"Do you think He's still in our part of the world?" a cafone asked. "When He arrives somewhere does He generally stay for some time?"

"He's in everyone who suffers. He told us so Himself. He's in every poor man."

"I'm poor, but He's not in me."

"You're poor, but wouldn't you like to be rich?"

"Well, of course I would."

"You see? You're not a real poor man at all."

"If He's living among us, why don't we see Him?" someone else asked.

"Because we don't recognize Him. They taught us to tell a donkey from a mule, a corporal from a sergeant, a priest from a bishop, but they didn't tell us how to recognize Jesus in the street or in the fields. The priests taught us to imagine Him in a completely wrong way, and on the altars in church they made Him look as handsome and dandified as a hairdresser, so that none of us would be able to recognize Him in the street."

"Please, please, tell me where I can find Him," an old tinker asked. "You know the state I'm reduced to, I so much need a grace."

"If you're in urgent need of money, you should apply to the devil, not to Jesus," the hermit replied. "Believe me, asking Him would be useless, it would be a waste of breath. He's poor, really poor, and not just in a manner of speaking. If he goes about dressed like a beggar, it's not playacting, and it's not demagogy, and it's not for the purpose of propaganda. He really has nothing but rags to wear, He's poor, actually poorer than you or me."

At this the consternation of these starvelings was complete. There might, perhaps, be more than one God, and it was said that every race had its own, but why in heaven's name should poor devils like us be saddled with a God like that?

"So if what you say is true, prayer is useless. If He's poorer and sadder than we are, what can He do for us?" the tinker wanted to know.

"He can help us to become even poorer than we are. That He can do."

The man went off in dismay. "Is that why we get poorer and poorer?" he complained.

A number of youths amused themselves by scaring the parish priest; they went to see him two or three times a day to warn him of the approach of a strange beggar.

"Take care, Father," they said to him, "a very doubtful-looking customer is coming to see you. You never can tell, he might be Jesus."

The unlucky priest did not know where to hide his head. He had just finished saying mass, had just finished sacrificing Jesus and washing his hands of Him, when the sacristan came and told him that a very badly dressed stranger was waiting for him outside the church. The priest, pale and distraught, escaped through a side door, hurried breathlessly up the steps of his house, and gave orders to the maid: "Never mind who wants me, say I'm not at home. Be very careful and let no one in. If it's a suspicious-looking type, lock the door and run and tell the *carabinieri*. After all, I pay taxes too."

But no one, either at Prezza or anywhere else, again saw the strange *cafone* with a silk shirt who had hoed the imprisoned Nicandro's land for nothing.

Pietro too went from village to village, searching for him in every valley in the area, but failed to find him. One night the temperature dropped sharply, frost destroyed the almond blossom that had yet again flowered too early, and the countryside was deserted; it was useless to look for him in the fields. Pietro went in his gig everywhere that Infante might have strayed to; he went along the Gizio, the Sagittario, and the Aterno, wandered like a lost soul about the streets of Prezza, Pratola, Vittorito, and Pentima, climbed all the way up to Roccacasale, questioned passersby in the streets, went into taverns, called on three or four peasants whom he knew. Many people had heard of him, and in the strangest ways, but no one had seen him. All his friends promised to let Cesidio or Pasquale the Cooper know immediately if they met him or heard reliable news about him.

His anxiety gave Pietro no peace, and he set off in the gig every day, resuming his pilgrimage without a destination; he went back to places he had been to before, went to see the same persons over again, and was given the same replies.

"My good woman," he said, stopping the gig, "my good woman, have you by any chance seen the poor devil whom everyone is talking about?"

The woman, dressed in black, was sitting on her balcony feeding her baby. "I stay here day and night in case he passes," she replied. "Several times I thought I saw him down there at the crossroads, but it wasn't he."

"Hey, my good man," he called out to a plowman, stopping the gig in the middle of the fields, "did the man everyone is talking about pass this way, have you seen him by any chance?"

The man stopped in the middle of his furrow; to protect himself from the rain he wore a sack over his head and back rather as if it were a cloak. "I may have," he called out in reply. "But the *carabinieri* are looking for him too, and to escape them he may have taken refuge in the mountains."

Pietro left the gig and the horse at an inn and continued the search on foot. He went up into the mountains and took a stony path that climbed between uncultivated fields and was interrupted every now and then by heaps of rubble, ash-colored rocks, abandoned hovels, disused churches. Anxiety, fatigue, fasting, dust, and mud made him almost unrecognizable, and outside a mountain farm he was actually taken for Him for whom everyone was waiting.

A shepherd fell on his knees and said: "Are you He who was to come?"

"Get up," Pietro replied, blushing, "I am not He for whom you are waiting; I am not fit to untie His shoelaces. But rest assured that He will come."

"And what must we do in the meantime?"

"Honor poverty and friendship," Pietro replied. "And be proud."

"What?"

But there was no trace of Infante. Pietro began to fear that something might have happened to him. In a tavern at Pratola he met Simone, who had also been searching in vain. They were disconsolate, and sat in silence. Peasants at a neighboring table were talking about a cow that for some days past had refused state fodder, a new product intended to compensate for the scarcity of hay. All the other cows ate it without giving trouble; this one alone stubbornly refused it. The authorities were worried; more

than anything else they were afraid of the scandal, the bad example it was setting. But Pietro was delighted.

"We ought to steal it, or buy it," he immediately suggested to
Simone. "Don't you agree that it would be treachery on our part
to abandon it?"

Simone was less enthusiastic and, without wishing to hurt
Pietro's feelings, pointed out some difficulties.

"A cow is bourgeois," he tried to explain, "it's sedentary, it needs
a good shed and a certain amount of cleanliness. Take it from me,
Pietro, having a cow is like having a wife and children, if not
worse. You can abandon a wife, but a cow? Suppose we had to flee,
how could a cow come with us with its archiepiscopal gait?"

"Flee, flee, always flee," Pietro exclaimed. "But perhaps next
time it'll be the others who will have to run away and hide."

"What others?"

"The police and their friends."

"That won't happen so quickly, I'm afraid."

25

RARE ARC LAMPS ALONG the main street swung in the wind and cast an intermittent light, rather like that of a provincial theater, on the houses. Don Severino, wearing a long, narrow, old-fashioned overcoat, defied the wind under the sign of the Victory (formerly Commercial) Hotel and looked closely at every passerby with the forward-leaning movement of the whole body that is peculiar to the nearsighted. His reflection in the glass door of the inn over the price list of the drinks reminded him of a character from a rooming house. But as soon as Pietro appeared he recognized him from a distance in spite of his nearsightedness and went to meet him.

"My dear fellow, I'd have recognized you with my eyes shut," he said, embracing him. "Come here, under the light, let me have a good look at you. But of course, you're not Pietro, or Saverio, or Berardo, you're just typical Spina."

To be able to talk undisturbed the two men walked down a road that led straight out of the village.

"I say this not to depreciate your merits in any way, but your forefathers were always slightly crazy too."

"How's my grandmother?" Pietro asked.

"She took to her bed on the day you left Colle," said Severino.

"Is she ill?"

"I went to see her that day, and she said to me quite simply: now there's nothing more for me to do down here below, so I expect that the Lord will be calling me back to Himself at any moment. She didn't feel unwell, she was not in pain, her pulse was regular, so she refused to call the doctor, who would not have found anything wrong with her. But she stayed in bed. I went to see her several times during the next few days, and once I went there with a notary; she wanted to settle all the family affairs calmly and carefully. I'll tell you about that later, there's no hurry now. She was delighted to hear you received the underwear she packed for you, but she added rather sadly that it was the only thing she could do for you, because you didn't need her for anything else. All mothers were good for nowadays, she added, was underwear. I shall not conceal the truth from a man like you, Pietro. Everything she told me about her long life in those last few days was heartbreakingly sad. The last time I saw her she was rather calmer and talked to me of the life to come. She said she hoped to be received in heaven, not for her merits, of course, but because of the redemption that is open to all. She told me of a minutely worked-out plan of hers about her life in the next world. If I tell you about it, Pietro, it's because it concerns you personally. She felt sure of meeting your mother, who was a good Christian, in heaven (she hoped to meet your father there too, but men were no good for what she had in mind) and she was also sure of meeting your other grandmother, whom you never knew. She told me that if the Almighty did not take you directly under His wing, the three of them would make such a fuss that heaven would be turned into a veritable hell, and that they would not stop until they got what they wanted. You may laugh now, Pietro but, as I know your grandmother very well indeed, I haven't the slightest, the faintest, doubt that she will keep her promise."

"Now tell me about her health. How was she when you left her? If I leave at once for Colle, shall I be in time?"

The two men were walking down a narrow path between vegetable gardens, where they were sheltered from the wind. Severino took some time to reply.

"My dear friend," he said eventually, "you'd be two days too late."

They both walked on in silence. There was a great peaceful-
ness in the air and on earth, and the very sorrow that gripped the
heart took its place like a natural thing among other natural
things. The night was cold and clear. The sky slowly became populated with carts, plows, mattocks, crosses, dogs, snakes, rats, and
Berenice rose in the east with her beautiful silvery hair.

"So far as the life beyond is concerned," Severino confessed,
"my faith has always been wavering. I have no difficulty in believing in it when a good person who is dear to me dies; but I believe in it much less in the case of the half persons who never
managed to be completely alive even when they were in this
world. It would certainly be interesting if Donna Maria Vincenza
could explain in heaven how sick unto death we are."

The path followed the ups and downs of the hill; at first it was
enclosed between a wall and a hedge, and then it was in the open.
All that could be seen of the two men in the darkness was their
faces lit by a whitish light. For some time they walked in silence.

"How is Faustina?" Pietro asked hesitantly.

"I came to talk to you about her too," Severino said. "I should
so much have liked her to have come with me, and she would certainly have been delighted to see you again; all this time she has
been thinking about nothing else. But at the last moment she did
not dare to come; she's afraid she left a bad impression with you.
Her misfortunes and her pride have given her a dreadful timidity;
incidents that to others would be trivial have always assumed
crushing and irremediable proportions."

"It was I who was most at fault," Pietro interrupted. "I should
have kept her here, and then I should have written to her to ask
her to come back, I should have explained what she means to me,
but I've been stupidly putting it off from day to day."

"Let me tell you frankly as man to man," Severino said, "that I
too had to overcome a strong reluctance before talking to you

about her; but the reluctance is only at the beginning, and it's only to telling you this: the gossip that has surrounded the friendship between me and Faustina lacks all foundation, except in appearance. The deception was certainly not premeditated, but it has been nourished, maintained, and exploited by Faustina. Vice is often concealed, of course, behind a hypocritical semblance of virtue, but it is my duty to tell you that in Faustina's case the opposite occurred: virtue has been concealed behind a semblance of vice."

"Never mind the details, Severino, they're not necessary."

"Wait a minute, there are certain things that I have to tell you; in fact let us take a step backward. When Donna Maria Vincenza threw her out my sister offered Faustina a temporary home, partly in memory of her mother and partly so that she should not be left in the street. At first she could never leave our house, because she ran the risk of being stoned. Neither then nor later did we ever discuss what happened in the Spina house, but in the course of everyday life we soon learned to appreciate her, and so my sister, with my consent, asked her to stay with us permanently. When my sister died she looked for somewhere else to live and wanted to move out, to spare any gossip at my expense, but I persuaded her that people's talk couldn't harm me; in fact, I had been considering for some time what would be the best way of bringing about a breach between me and the respectable families of the neighborhood, and I had been looking for something that would save me from being greeted by the devout, so I told her that if she stayed she would be doing me an invaluable service. So she stayed, and a great and discreet and gentle friendship arose between us. She still knows nothing about my most intimate life, and I still know nothing about hers, but we have shared the same bread and live in the same disrepute. To a proud, honest person who refuses to bend but does not dare to live a life of jeopardy as you have done, the appearance of vice and wildness is the only refuge tolerated by the law and by conventional morality. I thought I had found a plausible explanation of her ingrained resignation; I confess that until a few days ago I believed that it was based on the unhealed

wounds of early experiences, and I deplored seeing her tor-
menting herself because of errors committed many years ago. I
could not imagine — how could I? — that in the scandalous
events in which in the opinion of respectable people she was involved she was in fact merely a victim and not the diabolical se-
ductress that she appeared to be."

"Why stir the dust in a grave, Severino, is it really necessary?"

"Your grandmother told me to, and when you hear the story
you will see why. Let me tell you what happened. When Donna
Maria Vincenza felt that her end was approaching she wanted to
say good-bye to all her relatives, and in the case of her dead children she asked to be shown their portraits. When Donna Clotilde,
your Uncle Saverio's widow, came into her room, your grandmother (according to what she herself told me) meant to ask her
whether she had brought her husband's photograph, but absent-
mindedly she said: have you brought me that letter, Clotilde? At
this unexpected question by the dying woman Signora Clotilde
felt she was lost; she fell on her knees and begged forgiveness in a
flood of tears and moans, muttering confused and contradictory
excuses to justify her long concealment of a letter that no one else
knew about, and ended up promising to bring it to her that same
day. Your grandmother waited for the letter with a certain amount
of curiosity, having no idea what it might contain, but as soon as
she had read it she was seized with an indescribable agitation, ordered Venanzio to get the carriage ready immediately, and called
Natalina to help her to dress. She said she must go to Orta at once
to beg Faustina's forgiveness for having ruined her life by her own
blindness and hardness. Faustina's mother had been her best
friend, she said, covering her face in shame, she had promised to
look after the girl, and how had she kept that promise? She had
thrown her out of the house and dishonored her in the eyes of the
whole neighborhood, though she was innocent. Venanzio, as he
told me, was at a loss what to do. It was impossible to argue with
her, because she was in a state that brooked no reply, but doing as
she said would almost certainly mean her death. When I arrived
the poor old groom was wandering around in the courtyard,

weeping and trembling like a child, inventing futile excuses to delay their departure. To repair the wrong done to that poor creature, Donna Maria Vincenza said, I should need to live for another eighty years, and perhaps I may not have even eight hours left. I found her already dressed, sunk in an armchair, with her rosary beads in her hand. She made an effort to rise to her feet but could not. Is the carriage ready? she asked me. If I died now, Severì, if I died without Faustina's forgiveness, I should deserve everlasting punishment; the prayers for the dead would not work in my case. I had tremendous difficulty in persuading her to go back to bed, and in the meantime I told Venanzio to fetch Faustina in the carriage that was ready and waiting. It is I who must beg for forgiveness, Donna Maria Vincenza said, why should Faustina have to take the trouble to come to me? To enable me to understand her agitation she asked me to read the letter, which Saverio had written about ten years previously in the military hospital at Benghazi, but had been given to her only an hour before.

"Your uncle Saverio," Severino went on, "was not a banal person; perhaps he was intended by nature for the monastic life or, like you, for life in an underground sect. His greatest mistake was marrying Donna Clotilde, who had all the minor qualities of a good wife and bored him to death for that reason. He was, in short, a real Spina, that is, a hard man to satisfy. It was obvious from the letter that the only person whom he respected and feared was his mother. He had always tried to conceal from her the difficulties of his married life as well as his blind, obsessive, unrequited passion for the adolescent Faustina; and that was why he embarked on a course of dissimulation and intrigue that was not in accordance with his character. But his letter was intended to be a complete *Mea Culpa*, an exhaustive and detailed confession of his relations with Faustina, to exonerate her from the accusations and suspicions to which he knew she was subjected after his departure. The tone of the letter left no possible doubt about his sincerity. If I may take the liberty of mentioning it, Pietro, the letter did not contain the slightest reference in relation to Faustina that could bring a blush to the cheeks of the most modest girl. Her feelings for Saverio had never gone beyond the limits of family affection; and if at first, not yet realizing that she was playing with fire, she indulged in almost schoolgirlish jokes and familiarities with him, later she coldly and firmly rejected his passionate and embarrassing advances, when necessary actually with horror and disgust. This unrequited passion ended up completely dominating Saverio's mind; it became a tyranny, an exaltation, a monomania. His humdrum family life became intolerable to him, and because every wife, rather than admit her own or her husband's shortcomings, suspects and actually seeks out a seductive rival, it did not take long for Donna Clotilde to convince herself that the girl bore the whole responsibility for her unhappy marriage. In fact a great many clues seemed to justify the suspicion. As you know, Faustina then lived with your grandmother and, out of respect for her and an aberrant concern for Saverio, she made the mistake of not telling her about the molestation to which she was exposed. And your grandmother did not fail to notice the complicated precautions Faustina took to keep the secret, to hide Saverio's letters and her replies rejecting him. However, until the end Donna Maria Vincenza was uncertain whether to believe her daughter-in-law's bitter accusations, which were taken up and became the accusations of public opinion. But an unfortunate incident finally convinced her. Saverio had left two or three days before for Naples, from where he was to sail for Cyrenaica, and during the night Donna Maria Vincenza heard the sound of footsteps and voices coming from Faustina's room. It was Saverio, who had come back secretly to try to persuade the girl to elope with him. When your uncle heard Donna Maria Vincenza's footsteps outside in the corridor he implored Faustina not to open the door and betray his presence. She promised, and refused to open it. Next morning she was thrown out, and her fate was sealed. But she suffered her most painful mortification during the past few months, when she tried in vain to approach Donna Maria Vincenza in order to make contact with you and help you."

"What a marvelous girl," said Pietro. "So, but for the chance of my aunt Clotilde having been taken by surprise like that, she would have carried her secret to the grave."

The two men had completed a wide semicircle around the hill on which Acquaviva was built, and reached the small grassy space outside the abandoned little country church dedicated to San Martino where Pietro and Faustina had stopped during their walk.

"There's no wind here," said Severino, "let us stop and have a rest for a moment."

"I'm shattered at the thought of my grandmother's dying in an agony of remorse."

"Yes, it's dreadful that even honorable people cannot avoid making others suffer."

"Let us go back," said Pietro, "it's late. I'll wake Sora Olimpia and ask her to make us some coffee. On a night like this it's impossible to sleep."

Severino stayed at Acquaviva for several days. He did not want to go back to Orta without an invitation to Faustina from Pietro but, by agreement with Simone, he waited for it to come spontaneously from him. But Pietro said nothing. The weather had grown warm. In the evening people sat outside their houses and talked to each other from door to door. When they went to see Cesidio the friends made a long detour and went in by the back way, like conspirators, to avoid attracting the neighbors' attention. As soon as evening approached the air began to smell of soup, garlic, and onions. Severino was delighted with the place when Pietro took him there. In particular, he was delighted by the bread with a cross on the crust; it was homemade, was still good when it was a week old, and, as it was made without salt, retained a taste of wheat. It reminded him of the bread of his youth.

Don Severino was like a schoolmaster playing truant on a spring day. When the three of them, he, Pietro, and Simone, walked down the street, women hurried to windows and balconies to look at them. In his skeptical maturity Severino was tempted by the idea of returning to the happy dreams of his youth.

"My life has suddenly found a meaning," he said to Pietro

without concealing his emotion. "Somehow or other your way of living, which I used to think crazy, now strikes me as the only really decent and sensible answer."

"Then stay here with us and send for Faustina," replied Pietro, beside himself with pleasure.

"It's wonderful," Severino said, "my life seems about to make sense."

"You could try explaining Bach to the *cafoni*," Pietro suggested as an additional argument.

The two men went on talking until late at night, and by the time they went to bed they seemed to know everything about each other. But next morning Severino seemed disturbed.

"Do you feel ill? Didn't you sleep well?" Pietro asked him anxiously.

"I must tell you frankly," he said to Pietro, "that some serious doubts about your way of life occurred to me this morning. It's not the major difficulties I'm worried about, it's the minor ones. Let me give you an example. A few years ago an old friend of mine, a banker and a man of the world, became a monk. After a while I went to see him, to find out how he was putting up with the discipline. He talked to me with complete frankness. He told me he didn't regret the mistresses he had had in his past life, though he had had many beautiful ones, nor did he miss the social life, nor the excitements of business life, nor his friends and colleagues. What he missed was the breakfast in bed that the maid used to bring him every morning. He asked me to find out whether communism respected the right to have breakfast brought to one in bed every morning."

"If that's the difficulty, we'll bring you breakfast in bed every morning," Pietro suggested with a laugh.

"No," said Severino. "The fact of the matter is that my life has been all wrong, but now it's too late to change it."

"Won't you come and see Cesidio this evening?"

"Don't take it amiss, Pietro, but your friends bore me. I don't deny that they're excellent people, but they're boring."

To avoid leaving him alone, Pietro kept him company. They

went out together, and the conversation inevitably came around to Faustina.

"Shall I write to her and tell her to come?" Severino eventually asked.

"No, wait," said Pietro. "First I must find Infante and see him properly settled."

"Is your liking for Infante greater than your love of Faustina?"

Pietro looked at him with his eyes full of tears.

"Forgive me," Severino said. "That was a really stupid question."

26

FRIEND FROM POPOLI told Pasquale the Cooper that Infante had been under arrest there for several days and, after a brief discussion, Don Severino was sent to testify in his favor. Overcoming his reluctance, he went to the *carabiniere* barracks, and, after showing his papers, made a small speech, presenting himself in the guise of a noble benefactor explaining his pious interest in the unfortunate deaf-mute. He also had to show surprise and horror on being informed that Infante had been charged with adding seditious interrogation marks to slogans in public places.

"But it's impossible," Don Severino exclaimed. "He's illiterate."

"You don't have to have an arts degree to be able to scrawl an interrogation mark," the *carabiniere* warrant officer pointed out.

Fortunately inquiries had established that Infante had been writing interrogation marks indiscriminately, under all the signs and notices he came across, that in fact it had become a mania with him. He had not spared street signs, notices saying UNAUTHORIZED PERSONS NOT ADMITTED, and movie advertisements, with results that were sometimes unintentionally comic.

"Systematic doubt is not an offense," Don Severino plucked up the courage to point out. "At most it's a philosophical deviation."

"It's the only instance in which an offense is canceled out by its own excess," the warrant officer admitted.

Don Severino, after expressing appreciation of this perspicacity on the part of the *carabiniere*, asked that Infante should be handed over to him so that he might take him back to Pietrasecca, but the warrant officer told him that an order had come from Lama dei Marsi, the headquarters of the local authority area in which he was born, that he was not to be handed over to anyone but his father.

"But his father is in America, and there has been no news of him for many years," Don Severino pointed out with a slightly ironic smile at the fumblings of bureaucracy.

"Apparently he came back some weeks ago," the warrant officer said. "Actually he's coming here to fetch his son tomorrow."

Don Severino was unwilling to leave empty-handed. "But Infante isn't a minor and isn't subject to paternal authority," he pointed out.

"He's a deaf-mute, and so is legally subject to tutelage," the warrant officer explained.

Musicians know less than children about the law. The warrant officer dismissed the disappointed benefactor with the most benevolent of smiles; it inflated his cheeks in a way that recalled the smile of players of wind instruments that comes from continual blowing into them; and that was the news that Don Severino had to take back with him to Acquaviva.

"If Infante is returned to his father, that will be a load off your shoulders," he said to Pietro, "and now we shall be able to write to Faustina, I think."

"First we must see what sort this father is," said Pietro, not completely reassured.

"He certainly won't be anything but a father," Severino admitted. "He certainly won't be a mother or grandmother. But in times like these one has to put up with what there is; and for Infante he'll be better than nothing."

"First we must see what kind of father he is," Pietro repeated mistrustfully. "Then we'll consider the next step."

"His father will make him work, and sometimes he'll beat him," Severino said. "If one is a father, one has to demonstrate the fact; life is like that, and one has to put up with it. But living with his father Infante will no longer be on his own as he used to be, and that's the important thing."

"First I want to see the man," Pietro insisted, "and then we'll talk it over again."

Severino and Pietro arrived in Popoli in the gig drawn by the aged Belisario and tied him up in the corner of the market square. On the other side of the square a funeral procession was being formed. The militiaman who was controlling the traffic with extended arms resembled a uniformed travesty of a crucifix. Peasants looking like captured animals arrived in small groups and were lined up in fours. The flock extended as far as the eye could see, and officials walked up and down like guard dogs, barking here and there to keep the tired, docile, resigned men in line.

"Whose funeral is it?" Pietro asked one of them, his curiosity aroused.

The size of the crowd made him hope that it was that of some highly placed personage.

"I don't know," the peasant replied. "Do you know whose it is?" he asked his neighbor.

He didn't know either. The question made its way down the whole length of the procession. But nobody knew the answer.

"What?" Pietro exclaimed in disgust. "You attend a funeral without knowing whose it is?"

"They told me to turn up without fail," a peasant explained. "They said there was going to be a good speaker, that's all I know."

The talk caused one of the men responsible for marshaling the procession to appear on the scene, and he too was asked who the dead man was.

"Nobody's dead," he replied indignantly. "This isn't a funeral, it's the government's spring festival."

Severino dragged Pietro away. They went to the station to

meet every train in the hope of finding Infante's father.

"I'll recognize a man from Pietrasecca straightaway," Pietro said with confidence. "I'll spot him at once, even if he has been in Philadelphia for twenty years."

But many people got out at the station because of the spring festival and, strangely enough, they all seemed to be from Pietrasecca. So Severino and Pietro were obliged to walk up and down the road outside the station, scrutinizing and interrogating every passerby with the insistence and ham-handedness of amateur policemen. If they missed Infante's father on his arrival, they could not possibly miss father and son on their departure. But their efforts were unrewarded, and when they seemed protracted beyond due measure they gave up and went back to the square to get into the gig again.

They found Infante almost embracing Belisario, and with him there was an elderly, one-armed *cafone*, obviously his father. It was also obvious that father and son had already quarreled. His father had not been able to detach Infante from the horse he had run into by chance, nor could he understand what linked him to the animal, or how long he proposed to remain clinging to the creature's neck. He did not know how to communicate with him, and was not even sure of having made him understand he was his father.

Infante had followed him willingly from the prison as far as the square, but from the moment he set eyes on the horse his father had been unable to do anything with him. He tried taking him by the arm and dragging him away, but Infante was the stronger; he had dug his toes in and ended up giving him a powerful kick on the shin. His father was in the embarrassing and also ridiculous situation of a peasant who has bought a mule at a fair and has to show a great deal of patience before the animal gets used and submits to the voice of its new master. If it's a mule that kicks, one can't be too careful.

Infante was dirty and unkempt and in a worse state than ever, worse than a beggar; he looked resentfully and with obvious hatred at this unknown *cafone* to whom the *carabinieri* had handed him over as if he were his property. But on Pietro's appearance he dashed toward him, laughed and wept with pleasure, made a fuss over him, begged for his forgiveness like a lost dog that has found its master, and wanted to go off with him and never leave him again. He also greeted Don Severino since, being with Pietro, he too must be trustworthy. Infante's father was amazed at the affectionate familiarity that evidently existed between his wretched son and these two so distinguished-looking persons.

"Are you benefactors?" he asked in humble, servile fashion, taking off his hat. "I'm his father, my name is Giustino, Giustino Cerbicca."

To be able to talk more comfortably the four went into a small café, but Infante did not seem to like this stranger who kept close to him and sat beside him. He rose, said *pietra simonia*, changed places, and sat with his back to him. The café was deserted; a dish of cakes in the middle of the table was covered with a red cloth to protect it from flies.

"When I heard that after many years' silence you had come back from America, I couldn't guess why," Pietro said to Giustino. "But I understood immediately when I saw you have only one arm."

"Of course," Giustino said, sniggering as if to inspire sympathy. "A shortened tail can't ward off flies, but no doubt you are notables, persons of importance in the government party?"

"So you remembered you had a son only when you were disabled," Pietro went on. "Didn't you ever think of him before that?"

"Of course I did," Giustino protested. "He's flesh of my flesh, I often thought about him, but what could I do for him? I knew he was born deaf."

"But now, in spite of his deafness," Pietro went on, "he's a good beast of burden and could be useful to you."

"Well, I'm his father, after all," said Giustino, in the tones of a wretched victim. "If a son isn't to look after his needy father, who will? You are educated persons, you know the law."

The poor devil behaved like a *cafone* facing his judges, and he uncovered the stump of his arm to gain the court's sympathy.

"We are friends of your son," Pietro finally said.

Giustino smiled, but didn't understand.

"If you crossed the ocean for the purpose of using Infante as a donkey," Pietro said, "we shall prevent you, without worrying about the law. And besides, your son is now more independent than you might imagine."

Severino was tired of wasting time and tried to conclude the discussion, but Pietro went on: "He won't put up with ill treatment, you can depend on that. He'll beat you up, or run away. What it boils down to is that if you want to keep your son, you must deserve him. You must be more than a father, you must be a friend to him."

Giustino of course was not taken in by a word of this; he was not a child, and he knew the world, but it was so well said that tears came into his eyes. "Excuse me," he said to Pietro, wiping his eyes, "are you a public speaker? How well you speak."

He did not expect this question to produce such hilarity among his son's patrons. Since it was not a question of oratory, there was only one possible explanation, which was easy to guess.

"If the reason that you talk to me in this fine fashion," he said in alarm, "is that you're hoping to get money out of me, I must disappoint you. I swear to you that I came back from America with nothing but a hole in my pocket."

"Your son has some clothes to fetch in a village not far from here," Pietro said to cut matters short. "Come with us, and in the meantime perhaps you'll begin to understand what kind of persons you're dealing with. Don't be afraid."

So the four of them went back to Acquaviva. After a couple of days in the company of Simone and Cesidio, the "American" began to have a vague idea, a glimmering, of this strange, new, and absurd way of being friends. But he could not understand everything, among other things because no one explained to him who Pietro was. Apart from the suspicion that these people were members of a gang of swindlers, it occurred to him now and then that perhaps after all they were nothing but agreeable lunatics. At any rate, he was very sorry to have to disillusion them.

"You mustn't believe that because I've just come back from America I have a suitcase full of dollars, I appeal to you not to believe that," he told them every so often.

Simone was mistrustful. "As soon as he realizes who you are, he'll denounce you to the *carabinieri*," he said to Pietro.

But Pietro would not listen to him; nowadays he was often distracted or lost in reverie.

The friends met in Cesidio's house to hear what Giustino had to say about Philadelphia, which is the capital city of people from the Abruzzi on the other side of the ocean.

Severino did not come; he was impatient with Pietro's attachment to Infante, and upset at the delay.

"You must make up your mind, for heaven's sake," he said to Pietro. "Think a bit about the girl too."

"Please be patient," Pietro said. "Simone doesn't trust Giustino at all, and I should have no peace if I knew Infante to be in bad hands."

Cesidio had filled a bottle in honor of the friends, and it was passed from hand to hand; but it stopped when it got as far as Pietro, and Cesidio called out: "Drink and pass it around. What are you thinking of, I should like to know?" Giustino had with him in his suitcase a calf horn, which he showed to the company; years before he had taken it from Pietrasecca to Philadelphia, and now he had brought it back.

"It was this that saved me," he announced with conviction.

"It didn't save your arm," Cesidio pointed out.

"No, but it saved my life."

In his suitcase he also had an artificial arm with a hand in a black glove, and he showed it off with childish vanity. It had been presented to him by the firm of builders for which he worked; it was the compensation they gave him after his accident.

"No *cafone* has ever had an arm with a gloved hand like that," he said.

He held it on his knees the whole evening, and kept stroking it with his remaining hand.

Simone sat next to Pietro, smoking his pipe in silence. Occasionally he took the pipe from his mouth as if he were about to say something, but then put it back and went on smoking. There was no longer the serenity of earlier evenings after work in the vineyard.

Infante sulked because of the excessive attention his friends paid the new arrival, whom he hated without disguising the fact; on every occasion he called out *pietra simonia* and put out his tongue. While the others talked and laughed he squatted in a corner of the fireplace with the dog Leone, who was in a bad state, with infected scars on his skin.

"It's homesickness," Simone explained, *"amor patriae."*

In the course of his description of life in America Giustino explained at great length to Carmela that in Philadelphia Americans did not crack nuts with their teeth or with stones. No, indeed, they had a special little implement that they used for the purpose; he, Giustino, had himself once had occasion to use that implement to crack a nut. It had been a very curious experience, and the result had been that he hurt his finger and the nut emerged so crushed as to be inedible. But that was for lack of practice, of course; with any kind of mechanism practice was more important than theory. During his twenty years in Pennsylvania he had never had close contact with Italians who were not from the Abruzzi or with Abruzzesi who were not from the Marsica, and only with a few Marsicani who were not from the Fucino basin. The various families with whom he boarded were all from his own locality, and so were the bosses who engaged him and gave him orders on the job, and so were those who worked with him on the job; and so too was the banker D'Ambrosio, who had a place at the corner of Eighth Street to which poor *cafoni*, including Giustino, took their savings, which they never saw again; and so too was the Hon. Tito Macchia of Nineteenth Street, who out of philanthropy rather than anything else, sold speculative plots of land, "real estate," as it was called, on excellent terms to help his poor compatriots, with a guarantee of 100 percent profit; Giustino too had bought his plot, but it was not of this world, actually it didn't exist. The religion practiced was Catholic, but local; the only saints involved were Marsican saints: the Holy Martyrs of Celano, San Berardo of Pescina, San Cesidio of Trasacco, and others besides. In the basement of the church, where here the bones of martyrs are preserved, the priest for lack of sacred relics organized "spaghetti parties," as they are called there. After the swindle by his honorable compatriot Tito Macchia, Giustino was left without a cent, just as he had been twenty years before when he arrived in the promised land; that was the sole result of twenty years of toil and privations, with bread and sleep doled out as to a prisoner. He had then decided that his misfortunes were the result of living a life confined to his own kind, like an ant or a sheep; and without mentioning it to a soul he devised a hazardous plan of escape into the unknown: he decided to turn his back on the Fucino basin and try his luck among Lombards, Sicilians, or Piedmontese. After making careful and cautious inquiries, one night he left Philadelphia and went to Kingsview, in Scottdale County, still in the state of Pennsylvania. In Kingsview he was surrounded by Piedmontese, men from the Marches, Calabrians, and no Abruzzesi, with the result that for the first time in his life he felt himself to be abroad. His anxiety was easy to imagine. He boarded with a Piedmontese family, only a few words of whose language he understood; and a man from Calabria got him a job with a demolition firm. The work had not been heavy, pick and shovel had always been his specialty, but he was more depressed than he had ever been in his life, because after the day's work he had no one to talk to. In sheer desperation he got into the habit of talking to himself. One day he noticed a mouse in the rubble of a wall he was demolishing, a tiny, thin little mouse that he immediately recognized as coming from the village where he was born, and the sight made him dizzy with emotion.

"But how could you tell that it came from your village?" Cesidio's wife interrupted. "How did it cross the ocean? Did it swim?"

"If you had seen it, my good woman, you too would have immediately recognized it as coming from my home," Giustino replied. "There was no possible doubt about it. Gracious heavens, I said to it, how did you manage to come all this way? It vanished down a hole, and I wanted to tell it not to be frightened, to trust me, but I felt the ground disappearing under my feet. When I came around I was in the hospital, and two days later they amputated my arm."

"Drink," said Cesidio. "At bottom all stories are the same."

"It's certainly not worthwhile spending twenty years in America only to lose an arm," said Cesidio's wife. "You could have stayed at Pietrasecca and you could have lost your arm just the same, since that was your destiny, but at least you'd have saved the fare."

Infante sought out the dog's eyes; the two spent the whole evening looking at each other, talking to each other in their way, perhaps complaining. Pietro did not take his eyes off them for a moment. At one point Simone rose and apologized for leaving earlier than the others, but he was expected by Severino.

The result of this meeting was that Simone changed his mind about Infante's father and told Pietro so.

"He's a poor devil," he said, "and I now believe that he and Infante will end up getting on with each other. Not because Giustino is his father, of course, but because he has one arm and needs him. If it comes to the worst, Infante can always run away again."

"All right, all right," Pietro replied as if lost in reverie.

Simone undertook to persuade Infante and promised to come and see him from time to time at Pietrasecca. Infante listened and seemed to understand and be resigned.

With Infante's future thus settled, Don Severino left for Orta after agreeing with Pietro about arrangements for him and Faustina to meet again. The girl would wait for him at Caramanico, where an elderly woman cousin of Severino's lived alone in a big country house. The idea had been mentioned to her, and she had said that she would be delighted to have some company, without even asking who was involved or why. Faustina and Pietro would be able to stay there undisturbed and get to know each other better at their leisure and quietly and calmly make up their minds about their future. There would be no material difficulties, as the fortune left to Pietro by Donna Maria Vincenza assured him of a comfortable living.

"Do you think we'd be willing to live on unearned income?" Pietro exclaimed. "We'd rather work."

"You can live as you think best."

Severino encouraged Pietro to go back abroad, taking Faustina with him; he would undertake to get him a passport, which he did not think would be difficult, and he actually went off into a passionate eulogy of graft, palm greasing, and the use of influence.

"I know I'm offending against your most sacred principles," he said to Pietro, "but I'm convinced that corruption is the only kind of democracy possible in this country. It humanizes the state, mitigates the severity of laws and customs."

Pietro barely smiled. He had no desire to listen to paradoxes; he was thinking of Faustina. The love that had been long held back now flooded into his mind and brimmed over, like water in a spring.

He spent his last day at Acquaviva working in Cesidio's vegetable garden with Carmela. He wanted to avoid good-byes and sentimental effusions; between him and Infante and Simone words would be inadequate, so it was better to be silent.

He spent the whole day staking and pruning tomato plants, following Carmela's instructions. A tomato plant left to itself on irrigated land would grow more than six feet high, but this would not help the fruit, so it was better to keep it down to about four feet. Apart from the principal shoot, tomatoes also put out side shoots, sterile or hardly fertile auxiliary branches known as suckers, and it was better to remove these too.

"Many suckers are ruinous," Carmela explained. "At most you can leave one per plant."

The work left a light green coloring on Pietro's fingers that pleased him greatly. That evening he had a short and unexpected talk with Cesidio.

"So you're leaving?" Cesidio said without looking at him.

"Yes," Pietro replied in embarrassment; he would have liked to say more, but could not.

An awkward silence followed.

"I've calculated the number of days you've worked for me," Cesidio eventually said to him, showing him a piece of paper.

"I'm sorry," said Pietro, who was taken by surprise, "but I haven't calculated how much bread you've given me and Infante."

"Bread," Cesidio exclaimed resentfully. "You don't count how much bread you offer people. I don't see why you should try to offend me just when you're leaving."

"My work isn't for sale either," said Pietro. "Oh, Cesidio, I've always wanted to work for nothing and to live on charity. I know, Cesidio, that that's an ideal that can't yet be realized, that it's utopian. But please allow me to have spent some utopian days with you."

"If that's the case," said Cesidio, "why do you want to leave? Who's sending you away?"

Pietro seemed struck by that remark. Cesidio left him alone. Simone was nowhere to be found. Pietro wandered aimlessly around the village. Several times he said to himself: who is sending me away?

Sor Quintino had planned a small celebration on the occasion of his guest's departure, but when the latter appeared he dared not even mention it. The captain sat at his table preoccupied, hostile, as taut as a clenched fist, not replying to any greetings. What could he be hiding, a medal, a weapon, stolen property? His appearance among the notables who were already having dinner was like that of a stranger appearing on the stage while a performance was in progress. The notables were crushing the bones of small, rachitic birds, spreading pungent cheese on bread, licking their mustaches. On a table there was an old-fashioned gramophone with a dented blue horn.

"An event that will give you great pleasure has just been announced on the radio," the *podestà* said to the captain.

"The only news capable of giving me great pleasure is what would be called disastrous news on the radio," the captain replied.

"Excuse me" said the *podestà*, losing all self-restraint, "but it seems to me that sometimes you go rather far in what you say."

"I congratulate you on your perceptiveness," replied the captain.

Sor Quintino arrived with food to serve him, but he rose and walked out.

He wandered down the streets for a time, and then someone called him. It was Pasquale the Cooper.

"Where are you going? What are you looking for?" he wanted to know.

"I don't know," he replied, embarrassed. "I want to be alone, please excuse me."

The evening was full of the bittersweet smell of cut grass. He took the shortest way out of the village. He saw the lights appearing in distant villages and hamlets; halfway up the slope on the other side of the valley he saw a train making its way between the trees like a luminous caterpillar and then plunging into the mountain and disappearing. He went down a path flanked by the whitewashed trunks of fruit trees; he wandered among the vineyards, bemused and aimless and in the grip of a strange restlessness. Meanwhile the sky became populated with stars. He looked at the sky and smiled. Had his grandmother persuaded the Almighty to take him under His direct protection? He shuddered. It was terrible to fall into the hands of the Lord. He reached the edge of a stream. The waters were swollen and yellow, and carried along branches of trees, boards, planks, and household objects. There must have been a storm up in the mountains; in the foothills no one had yet noticed it.

"Praised be Jesus," an old woman said to him, emerging from the darkness.

"Good evening," he replied.

"The flood has carried away the footbridge," the old woman said. "If you take my advice, you'll turn back."

He turned back, and wandered about indecisively. The streets were full of complaining voices; they were like prayers, litanies, but they were the cries and complaints of women and children and the bleating of sheep.

It was late when he got back to the inn and packed his bags. Those containing his uncle Saverio's uniforms, brought there by mistake, had already been taken back by Severino, but even among his own clothes he found some that were useless and unnecessary. He made a parcel of them and left the inn to take them to Infante. Perhaps it was also an excuse to see him again, to say good-bye to him, to convince himself of the reality of their separation, and give a final word of advice to Giustino.

Since the day before Giustino had slept in the same house as his son, taking Simone's place. In the dark and irregular alley that was dug out like a trench and flanked by hovels, sheds, and pigsties there was still a light in the window he was looking for. He stopped and listened for a moment on the steps outside the door, but no sound came from inside. He knocked, waited for a moment, and then knocked again, but no one opened. In the distance he heard the long, doleful barking of a dog; he thought he recognized it. He pushed hard at the door, and it opened. On the tiles in the middle of the floor Giustino lay half dressed in a pool of blood, leaning slightly on the stump of his arm, obviously dead. There were dark, bloody gashes on the left side of his bare, hairy, almost simian chest. Near his bare feet there was a big knife with a red blade. Hiding behind the door and with his back to the wall was his son, quivering with terror from head to foot, with hanging head and his tongue between his half-open lips.

"Infante," Pietro exclaimed in horror. "Why? Why?"

Infante dared not look him in the face and replied with a hoarse, submissive, painful mumble, like the whine of an animal appealing for pity.

"Oh, you poor fellow," said Pietro, seized with compassion.

He opened the door to see whether anyone was passing.

"Go," he then said to Infante, taking him by the arm. "Go," he said. "Run, quickly."

The deaf-mute vanished into the darkness with an animal-like leap. Pietro remained for a moment looking after him, and then shut the door.

In one corner of the room a small fire of twigs was still smoking. The few, wretched things in the room, the straw mattresses, the jug, the washbasin, two chairs, bore the marks of a violent quarrel. Pietro stayed listening, trembling with horror and revulsion.

No sound, no sign of alarm came from the neighboring houses. All that was to be heard was the painful howling of the dog. Pietro covered Giustino with a blanket, but it was too small and left uncovered his big, black, gnarled feet and his hairy face, which was contracted into a horrible grimace. Pietro bent over to shut his eyes and thought he detected a slight death rattle. Could he be still alive? Every now and then a slight, almost imperceptible breath emerged from his dry, earthy, cracked lips.

Pietro called for help through the open window, called for some neighbor to hurry to fetch a doctor for a gravely wounded man. After a time there was the sound of a window being opened in the dark alley and a door being slammed. But when Pietro went back to Giustino and bent over him, he was dead.

"Of course," Pietro murmured, as if observing something that was only to be expected.

Time passed more and more slowly and eventually stopped. The *carabinieri* found Pietro sitting on a straw mattress with his head in his hands.

"It was I who killed him," he said, rising to his feet.

And he held out his hands for the handcuffs.

It was the hour when night fades and dawn reabsorbs the last stars, when mice return to their holes and *cafoni* load up their donkeys to go out into the country to work. The streetlamps were still alight; in the brightness of early morning their light was like that in the eyes of feverish persons after a sleepless night. Pietro was taken to the barracks handcuffed between two *carabinieri*. He walked silently and quickly; the hat on his head was tilted slightly, and he couldn't adjust it because of the handcuffs; he obviously found this very annoying. He looked like a man who had had an accident, had been run over by a horse or fallen down a staircase and was being taken to hospital for observation.

The two *carabinieri* were taller and stronger than he; they had big, massive faces like pumpkins or eggs, eyeless, noseless, mouthless, great smooth, oval shapes topped by lantern-shaped hats. Behind them a street sweeper appeared with a long broom; he advanced quickly, with the broad, graceful movements of a man using a scythe. And then the first shopkeepers came hurrying toward their shops, asking one another: "What was the matter with that dog that barked all night?"